ASHES OF THE SOVEREIGN

THE PHOENIX PROJECT OMNIBUS SERIES

BOOK TWO

M. R. PRITCHARD

Midnight Ledger
Publishing
14391 Spring Hill Dr. Suite 203
Spring Hill, FL 34609
MidnightLedger.com

12th Anniversary Special Omnibus Edition 2025
ISBNs: 978-1-957709-71-0 (paperback)

Printed in the United States of America

About Ashes of the Sovereign (The Phoenix Project Omnibus Series)

Love, deception, and conspiracies.

There's no time to grieve or make amends. The Entities demand loyalty — and Andie's role as **District Matchmaker** ties her fate to the survival of their crumbling world. As enemies stir in the shadows and her family's safety hangs in the balance, Andie must decide how far she's willing to go to protect those she loves.

With the rising storm of war and whispers of rebellion, one truth remains: **Crane always unleashes his worst havoc when Andie's away...**

This collection is a rollercoaster of action, suspense, and unexpected twists. It includes books 4-6 in The Phoenix Project Series titled: Inception, Origins, and Resurrection.

For the rebels.

INCEPTION

ONE

MY BREATHS ARE COMING IN A RAPID SUCCESSION, MUCH faster than they should and much faster than I have been trained to allow them. Breathing fast means those demons in the shadows of my mind are getting to me. I can't let them. Killing Andie and Ian wasn't part of the deal. Scare them, yes. Scare me, no. Nothing has ever scared the shit out of me as bad as seeing that man from the Swamps with his arms around Andie, holding her still so she could watch them kill Ian. Even if she never speaks to me again, I couldn't let that happen. Half a heartbeat was all it took for me to stop them. And then, watching Andie soothe her husband's wounds by the stream. Shit. I wanted it to be me. I want it to be me. And now this thundering in my chest, it's not helping. I need to clear my head; forget her, forget him, forget the children, forget my own son. I wish I could.

Mack watches me as the train to the Phoenix District pulls away. "So you weren't lying?" he asks.

"About what?"

"You and her."

Shaking my head, I turn toward the trail that leads back to Romney. And then, I run.

"Where ya' going?" Mack shouts.

I don't answer. There's no point. She's gone and she won't listen to me or a word I have to say. But maybe in time she'll listen. One day. Time may be my friend. I have all the time in the world now. Veering off the trail, I head for the dense forest. Leaping over downed trunks, splashing a step in the stream, I follow the whisper quiet sound of the train until it's gone. I run for it all; to stop this feeling, to stop knowing what's going to happen, not being able to control it, and losing. I run for losing her until I can't feel anymore and my heart beats so hard in my chest I think it might explode. Since I can't change any of it, I run.

When the day starts to darken to night, I stop. Unable to quell this feeling in my chest, I send my fists flying into the nearest West Virginia Pine tree, beating it like a punching bag until my knuckles split. Only then do I stop, turn, and head back to Romney, my only light being the moon. I'm not scared of the dark, or what now lingers in the shadows of the forests. My knuckles tingle as they heal. It's an annoying feeling, like ants crawling across my skin. I envision the nanocytes going to work–weaving and growing new tissue–and shudder. There's something creepy knowing that your body is filled with nanoparticles that resemble spiders. I should be used to them by now. I've had them long enough.

I follow the train tracks back to where the attack took place. Just as I reach the trail that will bring me back to Romney, a dark figure steps out of the forest. Perfect. I love being offered an opportunity to teach these sick freaks a lesson. I move fast, a few quick steps and I'm on him. "You were instructed not to harm them." Reaching for the bow and arrow at my back, I aim it at the Swamp man's face. "You overstepped your bounds."

"Seems you killed our leader. Scarface be dead." The man smiles, turns and spits on the ground.

"Scarface be stupid." I take a step closer. "You were instructed to just threaten them. You almost killed them. We had a deal."

The man shrugs. "We hungry." He turns his vacant eyes on mine.

"I don't give a shit that you're hungry. I've given you more than enough."

"Not enough." The Swamp man shakes his head, nods toward the direction that the train went. "We seen where dey went. We know dere's more up dere."

"Stay away from them." I tilt my head to the shadows of the trees; raise my voice so they can hear me. "All of you. Stay away from all of the Districts, especially Phoenix."

The man walks closer, until the point of my arrow touches the skin of his face. "What you gon' do 'bout it? Yer nothin' but a fallen soldja wid a broken heart–"

"Shut up."

"Dat's de worst kinda man. De most dangerous–"

"Shut. Up."

"Whatchu gon' do, broken man? You gon' kill me?" He smiles, all rotten teeth and putrid breath.

"No."

"Naw." He smiles again, mocking.

"No. I will kill every single one of you." My eyes sweep the treeline. There's at least twenty of them out there. I push the arrow against the man's face, watch as blood seeps out.

He steps away, wipes at the blood dripping down his face. "You gon' save dat lady wid all dat pretty hair? Live happy forever, like in dose movies? We had one dos' picture boxes before. Bet you kiss her if you could."

I don't know why I keep talking but the words come flooding out of my mouth. "She's gone. I'm dead to her now."

The man steps back toward the dark forest. "Well, now you def'netly de worst kinda man."

I shouldn't engage. But I can't help myself. "Why?"

"Cause you got nothin' left to live for." His lips split into another grotesque smile.

With that, I release the arrow, watch as it pierces his skull. He drops to the ground, dead in an instant. "Dumb shit." I reach forward and jerk the arrow from his head, press it into the dirt to clean the blood off. "I've got plenty left to live for." A certain red-haired dictator made me a promise, and since I have all the time in the world now, I plan on collecting when the time is right.

The forest shudders with the movement I've come to recognize as the Swamp people stirring. Turning, I find Mack standing there in the dark. Placing the arrow in its holster and the bow across my back, I stalk toward Mack, weave around him, and head toward Romney.

Two

IAN PARKS NEXT TO THE LARGE BARN ON THE GROUNDS OF the Pasture. The ride back here from our last meeting with Dr. Akiyama was tense. I want to say something to him, but I can't figure out the right words. How do you ask your husband to forgive you for withholding a secret like that from him for so long? Ian is married to a killer. I killed a man. Dragged Ian into this and he was forced to kill even more. I'm sure the only thing on his mind is that he's going straight to hell.

Neither of us makes the move to get out.

"I told you–" I start.

"Just stop," Ian exhales loudly. "Just stop, Andie."

I turn to look at him. "Stop what?"

"Stop trying to force me to be angry with you. I already told you that I can't hold those things against you. Whatever you had to do. I won't judge you for them."

"But, you changed, right after Dr. Akiyama told you that man I killed was unarmed. I could feel it."

He turns to me, "No, Andie. I didn't change. I needed a moment to take it all in. But you, whatever went through your body when Akiyama said what he said, your mood flooded that room. Not mine. I told you before, the world is different now, we do what we have to do to survive. My beliefs before..." He pinches his eyes closed for a second before looking at me again. "What I believed before about right and wrong, about God and Heaven and Hell; it doesn't apply to this life anymore. It can't."

Can someone just change like that? Can Ian really put all of his values behind him and move on with me, with what we've done? I think I've ruined him. Rubbing my hands across my pants, I dry my palms and take a calming breath. "I'm sorry. It's just, whatever Crane did to me–"

"The nanocytes?"

"Yeah. I think they...I don't think they're just rebuilding my DNA, it feels like they're changing me."

"But it's only been a few weeks."

"I know."

Ian's hand moves, brushes a piece of hair away from my face. "You look the same." He reaches forward with both arms and pulls me to him. "You smell the same." He tips my chin, then presses his lips to mine. "Taste the same."

For just a few moments I enjoy the warmth of him wrapped around me. "I have to stop it," I whisper.

"I know," Ian replies, squeezing me tighter. "Where will you start?"

"I think–"

We are interrupted by a sharp rapping on the window.

"Come on, lovebirds," Elvis shouts. He backs up and waves for us to get out.

Untangling ourselves from each other, we get out of the SUV.

"Would expect this from Sam and Blithe, but you two?" Elvis clicks his tongue and shakes his head.

"What do you need?" I ask Elvis.

"The boy is here."

"The boy?" I ask.

"Isaac." Elvis looks between us. I look at Ian. "Isaac Somers. Ian's... son."

"Oh." I look away.

"He's at the school house with the other children and Ms. Black."

"But, we haven't had time to get ready for him." I look toward the house, mentally calculating how many chairs and beds we have.

"Got you an extra dining room chair and Sam is bringing a bed for him," Elvis says.

"Well, I guess you've all got this covered," I reply.

Ian moves so he's standing next to me, his warm hand closes over mine. "Let's go meet him, together."

Walking beside Ian, trying to hold down an ever growing lump in my throat, I push away all those memories of the day this child, Isaac, was born. I push away standing there watching as his mother pulled down Ian's mask and revealed him as the father to me. I try to ignore that stabbing pain in my heart.

Ian squeezes my hand, brings me back to the present. "You're doing it again," he warns.

When I look at him I notice his features are pinched. "What?" I ask.

"Whatever you are thinking, it's radiating off of you like a storm."

"Sorry." It comes out as an annoyed mutter.

Ian stops me just steps away from the porch of the school house. "I don't want you to be sorry." His hand moves up my arm and squeezes my shoulder. "Just remember Lina and Raven are in there with him. They don't need to feel whatever it is you are harboring."

"I'm not harboring anything."

"Why don't you take a deep breath," he suggests with a small smile, "and tell me what you're feeling?"

Closing my eyes, I inhale a large breath of the early summer afternoon air. It should smell like dandelions and cut grass, it should be dry and warm. But instead the air is soggy, chilled; more like spring. We thought the spring blizzard was a fluke when we went to rescue the children in Romney, but it seems the seasons have shifted. I breathe out, emptying my lungs of the cool air.

"What was in there?" Ian asks. He's so patient.

"Just a little..." I look away from him, "hurt, pain, sadness."

"That's not a little anything. Do you feel better?" I nod and he leans forward and brushes a swift kiss across my lips. "Andromeda Somers, I love you. Now, let's meet this child."

Ian turns the doorknob and lets us into the school house. The noisy chatter of children fills our ears. Blithe waves from the other side of the room and walks toward us, smiling. "He hasn't stopped talking since he got here."

"Really?" Ian asks.

"Really. He seems older than Alexander said he would be."

"How so?" I ask.

"He's taller that most kids his age, and... well, you'll see for yourself. Isaac," Blithe calls quietly.

From the center of the circle of children, a boy steps out. I know he should be around three, but he's taller than Astrid, who's close to five now. He has pale skin, shaggy blonde hair and deep brown eyes. He walks right up to us, holds out a hand to Ian, and says, "You must be my father, Ian. Can I call you Dad?"

Perfect speech, perfect posture. He carries himself like an adult. Strange.

Ian takes his hand, kneels down, and studies the boy for an instant. "If you'd like," he responds.

When he is done shaking Ian's hand, Isaac turns to me and looks me up and down. Strangely, he steps forward, throws his arms around my waist and presses the side of his face to my stomach in a hug.

Not quite sure what to do, I move my arms from their shocked position and run a hand through his hair. Ian watches with wide eyes, smiles and shrugs his shoulder.

"Mom! Dad!" Lina runs to Ian's arms and he picks her up. "I have another brother. Isn't this great?" She smiles widely, pumping a fist in the air. "Now I have two brothers and Astrid. It's like we're a real family."

I look around the room, searching for Raven. I find him on the other side of the room, watching us silently. "Come here, Raven," I call to him.

He takes his time crossing the room to us while the other four boys play with toys that are on the floor. I pick him up, press my cheek to his. "What is it, Raven?" I whisper in his hear. Silently, he reaches out and runs his fingers across my brow. Something worries him. "Okay. It's okay," I tell him.

We collect the children, their coats and boots, and head for home. Just as we're crossing the courtyard, Sam opens the front door of our house and waves. He jogs toward us, dressed in full Volker garb. "I brought the bed for...er..."

"Isaac," I tell Sam. "His name's Isaac."

"Hey!" Isaac waves at Sam.

"Isaac, this is...well...your Uncle Sam," I introduce them.

"My uncle is the Volker Sovereign?" Isaac asks, his eyes wide with excitement.

"Yes," I answer.

"Cool."

"Come on, Isaac." Lina grabs his arm as she runs, pulling him along with her. "Me and Astrid will show you the house."

The children disappear into the house, all of them except for Raven, who remains on my hip.

"I wasn't sure where to put the bed so I set it up in Raven's room. I figured two boys, two girls," Sam says with a shrug.

"Sure," I reply, catching the scowl from Raven out of the corner of my eye.

Ian's hand makes contact with my back. "Well, we'd better make sure they don't burn the house down."

"You want to stay for dinner, Sam?" I ask.

Sam glances toward the school house and shifts on his feet. "Already have plans."

"Fine, fine, fine," I say. "Blowing us off for Blithe."

"It's nothing personal," Sam shrugs.

Ian reaches over and smacks him hard on the shoulder. "Sure it ain't."

We split up, Sam jogging toward the school house and Ian and I headed toward home.

Home. It's strange to think of it as home, finally, even after everything that's happened. But I have my family here, all of them. We are together. A mishmash of children from various paths our lives have taken. Parents who fell apart and then found each other again. Parents who have blood on their hands. As though he can read my thoughts, Ian reaches out and brushes his hand across my arm. He's so patient, so forgiving. I don't think I deserve this man in my life.

--

IAN CLOSES the door to our bedroom. "Four kids," he says as he walks to his dresser.

"Four kids," I repeat. "All in bed before ten."

I search my dresser for something to sleep in.

"I like this." Ian's clothes rustle as he changes. "More kids like we always wanted."

"We didn't want them like this," I remind him, absently searching yet finding nothing.

"At least we have each other. We're together."

I pull out a pair of sweatpants and an old sweatshirt. "Yea–"

Before I finish, Ian is behind me, close. I turn. "You're distracted," he says.

I hold up my sweats. "Was looking for something to sleep in."

"I see."

Ian reaches for the hem of my shirt, his hand brushes my hip and there is a fluttering in my stomach. The shrill ring of the telephone tears through the house. "What the..." We both leave the bedroom, headed for the living room.

Ian gets to the phone first and answers it. "Hello?" His eyes widen, brow furrows, he holds out the phone. "It's for you."

I take the receiver from him. "Hello?"

"Ah, Andromeda," Crane's voice greets me on the other end of the line. "I hope I didn't interrupt anything."

The fluttering in my stomach from Ian's touch is replaced by a severe annoyance. "Actually, you called a house filled with children in the middle of the night. That's kind of rude."

The asshole actually laughs on the other end. "Oh, so sorry. You see, I forget how late it is there. With the time difference and all."

"Why, Crane, what time is it where you are?" I ask.

"I bet you'd like me to tell you, wouldn't you?"

"I could care less." I sit at the nearby computer chair. Ian watches.

"I think you'd like to know."

"No." I hold back a yawn. "As long as you are nowhere near me and my family, I don't care where you are."

"Well, now the reason for my call."

"What's that?" I ask.

"You have five years."

"Five years for what?"

"Five years," he repeats. "You need to designate another Sovereign member to sit in my place. I would like to suggest Dr. Akiyama. And since you will be training the next generation of Sovereign, you need to be aware that Ms. Black is only capable of teaching the children up to a certain level. After that they will be sent to Hanford to resume their schooling."

"But..." As usual this makes no sense. "Blithe taught Sam when he got here. Why can she all of a sudden not teach the other children?" There is silence on the other end of the line. Strange. "Aren't you going to answer my question?"

"Sorry, but no."

"My children aren't going to another District to complete their schooling," I tell Crane. "We can teach them all they need to know here."

"Quite the contrary, Andromeda. They will go by the age of sixteen, or sooner or later depending on their individual academic achievements."

I mutter a few choice words under my breath before asking, "Why Hanford?"

"Well, you see, they have the best minds, the best resources and, thanks to you, an abundance of classroom space."

Oh, yes, I did tell them to stop having children there. Showed them the marks on my back, told them the stories of my broken family. Locked their reproductive organs right up. Still, I'm not sending my children across the country alone. "Fine, then I'll go with them," I tell Crane.

"Not while you are in control of Phoenix, you won't. You wanted me gone now you deal with the consequences."

I exhale a frustrated breath, feel the heat rising from inside me. Ian steps toward me, his hands out as though he's going to quell an explosion.

"Then I don't want control of Phoenix. I will go where my children go," I tell him.

"Well, we might be able to work something out. You see, I desire to return to my home, to Phoenix. If you agree to relocate, I will resume my seat on the Committee and all will be well in the world."

"And Sam?"

"Sam is an adult. Let him decide his own fate."

My free hand rubs my temple. Ian drops to his knees beside me, grips my legs and mouths, "*Calm down.*"

"I take it you are still a bit emotional with all that has happened over the past few weeks?" Crane asks. "I was hoping the incident with Adam–"

"Leave me alone," I snap at him. "And don't mention his name. Ever."

Crane laughs lightly.

"Are you done?" I ask.

"Yes, well, almost. I would like to wish you well and Sam well with his wedding."

"Thanks," I respond, flatly.

"Just remember, Andromeda. Five years."

"Whatever," I mumble.

"Oh, and don't try anything rash. I'll be in touch."

I slam the phone down, feel the heat rising in my cheeks. Ian grips my hands between his, brings them to his mouth and presses his lips to them. "What did he say?" Ian asks.

"In five years, Lina will have to go to Hanford to complete her schooling. The other children when they are around sixteen."

"So what's the plan?"

"We move."

"We move?"

"In five years Crane will return to this place and resume his seat on the Committee. I don't plan on being around for it."

"What did he say about Sam?"

"Nothing. He said nothing. Which leads me to believe Sam was allowed to join the Sovereign Children's training program for other reasons."

"Like?"

I shake my head, too tired to think about it right now. "I'll have to figure that out later." I focus on Ian's brown eyes, crinkles of concern marring the corners. "What?"

"You were getting so angry, and, I swear..." Ian scoots closer on his knees. "Andie, it was like the temperature in the room went up ten degrees."

"That's impossible." I run my hand through my hair and rub the back of my neck. I can feel my body trembling a bit. "Impossible." I shake my head.

"Maybe. But..." He moves closer, pulls my hands away from my face. "Let me just try something." Ian's hands are in my hair, running down my back, pulling me to the edge of the chair I sit on, pulling me closer to him. His lips are on mine. Warm and soft, familiar. For a second I begin to melt into him and forget everything else. I forget the words of Crane and his five year warning. I forget this other child that has come into our lives. I forget the fact that Crane has altered the biologics of my body. And then, I remember we have a houseful of children.

Stopping, straightening my back and pulling away, "Are you trying to seduce me in the living room, Ian Somers?" I ask.

"Perhaps I was." He curls a strand of my hair around his finger.

Standing and pulling him up with me, I say, "Let's go to bed."

As we return to our room, I notice a lump under the sheets. Ian must also; he takes a few quick steps, reaches for the blanket and pulls it back. There lays Raven, curled up in the middle of the bed, sound asleep. A sleeping Guardian shifts in the corner of the room.

"At least we were alone in the living room," Ian points out.

--

"So, a wedding," Dr. Akiyama brings his hands together on his knees.

"First Sovereign wedding in the District." I nod at him.

Ian stands near the window, watching the Residents mill about below us with their daily duties.

"I'm assuming you will be holding a Committee meeting not long after that?" Dr. Akiyama asks.

I stand from the couch and pace to the back of the room. "About the Committee meetings, Doctor. Crane told me he would like you to take his seat until he returns."

Dr. Akiyama smiles and leans back in his chair, rolling his pen between his fingers. "And if I told you I had no desire to sit in on a Committee meeting?"

"I would say you're a liar," I reply, probably too confidently.

"You could say that, Andie. But the truth is that I have no desire to claim Crane's seat. I am happy where I am, with what I do."

"But you are the District Physician. You know the Residents, the Sovereign, you've been answering Crane's wishes since the beginning."

Dr. Akiyama tips his head in a slight nod.

"Why won't you?" I ask.

"Perhaps it's not the request to join the Committee that's deterring me, but the seat you've asked me to fill."

"Crane's?" I ask.

"Perhaps if you had asked me to fill another's seat, say, Morris' seat, I would have a different answer for you."

"I took Morris' seat." I walk toward the couch I was sitting on and grip the back of it.

"Yes, well, does it really matter what seat? A seat is a seat is a seat. When it comes down to it we're really just playing ring-around-the-rosie." He taps his pen on his knee.

I watch him as he flips through his papers for a second before making eye contact with Ian. We both move and sit down on the couch, next to each other. I take a deep breath, plant a smile on my face and ask, "Dr. Akiyama, we would like for you to take a seat at the District Committee meetings."

He looks up from his papers, smiles and says, "Yes, I would be honored." Dr. Akiyama's eyes flick to the clock on the wall. "Well, let's get down to business, shall we?" He flips through his notebook. "How is young Isaac adapting to life at the Pasture?"

"Everything seems to be fine. He seems happy. Does well in school. Doesn't cause any trouble," I reply.

"Well, he sounds like a good boy then," Dr. Akiyama writes something in his notes. "And you, Andie, how are you coping with this change?"

"I–"

"She's been perfect," Ian interrupts me. "Loving, motherly. Treats him like her own son."

"Like you treat Raven?" Dr. Akiyama asks Ian.

"Yeah," he says.

"Good," Dr. Akiyama responds.

"He doesn't seem to miss his mother," I point out. "He's very young. Most children his age would be showing some effect of being taken away from their mother and transplanted in a new family."

"Well," Dr. Akiyama shrugs. "Perhaps his mother was not very motherly."

"Oh," is the only response I can get out.

"Very good." Dr. Akiyama slaps his notebook closed, stands and says, "It seems, for now, that you no longer require my services." He gives a slight bow, checks his watch. "You have a wedding to attend soon, do you not?"

"Yes, later tonight, but–"

"Well, have a good evening. Give my wishes to the newlyweds and I will see you at the next Committee meeting."

"Okay." I stand and look at Ian.

"Okay." Ian stands and takes my hand.

"Good day," Dr. Akiyama walks to his desk, places his notebook inside and pushes his arms into his white coat. "I have patients to attend to." He nods and leaves the room.

Ian and I walk out of his office.

"That was strange," I say.

"A bit," Ian responds.

As we walk to the SUV, I can't scratch the strange conversation with Dr. Akiyama. It went up and down and full circle. I can't make sense of it or the fact that he agreed after stating so strongly that he had no desire to sit on the Committee.

Ian asks, "When do you plan on holding another Committee meeting?"

"I'm not sure. I'd like to never do it." The last thing I want is to be in charge of this place. But it's the only way to get Crane to go away. It's the only way to keep him away.

"You can't ignore this entire place. You're in charge. Crane left you in charge."

"This place runs itself, Ian. Look around us. The Residents do anything they're told. The Factions have managers to assign duties, the Volker have their rounds, and everyone does what's required of them. The Residents have been paired. Akiyama manages the ill and the expecting. I do what I can do from the Pasture."

"Just like a–" Ian starts.

"Rockwell painting," I finish for him.

"Well, no. I was going to say a creepy robot town."

"Oh." I continue our walk to the vehicle.

"What about the Survivors?" Ian asks, "And those Swamp people that we ran into?"

"As long as you maintain the fence at full power, we'll be fine." The Swamp people know what happens when they touch the fence. "Can't you just override the programming so it doesn't shut off when someone touches it?"

"Well..." Ian rubs his hands together as he thinks for a moment. "We could do that, but, right now the fence turning off is kind of like a security feature. It shuts off so the person touching it would have a chance at survival."

I remember when the man in Crystal River touched the fence. It shut off and he still fried to death. It's too much electricity flowing through the metal. "Override it. No one survives anyways."

"What if we need to leave or someone needs to get in?"

"Crane won't be showing up for five years. And he will be entering through the gateway near the train platform. The fence doesn't shut off when that entrance is used. Plus, we are self-sufficient, just like the Entities want. We grow more than enough food now that the greenhouses are up. We don't need to open the gates."

"Is that an order?" Ian asks.

I think he's half-joking but I'm serious. I stop next to the SUV, reach for the passenger side door handle. "Yes. That's an order. No one is to open the gates for five years."

Ian stops next to me. "But Marcus and Cashel are older than Lina."

"I know." That familiar unease fills my gut. But I'm in control now. I don't have to fear the repercussions of Crane in this place. I hope.

"They will need to go to Hanford before she does," Ian points out.

"They will go late, when we bring Lina. I'm not opening those gates before Crane returns."

THREE

Adam

Restless, I tap my foot on the laminate floor, trying to remember a good song to sing in my head to pass the time. Unable to decide, I turn to clicking the light on my desk on and off. Electricity. I owe Sam big for managing to secure a line of electricity from the base camp outside of Phoenix to Romney. The nuclear reactor in Phoenix puts out enough power to light up New York City, so they could spare it. Even though his sister apparently hates my guts, he still has some allegiance to the person who saved his life. She still has every right to hate me.

Annoyed with the lack of activity around here in the evening while the men eat and change shifts, I stand, ready for a long walk in the woods. Closing the door to my office and turning to leave, I stop. The formidable door where I kept her waits before me. Against my better judgment, I walk forward and kick the door open with the toe of my boot. Holding my breath, not wanting to be reminded of her smell–a bit like honey and basil, fresh baked bread–she smells like the home I haven't experienced since I was a child. The empty cot stares at me; the rust stained sink, the cool tiles of the wall. *Guilty*, it all says.

I had to do it, I tell myself. I take a shallow breath in, a bit pissed when I can't smell her. The scent lingered for a few weeks after she left, but now it's completely gone. *I need to forget them*, I remind myself.

"Boss?" Mack's hesitant voice pulls me away from the regrets I see before me.

"What?" The word comes out clipped, short. I leave the room, slam the door and vow to have it covered by a wall before next week.

"They want a meeting," Mack says, a tick in his jaw. *They*, the Swamp people. He hates them worse than I do.

Grateful for the distraction and the opportunity to pound my fist into another one of their faces, and with a new kick in my step, I head for the nearest exit. "Let's go."

We meet them at the tracks. Mack holds back, hidden in the shadows of the West Virginia forest. He's the backup I don't need, he just doesn't know it.

"We hungry. Mo manje," the one I've come to know as Glane says as I approach.

I guess it didn't faze them when I killed the last two. But this isn't the first time they've visited. I doubt it will be the last.

"I have no food for you people. You've taken too much already."

"More." Glane tips his chin.

"Find your own food."

Glane smiles. "Dem peoples up nord, dey gots food. An chil'ren." Glane licks his lips. "Dey de mos' tender. Good for eatin' off de bone."

The thought of them going near Lina and Raven, ignites a rage in me like no other. No, I can't forget them no matter how hard I try and especially not when their lives are in danger.

"Dat pretty lady dere too. Her hair be longer now. I seen her."

That's it. I grab Glane by his scrawny neck. "Stay the fuck away from them," I threaten, and at the same time I wonder how he can be so scrawny with all the food I've given them. What the hell are they doing with it all? My men are already half starved.

Glane smiles, what appears on his face is mostly black and void of teeth. "Got me lots of men who'd touch dat fence and turn off de power." I squeeze his neck. His voice becomes clogged sounding. "Mo manje." Glane's hollow eyes bore into mine. I drop him and with a feline grace he lands on his feet like I never had him strung up in the air with one hand.

"Mack!" I shout as I turn to leave.

"Boss." Mack meets me near the path that leads back to Romney, quick and silent, the reason why I chose him as my right-hand man.

"Get them half of everything we've got left. Leave it near the tracks."

"Boss, half? But there's barely enough to survive the winter," Mack replies in a controlled voice. So close to the last straw, I'm a bit surprised he's so controlled right now. I've watched him tighten his belt over the last year. All of my men have. They can have my rations since it seems I no longer hunger for food. It brought comfort for a bit, but now nothing seems to be able to fill the empty void in my center.

When we get back, I head to my room and grab my pack off the floor, a few weapons. Then it's back to find Mack and give him my orders. "I'll be back in two days. You're in charge."

"And if that cretin Glane comes back?" Mack's irritated. He knows we won't last long during the winter without that food.

"He won't. They won't."

"Adam, you're going to get yourself fucking killed, man," Mack says.

Must've pushed him over the edge. It's about time. All the times he's had to clean me up from another run in with the Swamp people and cover for my ass while I go off to recover, his expressions are past due.

"I'll be fine." I pat him hard on the shoulder. "Promise. I have to go barter."

"And if Christian Whitmarsh shows while you're gone? I mean, he's never showed his face in these parts before, but what do I tell him? You're working on his clock. We all know he's killed men for less."

"He won't show."

"How can you be so sure?"

I head for the door. "Just am." I hold up two fingers. "Two days. I'll be back."

Mack's clearly annoyed, but he nods and returns to the list of inventory that's in his hand.

I make my way toward one of our old trucks. It's rusted, a mixture of old red paint and oxidized metal. I check the gas gauge; retrieve a few gas cans from the storage garage. Unable to control the need to make sure they're all okay, I head north toward Phoenix. It's a long, lonely drive with nothing but the fight in my head to worry about. As I near Phoenix, that familiar anticipation floods me. They are all here; family, home. What I wouldn't give to have all of that again. The few short months that it was mine weren't enough.

Leaving the truck hidden in the woods a few miles away, I approach the gates of Phoenix on foot, plucking a tall piece of grass from the ground and then a large stick. I pause to pull a pencil and paper out of my pack and I write: *Get me Sam*, then secure the paper to the stick, tying the blade of grass in a simple knot. I throw it over the fence, hitting one of the Volker on the shoulder.

I wait, pacing, remembering all too well the long days during which Crane sent me to monitor the integrity of the fence. The entire fence. Miles of fence. That was a long and lonely time. Lots of time to think.

Before long Sam's tall frame appears. He gathers the Volker and sends them away so we can have some privacy. Since the hum of the fence is so loud, this is how we communicate. Otherwise I'd be bleeding from the nose and mouth trying to get close enough to hear him. Sam pulls out a piece of paper from his pocket and a pen, writes on the paper that his Volker gave him, secures it to a stick with a piece of grass and throws it effortlessly over the fence. It lands at least two hundred feet behind me. I'm surprised he didn't play football in some state college instead of going to med school. I think he was on the wrong path. I mouth, *what the hell,* to him before turning to retrieve the stick.

Pulling the grass away, I read the note he wrote.

Crane is gone. Andie's in charge. Gates are closed for five years. No one in, no one out. We'll keep the power on for you. Ian's on board. He still hates you. Just remember the deal: You keep the Swamp people away. PS. Andie's ready to crack. Why did you have to piss her off so bad?

I pull a pencil from my pack and write: *I didn't want to. Wasn't much of a choice. The deal's still good.*

Ripping a new blade of grass from the ground, I secure the note, back up and pitch it over the fence. It lands at Sam's feet. Perfect shot. He gives me an unimpressed look before bending to retrieve the note. He reads, nodding his head. Smiling, he starts writing a response.

Judging from the grin on his face, this ought to be good. Sam's always joking. He wraps the note and tosses the stick.

Retrieving it, I open the note and read: *I'm marrying your sister in three days.*

What the shit? I swallow down whatever it is that's brewing in my chest. It's not anger. Shock maybe. My baby sister, marrying Sam... Jesus Christ. It takes me a good long moment to recover, but one thought comes to the forefront of my mind: Sam's a good guy, one of the best. I couldn't have picked a better man.

I write: *Be better to her than I was. She deserves it. Keep her safe.*

I chuck the stick over the fence. Sam reads the note, and when he is done, nothing more passes between us besides a knowing look and a quick nod. I get close enough to the fence to look him in the eye good and hard then give him a thumbs up. Then I return to the truck, part of me wishing I still had a home on the other side of that fence. What man misses his baby sister's wedding? Better question, what man does what I did to the only woman he's ever loved? What kind of a man gives up on his first born son?

--

I STOP at the settlement near Phoenix before heading back to Romney. With winter coming I need an inventory from everyone around me. If they have stock to share, I need to move it around. With the Swamp people running through our rations faster than ants on honey, my men will starve this winter.

"Hey, Mr. Whitmarsh," one of the Survivors at the barricade greets me. His name's Ben. He's young, much too young to be holding a rifle and have that look about him. He's younger than I was when I went into the military.

"How are things?" I ask, gripping his hand and shaking.

"Gettin' colder. Steven says this winter'll be a bad one."

I nod. "I need to talk to Betsy and Steven about that."

"Sure, man." Ben moves the barricade out of the way.

I go back to the truck and drive through. Headed for the door of the old gas station, I glance at the sign: *Buy, Barter, Trade.* How about demand? I swing the door open, the bell on the frame jingles.

Steven looks up from behind the counter. "Long time no see."

I move to greet him. "Don't be so happy to see me just yet," I warn.

Steven takes his hand away from mine. "What now?"

"I need more food for my men."

"This is crap," Steven shakes his head. "You know we barely have enough for ourselves."

"I know. But we're keeping the Swamp people to the south. It's payment for protection. I'm just doing my job."

"Shitty job." Steven frowns.

"You have no idea."

"Betsy!" Steven hollers.

Betsy appears from the back of the store. "Yeah?" she notices me. "Oh, hey, *Adam.* How ya been?" Seems Andie calling me Adam last time we crossed through these parts wasn't lost on her. The woman has a mind of steel.

"Bets, go get Jill."

Betsy drops the smile. "Why Jill?" she asks.

"Seems Whitmarsh wants more food for his thugs."

"We're not thugs," I say.

"But Jill–"

"Get her!" Steven demands.

Shit, who the hell is Jill? I imagine it's some preteen they've been hiding away. It's not the first time one of the settlements has tried to pay me with a woman. They used to do that a lot up and down the east coast. Skin trades. I put a stop to that. If I were another man, the offer of a woman–young or old–might be a fruitful one. Too bad for them that offer is so easy for me to turn away. "Steve, man," I take a step toward him. "I don't work in the Skin trade. I put an end to that. Remember? Now I don't know who this Jill is, but I'm not taking her. I just need an inventory. Anything you can spare. That's it."

"Don't worry, *Adam.* You'll like Jill. She's got real soft hair," Steven promises.

"Jesus, Steven–" Before I can protest further, I'm interrupted by a soft bleating. Turning, I find Betsy standing at the door with a twine rope in her hand, tethered to a goat wearing a pink sweater.

"Is that a goat in a... coat?" I ask Steven, relieved it's not a fourteen year old girl at the end of the twine.

"Best damn goat in a coat you could find in these parts," Steven replies with a smirk.

"What the hell am I going to do with a goddamned goat in a coat?" I ask.

Betsy speaks up. "We've sent you goats before. Mack said the last female you had down there broke its leg and died. Lucky for you, Jill here's a female. Produces lots of milk. Find her a boy goat, feed her your front lawn, let the goats fall in love, and before you know it they'll be making baby goats. Use their milk, use their meat."

I shake my head. I don't have time for goats. "I can't take a goat."

"Take her. You'll like her," Steven promises. "Besides, our other goats don't like her. That's why she's wearing that ridiculous coat Betsy knitted for her. Can't keep her in the barn, the other females kick at her."

I shake my head. It's a good thing I brought a truck. "Fine." I shake my head. "I'll take the goat in a coat."

Fucking goat in a coat. I don't have time for this shit. Pulling the truck up to the store, I reach behind the front seat and pull out a black bag. Bartering supplies, my last. I make my way inside as Betsy leads the goat toward the truck. Steven looks at me expectantly as I set the bag on his counter.

"What's this?"

"Trade," I say, opening the bag to reveal an old pistol and a box of bullets. "I feel bad just taking the goat."

Steven frowns, pushes the bag away. "Keep it. Going to be a bad winter. You're going to need all the weapons you have."

"But you're giving me a goat."

"You're going to tell *Whitmarsh* that our inventory is zero." I don't miss the acid in his tone. Unfortunately, Steven and Betsy are now one of the few who know my alias. "We've got nothing to spare. And you're keeping those damn Swamp people out of our neck of the woods."

I freeze. "Have they been up here?"

Steven shakes his head. "Nope. But when things get rough, I'm guessing they'll come like crows to the garbage piles."

"I'll keep my eye on them."

"I'm sure you will."

I leave the store only to find Jill standing on the passenger seat of the truck.

"Jill doesn't like truck beds," Betsy says from behind me.

"Wonderful." Stomping toward the truck, I open the driver's side door and replace the bag with the gun behind my seat. Jill lets out a soft bleat as I get in. "Sit down and shut up, Jill." The goat is silent as I start the engine. I look up to see Steven and Betsy watching, and then I feel a warm, wet tongue in my ear. Steven and Betsy break out into laughter. They know who I am. They shouldn't be laughing and watching Christian Whitmarsh getting licked in the ear by a fucking goat in a coat. If this gets out it will ruin my credibility. I mime them a gesture that implies they shut their mouths, then push Jill away and drive for Romney. "Don't crap in my truck," I warn the goat.

--

"WHAT THE HELL am I supposed to do with this?" Mack asks as I hand him the free end of the twine.

"Milk her."

Mack bends, inspecting the goat. "It's wearing a sweater."

"Goat in a coat," I correct him. "Her name's Jill. Treat her real nice."

Mack straightens and glares at me. "What the hell, Adam?"

I shrug. "It's a gift from Betsy and Steven. We need food. They had a misfit goat. Have fun learning how to milk her. Maybe there's some books in the library of this place. Or find that kid who was taking care of the last one we had." The goat rubs its head against Mack's pant leg. "I think she's in love with you already, Mack. Didn't know you were such a ladies' man."

"Screw you." He turns to leave, goat in tow.

"Hey," I stop him. "Have you heard anything about what's going on south of here?"

"One day we got a newspaper from the south. Word is someone set up a printing press in their house, using it to inform people of what has been going on and where. They're taking word of mouth stories and writing them all down. Not filled with propaganda like the papers used to be, you know. This is just local stuff. Nothing about the tsunamis in Japan or the industrial revolution in China or nuclear bombs in Russia. Just stuff from America. Pretty good idea. Usually they're wrinkled and ripped by the time they get this far north. The last paper we got had a story in it about a bunch of guys down in Texas getting a rig moving over some of the oil wells. Maybe get production going again." Mack pauses to shake his head. "Shame about Canada though. Their Reformation backfired. Something about the weather, the paper had said. When the missiles hit there, what followed was a winter that an industrialized nation could barely survive. Wonder what happened to the weather? Maybe the next paper will have an explanation. So here we are. Starting over from the ground up."

"The ground up." I agree. "When's the last time we got one of those newspapers in these parts?"

Mack squints his eyes in thought. "Been a few months now."

"Okay. Thanks. Oh, get someone to clean that truck out, smells like a barn. And Jill crapped on the front seat."

Mack flips me off as he leads Jill away.

I chuckle to myself for the first time in a long while.

FOUR

Sam

Blithe's back is to me as she looks at herself in the mirror. "You sure you want to do this?" she asks.

"Yes." She twists and drapes her hair before pinning it into place. I just want to pull it all down and run my fingers through it. "Now, stop asking me that," I warn her. I know I want to do this, but I can't help but feel she's only doing it because in the game of *if-you-were-the-last-person-on-earth-who-would-you-marry?* I'm her choice. I'm not sure if I'm her first choice, her last choice, or her only choice.

"Even though I'm slightly older than you?" she asks.

"Barely older." We never talk about age, but I'm guessing she's got maybe three years on me.

She turns away from the mirror and I am speechless, almost. "Holy hell."

"You sure?" She teases, twirling in a circle so her white dress flows around her like a cloud. "This is your last chance."

Last chance be damned. "Hasn't anyone ever told you?" I move to walk toward her.

"What's that?" She smiles so sweetly.

"It's every man's dream to sleep with his teacher." I reach for her, not caring if she's in her wedding dress and there are rules to follow before a wedding. I'm done with rules.

"Sam Salk!" Blithe reaches out to slap my shoulder. I catch her wrist midair and pull her against me. As I hold her still to kiss her on the mouth, she struggles in my arms.

"Sam!" She pushes me away.

I smile when I hear her breathless voice. "What?" I whisper.

"It's bad enough you're seeing me before the wedding. But to kiss me... you're going to bring us bad luck."

Although she is quite tall and strong, it's not enough to escape me. "There's no such thing." I give in and kiss her again, pull her hard against me, loving that I can do this now without worrying if others see us.

We are interrupted by the sound of eight feet running through the house, up the stairs and into her room. When the boys find us, the room is filled with the sound of moans, yucks and barfing noises. I reach out and swat at Cashel's baseball cap. "You boys better be good for Elvis while we're gone. Or you're all going to do a week of drills at the Volker training camp," I warn as they run out of the room and downstairs, hooting and hollering.

"Oh, Sam," Blithe pulls away from me and zips her bag. "They're boys. Of course they won't be on their best behavior. I think they're more excited to have two full days off of school than the wedding."

I adjust my Volker uniform in the mirror, now that it's free. I don't miss her reflection as she frowns. "What?" I ask.

"Why do you have to wear that?" Blithe asks.

"Couldn't find a tux, or anything nice for that matter, to fit me. I didn't think you'd want to marry me dressed in a pair of hand-me-down jeans and a shirt that barely fits." Finding clothes that fit me properly has been an ongoing battle here. Seems the Phoenix District has one size and it's not tall.

"Well, you are freakishly tall. And I know you have trouble finding clothes that fit." Blithe moves to the closet and opens the door. "But if you had something nicer to wear, would you wear it?"

Watching myself in the mirror, I run a hand down my chest to flatten out my shirt. "Maybe."

Blithe appears at my side, holding a hanger. "Say there was a suit in here that might fit a man of your freakish height." She motions to the garment bag. "Would you wear it?" She smiles that innocent smile she's so good at and reaches for the zipper. "I've been saving this. Figured you might need it again in the future." She unzips the bag and pulls out the suit I wore years ago at Andie's speech to unite the Residents. The first glimpse of that suit brings a flooding of memories and it's like I am no longer standing next to Blithe on my wedding day...

--

THEN

I'M STANDING at the county line, screaming at some military woman who keeps telling me I can't cross the dividers. "You haven't sent one vehicle in there to help!" I argue.

"No one in, no one out. President Berkley's orders."

"My family is there—"

"Your family *was* there," the tight lipped woman in uniform says. "I am sorry, young man, but there are no survivors. You cannot pass."

"I have to. I *have* to. They are all I have." All I can envision is my niece, Lina, hurt or lost, and she's too young for any of this.

The lady in uniform holds her hands out as I walk toward her, ready to jump the barricades. "You cannot pass," she barks with authority.

I don't care about the words coming out of her mouth. She has to be almost a foot shorter than me, tall for a woman, but short next to me. I advance. I will pass. "I'm going," I warn her. "I will pass."

"I need help over here!" she shouts.

I run, push her out of the way and leap over the barricade. All I can hear is the wind in my ears and the sound of military men's footsteps pounding the ground as they run after me. A smile starts to spread across my face when I realize they are slower than me. I can make it. I can make it! The sharp pinch of steel piercing my back sets off a warning in my brain. And then the stinging zap hits me. The fuckers tasered me. I drop to the ground, feel my body shudder. The shadows of six men advance on me. I laugh. Six to one. I laugh harder, the adrenaline and the shock converging and making me sound a bit mad. And then I'm out.

Focusing on the drop ceiling and florescent lights above me, I wake to find that I am in a mall department store, handcuffed to a cot that's tucked between a row of washers and dryers.

"Hey!" I shout. "Get me out of here!"

After a second someone shows up. Uniform, buzz cut, wrinkled face. Military. Perfect. "What's your name, son?" he asks.

I reply with a scowl.

"Look," he exhales, "We don't really have time for this. I've got plenty to manage without one punk getting in the way. Now, what is your name?"

"Sam Salk."

"Look, Sam, I'm sorry to have to break this to you, but that entire county is a loss. A complete loss. A nuclear disaster. No one in, no one out. Berkley's orders."

"My family..." I move to sit up.

"I'm sorry, son, but there's no one left. All we can focus on now is keeping people out of there. You seen the pictures of Chernobyl in history class?" I nod, bringing my hands to my face. Only one makes it, the other is cuffed to the bed. "That's what we're looking at here. Chernobyl in upstate New York." He pauses as I rub my free hand over my face. "Who was there?" he asks.

"My sister, brother-in-law, my niece. She's only four." I cough and clear my throat, correct myself. "She was only four."

"I'm sorry for your loss." He pulls a key from his pocket and unlocks the cuff. "Come with me."

I stand, towering over this man who is supposed to be in charge. He looks up, approvingly, before leading me past rows of refrigerators, appliances and clothing. He leads me out into the main hallway of the mall.

"You want to do something? Need a place to focus all that energy?" He points to a table down the hall. "Go sign yourself up for the National Guard. We could use a big guy like you here. Plus you'll be the first to hear of any changes."

I rub my wrist and look in the opposite direction of the table. There's a whole row of military men at the door out of this place. As though he were sensing my hesitation, he says, "If you decide not to sign up, a few of my men can escort you home. And if you cause any more trouble, I'll have to ship you out, in custody. Catch my drift?" He tips his head.

"Sure." I head for the table.

--

Now

"SAM? SAM?" I hear Blithe's voice in my head. "Are you okay?" She shakes me a little. "Sam?"

I blink hard. "Yeah?" I focus on the room and bring myself back.

Blithe looks up at me with worried eyes. "You did it again," she warns. "Are you sure you want to do this? Are you sure you're ready?" She takes my hand away from the smooth fabric of the black suit.

"I'm fine." I reach for the suit with my free hand and start to change.

"Are you sure? We can wait. We don't have to do this today."

"Yeah. I'm fine." I'm not putting this off for another day. Not for another second. Whatever her reasons are for actually agreeing to this, if she loves me or not, I want her. Since the first second I laid eyes on her, I've wanted her. And a Sovereign pairing is required of us, why not make it enjoyable? At least I know my own reasons; I'm still on the fence about hers.

Blithe backs away, toward the door. "I guess I'll meet you downstairs?"

I focus on her and smile. Smiling usually settles a room. "You better."

The suit fits better than anything they've ever given me to wear here. But then, it fit perfectly on the day of my sister's speech. Walking down the stairs, the boys greet me all dressed in their nicest clothes.

"Are you ready?" Marcus asks as I reach the last step.

It's so strange the way these children talk; no slang, no mumbling, everything perfectly pronounced. You can't even hear the harsh pronunciation of vowels that's typical in upstate New York. But this is what is expected of them, the next generation of Sovereign.

Blithe isn't in the room. "Where is she?" I ask Marcus.

"Come on," he waves, "we're supposed to bring you to her."

I follow Marcus, Cashel, Ira, and Lex out of the house, down the steps of the front porch and toward the courtyard. There, in the twilight, in the center of the courtyard, stand the few people that mean the most to me: Blithe next to Elvis, her white dress flowing in the evening breeze; Andie, Ian and Lina, all standing in a row.

Astrid runs toward me, dressed in pink, one of Lina's old dresses. Her dark hair pulled back in some fancy braid that Blithe probably did. "Sam!" she whispers, her eyes wide with excitement. "They said I can walk you down the aisle!" She shoves at Lex, pushing him toward everyone else. "You boys are supposed to go wait next to Elvis."

And then I am no longer staring at the courtyard, it blurs away...

--

Then

. . .

ALL I SEE IS an empty highway, barricades built thick enough to stop a semi and our relief getting report.

"You want one?" the other guy working night shift asks me, holding out a pack of cigarettes.

"No." I wave him away.

"You s–" He stops short, eyes move to the sky and he drops the box of smokes.

I can feel it before my eyes move to the sky, a thunder that starts at my feet and moves to my chest.

"Holy shit," the other guy says just before he starts running.

The deep rumble deafens my ears. I look up and see that there's something falling out of the sky. I saw video of these in the five minutes of Guard training they rushed me through. Missiles.

Frozen, I watch as they hit the ground miles away. The reverberation through the ground knocks me to my knees. There is yelling, screaming. Getting to my feet I take a step forward ready to run.

"You are not to leave your post, soldier!" my commanding officer screams in my direction. He pulls his weapon from its holster and I know he's not playing.

Holy shit. I step back. My fight-or-flight response is off the charts.

He nods, picks up his radio and starts speaking into it.

I listen. I watch. The entire time I realize that not once do any of the missiles come within a mile radius of the barricades. Dust fills the air. The sun goes down. I stay at my post, gut twisting, afraid to be sent away and afraid to die. I can't even buy alcohol legally. I could die tonight before I ever need to get rid of my fake I.D.

I've tried to forget everything that happens next.

Walking toward my apartment, half-asleep yet half-awake, I turn onto the street only to find my building gone–demolished; a pile of rubble, dust, glass and... a figure stands there. Tall, but not as tall as I am–since few are–dark hair, shoulders slumped, head tilted down to something in his hands.

"Who are you?" I demand when I get close enough for him to hear me. It's bad enough that all my shit is wrecked, but to see this douche looting it... After the night I've just had, I might just kill him.

He turns. He's wearing black cargo pants and a black shirt, professional like SWAT or something. "Sam Salk?" he asks.

"Who are you?" I repeat. "And what are you doing here?" I walk into the rubble and reach toward him, ripping the picture out of his hand.

"Colonel Waters," he says. "I have some information for you."

"That's bullshit. Get out of here." I reach for the pistol at my hip.

"Sam, we need to talk. I know your sister, Andromeda, and your niece, Catalina. I need you to come with me."

I pause. Andie, Lina... I size this man up, my hand hovering over my weapon. He has two of his own that I can see. "I've been searching for them since the earthquakes," I tell him. "I was told they're dead." I look at the photo in my hand. The last photo I have of my dead sister. Forgetting about pulling my weapon on this guy, I twist the frame, breaking it, and pull the picture out.

"They are very much alive," Colonel Waters says. "If you want to see them again I need you to come with me."

"Where are they?" I look for any indication that he might actually be a Colonel. He's built, has a cocky air about him, commanding. He could be a Colonel.

"In Phoenix," he responds.

"There's nothing left of that town. Didn't you hear there was a nuclear meltdown after the earthquakes?" I fold the picture and start to tuck it into my shirt.

"Lies, Sam. The town is there. The people are as well. They weren't earthquakes."

Impossible. But... "How do I know you're telling me the truth? Why should I trust you?"

"Because your sister once did, and your niece, Catalina."

Pulling the picture out of my pocket, I eye the photo again, rubbing the dust off it. "You had better be telling me the truth," I say through clenched teeth, moving my arm and pointing my finger at his chest.

"You can trust me, Sam." He gives a wary look around us. I wonder if he saw the same things I saw last night. Missiles falling, our country blasted apart as I stood at the barricades and held my post like a good Guardsman. "We need to go now." He pauses, glancing at me, figuring out if he can trust me. "And you can call me Adam," he adds.

I feel something when he says those words, a tiny spark in my chest. Hope. Right now I have nothing. I have nothing left to lose. "Now," I repeat.

"Now." He nods.

And then we are running, side-by-side, around the rubble with the sounds of gunshots and screams coming from the nearby suburbs. Adam talks, telling me some crazy story about a man named Burton Crane who is using my sister to help him genetically engineer humans, humans that will be completely cooperative and docile. I want to tell him that she left the genetics field forever ago to be a nurse, but he says it again, and that hope swells a little more in my chest. Phoenix is there but he keeps calling it the Phoenix District not the town of Phoenix that I grew up in. Words fly out of his mouth; Sovereign, Residents, Volker, Factions, mind altering medication and some electrified fence. I can barely keep track of it all. And I barely give a shit about any of it since it all sounds fucking crazy. All I want is to see my sister and my niece.

This man named Adam, he stops at a train, a fucking train in the woods of all things. We stand next to it as the sun sets. "I'll get you in," he promises me. "But I have to hide you. The Volker might check the train. Come on." He leads me to the last car and opens the door. It's packed with containers labeled *rice* and *oats*. It smells like oatmeal, like someone opened a brand new container of it. It smells better than the shitty rations the Guard has been paying us with all these months since the earthquake. The Guard brought in a truck once a week and we got whatever they brought. Smelling dry oatmeal now, my mouth waters. Of all fucking things, dry oatmeal smells like a goddamned steak dinner. I look at Adam.

"You see," he says. "Food for the Residents. They're there, hundreds of them." Adam jumps up into the train car, shoves around a few of the barrels and boxes. "Back here I think will be good." He looks me up and down. "I wasn't expecting you to be so tall. Since Andie is so... short."

Yeah, he must know something about her. You can't fake that type of shock. I nod and climb into the train car.

"They might want to search the back, but I'll distract them. Just stay hidden," Adam warns. "Should be about thirty minutes until we're there."

I turn in a circle, the hope swelling a little larger. "You better not be fucking with me, man." I point at him. Then he looks at me, blue eyes blazing, serious as shit. And in that second I trust him. I trust him with my life, Andie's life, Lina's life. I trust him to take me to them.

Everyone packed up their shit and left town. Stores, people, jobs. They were scared of the radiation, they said. It could leak into the groundwater, they said. I drank the water, straight from my tap. It was fine. My brother-in-law, Ian, he works... worked at the nuke plant, said that place was built to withstand a direct missile hit. A missile never hit in that direction–everywhere else, not there. I don't believe what these people are telling us.

--

Now

"Sam!" Astrid pulls at my hand. "Sam, come on. Ms. Black is waiting for us."

I look up to see them all watching me. I focus on each of them and when I finally reach Blithe, she looks a little concerned, like she always does when this happens. It's been over a month since I've had a flashback, over a year since I've had more than one in a day. I know they worry her, so I do the thing I always do, I smile at her. And all the hope I had when Adam found me and brought me to this place, it fills my chest again, reborn as hope for the future, my future, with my wife.

"What will we call Ms. Black after you marry her?" Astrid asks.

"Mrs. Salk." I'm not taking my wife's last name like my grandparents and parents did.

"Mrs. Suck?" She twists her little face. "That's a weird name."

I laugh. "No, S-a-l-k, Salk."

"Oh." Astrid turns toward the courtyard, the boys run and stand behind Blithe in her white dress. "I guess we should go now."

"Astrid?" I ask her. "Isn't the lady the one who walks down the aisle?"

"I think so, but Andie said this would make it more special for you."

Somehow, between the time it took me to walk from the house, and the words that Elvis said, I became married. Blithe stares up at me, eyes wide. I focus. She's never looked more beautiful. Elvis cracks some joke about second thoughts.

"Hell no," I mutter. Blithe's eyes widen a bit more, she smiles. Before anyone can say anything, I kiss her; pull her off her feet and into my arms. I twirl us in a little circle while the children clap—chicks love that shit. If we had a camera, a picture of this would sit on her nightstand. Me twirling her, our lips pressed together, the little girls giggling.

Now I'm married. Now I have one more person tethered to me, one more person to protect with my life. I always planned on protecting Blithe though. I guess the only difference now is that she knows it for certain. Andie and Ian move in for hugs. Elvis slaps me hard on the back. In the distance, music starts playing. It's been so long since I've heard music. I stand there for a moment, listening to the words of some female vocalist.

"You're supposed to dance with her," Lina announces.

I laugh, pull Blithe close to me and press my forehead against hers.

"You okay, Sam?" she whispers to me. "You seem a little off."

"I'm fine." I kiss her again. "Perfect."

Out of the corner of my eye, I catch Andie whispering something in Ian's ear. He smiles. They're all smiling. This is all so goddamned fake. Before I can think anymore about it, a wonderful smell fills the air. I turn to find Elvis at the fire, laying steaks over the grates. I fucking love steak.

We eat our meal, dance some more, eat cake, and when it's time to go Elvis pats my shoulder. "Enjoy your trip," he says with a smile.

--

. . .

Then

THE TRAIN STOPS, there are voices outside. I sit and wait until the door finally opens. I think I'm going to have to start making tough decisions. From the second I stepped on this train, I left all my thoughts of still being a kid behind. In the world we lived in before I could be selfish; do what I wanted, sleep around, pay my bills late. But the Reformation, it changed me. I flex a muscle in my bicep, thankful for years spent competing in sports.

"Sam?" a hushed voice I recognize as Adam's asks.

I push a stack of boxes out of the way and stand.

"Come on," Adam motions for me to get out.

It's dark now, an almost pitch-black night. I follow Adam behind the back of the train car, to the tree line. Leaves shuffle as he pulls back a branch and walks into the forest. I follow and find that we are walking on a well-beaten path. Adam clicks on a flashlight to light the way and we walk through the forest. When we finally get to the end of the trail, he walks to an SUV parked in a small clearing.

"Get in the back," he says.

I hesitate.

"You can trust me," he promises. "Let's go."

Soon he is speeding down the road, headed for Phoenix. I watch out of the tinted windows, see all the familiar landmarks, the stores, gas stations, houses, schools. Except... it's all so dark now. Not a soul on the street, not a light on in any of the stores. As I notice the bridge ahead of us, I ask, "Hey, they don't live across the bridge. You missed their street."

"Nope." Adam shakes his head. "She's not there anymore."

"Then where is she?"

"The guy that's running this place, Crane, he's holding her in one of the campus buildings. The chemistry building. He built her a nice little apartment. Keeps her busy with research shit."

Adam speeds in that direction. He pulls into a parking lot and parks in the shadows under a tree. I follow him into a building, down stairs, down a hallway, and up another set of stairs. Just before he opens the door at the top of the stairwell he warns me, "There's a camera. If you stay tight against the wall, you'll be out of range."

I nod. When he opens the door, I press my back to the wall and follow him to a set of glass doors. The door is open and as we enter, it looks like an apartment, but the cupboards and drawers are open, blankets and pillows litter the floor.

"I thought they were supposed to be here," I ask, annoyed.

Adam runs through the space, opens doors. Somehow through it all he maintains his composure.

"Where are they?" I ask.

"They were here, but I've been gone for weeks. The last time I was here Crane caught her trying to escape. I didn't think that he would do anything to her. She's too important to him and to his plan. Then I was sent to gather supplies, food for the Residents."

I take a step into the living room, my foot falls on something soft. I move and bend to pick it up and find myself holding a small doll. "You never told me that she tried to escape," I say.

"I'm still pissed that she got caught." Adam is suddenly tense, an anger radiating off of him. "I tried to get them out of here. I tried to do something right for once. I swore I would protect them. That is what the Volker do here. We protect all Sovereign, with our lives." He stands there; still, seemingly unsure of what to do next.

"Now what?" I ask.

"Now I take you to Crane. You're officially the first Survivor to pass through the gates of the Phoenix District. It helps that you're Andie's brother. Still, you need to prepare yourself," he warns.

"For what?" I shove the doll in my pocket.

"For life inside these walls," Adam responds. "Welcome to the Phoenix District."

Something stronger than unease crashes into me.

--

. . .

Now

"Sam?" Blithe's voice breaks the memory. "Sam?" When I focus on her, her face is twisted in concern. "How many times has this happened today?" she asks, pressing a hand to my forehead. "Two?"

"Three."

Blithe frowns.

"I'm fine. It's just stress from the wedding," I say.

She steps away from me. I don't like it. I want her close, like I've always wanted her close. I check the clock. "We better get going."

I look down at her. She changed into jeans and a sweatshirt just like I asked. No woman has done that before. All the other ones were like: I'll wear this mini-skirt instead, and I always had to change my plans from nature walks and picnics to the movies. I guess she didn't really have a choice. It's not like I'm bringing her to the airport or the mall. We're going into the forest. I collect our backpacks.

We get in my SUV and I pull away from the Pasture, our hands intertwined, our bags on the backseat packed for two nights in the wilderness, alone, without children or Volker or anything Phoenix District. Just two nights, two bags, a little food and a few changes of clothes.

"Camping isn't really my first choice," Blithe says. She squeezes my hand.

"Well, there won't be much camping going on. It is our honeymoon."

"Yes, a honeymoon in the woods, every girl's dream." If I didn't catch the sarcasm in her voice I might be concerned.

The drive is short, twenty minutes after leaving the Pasture, which is good. The District is short of fuel, real short. Soon I'll be walking into town or riding a horse. I don't look forward to those days. But that will be the price I pay for living at the Pasture. At least out here I feel less like a caged animal, when I can forget about that damned electrified fence for a few minutes. I pull over to the side of the road and stop the vehicle. Checking the map one last time before reaching for the door handle, "We're here," I tell my new wife.

As we get out Blithe asks, "Where's here?"

"Camp, about a mile into the woods." I hand her a backpack and pull mine on.

"Are you sure we have enough stuff?" she asks.

I close the hatch to the SUV and lock it. "Yeah, plenty."

Taking my new wife's hand, I lead her into the woods. Side by side we walk over fallen trees, soggy ground thick with mud, soft patches of fallen pine needles. A deer watches us from a few yards away before running off. Finally we are there, the tree trunk with the ladder hammered into it. The tree house looks just like Andie described it. Up in the canopy, round and large, and definitely not a child's tree house.

Blithe and I climb the ladder.

"So what is this place?" Blithe asks as she circles around the large tree house.

I inspect the place, swipe at the cobwebs with a broom from the corner. "An old hunting camp."

"So why are we here?" She opens a cupboard and pulls out a book. "We should bring this back for Elvis," she suggests.

I glance at the book, knowing well what it's about. My mother gave that to Andie as a gift, she had an affinity for odd books. "We are here because it's the only place with some real privacy. And no. Elvis knows his stuff, bringing him that would just insult his intelligence."

She shrugs and replaces it, sighs heavily as she turns to face me.

"Just pretend it's one of those huts over the ocean in Bora Bora," I suggest as I pull out the foam sleeping mat and sleeping bag.

Blithe kicks off her boots, kneels in front of me and starts searching her bag.

"What are you looking for?" I ask.

"My vitamins."

"Vitamins?"

"Yeah."

"Where did you get vitamins?"

"Dr. Akiyama," she replies.

"Blithe," I reach out and hold her hand still. "Vitamins?"

"Yeah, you know, in case I get pregnant. I don't want the baby to have any neural tube defects or anything. Don't want to risk any serious genetic issues. You know how Crane is…"

I stand and step away from her. "Is this the only reason why you married me? So you could have a baby?" I should have known better. I didn't know her reasoning when I proposed. I didn't even give her a damn ring and she agreed in a heartbeat. I barely know who she really is. A fucking baby. I hate this place. Even if we are safe from the Survivors, the people that designed and run this place are no better.

Blithe scoots toward me. "No, Sam. Definitely not." She takes my hand. "But I have a timeline. Didn't Andie tell you? If I don't add to the Sovereign population soon, I'm out of here. They'll kick me outside the gates, or worse."

I freeze, chest numb.

"She never told you?" Blithe asks.

"Never," I say. Now I wonder if we rushed into this way too fast. My heart beats a little faster. Maybe I made a mistake.

"Everyone has their purpose in these Districts. A dual purpose. Keep the Sovereign levels adequate and do your job. If you can't do both of those, then you are no good to them. You're replaceable. I think I know why Burton Crane brought me here. It was more than just because I could teach. I was young, unmarried. And… well… you know who my brother is."

Yes, I do know who her brother is. I just watch her, wait for her to say more.

"Crane always has an alternate agenda. Before, I was pretty naïve. But now I'm beginning to see it. Sam," Blithe starts, reaching for the bottom of her sweatshirt. "I didn't just marry you to have a baby. I genuinely like you." She pulls off the sweatshirt, revealing her pale skin and a pink bra. "I have liked you for a long, long time." She moves closer, reaching for the button of her jeans. "Ever since you showed up here all busted up from the Reformation." She stands, drops her jeans and kicks out of them. "I've never felt that way about one of my students." She stops in front of me, tugs on her bun, releasing all of that long blonde hair that she always keeps pinned up. Then she reaches behind her back. I stand, grab her arm, stopping her distraction.

"One thing, Blithe." Her eyes widen at the seriousness of my voice. "You are Christian Whitmarsh's sister. I am the Phoenix District Volker Sovereign. We should be natural enemies. So tell me, my new bride, tell me why I should trust you for the rest of my life."

Her arms drop to her sides. "Oh, Sammy, you should trust me because I love you. I've loved you for years."

Is that enough? Is her confession of love enough for me? I'm not sure, I press on. "Why don't you have the same last name as him?"

She gives a little shrug. "Have you ever just wanted to disappear? Change everything and start over? My parents died. I thought my brother had died. I wanted a fresh start. So I changed my last name to Black. You know, it was simple, common. It was how I felt inside. Alone, dark, void. I had no one."

I take a step back, hold her at arm's length, try to get control of myself even though it's hard with her standing in front of me, almost naked with that lacy underwear just like I've dreamed of for years. "Just one thing," I warn her. "You're with us. You are Sovereign." I twist her arm, revealing the Phoenix District tattoo there. Holding out my wrist, I place mine alongside hers. We are Sovereign. Only the second married couple in this District. That's kind of a big deal.

"Yes. I know." She nods. "And to answer the question that you haven't asked, I hadn't spoken to Adam for years. When he showed up here I barely recognized him. We are almost ten years apart in age. He was more of a ghost than a brother. I was told he was dead, died overseas in the war. He's dead to me. Has been for years. That person he is now, I don't know him. I don't trust him. You are my family now. You and Andie and Ian and the children. Forever. I promise."

"You promise?"

"Always," she whispers.

I'm not sure if it's my crotch or my brain, but in this instant I trust her with my life. "Good answer," the words come out in a Neanderthal-like grunt as I pull her close and take her to the floor with me. I can't give her much, but this... I can give her this. I can give her love with my body, and hopefully that is enough.

. . .

--

Then

"Andromeda's little brother?" A strange smelling, orange-haired man in a suit circles me. "What did you say your name was again?"

"Sam Salk."

"Ah, yes, Sam." He stops, crosses one arm over his abdomen, his free hand scratching the side of his head. "Now what will we do with you?"

"Shouldn't we contact the other Sovereign?" Adam asks.

"No. They aren't very happy with me right now."

"May I ask why?" Adam tips his head.

"No," the man named Crane replies to Adam. He continues to watch me. "We can use you here. I can use you here."

"I want to see my sister."

"In time," Crane promises.

"How much time?"

Crane shrugs. My eyes flick to Adam, who is watching Crane intently. "There are certain rules here. Protocols that need to be followed. It seems Colonel Waters failed to follow any of them when he brought you here."

"Cra–" Adam starts.

"Enough!" Crane silences him. "Take Sam with you to your home. We will meet with the other Sovereign in the morning."

We leave the building.

"I want to see them," I urge Adam, as we walk toward his vehicle.

"I know. I do too. I just have to find out where they are."

"Wait," I grab his arm, "What about Ian?"

Adam stills, focuses on my hand. "He's not who you remember him as."

I drop my hand. "What?"

"He's at the nuclear plant. That's where Crane keeps him. But he's not the same. The medication he has been given affects the brain. He doesn't remember any of them." Adam looks up at me. "He doesn't remember Andie and Lina. He won't remember you. I've seen him. And I've seen him stand in front of her and have no idea who she is."

I pause. "What the fuck is going on here?"

"I told you most of it. You're about to learn more. Come on."

Adam brings me to the student housing on the lake. There are lights on at the homes here, men and women in uniform coming and going. "Where are we?"

"Volker housing." Adam pulls into a driveway and turns off the vehicle. "This is my place."

"Your place?"

"Yeah. Come on." He opens his door. "I'll explain what I can and in the morning we find your sister." We head toward the townhouse and as Adam opens the door he asks, "Are you hungry?"

"Starving."

I sit at the table and watch him while he moves around the kitchen cooking a dinner of frozen chicken and vegetables. My third glass of water does nothing to slow the rumbling of my stomach. Adam talks the entire time, filling me in on Crane and what Andie has been doing. It all sounds so strange. But considering the state of our country, it almost makes sense.

"In the morning," he sets a plate of food in front of me, "I have to go to Volker headquarters for a few things, then I'll take you to Morris. He'll know what to do."

"Who's Morris?" I ask around a mouthful of food.

"Another Sovereign, the sanest one of them all." Adam sets his fork down and stares at me. "How old are you, Sam?"

"Twenty." I shove a chunk of chicken breast in my mouth.

"That's good." He takes a few bites of his food and it's easy to see the wheels turning in his head. "Are you smart like your sister?"

I shrug. "I was in med school."

"Good."

"Why?"

"To get you to Andie, we need to prove that you can do something for the District. That's how we separate you from the Residents. You're young enough. Let's hope Morris can get you into the Sovereign Children's Training Program. That will get us to Andie."

"But I'm not a child." I set my fork down.

"I know that."

We finish our dinner.

"There's a bathroom upstairs on the left. A spare bedroom on the right." He looks at my Guard uniform. It's wrinkled and dusty from the run through the woods and the train ride. "I'll try to find you some clothes but you're a big guy. It might take a while to find something."

Rubbing a hand over my face, "Sure," I tell him, exhausted. "If you don't mind I'm going to crash. I've been awake for days."

"Go on," Adam says. "I'll clean this up."

I use his shower and stand under the hot stream of water for much longer than is acceptable when you're a guest at someone's house. I hope he didn't want to shower. When I'm done, I lie in his guest bed and wonder where my sister is. Unable to sleep, even though I'm exhausted, I stand, move to the window and open it. The familiar sounds of the water lapping against the rocky shoreline fills the room. I stand there, staring over the lake. Hearing a boot scrape across wood, I tip my head out the window and look down. Adam stands on his back porch, doing the same thing I am. Watching, thinking, planning.

--

THE NEXT AFTERNOON, Adam takes me to meet the old man named Morris. We walk to a nearby campus building. "What is this place?" I ask.

"School. For the Residents' children."

"They go to college?"

Adam shakes his head, tucks his hands into the pockets of his uniform. It may be gray and drab, but it looks professional and he looks serious as shit in it. "They moved all schooling out here. Little kids, big kids, job training."

I look around. The building we are headed to is large, but it doesn't seem large enough to house every kid in the county. "They cram them all in here, huh?"

"There's not as many as there used to be. In the past two years there have been a lot of deaths from illness and disease. No more medications, no more immunizations. They never told Andie when she was locked up in the chemistry building, but there was a flu outbreak the first year. Measles and pertussis next for the kids that weren't immunized. People with diabetes and heart problems didn't have their meds. They died."

"Andie and Lina didn't get sick?"

"They were locked up."

"You didn't get sick?"

"I was military. I've been loaded with vaccines that hadn't been approved. Things that can only be found in the middle of the African jungles and the gutters of India."

The wheels start churning faster in my head. "But... this won't be good. All these people, they will have primitive immune systems. They'll be like that family in the woods of Russia in the seventies, or the Native Americans, one disease from the normal population could wipe them all out."

Adam shrugs. "I don't make the rules. I just enforce them here and protect the Sovereign, make sure the fence is secure."

"That's a cop-out," I mutter. Adam glares at me so I change the subject. "So what's to stop all these people from making a million babies without birth control?"

"The population is controlled. That's what Andie does, she matches the Residents based on their genetic data. Now the population is limited. That medication they've been giving all the adults, it makes the mothers deliver early. We've had very few births in which the infants survived."

"I thought there was more to what she does?"

He raises an eyebrow. "She also makes sure the ones that are born in the future will listen to orders and do what their told. Without question."

"So they're dumb?"

"No. Just... cooperative. Very, very, cooperative."

"Seems strange."

A group of men wearing Volker uniforms jog by us.

Adam reaches for the door to the building. "I warned you. I even gave you that damned Manifesto to read. Did you read it?"

I think about the thick booklet he left on the bed. I was too tired to read last night. "Not yet."

"You better. You need to."

Our footsteps echo on the linoleum floor that's waxed within an inch of its life. There is not a speck of dust or a dirty crevice on the length of hallway we walk. "How do they keep this place so clean?" I ask.

"Everyone has their job here," Adam replies. He stops at a plain looking door and knocks.

From the other side, an aged voice answers, "Come in."

He opens the door. We walk through and are greeted by an old man. He's short and balding. What remains of his hair is grayed. He smiles one of those smiles that you can't help but trust. The wrinkles of his face reach his eyes. He stands, holds on to the desk for support as he rounds it.

"You must be Sam." He holds out a hand. When I place my palm over his, he gives a hearty handshake and doesn't let go. "I'm Morris." He stares at me a moment too long before turning to Adam. "Colonel Waters," they shake. "Seems we've got a new Resident here?"

"No. I'm thinking more of a Sovereign," Adam replies.

Morris looks at me one more time. "Well," he heaves the words out as he leans on his desk for support. "This can go two ways, good or bad." He scratches his chin, seems to drift off into though. "Crane didn't tell me he's here."

"Why not?" Adam asks.

"Let's just say, his sovereignty has been overruled for the time being. He's in a bit of a time out."

"Why?"

Morris does nothing but stare at Adam, lips pressed closed. Whatever happened while Adam was gone, he's not telling. "You think Sovereign?" he finally asks Adam.

Adam tips his head yes.

"Well, let's test him and find out." Morris reaches for the phone on his desk. "I'll call for Ms. Black."

"Who's Ms. Black?" I ask Adam.

"Sovereign teacher."

"What is this teacher going to do to me?"

"Give you a test," Adam replies.

Morris talks into the phone.

"What kind of a test?"

"To figure out if you're smart enough for the cool kids club."

"Club?"

"That was a joke." Adam crosses his arms over his chest. "Guess it wasn't funny."

"No. No it wasn't."

"Relax kid. Ms. Black is just going to test your mental abilities. I'm guessing you'll score high. Every Sovereign does."

"Let's go down the hall," Morris suggests, interrupting us as he hangs up the phone.

We leave the office, shoes echoing as we walk the length of the hall to a room at the end. Inside there are tables with chairs.

"Take whatever seat you like," Morris offers.

I sit at a table in the middle. There is a knock at the door.

"Ah, welcome!" Morris steps out and speaks to someone in the hall. After a minute he turns toward me. "Sam, this is Ms. Black," Morris introduces us.

A lady steps into the room and smiles at me. I stop, frozen in my seat. She's not really a lady; she can't be much older than me. She's tall, her hair pulled into a tight bun, eyes blue as the sky, red lips, no makeup. She's the most beautiful woman I have ever seen. And she's my teacher. Fuck. Mental abilities my ass. I'm going to fail this exam.

"I need to return to my office. Stop in and see me when you're done," Morris tells Ms. Black before leaving.

Ms. Black turns to Adam, scowling. "I need you to leave. Now," she demands.

"No." Adam crosses his arms.

"Get out of here." She waves a hand at him. "You're distracting."

"To whom?" Adam asks.

Ms. Black glares so hard it scares me. "Everyone."

Adam turns on his heel and walks out of the room, slamming the door behind him.

Ms. Black faces me. "Sorry about that." She smiles. Reaching into a bag, she pulls out papers and a pencil and sets them down in front of me. "Take all the time you need." She moves to the front of the room and sits in a chair, crossing her legs all prim and proper. Back straight, head tilted just so as she reads from the papers in her hands.

I look down at the papers she handed me. Math. Good. I'm good at math. I do the math. All fifteen pages of it. It's when I get to the reading that I start having trouble. I glance up, Ms. Black still sits there. One piece of long blonde hair has fallen out of her bun. Dear God, I can't stop imagining her naked. I shift in my seat. Hardest test ever. Then it happens, she catches me looking at her.

Who am I kidding? I wasn't looking. I was ogling, staring like a creeper, taking mental pictures.

"Is there a problem, Sam?" She pushes that piece of hair away from her face.

Not trusting myself to talk, I shake my head from side-to-side and focus on the paragraph in front of me. I close my eyes. Breathe deep. Remember that I'm here to find my sister and my niece, not a girlfriend. I've had plenty of those but none of them have ever hit me in the gut like Ms. Black.

The remainder of the test is hard, for the sole reason that I'm so distracted. I start to wonder if the test is the real test or if the other person in the room is the test. Finally, I finish. When I look up, Ms. Black is gone.

"That was fast," a soft, feminine voice says from behind me.

I stand fast and spin around.

She looks up at me. "I wasn't expecting you to be so tall. Andie is so—"

"Short." I step away from her. "I know."

She looks me up and down. "Come here, Sam." She beckons me closer with her index finger.

Dear god, I think I'm dreaming or this is a really, really bad joke. I step closer and try to shove away all those naked images of her out of my head.

"Closer," she whispers. "I have a secret to tell you and you're too tall."

I take another step closer and bend down. She is so close and she smells so good. I want to pull her hair out of that bun and sink my fingers into it. "Sam," her warm breath is in my ear. I grip the table next to me and squeeze, try to focus. "Andie and Lina are..." And then she whispers exactly where they are being held into my ear.

Ms. Black smiles, weaves around me and walks toward her bag. She opens the door. Adam is standing in the threshold, looking pissed. "Excuse me." Ms. Black brushes by him.

Adam reaches out and grabs her arm. "We need to talk."

She rips herself out of his grip. "Like hell we do." She glares at him for a half-second. "You are dead to me," she whispers under her breath.

I get the feeling that I just witnessed something personal that I shouldn't have seen. The sound of Ms. Black's shoes echo down the empty hallway. "Come on," Adam waves to me. "Let's get the hell out of here. This place gives me the creeps."

As we walk out of the building a bus pulls up and a load of children all dressed in uniform get off. They push, play, and shove. They're loud, just like normal kids.

"Why don't they act like the adults?" I ask Adam.

He glances toward the children as they enter the school. "They will. When they get old enough, if they haven't been pulled into the Sovereign Children's Training Program, they will. They're the first wave. They'll change."

We walk toward the cluster of townhouses where Adam lives. "Now what?" I ask.

"We wait."

"Wait for what? Ms. Black, she just told–"

He holds a hand up, silencing me. "Don't tell me. If she told you where they are don't you dare tell me, Sam. Not until I'm ready."

"What?" I stop. "Why?"

He stops and turns toward me. "If you tell me now, I'm going to go wherever they are. I'm going to break rules. I'm going to get us in trouble." He starts walking again at a faster pace.

"And you don't want to do that?"

Adam turns his intense gaze on me. "Hell no."

"Why? I want to see them. I have–"

"I want to see them too. But I already broke the rules bringing you here. One more slip up and it will get me nothing but dead. You don't fuck around with Crane. You wait for the others like him to fuck him over and tell you everything."

I shove my hands in my pockets. "Others..." I don't understand.

"You'll see," Adam picks up his pace, eager to get away from the campus. "Eventually you will see."

Weeks pass as Adam waits for the perfect time to bring me to them. He keeps telling me that we have to wait just another day, or just until he gets this done or that done. He's on edge the entire time. And with nothing to do I'm on edge the entire time too. Finally, when he says the moment is right, I tell him where they are. I tell him exactly what Ms. Black whispered in my ear weeks ago and Adam is out the door in a heartbeat. He doesn't even wait for me; he doesn't even close the door to his place. I run after him, swinging the front door shut as I exit the townhouse. His vehicle is already moving. I leap down the steps and run after him as he's backing out of the driveway. Pounding a fist on the hood of his SUV, I yell at him, "Wait!"

He stops, glares at me. "What the hell is taking you so long? Get in."

Ripping open the passenger side door, I throw myself into the vehicle. "What the hell, Adam? That was an asshole move, leaving me here!"

"It's not my fault you didn't move fast enough."

Adam drives down the winding country roads until we come upon a barely visible driveway, just like Ms. Black said there would be. We pass towering trees thick with leaves that block out the sun. He stops at a gate.

"You see, Sam." Adam turns to me. "I needed the code. Morris wouldn't just give it to me. He made me wait. He wanted to make sure he could trust me not to hurt her. Something happened while I was out scouting for supplies and finding you."

Adam parks the SUV and we both get out. Instantly I can tell that there is more than forest on the other side of that gate. The pungent scent of manure mars the summer air; there is a distant bleating from a goat or some other animal. As Adam rushes to open the gate it hits me, everything comes together at once. "You're in love with her, aren't you?"

He just stares at me. Blue eyes blazing, face set. He's not going to say it out loud but I can tell. He acts the same way Ian did, but... worse.

"Just promise me, Sam," Adam says. "If I don't do it, you will."

Even though I spent weeks at his place, he was hardly ever there. "I barely know you," I point out.

"You know me enough."

I take a deep breath. He's right. "Okay."

--

Now

"Sam?" A small hand is pushing at my arm.

My eyes flick open to find Blithe looking down at me. Feeling the rough boards under my back and the smooth sleeping bag around my body, I remember where I am. "What's wrong?" I ask Blithe, pulling her down to me.

"I think you were dreaming," she says, one hand trailing across my chest.

"Probably."

"Maybe you should see Dr. Akiyama when we get back," she suggests.

"No." I shake my head, pinch my nose. "No. I'll be fine."

"Sam," Blithe kisses my shoulder, "You kept saying his name."

"Whose name?"

"Adam's. You know his real name is Christian. Why do you still call him Adam?"

I focus on the ceiling and try to pull myself together.

"Sam?" she asks. "Why were you dreaming about my brother?"

Moving to sit up, Blithe moves with me, since we are tucked into the same sleeping bag. "I promised him something."

"You promised your enemy something?" she asks.

"Yeah."

"What?"

"I promised him that I would kill Burton Crane."

Blithe sighs and nods. I lie down and tuck her close to my side. "It seems everyone wants to kill him," she whispers.

"Seems so," I agree, moving my hands over her freely, possessive, just like I've always wanted to. "Blithe?"

"Yeah?"

"If you knew Raven was your nephew, why would you submit those reports to Crane?"

She stiffens. "Have you ever been so afraid that you feel like you have no choice but to do what you're told?"

My time standing at the barricades watching the world explode rushes through my mind. Yeah. I know that feeling. It's not a good one.

"I'm not proud of doing that. I didn't want to do it, but I had no one, Sam. I had no team. I had no one on my side. I only had Crane, who was threatening me every step of the way."

"What about Adam?"

"We were never close. I guess that's what time and distance did to us, we forgot who we were." She pauses, probably reliving some memory in her head. Chicks do that kind of thing while they're talking. "We barely spoke when he was here. We barely spoke when he took us to Romney. He went off and did his thing. That's what he was always doing. Off at war doing whatever they trained him to do. Killing, I guess. He never had time for me. And after our parents died, he didn't even come back to say goodbye to them. I had to handle everything myself. And then he died himself and I was free. I had no family left."

"Maybe he thought he was keeping you safe by being distant."

"I think I would have rather had a real brother. Someone I could trust. Someone to keep track of me and watch over me like Andie did for you."

Absently twisting her hair around my fingers, I ask, "Why would Crane bring you both here?"

"I don't know." She shrugs. "I can teach. Adam can kill. Two types of people that he needed here. And we're local."

Something flashes in my mind. "Are you related to Crane?"

She shakes her head. "Not that I know of. But you know people in our town. Somehow, everyone is related to someone else. So I guess it could be a possibility."

"Hm." There is a long pause. And then I say something that's been weighing heavily on my mind. Something I should have said before we got married. "I don't want children, Blithe. I don't want to see them go through what we have gone through."

She looks up at me, eyes watery. "I can understand that, Sam. But then you lose me."

I move my hand to her face, run my finger down her jaw. "I don't want to lose you."

"Then we have no choice."

--

Then

When the gates open Andie is standing there. Oversized clothes, skin yellowed, a bruised and broken nose, and... her fucking arm in a cast. There are huge ass dogs everywhere watching us, standing next to her. An army of canines. I've never seen anything so strange in my life. Andie is scared shitless. I can tell by the look on her face. I've never been so angry and I've never felt the anger flowing off of Adam as it is now. Seeing her like this, I know I will kill Crane. I will race Adam to kill Crane. And I will kill him right now if he laid a finger on my niece.

There is another man there, older and holding a gun. Adam moves toward him. I assume he is safe and ignore him for now.

"Andie," I force the word out, run toward her and pull her into my arms. "Oh my god, I thought you were dead." I crush her to my body, probably a little too hard. She lets out a squeak. At first I think it's from laughter or joy, but then I feel her through the baggy clothes she's wearing. She's skin and bones, lumps along her ribs. They're broken. She's full of broken bones. What the hell happened to her? I pull myself together. I'll wait for answers. "Where's Lina?" I move her away from me, look down at her eyes, and it's so easy to see that something is not right.

"She's in school," Andie replies, turning and pointing at a small house not far from us.

She's alive. The excitement is too much to contain. "Let's go. I can't wait to see her." I take Andie's hand and run, and that second in which she turns around to glance at Adam, I don't miss that.

We run for the house, leaping up the steps. Andie opens the door.

"Uncle Sammy!" Lina leaps from her desk, all blonde hair and green eyes and... tall. When did that happen?

"Lina! You're so big." I lift her and spin her and hug her so close. "I can't believe it. When did you get so big?" Her giggles are like Christmas bells, filled with joy. I know dudes aren't supposed to think that crap but I can't help myself. I'm just so glad she's alive! I stop, set Lina down and take a look around. Holy hell, it looks like I'm going back to elementary school. All these kids are under the age of ten and the desks are tiny. Looking toward the front of the classroom, Ms. Black stands there, her hair twisted into a tight bun, wearing slacks and a dress shirt, looking like a sexy librarian. Shit. I'm in big trouble.

"Welcome, Sam." She crosses the room and holds out a hand.

I take it, give two shakes and let go. Her skin is too soft, her hand fit too well in mine. All those horny images come flooding back. "Thanks," I reply and move away from her. At what could almost be considered a near run, I get the hell out of that Schoolhouse.

--

. . .

Now

THIS TIME BLITHE doesn't wake me up. My eyes flutter open to find the early morning sunlight filling the tree house. Blithe sleeps on her stomach with her side pressed tight against mine. I shift and move her hair away from her neck. She's all smooth, pale skin. Not all marked up like Andie. I wonder how long before they do that to another Sovereign woman, mark her up with all the District images. Even though it was months ago I can still smell her burning skin. To this day Andie's never told me why. Closing my eyes, I shake my head and try to rid myself of those memories right now. I wrap my arm around Blithe's slender waist and rest my cheek on her back.

She stirs. "Sam?"

"Yes." I press my lips to her shoulder.

"There's a giant spider over there." She points to a large black spider a few feet away that seems to be staring at us. "You need to kill it."

"Why me?" I tease, already knowing she hates spiders.

"Because you have sworn to protect me, Volker."

Reaching out, I grab my boot and slap the sole down onto the spider. "Sovereign duty fulfilled." I pull her shoulder and roll her over to face me. "Now where were we?"

She smiles as she reaches up and runs her fingers through my hair. "I think you were about to get up and make me breakfast."

"But I killed the spider," I kid. "So you should be making breakfast."

"Hm." Blithe wiggles closer to me and pulls the sleeping bag up and over her shoulder. "Guess we'll starve to death right here in this sleeping bag."

"Fine with me."

Her face turns pinched. "You were doing it again last night. Saying his name. I'm worried about you."

"I'm fine. It's just..."

"What?"

Not wanting to burden her with my thoughts and dreams, I say, "I left that guy, John Jones, in charge. I'm afraid he might burn down the Volker Headquarters."

Her hands are on my face. "You are a better liar than that, Sam," she whispers before kissing me. When she pulls away from me, her eyes are glossy. "You need to be a better liar than that if you want to survive this with me." And then a tear starts to slide down her cheek.

PART ONE

Five years later

FIVE

ANDIE

As I pull a roast out of the oven I hear footsteps in the living room. "Ian?" I shout. "Can you get me some vegetables from storage?"

"It's Isaac," a young voice so similar to Ian's answers.

My back straightens. I turn. "Oh, sorry, Isaac. You just... walk the same as your father."

Isaac shrugs and leans on the doorframe between the kitchen and the hall, studying me as I try to busy myself with getting dinner ready. I don't like being alone with Isaac. He's nine but he still carries himself like an adult. He's cocky, confident, much larger than a normal nine year old should be. And by larger, I mean he's the size of Lina and she's going to be sixteen in a few days.

"Shouldn't you be in class?" I ask him.

"Another testing day. I finished early." He steps into the room.

"Oh. So Blithe just let you go early?"

"Yeah. I told her I was going to help Elvis in the barn."

I stop reaching to get plates out of the cupboard and turn to him. "Then why are you here, Isaac?"

"Not sure." He takes another step toward me, staring intently.

He's done this before. So, I do the same thing I've done in the past: take a deep breath, plant a smile on my face, reach out and touch his shoulder. I push away those feelings that warn me something is odd about him and I say, "Isaac, son, Elvis needs you in the barn. Go there. Now."

He blinks, tips his head to the side and as though his focus has changed, he says, "Yes, Mother," and walks out of the kitchen and through the front door.

Now that I'm alone, I check the clock. It's time. I put a lid on the roast for later, slip on my boots and head for the forest. An anticipation and excitement warms me, these results could be what I've been searching for. A cure. Finally.

--

IAN GREETS me the same as he does every day after he gets home from the nuclear plant. He walks toward me, smile on his face, looking like I'm the only person in the world he wants to see today. He wraps his arms around me, pulls me close, plants a kiss on my lips, smells my hair and holds me for just a few minutes. When he pulls away, I warn him, "Something is strange about your son, Ian."

"I know," he twirls a piece of my hair around his finger.

"He did it again today. Showed up in the middle of the afternoon."

"What can I say? He's a fast test taker. It's not like he lied. Blithe always lets him go early."

I kind of dislike it when Ian defends his son. But, it's his son. I'd do the same for Lina no matter how strange she was acting. I push those thoughts and feelings away. "I know, it's just strange." I look toward the fields. "Can you tell the boys to wash up for dinner?" I ask Ian. "The girls and Sam should be here soon."

Releasing my hair, he looks around the courtyard at the picnic tables before focusing in the distance at a garden where all six boys are working. "I didn't know when I grew up I'd be living the Amish life," he says with a smirk.

"It's not the Amish life, it's the Sovereign Life," I correct him, squeezing his arm. He's still too thin, but lean with muscle. Sometimes I hear him get up in the middle of the night and leave. Just like he used to. I don't ask him where he's going. I assume it's to blow off steam, to work out or run.

Before Ian leaves, Elvis' footsteps echo behind us. "It's a good life. The boys need the labor of the fields. They are teenagers, nothing but pressure cookers waiting to explode. Sitting at a desk all day isn't helping them," Elvis says.

"Boys!" Ian shouts as he walks away from us. "Time to wash up." He looks at his watch. "Dinner's ready and Sam will be here soon with the girls."

"That will get them moving," Elvis warns with a dash of humor in his voice.

I shake my head.

"Lina's going to be sixteen soon."

I turn to him, stiffen. "Don't remind me."

"Five years is up, Andie."

"I said, don't remind me."

Elvis crosses his arms. "What's the plan? You've refused to talk about it all this time. You locked the gates for five years, refused to open them, refuse anything. Alexander is coming tonight. It's the perfect time to talk."

"I don't want to talk," I say.

"I know. But Alexander's not happy that you trapped him here for an extra five years. He wants out. He wants answers. You promised him he could go–" Elvis looks beyond my shoulder and tips his hat. "Well, if I ever saw a woman glow." His face breaks into a smile and I turn to find Blithe has walked up behind us, her stomach extended in her third term of pregnancy.

"Hey, Elvis." Blithe holds out a salad bowl and rests a hand on her stomach. Elvis takes the bowl and brings it to the table.

"How are you doing, Blithe?" I look her over as she smiles and sits.

"Fine. Great. I feel great." She shrugs.

I sit next to her. "Did Dr. Akiyama tell you if it's a boy or a girl?"

"Yeah," she smiles, "but I was going to wait until Sam has a few days off to tell everyone. He'll be upset if I tell everyone else before him. He's been so busy, you know, preparing. He hasn't been home in two nights." She frowns and twists in her seat. "Oh, he's here!"

As we stand and head for the driveway, I say, "I didn't even hear him come down the driveway."

"He's got the girls with him," she says as we walk. "He always drives excessively slow when they're in the car with him."

Lina and Astrid get out of the vehicle. Lina's carrying a bucket, most likely filled with her catch from an afternoon spent fishing at the lake. Sam gets out and jogs to Blithe's side, pulling her close and kissing her hard. "Oh! Sam," Blithe wraps her arms around him and as he nuzzles her neck she whispers in his ear.

"Mom!" Lina holds up a bucket. "We caught ten bass." She walks toward me, the wind blowing at her long blonde hair that has turned just a shade darker with her age. She's already taller than me by two inches at almost sixteen and totally oblivious to how beautiful she is.

"Great, Lina." I pull her in for a hug. "How many did Astrid catch this time?" I ask, releasing her.

Astrid shrugs. "None. I never catch any fish." She pushes a lock of dark hair behind her ear.

Reaching for Astrid, I wrap my arm around her shoulder, kiss her cheek. "One day you will. Practice makes perfect."

"Are you serious?" Sam's voice shouts. "Really?"

The girls and I turn to find Sam gripping Blithe's shoulders. She's smiling wide and nodding yes. Sam turns to us. "A girl!" In one large step he pulls all of us together into his arms. "She's having a girl, sis," he whispers in my ear. "Oh my god." His voice drops to a timbre I recognize from him as one of fear and dread. "Oh my god, it's a girl. Andie, what the hell am I going to do?"

Instantly, I know why he feels this way. He's watched what I've gone through trying to keep my own children safe. Glancing over Sam's shoulder I notice Blithe's face as her smile starts to drop, a hand moves to her stomach, her bottom lip quivers. I pat Sam hard on his back and whisper in his ear, "You're going to pull yourself together, for Blithe.

You can't let her know you're feeling like this. You're going to upset her. Now, go to your wife before she starts crying."

Sam stiffens, stands straight, a change washing over him as he pulls away. And then he is moving toward Blithe, pulling her into his arms, kissing her, whispering things that I'm sure I don't want to hear, being his sister and all.

"Come on, girls." I motion to Lina and Astrid. "Let's get ready for dinner."

We leave Sam and Blithe, heading toward the courtyard. Ian and Isaac are at our sides before we get there. "Hey, Lina! Oh, wow, look at all the fish," Isaac takes her bucket out of her hand. "When are you going to bring me with you?"

"When you're older." She ruffles his hair and shoves him away. "And not as annoying."

"That's not fair! I'm as big as you are," Isaac replies.

Ian and I exchange a quick glance.

"Yeah, but you're not old enough to be out of the Pasture without supervision." She punches his shoulder.

I look toward the picnic tables and see Raven standing there, watching. He's still never spoken a word. Never once. He passes all his tests, reads all the books that Blithe assigns and more. He spends more time in that library house than any of the other children. But still, no words. I smile at him. He focuses on Isaac, presses his lips together. Raven may look like his father, whose name I will not mention, but like me, it seems he can sense something is off with Isaac. Walking toward him, I bring him in for a hug. At eight, he's too independent, always studying and locked away with his books. Brushing his shaggy dark hair off of his forehead, I tell him, "You need a haircut, Raven." He softens, looks at me and nods. Rubbing his back, I lead him along with the rest of us toward the picnic table laid out with food.

Lina and Astrid are in line behind Elvis, filling their plates with dinner. In just a few short minutes the boys, Cashel and Marcus, are tailing her, filling their plates and following the girls to an empty picnic table. Both boys are older than Lina and Ian has already delivered a speech to them about keeping their hands off of his precious daughter. Right now they don't seem to remember a word of it. Ira and Lex trail behind the older boys but settle at the table with Elvis. Thankfully, they're a bit younger, both thirteen, and their interests still lie in Elvis's stories of Australia and the Outback. Ian and I sit down with Raven at another picnic table. Isaac wanders over to Lina's table but the older boys crowd the seats and won't let him sit.

"Call your son over here," I warn Ian. "Before he gets in a fight with the big boys again." Ian gives me a knowing look before calling him over to our table.

Isaac mopes. "I just wanted to sit with the guys." He plops down next to me and scoots very close to my side. Raven watches, chewing his dinner slowly.

"That table is full, Isaac," I point out. "Besides, your father and I would like to spend some time with you before bed. You did spend half the afternoon in the barn."

Isaac digs into his dinner. Whatever reason he had for wanting to sit with the older boys seems lost as he eats. Sam and Blithe join us. Raven's focus moves from Isaac to Blithe's abdomen that's full with child.

"You want to feel the baby?" Blithe asks Raven. He just stares. She sits next to him, takes his hand and presses it to the side of her stomach. "She's kicking." A slow smile spreads over Raven's face. Blithe removes her hand from over Raven's, he keeps his hand on her stomach, eyes wide with wonder.

When I look away from them, Ian is watching me with a smile on his face. "What?" I ask, dropping the smile.

"Number five?" he suggests, one dark brown eyebrow tilting up suggestively.

My stomach flip-flops. "Not funny." I shove a forkful of food in my mouth and chew. I swallow. "I'm too old. We're done. No."

"No what?" Sam asks around a mouthful of food.

"None of anyone's business." I fill my mouth with more food, probably too much. But it keeps them all from talking to me. I can't believe Ian would even suggest that, another child. We've had this conversation. Years ago. And now he brings it up again. What has gotten into him?

Six

ALEXANDER

THIS IS NOTHING COMPARED TO MY LAST OFFICE. IT'S spacious, but lacks the newness and brightness of the last one. But I guess that adds to the charm. My old office had a mini-fridge next to the door where I always kept a six pack of soda and an array of liquor. But thanks to Crane's rules these Districts are dry. I rub a hand over my stomach. Probably better this way. The way I drank before, I'd probably have cirrhosis by now.

There is a knock on my door.

"Come in," I yell, adjusting my cane against the desk so it doesn't fall. It seems my body has not welcomed old age.

A middle-aged man named Bob Burke walks into the office. He's dressed in the uniform of his Faction. Blue. He is a Current, manager of the hydroelectric plant on the river and medicated within an inch of his life. "Sir?" Bob asks.

"What's wrong, Bob?"

"The river level is too high. It's flooding the turbines. What do you want us to do?"

"Close the intake, Bob. And get a crew building another turbine and pipe system to handle the excess. The river will probably be high for the next few years. We can use that power in the greenhouses." He stands, question twisting his face. "What?"

"It's just..."

"What?"

"Everyone is already working. To build another turbine I'd have to–"

"Bob." I interrupt him. I could tell him to go jump off the bridge right now and he'd happily do it. This is what we've created.

"Yes, sir?" Bob asks.

"Your workers only work six-hour shifts, right?"

"Yes."

"Tell them to work nine hour shifts for the next few months. You'll have it done in no time."

Bob's face brightens as he sees the solution with clarity. "Oh. That will work. Good day, sir." He leaves the room.

I lean back in my seat and stare at the piles of papers on my desk before turning my focus out the window to watch the high river waters flow. Just a few more days, that's all I have left. Opening the drawer to my right I pull out a faded picture, the edges ragged and bent. "Soon, Janice," I whisper to the photo. "Soon I will join you. Soon I will be done. Once I say goodbye to our children."

--

THE PASTURE, as serene and beautiful as I would imagine the Elysium fields to be. This place, although it's nice to look at, it is not my Elysium, it is not my Heaven. It is meant for someone else and like the Entity she will become, Andromeda loves it here. This is her Heaven, this is her Elysium field, this is her place of solace and peace. Leaving my vehicle, I gather my cane and hobble across the crushed-stone driveway toward the courtyard. They all stand there. A roaring fire to the right, a bank of picnic tables to the left, a billion stars in the sky above them.

Oh, it is peaceful.

They are all here: Andromeda, Ian, Sam, and Elvis. The children must have been sent to bed, and Blithe, now that she is pregnant and has solidified her term here with her addition to the Sovereign population, must be sleeping as well. Part of this seems wrong, part of it seems right, but so far Crane's theory proved correct. It's too bad it all has to change so soon.

As Andromeda Somers walks toward me, her face flexed in thought, all I can think is that it's not right that she should look so young. At the age of thirty-five she should have crow's feet around her eyes, her stomach should be soft and pouched from pregnancy, there should be a hint of age to her. But as I stand here wobbling on my cane, having waited an extra five years to see the ones I love because of her, she walks toward me having no clue what she is actually capable of. And yet, it is hard to tell that she's capable of anything, as short and innocent looking as she is. She looks exactly how Crane wants her to look: appealing to the Residents and trustworthy to the Sovereign. If only they knew what she harbors inside. It is more than the pain and grief he has made her endure. Much more. And then there's the problem that she's soon to discover, Adam cannot keep away from her. The longer he is without her, the worse he becomes.

This was an unexpected factor, which almost dismantled Crane's plans. It seems there is such a thing as fate. And as much as Crane has tried to alter and flex and control it, the fibers of our being can only be stretched and twisted so far. Still, her story is one that this new world will follow for years to come. They will trust her, they will love her, they will fear her. Men will bow to her, women will live her word, and those that cross her... we have yet to see the response. I fear it will not be good.

I almost wish I hadn't come here, but it is necessary. Whatever she decides, I know I will agree to. That is what she does now, she makes people agree, she makes them bend to her wishes, whether she knows it or not. Dear God, I cannot wait to go home to die and be done with all of this.

"Alexander," she holds out a hand to greet me. Finding it hard to ever be angry with her, after all that's happened, I take her hand.

SEVEN

Adam

Hearing Jill's subtle bleating from the hallway, I move to the door and open it. Just as I suspected, Mack is headed toward me, Jill trotting behind him. "Think your girlfriend's hungry." Jill nips at Mack's fingers. He brushes her away and shoves his hands in his pockets.

"Fed her already."

"What did you feed her?"

"Vienna sausages. Last can in the place."

"Uh, I don't think that's a food goats normally eat."

Mack shrugs. "She likes them."

Jill rubs her head against Mack's leg. Mack shakes her off.

I crouch and hold a hand out. Jill trots forward, nuzzling my hand. "Aw. She just wants some love." My focus moves to the damned pink sweater she's still wearing. The neck is frayed. "Think you need to knit her a new sweater, man."

"Screw you." Mack crosses his arms. "It's a goat, not a goddamned dog."

Standing, I chuckle. "What's up?"

Mack gives me a grim look. "Ben went missing up in the settlement near Phoenix."

Damn it. "Shit."

"Yeah."

My eyes move to the boards hammered into the wall across the hall from us. I've finally stopped myself from going in there, but nothing has stopped me from thinking about her, and them. Jesus. I run a hand through my too-long hair. They're making their way north. The settlement isn't far from Phoenix. For all I know they could have already made their way there.

"What do you want to do?" Mack asks.

My focus turns to the snowstorm out the window. I can't risk a trip with the men in weather like this. Fuel's low and so is food. The weather's real screwy. North of here it's warmer, no snow. "Get a team ready just in case." The Survivors inhabiting the remains of the city will fill their stomachs for a while. I get the gut feeling that Ben was just a threat. "If anyone else goes missing let me know."

"We're not going out?" Mack actually looks disappointed; he's probably jonesing for some time away from Jill.

I point to the window. "Can't risk it in this. If it clears we'll head out. But you know the probability of recovering someone alive from them is pointless. Swamp people'd eat them alive if they're hungry enough."

"Sure, Boss. Ben was just a kid."

"I know." A kid with a gun, doing a job his family would've never let him do before the Reformation.

"Can't stand the thought of those freaks eatin' kids."

An image of Lina and Raven cloud my vision. "Me either." Somehow, I'm going to have to put an end to the Swamp people, even if I do it one by one.

Mack turns and walks away, Jill trotting at his side.

Crossing the hall, I reach between the boards hammered across the doorway and push the door open. Setting my forehead on the rough wood, it's the perfect position to look into the room and regret every decision I've ever made.

EIGHT

THEY ARE ALL HERE, WAITING FOR ME TO SAY SOMETHING, but truthfully, I have nothing left to say. I have no idea what happens next. All I know is that Crane is returning in a few days, which one exactly I am not sure of. But I do know that I will leave this place and move on.

Now I'm antsy. There are other things I'd rather be doing since the children are in bed. Things I have been doing for a few years now. Things no one else knows about except my husband. It seems I have found death. I have found a way to release myself from the curse Crane has bestowed upon me. I look them all in the eye before I speak.

"So, we open the gates when Crane shows up." Not the best way to start a speech. I clear my throat in an attempt to start over. "Five years ago, Burton Crane informed me that he would be back and that the older children will be sent to Hanford to further their education as future Sovereign. Since Lina will be sixteen in a few days this means she will go to Hanford." I look at Ian, then Sam. "Ian and I will be going with her and bringing our children."

Sam scowls.

Alexander's face is blank.

Elvis rubs his chin.

Ian takes my hand. "You all know that I can't let her go alone and I will not split my family." Alexander leans on his cane and watches me intently. "Alexander will leave with us as promised. That leaves Crane, Elvis and Sam to run the Phoenix District."

"He'll recruit more," Elvis says. "You know it."

I nod. "I'm sure he already has people. Probably from Tonopah."

"Why Tonopah?" Sam asks.

"Crystal River is still too small. So is Wolf Creek. Galena... well, I haven't been there and I haven't heard from Berkley in years. And he doesn't want anyone from Hanford."

"Why do you think that?" Alexander asks.

"Because you're all too strong willed and independent there. I'm thinking Tonopah. They are the easiest to control, even if they are designated Sovereign. They're on the Halcyon protocol. They will do whatever he wants."

"So what's the plan?" Sam asks. "Just wait for his train to show up?"

"Yes. We will pack our things. Get the older children ready to go. And since I have no desire to see Crane, we'll leave soon after he arrives." For some reason an irrational fear of opening the gates strikes me.

"You're not taking Sam?" Elvis asks.

"We can't go," Sam says. "Blithe is too close to delivering the baby."

I already spoke with Sam about coming with us, but he adamantly refuses. He keeps saying it's because Blithe is pregnant, but I can tell he's keeping something from me.

"And after she delivers?" Elvis asks.

"Sounds like you're running us out," Sam replies.

Elvis looks at Sam, then me. I know that he wants to ask why Sam won't leave, especially when he has the perfect excuse to leave. Elvis tips his hat in defeat and drops the conversation.

"So after all this and trying to force him out," Alexander asks. "Seems we've failed. He's coming back." Alexander knocks his cane into the ground a few times, thinking. "And now you're leaving, Andie. So you're giving up on this place. These Residents you've created. You're abandoning them. God knows what Crane will do when he gets here. What changes he'll make. Who he will bring to replace us all as Sovereign."

I look at Sam. Even with all of Alexander's points, I know he won't leave.

"So, Andromeda, we've failed," Alexander says.

I shake my head. "No, as long as I am nowhere near Crane, I have not failed."

"Selfish of you. And the others?" Alexander asks.

I cringe; there is a sharp pang of guilt in my chest. "I can't control every factor. I can't do it all. As long as he stays away from my children–"

"And the Residents?" Alexander asks.

"They will be fine. Crane invested so much in them he won't risk anything happening. It's his dream, after all. They will be fine. They will be fine," I repeat, more for myself than them. I don't tell him that since there is a chance I may live forever I will always be able to keep track of them.

Fed up with the direction of the conversation with Alexander, I turn to Elvis. "You think you'll be alright with us gone?" I ask him.

"Of course," he nods toward Sam. "Not being left alone or anything. Sam's here, Blithe, the younger kids. It will be good."

"Okay, there's our plan," I say, eager to end this meeting.

"We split," Sam says, crossing his arms.

"We split." I nod. "We'll make it work. We still have a way to make it back here if there's a problem."

"Well," Sam speaks up. "You'll need to come back when Blithe delivers."

Ian squeezes my hand. This is a surprise request. Sam's never mentioned it before. "Is that what you want?" I ask Sam.

"It could be nice. You could come get us after she has the baby, bring us to Hanford."

"Oh, of course." I just figured he would never want to meet us in Hanford, that he would stay here. "Of course we'll come get you."

Sam smiles. "Good." He looks toward the house he shares with Blithe. "Well, since I haven't seen my own bed for two nights, I'm headed home." Sam waves and turns to leave the group.

Elvis and Alexander say goodnight and take off, Elvis for his house and Alexander for his vehicle. Ian and I sit around the fire and wait for everyone to go to bed and to be certain that Alexander has left.

Ian stretches an arm behind me. "Sam's changed his mind?" he asks.

"Yeah."

"Nice surprise."

"I guess so. I thought he was going to stay here." I run my fingertips across my pants, itch the skin underneath. It feels tight, awkward, wrong. I want to run into the forest and swallow what I've discovered so I can feel like myself again.

"Maybe he really just wanted to wait until she delivered."

"Um hm." Elvis's lights click off. A cow from the barn bellows. "I think it's time."

"Time?"

"Come on." Standing, I take Ian's hand and lead him away from our house, toward the fields and the forest, our path lit only by the glow of the moonlight and the stars.

"Where are we going?" Ian asks.

"I have something to show you. Something I've been working on."

He pulls me to a stop. "A cure?"

"I think so."

And then we are running through the fields, past the water tower, past the graves, past the sleeping trees and the Guardians who are always watching from the forest. I pull a small flashlight out of my pocket and click it on to light our way. It's not long before the old ruins are in front of us. We slow, both of us out of breath as we walk toward the third house, the one with a roof and a hidden room underneath the floorboards. We descend the steps and I move to light the oil lamps. There's an old table that was already down here, a microscope, medical supplies from the hospital, a few crates that I was using to hold the Guardians. He knows everything that's here, he helped me stock it. Moving toward a box on the table, I open it and pull out a vial. The only one that's worked so far. All the others did nothing. But this one last vial, injecting this into a Guardian, resulted in the Guardian on the floor dying.

"I've figured it out." I hold up a vial filled with amber liquid to show Ian. "This chelates the metals of the nanocytes. Binds them together and pulls them out of the cells, then excretes them out of the body."

He turns to the deceased Guardian on the floor. When he looks to me his brow is wrinkled with worry. "How long did it take for it to die?" he asks.

I open a notebook and flip through the pages. Run my finger down the page until I find the data he's asking for. "About seven days. There was an exponential ageing rate and then death."

Ian crouches and runs his hand over the Guardian's grayed fur. "How old was it?" he asks.

I shrug. "I'm not sure."

"You don't know?"

"No."

"How did it die?"

"It just, laid down and... passed away. Peaceful and quiet."

"How long for a human, then?"

"I'm not sure," I say again.

"So you are ready to inject that into your body without knowing how long it will take for you to die?"

My jaw snaps shut. My fingers tremble over the open notebook pages.

"Andie?" Ian stands still.

"What?"

"You are ready for this? Are you ready to end all of this now?" he asks.

"Yes." I nod.

"And what if you take that and you die in one week?" He pauses. "That's all the time you want left with us? That's all the time we'd have. One week, two weeks, six weeks. You don't even know. You could die in your sleep tonight. You could die in your sleep tomorrow."

I set the vial down on the weathered table I've used as a desk. "I could die in thirty years, fifty even."

"Can you be certain?"

"No."

"Then how can you do this?" His expression is pained as he motions to the dead Guardian on the floor.

"I just want it to be over."

"Don't you want to see Lina turn sixteen? Don't you want to see Raven turn sixteen? Don't you want to see–"

"Stop it! Of course I do." I focus on the dead Guardian. It wasn't in pain as it died. I could tell. It just seemed to wither and go silently. I couldn't wish for a better, more serene death.

"Then why are you so willing to hurry this along? Why are you so quick to end this?"

"Because I can't take it anymore. I don't want Crane to be able to threaten the ones I love. He's coming back. You know what that means? You see what he's already done to us."

"But, we are leaving this place. Don't you want more time with us in Hanford?"

"Of course I do." And then my head is filled with all the images and dreams I had when I was being held in Romney, when I was so ready to go, when I was so ready to give up, when it felt right.

I take a deep breath.

When I open my eyes, Ian is walking toward me. He places his hands on my shoulders, frowns. "If you think that's best. Go ahead. But I don't think you should do it. I don't want you to do it." He is so calm as he speaks. He's always so calm. The only time I've ever seen him really worked up was the day he saw Adam and pressed a gun to his chin and threatened to kill him.

Staring at the glass vial, I only have enough for one cure. Perhaps he's right, I should make more, I should wait just a little bit longer until the children are grown and they can take care of themselves.

"You would let me do this? Now?"

He tips his head to the side. I want him to yell at me. I want him to grip my shoulders and shake me and show me that he really means it. But instead, he squeezes my shoulders and says, "I just want you to be happy. I just want you to be right."

I pick up the vial, hold it up to the light and watch the amber liquid flow as I tip it from side to side. He's right. I should wait. Placing the vial in the lidded box, I move to the soil wall, dig out a space, and press the box into the hollow space. When I turn Ian is smiling.

"What?" I ask as I flip my notebook closed.

"I'm just glad you chose us." He holds his arms out and I walk to him, just as I have the past five years.

NINE

THE DAY IS COOL, CRISP—AN OUT OF SEASON TEMPERATURE
for June. It should be hot and humid. We should be watering the fields
by the bucket. But we're not. Instead there has been a steady cool driz-
zle, much like spring. As Sam drives, leaving the comfort of the Pasture
headed for the gateway and the arrival of Crane, I can't help but feel a
stirring in the pit of my stomach, one that warns me this won't be good.
Facing Crane is never good. I rub my finger over my forearm where he
injected me with the tracking device. It turned out to be a seed pod of
nanocytes, there is no scar, no lump, just smooth skin that shows no
indication of the night I cut the device out of my arm with a paring
knife. I have yet to come to terms with my inheritance and I have yet to
tell Sam everything that Crane told me the day he released the nanocytes
into my body. Being my brother, a small part of me feels like he should
know that Crane was our great grandfather's best friend.

"You okay?" Sam asks, gripping the steering wheel.

"I think we should have brought Ian." I gaze out the window at the
passing fields.

"He's with the kids in case something happens." Sam looks at me.

"We discussed this already, Andie. We can't leave the children alone, and especially not with Blithe being so pregnant."

I nod and shift in my seat. "I know."

"Then what's wrong?" he asks.

"Burton Crane."

The rest of the ride is in silence.

Sam parks next to three other Volker SUVs. "I thought we were almost out of fuel?" I ask.

"Yeah." Sam puts the vehicle in parks and unbuckles his seatbelt.

"Why the caravan?"

"Crane is supposed to be bringing a shipment of fuel and some other things."

"Whose train is he coming on?"

"Crystal River's."

We walk toward the tree-covered trail that leads to the train platform. The Phoenix train has been moved back to make room for Crane's arrival.

"Any movement outside of the fence?" I ask Sam as I watch the tree line for the movements of the Swamp people. Since I closed the gates five years ago, we've seen evidence of them; rustling trees, dead animals thrown against the fence, piles of rocks in odd places. Since Ian changed the programming of the fence, it no longer turns off when something touches it. The squirrels and small animals that were thrown up against it barely made the lights flicker.

Looking out at the expanse of dirt before the forest, I notice none of that evidence right now. Good. I'm not sure I could deal with anything else besides Crane's arrival. If one more thing were thrown into this day, I might crack.

The dull whistle of the train pierces the air. The Volker move into place. Sam stands at my side, his hand on his weapon. The gates open, the train glides into place. I wait for the gates to close before I look away, finally able to take a breath once they are closed and the threat of the Swamp people or the Survivors is over.

The train brakes. The door opens. I hold my breath again. Burton Crane steps off the train; crisp suit, pink shirt, red hair trimmed neat and short, too short to curl. He smiles and steps aside, the shadow of another person behind him becomes visible. The shadow walks toward the edge of the train door.

"Richard?" I ask as Richard Ruiz steps off the train.

"Andie!" Richard smiles and moves toward me. "It is cold here." He says with his familiar thick accent as he stops to pull on a wool pea coat that was draped over his one arm.

When Sam nudges me with his elbow, I realize my mouth is hanging open. I snap it shut and move to hold my hand out and greet him. "Richard, what are you doing here?"

"My services were no longer required in Crystal River. And so, Mr. Crane thought it best that I relocate."

I look at Crane.

"I see you're well, Andromeda." He nods at me, making no attempt to move toward me. "And Colonel Salk." Sam moves to greet Crane and a tiny part of me wants to reach out and grab him and pull him away.

"Welcome back," Sam replies, shaking Crane's hand.

Unable to come to grips with facing the man who gifted me with immortality, I stand there in the shadow of one Richard Ruiz who looks ridiculously out of place here. I feel my cheeks redden, my heart rate pick up, an anger flows through my veins strong enough that my body is almost willing me to finally wrap my hands around Crane's speckled neck and wring it tight. It's been five years and still my dislike for him is strong.

Noticing me watching him, Crane steps away from Sam and tips his head at me. "Are you feeling ill, Andromeda?" he asks.

With perfect timing a swift wind blows, bringing the sickeningly sweet musk of Crane to my nose, and I think to tell him yes. But when I look around I notice that the Volker, Sam, and Richard are watching me closely. "I'm fine."

"Let's meet at Headquarters and we can discuss what's been going on here since I left. You," Crane points at one of the Volker. "You will drive us. Colonel Salk, you drive Andromeda."

Richard nods and heads toward Crane. Sam moves to my side and we wait until they have exited the platform and are walking to a Volker vehicle.

"Ready?" Sam asks.

I shrug. "It's not like I have a choice." I walk down the steps of the platform and make my way to Sam's vehicle.

As Sam pulls away and begins driving to town, my head floods with facts and memories and things I want to tell him. I can't stay here long.

"Sam," I start.

"What?"

"There are things I need to tell you. About Crane and our family. Important things."

"I knew you were keeping something from me. So are you going to tell me?"

"Later. Let me get this meeting with Crane over with."

"Sure."

--

SAM PARKS in front of Headquarters and I notice Crane is outside of the building, motioning to a Volker to take down the tattered Phoenix District flag. In five years I never bothered to even glance at it. But I warned him that it would get ruined being this close to the lake. When we get out of the vehicle and walk toward the building, Crane is inspecting the frayed stitching, frowning.

Richard waves, pulling his wool coat tighter across his neck, trying to ward off the cool wind coming off the lake. He stands out like a sore thumb against all of us pale northerners. He's too tan for this place.

"I was hoping you would take your assignment seriously," Crane mumbles as we come up behind him and follow him inside.

We board the elevator, Crane continuing to run his fingers over the frayed flag. An unwelcomed sudden twinge of guilt hits me. I push it away and tell myself I don't care if he's upset over the frayed flag, not after all he's done to us. The elevator dings, we exit to the familiar cubicle-lined room, the single walking lane down the middle of the room leading directly to the Committee room. Sam nods at his Volker and moves to speak to them. How boring it must be, keeping track of an entire building that is empty.

Crane opens the door to the room, we follow him inside.

"Leave us," Crane motions to Richard and Sam.

Sam's worried gaze meets my eyes. I tip my head and nod toward the door, watching as they leave, my heart beating fast. Sam won't go far. If I know him he probably has his ear pressed to the door right now. And I think I know my little brother pretty well.

Crane runs a finger across the table coated in a thick layer of dust. "Seems this room hasn't seen the light of day in a long time," he mutters before moving to open the window blinds. "Where have you been holding your Committee meetings?"

"We haven't had one in a while." I move toward the glass walled children's play area, remembering all the time Lina spent in there while Crane held his hours long meetings to decide the fate of our Residents.

"And why not?" Crane asks, obviously annoyed.

"Had no need. Everyone's on the same page. The District runs effortlessly."

"You should still be meeting monthly if not weekly. This place looks like it hasn't been touched in over a year."

I try to remember the last time we actually held a meeting here. The only person who I think has been in the building has been Sam. The last time we all met was around a roaring fire out at the Pasture. I look around the dark room. I prefer the Pasture to here.

"We will hold a meeting immediately." Crane snaps the window blinds into place and gazes over the buildings and walkways of the campus. "Call your other Sovereign," he demands.

"That won't be necessary." I walk away from the play area and rest my hands on the back of an office chair as Crane leaves the window and moves to switch on the computer at his old seat.

"Why not?" Crane asks.

"Because we are leaving."

Crane stills, his finger hovering over the power button on his computer. The corner of his mouth tips up for just a nanosecond before becoming straight again. I didn't miss the motion. He straightens. "And where do you think you are going?" he asks.

"Hanford."

"Hanford?"

I nod.

"What's in Hanford?"

"Lina turned sixteen last week. She needs to go for her schooling. I'm not sending her alone."

"I take it you haven't sent Marcus or Cashel?"

"You know I haven't. We are all leaving together."

"Why didn't you send the boys when they turned sixteen?" Crane asks.

"I closed the District gates. Forbid them to be opened. Alexander was not particularly happy with my decision. He wants to go home." I stand up a little straighter, needing to emit a bit of confidence. "Your arrival is the first time the gates have been opened in five years."

Crane's face shows a hint of surprise for just a second. "Five years and you didn't open the gates, not once?"

"Correct."

"Well, that's... that's..." I wait for him to add a word of negativity or reprimand and I steel myself for his backlash. "That's quite amazing, Andromeda." He laughs lightly. I find it hard to control my look of confusion. "I mean, five years. Crystal River almost ran themselves into the ground with their gates closed for just two years, but five... five years with nothing in and nothing out. I mean that's been unheard of in any of the Districts without oversight from me."

I cringe at his comparison of us.

"The others helped. Alexander, Sam, Ian, Dr. Akiyama."

Crane straightens. "Dr. Akiyama?" he asks. For the first time I hear surprise in his voice.

"Yes. You said he needed to be designated Sovereign."

"Yes, I did."

"So I did it."

"Hm." Crane smiles and finally pushes the power button to his computer. "So you did."

"What is Richard Ruiz really doing here?" I ask.

"What do you think he's doing here?"

I find myself squeezing the back of the office chair that's under my hands. I almost forgot how he speaks in riddles and clues. "I have no idea."

"None?"

I shake my head.

"Has Richard ever told you where he's from?" Crane asks.

Memories of our past conversations run through my mind.

"Aren't you dying in that suit?" I ask Richard.

"I'm used to it," he smiles. "I'm originally from Rio de Janeiro." His accent suddenly turns thicker, his voice dropping a few octaves as though he's just revealed a deep secret.

"Rio de Janeiro," I respond to Crane.

Crane's eyebrows rise. "And..."

Something clicks in the back of my brain and I remember that not long enough ago I stood in the principal's office at a High School in Romney, West Virginia, and Burton Crane told me a story:

"We also had to travel a lot, which made that danger uncomfortably close at times. This became apparent as Arthur and Andrea traveled back to the states to solicit a very prominent scientist and bring him back. It seems there was a drug lord in Rio de Janeiro who was rather unhappy with the intellect of his son whom we genetically altered for him. This drug lord wanted a smart son, someone to take over the family business, but what we gave him was a genius brain and drug lords have no time for a child with book smarts, they want the street smarts kind. If only we had realized this before. Sadly enough Arthur and Andrea never made it back from their last trip. They were murdered in their hotel room as they packed to leave."

"A drug lord's unwanted son," I say softly.

Crane nods.

"So how old does that make him? And... since when have you pitied anyone enough to take them under your wing? If he is the discarded son of that drug lord... he's old enough to be my grandfather. And he's the son of the man who killed my great great grandmother. How can you trust someone with such a tainted history?"

"Well, you know what they say. It's really something you should internalize; keep your friends close and..." he flips his wrist in the air, motioning away the rest of the phrase as though his words were a butterfly flitting away instead of finishing what he was saying.

I cross my arms and scoff. "Seriously. You take pity on no one. You expect me to believe that you have been dragging him around for a hundred years because you feel bad that you genetically engineered him to be too smart for his drug dealing family?"

Crane shrugs and continues to watch me.

"No." I shake my head. "You brought him here because you want me to think that you might actually have an ounce of compassion in your body." Feeling my cheeks redden and my fingertips tingle, I take a deep breath to try and calm myself. It doesn't work. I look at my hands, discouraged with this sudden inability to control my emotions.

"Are you feeling ill, Andromeda?" Crane asks, tipping his head to the side as though he's studying me.

"Stop asking me that!" I run a hand through my hair and take a few quick paces around the room. Turning to face Crane, I point an accusatory finger in his direction. "I don't care who you drag around with you. You do not have a heart. You don't care about a soul. You killed millions of people. You tried to ruin my family. I rid myself of you for five years..." Oh, the anger rises in my chest. "Do you know what it's like to feel freedom for five whole years and then to have you return and screw my life up again?"

"Are you sure you're feeling all right?" Crane asks, smiling.

"Shut up!" I make my way to the door. "I can't look at you. I can't be around you. I hate you, Crane. I hate you with every fiber of my being and I will never forgive you for what you've done to us! You've taken away the only home I've known." I whip the door open only to find Sam and Richard standing there with surprised expressions. "I'm taking my family out of here. Right now. We are leaving."

"If that is what you think you need to do, Andromeda." Crane's voice is irritatingly composed. "You may go to Hanford. Take your family. But you cannot rid yourself of Phoenix. It is your home after all. You belong here."

"I'm sorry, Richard," I say as I pass him, knowing that I am cutting a reunion with him short and I will probably never speak to him again.

"Let's go." I take Sam's sleeve, dragging him past the empty cubicles and toward the elevator.

As the elevator doors close, I notice Crane and Richard watching us go. I don't miss the moment that Crane reaches out, patting Richard on his shoulder. A fatherly gesture? I'm not sure. But I am sure that Crane does not have a heart. He's a sociopath. There's no way he gives a crap about Richard, even if his parents filled their order form out wrong for their genetically modified baby. Crane would never take responsibility for him out of guilt. There has to be something else.

"You done fuming?" Sam's voice breaks my thoughts. He rubs his chest and grimaces.

"What's wrong with you?" I ask.

"Nothing. Must've done too many push-ups. So what's wrong with you?"

"I'm not talking in this building." We exit the elevator and head for Sam's vehicle. "Let's go home. We have a lot of packing to do."

Crane has no heart. He is heartless. That is my mantra for the drive home. Sam pulls into the Pasture and puts his vehicle in park.

"You can't stay here with him, Sam," I say as I unbuckle and reach for the door handle.

Sam grabs my arm "I'm not going with you, Andie," he says, serious as ever.

"You can't stay here with him. He hasn't changed. Five years and he's still the same. I bet if I stayed in that room any longer he would have been worse. He would have been doling out punishments and screwing up our lives even more."

Sam shakes his head from side-to-side.

I move to get out of the SUV and meet Sam as he's exiting the driver's side. "Sam, come with us," I beg him.

"I can't." He stills, crosses his arms in the intimidating manner I instructed him to years ago. "I have to stay here and kill him."

"He can't be killed." I shake my head. "You can't kill him, Sam."

And then everything comes flooding out of my mouth. The story Crane told me in West Virginia about our family, the nanocytes, and who Richard really is. When I'm done, Sam just looks at me, unsurprised. There's a beat before he speaks and says, "Then I'll wait. I'll keep track of him. He can't be loose and free to do whatever he wants. You need someone on the inside, Andie. And that guy's going to be me. For as long as I can do it."

"Don't sacrifice yourself for his cause. It's not worth it. Get Blithe and your unborn daughter out of here."

"For the fate of the world, the fate of my family, I'd say it's worth it. I'm not going to stand by and watch him ruin us all."

"I'm leaving," I warn him.

"I know." Sam pulls me in for a tight hug. He presses his lips to the top of my head and squeezes hard. "You better go pack your shit. I'll go get Alexander. He's been waiting for this day for five years."

Tears threatening at the corners of my eyes, I take off running for the farmhouse where Ian is awaiting my return.

TEN

I CAN NEVER GET OVER HOW DESOLATE HANFORD LOOKS AT first glance. There's nothing but barren land, miles and miles of sand, and that half-burned school. Having not left the gates of Phoenix in years, the children spent the train trip glued to the windows and hyper. We've brought eight Guardians. One for each of us. And then there's Alexander, sitting still the entire time with a blanket across his lap and his cane in his hand. He hasn't said a word, but a few times I've noticed the corner of his mouth twitching, threatening to display a small smile. It seems he is as grateful as I am to get out of Phoenix.

George greets us at the train platform. Khaki pants, red shirt, glasses that seem to melt down his nose. Good old George. He smiles, same row of crooked teeth, same Hanford District brand of the atom on his right wrist. "Andie!" He greets me with a tight grip of a handshake. "It's been too long."

"George," I smile at him. Ian is at my side in a heartbeat. I introduce them. "This is my husband, Ian. Ian, this is George Crossbender." They shake, and afterwards I introduce the children, all six of them.

Alexander steps forward and extends an arm. Leaning heavily on his cane, he looks exhausted.

George doesn't move to take his hand. "Alexander." He nods. "Welcome back. Well," George pushes his glasses up and starts for the stairs. "We better get you all settled before bed. I'll send someone up to get your things."

"There's not much, George," Ian says. "Just clothes and a computer. We can probably take it all now."

George turns. "Oh, that's all?" He looks at me.

"That's all we brought. Clothing. That's all we really had," I say. "Is that a problem?"

"Well, no, we'll just have to get some furniture together. Shouldn't be a problem."

We get our bags and George takes the box with my computer. We follow him to the elevator hidden in the ruins. And to my surprise he pushes the last button. The elevator drops. Being full of humans, bags, and giant dogs, we barely budge as the elevator jerks to the left just before coming to a complete stop.

"Here we are." George holds the door open as we unload. "Let's just set your things here." He bends and leaves the box with my computer on the floor next to the wall. "And the children will need to go to the testing center."

The children walk to the center of the large open hall where we stand and look up. It's open, all the way to the top level. I move toward them and follow their gazes. Hundreds of faces stare down at us. "But we already sent their test scores," I tell George.

From the corner of my eye, I catch Alexander wandering away just like he did last time we were here. He doesn't even say goodbye.

George doesn't get to answer, the open area is filled with the sound of voices shouting *hello* and *hey* and *welcome*. I wave, they get louder. "Say hello," I urge the children. They wave, all of them except for Raven. The crowd above us gets even louder. Ian moves behind me. When the noise finally dies down, we move away from the openness.

George clears his throat. "We're excited you're all here. But we have different testing and schooling methods from what you've had in Phoenix. Follow me." He heads down a hallway, turns a corner, opens a door. It's all concrete. Gray, dull concrete. However far we are under-ground it's hard not to think of everything above us. The Guardians follow us as we move down the hall.

"Mom," Lina says from my side. "You're not going to leave us alone down here, are you?"

"You'll be fine. We'll be close," I assure her. "Promise."

Raven stares. Isaac walks around the room excitedly. Marcus and Cashel look a little lost. I think they miss Blithe and Sam and home. There is a lady there who George introduces as the proctor for their exams, a plain looking lady named Janet. As we leave the room I can't help but feel each of their eyes on us, begging us not to leave them.

"Come," George directs us down the hall. "I'll show you to your living quarters."

George makes small talk, and as he and Ian talk nuclear reactors I take in my surroundings. The windowless, gray walls and the dark cement flooring. Sterile and cold. I already miss the openness of the Pasture. We take the underground rail, walk into the depths of the earth a little more before George comes to a white door. Pushing it open, we walk inside. It looks like an apartment. An underground apartment.

I stop in my tracks. "I can't live underground, George."

"It's safer underground." He pushes up his glasses. "Closer to the school and the rail."

I shake my head, look to Ian. "No. I can't do it. I won't." I feel my cheeks getting red.

"It's not a good idea," Ian adds.

George crosses his arms and looks around the hallway. "Okay, well..." One hand moves to his chin and rubs the skin there. "There is one place, but, I'm not sure if you'll like it."

He takes us along the rail, back to the mall-like portion where all the classrooms are. We follow him to the top level, the level just below the ground. George takes us down a long hallway.

"I'm not sure if this might suit you. It was really meant as more of a scientific classroom. But it's equipped with water, a kitchen, lots of space. The offices could be used as bedrooms." He stops at a plain looking door, inserts a key and turns. "If you can get over the ceiling. We needed the room to have a lot of natural light. But it doesn't really let in a lot, just enough to not really need electric lights."

We step into the room which it seems to be illuminated by an amber light having no source.

I look to George, he points up with a shrug. The entire ceiling is just the same as it is in the Artillery Research Unit, some thick Plexiglas material with a thin coating of sand above it.

"So, what do you think?" George asks. "There are private offices along that wall," he points across the room to where I see six brown doors. "They could be bedrooms. Some wall dividers to separate the space. It's still close to the schools. Ian will have to travel a little further to the nuclear reactor, but..."

Ian grips my elbow and nods his head in approval. "Yeah," I tell George. "Yes, I think this could be perfect."

"Okay," George smiles. "Great. Well, let's get your things and the children should be done with their testing by now. I'll put in the call to get some furniture moved in here for tonight. There's already two bathrooms in the lab... I mean apartment, and the safety showers can be easily converted into regular showers. We'll have your living quarters set in no time."

We walk toward the elevator. I pull the neck of my blouse away from my body as he presses the button for the bottom floor. "I didn't know you were claustrophobic," George says as he turns to face me. "Didn't notice that last time."

"I'm not usually..." I don't ever remember being that way. Maybe it's the two times I've been held against my will in small spaces and the openness of the Pasture. Maybe that's why.

The elevator dings and we get off.

"Well, why don't you both get the children and I will make some calls and get some furniture up there before nightfall."

"Sure," Ian says, taking my hand as we walk down the hall.

"I'll stop by soon," George waves before he turns and walks down the hall in the opposite direction.

Ian and I walk toward the room where we left the children. It's still closed. From the hall we can hear Isaac's voice. "Why won't you let us go? All we had to do was take a test. We want to leave." We can hear the hushed tones of an adult speaking. Then it's Isaac's voice again, "Where's my Dad? I want to leave. I'm done."

I give Ian a look. "He must've finished," Ian says. "He's used to Blithe letting him go early."

"I guess–" I start to say, but there is a loud thud from against the door.

"Where's my mom?" Isaac's voice shouts. "Open the door!"

Ian and I both run for the door. Ian turns the door handle. "It's locked."

I pound on the door with my fist. "Hey," I shout, "Open up!" Ian bangs on the door and twists the door handle. It opens with a sudden jerk. The proctor, Janet, stands there, a grim look on her face.

"What's going on in here?" Ian demands. We step into the room. Isaac rushes us and throws his arms around my waist. I look around to see the other children staring at us. Astrid's bottom lip quivers and Marcus glares at the back of Janet's head. "What happened?" Ian asks.

I run a hand over Isaac's hair. "Why was the door locked?" I ask.

Janet takes a step back and straightens her shoulders. "Well we couldn't have them all running loose in the hallways. Not without a proper guide. There are rules here that are meant to be followed."

"Why do my children need a guide?" I ask. "The other children roam free here. I've seen them."

Janet smoothes her hands over her shirt, in an effort to calm herself it seems. "These children are not to be left without a guide. Not yet. They are too new here. They don't understand the rules."

"George never mentioned any rules to me." I shoot a concerned look at Ian.

"Are they done with the testing?" Ian asks.

"Why, yes–"

"Good." He doesn't let her finish. "Come on, let's go."

The children rush out of the room, making extra effort to weave around Janet. When I am the last one standing in the room, I turn toward Janet. "What happened in here?"

"What makes you think anything happened?"

I take a step toward her. "Don't lie to me. Don't you know who I am?"

"Of course, you're–"

"I suggest you stay away from them." I pause, take a deep breath. "Stay away from my children. All of them."

"Why... why yes, of course, whatever you want." Janet backs away from me.

I turn to leave, stopping just as I close the door. "I will be discussing this with George."

Janet just watches me, not saying another word.

Leaving the room, I catch up with Ian and the children, who are already halfway down the hall.

"What happened in there?" I ask Lina.

She opens her mouth to speak, but Marcus interrupts her, "We just took a test. That's all." He gives Lina a look as we reach the elevator. Isaac pushes the button to call it.

"And?" Ian asks.

"They said they are assigning us Apprenticeships," Cashel adds. Marcus glares at him.

"Apprenticeships?" Ian asks.

Lina nods. The elevator doors open and we all get on with one of the Guardians trotting behind us.

"They're splitting us all up," Astrid blurts out, her eyes glistening with impending tears.

"What do you mean?" I ask.

"Making us go to different classes. That's what Janet said. Since we're all different ages, we can't be taught in the same classroom anymore," Lina says as she puts an arm around Astrid's shoulders. "They are splitting us up. It's not fair. We don't know anyone else here."

Feeling a hand wrap around my arm I turn to find Raven standing close by my side, staring up at me with those blue eyes. I've come to understand his actions, the looks he makes. Even though he doesn't speak, it's enough for communication. He's worried. And I'm betting there's something the children aren't telling me.

We get off the elevator and bring the children to the new apartment.

"Okay, kids," Ian says as he opens the door. "Welcome to our new home sweet home."

The children filter in; Raven, Astrid, and Isaac seem slightly impressed with the place. Marcus, Cashel and Lina look a little disappointed. I can understand why. It looks cold and sterile, not comfortable like the farmhouses we've been living in for years.

I notice our belongings are sitting in the middle of the room with the boxes with my computer. I pick up my computer and move it to the kitchen countertop. The kitchen is really nothing but poured concrete and laminated cupboards. It reminds me of my college labs. I run a hand over the dark countertops.

Ian knocks on the island counter. "Concrete. Sturdy."

"Better than living twenty stories underground," I say.

"They were going to make us live underground?" Astrid asks.

I nod.

"How did we wind up in this place, then?" Marcus asks.

"I told George I wasn't living underground," I say.

"Thank God," Lina sighs.

Raven searches the open space. I know what he's doing, looking for the quietest spot, a place to read and store his books. Well, the few that he brought with us. He searches the pile of bags for his belongings, pulling out his bag; he takes it to the office on the far side of the room, away from everyone.

There is a knock on the door. Ian answers it. When he steps to the side, a steady stream of people brings in tables, chairs, beds and mattresses, desks. Everything a family of eight would need. George shows up last. "We have a dining hall. For dinner. Almost all of our members converge there in the evenings." He looks around the space. With all the furniture it now looks a bit cluttered and askew. "But, if you want to take tonight to settle in, I had some foodstuffs delivered."

"Thank you, George," Ian says as he moves to shake George's hand. "You've done so much for us already. But I think for tonight we'll stay in."

"Fine, fine," George responds. "It's open for breakfast and lunch also. There's a map of the place next to your phone. Not the entire District, but what you need to know about." I give him a questioning look since I didn't notice a phone. George points to the wall. "Over there." I notice near the front door there is a white wall phone with a pamphlet pinned next to it.

Smiling at him, I reply, "Great, thanks so much."

George pauses just before he closes the door. "Oh, just one thing. The curfew."

"Curfew?" Ian and I ask at the same time.

"At nine. All Sovereign and the few Residents we have here are to be secure in their living quarters."

"Why is that?" I ask.

"We can discuss it later." He glances at the children.

"I expect to."

"And I'll have someone deliver uniforms by morning."

"For who?"

"The children. Everyone else here wears uniforms. They look out of place in the clothing you brought from Phoenix. We try to keep things as consistent as possible with the least amount of distractions."

"Well... do you need to know their sizes?"

"No. Those were sent along with their educational records."

"Oh." That's a bit strange that none of this was ever mentioned to me. I shake it off. Of all of the things to worry about, what size clothing the children might wear is the least of it. "Okay." I nod.

"Goodnight," George waves and closes the door.

"Goodnight," Ian and I both reply before the door closes. Ian takes two steps and reaching forward, he locks the door.

Marcus and Cashel, being young strong boys, help us move the furniture around. Lina searches the bags that were dropped off, stocks the refrigerator and cupboards. After a few hours there is another knock on the door and when I open it, there is simply a box sitting there. I open it to find khaki colored pants and dark blue shirts. Uniforms for the children.

When all the children are in their own beds, Ian checks the lock on the front door. I move to switch off the lights. The action does not leave us in darkness. The glow of the moon fills the room, shapes play across the floor as the wind pushes the sand around on the Plexiglass-like material that is our roof. Ian walks toward me, the shadows now playing across his face, distorting his features.

"Six kids," he whispers.

"Six kids," I respond.

"And us." He reaches out and touches my cheek. "Aren't you glad you chose us?"

I tip my head in question.

"Instead of the vial," he says.

"Of course." I step forward and press a kiss to Ian's chin. "Always." But I haven't forgotten about the vial. I need the vial. And my notes.

--

THE MORNING BRINGS a flurry of activity. The pamphlet George left indicates that the cafeteria is only open for breakfast from seven to nine but we are still on our old schedule from the Pasture, used to doing our own thing and moving at our own pace. By the time everyone is dressed it's already ten to nine. We settle for toast and some boiled oats.

As Ian hands out everyone's plates, Isaac looks at his oats and makes a face. "This is gross."

"It's oatmeal," Astrid says.

"Not like we usually have," Isaac argues.

"There's no honey," I add. "Or milk." I exhale a frustrated breath and close the small refrigerator.

"No coffee, either," Ian says.

I run my fingertips across my forehead, already feeling a headache from a lack of caffeine. Maybe they'll have some in the cafeteria. If not... I guess it's about time I drop that addiction. It's surprising I've kept it up this long, considering the state of the world.

There is a knock at the door. Ian moves to open it and as he swings the door wide, over his shoulder I can see George's shaggy brown hair. There's someone else with him. As I get up from the table and walk toward them, Ian steps aside and I see George there with a young man.

"Good morning, Andie. I want to introduce you to Kevin. He will be the children's escort until they become familiar with this place. And well, I was planning on Janet doing it, but for some reason she adamantly refuses."

Kevin waves. He's young, probably the same age as Cashel and Marcus.

"Nice to meet you, Kevin." Ian reaches out to shake his hand, squeezing it for a second too long.

"No need to worry," George says as he focuses on Ian and Kevin's clasped hands. "Kevin is one of our brightest young minds here. He can be trusted."

Ian drops Kevin's hand. "Good."

"Let me get the children," I say. As I turn my back, I hear George talking to Ian about the location of the nuclear reactor.

When I get to the table, barely any of the kids have touched their breakfast. Hopefully their lunches will be more appetizing. "Come on guys." Raven leans around the side of me to get a good look at everyone standing near the door. "Time for school."

We all move toward the door, Isaac chattering away as usual, "Who are you?" he asks as he walks toward Kevin.

"I'm Kevin." Kevin waves, a pink flush spreading across his pale cheeks as he focuses on Lina.

Ian slaps Kevin hard on the shoulder. In an instant it seems to bring him back into focus. Kevin looks at all the other kids. Marcus steps up to him and crosses his arms. Marcus is taller by at least three inches. And just as Elvis warned, it seems Kevin noticing Lina has done nothing but bring out the protective nature of Marcus and Cashel. "You're Kevin," Marcus says, sizing him up.

Kevin's cheeks blush again.

Cashel steps next to Lina, knocking Astrid out of the way.

"Stupid boys," Astrid complains.

Lina stops. I tug at her shirt and when she turns I pull her in for a hug. "I'll see you tonight." I kiss her cheek and then do the same for Astrid, Isaac, and Raven. When the teenage boys are done doing whatever it is teenage boys do when they meet for the first time–assessing their ranks, I assume–the children file out the door.

"Have a good first day at school!" Ian tells them.

A few of the Guardians follow the children down the hall.

George turns to us. "Are you ready for work, Ian? I can walk you to the rail platform. Andie could come with us, unless…" he glances around our living space, "she wants to stay here and settle in."

Ian presses a hand down his chest, flattening his button-down shirt. It's an old plaid shirt in hues of blue, with the worn jeans and boots. He looks a bit country. He looks at me and tips his head, inviting. "Sure," he says to George.

"I'll go. Just let me put these plates in the sink." I move to clean up the table, feeling a little guilty about the wasted food. We never wasted anything in Phoenix and whatever wasn't eaten was fed to the pigs. That makes me wonder. "You have any livestock here?" I ask over my shoulder, scraping the oats and toast onto one plate.

"Of course we do," George replies.

I set the plates down and turn to leave. As I dry my hands on a towel I look down at myself. I look no better than Ian in my jeans, boots and a black shirt. "Maybe we could get some bins for the scraps?" I ask.

"If you'd like," George replies. "We have them in the dining hall. But I see you didn't make it there this morning."

"Maybe for dinner," I reply as we walk out the door. "Getting organized this morning took a little longer than usual. We aren't used to the time change." Ian takes my hand as we walk; he gives it a light squeeze. "It's not easy moving across the country with six kids. I think they miss home."

"I think the boys miss Blithe," Ian adds. "And Sam."

George uses an index finger to push up his glasses. "Understandable. And you both? How has the move been?"

"It's the first night," I say. "We'll see how it progresses." There is a moment of silence between us as we walk, and I say, "There is one thing, George."

He slows a bit as we walk as though he's expecting this.

"That lady, Janet, she locked the kids in that room. They couldn't get out and we couldn't get in."

"Well, that explains why she refused to escort them to their classrooms today. What did you say to her, Andie?" George asks.

"I told her to stay away from my children."

"Well then," George replies. "I guess she listened."

We walk down the hallway, coming to the portion I recognize from the first time I was here. I peer into what I thought were store windows then, each space is filled with people sitting at desks.

"The older students are on this level. No doubt Marcus is in one of these classrooms," George says. "The other children will be on the lower levels. Cashel is one floor down, Lina the next under that. It goes in order of grade level. But since the birth rate has been zero the past eight years the lower levels of the educational facility are empty. We've converted that space into work spaces and rooms for training."

The hallway seems to extend forever until we come upon an elevator. George presses the down button and we descend further into the earth. This time, when the doors open, we are at the underground train platform.

"The last stop on the train is the nuclear power plant," George tells Ian. "One of the engineers will be there to meet you. His name is James Ford, about your height, brown hair, red shirt. He's expecting you."

"You want me to go with you?" I ask Ian.

He leans in, kissing me. "No, I'm a big boy. I'll see you tonight."

There is a deep rumble as the train arrives. A few people get off before Ian steps onto the subway car. He turns and waves. I watch as the subway train pulls away and disappears into a tunnel.

"So, Andie." George smiles. "What would you like to do? See the labs? They could use you, or you could teach."

Narrowing my eyes on him, I say, "I want you to tell me more about Hanford. It seems things have changed since I was last here."

George shifts on his feet. "Come with me. We can talk in my office."

We return to the elevator. George presses a button for the fifth floor. When we get off, we walk side-by-side down long hallways with closed doors. A bell rings, the doors open and the halls flood with children.

"Change of class," George says as he weaves around the children.

"Hey, hey," I hear a familiar voice. Turning I find Isaac running toward me. "Hey, Mom!" He throws his arms around my waist. "I didn't know you would be here."

"I didn't plan on it." Patting his back, I notice Raven walk up behind him.

"Are you in the same class?" I ask Raven. He just stares and presses his lips together. I never knew an eight year old could be so brooding.

But that's been Raven, since the day he was born. "Well, you better get back to class, Isaac."

"Yes," George adds, looking at his watch. "They only have three minutes between classes."

"Okay." Isaac looks up at me with a smile. "See you when we're done."

The boys walk down the hall and both enter the same room just as another bell rings.

George clears his throat. "So," he starts, "can you tell me why Isaac is so tall for a nine year old?"

I shrug. "I have no clue."

"But he's your son."

"I didn't give birth to him." I turn and start walking in our original direction.

"But he looks just like Ian," George says. "I mean, *exactly* like Ian."

"I know this."

"And he's a little–"

"I know," I cut him off. I don't need him to finish. I could fill in that blank with a variety of words: strange, odd, peculiar. It's like there's something inside him waiting to be released. I could feel it each time he showed up at the farmhouse home early from class, standing in the doorway and staring at me.

We start walking again. George adds, "And Raven, he still never speaks?"

"Never."

"Never?" he asks.

"Never."

George pulls a key from his pocket, unlocks the door and opens it. "My office." He waves me in.

"Have you heard from Alexander?" I ask as I walk into the room and George closes the door. "He just took off when we got here. I haven't heard from him since."

"Probably won't," George replies.

"Why?"

"Alexander came here for one thing and that's to tell his children goodbye before he dies."

I flinch.

"What's wrong?" George walks around the side of his desk.

"I was just thinking how I made Alexander wait an extra five years before he could come home. I feel a little guilty about that. He could have spent that time with his family."

"You know Crane would have never let him leave," George points out.

"Yeah, I know."

Looking around, the room is the same as the last time I was here. Except I think his office was above ground then, it's hard to remember. All that time seems to blur together. Small, cluttered, papers strewn about his desk. The map of North America still hangs on his wall. It's different now, the Districts are indicated with red lines around their borders. I recognize that much.

"George..." I start to ask, stepping toward the map. "What happened to Canada? You only have the U.S. Districts marked here." When he doesn't answer, I turn and find him staring at the map with both of his index fingers pressed to his lips, creating a V-shape. "George?"

He waves a hand. "It was bad."

"What do you mean by *bad*?"

"Too sparsely populated, the places that had a dense population were taken out. Just like in the U.S. That left a few stragglers out in the territories, tiny towns... and that first winter." He makes a strange quirky motion that suggests something between grief and anger. "It was bad here, it was bad in Phoenix." I remember the snow piled up to the second story of our farmhouse. "It was not survivable there." He points to Canada.

"What about Galena?" I ask.

"They're fine."

"But an entire country gone?"

"For the most part."

"Was that part of the plan?" I ask George. "I mean, what were you people thinking?"

He slams a fist down on his desk so hard it startles me. "It's not what we meant! It's just..." George shakes his head. "It's just that damn scientist, Norman Eckstein, he seeded the ocean water with all that iron, created that algae bloom and turned the ocean red. It's still red. Not as bright as before, but it's there, still disrupting our weather. I know it has affected Phoenix. Galena seems to be just out of reach of many changes. Tonopah too far south, so is Crystal River. But here and Phoenix, the jet stream shifted just so and screwed up our weather real good. We've had to move everything underground here."

I hold up a hand to stop him. "Underground?"

He nods.

"Everything?" I ask.

"Yes. Everything."

"Why?"

"Because we get tornadoes now. Giant, F-5 tornadoes like you used to only see in the movies."

My back stiffens and my stomach drops. I can stand snow. That's why I put up with the weather in upstate NY for so long, because I can stand snow. You can shovel it, move it around, play in it, build an igloo. But a tornado... I've had nightmares about those since I was a kid, not that I'd ever been near one, but they've always been one of my fears. "Are you serious?" I ask.

"Dead." He tips his head. "Serious."

"Why didn't anyone tell me? I would have never come here." I feel my head shaking from side to side.

George tips his head, his eyes narrow on me. "You would have stayed in Phoenix with Burton Crane living down the street from you if you had known we get tornadoes here now?"

"I think so. At least I could wrap my hands around Crane's neck. I can't do that to a tornado."

George chuckles a bit. "Well, we've found ways to get around them. Everything's underground. We have a strong meteorological team, sirens, the curfew–"

"But you had buildings up there before." I point above us. "I saw them. The birthing center, shops, the molecular research laboratories."

"Gone. Three tornadoes was all it took. Now there's nothing but debris. Thankfully we got the research laboratories relocated before the worst hit. Lost a few men, a few women." He focuses on the map again. "We have everything we need underground. It's safe."

I think of the transparent ceiling in our living quarters. "Is our roof stable?" I ask.

He nods. "Yes. You could drive a semi across that roofing. It's the same as in the Artillery Research Unit."

"Good," I sigh. I have to get off of the topic of tornadoes. "So the children said that they will be assigned an Apprenticeship?"

George's face seems to light up. "Yes! We just implemented the program. Well, you know, since our population is static for the time being. We thought it was best to team up the new graduates with our doctors, scientists, chemists, and engineers. Keep everyone busy and learning."

"Preparing for the next generation of Sovereign?" I mock.

"Yes. But we have too many here. We've always had too many. Even with the lack of a birthrate right now. You have to know what's going to happen, Andie."

"What?" I know before he says it.

"Sovereign in the other Districts are hard to come by. We're going to have to start shipping people out."

I nod. "I'll need to know who. So I can update the pairings." I don't need to remind him that as the sole District Matchmaker I have files of each District's inhabitants and their genetic data. And while matching the Sovereign has been a task that I have declined in the past, I felt the need to continue with it after checking Sam and Blithe's data.

"Thought you didn't match Sovereign?" George asks.

I shrug. "You know it's only a matter of time before he requires it."

"I bet."

I focus on the stacks of loose papers on his desk top. "Do I get an Apprentice?" I ask George.

"No." He shakes his head.

"Why not?"

George smiles, tips his head to the side. "You and I both know why." He tips his head knowingly. Because I will never die. Well they're wrong. "But... Lina, Raven, the other children, they will be assigned someone."

"Lina?"

"Yes. I have high hopes that she might follow into the genetics field like her mother."

I shoot him a look. "I don't."

"No?"

"Definitely not."

"Why?" George pushes his glasses up on his nose.

"Look at the trouble it got me. Of all the people in the world, look where the genetics field got me."

He leans back in his chair. "Well, that was due in part to *your* genetics, not the field of study. And, well, you could have suffered the same fate as the rest of the U.S. It seems like the genetics field has been good to you and your family."

"I used to like you, George. But now you're being sneaky. Please tell me that you're still someone I can trust."

He smiles. "Of course you can trust me. I've helped you in the past. I wouldn't have done that if we weren't on the same page."

"Then what's this talk of genetics and Lina?"

He shrugs. "I was just hoping that whatever she does here will solidify her future here with us."

I take a long glance at George. "Don't push her. You let her gravitate toward whatever interests her. I want her safe, but I don't want her following the same path as me." I give him a look. "I want her and the rest of my children to live as normal lives as possible here. That is why we moved."

George nods. "Understood."

There is a long pause as both of us stare at the map on the wall.

"So..." I say, "The nanocytes."

George shifts in his seat. "What about them?"

"I don't want mine."

"I figured as much." George stands. "But we can't do anything about them. Why worry about it now? It's too late."

I raise an eyebrow. "Are you sure about that?"

George walks around the desk, stopping in front of it and leaning a hip on the dark wood top. "Getting yourself into trouble again, are you, Andromeda? What have you done?"

"It's Andie." I do nothing but give him a smile. I don't tell him my secret, that I figured out a way to draw the nanocytes out of a body.

George looks at me for a long time before speaking again. "So, would you like a job in one of our labs?"

I shake my head. "No."

"No?" He seems almost surprised.

"I have my family to take care of. Actually, six kids now and my husband. Plus the pairings. I don't have time for more work." I secretly wish I had brought my notebooks on the nanocytes. I have time for that. When I return to get Sam and Blithe, I'll have to get the vial and my notes.

"Your husband," George starts, "seems like you both haven't missed a beat. It's like you were never apart for those years after the Reformation."

My stomach sinks, just like it always does when I think about what I did to Ian. And then with just a glimpse of Adam in my memories, a flaring hot anger rises. Not wanting to talk about my infidelities toward my husband, I step toward the door.

"Are we done?" George asks. "I thought we were having a conversation." He takes off his cardigan. "Is it hot in here?" he asks offhandedly as he sets the sweater on his chair.

"We're done. For today." I reach for the door handle, pause. "George?"

"Yes?"

"Do you feel different, since the nanocytes?"

"What do you mean by *different*?"

When I turn to look at him, he pushes his glasses up, so innocently. Just like the George I knew at the beginning, before I knew that he would be living forever. I think it's changed him, a tiny bit.

"I'm not sure how to describe it. I feel..."

"You seem fine to me," he says after I can't find the right word.

"Okay. Forget I asked."

He stands up. "You want me to walk you back to your place?" he offers.

"Nope. I can find my way."

As I walk out of his office, he moves to close the door behind me. "Will you all be making it to the dining hall for dinner tonight?"

I nod. "Yes. See you then."

Leaving George Crossbender, I make my way for the elevator, secretly wishing the bell would ring again so I could get a glimpse of Raven and Isaac. The thought of checking the upper levels for Lina and the boys runs through my mind. It's a bit distressing, not knowing exactly where they all are and who they're with. I control the urge and head for the elevator.

Opening the door to our new living space, I look up at the sand covered ceiling and hope to God I never witness a tornado blowing across it. After closing the door, I start washing the dishes from breakfast. When the dishes are done, dried and put away, I move on to straightening up. The living space is large and it seems sparse. The box holding my computer catches my eye, and then the empty desk in the corner. With a sigh, I move toward the box and start unpacking the computer. As I move the desk to the room I share with Ian, plug in the wires and arrange my workspace, one thing consumes my mind: I should have brought my notebook with my research on the nanocytes. We left in such a hurry I didn't have time to run out to the ruins and collect it. I still, turn, and find a Guardian sitting in the corner of the room watching me. Part of me thinks I could start over, but another five years and I only have eight Guardians here. People will notice if they start to go missing. Plus, I feel guilty for causing the death of that one in Phoenix. I wish there were another way for me to solve this. Waiting the few weeks for Blithe to deliver so we can go back to Phoenix and bring her and Sam and their baby here, it feels like years away.

I give up thinking about the nanocytes and resume setting up the computer. Thankfully this place is equipped with a bunch of electrical and ethernet outlets. Just like a laboratory should be. Once everything is plugged in, I pull a chair over to the desk and turn the computer on. It's when the small green light above the screen blinks twice that I think to get a piece of tape to cover the camera with. I rip off three more strips of tape, used to keep the computer box closed during our travels, and press them over the camera, just to be certain. As I'm leaning back in my chair, satisfied with my workspace, there is a loud thud from the other side of the living quarters. I stand abruptly, leave the bedroom and look around.

"Hello?" I ask the empty living room. This is followed by another thudding sound coming from the farthest end of the apartment, Raven's room. "Raven?" I ask as I start walking toward the door. A thin strip of light glows from the crack between the bottom of the door and the floor. I didn't hear him come in; I didn't see him at all. But I guess he could have been here while I was gone. "Raven?" I ask, reaching for the door handle to his room. The door whips open before I can touch the handle, and Raven stands there, hair disheveled, face pale, his room a mess with books strewn all over, and his eyes watery with tears. "What's wrong?" I ask, taking the scene in.

Raven scowls, his bottom lip quivers and one tear slides down his cheek. As I reach out to touch him, he steps back and picks a book up from his bed, thrusting in my direction. Taking the book, I read the cover. *Mathematics for the Third Grade* is what it says. I flip through the book, which is more of a self printed and bound booklet.

"Where did you get this?" I ask Raven. I know I sent his records and I know they clearly indicated his mathematical capabilities are much further along than basic multiplication and division. He just stares at me before wiping at another tear. "Raven, why do you have this?"

He crosses his arms and leans against the wall.

"I'm going to guess that they put you in this class and you're not very happy about it."

Raven nods.

"So you just left?"

He nods again.

"Did you tell anyone? You're not supposed to be wandering around without a chaperone."

He shrugs.

I watch him for a long time. He may not speak, but I know his body language, his facial expressions. "There's more, isn't there?" I ask. He nods. Before I can ask another question, I hear the sound of the front door crashing open. "I'll fix this," I promise Raven as I leave his room. "Tomorrow, I promise. I'll fix it."

As I make my way toward the front door, Isaac runs toward me, a yellow piece of paper in his hand. "Look," he shouts. "Look, they advanced me!"

Taking the paper from him, I read the handwritten note. It says "upon further consideration" they advanced him two grades and it's signed by one Janet Jones. Then it hits me, Raven is not only angry, he's jealous. I look up with just enough time to see Raven smack his bedroom door, slamming it shut.

"Congratulations, Isaac." I say. "Wait until everyone else hears." Isaac beams, his dark brown eyes glistening with cheer. Behind him, the older children trail inside, followed by Ian. "Welcome home," I greet them all. "How was everyone's first day?"

And then the room erupts with the sound of five voices talking, shouting and trying to be heard. I make eye contact with Ian. He stops talking and within a few moments the children settle.

"Okay, well, who's ready for dinner?" I ask.

"But we have homework," Astrid bemoans.

"I have a report due in the morning," Marcus says, his voice sounding distracted.

"I have a test," Lina says as she throws herself down onto the couch.

"I'm tired," Cashel says.

"Well, you're all not going to do much on empty stomachs. So go wash up. We'll head to the dining hall for an early dinner." As the children make their way for their rooms, I motion for Ian to come closer. "How was your day?" I ask, stretching up on my toes and pressing a kiss to his chin.

"Just got a whole lot better," he grins down at me.

As his arms wrap around me and he steps closer, I tell him, "Raven came home early today and upset."

Ian straightens. "That's not like him."

"I know. He was crying, tore his room apart. They dropped him down to third grade math."

Ian makes a face. "Eh."

"I know." Then I hold up the note Isaac gave me. "And Isaac got to skip two grades."

"Hmm." Ian moves a hand to his chin as his eyes glance over the letter, a smile playing with the corner of his mouth. He's obviously proud, but then he's always been with all of Isaac's achievements. "Who is this Janet Jones lady?" he asks.

"The lady who proctored their exams when we first arrived," I say. "There's something about her..."

Ian looks up and I turn to find Raven walking toward us. Lips pressed together and face red, he pulls the letter from my hand and begins tearing it into tiny pieces, littering the floor.

"Raven!" I gasp. He's never acted like this.

"Hey," Ian reaches for Raven and stills his hands by gripping his wrists. "What do you think you're doing?"

Raven stands there, flicking the tiny bits of yellow paper from his fingertips and breathing heavy. "He's not going to answer you," I point out.

"He doesn't need to answer me." Ian releases Raven's wrists. "Unacceptable, Raven. You may be upset but acting like this is not allowed." Ian bends to scoop up the bits of paper. When he stands, he takes Raven's hand and pours the bits of paper into Raven's palm. "We will figure this out, but you can't be tearing this place apart because you're mad. Now, take this to the garbage."

Raven turns and walks toward the kitchen, but not before throwing one disdainful glance at me.

Even though I know Raven was acting a bit out of control, seeing him get scolded for the first time ever breaks my heart a little bit. I've never had to yell at the children, or punish any of them.

--

Lina leads us to the dining hall. It seems those years of me making her memorize maps and routes out of Phoenix stuck with her. We travel to the elevators, descend ten levels, walk down a short hallway, and just like high school, the double-doors of the dining hall stand in front of us. Marcus holds the door open for us to pass and as we walk through I catch him staring a little too longingly at Lina.

Ian smacks Marcus in the back of the head. "Uh, uh," Ian warns. A red flush breaks out over Marcus's cheeks.

We all come to a standstill in the middle of the dining hall. There are rows of tables, and rows of buffet style dining. There are just a few people here, less than one quarter of the tables are filled. From across the room, I notice a man stand and walk toward us. It's George. He smiles widely. "Early to dinner I see." He offers Ian a handshake. "How was your first day in the nuke plant? I trust James was good to you?"

"Yes," Ian answers.

"So, welcome to the dining hall. Get yourselves some dinner, and," he turns and points to a far table, "come have a seat with me and my wife."

My head snaps to the direction of his table, where a woman with short blonde hair sits, patiently waiting and watching us. Of all the times I've met George, I have never met his wife. And he's only hinted at her once.

"Sure," Ian offers.

"Good, then." George smiles. He stops before he gets five steps away. "Oh, I would suggest the eggplant dinner. It's delicious."

We make our way to the buffet and examine the dishes.

"So, which one's the eggplant?" Ian asks.

As my eyes roam over the stainless steel dishes I find it hard to identify much of anything besides salad and a pile of small, round dinner rolls.

"Yuck," Astrid wrinkles her nose as she pokes at a dish of gray matter with a serving spoon.

As we fill our plates the dining hall starts to fill with the locals of Hanford.

"They all wear the same thing," I hear Cashel mumble.

Turning around, I notice Cashel's right; everyone is wearing khaki pants and red polo shirts. We look out of place, and for the first time since we've arrived in Hanford, I think to myself that we don't fit in here. "Come on kids." I pile their plates with salad, something that looks like a slab of meat with gravy and dinner rolls. "Follow your father to George's table."

I follow behind Ian and the children, ensuring everyone makes it to the table as the room fills up.

George smiles as we sit. "Andie, Ian, I'd like to introduce you to my wife, Maryam."

"Hello." The woman stands and holds her hand out to us. "I've heard so much about you both."

Maryam has a pinched looking face but her smile is pleasant. And then, as she reaches to shake Ian's hand, the sleeve of her cardigan creeps above her right wrist and I notice that she does not have a Sovereign marking there. Unable to hide my surprise, my eyes flick to George. He simply smiles and gives the slightest shake of his head, indicating for me not to ask. I press my lips together and sit down in my seat.

"I trust your first few days here have been satisfactory," Maryam says as she sits.

"As well as to be expected," I reply, at the same time pressing my fork into the slab of meat I doled out to myself and the children. I move the fork to my mouth and chew. Whatever it is, it tastes nothing like meat. It's spongy, tasteless. I look quick to the children, who are all waiting for my reaction, their plates still full of whatever it is I put there.

"You chose the Smelt. You didn't try the eggplant," George points out. He motions to a square shape on his plate.

"Um…" I swallow what's in my mouth. "Exactly what is Smelt?"

George replies, "Simulated meat proteins mixed with a little tincture."

I freeze. "What is a tincture?"

Judging from the surprised look on George's face, he must realize that all I can think is that they dose this food with the Halcyon. And I just broke my golden rule of traveling to the other Districts: don't eat their food. I never even considered what we would do here, I wanted so badly to escape Crane.

"Oh, don't worry, it's just electrolytes and vitamins. You should have gotten the eggplant." George raises his fork.

"I couldn't tell what was eggplant," I say. "And eggplants are circular. Whatever is on your plate, George, it doesn't look anything like eggplant."

George pushes his fork into the square shape. "Well, it's made with eggplant." The shape separates into a formless gray and green. Scooping a mouthful onto his fork, George chews it and smiles as though it's delicious.

A shiver of disgust runs up my back. I turn to the salad. Thankfully, it tastes like real lettuce. Next I try the roll. It's dry, crusty, salty. Dear God don't these people know how to cook?

"Good, aren't they?" Maryam asks. "It's an old family recipe." A pleasant smile plasters her face again.

"They're amazing," I lie, shoving the rest of the roll into my mouth. I can sense Ian chuckling from next to me.

--

"So TELL me more about this Janet Jones lady," I ask George. Maryam stands, taking the empty dishes and heads toward a pair of double doors.

George runs a hand down the front of his shirt. "She's in charge of some of the aspects of schooling here at Hanford. Much like Ms. Black is in Phoenix."

"She dropped Raven down a grade and skipped Isaac forward."

"Well, she makes decisions based on their academic abilities."

"If you've seen Raven's records then you know he doesn't deserve this."

"Perhaps it was for another reason." He pauses.

"Because he doesn't speak? Is that her reason?"

"I'm sure whatever reason she has it's a good one."

"Listen, George, we came here to seek refuge from Crane. We don't fit in. That's apparent. But I will not have your people doing their best to point out that the children aren't from here. I'll pull them from your Sovereign Children's Training Program. I know it's the largest of all the Districts, with the best teachers, but I can teach them at home."

"We can't have that," George says. "No."

"It's barely any different than the schooling they went through in Phoenix. They were all together in a one-room school house."

"Yes but this is different, and there's more, there's the integration into all the research Hanford does. And there's the socialization–"

"Socialization?" I interrupt. Ian pats my arm and I know I'm raising my voice, but this is a bit ridiculous. "We're not talking about pets here, George. We're talking about human kids."

"Very important human kids. The next generation of Sovereign. It is bad enough they stand out amongst the others. Even with the uniforms the other children know that they're different, special even."

"Because they grew up on a farm and got individualized instruction?"

"No. Because they are children of the Matchmaker."

I wave a hand at him. "That means nothing."

"Oh, it means plenty. You decide futures and fates–"

"Of the Residents, not the Sovereign. What I do barely impacts anyone here. You scarcely have Residents and you have even fewer Volker. Your District population is the only one out of all the Districts that gets to make the majority of their decisions themselves."

"You know he's going to ask you to pair the Sovereign, soon enough," he reminds me.

I shake my head, refusing to think about when that day comes and what I will say to Crane. I'm not discussing it now. Directing the conversation back to where it started, I say, "I want Raven accelerated based on his abilities, not because he doesn't speak."

George tips his head. "Why doesn't he speak?"

"I don't know. He just never has. He never made a sound as a baby; never spoke a word as he got older. Ask him why. All my questions are met with silence from him."

"Hm." George scratches his head and pauses for a bit before speaking again. "I'll talk to Janet Jones and have Raven moved back to his original classes."

"Thank you," I respond, with the thought of visiting Janet Jones myself sticking in my head.

I turn to catch Ian and all the children watching me. "What?" I ask.

"It's getting late," Ian offers. "I think it's time to get you to bed." I don't catch that Ian winks at George.

I sigh, and realize maybe I am a bit tired. A cross country move and no coffee, that might kill some people. I stand, gather the children, say the most polite goodbye I can muster to George and Maryam when she returns, and then we leave.

As we walk back to our living quarters the children grumble about the lackluster dinner.

"What I wouldn't give for one of Elvis's steaks right now," Ian says as he takes my hand.

"I can't believe these people eat that stuff," I reply.

"I can't believe they were playing that stuff off as meat. What did George call it? Smeat?"

I giggle. "No. Um. I think it was Smelt."

"What does that even mean? I can't remember what George said. Either way, it was disgusting. I'd eat a hundred cans of Spam over that stuff any day."

Disappointed in myself, I reply, "Well, it's not like we can do much about it. We live here now. And short of growing our own food and asking for our own livestock, we have to eat it."

"I'd rather go back to growing our own food and asking for our own livestock."

"And where would we keep it all?"

"I'm sure they have some secret space here, all lit up with growing lights."

"Well, they must."

"Maybe you could teach them how to cook." Ian suggests. "Or at least how to make bread."

"Didn't you hear Maryam? Those rolls are an old family recipe."

"The rolls were gross," Isaac shouts to us.

Ian and I burst out laughing.

Once the children are in bed, I sit next to Ian on the small couch in the living room. "What did you think of Maryam?" I ask him.

Ian shrugs. "She seemed nice."

I drop my voice to a whisper. "She didn't have a Sovereign tattoo on her wrist."

"I saw that."

"What do you think about it?"

"Well," Ian stretches his arms above his head before settling them across the back of the couch. "She didn't pass the test to be Sovereign, or maybe she's from outside the gates."

"A Survivor?" I ask.

"Who else would make such a terrible dinner roll?"

"Hm," I ponder the thought. George married to a Survivor. Crane wouldn't allow it. Not in a million years. And she didn't resemble a Survivor. She was petite, healthy, her teeth looked good–I'm not sure why I thought of her teeth. There has to be some other reason as to why she doesn't have a Sovereign marking. One of these days I'll have to ask George. But in the mean time, I snuggle close into Ian's side, lay my head on his shoulder and close my eyes. I try to revel in the fact that I have him and my children and we are safe, far away from Crane, together. Even if this place seems strange and we don't fit in, at least we have each other here. And as though Ian knows the thoughts running through my head, he moves one arm off of the back of the couch, wrapping it around my side and pulling me close to him. I feel him sigh under my cheek.

"Do you think it was a mistake?" he asks suddenly.

"What's that?"

"Leaving the Pasture. Do you think it was a mistake?"

I lift my head and look into Ian's deep brown eyes. And as he looks back at me, waiting for my answer, I can't help but wonder what else he thinks might have been a mistake. Did I make a mistake years ago when he asked me to marry him and I said yes? Did he make a mistake in asking me? Does he regret the life we created together? It doesn't seem like he does, but then there's these moments where he pulls away, or he hesitates and doesn't jump in with both feet. Maybe he's just reacting with his brain instead of his heart. Maybe that's what I should try to do more of, using my brain instead of my heart. He could have left us and chosen a different path. Did he even want to come back to us, or was it forced, or was it the only option he had? I wait for Ian to do something that shows me he doesn't regret any of his choices. His hand cups the back of my head and he pulls me to him in a long deep kiss. Just like I want him to do. When he pulls away, he says, "Forget I asked."

--

IN THE MORNING, after breakfast in the dining hall, I walk with the children as Kevin escorts them to all of their classes. I take note of what levels they are on, what plain doors they enter first. I'm not sure why I have this urge to know where they are at all times. Having them floors away and not just across the courtyard in the school house bothers me. I want them close. I want them near me. I want to be able to scoop them up and run out of here if we need to. Even though I know Crane is not here there's just something about Hanford that I don't trust. I can't put my finger on it. Five levels under our living quarters, Raven and Isaac exit the elevator. Isaac gives me a tight hug before leaving, Raven just stares as though I've been soiled and he can't be bothered to touch me. I pull him close anyway.

Now it's just myself and Kevin in the elevator. He pushes the button for the top floor. "So what do you do now?" I ask him.

He seems startled and a little nervous. "Well, Mrs. Match–" he clears his throat, "I mean Mrs. Somers. I have to check in with Ms. Jones and let her know that all of your children made it to their class and then I go to my Apprenticeship." His eyes flick to the elevator door.

I try to ignore the fact that he almost called me Mrs. Matchmaker. I wonder if that is how these people view me and if the one person responsible for escorting my children to their classes uses the term, it makes me wonder how many others do also. I wonder what they must think of us.

"Where are you doing your Apprenticeship?" I ask.

The elevator stops on the top level and we step out.

Kevin takes three steps back, away from me as he answers, "In the Atmospheric Chemistry department."

"That sounds interesting." I say.

Kevin just stares wide-eyed, like he's scared or intimidated or something.

I give up on the conversation, nod and smile at him. "Have a good day, Kevin."

Kevin leaves, walking straight-backed down the opposite hallway, which I know has three more hallways extending off of it. And they are all gray and dull. What I wouldn't give for the openness and greenery of the Pasture right now, filled with life and color at every turn. The only things that were gray there were Elvis's sideburns and the Volker uniforms.

When I make it to our living quarters I find a Guardian lying in front of the door. Bending to pet it, I ask, "Do you need to go out?" I realize that no one has ever let them outside since we arrived here. But the Guardians seem to always take care of themselves somehow. "Come on," I tell the Guardian. It trots beside me as I return to the elevator, my finger hovers over the button labeled for the ground floor. My nerves hit me as I recall what George said about the tornadoes. But we've been here for days now and we have yet to experience one. How bad could it really be? I push the button.

The Guardian stares at me.

"What?" I ask it. "Don't you want to go outside?"

We ascend.

When the doors open the Guardian follows me through the broken down High School and outside.

The first thing I notice is the sun. It beats down on me with a heat I haven't experienced in weeks since summer never seemed to show up in Phoenix before we left. I walk around the building and face west. That's the direction George drove when we came here for guns five years ago. It might be a mile or two away but I can see structures, dark shapes that make it look like the buildings are just as they were before.

"Come on." I start jogging with the Guardian at my side.

It feels good to run and stretch the muscles that haven't been used for more than long walks in the fields. Even better is the sun and the fresh air. I'm not sure how long we can stay here in Hanford living underground.

The wind picks up. As I jog toward the buildings in the distance, I look toward the sky as it fills with clouds. The temperature seems to drop. I look behind me and see that I'm about halfway between the High School ruins and the buildings. A feeling of unease floods me as the clouds thicken, blotting out the sun. I run faster. The Guardian runs faster. A few minutes pass before the wind picks up, stronger than I've ever felt it, stronger than the winds blowing off of the lake ever were. When I look up my stomach drops, panic fills me and I instantly regret leaving the underground levels of Hanford.

There is a funnel cloud in the distance.

Looking around, I see that George was right. From the distance the shadows did nothing but obscure what is left. There are pieces of structures, portions of buildings, but none are whole. Fortunately the beams look secure but a beam won't help me with a tornado. The wind blows faster, harder, whipping my hair across my face. The funnel cloud is moving closer. I should have never come up here. The Guardian bites the sleeve of my shirt and starts pulling me back in the direction we came. Looking over the expanse of sand that we just covered, I wonder if we'd even be able to make it back to the elevator in time.

Shaking my arm to get the Guardian to release, I move toward the first building, thinking that maybe I could find shelter from the tornado. The Guardian growls and tugs harder at my sleeve, pulling me in the opposite direction. For a second there is a tug of war, me pulling, the Guardian growling and pulling back. The wind whips. I look up to see the funnel cloud ambling toward us.

"Okay!" I give a frustrated shout at the Guardian and we take off running for the abandoned High School.

The air is filled with debris and a strange noise that sounds like the dull whistle of a train. If I didn't know better I'd say someone was nearing arrival at the train platform. But I know better. Sand stings my face. I run harder. The Guardian never leaves my side. As the abandoned High School nears, the wind gets stronger, pulling and tugging me away from my destination. Sand slips under my feet. I jog up the two steps to enter the building and as I raise my left foot to take a step the wind blows so hard it knocks me off my feet. I hit the cement of the entryway on both knees, a shot of pain courses through my bones from the jarring. I reach out and grip the doorframe. My fingers stretching, the pain in my knees throbbing, and I swear to God I feel my feet lift off the ground. The Guardian is at my back, pulling on my shirt with its teeth as though it could ground us, but I can feel it being pulled just as I am. Arms aching, I try to pull us closer to the door frame, and through it all I notice that my feet are definitely not on the ground anymore.

I open my mouth to scream but it is filled with a sandy current of air, sucking the breath out of me.

A warm hand wraps around my wrist. I look up to see Ian there, just past the threshold of the building. He grabs me with two hands now, reeling and dragging and pulling, fighting with the wind. He pulls us into the depths of the building, which barely seems to be affected by the storm. Strange. I stumble to stand, the Guardian shoves at my legs, moving me deeper into the structure. Ian starts running for the elevator dragging me along with him. The doors of the elevator car are propped open with a brick. We run inside, Ian kicks the brick and presses the button to bring us underground.

He turns to me, panting, sweat dripping down his face. "Holy shit, Andie. Can't you stay out of trouble for five minutes?" Ian tugs me close, crushing me to his chest. "I almost lost you." He squeezes me so tight I can barely breathe. "I can't lose you again. Not again." I feel the pads of his fingertips pressing into me, hard, like he's making sure I'm here and real. It makes me wonder how I could have ever thought he might have made a mistake in choosing me.

When my breath settles and my knees are only slightly shaky, I ask, "How did you know I was out there?"

He holds me away from him, his grip tight on my shoulders. "I forgot something at the apartment. Had to go back. You ran across our roof. I saw you running. Didn't they tell you about the tornadoes?"

"Yes, but–"

"Then why were you out there?" Ian's almost yelling, he wraps his hand around my upper arm and steps closer to me. I see the ring of sweat around his neck, the damp spots on his shirt. "Andie?" he asks again, waiting for my answer.

I shake my head a bit. "I just was letting the Guardian out. And then I wanted to see the remains. I wanted to make sure that George was telling me the truth about the tornadoes damaging the buildings out here. They're always lying to me. I just wanted to make sure. I just wanted to see the truth with my own eyes." I turn to look at him, place a hand on his warm arm and feel the muscle twitch underneath my touch. "If you hadn't come... I... I don't know what would have happened."

Ian drops his head. The elevator doors open on our floor and we step off, the Guardian following. We head for our living quarters. Ian opens the door and ushers me inside. The Guardian lies down outside the door.

"Maybe you should have an escort," he warns as he walks toward our room. I follow him, watch as he opens the drawer of his night stand and pulls out a folded piece of paper.

"I don't need an escort," I huff at him. Looking down, I notice bloody marks on my knees. I bend and pull my pant legs up. There are faint pink marks there and some smeared blood.

When I straighten myself, Ian is standing in front of me, tucking the piece of paper into his pocket. He kneels, runs a finger across my knee and inspects my bloody pants. He looks up. "I don't know what Crane did to you. But you're not invincible. Those nanocytes might help you heal, Andie, but a tornado... It could have whipped you up into the atmosphere. Imagine what a fall like that would have done to your body. Next time call George before you venture outside, and get a weather report." He looks at me for a long time, concern marring his face. "Please. Just please, do it and think for once."

I should be pissed at him. Think for once. I'm always thinking, can barely shut my brain off half the time. But I nod. "Okay," I say.

"Serious."

"Okay! I promise."

Ian looks me over quick. "Good." Pressing a quick kiss to my lips, he makes his way to the door. "I'll see you soon," he says as he leaves.

I throw myself down on to the couch and look to the sand blowing across our transparent ceiling. Pulling my knees to my chest, I inspect them. Pressing my fingers to the pink areas I feel for any bruising or pain, but there is none. And as I sit there I wonder what kind of injuries the nanocytes can take care of. The night I cut my arm it healed almost instantly and with this most recent injury the healing was done in a few minutes. If that tornado did whip me up into the sky and I fell twenty miles to the ground, I wonder how long it would take for me to recover. Would I lose consciousness? Would I feel pain? Would I remember any of it? Looking up again, the sand swirls faster, blowing and drifting in some fervent nature dance. I decide not to test out any theories on how bad I could injure myself and survive. Instead, I stand and head to the shower to clean off the sand and dust and memory of near death.

ELEVEN

IAN

Taking my folded up piece of paper, I leave Andie in our living quarters hoping to God that she can stay out of trouble. I ride the elevator to the lowest level, walk to the underground rail platform and wait for my ride. An old man in a dark green shirt and matching green pants sweeps the platform as I wait. The rail vibrates and hums as the train nears. When it stops, I board, take a seat and sit alone. As the minutes pass I have nothing but my thoughts until the train reaches the nuke plant. I want to think of my wife and how I almost lost her again just a few moments ago, but instead I think of the man in the green shirt. All of the Sovereign here wear red, the children blue. The green stands out. In Phoenix our Orderly faction that cleaned the halls wore dark red. I have never asked Andie what color the factions of other Districts wear. It must be green here.

The train slows to a stop. I get off and head back to the reactor room. James turns to look at me when I walk into the room and sit behind my designated computer. He smiles. I wave, then focus on my computer screen. I resume the list of tasks James gave me to complete for the day. Check status of the Phoenix reactor. Done. Check status of the Crystal River reactor. Done. Check the Status of the Tonopah reactor. Done. Check the status of the Galena reactor. Done. It was all done before I left, when I realized I forgot my sheet of paper. My cheat sheet.

Feeling the presence of someone behind me, I turn.

"Hey," says James. I didn't even notice him leave his desk. "Me and some of the guys have a gym set up. You look like you work out. Want to join us after work?"

I flash a smile. One of those innocent ones I used to give to Crane so he'd think I was an idiot still zoning out on Halcyon. I flex a bicep. They're not as big as they were at the Pasture, just a few weeks underground, and without the labor of the fields, has deflated my physique quick. I'm getting soft. I can't get soft. "Sure. Been dying to go running."

James slaps me on the shoulder. "Good man, we've got a track and everything."

I motion to my clothes. "I don't have any workout wear."

James laughs. "No problem. I'll order you some gym clothes and running shoes. What size do you wear?"

I tell him.

"Should be up before the end of the day."

"Where does it come from?"

He shrugs. "Dunno."

"You just order clothes and shoes and you don't know where they come from?" I ask.

"Not my problem. I run the reactor. I don't make clothes and shoes."

"Sure. Sure." I watch him make his way back to his desk. So they can just order clothes and they show up. Andie told me that the Sovereign here pretty much run this place by themselves. There aren't many Volker, and there are even fewer Residents. But it seems to me that the clothing has to come from somewhere.

I stare at the computer screen, thinking. There is something that's been on my mind since we got here. I know what's in Crystal River, Phoenix, Tonopah and here. But Galena, I think there are secrets in Galena.

Looking around, ensuring that my co-workers are busy, I pull the piece of paper out of my pocket and open up Galena's database on my computer screen, then start searching the files on my list. It's amazing. These smart people. Just because they're all intelligent they trust each other beyond belief. There are no locks. No passwords. In Phoenix we locked ourselves behind the walls of the Pasture to feel safe. Here there's nothing. Only trust. I wonder if Crane knows the Hanford District is running on brainpower and trust.

--

"Ready, Ian?" James shouts from across the room.

My eyes flick to the clock. No. I'm not ready. I need ten more minutes in Galena's database. Unlike Hanford, there are firewalls everywhere. Blocked access. I've never encountered this before, not even when I had to fix Crystal River's reactor back when Andie was down there and the fence shut down. We can get in and check the reactor but that's about it. I shut my computer down and stand. Maybe a run would be good. Clear my head. I can come back and finish this later.

James throws a package of brown paper and twine at me as I walk toward him. "Gym clothes," he says. I follow him out of the room. Two other guys wait in the hall. "Frank. Ed. This is Ian. He's joining the gym."

Frank and Ed each give me a hearty handshake. The one named Frank has red hair that almost matches his red shirt. He's pale and freckled. "Hope James told you the gym is invite only." He squeezes my hand tighter.

I nod. "He didn't. Thanks."

Ed's next. He looks like an Ed. Aged, bald, a paunch belly. "Bet you'll do laps around us," he murmurs as he shakes my hand.

"Let's get moving before the dinner hour catches up with us." James starts walking down the hallway.

Thoughts of Andie flash through my mind. She's probably busy, won't even notice I'm late. She's like that. Gets caught up in her work and forgets about the world going on around her.

The four of us take a few turns before James reaches for an unlabeled door.

It's a crude gym. A green track painted on the floor. A few benches and bars and weights. I change in the corner before stretching and starting out at a slow jog on the track.

"So," James asks as he runs next to me. "How is it to be famed?"

"Famed?"

"Yup." He motions to the Phoenix District mark on my wrist.

"I'm Sovereign, just like you, no different," I say.

"Oh, you're different."

"How so?"

"You're married to the Matchmaker."

"She's–" I start.

"Going to find me a new wife." Ed jogs on the other side of me now.

"Me too," Frank says from behind me.

"Can you put in a good word for us?" James asks. "Can you take notes? I want a blonde. Skinny legs, big rack." He motions to his chest.

"She doesn't pair Sovereign, guys," I say.

"Sure she doesn't," Ed laughs.

"The women here have been talking about her already. Waiting for her to pull something like the last time she was here," Frank says.

"What happened the last time she was here?" I ask since I was a ward of Crane at the time and I have no idea what they are talking about.

"Last time she was here," Ed starts breathing heavy from exertion, "she was pregnant. Told all the other women they had to stop reproducing or Burton Crane would show up and take the children away." He slows, reaching out to grab my arm and stop me. I pull it away from him. "That's quite the threat to make. You know how hard it is to get a woman now? No one wants to risk getting pregnant. They all saw what Crane did to the Matchmaker. Her marks."

They all stop running and watch me. "You didn't know she was here when she was pregnant?" Frank asks.

I say nothing. I know of the marks on her back. She's told me of them. But she's ashamed of them. Doesn't show many. Keeps them covered.

"How can you not know where your pregnant wife is?" Ed asks.

If only they knew the secrets we Sovereign from Phoenix keep.

I force out a laugh. "Just joking, guys. Of course I knew she was here."

I start running faster just to get away from them. Rounding the track, I stop when I get near the door and my clothes. "I gotta get going," I shout to the guys. They haven't even attempted restarting their run. I grab my clothes and the bag James gave me the gym stuff in and leave.

Weird dudes. Wiping the sweat off my forehead, I make my way back to the reactor room with one thing on my mind. Finding out Galena's secrets. Pushing open the door I am relieved to find the room empty. Figures. These people run like clockwork. Arrive at the same time every day. Leave at the same time every day. I close the door. Set my bag down in front of it. Making my way to my computer, I stop and zone in on James's computer.

Why not? I sit at his seat and fire it up. No password. Again, figures. I open up Galena's files. Check their reactor status, just to make it look like I'm doing my job. And then I start searching, opening files with strange names, icons of the Galena District Image, a small flame. There is nothing.

"State your name," a voice from the computer suddenly asks.

I look around the room.

"State your name," it repeats.

I clear my throat. Panic a bit. I'm at James's computer. Shit.

"James Ford," I lie.

The computer screen goes blank for a moment. Then it flickers. Once, twice, three times before an image comes into view. Holy crap, it's President Berkley. But he's not the President anymore. We no longer live in a democracy. He looks the same. Dark skin and blue eyes that seem too light for his heritage.

He blinks at me. "You are not James Ford," he says with his deep voice.

"No," I reply. I want to launch from my seat and make my way out of here but I'm already headed toward trouble, I might as well get some answers.

"What's your name?" Berkley asks.

"Ian Somers."

His dark handsome face breaks into a wide smile. "Oh, I know you." He clucks his tongue. "Ian Somers. Ian Somers. Are you looking for trouble intentionally or did you just stumble upon it?"

What the hell? "I'm looking for a few answers."

"Isn't everyone." He leans toward the screen. "Tell me, precious Ian. How is that lovely wife of yours? She like her nanocytes?"

I feel my hand curl into a fist in my lap. I don't answer.

"I'm sure she doesn't. Could tell that about her the moment I met her years ago. But, she is so important to Crane." His eyes turn stony. "Now. Pawn. Tell me what you want."

"Galena has an abundance of inaccessible files."

"Oh, you've been snooping. We do."

"What's in them?"

"A little bit of this, a little bit of that, a little bit of information your wife might very much like to have. Especially if she's working as hard as I think she is to get rid of those nanocytes. Has she injured herself yet? Tried to cut them out? Drained herself of her blood? What's the worst she's done? Tell me. I'm dying to know."

Both my hands are fists now. The thought of her going to such extremes. She almost tried with that vial. "You have what she needs, don't you?"

He nods.

"How can she access it?" I ask.

"She needs to visit me. Bring her up here to the frozen arctic. I'll give her everything she needs. All she has to say is please."

I wait.

"The code is *B. C. Bertrand*," he enunciates obnoxiously. "The password is *15398genesis*."

I pull out the folded piece of paper from my pocket and write it all down. When I am done, I look up to find Berkley watching me. "I'm guessing you're finding out that Sovereign from Phoenix don't exactly fit in there. Aren't you?"

I shrug.

"Well you don't. That's why Crane locked you all away at the Pasture. You should have never left."

"Why?"

"The Reformation was planned for decades before that first missile struck American soil. Things are not as they seem in Hanford. It may seem very proper and happy and trusting, but Crossbender has his secrets that keep his District running. Maybe you'll snoop around long enough to find out." There is a noise in the background. Berkley leans away from the computer screen. "Duty calls. Goodbye, Pawn."

With that the computer screen goes black for an instant before returning to normal. I press the power button to turn it off.

Leaving the reactor room, I head home. Deep in thought after my conversation with Berkley, and as I wait at the underground rail platform, I hear movement. I turn to see the old man in the dark green shirt from earlier in the day. A Resident? The rail vibrates as the train arrives and I get on. When the train stops, I exit and notice another man in a green shirt walking down a dark hall. Andie's going to kill me. I'm already late. But with the things Berkley just said to me... Curiosity is a stone cold bitch. I follow the man in green.

Moving fast, I pull the small duffel bag James gave me to keep my work clothes in over my head. The man in green walks down the hallway. They seem endless here. All gray, unlabeled. Like a beehive or an anthill.

I follow him and he doesn't seem to notice me or care. He pushes open a door. It's a stairwell. I lean over the railing and see him descending. I follow. I thought I was already on the lowest level. That's where the underground rail runs. The lowest level. That's what Crossbender told me. But as I follow the man in green down, I pass a door on each level. Now we're at least seven down and he shows no sign of slowing. I pick up my pace, following him deeper and deeper until finally there are no more stairs. We must be another fifteen stories underground.

He pushes open a door. I follow.

Holy crap. There are no more hallways, just a great expanse of openness. My eyes focus in the dim light. There is rock everywhere. And it's hot. Even in my shorts and T-shirt the air feels heavy and heated as if I were standing in front of a furnace. There are people here milling about. Tables and tents set up, a market it seems, and built into the walls of the caverns I can see cutouts of windows and doors, stairs and balconies.

What is this place?

The air is thick, hard to breathe. I cough. The man in green appears at my side.

"Your kind is not allowed here," he says, voice rough. He grabs my arm, his grip stronger than I'm expecting. He twists my wrist and inspects the mark there, my Sovereign mark. "Definitely not allowed here. You especially."

"What is this place?" I ask.

He pauses. Tilts his head to the side and studies me. There is a long passage of silence before he scoffs and opens the door to the stairwell with his free hand.

"What is your Faction? Are you an Orderly?" I ask, desperately trying to get something out of him. In Phoenix they would just answer. No questions. Nice and polite.

He laughs and pushes my wrist away. "None of that Faction and District crap down here."

"I saw you cleaning."

"You saw me nothing. I am a ghost. A magician. A serpent of the night. I *work* while you people aren't looking. While you're sleeping." He throws an arm out to the expanse of underground. "We all do here." He opens the door with a force I wouldn't expect from him. "Now. Drag your ass back up those stairs to the top of your pyramid where you belong. Forget this place."

I wait. I want answers.

The man in green takes a step toward me and pulling a knife from his pocket, he holds it to my chest. "Run, Pawn," he sneers. "Before I cut your heart out."

Not wanting to leave my children fatherless and my wife to mourn again, I turn and run up the stairs faster than I ever have in my life. By the time I reach the fifteenth floor where this all started, I'm soaked with sweat. I push the door open and run to the elevators that will bring me to the top floor. Something strange is happening in the bowels of Hanford. The roots of this District run deeper than I originally thought. And why the hell do people keep calling me Pawn? None of this can be good.

Twelve

Andie

"So, you had some weather trouble." George gives me a look and frowns. He doesn't even bother to push his glasses up as they drift down to the tip of his nose.

I think he's scolding me. It's kind of hilarious, really, George trying to scold. He's got nothing on the intimidating looks Burton Crane could pass around a room. "How did you know?" I ask. Ian was the only one who knew, I told no one else. But Ian wouldn't tell on me.

"Cameras." He pauses and finally pushes his glasses up. "We have cameras here, above ground, just like you have in Phoenix and the rest of the Districts."

"Oh." Feeling like an idiot I brush a piece of hair out of my face. "I didn't really think the weather would be that bad. It seemed fine when we arrived a few days ago."

"I told you," George tips back in his office chair, "ever since Norman–"

"I know." I interrupt him. "I know about the ocean and the weather. I just wasn't expecting it to be that bad." I don't want to hear that name; it just makes me think of that trip we took to Galena.

"Did you get hurt?" he asks. "I saw you fall on the video. It's a good thing Ian went home to retrieve something he had forgotten. And a good thing the Guardian was with you."

I stare at George for a long time before answering, remembering the bloodstains on my pants and my instantly healed knees. "I'm fine." He should know this.

Looking to change the subject and searching for answers, I ask about the District I've heard the least about in the past few years. "What's in Galena?"

He sets his chair right and picks up a pencil, twisting it between his fingers. "You know what they do. Oil production and alternative energy research."

"What else?"

He takes a deep breath. "Things are... stored there."

"Stored?"

His eyes flick to the door. "I shouldn't be telling you this."

I take a deep breath, wanting to know so badly. "Tell me," I urge.

"I shouldn't." He sets the pencil down and folds his hands.

I wait.

He gives up, and finally says, "Before the Reformation, the world's data was stored in locations where people could access them online. You remember this. Libraries, hospitals, research facilities, all those research papers, years and years of discoveries, it was all out in the digital world. Reachable by just a few keystrokes. And then there was the Reformation and it all went away."

"But I have access."

"Yes, *we* have access. But, think about those Survivors. Did you ever once see a computer while they had you? You didn't, because that's all been removed. Only we have access to the discoveries which haven't been printed in books. The structure of the internet was destroyed and most of the power stations. The Funding Entities all knew where the data clouds in the sky were, they knew where all the remote servers were and they destroyed them. *After* they backed the world's data up to their own remote server." He pauses. "And that server is in Galena."

"Holy crap."

George nods.

All I can think of is how I need to get my hands on that server and find Crane's original data on the nanocytes. Then I can get them out without killing myself. Is it selfish to only think about myself and not returning all that information back to the Survivors? I don't know and I can barely contain the thought of finding it all and figuring this out.

"Whatever you're thinking, I'll warn you to stop right now," George says.

"I can't." I stare at the map. "I want these out of me so badly."

George stands from his desk and takes a few steps toward me. "Surely it can't be that terrible."

What does he mean it can't be that terrible? He should know what it's like, no longer feeling yourself, no longer trusting half the people around you. He should understand, he's just like me. I start to say, "You have the nanocytes, like me–"

He raises a hand to stop me. "No, I don't."

"But... Crane said–"

George shakes his head. "I told Crane I didn't want them."

"He gave you a choice?" I step back, shocked. "He didn't give me a choice."

"He has never given you a choice, Andie." George steps closer, drops his voice a bit. "The only reason I got a choice was because I'm not important to him. He doesn't care what I do as long as I uphold the rules of the Funding Entities. I have no desire to live forever."

"Neither do I."

"I know this."

"Then get me on Galena's server."

"It's not that easy. We can only access a portion of it from the Districts. You'd have to be in Galena and physically touch their computers to access it all."

I walk a tight circle around the room, thinking. "I need that data. I need the data on the nanocytes. I have to get rid of them." I stop in front of George. "I need to go there."

George frowns. "Good luck."

"What? Why?"

"Because after the last time you were there Galena's borders were closed. We are forbidden from going there. We drop supplies when needed and that's it."

"But I don't want *this*." I clutch at my shirt. "I don't want to be like this!"

"I know."

"You don't know. You have no idea how it feels to know that everyone I love is going to die and I will live on without them."

George's eyes soften for an instant. "We had a child. Maryam and I. A boy. He died when he was five. So I do know a little bit about living on after your loved ones are gone."

"Oh, I'm sorry." Well that answers one question we had about Maryam, if they had a child in the past, she couldn't be a Survivor.

He turns away from me. "Couldn't do anything about it. He was sick. He found peace in his death. But that doesn't make us miss him any less." George sits down behind his desk. "Living on without your loved ones isn't so bad. At least you know they are safe in heaven."

"I would rather be in heaven with them. I don't want to be here doing this dance forever with Crane."

"I'm sorry then."

The silence between us is so strong at that moment that all I hear is the tick of the clock on his wall.

"Why doesn't Maryam have a Sovereign tattoo?" I ask.

"I figured you'd notice that." George looks away.

"Is she a Survivor?"

George shakes his head. "No. She was here for everything. For it all."

"What happened?"

"She just gave up. Not long after our boy died. Lost her will, her drive. She was a doctor, a damn good one at that." George rubs a hand down his face and pushes his glasses up. "Well, now she just reads books. Fiction. Romance and fantasy novels. I think it's the only thing keeping her right, getting lost in her books all day. She lives in a fantasy land in her head. But she gets by. And she still loves me. That's all that matters in all of this, right? Hidden in all that the Funding Entities were trying to do, changing the world, making it a better place, we're no longer staring at televisions and smart phones, we're back to interacting, we're back to being human."

Not sure what to say, I nod, absorbing what he's just told me. So Maryam and George are just as broken as the rest of us. A dead child. I'm not sure how I would react to finding out one of my children died. Perhaps I'd push everything away and turn to a fantasy in my head like Maryam, perhaps I'd do something rash, perhaps I'd end my own life. If I could end my own life. But they will die. Eventually all of my children will die and I will go on without them. If I don't figure out these nanocytes and that day comes, it could wreck me. I'd never be the same. I know this deep down in my soul.

Looking up, I realize the children will be done with their schooling soon. I make my way for the door. Just before I close it I tell George, "I want access to the servers in Galena. And I'm going to get it. I'm going to end this."

George nods. "I'm sure you'll try. Good luck."

--

THROUGHOUT THE AFTERNOON, I can't stop thinking about the servers in Galena. For five years I worked in that underground lab only to discover a solution that might kill me overnight. All those wasted years. If I had known Galena held the data I needed, I might not have closed our borders. I might have tried to get to it sooner.

I think it's time to visit Alexander.

Turning from my computer screen I check the clock. Ian's late. I sent the kids to their rooms to do their homework before we go to the dining hall; I was so busy matching the Residents' data that I didn't even realize how much time had gone by.

Saving the data and shutting off the computer, I head for the phone, pausing when I get there and realize I have no phone number for wherever Ian works. I don't even have an extension to reach him at. One of the Guardians from the corner of the room stands and faces the door. The handle jiggles before opening and Ian steps into the room.

"Hey," Ian flashes me a smile. I notice he's wearing different clothes:

a T-shirt, shorts and athletic shoes. He's carrying a small duffel bag with him.

"Where have you been?" I ask. "You should have been home hours ago."

"Running." He sets his bag down and moves toward me. "Some guys I work with, they set up this gym in the lower levels and invited me to go with them after work."

A bit of mistrust swirls in my brain. "Where were you really? I mean... running?"

"I've been running for years, since Crane released me from that–" he pauses. He's never told me where Crane kept him all those years. And it seems he doesn't want to, still.

"Why don't you ever invite me to go running with you?" I ask.

Ian gives a half-laugh, pauses, looks into my eyes. "You would want to?"

"Why not?"

Ian steps back. "I just thought..."

"What?"

He shakes his head. "Never mind."

"What, Ian? You thought I'd rather sit around and wait for you to come home? Because maybe I'd like to escape these four walls and get some exercise. I've already been forbidden from stepping foot outdoors. You know how hard that is? I used to spend half my day outdoors and now all I get to do is watch the sand blow across our ceiling."

"You can come with me any time you want."

"This is the first I've heard of it!"

Ian's eyes widen a bit and he closes the space between us. "You're mad."

I search his features for some truth in this, unsure of why I don't trust him. He looks like he's been running, there's damp ring around the neck of his shirt and his blonde hair is mussed on top and matted to his neck in places. Maybe it's not trust, maybe I was just worried. Maybe that's my problem. "I was worried." I cross my arms. "You didn't call. You never mentioned this. What am I supposed to think? For all I know you have a girlfriend down in the sub-basement waiting on you."

Ian chuckles a bit. "Seriously, Andie, after all I did to get you back? What I did to myself to escape that–" he pauses and shakes his head.

"Why have you never told me about that?" I ask. "I've told you everything. All that has happened. You know my darkest secrets. What I did to that man, and Raven." I stop myself.

"And I have Isaac." His hands grasp my shoulders, kneading the tense muscles there. "We've done things we are not proud of, but we have each other. And as far as where Crane was keeping me," he pauses, drops his head low and I see his own shoulders tense, "if you really want to know I'll tell you. But not until after dinner and the kids are in bed. I'm pretty sure three of those six doors are open and we're being watched."

I lean around him and see he's right. The doors slam closed.

"There's no one else. There will never be anyone else," Ian says as he leans in and kisses me hard. "Now, let's go get some sludge for dinner. Have I mentioned I hate the food here?"

"Only a hundred times."

I holler for the kids and we head to the dining hall.

--

LAYING IN THE DARK, waiting for Ian to finish his nightly routine, I wonder if he'll actually tell me what happened for those years he was gone and I considered him dead. Ian sits on the bed and rolls to face me, pulling the covers over my shoulder.

"He kept me in a tiny little trailer out by the nuke plant."

I watch him and wait for more.

"They brought us breakfast, lunch, and dinner. I don't even remember what the food looked like or tasted like." I don't remind him that it was some strange canned rations. "There was this one time, I remember, just sitting there staring at my plate. I was so busy trying to fix a problem with the reactor programming that I forgot to eat lunch. And this strange feeling came over me that I was missing something. I found an old vending machine at the plant; it still had snack foods in it. I got them out, ate them. I started skipping meals. Flushing them down the toilet and stuff. Eventually I stopped eating the food and the drinks they provided altogether. Every day I went from this tiny trailer to my job. Back and forth, back and forth. Then one day Burton Crane showed up. Another day he brought in a child, Isaac, said he was mine."

Ian pauses and frowns.

"I don't know where he came from, Andie. I swear. I would think I would remember cheating on my wife." He pauses and my breath catches in my throat. "Sorry," he says quickly as he takes a deep breath and continues. "Another day he brought out the Manifesto and told me to read it. I found your picture in there. *Andromeda Somers, District Matchmaker.* I had skipped enough meals to remember I was staring at a photo of my wife. I just knew it, looking at that picture of you, that you were mine, but I couldn't remember how I lost you. And I didn't know where to find you. It was all so confusing. I remembered nothing about Lina until I saw her out at the Pasture." Ian moves his arm and tucks a piece of hair behind my ear. "And still I knew I was missing more. I remember seeing you, pregnant, wearing that blue dress. Knowing that the child in your belly wasn't mine. I wanted so badly to break away. But it wasn't the right time. When Crane guided me away from you... I should have done something. But I saw what was going on. People had gone missing. That old fat guy I worked with, Jeff Olson, he died in the reactor room one day. He looked sickly for a while, a few days at least, and then one day he just grabbed his chest and tipped over in his chair. The Volker carried him out. And Alexander was there saying something about they'd lost too many because the Residents weren't getting their normal medications. He had a heart condition. Remember that year he had a heart attack?" I nod, remembering Ian telling me over dinner years ago. "So I told myself that I had to pace myself. I had to pretend I was still eating their food and taking whatever it was laced with. The guys at the plant, they acted so strange. I mean, their mental abilities were all there, the logic and critical thinking, but they listened to whatever Crane said. They did whatever he told them to do. And I knew I had to act the same until the time was right."

The backs of my eyes burn realizing Ian was there watching as everything went on. As I gave up on him, as I moved on with another man. He was there for it all. I did it all right in front of him. My chin quivers, the guilt and regret stinging me hard.

Ian reaches out, one hand resting on my cheek. He shakes his head. "Don't cry for me. We had to make choices, Andie. But we survived. We got back to each other."

It's when he leans forward to kiss me that those tears come flooding out. God I hate crying, it makes me feel so weak and stupid.

"We did what we had to do to survive." His hand moves to my neck, brushing away the hair there and laying a sweet kiss on my shoulder. "I would have hated you if you sat back and did nothing. You did something. You kept our daughter alive. We found our way back to each other. And now look at us."

I squeeze my eyes tighter together and move my hand to swipe at the tears.

"We have each other. We have a future together."

Thirteen

Ian

Waiting until she's sound asleep, I watch her. Dr. Akiyama told me she used to have nightmares every night from whatever Crane did to her. I have never witnessed one and I never saw her bruises or broken bones, just the healed bump in her nose. Now, she sleeps peacefully, the only movement being the rapid motion of her eyes behind her eyelids. She may not have nightmares but she still dreams. Her breaths become shallow; a tiny sound escapes the back of her throat. She shifts and rolls away from me. Propping myself up on my elbow, I watch her as I pull the blanket to her bare shoulder. She makes a sound. She has a bad habit of talking in her sleep. I lean closer.

Adam, exhales off her lips. It's like Elvis punched me in the gut. She dreams of him and this isn't the first time I've heard her whisper his name in her sleep. He will never be dead to her, no matter how much he deceives her. I wonder if she dreamt of me as she lay next to him in bed. The anger and hurt are hard to ignore. I've tried so hard to ignore it and keep my calm. And while she chose me, I don't think I was her first choice.

I have never forgotten the day I killed those men and Andie kissed me by that cool stream after wiping the blood from my face. "*Be here now. I am here, our children are here. I will not let this ruin you,*" she promised me as she stared into my eyes and it felt like there was no one else by that stream but us. Self-consciously I knew he was near. I could feel his icy gaze on us as she brought me back from whatever dark place it is you go to after you've killed someone for the first time. She brought me back. It was her. She saved me. And I love her, but this... her saying his name in her sleep. It stings, hard. And that blackness that gripped my chest when I saw another human's life fade by my hands starts to creep back.

Part of me wonders if she remembers those words, or all the words of love we've shared over the years. If she's dreaming of him I find it hard to think that she does. Maybe I was ruined before all of that. I gaze down at her. No. One thing Andie doesn't do is lie. She may omit, or keep secrets, but she does not lie. If there's one thing I know about her, this much is true. If she says she loves me, she loves me. That's her problem, she mostly thinks with her heart and it's easy to see when she's withholding something, something about her looks ready to burst and then she spills it. She wasn't supposed to tell me the secrets of the Reformation that day at the water tower, but she did. She runs on pure emotion; guilt, love, and whatever else is coursing through her body.

Rolling onto my back, I wait a few more minutes and contemplate my plan. Now that she's asleep it's clear in my head again. It's strange that the only time I don't feel completely overwhelmed by her is when I'm far away or when she's sleeping. I wonder if she feels the same about me. Overwhelmed and attuned.

I roll out of bed and make my way to the gym bag. I pull out a green shirt. It's not the same shade as that man I followed. It's faded from years of wear at the Pasture. There is movement from a Guardian in the corner of the room as I slip the shirt on then leave the bedroom.

I check each of the children's rooms. They sleep soundly, tucked in their beds. Safe and sound. Making my way across the living space, I reach for the door, open it and slide out. I did this plenty of times at the Pasture. Slipped out at night, returned in the morning. This is something I'm skilled at. The door clicks closed behind me. A Guardian looks up from its post outside the door to our living quarters. "Stay," I whisper to it.

And now, time is frozen. At least that's how it's always felt the other nights I've snuck away to run or box with Elvis when we were at the Pasture.

I run down the long gray hallways. I skip the elevator and take the stairwell that I followed that man down. The only problem is that I'm at least twenty stories above the underground train platform, which means I have thirty-five stories to run down. I don't hesitate, I run. I don't slow until I hear the door below me open. Men and women in green clothes enter and exit at what I thought was the lowest level. Fifteen more to go. I fall into line behind a tall man and follow him down. More exit and follow me. I try to keep my heart rate steady, my eyes to the back of the man in front of me. They make no sound, there is no talking. Just silence. If they've noticed I don't fit in, they say nothing.

Finally, we reach the bottom level.

The hot, heavy air hits me as soon as we exit the door. I follow them, a straight line that extends to the rows of tables and tents I saw the last time I was down here. The ground is hard, a smooth polished stone with no dust. This place is bustling now. I step out of line and behind a nearby tent. From here I watch. I recognize none of their faces. They don't have the glaze of the Residents from Phoenix who are on Halcyon. These people have their own minds and they move with purpose.

I sniff the air, smell the most wonderful scent. Just like our kitchen at the Pasture when Andie spent the day baking bread. Real bread. Not that crap they serve us in the dining hall. "Two loaves," I hear a woman's voice from the tent next to me.

A man's voice answers. "Two dollars."

I lean around the tent. The woman hands over two bills. Two American dollar bills. I haven't seen American money in years. Not since before all this.

"Thank you," the woman says as she takes two paper packages. As she turns she catches sight of me.

Crap.

Her face goes from sunny smile to severe disappointment. She sets the bread down and walks straight for me. I back away, but she follows. "Nice shirt," she says, backing me further into the shadows of the tents.

I move away from her, looking to either side to find a way out. There's no escape. I check her out. She's just a few inches taller than Andie, maybe five foot five. She looks thin under her layers of green. I could push her over and run. But then where would I go? Thirty-five stories up is my only option. I'd crawl back into bed with my wife, a wife I fought so hard to get back. She doesn't even dream of me.

"Stop," the woman demands, brushing pale blonde hair out of her face.

"Why should I?"

"Because you don't belong here."

I give her a quick smile.

"What are you doing here?"

"Curious."

She reaches out and jerks my wrist forward. "Shit," she spits. "Of all goddamned people to wander down here, it has to be *you*."

"What's wrong with me?" I ask, a bit offended. Usually my wife is the one that gets noticed, not me–I stand in her shadow.

The woman glares like no other. She turns, still holding on to my wrist, dragging me along with her, muttering something about rules and greens and stupid men. I'm strong enough to break her grasp but because I'm curious, too curious, I let her drag me out of the shadows and down the rocky path. We pass tables and tents which now I can see are selling wares and clothing, food and shoes, packaging them up in brown paper, just like when James ordered me the gym clothes. Hands are dealing with money. American bills and coins which I used to have a wallet full of. This woman in the green skirt and top leads me to the far end of this cavernous place, stopping at a large door. When she pushes it open I see another stairwell. Anticipating my climb to the upper levels of Hanford, I don't look forward to climbing any more stairs. She turns and starts going down, dragging me along with her.

"Aren't you going to tell me your name?" I ask, tugging back on my arm to stop her.

She stops and glares at me. "As far as you're concerned, I'm your goddamned savior. That stupid mark on your wrist won't protect you down here. It will get you nothing but trouble." She looks me up and down. "Pawn."

I rip my arm out of her grasp. "Why do people keep calling me that?"

"That's what you are." She reaches forward and grabs the front of my shirt, tugging me down the few inches to meet her nose. "You are in a crapload of trouble." She releases my shirt and pushes me away, and grabbing my wrist again, throwing my balance off kilter for a second, it's all she needs as she tugs me five flights down. She's stronger than I expected.

"You're telling me, in all these years, one of us hasn't wandered down here?"

"No." She pushes a door open. "There are curfews for a reason. All you stupid Sovereign are supposed to go about your jobs and families during the day, and go to your homes at night. The others listen. But you. They already have you on camera sneaking down here the first time. If you were someone else, besides *her* husband, you'd be dead by now."

The door closes behind us and a violent rush of heat hits me. Instantly sweating, I ask, "How far underground are we?"

"Far enough to not need heat."

I wipe at my forehead. "Will you at least tell me your name?"

She smirks. "Jenn." She tugs my arm again. "I'm taking you to meet Crossbender. I can't let you go back up there without being debriefed."

"Crossbender?" Crap. Simple George is down here. No doubt he'll be muttering and pushing his glasses up.

Jenn knocks on a door and opens it. Inside there is what looks like a waiting room from the mid-twentieth century. Everything is burnt orange and dull green. There's even shag carpet. White and gold walls.

"What is this place?" I ask.

Two men look up from their seats near another door.

"Need to see Crossbender," Jenn tells them. She holds my wrist out. "We've got a wanderer."

One of the men, never rising from his chair, reaches behind him and knocks on the door. A soft voice from inside says something. The man twists the door handle and shoves the door open. Jenn drags me through. Taking my focus off of the room around me, I look up and see sweet, quiet Maryam Crossbender sitting behind a large desk.

--

"Ian Somers." Maryam stands. "Give me a moment with him, Jenn."

I hear the door close behind me and wonder, *does George know where his wife goes at night?*

"What the hell are you doing snooping around at night, Ian?" Maryam is no longer the sweet wife of George who I met weeks ago, making big eyes at her husband and smiling lovingly at my children.

"What is going on down here?" I demand.

She smiles sweetly. "Answer my question first."

"I was curious."

"People die from curiosity, Ian. You should have obeyed the curfew."

I could care less about the curfew. "Who are you?" I ask her.

"That's not important right now." She looks me up and down. "The first threat from my people wasn't enough to keep you away? Some of them will cut your heart out."

Little does she know, my heart was already half cut out the second my wife whispered the name of her ex-lover as she slept in our bed. And I can tell Andie that I forgive her, but no matter how many times it comes out of my mouth, the fact is; watching her, it broke me like nothing ever has. "I'm not scared of an old man with a knife. I've been through worse."

"Hmm." She taps a finger on her chin. "I think... we could use you. Tell me now. How did you manage to escape Crane's clutches? I know he had you all drugged up, doing his dirty work." She steps toward me. "How did you do it?"

"I stopped eating their food."

"That's it?"

"Yes." I don't bother telling her how I stared in a mirror for hours, practicing that complacent look that the Residents have.

"Hm. I think you've got more drive than I gave you credit for. Strong will. That will get you further than brains nowadays. I've seen it in your wife. It's the only reason why she's survived this long. No matter how bad Crane wants her for his little experiment. All this would have killed a lesser willed person." She pauses, tilts her head as though she's posing for a picture. "I've told you too much. George always says I have a problem with talking."

"You've barely told me a thing." I look around her office. "What is this place?"

"You're not ready to know." She walks around the desk toward me, reaches out and lays a hand on my shoulder and squeezes. "You're strong. Good looking. Innocent looking. No wonder Crane gave you back to her. Nothing to grind on her guilt like such an innocent looking man who'll do anything for his family. He controls her with her guilt. I bet she hates herself for what she did to you." Maryam removes her hand from my shoulder. I feel myself sweat. It's so hot down here. "How do you feel about death, Ian Somers?"

A sensation consumes me. One I can't quite explain. "Whose death?"

"Anyone that you love. Your family. Your children. Your wife. How do you feel about death?"

"I will do anything for them. I would die for them. For her." I was dead when they were taken away from me. Maryam sounds so innocent in her questioning, but asking a man how he feels about the death of his wife and his children cannot be taken lightly.

"Good." Maryam circles me. A wolf stalking its prey. How deceptive she is. "You will not mention this place to anyone. Ever."

That will be easy. If Andie knew what is dug under Hanford, she'd be down here in a heartbeat investigating. "Does George know?" I ask.

She laughs. "Of course he knows. He's one of the Originals."

"Originals?"

"Original Entities who want Crane gone. You know this already. Not so long ago our dear friend Elvis tried to start a revolution. He told you what Crane does. He kills families to get what he wants. He will use you to control her by guilt. And then he will kill you. He has done it to all of us."

"But..." I shake my head. "What is the point of all of this then? The Districts, Andie pairing the Residents, the Survivors, the Swamp People, the Funding Entities..."

"Wouldn't you like me to divulge all the secrets to you right now? Pawn."

My fists clench. "I am not a Pawn."

"Prove it."

"I will."

"Good. I'll look forward to it. Until then, I have a task for you, Ian Somers."

I didn't plan on coming down here to get an assignment, just to snoop around a bit. Still, I ask, "What?"

"I want you to kill your wife."

"No."

"Hm. Quick to answer. She's done her job you know. Paired the Residents, inserted the Subordinate gene into the human race. She even created a computer program to do it all for us. She is no longer needed."

They must not know that that computer program has an expiration date. Andie inserted a virus into the code. It stops assigning genetic pairs two years out. Without the encrypted password, the program will not continue. Three wrong tries at the password and it wipes the program. I think they still need her if they want to continue selectively breeding the human species. She is a mother and a wife; my wife, mine no matter how many times she says Adam's name in her sleep. She is still needed.

"If I asked you to kill George, would you say yes?" I reply.

Maryam smiles and then says the strangest thing, "I would never need to kill George. He's not as dangerous as your wife. This is your first warning; she will be the death of you. Pledge your allegiance to our army. Be a Sovereign of the Underland."

Sovereign of the Underland? No thanks. "You say this is an army and you want me to join." I cross my arms. "Yet I have no idea what you are fighting for."

"She clouds your vision," Maryam says matter-of-factly, with the flick of her finger toward me. "That is what she was engineered to do. Did you hear that, *she was engineered*? She is not the woman you married so long ago. We are deep enough that she can't affect us here.

But I can feel it in the dining hall. Her will. People bend to it now. I bet you feel quite free being away from her like this." Maryam's finger moves into her hand and forms a small fist. "Now, you are going to fight for your life and future generations."

I say nothing because not so long ago I was lying next to Andie in bed thinking something so similar. When I'm next to her I want nothing more than to please her and do what she wants me to do. Still, I say, "You're wrong. Andie would never hurt us. I feel fine around her." I lie.

"*You're* wrong. And you have no idea what you think you are fighting for," she says, a sardonic arch in her voice.

"I'm fighting for my family. To keep them safe from Crane. We were supposed to be safe here. It seems we've just nested in another snake pit."

"The children, they're safe. We need them. We need the ones who don't remember the world as it was before the Reformation. When the old die with their memories of America and the free world, and the young ones forget what the world was like, it will be much easier to rule over them. And when no one remembers anymore, it will be much easier to mold new societies. They won't argue because they don't know better, and your wife will keep them oh-so-peaceful, even better than the ones whose brains she genetically engineered. She will give peace and we will give change, again. There won't be the chaos of the first Reformation. Those that remain will be easily herded into their respective places. You cannot change and reform society overnight, it's a process: break, mold, break, mold, control."

I cross my arms. Jenn was right, whoever she is, I just stepped in a pile of shit.

"What about Crane?" I ask.

"Like I said, your wife is dangerous. She will take care of him. No doubt after the events which are about to occur. We let him believe he's been in charge. Let him design all that's going on above ground. He doesn't know about what's been going on down here." Maryam sits behind her desk. "You wonder how long this has been here?" She waves a hand across the room. "Like the décor? It's been here for a hundred years. We've been here for a hundred years."

"You people have been living underneath Hanford for a hundred years? I find that hard to believe."

She shrugs. "Believe what you want. But what you did believe is now going to change. From this second on, whatever you look at up there," she motions to the ceiling, "it will never look the same. People you knew will never look the same. Your wife will never look the same. The future of your children will never look the same. Continue on with your brainless tasks of checking nuclear reactor statuses, sitting back and watching your wife pair up the Residents and eventually the Sovereign, manufacturing Halcyon to control your Residents, and designing the strongest weapons mankind has ever seen in the ARU, which, by the way, I will thank you for in the near future."

Being a nuclear engineer, I have never been described as brainless.

"You should have stayed in your Pasture. All of you. Like happy, brainless cows. Your life could have been much easier, Pawn."

"Stop calling me that," I growl through gritted teeth.

"Jenn!" Maryam shouts toward the door. It opens and the familiar face of the woman who dragged me down here walks into the room. "Take him above." Maryam turns her focus to me. "Don't let me find you wandering down here again. If I do you will never be allowed above ground again. You will disappear. It's happened before. It will happen again. And, Ian, take a look around you while you're milling about Hanford, you'll start to notice a few kinks. That is, if you can get out from under your wife's influence." Maryam waves a hand at us. "Go. Now."

I follow Jenn out of the room. She leads me down the hall, up the five flights of stairs to the cavernous area. The place is packed now. There must be hundreds, thousands of them down here. Jenn weaves through the people, all dressed in green. Being tall, I don't miss the few guards standing on the outskirts of the tents and tables. Volker.

"Keep up, pretty boy," she shouts over her shoulder to me.

Seems the lies of the Reformation run deep.

When I get to the stairwell door, Jenn's there, holding it open. She has a look of humor spread on her face. "Bet you wish you never jumped down this rabbit hole."

She couldn't be more right. Still processing everything Maryam

Crossbender just told me, I don't bother with a reply. As I make my way up the stairs, Jenn follows. "Don't trust me to go home?" I finally ask.

"Crossbender told me to escort you out. You only need to go as far as the underground rail level. We call that the basement level. Then you can take the elevators the rest of the way."

More people in green pass us. "Maybe I want the exercise of the stairs," I say.

"You probably do. But from my view, I'd say you don't need it."

Red seeps into my face. I'm glad my back is to her. I hear her chuckle. What is wrong with this woman? I'm married. Happily married. Deceptively married.

When we reach the fifteenth floor, the space where Hanford ends and something else begins, I open the door. Jenn stays in the stairwell.

"They're going to lock these now. Because of you."

"Good," I mutter.

"Go crawl back into your warm bed with your little wife. Crossbender will call on you when she needs you."

I run for the elevators, trying to put as much space between me and whatever the hell it is that lies under the Hanford District. With Berkley's taunting fresh in my mind, all I can think is that I need to get her out of here. One Funding Entity wants her dead and another wants her in Galena. We've been living in these Districts and thinking we were safe, special even, better than the Residents and the Survivors and the Swamp people. We are nothing but lambs waiting for the slaughter.

I will not let this ruin you.

I will not let this ruin me.

FOURTEEN

ALEXANDER

IT TOOK ANDROMEDA LESS THAN A WEEK TO COME LOOKING for me. No one needed to tell me she was walking down the wing of my living quarters. I could feel her presence, no doubt like the rest of the Sovereign here and the entire Phoenix District. She doesn't realize this though. Someday she will. Someday she will realize what she is capable of and she will do the right thing. Andromeda will set all of this right. She will fix our mistakes. Crane was wrong in trying to break her. He thought she needed to feel the world's pain; that it would help her lead. Let's hope the world does not need to feel her pain since it is so easy to feel everything else that radiates off of her. I can imagine her dragging her pain across the plains of the planet will be enjoyable for no one.

I expected her to arrive sooner, maybe a few days after arriving here. It doesn't take her long to start investigating when something impacts her family in a negative fashion. There's no doubt in my mind that they're being treated differently. She is the Matchmaker, after all. They are intimidated by her, feared by some. Eventually she will decide all of their fates. I hope they are nice to her children. Maybe I should warn

George Crossbender about being nice to her children. There is something fierce in her when it comes to them.

I'm sure she's noticed how different this place is from the last time she visited. It's even different to my eyes; it seems the Reformation changed everything. It was meant to change everything. That was our plan. And in the end, all I wanted was to go home to die. But we can never go home. Not now.

"She's here," Will tips his head in my bedroom door. "You need help getting up?"

"No. Thank you, son." Through the pain I force a smile. It's the least I can do, fake it, even when it hurts so bad. After watching Morris suffer for his last few years I was hoping my ending wouldn't be the same. It seems it will be. I have caught the Funding Entity curse, a slow painful death in a time in which we have eliminated all the medications that might help. Perhaps Karma is real. It must be real. I never thought much of the supernatural, but now I'm wondering if there is more in this world, something stronger than the sciences, that cannot be explained. The forces of the earth are punishing us. That is all I can think.

"Alexander?" Andie enters my room in a hurry, pausing and paling at the foot of my bed. It is no doubt that she is remembering her time with Morris as he shriveled away to the heavens.

I wait for Will to close the door. "Andromeda, have you found Hanford comforting?"

She tips her head in question. Perhaps I said the wrong words, that sometimes happens now. It seems I am not the well spoken man I used to be. The words get jumbled sometimes.

"I'm not sure *comforting* is the right word. And I've asked you to call me Andie." She pulls the chair away from my desk and moves it, sitting down next to me. "What's wrong with you? We've been here a week and you go from walking with a cane to bedridden." She stares at me, her eyes taking it all in, assessing, looking for clues. I've seen her do this before. It's another reason she was chosen.

"I am dying."

"Why?" She reaches out and places her hand over mine.

I don't bother forcing a smile or letting her know that I can feel her index finger over the pulse on my wrist, her eyes still for a few seconds as she counts how many times my heart beats and I give her a few uninterrupted minutes as she finishes her assessment. It seems the urge to nurse others is still strong, even after being out of the field for all these years.

"We will all die. It's part of life. There's just less of an urge to prolong the death now. I am grateful that I have spent my last week with my children instead of rotting away in a nursing home for nine years."

Andromeda frowns and moves her hand away from mine. "Not all of us have the comforts of death." Her features morph, her eyes narrow, brow furrows, lips pinch.

"I didn't do that to you," I remind her. "Don't punish me in my last days for what Crane did to you."

"Then what should I punish you for?"

"For not telling you everything."

"So tell me everything now."

"I cannot." I truly regret this. There is nothing more I would enjoy than whispering every secret to her.

She sighs, frustrated. "Then tell me one thing. Does Galena hold the world's data?"

Oh, she is so drawn to the facts, research and numbers, like a moth to the flame. It will be her undoing, trying to figure out these puzzles. When she has an empty nest Crane will regret this.

"I need to go there. I need my great-grandmother's data on the nanocytes. How do I get into the Galena District without them knowing?"

"You simply ask."

"I ask?" she straightens in her seat.

"When you are ready. You will know how to ask and then the world's data will be at your fingertips and you will do what is right."

"What do you mean *I will do what is right*? I just want to get these nanocytes out of my body."

I give her an uncomfortable stare. Her eyes give a subtle twitch from side-to-side as she processes what I've told her.

"You know what to do. You know who to stop. You've always known. Galena will help you achieve this. Perhaps you can reverse the disappointments of the Funding Entities," I say.

"You want me to kill Crane. That's good, because I want to kill him myself. It seems everyone wants to kill him." She moves a hand to her temple and presses two fingers there. "Everyone wants to but no one will, no one can."

I force a smile, the strongest pain I've ever felt ripples through my left hip. It's as though Burton Crane can hear me, imparting a punishment from afar. The pain ripples to my chest, grasping my heart. I still and wait for it to pass. I was wrong; I don't have days or weeks. I have today, that's all I have left.

"So the Funding Entities have failed. That's great, Alexander. You've all killed millions of people for no reason at all. Wonderful."

As the pain begins to die down, I grip her wrist, squeezing, wishing she could give me some of her youth to stop this hurt. Her widened eyes force me to stop and focus. "It's amazing what can happen to the world when people stop caring. Do you think it mattered to all of those souls in the suburbs that running their air conditioning on high was only making the summers hotter? Do you think they realized they would all get some form of cancer because they ate and drank out of plastic containers that did nothing but leech chemicals into their bloodstreams? I will not apologize for trying to make the world a better place. I will not apologize for trying to save mankind."

"Save mankind?"

"Look at you." I stare at her for a long time. "It has been under your nose the entire time."

"What?"

"The solution."

"I figured out a solution. How to end the nanocytes."

I pat her hand. She probably thinks I am nothing but a crazed old man. "Good. Just remember to use it on the right person." The pain grips my chest, spreads across my shoulders, up the back of my neck. I still, grit my teeth and wait for it to pass. As I lay there, the pain a bright blaze behind my eyes, I focus and realize I will not last the day. "Now, Andromeda, ruler of men, chosen leader–"

"I'm not a leader or a ruler." She shakes her head, frustrated with me.

I force a smile. "If that's what you believe. I need you to take a deep breath and tell me it doesn't hurt. Tell me there is not pain in my bones and my soul. Tell me I am happy and content. Tell me I am loved and forgiven. Tell me all is well–"

"You want me to lie to you?" she scoffs.

"If you say it I will believe it. Cannot you do this one last thing for me? I am dying after all. This is my last wish. My dying wish."

Her features soften and for a moment I get a glimpse of the young woman Ian must have fallen in love with, bright green eyes, pale smooth skin, long curling brown hair. Appropriate that today she is wearing white. Beautiful. I prefer her over the hell hounds, which is what I expected to come for me. I wait.

Andromeda takes a deep breath, she closes her eyes and says, "Alexander, you are loved." She takes another deep breath and clears her throat. "Alexander, you have no pain, there is no ache in your bones. There is no regret in your heart. Your body is light, free and buoyant. Vibrant. Alexander..." An ache enters her voice, but for some reason I do not care. I am so selfish in my last moments of life. "Alexander, you are filled with contentment. You are forgiven of all you have done wrong. Your heart is light and filled with love." She chokes back a sob, presses her hand across her mouth for a moment before removing it. "Alexander," she whispers now, "Alexander you are loved and your Elysium fields are waiting for you."

I think I have thought that before, the memory flutters across my mind but I push it away, reveling in the lightness I haven't felt in months. There is no pain.

"You are loved. You are forgiven," she whispers.

The only words I have wanted to hear. The words I have been dying to hear. And I believe them so strongly. As though she speaks the truth and at this moment and I could care less about anything else. Reaching out a weary hand I swipe at the tear sliding down her cheek. "Why are you crying, angel?"

She says nothing.

When I close my eyes, I know it will be for the last time. But I am content. I am full. I am ready to join Janice. Perhaps I was wrong, maybe we didn't fail.

Fifteen

Andie

Today I lied to a man on his deathbed. I told him lies just so he could die with peace in his heart. A peace he didn't deserve. Actually, maybe he did deserve it. He was better to me than Crane. What is wrong with me?

I walk the long hallway to my living quarters. Sensing a presence behind me, I turn to find a Guardian trotting after me. "Oh, it's you," I tell the Guardian. "You need to go outside?" I ask.

The Guardian growls at me. Remembering my mishap with the tornado, it's probably best I don't go outside. But it's so hard to stop longing the fresh air and open space. We weren't meant to live underground. Soon I fear the walls here will start closing in on me. I stop outside the door to our living quarters. I need to do something. I need to do something and not sit around and think about Alexander's death over and over and over again. I turn around and head for the elevator. I press the button for the dining hall level and then I busy myself with searching for the kitchen. Gray, lifeless walls and halls. I head toward the dining hall and from there I scout the halls, hoping to smell the cooking of food.

I can hear the scraping of pans, the sound of a knife chopping hard against a cutting board. This sounds like a kitchen. I push the door open just a crack. Jackpot. The kitchen lies before me, all silver appliances and cookware. I push the door open and let myself in. My eyes focus in the bright lights. I step further into the room, notice shelves stocked with flour and sugar, see a door that can only be a cooler and an open space that looks like a pantry. My mouth waters at the thought of a home cooked meal. I step forward only to be stopped by a voice.

"You can't be in here," a young woman in a white apron says from near the stove. She holds a knife in her hand and is cutting carrots on a wooden cutting board. So the food does look real before they turn it into sludge.

"I just need to grab a few things. I'll be quick. Promise."

She shakes her head, waves her knife in my direction. "Uh uh. No one is allowed in here during working hours except the chefs. You should be at your assigned job." She takes a step toward me.

"Oh, well." I hold up my wrist. "I don't have an assigned job."

The young woman freezes and a look of shock covers her face. "You," she whispers.

What about me? "I just need some groceries. Don't take offense when I say the food here is less than palatable." I take two more steps into the kitchen and get a good look around, already planning what to take. George did bring us some food on our first night here, so this can't be so bad.

The young woman shakes her head from side to side before resuming her chopping. I watch her for a second before I start. She's not happy with me being here, but she's not making a move to stop me. Game on. I notice the shelves and coolers are lined with fresh food, and it makes me wonder how the hell they manage to turn it into sludge. I take a large metal bowl that's hanging on the wall and start filling it with potatoes, carrots, lettuce, real eggplant, squash and onions, a slab of beef, a whole chicken, a package of flour, another package of salt, a small shaker labeled as baking powder. As I fill my shopping bowl, I imagine how angry this will make George. Hopefully it will be nothing like his anger for going outside. That was almost laughable.

The young woman in the apron scowls at me as she stirs a pot at the stove.

"Almost done," I tell her, reaching for a stick of butter and a small baking tray to add to my stockpile. By the time I'm done, the large bowl feels like it weighs fifty pounds. I head for the door to take my spoils home.

"You're not supposed to be in here," the young woman says from her place near the stove. "I'm going to tell Crossbender." She now waves a wooden spoon at me. "It doesn't matter if you're the Matchmaker. You can't just do whatever you want without regard to Hanford's rules. The rules still apply to you people. You can't just walk around here like you own the place. The others were right, what they said about you."

I stop in my tracks. "What did they say about me?"

The woman presses her lips together, refusing to say more.

"What did they say?" I ask again.

"I'm going to tell Crossbender," is all she says.

I pause. "You're not going to tell anyone."

Strangely, she shrugs and turns back to her pot without saying another word.

I think I've turned into a sociopath. Or something like that. Stealing food and intimidating an innocent woman who's just doing her job. Crane would be proud. I open the door and leave, my grip on the bowl tightens. It's so heavy I have to stop walking a few times and heft it higher into my arms. Ignoring the odd looks from the people I pass in the hall and the elevator, I make my way back to our living quarters.

As I open the door and close it behind me with my foot, arms full and out of breath, one of the Guardians gives me a look. One of those looks only a dog can give a person, it says something like: *No one else may have seen you, but I did. I saw you. Now, give me some bacon.* I'm certain if the Guardian could talk right now, that's what it would say.

"You saw nothing," I tell the Guardian, setting everything on the counter. How many times will I be able to rob the Hanford kitchen before I get in real trouble? Shaking the thought from my mind, too eager to indulge in a real dinner that doesn't taste like crap, I do what I do best before my family returns from their day–I cook.

The entire time I'm preparing the beef, seasoning it, searing it, and arranging it in a baking dish, I can't believe how this place takes all that food and turns it into the junk they serve on the buffet. I know they're adding vitamins and protein to everything but there has got to be a better way. Glancing around the kitchen I wonder if the other living quarters have kitchens. If they're expected to eat in the dining hall, do they have any food or appliances at all? When I think about the apartment that George showed us deep underground, I don't remember even seeing a kitchen in it at all. It's a good thing I threw a tiny fit and got us out of there.

Turning my attention to the carrots and potatoes I stole, I wash, peel, and slice them before arranging them around the meat. Topping it off with onions and salt, I yearn for the fresh spices of home. There's nothing better than fresh thyme on a roast.

As I'm mixing a batch of simple baking powder biscuits the children trail in through the door.

"Real food?" Astrid asks. Her eyes open wide and she smiles.

"Good, I'm starving," Isaac says as he walks in.

When Raven breaks the threshold, a smile splits his face. It's been too long since I've seen him smile.

"Why don't you guys go start your homework, dinner won't be done for another hour or so," I tell them as I spoon the batter onto a tray.

Feeling a little more normal, almost having forgotten what went on this afternoon with Alexander, I clean up and set out the plates this place came furnished with. If there's plates, George must've expected us to eat here. Unless they're just left over. I may never know. Maybe I'll ask George.

Ian opens the door. He doesn't acknowledge that the children are absent, in their rooms doing homework, or the smell of a home cooked meal. Instead, he walks swiftly toward me. I set dinner on the table and free my hands. He grabs my upper arm and whispers harshly, "We need to talk, now." I follow him to the bedroom, close the door and turn. He starts pacing, running his hands through his hair.

"What's wrong, Ian?" I ask.

"They assigned me an Apprentice."

"Already?" I ask. "That's strange. You're far too young to need one, they only assign those to the Sovereign that they know are going to–"

"Die. To the ones they know are going to die. To the old and the sick and the ones who are getting ready to leave the field." He stops in front of me. His emotions wavering between anger and fear.

"You know what this means, right?"

I shake my head.

"Crane is planning on me dying. It might even be Crossbender. They're preparing for my death."

"No," I wave a hand, dismissing.

"Yes."

"No–"

Ian grabs my arm, hard, jerking me to focus. "Andie, this is what he does. These places, these Districts, they are not our safe havens."

"I know exactly what he does. And it's just an empty threat, Ian. He can't touch us here. That's why we left Phoenix. We are fine."

"Are you sure?" He moves to place his hands on each side of my face. "I can't lose you and the children. I can't do that again, not so soon after I got you all back." And as though I wouldn't believe his words, he presses his lips hard against mine. Ian's hands move to my shoulders, his fingertips pressing into my skin. It's as though he's trying to hold me here, keep me here with him in this moment, like I might turn away from him and leave him in a time of panic. Guilt stings the center of my chest and I remember the last time Burton Crane gave me a choice and I didn't choose Ian.

When he pulls away, I say, "I'll talk to George in the morning."

Ian just stares at my face.

"What's wrong?" I ask.

"I'm not special like you, Andie. They don't need me here. They don't need me at all."

"Stop it. You are special to me, as a result you are special to them. I won't let anything happen to you. Not again. Never again." I place my hands on his chest; feel his heart beating fast under my right palm. "I won't let them touch us. I won't let him touch us here. I'll talk to George."

"Okay." He nods.

I take a calming breath. "It will be fine," I tell him. "Everything will be fine." I feel his heart rate slow under my hand. He pauses, focuses on my face.

"What?" I ask.

"What happened to you today?" he asks.

"I stole food from the kitchen so I could cook us dinner."

"No. There's something else."

I thought I wiped the tears from my face, but he must know, after all this time together. "Alexander died. I was there as he passed. He asked me not to punish him. What does that mean, what does that even mean? *Me* punish him?"

"What did you do?"

"I just..." I shrug my shoulders and drop my arms at my sides. "I just told him he was forgiven, he asked me to. I said things that he asked me to say and then he died right in front of me. At least, I'm pretty certain he's dead. I didn't check for a pulse." I hold down a sob that threatens to rack my body, press my hand over my mouth and try to stop my chin from quivering, squeeze my eyes shut.

"Shhhh." Ian tries to soothe me as he pulls me into his arms, squeezing me tight to his chest. I can't ignore the feeling of his bicep pressed against my shoulders, his broad muscled chest pressed to my face. Inhaling, mint and lemons, the scent ignites a deep charge in my center, there is raw need to erase death with love. Moving to my toes, I press my lips to Ian's, hard, harder than I need to. My hands move to his shirt, underneath, fanning across well muscled flank and abdomen, still unbelieving that this is the body of my husband. In a few short seconds of lips and bodies pressed together we are out of breath.

Ian stills, presses his hands against my shoulders to stop me. "The kids." His eyes flick to the closed bedroom door.

"They're all doing homework." I move my mouth to his neck, his ear, licking and kissing and whispering, "I love you. I want you. Now." I know he won't deny me, he never does.

Ian pushes me away, taking a deep straggled breath. "Just a sec." He moves across the room, picking up a chair and placing it under the door handle. He reaches for the hem of his shirt, pulling it off in the few short steps it takes for him to cross the room to me. Then his fingers are quick and nimble on the buttons of my shirt. In a rushed breath he asks, "Why are you wearing white? You never wear white." He pushes the blouse from my shoulders.

"I was out of clothes. It was the only thing clean." I reach for the snap of his jeans

His warm mouth is on my shoulder, deft fingers under the strap of my bra. "You look good in white."

"I prefer black."

A laugh that sounds more like a grunt emits from his chest. "You're a bit stubborn." He kicks off his pants before reaching for mine.

"You like me stubborn." I tease, pressing my fingers into his hair, kissing his nose.

"I like you." He pauses before pushing my pants to the floor. "I love you."

"There was never a doubt in my mind."

And when his eyes meet mine, there is a flicker of something in their deep brown depths; pain, memories, I'm not sure. I take a deep breath and whisper, "I love you, Ian."

His eyes clear. He moves swiftly, lifting me and sinking the both of us onto the bed.

Sixteen

Ian

Listening to Andie's soft breaths as she sleeps, I roll out of bed. I can't risk hearing her whisper his name again. I get dressed in the darkness of our bedroom and retreat to the couch to read a book I found in Raven's room. The kid is always sneaking them home from school.

It's not long before the silent Guardians in the corners begin to stir. They stand and four of them wander out of the shadows to stare at the front door. I didn't even know there were four of them in here right now. They're always so quiet and barely noticeable, unless there's a problem. There is a hushed noise, a shadow moves in the space under the door. I stand. The Guardians move closer. Turning, I check all the bedroom doors. They're closed. Everyone's asleep. I take a few steps toward the front door. There's the muffled sound again and a soft growl from one of the Guardians outside the door. Reaching for the door, I jerk it open hoping to surprise whoever is wandering the halls this late after curfew.

"Hey, pretty boy," Jenn says with a smile. "Think your beasts need collared." She motions to the two Guardians staring her down.

Stepping into the hall, I close the door behind me. "What are you doing here?" I whisper harsh through my teeth. Grabbing her upper arm, I pull her away from our door.

"Hey!" She rips her arm out of my grasp. "You don't touch me."

I push myself away from her. "What the hell are you doing here?" I ask.

She folds her arms across her midsection. "Crossbender calls."

"What?" It is the middle of the night, I have to work in the morning, and it is past curfew. "I don't think so." I run a hand over my hair, smoothing it down.

Jenn's eyebrows rise as she smirks. "Did I interrupt you performing your husbandly duties?"

I find it hard to control a scowl. This chick is all sorts of inappropriate. "They're sleeping. All of them."

"Good. Then they won't miss you." She starts walking down the hall. "Come now."

"I have to work in the morning," I remind her.

"It's brainless work. You can do it with your eyes closed." She whispers over her shoulder with a grin. "Let's go."

Taking one last glance toward the door, I follow her.

"Why does she need to see me?" I ask Jenn when I get close.

"Crossbender doesn't tell me why. She just tells me who she needs and where to bring them."

"You do this a lot?"

"No."

"Then why did you come for me?"

"I found you. I brought you to her. Now you're my problem." She slows her step to give me a look. "Don't think I enjoy this. There's plenty I'd rather be doing." Jenn picks up the pace. She's wearing all green again. But instead of a skirt like the last time I saw her, she has on a pair of tight pants and what looks like a green leather jacket.

"Won't the cameras see us?" I ask her, tearing my eyes away from her. I shouldn't be looking at this woman. Especially not after spending the night with my wife. *My wife. My wife. My wife.* I repeat it and keep my eyes locked on the dull hallway before us.

"We can cut into the cameras. Run a delayed feed." She motions to a tiny black box in the corner of the hall. "They won't even know we passed through here."

"Figures."

"We've been doing this long before you and your clan showed up. So while you have no idea what we're doing and what's really going on here, we do."

"About how long would you say?" I ask.

She gives a sidelong glance. "Wouldn't you like to know?"

Yeah. I would. But I keep my mouth shut. That's how I got free from Crane. Being quiet. Looking innocent. Jenn brings me to the stairwell I last took to the levels under Hanford.

"Thirty-five flights." She bends, stretching her legs. "You ready for this?"

"That's nothing." I ran laps around the Pasture for nights, boxed with Elvis so hard I could barely move the next day. Thirty-five flights down is cake.

Jenn pushes the door open. "The pretty ones go first." She motions to the stairs.

I walk past her without a glance and start my way down. When we get to the bottom and I push that door open, the heat that envelopes me is almost unbearable.

"How do you people stand it down here?" I mutter.

"You get used to it." Jenn shrugs off her jacket revealing a green tank top underneath. I should have changed into the gym clothes James ordered me. I'll be sweating through my jeans and T-shirt in no time.

This place is alive again. Bustling. People, they all wear green, stand in line at the tents and tables. Forking over money and taking away bags of goods. Food, fabric, clothing, trinkets and things wrapped in brown paper. Looking to the far walls I can see people entering and exiting the dwellings that are carved into the rock. I follow Jenn to the far side of the cavern. We pass the vendor selling fresh bread. The smell of it makes my mouth water. Andie's been cooking at home but she hasn't been able to get her hands on any yeast. The taste of bread fresh out of the oven and loaded with butter is one that I miss. A few wayward glances come my way. From my clothes to the mark on my wrist it's easy to see I don't belong down here. Jenn pushes open the door that leads down another five flights of stairs. And then we enter the waiting room. The two large men sit outside Maryam's door. Looking up when we enter, Jenn says nothing, but one raises a thick arm and knocks on the white door in front of us before twisting the handle and shoving it open.

Maryam Crossbender rises from behind her desk as we enter her office. "Welcome, Ian." She moves to greet me. "Haven't seen you and your family for dinner lately. Tell me, have you been eating elsewhere?"

"Andie's been cooking." Saying her name down here, knowing that I'm keeping this secret, I don't want to talk about her. I don't want to taint the image of her in my mind with whatever is going on in the bowels of Hanford.

"Cooking what, exactly?" Maryam asks.

I shrug. "Food." I'll be damned if she's going to pinch information out of me about our home life.

"And where is she getting it from? There are no farms above ground. And we know after her little incident with the tornado she hasn't ventured up there again."

"I have no clue. I come home from work each night and dinner's there. I don't keep tabs on what she does all day."

"Hm." Maryam rounds her desk to stand in front of me. "You should. Do you know what she does during the day?"

I don't respond. Of course I know what she does. She meets with George; she takes care of the kids and our new home. Somehow she finds food to cook us dinner. She pairs the Residents of all the Districts. She doesn't have time to do much else. But, there was that one time she ventured above ground and nearly got sucked up into a tornado.

Maryam eyes me for a moment before speaking again. "Have you thought at all about our last meeting?"

I assume she's talking about the last time I was down here and she asked me to kill my wife. "Haven't thought much about it. Not going to do it. Told you that before." I cross my arms over my chest and straighten my back. I'm not as tall as Sam, but pretty tall. I'm hoping Maryam will back off.

She doesn't. She steps closer. "I need your help, Ian." She sounds a bit desperate. "Before it's too late."

I laugh at her. "It's already too late. Your husband has assigned me an Apprentice." I pause for effect. "You know what that means? I do. Someone's planning on killing me."

Maryam smiles. "I told you she would kill you."

No, not her. Crane. I'm sure it's Crane. He's used me before to make her do things. I wouldn't put it past him to use me again. "She won't," I say. "Someone else will. And I'm pretty sure I know who."

"Ian." Maryam steps closer to me. "You're not made for all of the deception that's going on up there." She motions to the ceiling. "Just do what I've asked. And then you will be free. You can live out a quiet life. A normal life–"

"No." I shake my head and back away from her. "How many times do I need to tell you? I will not kill my own goddamned wife. No. No. No. No. No," I say a bit sing-songish. "What the hell is wrong with you people?"

Maryam crosses her arms over her stomach. "You're going to wish you did when you're six-feet under, Pawn."

"I can't believe you dragged me down here in the middle of the night over this. This is my final answer. No. Do not come to me again. I am done with you people."

I reach for the door, jerk it open and leave. When I get to the stairwell I hear Jenn's footsteps behind me trying to keep up with my pace. I have to get out of here. I can't spend one more second down here with these people asking me to kill her.

"It's just your wife," Jenn says as she catches up. "Do you even love her?" she asks. "I mean, we all heard what she did to you. Ditched you and moved on with that other guy. Had his baby. Played house for a bit. And you were alive the entire time. What's his name? Adam. If that were my wife I think I'd have killed her a long time ago. I mean, talk about a woman scorned, but a man..."

That's it. Something snaps inside me and stopping, I turn to her and before she can say another word I shove her against the wall, hard. "Shut. Up. Now." She smirks. If she were a guy I think I'd punch her in the face. "You people are screwed up. I love her. She loves me. We have children together. We are a family. And I wasn't raised like that. To kill people. It's bad enough..." I stop myself before telling her about the Swamp people that I killed near the train tracks that one day. That is a guilt I will never outlive. But that was in a moment of pure panic. That was live or die. They would have killed us all. They tried.

"How were you raised, pretty boy?" Jenn peels my fingers off of her neck.

Hands shaking, I can't believe I was holding her like that. "With decency and conviction," I reply, shoving my hands in my pockets.

"Well," she snickers, "both of those will get you nothing nowadays." She stops short. "Crossbender was right."

"About what?" I snap at her.

"You're too innocent. You don't belong in the middle of all of this." She smirks and winks. "Nice knowing ya, Pawn. I hope your death is painless. For your sake. See you in hell, pretty boy."

I take the stairs, all thirty-five flights, up, trying my damndest to work out the anger. These people are ridiculous. I can't kill my wife, the mother of my children. I won't. And there's no way she would ever harm me. By the time I reach the top level I'm out of breath. I push the door open, don't bother to be quiet. Making my way down the hall, I wonder if they still have the cameras on a lapsed feed. If not, I might be in a bit of trouble with simple George.

There are two Guardians outside the doorway to our living quarters. They watch me from under the thick hair on their faces. I slide in the door. Lock it behind me. I check on the children and make sure they are all in their beds sleeping soundly before going to the room I share with Andie. My wife. A wife that Maryam Crossbender wants me to kill. I could never do that.

In the dark, I slip my clothes off and slide into bed next to her. She's sleeping so soundly she doesn't even move as I get comfortable. Reaching out, I wrap an arm around her waist and pull her close to me. With a soft sound, she rolls and presses her face into my neck. Her life is in danger and I have to figure out a way to keep her safe. After all, we've worked so hard to be together. I can't give up now. No, I will not kill her and I will not let any harm come to her.

Seventeen

Andie

The next morning I meet George in his office. He's sitting behind his desk, buried under a mound of papers. What does he need all these papers for? What do they mean? Crane only had maps. But George, it's like he has paper records of everything and nothing electronically stored. Where does he even get all of this paper from? I have half a mind to walk over and pull a few pages off of the top of the stack to his left and read through them.

"Can I help you, Andie?" George asks as he pushes at his glasses.

I step into his office and close the door. "Ian has been assigned an Apprentice. Why?"

"Oh, well, it's just a necessity," he answers calmly, waving his hand at me in a gesture that suggests this is no big deal.

It's a big deal to me. "Don't screw with me, George." I take five steps toward him, just enough to get me to the edge of his desk. "Why does he have an Apprentice? They are only assigned to the old and dying."

"We don't have many old and dying here. But we do have a lot of youngsters ready to leave their nests and they need to work. I'm out of old people." George shrugs innocently. "That's all."

I sigh and control the urge to reach out and take a piece of paper off of his desk. "Ian's convinced this is Crane trying to kill him off." I sit in one of the chairs that are in front of his desk. "He was scared last night."

"He shouldn't be." George moves a stack of papers from in front of him to his left. "I haven't heard from Crane. This has nothing to do with him."

"You promise?" I ask.

"I promise." He begins sorting through a new stack of papers.

"I moved my family here to protect them. I came here because you are one of the last people I trust, George. Please tell me I can continue to trust you."

George stops sorting the papers on his desk. "You can trust me."

"Good."

Standing and wandering across his office, I stop in front of the map that hangs on his wall.

"Did you just come here to stare at that?" he asks me.

"I'm studying it."

"You have an obsession with it."

"You know I need that data."

"So what's staring at a map going to do for you in that regard?"

"I'm memorizing the route I'm going to take."

"What route is that–" George stops as the shrill ring of the phone on his desk interrupts us. "This is Crossbender," is how he answers the phone. "Uh huh." He nods. "Yeah." There is a hollow noise as he taps his index finger on his desk. "Yes, well..." George looks at me. "She's standing right here. That's why no one answered at her living quarters. Sure. Yes." He holds the receiver out to me. "It's for you."

"Who is it?" I ask.

"Sam."

I rip the phone out of his hand. "Sam?" I ask. "What's wrong? Is everything okay?"

"Andie?" Sam's voice sounds a bit off. "How are things in Hanford?"

"They're fine. Different, but fine." I avoid eye contact with George. "Why are you calling, Sam? What's wrong? Is it Blithe?"

"Well... yeah, actually she's in labor. Can you come? Can you come back to Phoenix and help..."

"Help what? Sam?"

There is the sound of a soft feminine voice in the background. "Sorry, Blithe says hi. What I was asking before, can you come get us? I think it's time for us to leave Phoenix."

Shocked, I still, not expecting this so early. We've only been here for a few weeks, which means Blithe isn't exactly due yet. But Sam has never been one to give up or run. He was going to watch Crane, he was so certain. And now he's calling. I cannot control the desire to have them here with us. The children miss Blithe and I miss Sam.

"Andie?" Sam asks on the other end.

"Yes, Sam. Yes. We'll come get you."

"Okay, great." He talks in the background, probably telling Blithe. "When will you leave?"

"Soon. Maybe in the morning." I finally look to George and he nods in approval. "Definitely in the morning. First thing."

"Okay. Great. We'll see you soon."

"See you soon, Sam."

There is a click on the other end. I hand George the phone and he hangs it up.

"So..." George starts.

"Looks like I have to go get my brother from Phoenix."

And now that I'm standing this close to George's desk, I get a good look at the papers he's been rifling through. There are names, lists and lists of names covering each piece of paper. Some have a red line through them, others a black checkmark. The corners are rumpled, like he's been sorting through these for a long time, years even. I pick up a top sheet.

"What is this, George?"

He reaches out, lightning fast, and rips the page from my hand, setting it nice and neat on the stack it came from. "Names."

"I can see that. Whose names?"

He gives me that sweet, shy George look before looking back to the stacks of papers. "The American census. From just before the Reformation."

"What?" I reach out to take another sheet but George slaps my hand away.

"Don't touch them." He pats the sides of the stack I was reaching for, making sure every sheet is straight and in place. "Don't mess them up. It took me years. Years. All these years." He seems a bit distraught, like I was about to kill his wife or something.

"What are you doing with stacks of names from the census?"

"Checking them," he replies, matter-of-factly, like it's no big deal and not the least bit odd.

"What are you checking them for?"

He stands straight, looks around his office, leans toward me and says, "For those who are dead, those who are alive, and those who don't belong."

"Don't belong?" I ask and it comes out as a whisper.

George nods energetically. "Or they were alive and have gone missing."

"Hm." I cross my arms and stare at the piles of papers. "But... George, this may sound a little odd but there were over four-hundred-million people in the US before the Reformation. And this," I motion to the stacks of papers, "this will take you the rest of your life to figure out manually. Why don't you have a computer program for this?"

He sets one hand down on a stack, fingers spread and says, "Because I don't want anyone to know about it."

"Oh." Well, that makes some sense. Crane was tracking what I was doing on my computer, I don't doubt that the Entities can track what goes on with the computers in all the Districts.

"I can trust you to keep this between us."

It's not a question. George is demanding something for the first time ever. Which tells me he's onto something that he thinks is very serious. I'm not sure if I find it as serious as he does. The Reformation killed millions and millions of American citizens, and that was the goal of the Entities. For George to be nitpicky now... I don't have time to think about it. I have to get ready for my trip to Phoenix.

EIGHTEEN

MACK

ADAM WATERS STANDS IN THE MIDDLE OF SIX SWAMP MEN. IT always seems to start in the same place, right where he killed their leader, on the train tracks that haven't been used in years. I think he meets them out here because he secretly wishes she'd come back. It's been years now. She's never coming back. Word has it from the settlement up near Phoenix that no one has seen her for months. The gates opened once and there's speculation that she left. Now they never see anyone besides the Volker. Adam's been worse since then. Taking risks, risks that a normal man wouldn't survive.

Christian, the leader of the Survivors, appointed Adam as a leader here. He leads all right, but methinks he's losing it. He doesn't sleep, he's always running. Everyone does what he says, which is good. I've seen what has happened to the few that haven't.

Now the Swamp people want more food. They always want more food. And this is what it always leads to. A fight to decide if he gives them more. Each time he tells them the same thing, "Kill me and you can eat me." They were right when they told him he has nothing left to live for. This has been going on for years.

I shift in my tree as the Swamp men step closer to him. Turning my head to the side, I try to catch every word.

"Still de worst kinda man." A lanky man with a missing eye spits on the ground as he speaks. "Tol' ya las' time. You got nothin' left to live for. Can see it in yer eyes." The man points his stained fingers at Adam. "Heard dat lady wid all dat pretty hair went up to de heavens. Now ya'll never live happy forever like in dose movies." He grins.

This is stupid. He could try to replace her. God knows more than enough women have thrown themselves at his feet. I've never noticed him with any of them. I hope they're lying, because that's all they have to say to him. Adam all but explodes. It's seven to one, dust and fists flying. I'm supposed to be his backup and I can't see a damn thing. I don't bother taking aim. I can't waste the ammunition. And then there's the part where he told me to leave him alone, and that he doesn't need backup. Usually he doesn't.

When the dust clears Adam is lying on his back, bent over the rail of the tracks. Four Swamp men are down. One looks pretty close to dead and another one is bleeding profusely from his head. The last one standing bends down to Adam and says, "Dis de las time. Mo manje. If dere be no food we start taking de young ones when yer not lookin."

Adam coughs and spits a mouthful of blood at the man's feet. "Go fuck yourself."

The Swamp man smiles a rotten-toothed smile. Others slither out of the forest and drag their injured home with them. "Dis de las time," the Swamp man warns again as he backs into the shadows.

I jump down from the tree I was perched in and make my way toward Adam. He rolls onto his side and groans, wiping blood from the corner of his mouth. This is the sixth time they've been here in as many weeks. We've given them all we can. If we give them the rest of our food we'll have nothing to last out the rest of winter.

"Really showed them."

"Screw you," Adam spits at me, his mouth lined in blood.

He says the same thing every time. I hold a hand out to help him off the ground. He grunts and rolls away, stumbling to a standing position.

"You coming back to Romney now?" I ask.

Adam grunts again and staggers off toward the direction that the Swamp people went.

I let him go and don't bother to ask. He'll disappear into the forest for the night and come back tomorrow for dinner looking like he never got into a fight with six other men. There won't be a single bruise or a cut. It's not normal for a man to heal so quickly and if Christian Whitmarsh could meet him, I'm sure Adam would take over this place. I just hope he brings back a deer, or any type of fresh meat. These men won't last much longer.

I make my way back to Romney, pass the school and head to the little apartment I keep behind a big old Victorian house. When we took over here a bunch of the guys claimed these huge houses that had been empty since the Reformation. Glorified bachelor pads. Not me. Too much space. I found a little in-law apartment in this backyard. Good thing too. The yard is fenced in and Jill likes to graze it when she's not following me around all day. Friggin goat. The last thing I need is a goat to keep track of. Hard enough running this place every time Adam decides to run off.

I walk to my place. Jill greets me with a soft bleat and trots to my side. I open the gate and let her out.

"Come on, goat." I head back to the school to inform the guys that Adam's on a mission. Hope Christian doesn't show. Rumors are he doesn't like when posts are abandoned. He took out unit leaders all over the east coast for abandoning their posts or participating in unsavory activities. The Skin trades. That's what was going on before. Hard to see your fellow man engaged in that. But after the Reformation there wasn't much else. Proud to say I never got my hands dirty in that stuff. Last unit leader did. He's dead now. Waters took his place. It's better now. Hard to turn a blind eye when they're bringing women and girls through here, talking about trading them and stuff. Mighty sick.

Jill bleats from my side. Wish I had seen the look on Adam's face when Steven offered her up. Hope it made him sweat, only because it seems like nothing else does. Would be nice to see him look shocked to shit like he did when we brought in that Sovereign woman from Phoenix. He can say all he wants but from the second he saw that mark on her wrist and the necklace, there was about three and a half seconds in which I registered pure shock and awe on his face.

By the time I'm done thinking about my boss and his lady troubles I've made it to a cluster of our men. I inform them that Adam's on a mission, again, and he left me in charge, as usual. Then I make my way to his office. This is where he lives, he never leaves. This is his Headquarters. I sit in his seat and click on the desk lamp. It has been pretty good here since Adam stepped up. He said he came from Colorado. Got injured on some bizarre mission near there. He doesn't talk about it much. Just what he knows about the Survivors out there. He said there's more food out there. Mostly just the big cities were bombed during the Reformation. Most of the farms weren't harmed. Then came the Great Panic. More death, disease. I think the only reason I survived it all was because I was on a camping trip in the Catskills and couldn't find it in my heart to return to civilization once I saw civilization had gone to shit overnight. Never liked hanging around big groups of people. Tried to stay away when they started rounding up men to form the militias, kinda got forced into this one. They were looking for big guys. And well, I'm a big guy. Stuck with it out of curiosity. And then it was for the food. The units always got fed. No matter what we were dealing with; good, bad, ugly. Whoever was in charge of the units, they always made sure we had food.

Heard from one of the guys on the unit, he's from down near New Mexico, he said tons of the Survivors from down there swamped the border, tried to cross into Mexico. They thought it would be safer there. It wasn't. The first site they bombed was the border crossing. Then a new Reformation began all over again in South America.

Jill jumps up on Adam's couch and makes herself comfortable.

"No shittin' on that," I warn her.

She replies with a bleat before tucking her head under the arm rest cushion.

Hope that's not where he sleeps. I'm sure if he comes home to his bed smelling like goat it'll get me some rough rounds during training. That's all we seem to do now. Train, keep track of the Swamp people and wait, then train some more. One day I asked Adam what we are waiting for, what the point is in having these units all over like some damned Militia in waiting that seems to never do too much.

Skin trade is over but that doesn't mean the bad guys are gone, he had replied. He was right. Haven't seen much of it but I'm sure it still happens.

Then there's the damn Swamp people. Trying to keep them from going any further north has been a pain in the ass. Seems they think that Phoenix District has something special. Adam didn't tell them about all the food and livestock out west. That's where we get our shipments from. If we can't grow it here, it ships in every so often. Seems to be less and less now that most of the oil and gas have been used up. Maybe if the Swamp people knew about the food stores in the west they'd leave us alone. I don't think that Phoenix District has much. Just electricity and people. What's the big deal with that?

Jill snores. Didn't know goats could snore.

There's a knock on the door and when I look up Chuck is standing there. Used to be quite the punk but he's turning out to be a good guy. Killer aim with his slingshot. He'll come in handy when we run out of bullets.

"Mack," Chuck says as he enters the room. "Got a paper in. Found one of the guys stuffing his boots with it. Thought you might want to see this."

"Is it a recent one?" I ask, standing to take the wrinkled paper from him.

"Says it's from last week."

"Hm." I scratch my chin through my beard. "Usually they're months old before we get them."

"Yeah, reckon you'd want to see one this recent. Wait until you read the story on the back page."

"You read it already?" I ask.

"Of course."

"Okay. Thanks."

"Sure, man." Chuck pauses on his way out. "Mack?"

"Yeah."

"Pantry's empty." He looks away. He's probably hungry. We all are.

I knew this was coming. Knew it when the Swamp people told us at the tracks that they wanted more. There's nothing right now. I look at Jill. "Take one of the goats."

Chuck looks at Jill. "Which one?" he asks.

"Not that one." I tip my head at Jill.

"Well, that's our last goat then. Last one that isn't a pet."

"Can't be avoided."

"Sure." Chuck pauses before leaving again. "Paper said there's a trade fair coming in two days over near the Ohio border. Might be able to get some rations from there."

I sit and flatten the paper over Adam's desk. "Get together some stuff to trade. We'll send a team out."

Chuck nods and leaves.

I start reading the paper. There's updates on that oil rig. Seems they got it moving, selling the refined stuff for twenty-five dollars a gallon or equivalent trade. Holy shit. Those numbers make President Berkley look like a saint. Don't know what they're doing asking for dollar bills, might as well wipe our asses with any leftover American money. It's worth nothing now. One day I caught a guy rolling tobacco up in a twenty. When I asked him why he said it was cheaper than trading for rolling papers and the bills burned slower.

There's a story about big Militias forming in the south, not little ones like we've got around here with twenty or so men, they're forming by the hundreds. Seems there's been a rash of people gone missing all over the coast. Disappearing from their beds at night or during the day. Strange. But if I had to bet on it, I'd say they became dinner for the Swamp people. They might have a chance with a unified force.

There's an update for the state of Arkansas, lists crimes and penalties. Most include death. About time. Lotsa crap probably wouldn't have gone on during the Great Panic if people knew they'd be held accountable for their actions.

There was a helicopter sighting over Washington State. Doubt that. Nothing's been in the air for years. Unless you count about a million missiles. Wonder who paid for all them? There was no warning, no motivation of troops, and our President just disappeared. Nothing like abandoning your own country and leaving them to fend on their own.

More deaths in Florida. Seems that state is a loss. They're begging for insecticides to be sent their way if any are found. And they're looking for people who can hunt alligators. Seems people got real dumb these past few years and keep feeding themselves to the wildlife. Idiots.

There's some stories of people sacrificing their children to that District in Arizona. The Tonopah District they call it. Seems they give away baskets of food and jugs of water for a child. Makes me sick reading that. Couldn't ever imagine giving up my own flesh and blood to fill my stomach. Makes me thank God I don't have a family. I'd rather die than do that.

Here's a story, someone said they heard and saw a train moving north near the Kansas border a few weeks ago. Hope they don't try to stop it. I've heard those Volker shoot first and ask questions later. Adam said the Districts were supposed to stay hidden, a secret even. They are like the white buffalo, we know they're there but we never see them and never seek them out. A bit sacred, a bit speculative. And there is something extraordinary and frightening about living behind those electrified fences and never being able to leave. I wonder what goes on behind those walls. The thought of that Sovereign woman comes to mind. Adam says they were together, was it before the Reformation? That has to be the only way he could know her. No one is allowed into those gated places. And the times that they take their train to go elsewhere are few and far between. I wonder how he knows her? And how could he still be so obsessed with her now that she's married. But, one of her children that was here, the little one with the dark hair and blue eyes, he looked just like Adam. Hm. Strange. Doubt he'll ever say a word about it.

Looks like in the middle of Virginia someone found an underground bunker. A family was stuck under there for years. Paper says they fled there during the bombings but a large slab of cement fell against the door and they couldn't get it open. They had enough food down there for ten years. A little generator. Article says they heard lots of strange noises coming from underneath the bunker. They were probably starting to go crazy. Wonder who stumbled upon that? Wonder if the family likes being above ground or if they prefer the bunker to real life the way it is now. Says there are three daughters, all grew up underground. At least they missed the skin trade. Well, probably easier for them to process everything not knowing what it was like before.

I flip the paper to the back page, there's a notice from the state of South Carolina. *Wanted on charges of murder and treason, Christian Whitmarsh.*

Seems I'm working for a wanted man. Not surprised. From the stories I heard he should be wanted in each state along the east coast. I wonder if Adam knows this. I fold up the paper, Wanted poster side up and tuck it into his top drawer. He'll see it when he gets back.

Nineteen

ADAM

I HAD HOPED THAT IT WOULD HAVE TAKEN LONGER THAN five years for something like this to happen. I make it north to Phoenix faster than I ever have before and when the Volker radio for Sam, I pace the cover of the trees waiting for him to show. Hearing the sound of an approaching vehicle, I stop and watch. I'm expecting Sam's tall frame to exit the Volker SUV and I am surprised when I see Blithe step out. I pause. Almost forget what I'm supposed to be doing here. She crosses her arms over her stomach and she... she's pregnant. What the fuck? Sam knocked her up. Shocked, I somehow find it in myself to write: *Where's Sam?*

I toss the stick. Blithe retrieves it. She pulls a pen from her pocket and begins writing. Sam must have sent her. She tosses the stick over the fence. I untie the paper, unable to take my eyes off of her bulging abdomen.

Her reply: *He's busy.*

That's it, he's busy. She's never been wordy with me, not since she found out I never died. I write back: *Where's Andie? Swamp people said she's dead.*

Blithe replies: *She went to Hanford with the children. Congratulations, you're going to be an uncle.*

I stare at her. She stares back. Not knowing what to say and barely even noticing when another stick drops by my side before I get a chance to write anything back to her. I open the note and read: *I'll never forgive you for dying. Twice. It was bad enough all those years ago when the military officers came to our house and told us you died in combat. Mom packed away all your things. Dad was never the same. We tried to erase you from our lives. It was never the same, living with a ghost. When they died I had no one. I was alone for all those years. Finding out you were alive all that time... and then you do it all over again! The third time I find out you've died you better stay that way or I'll kill you myself.*

She must have written this before coming out here. When I finally look up at her I can't help but see the little sister I left home so long ago. She was headed off to high school with a new haircut and her braces off of her teeth and I was headed off to war. She seemed so grown up then. But I wasn't thinking of her. A good brother would have really protected his little sister like Andie did with Sam. I didn't even try. I even used her as my excuse that day Andie asked me why. I used her as a scapegoat when the truth is I didn't even think about her when I made all those decisions. Not her, but someone else. I'm the worst kind of brother there is, even if I'm not her true brother, I should have done better. Mom and Dad, hers and my blood ones, are probably rolling over in their graves. They didn't raise me to be like this. No, they raised me to be the All American boy next door. To be a small town cop or a banker or a principal, or some white collar job with a house and two-point-five kids, big Christmases at home and birthday parties in the backyard. That backfired. They didn't raise me to be like this. Everything I did, the choices I made, they were all for myself. I don't know when I became so selfish and started putting my country before my family. Then it all went and backfired to shit. Now it's so hard to figure out who's telling the truth or which side to fight for. Too many times I've found myself staring off into space, wondering what I'm fighting for. I used to know. I don't think I do anymore.

I fold the paper and tuck it into my pocket before turning around and walking away. Blithe doesn't need me to mess up her life anymore. Andie will be safe in Hanford. As long as Sam keeps his side of the deal and the power stays on, I have no reason to visit this place again.

Twenty

Sam

Now

"You sure you want to do this?" Blithe asks, her face masked by the shadows of the room.

"Yes." I know it's not the answer she wants to hear. And I am sorry to say it and disappoint her.

"Okay," is her soft response as she looks away.

Gripping her chin between my fingers, I draw her gaze back to mine. "She can do good. I was going to risk my life for my country anyways. I'm just not going overseas to risk my life on a battlefield in some foreign country. I'm doing it at home." Home, it seems like a foreign country now. My eyes drift to her belly. "You sure you want to do this?" My hand moves away from her face and toward the round abdomen jutting between us.

Blithe looks down. "I have no one without you, Sam. My brother gave up on me. My parents are dead. I have to do this because without you... I am hopeless."

"And the baby?"

"There's still a chance we might make it. We could come out on the other side of this alive. She'll be fine without us." I don't miss the disappointment in her voice. Six kids and a house in the country. Growing old together. That was our dream. Too bad that's all it was, a dream.

I search for something to say to her. Something that might make this easier. Chicks like those flowery words. But at this moment, knowing what we are about to do, I cannot think of one of them. Instead I pull her close, kiss her and tell myself that in the end all of this will be worth it. Even if I lose, if I fail, it will be worth it. I'm not going to bore her with bullshit. She knows how I feel about her. We made this decision together. Someone has to put an end to all of this.

Her jaw twitches as she grinds her teeth and I remember what she was doing earlier today while I was making preparations. She went to face her brother. "What did he say?" I ask.

"Adam said to keep the power on. He won't be back unless it goes off," she says.

"Good."

"You sure you don't want his help?"

"If there's a problem, he'll show up."

"How can you be so sure?"

"Just am." I move away from her, toward the closet and pull out a bag, and start packing some of our clothes. We have to make it look real. A few nights in the hospital. That's what we're planning on.

"Lex and Ira will never forgive us for this. Abandoning them," Blithe points out.

"When they're older they'll understand." I throw some of my clothes in the bag. "They are the next generation of Sovereign. They have to grow into men someday. It's just happening sooner rather than later."

"But they're so young." Her voice softens as she moves to her dresser and begins removing clothes.

"Elvis will take care of them. He has a soft spot for kids ever since he lost his own." I pause, and for the billionth time think of losing the baby that Blithe is carrying.

And as though she senses my thoughts she says, "I think we should name her Norah."

I feel my body tense. This is so much harder with her having a name now. Before I could just separate myself... No. That's a fucking lie. No matter how many times I've tried to tell myself it's different; the baby isn't born, not seeing her barely makes her real... it was all lies. And now she has a name. Fuck me. This task just got infinitesimally harder. "I like that name," I tell Blithe.

"Are you going to call your sister?" she asks.

"Yeah." I head for the phone, pausing as I reach the threshold of the doorway. "I love you," I tell Blithe.

"I know." She smiles.

"If things were different..."

"I know." She turns away from me and starts packing her clothes.

I make the call, watching Blithe the entire time from the doorway. "Tell Andie I said hello," Blithe interrupts.

She's digging in the closet when I hang up the phone. "How long before they get here?" she asks.

"Probably within forty-eight hours." I look at the packed bags at the foot of the bed. "What are you doing in there?"

She pulls out a black vest. "The one thing my brother ever asked me to do while he was here was hold onto this for him." She shakes the vest out and unzips it. "He said this was extra, that I might need it someday." She takes a few steps toward me. "Thought it was just a vest until I saw him come back from the dead. One day I pulled the stitching apart. Right here." She motions to a frayed corner. "I couldn't even cut the material inside with a pair of scissors. It was so strange..." She laughs a little. "The one thing my brother ever gave me was a bullet proof vest. What brother gives their little sister a bulletproof vest? He couldn't give me a hug, or a phone call, he faked his death twice–" The last word comes out with as a sob.

God, I hate it when she cries. Everything that makes me a man seems to melt. I want to tell Blithe that there are a few people Adam cares about and if he's keeping his distance from her there's a reason why. It doesn't mean he thinks less of her. He's just decreasing his blast radius for when the shit hits the fan.

Blithe clears her throat. "Anyways. It was too big for me before. And I was never in the line of fire. But," she holds the vest out, "He's a bit shorter than you. I think this will still fit. Take off your shirt."

Reaching for the bottom of my shirt, I pause for just a second. "You know, usually when you tell me to take off my clothes, it's not to put more on."

She smiles, but it's a sad one that breaks my heart. "Since Burton Crane has a habit of shooting people I want to make sure this fits you."

I take the vest from her hand and put it on. Pulling my shirt over it, it's barely visible underneath.

"Just don't get shot in the head," Blithe warns.

"No one would dare shoot the Volker Sovereign in the head. They haven't got the balls." I pull off the shirt and the vest. "Now, I'd say we have about twenty minutes before the boys get done with their chores." Reaching out, I take Blithe's arm and pull her to me.

"I don't want to let you go," I whisper in her ear.

"I know." She nods, a single tear dripping down her cheek. "But we don't have time for that."

"I'm sorry." I squeeze her tight against me.

"Me too."

We stand like this, husband and wife, mother and father, alive and ready to die, until we hear the sound of children's footsteps enter the house. Feeling the movement of baby Norah in her mother's belly, I squeeze her one last time before releasing her. "Let's go have a baby and change the world."

She nods.

I grab our bags and head toward the sound of the boys.

--

THEN

. . .

IT LOOKS like I'm back in elementary school. I shouldn't be here. I've got at least fifteen years on each of these kids.

"Sam?" Ms. Black's voice is a bit too close to me.

She's probably hanging over my shoulder again. I shift in my seat and catch a glance of her out of the corner of my eye. "Yeah."

She says nothing.

"Yes, Ms. Black?" I finally ask. She's all about formality.

"Are you finished with that?" She points to the book in front of me.

It's a physics text. Something I read in college already. "Not yet." I turn the page before something comes to mind. "Ms. Black," I turn in my seat to face her, "Why don't you teach history?"

The children continue with their reading, except Lina, I catch her pausing to glance at me before looking away.

Ms. Black clears her throat before moving to stand in front of me. She lowers her voice to a whisper. "The history texts are not allowed."

"But... all that we've accomplished, all the history–"

"They don't want the children learning about it," she cuts me off.

"I don't understand."

"You and I, Sam, we know what the world was like before the Reformation. But the children, the people running this place don't want them knowing."

"Why?"

"If they don't know what it was like before and the freedoms we once had, if they never knew it existed then they won't bother wanting it back. It's called control by ignorance."

Ms. Black crosses her arms, it pushes her chest up and out. I try not to stare, but, oh Lord, every single day it's all I can do to sit here at this stupid chair and table and not envision her naked at least once. Blinking hard, I try my damndest to focus but it's so tough looking at her and... "What about us? I'm not going to forget."

She leans against my table. That's what I get here, a table and a chair, not one of those little desks that the kids sit at. "Eventually it will fade, Sam. All of it will fade and when we no longer exist it won't matter anymore."

She stares at me for a long time as I process what she's telling me. It's pretty screwed up when I can't focus on the topic for more than five minutes. All I want to do is bone the lady in front of me.

Stevie stands from her place next to Lina, barks once and runs across the room and out the doggie door.

"That's strange," Ms. Black says as she stands and moves to the window.

I watch her backside as she pushes the curtain away. Then she sucks in a breath, drops the curtain and turns to me, looking white as a sheet.

"What's wrong?" I ask.

"Volker–" Her voice is interrupted by the sound of car doors slamming shut.

"Adam's here?" I ask.

"No." She shakes her head and looks at the Guardians in each corner of the room. I've never seen her like this before. Shaken and nervous. A piece of hair falls across her face as she moves toward the children. "I think you better go put Stevie in Andie's house. Now."

I stand from my seat. This feels off. "Ms. Bl–"

"Go."

Adam warned me to stay in line. Do what they say. Worry about it later. So, just like when I was told to stand guard during the Reformation, I leave the school house. Stopping on the front porch, I notice the line of Volker coming across the courtyard. There are six of them. Stevie runs around them. One of the Volker swats at her.

"Stevie!" I call to the dog. She comes running over. I grab her collar and lead her to Andie's place. It's a quick walk and Stevie's not happy about it. She yanks herself away, tries to slide out the door as I kick at her to keep her inside. By the time I'm done, the Volker are in the school house. I make my way there, walking as fast as I can without running. One of those strange Guardian dogs rounds the building and starts following me. I hear one of the children scream and the sound of wood hitting the floor. I run, the Guardian at my heels. When I get to the porch I clear the steps with one quick jump and push the door open. Three Volker greet me.

"Uncle Sam!" I hear Lina's voice and she's upset.

"What's wrong?" I ask, trying to get around the Volker.

"Don't think so." One of them pushes me. "Out."

I push back. "What's wrong, Lina?" I hear her whimper, I push back harder. I'm bigger than all three of these guys and it's one hard shove to clear them away. I catch Ms. Black, she's holding out her arm, her pale skin marred with a black image on her wrist. "Sam, stop," she begs, hand out in warning.

The children are lined up in the middle of the room and a Volker is pressing a metallic device to their wrists, marking each one of them. "What the fuck…" One of the boys starts crying. And Astrid, that sweet little girl with the big eyes runs toward me trying to escape whatever they are doing. A Volker grabs her by the collar of her shirt and pulls her back.

"Don't touch them!" I run for the children. I don't get far before five Volker are on my back pushing me out the door, there's a gun in my ribs, a taser to my neck. I fight back. Whatever the hell they're doing here, I'm not going to let them get away with it. I punch the Volker with the gun, then the one with the taser. They let me go but only for a second.

"Sam!" Ms. Black shouts. She's standing so close. I didn't even realize it. I stop fighting. "You're just making it worse. Go back to your place." She waves me off. And at that second, watching her and watching the Volker take Astrid's wrist, marking her, watching what they could do to a group of innocent children, a bit of me turns black in this instant, watching all of this. And now, that blackened part of my soul, it wants revenge and to set things right, this day, this second, I know that I will do bad things.

I turn my back on Ms. Black. I can't stop them, but I can make them pay. I walk out of the school house, down the steps and to the Library house next door. I stop on the porch and turn. That Guardian is next to me. Why didn't they try to stop the Volker? They are supposed to protect us, that's what Adam told me. Must be whatever was happening wasn't bad enough to make them react. Maybe they only react when they can sense death is coming.

There are four Volker now. I think I can take four. Yeah, I can take four.

"You guys are dicks doing that to the kids," I say.

The one closest to me smiles. I punch him in his stupid face as hard as I can. He stumbles off of the porch, falls on his ass. The rest replace him. I hear one radio for backup. I punch another one that gets close enough for me to reach. On his way down, his arm shoots out with the taser. It's nothing like the military one I got hit with. Barely fazes me. And then one of the Volker pulls out a syringe with a needle attached.

The Guardian growls and moves to stand in front of me. I stumble from the taser. Maybe it was enough to drop me. Doesn't stop me from swinging. I get one of them with an uppercut, it's only half-strength, but it's enough. Oh... wait... shit. Nope. He's got my arm. Twists it. The other guy jabs me in the neck with the syringe. The Guardian growls and jumps in the air. Holy shit. There's a spray of blood, and that's the last thing I see before I'm out.

The next thing I hear is the sound of my sister's voice. She's pissed. How did I get in my bed? I don't remember walking up the stairs. All I remember was the blood, the Volker, the Guardian. My mouth is dry, my body feels like I've been hit by a truck. I roll out of bed and hang on to the wall to steady myself. My wrist burns. When I look down I see it's bandaged with white cloth. I rip away the bandage, the black image of a bird is tattooed there. A phoenix. Great.

"What do you want?" Andie's voice fills the house and she's pissed.

"We need to speak with Sam," I recognize Adam talking.

"Why?" Andie asks.

"I need to find out what happened here."

"You know what happened, Adam. Sam was trying to protect the children from this."

"There's more–" he starts.

"There's nothing, Adam, the Volker are suppose to protect us, which is your main task. Protect the Sovereign. Instead you let them come out here and brand the children, the *children* Adam!" She's near shouting now. She has been acting a little over the top lately. I wonder what's wrong with her. "I think you all need to leave. Let us at least recover from what happened here today."

"I'd love to, Andie. I really would. But I need to talk to Sam."

"No you don't. You leave him alone. He's been through enough today."

"I need to talk to him, now."

"Why?"

"Because I've got a dead Volker on my hands." Adam lowers his voice and I can barely hear him as I make my way to the top of the stairwell. "Stop. Now. You know I don't want to do this but I have no choice in the matter."

I make my way down, slow, still unsteady. Andie turns and looks at me. She turns back to Adam. "He's barely recovered from whatever they gave him. How do you even know if he remembers?"

"I have my ways."

"Don't touch him, Adam, I swear to God."

Adam looks at Andie, confusion cloaks his face. Whatever is going between these two, I have no idea.

Making it down the stairs, Lina looks up from the floor in the Library. I give her a wink and a smile. She smiles back and continues on with the giant book she's looking at. It looks like a book of maps. Wonder how long those will last here before they disappear. If they won't allow the history books, I'm sure they're not going to allow the old maps.

"It's ok, Sis," I say, gripping the banister to keep from falling. Whatever they stabbed me with is making me a bit woozy still. When my feet hit the ground floor, I step around her and head out the door to talk with Adam. One of the Guardians follows, trotting by my side. Adam waves me near the vehicles.

"Lina, stay inside with Stevie," I hear Andie say inside the house.

Elvis leaves the entrance to the main barn and starts walking toward us. Andie stands on the porch, watching.

"What happened?" Adam asks me.

"What do you think happened, Colonel Waters?" I keep my voice flat, calm. The Volker are watching. I recognize a few of them from earlier. The one that pulled Astrid by her shirt and the one that marked the children.

"I've got a dead man, blood on your porch, and no one wants to talk," Adam crosses his arms as he speaks. He looks so intimidating in his uniform, muscles bulging and eyes hard. He wants answers, but I want to give him a hard time.

"They should talk." I point to the six other Volker. "They were here, they know what happened, and they took part in it."

"I've been told there was a fight. They tried to subdue you. You fought back. And then some kind of scuffle ensued on the porch. The Volker responsible for injecting you with the sedative was found on the ground with a nasty gash to his neck. How did it happen?"

"I don't know. I was sedated. Remember?" I say.

"Sam, I don't want to bring you down to Headquarters. You're new here. You don't want to make a poor name for yourself. Let's get this over with. Speak."

I cross my arms over my chest. Just like him. We stare each other down for a few minutes. I find it hard to stop myself from smiling at him. But I'm pissed. And even though I'm pissed, I find it hard to control the urge to smile for some odd reason. Adam must notice the Guardian at my side. He crouches down so he is face-to-face with the animal. "Leave the dog alone," I step in front of Adam, blocking his view. "It's not involved. Your Volker are." I didn't miss that its fur is coated in blood.

Adam stands and frowns at me before turning to Elvis, who has made his way to Adam's side. "I need to use your phone." They walk to the barn where Elvis has his office.

"Sam," Andie whispers harshly from the porch. "Why are you risking your life for a dog?"

How the hell did she figure it out already? I turn to her. "They're more than dogs, Andie. I know you can tell. There's something different about them. They protect us. We need to return the favor."

A few minutes pass, enough for a quick phone call and a decision. Adam and Elvis walk back from the barn. "It has been decided," Adam announces to everyone. "The animal must be put down. It's not safe."

"No," Andie steps down from the porch and makes her way toward us, "it was only doing its job. They are here to protect us, it was protecting Sam. You can't kill it for that."

"My hands are tied, Andie. The Entities decided. Crane has decided. It needs to be done."

Elvis moves near Andie and puts his hand on her shoulder. "I'll take care of it."

The Guardian looks around, as though it understands the ongoing conversation, lingering on me for a few extra minutes, puffing its long hair from in front of its eyes. Elvis leads the dog behind the circle of houses. Andie follows. When they are out of view I turn to Adam and the Volker. It's then I make my decision. I'm going to be a Volker. I'm going to burn this place down from the inside out.

For weeks Andie starts pulling Lina out of school. I start going with them. Ms. Black whispered to me one day in the courtyard that she doesn't even know why I was allowed in the Sovereign Children's Training Program. I'm too old for what she agreed to do. Sixteen was her cutoff, earlier depending on the learning capacity of the children. The fact that they let me in raises an awareness inside me. I get the feeling that I was allowed in for other reasons. Well, whatever those were, I'm not going to let them use me.

Andie teaches Lina the maps and history she may not remember. After what Blithe told me, it makes me uneasy. Whatever these people have planned, Lina knowing these things could be a detriment. Still, she memorizes them, draws them out on blank pieces of paper. When we aren't reviewing maps and history, we head to the fields. Exercising, building muscle, training Lina how to use weapons. I practice with them too, until it scares Andie. I can't tell her that I'll never forgive myself for not protecting the kids from the Volker showing up and marking them. So I'm going to get them back. Andie has a plan to protect Lina. I have a plan for revenge. I just hope when all of this is over she will still recognize me as her little brother. I'm doing this for them.

On another late night, studying in my room, bright headlights interrupt me. I stand and move to the window, check the clock. Everyone's already here and home in bed for the night. A door closes, soft, I barely hear it. I recognize the form though. Adam's here. I haven't seen him here since tattooing day. He starts walking to Andie's place. I grab my coat, run down the stairs and out the door to watch him from the shadows. He waits on her front porch. When the door opens she lets him in. I make my way to his vehicle in the night and wait.

There are Guardians out here, dark lumps of dog sleeping on the ground. Sometimes, I think I see that one who tore out the Volker's neck along the tree line of the forest. It's supposed to be dead but I can't see Elvis killing an animal like that. The animals in the barn make noises and I am reminded of how strange it is, living on a farm out in the middle of nowhere, secluded from civilization. Oh yeah, civilization is no more. I lean against Adam's SUV and wait. It's only a few minutes before I hear footsteps and see Adam's shadowed figure. My eyes move to Ms. Black's house.

Adam walks up to his vehicle, doesn't even notice me. He's off his game. I step out so he can see me.

"What are you doing here?" I ask.

Adam jumps. "Shit, Sam." He pulls his key out of his pocket and drops it on the ground. Adam's all sorts of messed up right now. He bends and starts searching the ground for his keys. "What are you doing out here in the middle of the night?" he asks.

I don't miss the smell of alcohol on him. Last I knew it was banned here. Makes me wonder what else he's got going on if he's sneaking booze. "I'd like to ask you the same thing."

Adam stands, keys in hand, and just watches me, blue eyes blazing in the moonlight. He's always like that. So intense.

"What's your deal?" I tip my head at him.

He runs a hand through his hair, lets out a deep breath. "She's fucking pregnant."

"Who?"

"Your goddamned sister. Who else?"

Well, that explains a lot. I shrug. "Who's the father?"

"Who the hell do you think it is?" He takes a step toward me but I hold my ground. He leans against the SUV. "I fucked up. She won't talk to me. I didn't want to talk to her for a while, but I was just so... shocked. And she didn't even tell me, man. Fucking Crane told me. Of all people. She couldn't even tell me she's carrying my kid."

Shit happens. Wonder where Ian is, if he knew he might break that innocent demeanor and flip his shit for the first time in his life. That's probably why she didn't tell him, or me, or anyone.

"So what are you going to do about it?" I ask him.

"I have no freaking clue." He shakes his head.

I stand up a little taller. This is my sister. These people have ruined her family. Fucked her up real good in the head. I can tell she's close to cracking. And it's so much more than what a large coffee from Starbucks and a chocolate cookie can fix. Someone needs to watch over her because I won't be able to much longer with what I'm planning. "You need to get a clue," I say to Adam, stepping closer to him. "She needs someone. She's going to lose her shit having a baby in the middle of all this. The Reformation was bad enough. Whatever happens next with all of us... you think we'll survive? You think that baby in her belly will?"

Adam stills, looks at me for a long moment processing like I've seen him do before. "I know." He runs two hands through his hair now, gripping it between his fingers and pulling. "But this was not part of the plan–" He stops before he says any more, seems instantly sober with his loose tongue.

"Plan?" I ask, intrigued.

"Stay out of it, Sam." Adam reaches for the driver's side door of the SUV.

"You brought me here." I step closer to him. "You brought me into this. You owe me an explanation."

"No." Adam pushes his index finger into my chest. "I rescued your sorry ass from the wreckage of the Reformation. I did that. I brought you here for her. I owe you nothing. You're alive. Appreciate it."

"Yeah, you dropped me in the middle of this. And it's royally fucked up. I *appreciate* you bringing me back to my family. But when your men marked those kids. Fucking kids, man." I shake my head. "You weren't there. You didn't see how scared they were. It was so wrong."

"There are some things I cannot control here. Being the Volker Sovereign, I am only in charge of so much. You saw that when you were staying with me. How long did it take me to find out where this place was? Weeks. And *I'm* supposed to be in charge of the safety of the Sovereign." He thrusts a finger into his chest. "It took me weeks to find out where the most important Sovereign of this District were being hidden. They're going to mark every Sovereign. Including the one Andie's carrying. You think I want to see my own flesh and blood go through that? I can barely stand the thought of Lina going through it."

"What aren't you telling me?"

"It's not important right now." I don't miss it when his eyes flick toward Ms. Black's house, then Andie's.

"Maybe it's time for you to choose what's really important," I say.

Adam glares at me before wrenching open the door of his SUV, getting in, and leaving.

--

Now

"You okay, Sam?" Blithe asks, her cool fingers pressing into my forearm.

I rub my face. It's been weeks since I've had a flashback. "I'm fine," I reply.

Her eyes flood with worry. I smile before leaning down to kiss her. I know the distraction will make her forget for a few minutes at least.

We wait in a hospital room, Blithe lying on her side in the bed. I sit next to her in a chair and pull two vials from my pocket. They were given to me by Adam that day we went to pick up Andie and the children in Romney. If he knew I was using it on his sister he'd fucking kill me. But she agreed to this. She knows the risks. Plus, I promised Adam I'd kill Crane if he didn't. And he didn't. So that leaves me. And my wife. And my unborn daughter.

"How much longer until she gets here?" Blithe asks.

"Volker at the gateway radioed in about ten minutes ago. They'll probably head to the Pasture first. Then come here."

"So you think half an hour?"

"Give or take."

"And Crane?"

"He's been notified. Should be here soon. You know how he likes to make a grand entrance."

She nods. "I know."

There is a knock at the door and when it cracks open Dr. Akiyama walks in. I hide the vials back in my pocket. "Hello, Colonel Salk and

Mrs. Salk." He flips through Blithe's chart. "Contractions?" he asks. "Already. But it's a bit early. There shouldn't be any issues with this."

"I know," Blithe says, her hand moving to her stomach. "But they come and go. And there was bleeding."

Dr. Akiyama's eyebrows rise in concern. "Bleeding? Well..." A finger scratches his chin. "Barely thirty-six weeks. I'd like to see you go longer but if it's time then it's time."

I guess I never realized what a good liar my wife is. Makes me wonder... My radio chirps to life. Moving away from the bed, I hear the Volker on the other end inform me that Andie and Ian have arrived at the hospital.

Show time.

Twenty-One

Andie

"You're going to go back to Phoenix? But you just got here." George straightens his stacks of papers one last time before rounding his desk.

"I know." I make my way to the door. "But Sam said Blithe is going to deliver. I promised them I would go back and get them."

"How far along is she?" George asks.

I tip my head, thinking, calculating. She was in her third trimester when we left, and we've been here for a few weeks. She could be close, but not close enough. My heart thumps hard in my chest. "You don't think..."

He makes a gesture with his hands, palms up, expectant-like. What was I expecting? "What did you leave behind in Phoenix? Besides your brother and his wife?"

"Nothing." I shake my head. "Nothing. I brought the children, the computer, I've done the pairings, updated the programs I use to save everything on." The only thing I didn't have time to grab was my notes. Five years worth of research on the nanocytes that I hope to get back. But no one besides Ian knows about those.

"Maybe it's something you took?" he suggests.

"I took?"

George pushes his glasses up on his nose. "Did you leave any Sovereign in Phoenix? Do you plan on leaving any Sovereign there?"

Moving my arm, I look at the mark on my wrist, knowing I share it with the children and Sam and Ian. We are all Sovereign. Is it that obvious to him and not me? I never thought about leaving anyone behind. And now, going back to get Sam and Blithe and Lex and Ira. That will only leave Crane and Richard Ruiz if he hasn't recruited any more Sovereign. I took them all because they are all so important to me.

Without my asking, George moves to his phone and dials a number. "Send Ian Somers to my office as soon as possible." He hangs up and turns to me.

Unease fills me. I should have seen this coming. "He can get Sovereign from any of the other Districts. There's extra here. There's Tonopah..." No, no, no. I won't leave them behind.

George leans back on his desk. "Let me relay to you a bit of information, Andie. And while I'm saying this out loud, you must know that I know that I'm breaking some rules. But this has gotten out of hand; the rules need to be broken. The Funding Entities didn't just fund the Reformation and the building of the Districts, they funded you."

"Me?" I step back.

"Crane invested a lot of money in you and your history."

"I know the history. He told me about my great grandmother being some engineer who designed the nanocytes."

George nods. "And he's been tracking you your entire life. You think he'd let you slip out of his grasp just like that? You think for those five years he was gone that he wasn't keeping tabs on you?"

"I know Dr. Akiyama was still communicating with him. I expected that."

"A man doesn't spend as much money as he did on a project and watch it walk away, across the continent."

"I'm not some toy he developed." I shake my head. "And this makes no sense. There are others with the nanocytes–"

"Yes, there are others with the nanocytes, but there is something specific about your nanocytes. Your nanocytes can do something the others can't."

I focus on the map behind George's head. I need to get my notes and I need to get to Galena, then get these things out of my body. "What can they do?"

"You haven't figured it out yet?" he asks.

Of course I haven't. "What? Just tell me!"

"Some things are meant to be learned. You'll find out–"

George is interrupted by a sharp rap on the door. Turning quick, I open it and Ian steps into the room, slightly out of breath. "I got here as fast as I could." Ian looks at me, then George. "What's wrong?"

"Blithe's delivering. Sam just called and asked us to go get them."

"Isn't it too soon?" Ian asks. I nod. Ian looks to George. "What's going on?"

"We're not exactly sure, Ian. But George is thinking it might have to do with the fact that I took all of Crane's Sovereign out of Phoenix," I say.

"So are we going back to get Sam?" Ian's body is tense, ready to move.

"I have to get Sam. I can't leave him there. I have to try and get him out of that place."

"Okay. We can't bring the kids." Ian looks to me, worried. "They can't get in the middle of that mess again."

"I know," I reply, looking to George.

"They can stay here," George says without being asked. He moves toward the door. "Let's get you guys some supplies. I'll have the ARU bring up some weapons and ammo, but I don't think you'll be needing them." George gives me a look. I wish he would just tell me what's so special about these stupid nanocytes.

"Let's go pack and tell the kids." Ian takes my arm and we leave George's office, headed to our living quarters.

I've left the children behind multiple times, but there's something about this time that fills me with unease. Ian and I pack a few small bags, zipping them closed just as the children trickle in the door.

"Mom didn't make dinner?" I hear Isaac's voice, the disappointment evident.

I pause and stand up straight. "Let's go tell them," Ian says, taking my arm.

As we leave the bedroom, Lina takes one look at the bags in our hands and her face drops.

"No," she whispers. "No."

"It's okay, Lina. We'll be back before you know it."

She pales, shakes her head from side to side. I catch Raven's dark gaze from behind her. The other boys are simply silent but Astrid's eyes are already watery with tears.

"You can't go," Lina chokes out.

I move to her, pulling her close. "We have to get Sam and Blithe. She's having the baby. We're going to bring them here."

"But what about us?" Lina asks. "You can't leave us. Not now, not here in this weird place."

This is when I realize, they will all be truly alone. In the past I've always left them with Sam or Ian. Now I'm leaving them with no one. But there's no way to get around this. I need Ian's help to get Sam. And I can't bring four kids with me.

"George is going to take care of you all." I look over them all. "He's a good man. He's always helped me when I needed him. He'll keep you safe."

"Dad?" Isaac moves toward Ian. "You're leaving us?"

"We'll be back in a few days." Ian takes Isaac into his arms.

"What will we eat?" Isaac asks. "The food here is so disgusting, and without Mom here to cook who will feed us?"

"You'll just have to man up and eat the buffet food." Ian pats Isaac firmly on his shoulder before moving toward the other children. He talks intently to the older boys, Cashel and Marcus, and they stand up a little straighter, nodding along with Ian's words. He must be giving them a pep talk. Hopefully they'll take it better than his warning to stay away from Lina. They're good kids, all of them. I can't see them getting into any trouble while we're gone. I find myself gripping Lina harder to my side. I don't want to let her go. I don't want to leave any of them. But... I must. I promised Sam. I have to get him. And then we'll all be together again.

"We need to get to the train platform," Ian finally says.

We make our way to the elevator. And it's as we're piling in that I notice a few of the Guardians loitering in the hallway. One of them tries to get in the elevator and follow us.

"Stay," I tell it. "Stay here with the children." The Guardian sits as though it understood every word I said, along with all the ones I didn't.

--

THE CHILDREN FOLLOW us to the train platform to tell us goodbye. It's the first time they've been above ground since we got here. Instinctively, I check the clouds in the distance, the fear of another tornado hitting is strong.

"Weather's good for now," George says. He must've noticed my anxiety.

Lina gives me a questioning look. I never told her about the day I was nearly swept up into a tornado and Ian rescued me. I don't tell her now. Although, I feel like I should warn her about the weather here. Instead, I take the time to tell her goodbye one last time. "Lina, watch the boys." I hug her, crushing her to my chest for the last time.

"Mom?" she whispers and I feel her tremble under my hands. "Something's not right with this. I don't want you to go."

"It will be fine, Lina. Just a few days." I reach up and tuck a strand of hair behind her ear. I still can't believe that she's taller than me. "Your father and I will be back in a few days. George will watch over you all. He's a good man, true to his word. You're all grown up now; you'll be fine without us for a couple of days."

"I don't like this," she whispers to me, arms around my neck, refusing to let go.

"I have to do this, Lina. We don't leave family behind." With that she finally lets go. I pull Raven to my chest and kiss his cheeks and the top of his head. He says nothing, still, just stares at me with those intense blue eyes. "I love you, Raven. Stay with Lina." I move on to Astrid. "I know you don't need any warning. You're always good." I hug her. When I come to the end of the row of children, Isaac is standing there. I take a deep breath, place my hands on his shoulders and look deep into his brown eyes. "Isaac," I tell him, "you be good, Isaac. You be good for George, and you watch over our family." Even though I know it will feel awkward I pull him in for a tight hug. Whatever is off with him I hope he can keep it together before we get back. I don't trust Isaac and I can't trust that without me around he won't get into trouble. I walk up to George. "You watch them. Promise me you'll take care of them." I swipe at a tear that's collecting in the corner of my eye. "Promise."

"I will, Andie." He smiles that boyish smile and pushes his glasses up on his nose. "I won't let anything happen to them. They are safe here."

And then we are on the train pulling away from Hanford and George is taking the children back underground.

"They'll be fine," Ian says from the seat next to me with his arm draped across my shoulders.

"I hope so."

He squeezes me closer to him. "They will be."

"Do you think we'll make it back to them?" I ask. When Ian doesn't answer, I continue, "I feel like I'm... I'm going to war. I don't know how else to describe it." I think of the loaded pistol in my bag and the one in Ian's, the extra ammo and guns we've brought with us. "Why does it feel like I'm never coming back here?"

Ian is silent.

--

When we reach the Phoenix District we are not greeted by Crane as I would expect. There is a sole Volker there, standing on the platform, weapon drawn. He leans over to glance at the man from Hanford who drove the train, then me and Ian. I show him my wrist. Ian does the same. The Volker nods and motions for us to get off.

"I'll wait here for you," the driver says, pulling a book out of the bag next to him.

"Sounds good," I tell him. If anything happens to him I'll have Sam with me and he knows how to drive the train.

"Welcome back," the Volker says. "Burton Crane sends his regards. He said he was too busy to come here and meet you." The Volker holds out a set of keys. "He left a vehicle for you."

I hold out my hand and take the keys. "Thank you," I say before Ian and I take our bags and make our way toward the vehicle. The cool metal from the handgun George gave us digs into my hip. Ian has his in his waistband also. We loaded them and put extra ammo in our pockets. Just in case.

"This is strange," Ian whispers from behind me. "Just letting us walk in here, no escort, no Crane, no…"

"No Volker Sovereign."

"Yeah."

"I would expect him to be where ever his wife is." I look around. "But I agree, it is strange."

I turn and notice the Volker watching us just before he says something into the radio on his shoulder. My eyes scan the fence line. I don't see any movement that I might recognize as the Swamp people. But then, it's been so long since I've seen them, I guess they could be even more stealth in their movements now.

Ian takes the keys from my hand and throws our bags in the back seat of the SUV before we get in and he takes off for the Pasture.

--

IAN PARKS next to the large barn. This place is so familiar and the feeling of home is immediate. The large Guardians exit the barn as if to greet us. They are followed by a familiar face, Elvis. He waves as he makes his way toward us. Ian grabs our bags from the backseat as I get out of the SUV.

"Howdy, welcome back." Elvis greets us with handshakes and hugs. "Hasn't been the same without you all here." He looks toward the empty school house. "Kinda quiet without all the kiddos running around. A bit lonely too."

"There's lots of kids in Hanford," I tell him. And then I say no more, George's warning fresh in my mind. *Did you plan on leaving any Sovereign behind when you are done there?* "Where's Sam?" I ask, noticing his vehicle isn't here.

"Been some trouble in town," Elvis replies.

"Where's Blithe?" Ian asks. "Sam called and said she was delivering."

"Well, she's up at the hospital. Been there a few days now."

"What?" I ask.

"Sam didn't call you?" Elvis asks.

"Well, he called me to tell me to come get them. He didn't say she's been at the hospital for a few days."

"Oh," he replies with a look of slight confusion crossing his face before he continues. "Guess she's been feeling a bit sick and sad without all the boys around to keep her busy. Just Lex and Ira now." He thumbs toward the barn. "Doing chores before dinner."

I turn toward Ian. He moves to toss the bags back into the vehicle. "Let's head there."

"We'll be back, Elvis."

"We'll be here waiting," Elvis says.

I get in the SUV and buckle up. "Strange, don't you think?" I ask Ian.

"Yeah." Ian buckles himself in and heads down then gravel driveway.

"It feels so empty here," I say as I watch the fields and the farmhouses and courtyard disappear behind us. "I wish Crane wasn't here so we could come back."

Ian shrugs. "Maybe Elvis will send us home with some real food. Steaks and potatoes, or something."

"That would be nice." Then I could stop stealing food from Hanford's kitchen for a few days.

Ian moves one hand from the steering wheel and intertwines his fingers with mine. "Hanging in there?" he asks.

I nod. "It feels so strange being here without the kids. I feel so... wrong without them."

"Me too." Ian squeezes my hand. "We'll be back to them in no time." He drives past the stone wall that separates the rural areas of Phoenix from the town. The gate is open with no Volker standing guard. "Must be something good going on in town." He lets go of my hand and accelerates toward the hospital.

--

THE STREETS ARE CLEAN. Front yards prim and tidy. Houses all painted white. Ian slows to follow a bus that drops off Residents and picks new ones up. Dressed in uniforms, the color of the fabric dependent on their Factions, the Residents carry on their business, smiling and obedient, just like Crane wants them to be. We see no commotion, nothing that would cause the gate to be unmanned.

Ian parks in front of the hospital, in the same spot as when we would come here for our couple's therapy sessions with Dr. Akiyama.

"You okay?" Ian asks as he shuts off the engine.

"Fine." I unclip my seatbelt. It seems like there's nothing going on in town to warrant unguarded gates. It makes me think of the Swamp people. Makes me fear that they might be able to attack if our defenses are down. And although the familiar feeling of home fills me, it wars with a gentle unease.

Ian and I make our way into the hospital. We take the familiar route to the maternity ward where I spent so much of my time when I finally got the nerve to leave the Pasture. Dr. Akiyama is there, writing in a chart. He motions to a room with an open door without a greeting. We haven't been gone long. I guess I wouldn't expect him to miss us. When we enter the room, Blithe is there lying in a hospital bed and Sam is sitting at her bedside in a chair. Sam stands when he notices us.

Blithe turns. "Who are they?" she asks.

I reach out for Ian, stopping him.

"Who are they?" Blithe asks again, reaching for Sam.

Sam just watches us, his face complacent.

"Sam? Blithe?" I ask. "You called us. We came as soon as we could." The steps I take to the side of her bed are hesitant.

Blithe's eyes meet mine. "Why would we call you?" she asks. "We don't even know you."

How could she not know us? I look at Sam, reach out and touch his arm. "Sam? What's going on here?"

Sam looks at my hand, then my arm, then my face. His head tips for a bit, confusion and then recognition. "Sis?" he finally answers. "What are you doing here?" he asks.

"You called me, Sam." I move closer to him. Ian stays where he is. "You called me to come get you." I look between Sam and Blithe. "You're both coming back to Hanford with me." I wait. They say nothing. Blithe's brow furrows. She's totally confused. "Blithe..." I sit down on her bed; don't miss it when she scoots away. "Sam called me to come get you and take you out of here. We're going to Hanford. We'll be safer there. Away from Crane. Marcus and Cashel are there with Lina and Raven. We'll all be together again and away from here. It's nice in Hanford. Safe." She shakes her head, her hands flutter to her belly. "Is the baby okay?" I ask Sam.

"What do you want with my baby?" Blithe asks.

"I..." I start.

"You can't have my baby!" Blithe throws her covers back and stands. She's still tall and beautiful and a bit distraught at the moment. "You can't have my baby. She's mine. Not yours. I won't let you take her." Blithe's eyes fill with tears. Of all the time that I've known her I've never seen her like this.

"I don't want your baby," I say. "Sam, tell her. What's wrong with her, Sam?"

Sam stands still. Strangely still. Watching. And just as he's about to say something, with Blithe still yelling, Dr. Akiyama walks through the door and takes my arm.

"Andie," he says to me, "I think you need to give them some time. All of this is a bit overwhelming."

"What's wrong with them?" I ask Dr. Akiyama. "Why are they acting like this?"

Dr. Akiyama leads me out of the room, Ian follows. When we get to the hallway, Dr. Akiyama tugs Blithe's door closed and turns to me. "Did Sam call you?"

"Yes, of course he did."

"Are you sure?" Dr. Akiyama asks strangely.

"Yes. George Crossbender was standing right next to me."

I look at Dr. Akiyama. His response is simply the rise of his brows. I look at Ian, who watches me expectantly. What the hell is going on here?

"Are you sure Sam called you? It wasn't someone else?" Dr. Akiyama asks again.

"Who else would it be?" A choked laugh escapes my throat. The absurdity of it. Who else could call? It's not like the telephone system is set up like it was before the Reformation. At least... I don't think it is. "I think I know the voice of my own brother. And I would never come back here just to... to..."

"To what?" Dr. Akiyama asks, and in that second, I remember George's warning of Crane being angry for me taking all his Sovereign out of Phoenix.

I freeze, mouth open, frustration welling inside of me, unsure of what to say. "I just... I need a minute to clear my head." I need air, the openness. I need to breathe. I leave the hospital hallway, retreating outside. It's a feeling I can't get enough of, being out in the open, after being stuck in the confines of Hanford for all this time.

Something is very wrong with my brother and his wife.

"They're changed," I tell Ian when I get him alone. "Sam and Blithe. It's like they've been brainwashed."

Ian tips his head. "Or medicated."

"Shit."

"Yeah." Ian pauses for a moment. "Or maybe they're just pushing us away."

I look around us. "Why isn't Crane here?" It's unlike him to not show up. We've been here for at least an hour or more and I can't believe I haven't seen his speckled face yet.

"I figured he'd just show up whenever." Ian looks around. "It's strange though. We've been here for this long and he hasn't shown up."

"Yeah," I agree. After taking a few deep breaths, I say, "I have to talk some sense into Sam. Do you think we should go back in?" I ask Ian, unsure of what to do.

"Sure. But first," Ian pulls a piece of paper from his pocket, "the day of that tornado." He presses the paper into the palm of my hand. "I went back to our living quarters to get this. I've been doing some research."

"What's this?" I grip the paper between my fingers.

"Galena's passwords, schematics..." He runs a hand through his hair, shakes his head. "I was warned that I'm going to die soon, Andie."

"Would you shut up already? I'm not going to let you die. You're not going to die. No one is going to die!" I exhale a large breath. I'm so sick of people dying.

"Sure. Well..." He motions to the paper. "Been working on it for a while. Researching. You'd never believe the data Galena has on their servers. Galena has what you need. To get rid of the nanocytes. All of your great great grandmother's stuff, that's how you get to it."

I start to unfold the paper. "How did you know?" I ask, my heart beating with excitement. How could he know?

"How could I not know?" he replies with a smirk.

I scan the page. There's a detailed sketch of Galena. Their gates, their nuclear reactor, where the server room is with the world's data. And passwords. Every password I could need written there in Ian's neat handwriting. "Jackpot," I whisper.

"Knew you'd like it," Ian replies proudly.

"Will you go with me?" I ask him as I fold the paper and tuck it into my pocket.

"If you want me to. When we're done here."

"Yes. Yes!" I throw my arms around him and kiss his cheek. "You're amazing. You know that?" I kiss him.

Ian holds me at arm's length. "You ready to go back and see them?"

"Yeah," I nod, exhaling a breath. "Yeah."

--

WHEN WE GET to Blithe's room, Sam is standing outside her closed door. I walk right up to him. I don't even bother finishing our conversation from before since it seems pointless now. Something's wrong with Blithe if she doesn't recognize us. "Come with us, Sam," I beg him.

He seems to be back to normal again. Mostly. "I can't." He runs his hand through his disheveled hair. "I have to stay here. I have to kill him." He stills, looks around as though he's revealed a secret. He has. Voiced out loud in the middle of the hall that he wants to kill Crane. And even though Dr. Akiyama is standing just down the hall, he doesn't act like he heard. Sam grabs my hands and squeezes them between his.

"He can't be killed," I warn Sam. "He has these things in his body, nanocytes. They heal him. Keep him alive. He's been alive for hundreds of years, Sam." I pause, make sure he's listening. "Did he tell you any of this?" I ask. "He can't be killed. He won't die."

Sam shakes his head very slowly as he processes this and recovers from whatever is wrong with him right now.

I continue. "We had a great grandmother who invented these nanocytes. They keep a person living. Heal the body. Everything. I've been trying to figure out a way to get them out. I almost had it, not long ago. But... he can't die. It's impossible."

Sam stares at me for a long, long time before talking again. "Then I will wait and keep track of him," Sam says. "You take Blithe and the baby back to Hanford. She knows–"

Our conversation is interrupted by a gut-wrenching scream that comes from Blithe's room.

I run, pushing the door open, not caring any longer that she can't seem to remember who I am or what I'm doing here. Sam is on my heels. He pushes me out of the way. Hard. I stumble. Ian catches me by my shoulders and rights me.

"There's blood!" Blithe screams. "Blood. Blood. Blood!" She throws her blanket off of her and I can see that the bed underneath her is soaked.

"The baby," Dr. Akiyama's voice is behind me, filled with concern.

I hear the water running. The sound of the doctor scrubbing his hands. "Help me, Andie," Dr. Akiyama yells.

"Where are your nurses?" I ask.

"Not here."

"Wha–" I start but Ian moves me toward the sink with his grip on my shoulders.

"Help, Andie," Ian whispers harshly in my ear. "You know what to do."

"No. It's been too long. I'm out of practice." I push back against Ian's hands and as I do, I catch Sam out of the corner of my eye.

"Help them," Ian urges.

I scrub my hands. "Where is your medical staff?" I ask Dr. Akiyama. It wasn't so long ago that I had a c-section in this very place. Or was it? Raven is eight now. Gosh, it has been a while. Dr. Akiyama doesn't answer me as he finishes drying his hands and goes to Blithe's bedside and gets her to lie back as he examines her. Drying my hands, I walk up behind him and see the umbilical cord between her legs.

"I think the placenta abrupted," Dr. Akiyama says.

Oh, God. This is an emergency and this place isn't prepared or staffed or trained for this. She would need a c-section or risk bleeding out. She'll need a transfusion. Surgery.

"You need to take her to the operating room," I say.

"No. Can't. We no longer staff it. There's no one here."

"How can you not staff it?" I yell at him.

Dr. Akiyama turns toward me, sweat on his brow. "There's no one to do it. We don't do those procedures anymore. If you survive, you survive. If you don't, you don't. There's something to be said about those who can survive the inevitable, they're stronger, meant to live. We are done helping mankind limp along. We only want the strongest."

"What? That is the dumbest–"

Blithe screams and clutches her abdomen. Dr. Akiyama tips her bed back. "Here." He grabs my hands and presses them to her. "Keep the head off the cord. You know what to do."

I want to tell him I don't. I used to do this, years ago, but I haven't in so long. I'm not sure if I can remember...

Dr. Akiyama heads for the door. "Where the hell are you going?" I yell at him.

"I have to get a kit."

"A kit? What kind of a kit?"

He doesn't answer, he just leaves.

I look to Blithe's face. She's pale, too pale. There's too much blood. It runs over my hands in rivets as I hold the cord in place. "Ian." I feel his presence behind me. "Check on her, Ian," I say.

Sam is at her side, his hands on her face, whispering things in her ear. Things I can't hear. Things that I hope are soothing to her. I hope he's calming her. Ian touches her face. Blithe groans and then she starts breathing fast. I feel her body tense against my hand. She's pushing.

"No! Blithe, no! Don't push!" I crane my head around. "Dr. Akiyama!" I shout toward the door.

He comes running back, out of breath and carrying a surgical tray.

"What the hell are you doing with that?" I ask him.

"Just in case. You know." He's concerned. He washes again.

"She's pushing," I warn him. I want to scream at him to stop washing his hands and get his ass over here to help me. But some tasks that have been pounded into your head over the years are hard to break. It's probably best that he has clean hands.

"Tell her not to push!" Dr. Akiyama says.

I hear Ian whisper to her, "Don't push. Just wait a second. Just wait, Blithe."

The blood flows faster, more. Oh no! Not good. Not good. "Doctor!"

"Don't push!" Dr. Akiyama shouts.

There's so much going on. Blithe screaming. Ian telling her to stop. Sam whispering words in her ear. And then... it all stops. It's all quiet, soundless, like the noise of this emergency was sucked into a vacuum. I could hear a pin drop. I can hear Blithe's blood dripping onto the floor. Drip, drip, drop. The hairs on the back of my neck stand up and a terrible, horrible, eerie feeling overwhelms me.

"Get the baby out!" Dr. Akiyama shouts as he dries his hands. "Out, out, out! Get the baby out!"

I look to where my hands are pressed, covered in blood, holding the umbilical cord in. She's fully dilated, and there's a bulge, the bulge of a head. Ian presses his fingers to her neck. Sam slaps her pale cheeks. Her skin takes on a bluish hue around her mouth. Oh, it's too fast, it's all happening too fast.

Dr. Akiyama shoves me out of the way. "We have to get the baby out or we'll lose it too!"

I don't need to ask him how. I expect him to use the surgical kit and cut the baby out. But instead, he reaches into the birth canal with one hand and pulls. Oh my God, of all the things I've seen in my life. Never this. Never this.

Twenty-Two

Catalina

Descending the elevator, a fear fills me and it's worse than any other time that she's left us. I can't help but wonder if this is the time, and she won't come back to us. Marcus and Cashel are tense, their backs straight as boards. I feel Raven's small hand fit into mine from beside me. Isaac is smiling like an idiot.

"So, kids," Mr. Crossbender starts. "Your parents have left me in charge of you." He tugs at his collar as he turns to us. "I think it's best that we move you deeper underground. It's not safe having all you children alone, so close to the surface."

"No." It comes flying out of my mouth faster than anything.

"We're not moving," Marcus takes a step toward Mr. Crossbender. "We're staying together. All of us."

"I don't think you children understand how important it is for me to make sure you're safe. Your mother left me to watch over you–"

Cashel slams his fingers down on the button to the floor of our living quarters and the elevator comes to an abrupt stop. The doors open and the eight Guardians are sitting in the hall, waiting. Just like my mom told them.

"Strange..." Mr. Crossbender starts as he notices them.

"We're not going deeper," I say, taking Raven's hand and pulling Isaac along by his sleeve to get off the elevator. "They will be back in a few days. There's no point in moving us all."

Mr. Crossbender steps out of the elevator. "And if something happens? How am I going to explain it to your mother? You know who she is and how important she is."

"Do you plan on something happening?" Marcus steps closer to Mr. Crossbender. It's totally intimidating, and a small part of me fears he's going to get in trouble for it.

"We have eight Guardians. That's more than the number of Volker I've seen in this place. They protect us. They always have," I say, glancing at Raven. His fierce scowl is trained on Mr. Crossbender. "We stick together. We always have, Mr. Crossbender. We'll be fine."

There is a long period of quiet as Mr. Crossbender looks at each of us and then the Guardians and then the elevator. "Okay," he says. "For now. But none of you go above ground. None of you leave the living quarters outside of school time without your Guardian or your escort. I'll have to have Mrs. Jones find a few more escorts for your activities and meal times."

I shiver, remembering what that old hag said to us the day we showed up and she locked us in that room and wouldn't let us out. *You are not in the Phoenix District any longer. Here, you will follow the rules. You will do what you're told. If you don't, you'll disappear. If you tell your parents, they'll disappear.* I'm not a fan of Hanford. I'm not a fan of their people, my peers, or their food.

"It's odd that you're saying this," Marcus says, his voice deep. "It sounds like you're not planning on them coming back."

Mr. Crossbender pushes his glasses up on his nose and stands up a bit straighter. "You know Andie has a habit of getting herself into trouble. I'm not saying it's going to happen, I just want to be prepared. You children are our future. And with the country the way it is now, we can't risk anything happening to you."

"We stay where we are," I say. "We're not moving."

Mr. Crossbender focuses on me and seems to lose his internal battle.

He's kind of a pushover. "For now. Go back to your living quarters, children." As everyone starts to move away, he says, "Catalina, I need to talk with you."

I hold back.

"What?" I ask.

"I heard what you said to her on the train platform. That this feels wrong. It doesn't just feel wrong to you. Now, I don't want anything happening to your parents but I can't help but feel like Crane has something lying in wait. You know she's going to try her damndest to get your Uncle Sam and Blithe out of the Phoenix District."

I nod at him, understanding exactly how she is. She wants to pull us all together and keep us contained in a little box just like we were at the Pasture. That's one thing my mother has never been able to do, let us go off and away and be separated.

"How many times has she left you children alone without a family member to watch over you?" Mr. Crossbender asks.

"Never," I reply.

"Never." He scratches his chin. He sighs. "I'll see you all for dinner." He turns to leave, but pauses. "I haven't seen you all in the dining hall much lately. Where have you been eating?" he asks.

"At home."

"At home? Did she cook?"

"Yeah."

"Where did she get food from to cook?"

I shrug. "I don't know. We came home from school and dinner was ready."

"Hm." He checks his watch. "See you in a few hours for dinner." And then he walks away.

I turn and start making my way toward our living quarters. Marcus is standing in the doorway, arms crossed, scowling at Mr. Crossbender's back. Marcus is going to get himself into trouble giving looks like that. I'm sure it doesn't fall within Mrs. Jones's warning of following the rules.

"What did he want?" Marcus asks.

"Pretty much said the same as when we were all together. And he asked where Mom got the food to cook us dinner." I walk into the living room and Marcus closes the door behind us, flicking the lock.

I sit on the couch next to Raven. Astrid's already crying, her face buried in her hands. Isaac is staring off into space. He's always like that, a total space cadet or creepy as the mall Easter bunny. Yes, I remember the mall. I think I like him as a space cadet better.

"What do we do now?" Cashel asks Marcus.

Marcus looks at me, fierce and determined. "We stick together."

"They're coming back," I say.

"Isaac, Raven, Astrid, go to your rooms. The big kids need to talk," Marcus demands. They all scatter, just like they always do around Marcus. He's a bit intimidating to them, but not me.

I pull my legs up and sit cross-legged on the couch. Marcus sits next to me and Cashel pulls up a chair to sit close to us. Marcus drops his voice. "What if they don't come back?"

"I don't want to think about that."

"We have to," Marcus says. "We have to set a plan."

"What are we going to do? Leave this place? There's nowhere to go," I say.

A moment of silence passes.

"You remember the time before the Reformation?" Marcus asks. "I had a family. Cash had a family. Maybe we want to see what happened to them. You have your parents, Lina. We don't. They were taken from us. We remember the way the world was before. The parks and schools, McDonald's and Burger King, grocery stores."

"It's all gone now," I remind them. "If they're not Sovereign they won't remember you. Just like my Dad didn't remember us when he was on the Halcyon. That's what it does to them."

Marcus leans back, stretching his arms across the couch. I move away from him, so my back is against the armrest, and I wait for him to say more.

"I'm not saying I don't want them to come back–" Marcus starts.

"I remember my family," Cash interrupts. "We lived in a trailer out in the middle of nowhere. My mom was a drunk and my dad was never home. Lina's family has taken better care of me than they ever did. If there were no Reformation, there would have been no future for me." He looks away, his face pink.

I blink, shocked. Cash has never mentioned his family. I just assumed he missed them.

"Sorry, man." Marcus taps his fingers on the back of the couch. "I just… I don't know where I was going with that. I just wish there was somewhere we could go if they don't come back. Somewhere we could escape to."

"How about we just stick together," I remind him. "It's gotten us this far already. Family sticks together."

Marcus looks at me and frowns a bit. "Yeah. Sure."

"So we go to school, we go to the dining hall, we color within the lines," Cash says. "How many days do we do this for?"

"Mom said it would only be a few days," I remind them.

"So, three. Four at the most," Marcus says.

"And then what?" I ask.

"Then we start getting into trouble," Marcus says with a smirk.

"Trouble won't get us very far. I saw what trouble got my mom. Remember when she tried to escape? Crane brought in someone to make sure she never tried to escape again."

Silence. Again. They were at the Pasture when we were sent out there, and we may have been little kids but I remember the looks on their faces when they saw her cast on her arm. I remember the way I felt when I knew someone had hurt my Mom when all she was doing was trying to protect me. And the time after, before Uncle Sam showed up, I was worried that she'd never be the same. That she would only ever be the shell of the mother that she was to me before that incident.

"I think we should just lay low. Follow the rules. And wait for the right time," I say.

"The right time for what?" Marcus asks.

"I don't know."

"This is not a plan," Marcus scoffs. "To sit around and wait."

"We aren't spies, Marcus. We're kids. With three little kids to take care of. If something happens to us, what happens to them? We have to think beyond ourselves."

Marcus focuses on the closed doors at the far side of the living space. "Fine." He shifts in his seat, turning to face me. He looks at me like the way he did that one time when my dad smacked him upside the back of his head and told him to keep his hands to himself. He glances at the door to my parent's bedroom. "Has your mom done our pairings yet?"

"Uh..." Cash leans away.

"Go away, Cash," Marcus orders.

I sigh. "Mark, she doesn't pair Sovereign. And I'm only sixteen."

"I'm eighteen. You know what that means?"

"You'll get assigned to your Apprenticeship soon." I look away from him, bored with his antics.

"Not just that." He shifts a tiny bit closer.

"Please, this isn't the sixteenth century. You're not going to marry your sister."

"You're not my sister." Marcus leans toward me. "I like it when you call me Mark. It's cute."

"I can't watch this," Cash says. Disgusted, he stands and tips his chair over as he heads toward the kitchen.

"I'm also a bit too young to be thinking about being paired with anyone." I get up to move but Marcus grabs my wrist. Just as fast as Adam taught me, I bend my wrist, twisting his backward, and jumping up on the couch I press my foot to his throat. "My dad already told you once, Marcus, no touchy."

"I love it when you get all physical." He doesn't make a move to knock me off of him even though I know he has the ability to. Sam and Elvis taught us all of that stuff. Hand to hand defense, weapons, the shooting range, and I've got a map of the country in my head. We may have been here for weeks already, without practicing all that stuff, but it doesn't mean I forgot any of it.

"You're not going to love it when my Uncle Sam gets all physical on you," I smirk and twist his arm higher.

"He taught me a few things out at the Pasture too." Marcus winces as he speaks.

"He'll teach you a lot more, like no touchy his little niece."

"That's *if* he comes bac–" Marcus stops short.

I drop his arm and jump down from the couch. "You're a jerk." I head for my room and hearing Marcus stand and start after me, I spin, walking backward for a few steps. "I can't believe you'd say that."

He stops, one arm reaching out. "Lina, wait. I didn't mean it." Regret masks his face.

I step into my room and slam the door closed. Leaning my back against it, I hear the voices of Cash and Marcus outside the door.

"You shouldn't have said that," Cash says. "You know how she is. You know what she went through. It's messed up."

"I know," Marcus says. "I didn't mean it."

"And stop hitting on her, dude. It's weird and awkward."

Marcus makes some noise. "Jealous much?"

And then there is the sound of them beating on each other. Stupid boys. I throw myself on my bed. Reaching down with one arm, I pick up my chemistry textbook and start studying for my test in the morning.

I'm mid-chapter before I hear someone at my door. The handle turns and I wait. Marcus knows better, so that can only mean it's one of two people. A dark mop of hair and bright blue eyes enters the room. Raven. I scoot over and pat the empty side of my bed. He curls up next to me, his head on my shoulder. I kiss his cheek. "She'll be back," I tell him. I don't bother waiting for a response, he won't say anything, he never does. "Want to read advanced chemistry with me?" I ask, turning the page. His eyes scan the page and I go back to studying. Less than ten minutes pass before Astrid comes into my room, book in hand, and sits next to the bed.

She's only been gone for less than half a day and the little kids are already falling apart. Tears collect in the corner of my eyes. Clearing my throat, I swallow them down and focus on the chemistry textbook. If I get anything less than a B, they'll hold me back. And I can't stand that type of boredom. So I memorize the words, just like my mom taught me how to memorize all those maps when I was a little kid.

This is where we wait until my stomach growls. I can almost smell the last dinner she made here. Maybe if I check the fridge I'd find enough to scrape together an edible meal. Something better that the food they serve here. What I wouldn't give for a roasted turkey, or squash, or fresh berries from the fields. I can't scrape together a meal tonight. Mr. Crossbender is expecting us and I don't want to risk him finally getting upset and moving us. Checking the clock on my nightstand, I see that it's time to go. I close my textbook. "Come on, guys. Time to go to dinner."

When we arrive to the dining hall the Crossbenders are already there. Mrs. Crossbender waves at us from her table and Mr. Crossbender stands and crosses the room to us.

"Glad to see you could all make it on time." Mr. Crossbender smiles. "Why don't you get some plates and join us?" He heads back to his table as we all stare at the buffet.

"Yuck," Isaac whispers.

Marcus clears his throat and reaches for a plate. I do the same. Oh yes, we are so brave, eating this horrible food. And then we advance down the line, each of us choosing things that don't make our stomachs too upset. The salad is usually okay, which means our plates are loaded with it. And although the rolls are salty, they are easier to swallow than the other stuff that tends to slide down your throat without needing to be chewed.

As we make our way to the Crossbender's table, the dining hall doors open and the room starts to swell with the Sovereign of Hanford, here to get their dinner. Still in our school uniforms, we fit in much better than we did the first day we were here, dressed in our clothes from home. Working Sovereign wear red, students wear blue. We fit in by the clothes we wear. The only differences are the marks on our wrists. Right now. In class, it's another thing.

We sit with our plates. Mrs. Crossbender pours tall glasses of water for each of us and hands them out.

"Now, children," she starts as she sets a glass of water in front of me. "I hear you don't want to leave your living quarters." Her voice is so soft and meek. "We can only let this go on for so long." She looks right at me. "Your mother is a strong willed one, and while she was at the upper levels to watch over you, we cannot have you all living up there without an adult present. District rules." She nudges Mr. Crossbender with a sweet smile. And then she stretches one arm behind Astrid's back and hugs her shoulders.

Astrid's shocked eyes meet mine.

"We'll watch over you all. Mr. Crossbender and me. Always wanted a houseful of kids."

I turn to look at Marcus. His lips are pressed into a thin line and I can tell he's holding in whatever response he wants to give.

"We'll give them some time, Maryam," Mr. Crossbender finally speaks up as he forks the mass on his dinner plate then frowns at it. "Andie and Ian should be back within a few days." He looks up and smiles at his wife. "Just a few days. We'll give them that much."

The rest of dinner is filled with an awkward tone as Mrs. Crossbender tries to ask us about our studies and our homework for the night. When our plates are finally cleaned, she stands and takes them all. Walking to a set of doors, she disappears behind them.

"Well, children." Mr. Crossbender stands. "I think it is best that you get home for the evening. I'll walk you back."

We are silent on the walk to our living quarters. The Guardians watch as we make our way down the hallway.

"Goodnight now," Mr. Crossbender says just before he closes the door to our living quarters. "Sleep tight."

"Goodnight," we respond in unison.

I reach out and twist the lock on the door as soon as it's closed.

--

THE NEXT MORNING, dreading going back to the dining hall for breakfast, I stand in front of the small refrigerator in the kitchen and stare. There's a half-full container of milk. Some carrots and lettuce. I move to the cupboards and search. I find oats, some sugar, and a small package of dried cranberries.

Now I stand at the counter, bowls and spoons out, a pot on the stove cooking the oats, and the image of cooking spaghetti with Adam flashes through my mind. I push it away, like my mom's always told me to. I stir the pot and when the smell of fresh soap invades the room, I turn around.

Marcus stands there, adjusting his school uniform. "We're not on the farm anymore, Lina." He focuses on the items littering the counter.

I turn around. "I can't eat their food. It's so gross."

He sits down at the table. "I know."

"Where do you think she got the food from?" I ask as I turn off the stove and spoon the oats into six bowls.

"They have to have storage here somewhere." Marcus taps his fingers on the table. "They have to have a kitchen. In the lower levels maybe? I heard one of my teachers talking about openings for Apprenticeships in the agriculture department. That has to be below everyone's living quarters. Don't you think?"

I shrug as I pour milk over the oats. I add sugar, then the dried cranberries to the bowls. "There's only carrots and lettuce left," I say as I set out the bowls and spoons.

"Hm." Marcus stares into his bowl.

As I sit down to eat, everyone else trickles from their rooms. All in various stages of getting dressed and ready. "We're going to have to go back there for dinner," I warn Marcus. "Carrots and lettuce won't feed everyone for tonight."

There is a sharp rap at the door and Isaac runs to open it.

"Wait!" I start, leery as to who might be here this early. But it's too late. Isaac has the door flung open and he's smiling and talking to whoever is out there.

Mr. Crossbender walks in and we all freeze, caught in the act of eating. "You're all up." He smiles and focuses on the bowls on the table. "What's this?" he asks as he moves into the room.

"Breakfast," I say.

"Oh." He looks surprised. "I thought I'd check to make sure you're all ready for school and escort you to the dining hall for breakfast."

"We can take care of ourselves," Marcus mutters into his bowl.

I kick him under the table. If it were Crane running this District and Marcus was acting like this, he'd probably be dead by now, or sent off to wherever they send unruly children. Or unruly near-adults. He'll be assigned his Apprenticeship soon. They won't be able to wait much longer.

"Well," Mr. Crossbender looks around for a moment, "I can wait until you're all done." He sits in the chair that my mother last sat in for family dinner.

I feel Raven's gaze on me. No doubt he's glaring. I eat my oatmeal, hoping everyone else follows suit. There is no morning chatter like there was with Mom and Dad. Just silence, an uncomfortable silence that fills the room like a fog. I hate it. I hope they come home soon.

Mr. Crossbender opens the door when Kevin shows up to escort us to class. "How about you take the young ones?" Mr. Crossbender suggests. "I'll walk with the older kids."

Kevin leaves with Raven, Isaac, and Astrid following behind him. Mr. Crossbender blocks the door, holding me, Marcus, and Cashel behind.

"Now, children," Mr. Crossbender starts with a smile and pushing up his glasses. "I don't want you to worry about what Mrs. Crossbender had to say last night at dinner. I promised your parents I would watch over you. But creating distress in an already stressful situation is unnecessary. I know you're worried that my wife wants to move you to the lower levels. Just, don't be troubled by her. She's longed for children to fill our home. She just needs reminding that the children that fill the halls of Hanford are enough for us." Mr. Crossbender reaches out and lays a hand on my shoulder. "You'll stay together." Something in my soul relaxes. Finally. "For now," Mr. Crossbender adds. "You'll stay together for now." He squeezes my shoulder and that feeling of relief is gone in an instant. "Come now. Let's get you to class before the first bell." Mr. Crossbender waits as we file out of our home before leading us to the elevators.

We leave Marcus and Cashel on their floor and as the elevator drops another level, I fill the silence with a question. "Where do you get the food from here?"

"The food?" He pushes his glasses up with his index finger.

"Yeah, the food we eat. Where do you get it from?"

"Well, there are levels underneath us." The elevator dings and we step out. "Your mother said you are good with maps, did you ever look at the one I left in your living quarters?"

"Yes. But that only had a few levels and how to get to the dining hall. I know there's a nuclear reactor here powering this place, just like we had in Phoenix, and there has to be more than what is on that map."

"Yes, well, Hanford has twenty subterranean levels. The top level being where your living quarters are. It's mostly uninhabited. We don't like our people being that close to the surface. Then there are the schooling levels. Then more levels of living quarters. Under those we have the Agricultural levels where we grow food and house livestock."

"There's more though," I point out. There are hallways that seem to stretch in every direction and the majority of them we haven't explored.

"Yes, well, we have the ARU, the laboratories, research levels, etcetera, etcetera." He pauses to look at me. "You'll learn all this in your Apprenticeship. And you'll learn how to navigate our halls and levels when the time is right. Don't worry so much about it now."

"I was just wondering where I could get some food from. That stuff you serve in the dining hall is not good." I make a face. "I miss my mother's cooking."

Mr. Crossbender smiles and I see his crooked teeth. "We make it better for human consumption. Enrich it with vitamins and protein, to help you grow and to feed your brain."

"My mom made much better meals," I say to him. "And we grew up just fine on her food."

The bell rings.

"You should go to class now," Mr. Crossbender says, his voice rings like a warning. Crossbender wouldn't hurt a fly, but other people here would. Mrs. Jones would squash me like a bug.

As I walk down the hall, I feel his eyes on my back. I'm not sure how I feel about Mr. Crossbender. He seems trustworthy and nice, but at other times, I'm not sure I can trust him at all.

--

Sitting in calculus, waiting for our teacher, Mrs. Smith, to hand out another exam, there's a knock on the door. It opens and I recognize

Kevin standing there in the hallway. Every single girl's head in the room snaps to look at him. By sheer luck, or misfortune, my family was assigned the most eligible bachelor in all of Hanford as our escort. With his green eyes, light brown hair, and chiseled features, the girls have a hard time keeping their eyes off of him. Plus he's following the head of the Meteorology department. He's too pale, though. From years spent living underground I guess. It reminds me of those vampire movies my dad used to watch.

"Sorry to interrupt." Kevin flashes our teacher a swoon-worthy smile, all she does is frown. "Mr. Crossbender wants to see her." Kevin tips his head in my direction.

Collecting my bag, I stand and make my way for the door. I feel the other girls' jealous eyes boring into my back. Good thing I've gotten used to that feeling since we arrived here. It no longer bothers me like it used to.

"You make up this test tomorrow," Mrs. Smith says.

I hold in a sigh. Two calculus exams in one day, I'd rather just come back and take it late. "I understand," I say quietly as I close the door to the classroom and follow Kevin.

"What's wrong?" I ask.

"I don't know." He slows a bit. "But they sent escorts to collect all of you guys."

"All of us?"

"Yeah." Kevin stops at the elevator.

This can't be good. It's only been one day, barely even a full day. My stomach feels queasy, no doubt a combination of dining hall food and worry. When the elevator door opens, Marcus and Cash are there with another one of the Apprentice level escorts. We stop down a level to pick up Astrid. And then, as we're walking down the hall, we see another escort dropping off Raven and Isaac at Mr. Crossbender's office.

"No," escapes my lips.

Marcus gives me a worried glance as we walk down the hall. As we step inside Mr. Crossbender's office, all of our eyes immediately go to the large map on the wall. I didn't know he had this. I could have been memorizing routes out of this place for weeks. I'm surprised Mom never showed it to me.

"Thank you, Kevin." Mr. Crossbender stands from behind his desk and moves toward the door. "You can head back to the lab now." It seems that's the job of an Apprentice, keeping track of the strange kids from Phoenix and running errands all over these underground levels, figuring out who everyone is and what they do and where they can be found.

As he clears his throat, Mr. Crossbender turns to face us. I notice he's sweating a bit, his face pale, not with lack of sunlight like people usually are here, but illness or shock. His hair is all over the place like he's been running his hands through it for hours. His shirt is wrinkled. He takes his glasses off and rubs his eyes and I notice they're red veined.

My stomach drops. I feel like I'm being sucked under a wave. Taking a step back, I feel Marcus behind me; he doesn't back away to give me space. No, he stands there, strong and supportive, just like he always is under his teasing exterior. Better than I am, he's steeling himself, ready for whatever terrible news Mr. Crossbender is about to tell us. My mouth dries. I reach out for Raven's hand as he stands next to me, quiet and focused. He squeezes my hand twice. If I know anything about Raven, he's already figured out what Mr. Crossbender wants to tell us, somehow. I think he senses it from people's body language or something.

Isaac is staring off at the map like a fool. Cash stands near Astrid, and I feel Marcus take a small step toward me, closing what little space was left there.

Mr. Crossbender clears his throat again. "Kids..." he starts, his voice sounding thick. He rubs a hand over his face and moves his office chair so he can sit in front of us. "I'm so sorry–" His lips press together and he shakes his head, once, twice. Sucking in a deep breath he continues, "I'm so sorry to have to tell you this but..."

And then his lips are moving but I'm not hearing a sound. Yet, somehow I know what he's saying. I know what those words mean, and a strangled sound escapes my throat. Of all that I've feared, her never coming back to us is the worst, but this... I can barely comprehend this right now. And within that instant I am irrevocably and forever broken. I know I will never be the same. This moment will forever change me; it will forever change all of us. As my hands move to my face, my body collapses backward, only to be caught in the strong arms of Marcus. He holds me tight against his side, a solemn promise, I know. And then Raven is burying his face against my shoulder, I feel my shirt wet with tears. I see the look on Mr. Crossbender's face, a look I will never be able to scratch from my memories. Shock, sadness, fear; he expresses all of them.

What terrible news to bestow upon six children.

TWENTY-THREE

ANDIE

MY HANDS ARE COVERED IN BLOOD. BLITHE'S BLOOD. I SCRUB them off in the sink of our old house at the Pasture. We fled after what happened at the hospital, unable to look at any of them. My heart shattered with the thought of another life gone. I am so sick of death. It always seems to come to the ones who don't deserve it.

I will never forget the look on Sam's face when Dr. Akiyama wrapped up the baby and shoved it into his arms. I haven't ever seen a look like that on his face. He was stunned, scared. At six foot four and built like a brick house, it's not easy to make the Volker Sovereign look like that. Whatever just happened there, it's ruined all of us.

"I am never coming back here," I say to Ian, scrubbing off the dried blood from under my fingernails, it has an odd gleam to it as it trickles down the drain, like it's flickering out and away. Strange.

"Okay," Ian agrees. He sits patiently in the kitchen chair, no doubt trying to process everything he just saw. He was never in the medical field, never able to stomach the sight of so much blood. A scrape on the knee is one thing, but to watch a person bleed out... It haunts me, even with my medical background and all. I will never be able to scratch that from my memory. Ian's probably in shock from seeing it all.

I pause from the scrubbing to look around me. Even though we've been gone for weeks, this place is still the same. The furniture is all here. Plates and mugs. The sheets still on the beds. It's like we never left. It's like we were expected to come back. And now, I'm not sure I could ever come back, even if Crane were gone. There are too many horrible memories here. The feeling of loss wells up inside me. I press my lips together, feel my chin quiver. Before I make a noise Ian is at my side, wrapping my hands in a towel to dry them and pulling me against his chest.

"It's okay," he whispers. "It's okay. I'm here with you." I feel him sigh against me as though he can feel what I do. He probably does, after all that. Of course he does.

I swallow the sorrow down. Take a deep breath. "Why did we come back here?" I ask him.

"To get your brother and his family." Ian rubs my back as he speaks.

"No." I shake my head. "Why are we here in this house?"

"Because we have to wait for Sam to pack his things. Then we're leaving. We are taking him and the baby back to Hanford. He won't stay here now."

No, he won't. Just a few hours ago he was insistent on staying and killing Crane. But now, with his wife dead and a newborn daughter, he can no longer stay here. Just like I can no longer stay here.

"What about Lex and Ira?" I ask Ian.

"I'm sure they'll come with us. They were like Blithe's own children. Sam won't leave them here." Ian moves his hands to my arms, rubbing them.

I shudder. We are taking all of Crane's Sovereign. "Then Elvis will be alone in this place."

"Don't think he'll mind so much," Ian replies, quietly. "He likes the business of the fields and the animals."

But Elvis is a Funding Entity. He can't just spend the rest of his life working on a farm. My back stiffens and I pull away from him. He had an investment in this. Can he watch us all walk away?

"What?" Ian asks.

"Do you think Elvis knew?"

"Knew what?"

"Do you think he knew about Blithe and Sam acting so strange?"

"I think he would have told us," Ian replies. "We can trust Elvis. He's one of the good guys."

Are there really any good guys in all of this? My thoughts flash to Adam for just a second. I told myself that I would never think of him again, not after his betrayal. I thought he was a good guy. He's lied to me so many times. There are no good guys. There are few that I trust. And Ian, yeah, Ian is one of them.

I turn away from Ian and start scrubbing my hands again. "I'm not sure who to trust anymore. All of this... it all seems so screwed up. We were just supposed to keep the Districts running, keep our family safe. What happened to all of that? And why the hell aren't they staffing the hospital?"

"I'm not sure," Ian murmurs. No doubt he's been thinking the same things as I have. Ever since Crane came back and we left for Hanford, things have been... off. Very off. I scrub my hands harder, unsure if I'll ever be able to feel clean again after having that much blood covering them. I look down and see drops of blood on my clothes and my boots.

"I have to change," I say.

"Sure." Ian heads for our old bedroom and begins digging through my dresser. There are some clothes here, we couldn't take everything.

As I change into a pair of worn jeans and an old flannel shirt, Ian waits by the door. He keeps a distance as my emotions fluctuate between sorrow and anger. Sorrow for obvious reasons, the anger due to thoughts of Crane and thinking that this might have something to do with him. And anger with myself for being so stupid and coming back here without a plan. I can feel it welling up inside me. Ian sucks in a deep breath and backs away.

"What?" I ask.

He rubs a hand across his forehead. "Nothing," he whispers, bending to pick up my blood-speckled boots from the floor. "I'll go clean these."

When I'm done getting dressed, I sit down on the edge of the bed and try to get my emotions under control. Ian returns and passes me the boots. The blood is gone, but it stained the leather a darker hue.

"I have to go get my notes and things from my lab before we leave with Sam and the baby," I tell him as I pull my boots on.

"I'll go with you," he offers.

"I'd like that." I don't want to leave him alone in this place for one second. I know he's a grown man, but I can't fathom the thought of something happening to him.

We walk in silence through the fields on our way to the forest. It is finally like summer. The field is dry and the dandelions, buttercups and purple aster brush against our shins. We are surrounded by color here. And space. Wide open, breathable space. These colors are none that we will ever experience from within the depths of Hanford. I will miss this. Blinking a few times, I try to press the sight of the summer wildflower field into my memories. At least I will have those. At least I can escape to these fields in my head.

When we get to the ruins, I lift the door in the floor and descend the steps with Ian following me. As I begin lighting the lamps, feeling another presence in the room, I stop short. There in the shadows stands Burton Crane. Suit, tie, smug look plastered on his face like always.

Turning in anger, I face Ian. "You told him?" I ask.

"I didn't tell him." Ian's hands move up in a defensive action as he moves to stand next to me.

Who else could have? There was no one else that knew of this place. Only Ian. Only my husband knew what I was doing down here. Only Ian knew what I had created in an attempt to rid myself of these damned nanocytes. Would he tell? Of all people, would he tell the one person I hate the most? I turn to look Ian in the face. He's pale, shocked, just like me. He looks so innocent. There's no way...

"Ah, Andromeda, I have missed you so–" Crane starts.

"No!" I cut him off. "I came back to get the rest of my family. Sam and... and..."

"Yes." Crane smiles. "How very tragic."

I still myself. He must know that Blithe is dead. "How?"

"You won't be leaving here, Andromeda. No matter how bad you want to. You belong in the Pasture. You belong behind these locked gates. You are not meant to be out in that world we created. You are a Sovereign of Phoenix. Not Hanford. Others may be moved between the Districts as necessary. But not you. Your place is here. You only leave these gates when I need you to."

"I'm going back to my children," I tell him defiantly. "I will not stay here. I am done with this."

Crane shakes his head from side-to-side. "No."

"I will. I *have* to. I'm going back to my family and... and I have to find a cure." Shit. I shouldn't have let that slip out.

Crane smiles as he inspects my makeshift lab, the empty crates, the microscope, and the notebooks filled with equations and theories and results. "Information seems to be a drug for you, Andromeda."

"It is not a drug. It is my cure. The only way I can stop whatever it is you've done to me."

"From this point on I forbid you from touching a computer other than the one you pair the Residents with. And since you already know what you're doing, you no longer need access to the world's studies. All those research papers, data, we have pulled that access from the rest of the world and now I pull it from you. You have a job. Stop meddling."

A hot fury burns deep in my chest as he takes away every chance I will ever have at curing myself. "You can't–"

"I will. You are not in control," he says so calmly.

"No!" My fingertips tingle.

"Andie...," Ian warns. "You're doing it again."

"Be quiet." I silence him as I step toward Crane, and all he does is smile. "Give it back to me." I hold my hand out for the vial filled with amber liquid, my cure for when the time is right. I will end my life with that vial when I am ready. If I cannot find another method to get the nanocytes out, I will use it. "Give it back!" I demand.

"The fact that you think what I did to you is the same as these dogs," Crane holds the vial up in the air. "It's preposterous really. You are now more than a mere creature of the earth. You are more than a dog. But," he pauses, glances at the vial in his hand. "The fact that you have killed an innocent animal in the desire to rid yourself of this gift I gave you, it makes me think that you might be ready." He smirks. "I read your notes."

I ignore the fact that he rifled through my research. "Ready for what?" I jerk my hand, motioning for him to hand over the vial.

His red brows rise, his face lightens. "For the second wave. I spent way too much money on you to have you throw it all down the drain in a heartbeat. You will not kill yourself with this."

To my horror, he releases his thumb from the side of the vial and flicks the cap off. It drops to the floor and bounces into the shadows. Crane tips the vial before throwing it down and the glass breaks as the amber liquid soaks into the dirt floor.

"No!" I scream at him as five years of hard work disappear before my eyes.

"Andie," Ian's voice warns. I almost forgot he was in the room with me. When I turn to him, he is sweating, his face red with panic and... something else is wrong. He's holding his stomach, bent over like he's going to be sick.

Turning to face Crane, the white hot anger I felt for Crane the last time I spoke to him on the phone comes back with a vengeance. I let the fury radiate off of me as I advance on Crane, fists out, ready to punch him in the face like I've always wanted to. He just stands there, smiling. The rage radiates stronger, until it's all I can think about, killing him is all I can think about.

There is the sound of a soft thud from behind me.

"Uh oh," Crane says with a smirk.

I turn to find Ian on the ground.

I stop. "What did you do to him?"

"*I* did nothing."

Forgetting Crane, I run to Ian's side. There is blood dripping out of his nose and his ears. I touch his forehead and find his skin is hot, mottled and sticky. "What did you do to him?" I scream at Crane.

Crane takes one step toward me. "What did *you* do to him, Andromeda?"

My hand moves to his mouth, his neck. There is no pulse. My lungs deflate. "What the hell did you do to him, Crane?" I tear at Ian's shirt, ripping the buttons and pulling it away from his body. I try to remember the basic steps for CPR, but it's been so long, I'm so out of practice. I put my mouth over his, blow in a breath of air, count in my head. It is one or two? I can't remember. I move to his chest, knowing every inch of his body, I don't count ribs I just start pushing with the heel of my hand. I count, is it thirty or sixty? Jesus I can't remember any of it now. Stopping, I give him a breath then resume chest compressions. I continue the pattern until I am out of breath, until my arms are so weak and I can no longer press down.

I turn to Crane. He is standing there, just as he always does. But something seems off. Something... I sniff the air. He no longer smells musky and sweet and stomach churning.

Crane notices my observation. "It was a mask," he says, "to hide the pheromones. Mine. Yours are different. I can control it but you..." He tips his head and laughs. "Ah, Andromeda, your pheromones can do so much more. This is fascinating, really."

"Pheromones?" Impossible.

"That's all it is, pheromones. Bees use them, ants and other creatures, as a method for communication; warning, control. All it took was a tiny tweak to enhance the way the human body excretes them and their impact. Perhaps you've noticed the way you can control a room, get people to do what you want." He looks hard at me, as if he's trying to see something different. "The others can control, never more than a handful of people, that's why we needed you to unite the Districts before. But maybe there was more..."

"No. I haven't noticed. You're crazy." I hear my voice crack. My hands are on Ian's chest and I feel his skin cooling underneath my palms. What do I do? What the hell do I do to fix him?

"Really?" Crane takes a step toward me. "Let me tell you a secret, Dr. Akiyama never wanted a seat on the Committee. How long did it take you to get him to agree? Ten minutes? And Isaac, he should have done some very bad things by now. He's wired to, after all. And yet, he remains as quiet as a church mouse in your presence. Even your husband has been a little clingy and smothering. It's just too bad he wasn't strong enough to survive your body telling everyone around you to die. You just secreted a chemical strong enough to kill a person, Andromeda."

I still. Think.

"You see now, it's all in the pheromones. And they are your worker bees, perfectly constructed worker bees." He tips his head, looks down at Ian's body on the ground. "I wasn't expecting you to be able to do that though. Allowing yourself to angry enough to kill. You should really learn to control yourself, Andromeda, especially now that I know just how dangerous you are. I wonder if the others…" His finger moves to his chin in thought.

"Why the hell didn't it do anything to you?" I ask.

"Ah, the secret. All those gifted with the nanocytes are immune to the others. You can thank your great-grandmother for that little tweak. I'm sure you would have killed me just now if my own nanocytes hadn't blocked the chemical signals your body just released."

"I hate you," I whisper.

"I'm sure you do."

Before he finishes talking, I run one finger down Ian's cheek; feel a pain and sadness stronger than I ever have before in my life. Stronger than when I thought he was dead the first time. There, a stabbing in my chest; guilt, pain. It drowns me. I did this to him. Looking down at Ian's lifeless body, all I can think is what if this were Lina or Raven or Sam… It wouldn't be any less painful to know that I did this to them. I can't let this happen again. I can't risk hurting anyone else. One tear drops off of my chin and soaks into the dirt floor. "I love you," I whisper. Standing, I run for the stairs that lead out of this place. Leaping up the steps two at a time, hearing Crane's laughter as he begins to follow, I run harder, faster, deeper into the forest.

"Where are you going?" he shouts.

Ignoring him, I know what I have to do. I have to draw him out. I have to get away from him and the ones that I love. Oh, how my world has changed. I have to get away.

I run for the fence.

"Where are you going, Andromeda?" Crane shouts into the forest.

As I run, I recognize the sounds of the Guardians following. They used to do this years ago, follow me through the forest because I couldn't be trusted to take care of myself. That was a dark time. This second, right now, it's even darker.

Skidding to a stop, just as the buzz of the fence reaches my ears, I search the tree line, find the tallest, the thickest, the closest tree, and start to climb.

"Andromeda," Crane shouts up at me. "What are you doing?"

The Guardians bark. There's dozens, no-hundreds of them below me. I test a branch that arcs toward the fence, just clearing the height of the steel chain link. I test the branch, balance, let go of the trunk and walk.

"Andromeda!" Crane shouts, his voice laced with panic.

I inch further, a tightrope walk. The buzzing gets louder. I feel the warm trickle that I know is blood dripping out of my nose. Still, I continue on the only path I know can free me from him, from this.

"Andromeda!" Crane screams again.

He is no longer in charge. I am. I jump.

"NO!"

The buzz of the electrified fence drowns out Crane's voice. It is as though I am flying, falling, some strange sensation between the two. I cycle my arms and legs, try to pull myself over using the air thick with electrical energy. It doesn't work. I cannot fly. My left foot hits the chain link as I drop. I feel the arc of electricity run through my body, every muscle stiffens, my breath catches, my ears ring, every single nerve ending sizzles. And then I am falling, falling into the shadows and there is nothing, just darkness and silence and... peace.

Twenty-Four

Adam

There is a knock on the door. My eyes move to the window. It's dark, too early for anyone to be up.

"Come in."

Mack's form appears as the door opens. "Boss?"

I drop my feet from the desk and sit up. "What's up?" Noticing he's alone, I ask, "Where's your goat?"

"Sleeping." Mack frowns. "We're missing three men. Disappeared while doing night rounds."

I stand. "Fucking Swamp people."

"Yeah. I have a few men ready to go out and search."

"You won't find them." I stand to pull on my jacket. "Hold down the fort, Mack. I'll go find them."

"Alone?"

"Yea–" The light on my desk flickers out and we are purged into darkness.

The sound of Mack clicking the power switch on and off fills the room.

"Stop," I say.

"Power's out."

"No shit."

We wait in silence. Sometimes it flickers, but it never goes out. A ferocious unease fills me. "Something's wrong." The room lights up again.

"Boss?"

"Stay here. I'm leaving you in charge."

"Where are you going?"

"North."

"Alone?"

"Yes."

"Don't think that's a good idea, Boss."

"I don't care what you think, Mack. Sit down, shut up, and keep Romney running."

On my way out the door, Mack asks, "What do I tell Whitmarsh if he shows?"

"He won't show while I'm gone."

"You sure?"

I should just fucking tell him the truth. I'm going to tell him the truth. "I am Christian Whitmarsh."

Mack twists his face with disbelief. "You are?" He lets out a harsh laugh, sucks it in, and turns serious. "You're Christian Whitmarsh." It is no longer a question.

I nod yes.

"Goddamn."

"You will not say a thing to anyone until I return."

"But... you're wanted by the Militia in North Carolina."

I smile. "Let me know when you find someone who doesn't want my head on a stick." I leave without Mack answering, consider heading back to my room to grab a pack and supplies. I drop the thought, there's no time. Thanks to the nanocytes I don't need anything besides the clothes on my back. I learned that a long time ago.

The missing men will have to wait. There's little chance that they survived a night with the Swamp people. Going to look for them will only get me two things: their bare skulls and a fight.

I head north.

. . .

--

STOPPING in the shadows of the forest that edge the District, I watch and wait. The electricity is on. I can sense it, just as I could sense when getting too close would make my nose and ears bleed. Reaching into my pocket I pull out a pen and a piece of paper. I write a note: *We need to talk*. Pulling a long blade of grass from the ground, I wrap the note around a thick stick and throw it over the fence. It hits one of the Volker standing guard. Good, the less time I have to wait the better. The Volker pulls the note off of the stick, talks into the radio on his shoulder, probably speaking directly to Sam.

Seating myself at the base of a tree, I take in my surroundings. Something changed. There is a smell in the air, pungent and faint, but still detectable. It reminds me of the Swamp people's camps. The steady hum of the fence tells me that the power's still on. Something's off here. I scan the fence line. There's too many Volker out here, which can only mean something happened. My eyes focus on the black SUV advancing toward the gate. It stops and the door opens. To my surprise it's not Sam's giant frame that exits the Volker SUV. Shit, Crane's back.

There he stands, his face flushed, his brow gleaming with sweat. He never looks like this, out of sorts. "What happened, Crane?" I demand, shouting across the expanse of land between us. The Volker who I hit with the stick places the note in Crane's hand. He motions me forward, seemingly not wanting to play pass-the-note as Sam and I did, but we were doing it in secret, we couldn't risk anyone hearing us shouting back and forth.

Crane moves forward until I see him wince from the surge of the fence. I do the same. And then Crane shouts. "Not very long ago, I made a deal with you."

"And?" I holler back.

"It's time for you to collect."

I still. Waiting to hear the only words I've wanted to hear since all this started.

"She's yours. Go find her."

"Let me in."

"She's no longer behind these gates."

"Where then?"

He motions to the forest behind me.

This doesn't make sense. "What happened to her husband?" I ask.

"Dead."

I wait, not believing him.

"For real this time. He is truly dead," Crane says.

"The children?"

"They are in Hanford, where she left them."

"She would never leave them."

"Oh, but she has." As he talks, filling me in on the events of the past day, my mind wanders between the details, fear floods me, then an anticipation I can barely contain. Crane clears this throat, bringing me back. "Now, Colonel Waters, or should I say Christian Whitmarsh? Go. Fetch."

I turn to leave, running, mind racing. Failure was not an option. Those are the words I've been listening to Crane and his team of wannabe goons repeat for years, but it seems Crane just might have failed, especially if the Swamp people ate her, and they will eat anything; that is their purpose, the scavengers, the cleaners, the carrion hoarders.

From what Crane just said they pulled her into the forest. Wrapped their hands around her shoulders and slithered off with her body, just like they did with the dead at the other Districts. I watched them do it in Crystal River. Just like I watched the look of horror on Andie's face as that man touched the fence. If I know anything about her, she will be punishing herself until the end of time. If she survives. If they haven't eaten her already.

They probably ate her alive.

I run faster.

Preview of Origins (The Phoenix Project Book 5)

Sam

It has been months since I've seen Adam–not since before Andie's death. He used to trek up here every few weeks to check on the place, make sure the Swamp people stayed away and whatever else he did. Truth be told, I've been dreading this day.

When the Volker patrolling the fence radio me to tell me he is here, I have him sent to the Gateway, where the train exits and enters. Since I'm pretty sure he's going to kill me with the news I have to tell him, I left him a Volker vehicle with instructions to meet me at the Pasture. If I'm going to die today, I'd rather die at home, in comfort. Then Elvis won't have to drag my ass so far to my grave.

I wait outside on the porch for Adam to show. As the black SUV drives down the gravel road, I stand and make my way to him.

Getting out and meeting me halfway, Adam says, "I'm looking for your sister."

Can't lie about it. "She's dead."

"She can't be." He shakes his head before pinning me with a dark stare. "She's not."

Crane must have told him the same thing he told me. Hell, I even saw the video–can't scratch it from my head. Don't understand why he can't get it through his thick skull that she's gone forever, just like the rest of them. Just like Blithe. Crap, he probably doesn't know that yet.

"You know how siblings share a connection? When you share the same blood there's a link there, you can sense things. Andie's dead. I saw it. I feel it." I pause before adding the last bit. "So is Blithe."

"What?" Adam's voice is so low that I almost wonder if it's the wind. "What did you just say?" he repeats.

"Blithe's dead. She died the same day as Ian and Andie. They're all fucking dead, man. We're all that's left." Somehow, saying the words makes my life sound so much more fucked up and lonely than it has been these past few months.

"How in the hell did Blithe die?" The look on his face is one of disbelief, like she could never die. "Tell me now, Sam!"

I've never seen him like this before, ready to explode. Blithe thought he didn't give a shit about her. She was wrong. But... how could he not sense it like I could sense Andie? Maybe it's something different I'm feeling?

"In childbirth. The... vials." I don't have to say more. He gave me vials of medication to use on Crane; not his sister, not my wife.

The things that come out of his mouth, I barely hear them; I'm too out if it, drowning in guilt and fear. I don't even see his fists coming. Adam hits me in the jaw, hard.

And then I think of my dead sister, my lost niece, my dead brother-in-law. I know Adam has been involved in this since the beginning. I don't know how he's involved, but I know he brought her here. I start punching him back. He hooks his foot around my ankle and punches in rapid succession, knocking me onto my back. And then we are on the ground. I taste blood in my mouth, see a split along Adams cheek. One second it's there, another and it's gone. What the hell? I punch him harder, sure I'll knock out a tooth. No teeth fall, but it's enough to shove him back and grab his arms. He twists, frees one hand and grabs me by the throat.

"Boys, boys, boys," Elvis's voice interrupts us.

As my vision clears, I realize he has a shotgun pointed at Adam's head. Reaching down, he pulls Adam off me by the shoulder of his shirt.

"Got that out of your system?" Elvis asks.

Adam gives me a look.

I nod. A truce, for now.

"You two go and make up." Elvis points to my house. It used to be Blithe's but now it's just mine, and I hate it. "Can't get much talking done when you're rolling around in the dirt." He crosses his arms and waits for us to move.

Adam steps up and holds a hand out. I hesitate for a moment before taking it and he helps pull me to my feet. I brush the back of my hand across my mouth, a trail of blood staining my skin.

"Dick," I say under my breath.

Adam smiles.

I lead him to the house. Once we're inside he stops in the living room.

"Wait here," I say as I head to my bedroom.

There she is; a sleeping angel wrapped in white blankets. Elvis has showed me a hundred times how to wrap her, but it seems I can never swaddle her tightly like he does. I pick up the baby, thinking that I should probably change her diaper. It seems I can never do that enough, either. I look down at her cherub face and she is so small in my large hands. Tears sting my eyes, I swallow them down. I can't do this. I'm not meant to do this alone. I make my way back to the living room.

"What's that?" Adam stills, a statue rippling with anger still but not a bruise or bleeding wound visible from our fight. My face and ribs are throbbing.

"I need you to take care of something for me."

"What?" His voice sounds uneasy. It should.

I thrust the baby into his arms. "Get her out of here." I step away, afraid that I might change my mind.

"What?" He accepts the bundle of blankets and something in him seems to soften when he sees her face. "Why?" he asks.

"I'll rot her. She's not safe in this place. Get her out of here. Hide her."

"I can't do this." Adam stands still, his eyes wide. "I won't do this. You don't know what you're asking."

"I know exactly what I'm doing." I blow out a breath. "You were a shitty brother to Blithe. Make it up. Hide your niece where Crane and the other Entities will never find her. You know she can't stay here. They'll do something to her. They've already broken enough of us. She's too innocent."

Adam moves the blankets from around the baby's face and as he does, her tiny hand reaches out and grasps his finger. He sees her marked wrist and sucks in a breath. Images of tattooing day at the Pasture flood my head.

"This..." he looks up at me, "this is your baby. Hers. How can you give up your own blood?"

Shit, that stings. "Didn't you?" I step away from him. "You turned your back on Raven. You weren't ever there for him. What were your reasons? How could you turn your back on your firstborn son?"

"I..." Adam's jaw moves but nothing else comes out.

I back away, ready to run out the back door of the house before I change my fucking mind. I must do something. Make this world halfway livable for her when she grows up. I can't do it with her here.

"Is this how it felt?" I ask, my hand moving to that pinching sensation over my heart.

He nods. Frowns. Looks down at the baby. "Yeah." He shifts her in his arms. "It doesn't go away, Sam. Never gets better. Only gets worse."

I nod.

"What's her name?" he asks.

"Norah."

And then there is nothing but silence passed between us. Adam reaches into his pocket and pulls out two more vials. He sets them on the table next to the couch. I swallow hard. Man up. Adam nods once before turning and walking out the door. I radio the Volker at the Gateway and tell them to let him out.

Watching the clock, I give him twenty minutes. I shower, put on my Volker uniform. In the living room, I pick up the vials Adam left and put them in my pocket before heading to my vehicle and driving to Headquarters.

ORIGINS

For those who have hung on this long

ONE

SAM

IT HAS BEEN MONTHS SINCE I'VE SEEN ADAM–NOT SINCE before Andie's death. He used to trek up here every few weeks to check on the place, make sure the Swamp people stayed away and whatever else he did. Truth be told, I've been dreading this day.

When the Volker patrolling the fence radio me to tell me he is here, I have him sent to the Gateway, where the train exits and enters. Since I'm pretty sure he's going to kill me with the news I have to tell him, I left him a Volker vehicle with instructions to meet me at the Pasture. If I'm going to die today, I'd rather die at home, in comfort. Then Elvis won't have to drag my ass so far to my grave.

I wait outside on the porch for Adam to show. As the black SUV drives down the gravel road, I stand and make my way to him.

Getting out and meeting me halfway, Adam says, "I'm looking for your sister."

Can't lie about it. "She's dead."

"She can't be." He shakes his head before pinning me with a dark stare. "She's not."

Crane must have told him the same thing he told me. Hell, I even saw the video–can't scratch it from my head. Don't understand why he can't get it through his thick skull that she's gone forever, just like the rest of them. Just like Blithe. Crap, he probably doesn't know that yet.

"You know how siblings share a connection? When you share the same blood there's a link there, you can sense things. Andie's dead. I saw it. I feel it." I pause before adding the last bit. "So is Blithe."

"What?" Adam's voice is so low that I almost wonder if it's the wind. "What did you just say?" he repeats.

"Blithe's dead. She died the same day as Ian and Andie. They're all fucking dead, man. We're all that's left." Somehow, saying the words makes my life sound so much more fucked up and lonely than it has been these past few months.

"How in the hell did Blithe die?" The look on his face is one of disbelief, like she could never die. "Tell me now, Sam!"

I've never seen him like this before, ready to explode. Blithe thought he didn't give a shit about her. She was wrong. But... how could he not sense it like I could sense Andie? Maybe it's something different I'm feeling?

"In childbirth. The... vials." I don't have to say more. He gave me vials of medication to use on Crane; not his sister, not my wife.

The things that come out of his mouth, I barely hear them; I'm too out if it, drowning in guilt and fear. I don't even see his fists coming. Adam hits me in the jaw, hard.

And then I think of my dead sister, my lost niece, my dead brother-in-law. I know Adam has been involved in this since the beginning. I don't know how he's involved, but I know he brought her here. I start punching him back. He hooks his foot around my ankle and punches in rapid succession, knocking me onto my back. And then we are on the ground. I taste blood in my mouth, see a split along Adams cheek. One second it's there, another and it's gone. What the hell? I punch him harder, sure I'll knock out a tooth. No teeth fall, but it's enough to shove him back and grab his arms. He twists, frees one hand and grabs me by the throat.

"Boys, boys, boys," Elvis's voice interrupts us.

As my vision clears, I realize he has a shotgun pointed at Adam's head. Reaching down, he pulls Adam off me by the shoulder of his shirt.

"Got that out of your system?" Elvis asks.

Adam gives me a look.

I nod. A truce, for now.

"You two go and make up." Elvis points to my house. It used to be Blithe's but now it's just mine, and I hate it. "Can't get much talking done when you're rolling around in the dirt." He crosses his arms and waits for us to move.

Adam steps up and holds a hand out. I hesitate for a moment before taking it and he helps pull me to my feet. I brush the back of my hand across my mouth, a trail of blood staining my skin.

"Dick," I say under my breath.

Adam smiles.

I lead him to the house. Once we're inside he stops in the living room.

"Wait here," I say as I head to my bedroom.

There she is; a sleeping angel wrapped in white blankets. Elvis has showed me a hundred times how to wrap her, but it seems I can never swaddle her tightly like he does. I pick up the baby, thinking that I should probably change her diaper. It seems I can never do that enough, either. I look down at her cherub face and she is so small in my large hands. Tears sting my eyes, I swallow them down. I can't do this. I'm not meant to do this alone. I make my way back to the living room.

"What's that?" Adam stills, a statue rippling with anger still but not a bruise or bleeding wound visible from our fight. My face and ribs are throbbing.

"I need you to take care of something for me."

"What?" His voice sounds uneasy. It should.

I thrust the baby into his arms. "Get her out of here." I step away, afraid that I might change my mind.

"What?" He accepts the bundle of blankets and something in him seems to soften when he sees her face. "Why?" he asks.

"I'll rot her. She's not safe in this place. Get her out of here. Hide her."

"I can't do this." Adam stands still, his eyes wide. "I won't do this. You don't know what you're asking."

"I know exactly what I'm doing." I blow out a breath. "You were a shitty brother to Blithe. Make it up. Hide your niece where Crane and the other Entities will never find her. You know she can't stay here. They'll do something to her. They've already broken enough of us. She's too innocent."

Adam moves the blankets from around the baby's face and as he does, her tiny hand reaches out and grasps his finger. He sees her marked wrist and sucks in a breath. Images of tattooing day at the Pasture flood my head.

"This..." he looks up at me, "this is your baby. Hers. How can you give up your own blood?"

Shit, that stings. "Didn't you?" I step away from him. "You turned your back on Raven. You weren't ever there for him. What were your reasons? How could you turn your back on your firstborn son?"

"I..." Adam's jaw moves but nothing else comes out.

I back away, ready to run out the back door of the house before I change my fucking mind. I must do something. Make this world halfway livable for her when she grows up. I can't do it with her here.

"Is this how it felt?" I ask, my hand moving to that pinching sensation over my heart.

He nods. Frowns. Looks down at the baby. "Yeah." He shifts her in his arms. "It doesn't go away, Sam. Never gets better. Only gets worse."

I nod.

"What's her name?" he asks.

"Norah."

And then there is nothing but silence passed between us. Adam reaches into his pocket and pulls out two more vials. He sets them on the table next to the couch. I swallow hard. Man up. Adam nods once before turning and walking out the door. I radio the Volker at the Gateway and tell them to let him out.

Watching the clock, I give him twenty minutes. I shower, put on my Volker uniform. In the living room, I pick up the vials Adam left and put them in my pocket before heading to my vehicle and driving to Headquarters.

Two

Mack

Adam's couch smells like goat. He's gonna kick my ass when he finally comes back here, been waiting months for him to return. Haven't heard a peep since the lights went out and he spilled the beans. He's Christian Whitmarsh. Hard to believe I've been working for a criminal. But then, they're all criminals these days. At least he put an end to the Skin trades. First man to do that since the Reformation. Guess I could be working for a worse criminal.

The Militia men still don't know the truth about him. Said I'd keep my mouth shut and that's what I plan to do. Still, he's been gone for a while. Since then we've lost two more men. Swamp people been picking them off. I've been thinking of pulling them inside. Winter's coming, people speculating it's going to be a long one. Weather acts strange these days, patterns all shifted.

"Boss," Chuck opens the door.

"Not the boss," I remind him. "Just filling in."

"Sure. Well, someone's headed our way."

I stand. No one is ever headed our way. Unless it's someone who knows we're here. "Adam?" I ask.

"Could be."

I shoo Jill off his couch and tidy the place up. "Cover him, make sure he wasn't followed."

"Right." Chuck leaves; his slingshot hanging from his back pocket reminds me to run an inventory on ammunition. We've been running low on lots of things, seems the most important go the quickest: food and ammo.

I pace the hallways until he shows. He doesn't stop in the hall, but beckons me to his office. I follow him. Jill trotting at my side.

Adam closes the door as soon as I step inside.

"I need you to do something for me, Mack." He unbuttons his coat. His chest is wrapped diagonally in thick blankets. Shrugging off the coat, he reaches into the fabric covering his chest and pulls out... a baby.

I raise my hands up in the air. Pointing a baby at me is just as bad as pointing a gun at me.

"This is important, Mack. You're my first in command."

"Hey, Adam... er... Christian, whatever you want me to call you. I want nothin' to do with a baby."

"You know me as Adam, you call me Adam." He shrugs a pack that was hidden under the coat off his back. "You're the only one I can trust with this."

"A baby?"

"Yeah."

"You bring me a goat. I can deal with a goat but not a goddamned baby. What do I even feed it? This is a Militia outpost, not a daycare."

"Goat milk. Until she's older. Then regular food"

I glance at Jill who's now sniffing the bundle of joy in Adam's arms. "Goat milk, huh?"

"Yeah." He empties the pack; there are a few small garments, diapers and bottles. "Sorry. I didn't have time to gather supplies."

"How long you plan on leaving that thing here?"

"It's a baby, Mack." He sets the bundle on the couch. "And I don't know."

"How can you not know?" I wait for him to say something about the *eau de goat* scent that's all over the place, but he doesn't seem to notice.

Adam moves around the office, starts changing his clothes and boots. The stuff he's wearing looks well-used and dirty. "I'll get word to you when I can." He pulls a light jacket on over his fresh shirt.

"You leaving again?"

"Have to."

"Where you going?"

"I have to find someone." He walks over to the couch to check on the baby. "You keep her safe, Mack."

"Sure."

He walks over to me, serious as shit. "No one is to know she's here."

"Sure, boss."

"Not a goddamned soul, Mack. That kid is to be the best kept secret in the northern hemisphere." He glances back at the baby. Jill's sniffing her head.

"She got a name?"

"Norah."

"Okay, boss." I think I might vomit, being left in charge of a baby.

"She's my niece. Not a soul knows about her."

I nod. "We'll keep it that way."

"Good."

And then Adam storms out of the place, leaving me with a goat and a frickin' baby.

"No shittin' on that," I warn Jill as she sniffs the baby. "Definitely no shittin' on that."

The baby makes a cooing sound as it reaches out and touches Jill on the nose.

THREE

CATALINA

IT HAS BEEN TWELVE MONTHS, TWO WEEKS, FOUR DAYS AND nine hours since my father died and my mother went missing. People want to know where she is. The questioning is relentless. They don't believe me when I tell them I don't know. I haven't heard from her since the day they left for the Phoenix District on that ill-fated trip to bring my Uncle Sam and his wife and baby to Hanford.

Since they've been gone, I turned seventeen. That means I only have one year left until I'm assigned my Apprenticeship in the Hanford District. The Sovereign that run the Children's Training program here haven't let on to their plans for me. By now, most of the kids in my classes have some idea of where they'll end up. We don't get to decide on our own. There's a meeting of the Hanford Sovereign, the ones in charge I'm guessing, they look over our accomplishments and then they assign us based on where we test strongly.

My mother warned me to stay away from the genetics field. She didn't want me to wind up like her. So, I've kept my grades steady, never excelled in one subject but just an equal performance across the board. She wanted me to stay away from genetics, but... part of me is drawn to it. I can see everything so easily in my head. It's hard to answer a question wrong when I know so easily what the right answer is. I even failed a test on purpose a few months ago. That got me a lot of trouble. Failing is not an option. No one ever fails a test, ever. It got me nothing but a stern talking to from Mrs. Jones, extra work, and community service sweeping the halls. *If you don't want to be a Sovereign, you could be one of the janitors.* That's what she said. She even threatened me with a green uniform.

We get plenty of threats here, now that our mother is gone. It's just me, Raven, Astrid, Isaac, Cashel, and Marcus. When Mrs. Jones came to Mr. Crossbender's office that day they told us what happened to my parents, she smiled this awful smirk. And I remembered the words she told us on our first day here. *You are not in the Phoenix District any longer. Here, you will follow the rules. You will do what you're told. If you don't, you'll disappear. If you tell your parents, they'll disappear. District or die.* I wonder if Mrs. Jones had anything to do with their disappearance. Part of me knows the answer is no. I don't think to ask any of them. Crossbender wouldn't hurt a fly, but other people here would, they would squash me like a bug. I'm not a fan of Hanford. I'm not a fan of their people, my peers, or their food. None of us are. The other kids and me, we may not all be related by blood, but we're family and we stick together. Lately, that's the only thing keeping us all going.

"Two more weeks," Cash says as he stares at his lunch.

"Until what?" Astrid asks.

"Until I get my Apprenticeship." Cash sounds excited about the possibilities. He thinks he's going to the lower levels to work with the farm animals. That's what they have led him to believe.

I look down at my plate. It's the only meal we can stomach, so we barely pass this one up. They usually serve sandwiches. The bread is not terrible, but it's not like my mom used to make. They put cheese on it and some type of meat that tastes way better than the stuff they serve at dinner. We hate the food here. When I look up Astrid is watching me, her eyes huge and watery.

"What's wrong, Astrid?" I ask.

Her chin quivers and then her eyes are on Marcus's empty seat. "Everybody's always leaving me. First our parents, then Marcus, now Cash." She sets her fork down and stares at her food. "Then you, Lina."

"Hey, it's okay, Ash." I reach out to take her hand.

Cash slides closer to her and wraps an arm around her shoulders. "We're not leaving you. None of us are."

Through a whimper she says, "We never see Marcus anymore. He's always gone. We're supposed to stick together. That's what you all told Mr. Crossbender. We're not splitting up. But we are. It's only a matter of time before we're separated."

"That's not happening," Cash tries to calm her.

Raven looks away. Isaac squirms in his seat. When Astrid gets like this it seems to make everyone uncomfortable. I push my plate away, feeling sick. She's right, even if we tell her she's wrong a hundred times. She's right.

Her hands move to her ears and she presses her palms against her head like she's trying to block out some loud noise.

A foot kicks the legs of my chair. "See your baby's crying again, *farmers*," a tall kid from my class, Joe, snickers as he walks by. The word *farmers* comes out like a slur. It is around here.

One of his buddies shoves his hip into our table, spilling our drinks.

Raven follows the kid with a glare that would scare away an adult. But Joe's not looking. He sits with a group of guys who all whisper and look back at us. It's only gotten worse since my dad died and my mother went missing. They used to ask us about our life at the Pasture like they were genuinely interested, but now they just whisper things to us in the halls and the lunch line.

"It will be fine," I say to Astrid, reaching for her hands to pull them away from her head.

Isaac starts to stand, pushing his seat away from the table. "I'll take care of him."

"No!" I reach for his arm and pull him back down to sit. "No, Isaac. You can't get in any more trouble."

Last week he punched one of Joe's buddies for tripping me in the hall. A few days before that he tossed someone's schoolbooks over the railing and down the center of the Hanford divide—that's the open space between the hallways of Hanford, daylight spills from the transparent covering at ground level, shedding natural light to the floors below. Isaac will defend us with all his might, but then, sometimes, he gets super creepy. Like the way he's looking at Joe right now and smiling with his eyes dark and menacing. And then there's the fact that he looks like he's sixteen and he's barely twelve. I guess we are a bit different in some ways. None of the Hanford children look like a teenager when they should be looking like a child.

"Look." Cash holds out his wrist so we can all see the Phoenix District image that's been burned into his skin. Under the table, my fingers rub over mine, remembering that day we received them. Our commonality is our Sovereign tattoo: a dark image of a phoenix firebird. The others here, their Sovereign mark is an atom. The mark used to keep us safe and identify us as special. That's when we were home. Now it only gets us into trouble and sets us apart from the others here. It doesn't matter if we're all Sovereign children. Our mark is different and most here don't like that.

"We stick together," Cash says.

Silence passes between the five of us. I wish Marcus were here. This only got worse after he left for his Apprenticeship.

Astrid finally calms down long enough to finish her lunch. This place has done something to her, to all of us. When I look up, the guys at Joe's table are still snickering at us.

"Ignore them," Cash says.

"I'll try," I say as I catch the shadow outside the lunchroom doors. The door opens and a familiar face peeks in. Great, Kevin's here. This can only mean one thing; he's here to bring me to Mr. Crossbender's office for another round of questioning.

I shove the rest of my sandwich in my mouth, wash it down with the milk that remains in my cup, and stand to leave.

Astrid looks up at me with her big eyes. She has attachment issues, just like the rest of us.

"Kevin's here. See you guys later. Stay out of trouble." I glance at Isaac. "Stay away from Joe."

Isaac smiles.

As I walk across the lunchroom, I ignore the whispers and glances, and pull the sleeve of my sweater down over my wrists.

"Hey," I greet Kevin.

"Lina." He smiles, standing in the doorway for a few extra seconds, allowing the girls to get a good look at him.

"You're looking paler than usual today, Kev." I start walking away, unable to deal with the longing looks coming at him from the girls in the lunchroom.

Laughing, he lets the door close and jogs up next to me, green eyes twinkling as he looks at me. "Don't mock my paleness, girl. When I'm old and gray there will be nary a wrinkle on this handsome face."

"Subtle, the way you preen for them." I shove my hands in my pockets and walk a little faster.

Kevin tucks his light brown hair behind his ears. It's longer than most boys wear their hair here. The length seems to make his cheekbones stand out. "Can't help it if the chicks dig the weatherman."

"You are ridiculous."

He shrugs. "You're jealous."

I walk faster. I'm jealous of him, maybe a little jealous that they don't treat him like they treat us. They want him. Kevin belongs. The rest of us, not so much.

"Hey, wait up," he shouts. I didn't realize how fast I was walking. "How do you even know where you're going?"

"Kevin, when you show up, it's only to bring me to one place. I know exactly where Crossbender's office is. I don't even know why he bothers sending an escort still."

He flexes a bicep. "I'm the muscle. Supposed to protect you."

I stifle a laugh. "Nothing ever happens here."

The soft padding of feet begins behind us. I turn to see a Guardian following us.

"When did that thing show up?" Kevin asks.

"They're not things, they're living creatures." I turn down a hallway and stop at the elevator. There are lots of those here. Elevators and stairs all leading deep underground.

Kevin pushes the down arrow. When the doors open we step in, the

Guardian follows. I press the button for two levels below, where Mr. Crossbender keeps his office.

"Don't know why that thing is following us." He motions to the large dog.

I reach out to pet it on the head. "Maybe it doesn't trust you." I scratch behind its ear. "Beasts are the best judgment of character."

Kevin scoffs. "I'm nothing to be afraid of. And it's not fair that they let you people have pets here. None of the rest of us has pets."

"You people?" I cross my arms to hide my wrist. "We came here to seek refuge. Your Sovereign leader took us in."

Kevin looks away. "You're overreacting. I didn't mean anything by it."

The elevator door opens and I step out, not waiting for him. The Guardian stays in the elevator as the doors close behind us. I guess it's taking a ride.

"Hey, Lina." Kevin catches up to me.

"Go away." I'm annoyed with him now.

I stop outside of Mr. Crossbender's door.

"Maybe if you were nicer–"

"It's hard to be nice when everyone here is such a jerk," I snap at him.

Kevin's pale face reddens a bit and he pulls a hand through his hair. "I didn't mean to upset you, Lina."

"Sure."

Things are tense. Kevin's nicer than anyone else has been to us, but this conversation just solidifies my feelings about this place. They think of us as outsiders, even though we've been here over a year.

"Good luck," Kevin says as he leaves. He always says that. It's kind of like a joke since I have rotten luck here.

I knock and open the door. George Crossbender sits behind his desk looking a bit worn. His brown hair is all over the place, his shirt is wrinkled, and his glasses are off, lying next to his arm on his desk.

"Catalina." He stands and offers me a handshake. Out of courtesy I shake. It seems pointless. I see him every day at dinner where his wife threatens to move us underground. They don't have their own children, so Mrs. Crossbender wants us to live with them. He sits back down in his chair. "I have to ask you this." His voice has a warning tone.

"Is it the same thing you asked me two days ago?" I ask.

He nods as he puts his glasses on and adjusts a tall stack of papers to his left.

"Then you already know my answer. I don't know."

"Where is she?" he asks as he adjusts another tall stack of papers to his right.

"I told you. I don't know." I sit across from him in a wooden chair.

"Where do you think she could be?"

"I don't know."

"Please. Lina. If you have any idea where she might be I need you to tell us." He looks directly at me now. "She is so important to us."

"Mr. Crossbender, I haven't seen my mother since the day she left for the Phoenix District and I begged her not to go. Then you told me my father died and she went missing. I haven't seen her since. I don't know why you keep bringing me here and asking me the same question. She hasn't walked through any doors leading into Hanford. Don't you think you'd see her before me?"

"I was hoping..." He leans back in his chair.

"Were you hoping she'd walk into here and continue on with her life? I'd love for her to show up here, Mr. Crossbender. But I haven't seen my mother in over a year." I look away from him and focus on the large map on his wall. It's a bit different than the ones my mom had me study. The locations of the Districts are clearly labeled and so is the train railway.

"I have people searching for her," he whispers.

"Good. Because there is nothing more I would like than for her to come back to us."

He nods in silent agreement. "Let me get you back to your classes." Mr. Crossbender stands and opens the door. I follow him out and into the elevator. He's silent the entire time, seemingly deep in thought, and when the elevator stops, Mr. Crossbender waits at the open doors. "You go on," he says, waving me away. "I'll watch you from here."

He's a little too trustworthy, letting me walk away from him like this without an escort. I could disappear around the corner, or into one of the stairwells and he'd think I went to class. Heck, I could jump over the railing of the Hanford divide and plummet to my death. I haven't worked up the nerve to do anything yet, but one day, I'm going to do something like that—not jump over the railings, but escape. And Mr. Crossbender's lax attitude on the whole escort rule is going to pay off.

The Hanford kids are making their way to their next class. I pass Joe in the hall. He has a black eye and won't look at me. Suddenly the bell rings and classroom doors start closing. I'll have to thank Mr. Crossbender later for making me late. I run the rest of the way to my next class and knock twice on the door before letting myself into the Calculus III classroom.

"Miss Somers," the teacher looks over her glasses at me as I make my way to my seat, "I see you're late. Again."

"Sorry. I had to meet–"

"Punctuality is expected of all children here. I don't need to hear your excuses." The class erupts into murmurs. "I'm docking your grade five points. You'll have to make it up on the next exam."

Great. I say nothing as I slump down into my seat; it would just get me in more trouble.

Four

Catalina

When I leave Calculus, Kevin is waiting to escort me home.

"Don't you have a job to learn?" I ask as I walk closer to him.

He shrugs, pushing away from the wall he was leaning up against. "It's just the weather."

I don't bring up our previous argument. "Couldn't you be doing other things rather than walking me around these hallways?"

He looks past me at one of the girls in my class. She's smiling at Kevin. They always are. Kevin is a hot commodity. You would think that they would want to get close to me to get close to him. Nope. They dislike me even more because I'm close to him. I don't understand people sometimes.

"There's drool on your chin," I warn him.

Kevin smirks, turns around and hits the *up* button on the elevator. "Were you late to Calculus again?" he asks as he crosses his arms and leans his shoulder against the wall.

"Yeah. Ms. Smith is busting my balls."

"You should tell Mr. Crossbender. He runs this place you know."

I shake my head. "I don't need any more trouble. And what is he going to do? Ask her nicely to stop docking my grade?"

Kevin looks toward the ceiling and away from me. "There's a cluster of tornadoes coming our way."

"Oh yeah?"

The elevator stops and we step off. Kevin walks by my side as we get to the front door of my family's living quarters.

"You going to watch them?" he finally asks.

I push the door open and step into the living room. Looking up, through the transparent ceiling, I ask, "When do they start?"

"Right after dinner." Kevin walks into the room and looks up. We are the only ones who live this close to the surface. Most Sovereign here don't get to see the sun or the moon or the tornadoes. They're kept deep underground, where it's safe.

"You want to stop by and watch?" I ask, knowing he likes to see the tornadoes in person. Since he's working on his Apprenticeship in the Meteorology labs, it's right up his alley.

"Do you mind?" he asks.

"Us weird kids from Phoenix aren't like you Hanford people, we don't mind visits from friends."

He seems to cringe at the word.

A little sadness burrows in my chest. I've known him for almost two years now and he can't think of us as friends. I bet he's just using us to see the tornadoes. He wouldn't get a chance to otherwise.

I walk away from him, let him show himself out. "See you later, Kevin."

We go to dinner and sit with the Crossbenders. Maryam is still talking about moving us to the lower levels where it's safer. I avoid looking at Astrid, knowing that her eyes are probably filled with tears. Mrs. Crossbender doesn't say it out loud, but I know that she doesn't think my mother is still alive like Mr. Crossbender does.

Mr. Crossbender sits there with his same tired look and disheveled hair; he keeps staring off into space like he's working hard to figure something out in his head.

On our way back, Kevin is standing outside our door, two Guardians behind him, watching. I think that the Guardians are the only reason why we haven't been moved to the lower levels. The large dogs make the people here uneasy. Sometimes they follow us around, other times they just lay in the hall outside our living quarters. The Hanford people pitched a fit when they were following us into the dining hall, made Mr. Crossbender ban them from there.

Kevin smiles as we get closer. "It's starting in five minutes," he says, glancing at his watch.

"What's starting?" Cash asks.

"Tornadoes tonight," I say as I open the door and everyone files in.

Astrid makes a face. She usually hides in her room on tornado nights; they scare her.

"I can't wait," Isaac says, his voice sounding much more youthful than he looks. He runs to his room and comes back with his pillow and a blanket.

Cash gets his pillow, Raven gets his. I get mine and grab an extra one from the linen closet for Kevin. As they all get settled on the living room floor, I'm surprised to see Astrid bring her pillow out and lay down next to Cash. I turn the lights off and lie down on the floor.

"How much longer?" Isaac asks.

I hear Kevin move and his watch lights up. "About thirty seconds." He dims the light. "Listen... I think I can hear the wind."

Our eyes are fixed on the transparent ceiling. The sand starts swirling as the wind picks up. Tiny grains of earth whirling and dancing, smooth and lazy at first. And then it becomes a bit harsher, whipping from side to side in a torrent that lasts for long minutes before there's a pause.

"Here it comes," Kevin warns us with a whisper.

Astrid squeals and covers her face.

The sand starts swirling, faster and faster. Looking past the tiny grains, dark clouds are visible in the sky above us. Nearly black and angry, they rumble and swirl. Lightning flashes. Staring at the clouds, past the thin layer of sand that covers our roof, the storm reaches for us. A dark whirling, it stretches, closer and closer. Everyone is silent. Watching. Holding our breath. It's a rush, seeing one of these violent storms so closely. The clouds descend from the heavens and it's like they see us, watching through our only window to the world outside. Too far away to touch, but right there, separated by the transparent...whatever it is they made our roof with. The funnel cloud sucks up the sand, leaving the roof clear until the wind blows more across it, coating the roof. The tornado twists, stirring up twigs and debris and pieces of what is left aboveground. When it finally moves away, everyone takes a deep breath. My heart races, just like it always does when we watch these. There's something about staring into the eye of a storm, knowing that if there wasn't the protective shield of our roof, we could be sucked up into the atmosphere. It makes your heart stop and then start up again. It reminds me of the Reformation and the day my world stopped and started up again, so different, with so much lost.

"I'd say that was an F-3," Kevin says from his spot on the floor.

"We've seen bigger," Cash jokes.

"Wait until you see the next one," Kevin promises. "Radar and weather maps say we've got a big one coming."

The tornadoes continue until dusk begins to turn into night, the darkness encroaching on nature's entertainment until we can barely see anything. The promised F-5 never shows.

A Guardian shifts in the corner and the door opens. Marcus is home.

"Curfew's in ten minutes, Kevin," Marcus warns as he walks into the living room and sees us watching the show. His voice is tired, heavy.

Kevin moves to stand. "Almost over anyhow." He nods at Marcus as they pass. "See you guys in the morning."

Marcus shoves the door closed behind Kevin, gives us all a glance as we lay on the floor watching the storms, and then heads to his room. We don't see Marcus much since he started his Apprenticeship. Every day he comes home looking like he's been through the wringer, but he doesn't talk about it. Not the way Kevin does. Actually, Kevin talks a lot about his Apprenticeship sometimes. It makes me wonder what's going on with Marcus and what he's learning.

"Let's go to bed, guys," Cash suggests as he stands.

We pick up the pillows and blankets, returning them to their rightful places before heading to our own rooms. We won't be sleeping anytime soon. Well, maybe the younger kids, but me and Cash will be up studying and doing schoolwork for the next few hours.

After I get the younger kids in bed, I close the door to my room and pull the books and notes out of my bag. A small piece of white paper flutters out and onto the ground. I bend to retrieve it, opening the folds as I stand. It's a handwritten note.

Matchmaker Matchmaker make me a match,
Matchmaker Matchmaker open my hatch,
Matchmaker Matchmaker scramble my brains,
Matchmaker Matchmaker... you're dead.

I RECOGNIZE THE HANDWRITING. It's Julie Rubie, she sits next to me in Calc. Julie has short dark hair, large, almond-shaped brown eyes, and thin lips that make her look like she's always smirking. She's one of the few with color to her skin. She doesn't look pasty-white like most of the others here. She has proudly announced that her mother came straight from the islands of Indonesia; I've seen her in the dining hall at dinner time. Julie is lucky to have both of her parents here with her. All the kids here, they've never known loss, had their parents at their sides their entire lives. Of course they tease us; they don't know what it feels like to be completely abandoned. I look at the note in my hands. This isn't the first time she's slipped one of these in my bag. I crumple it in my hand and leave my room to throw it in the garbage.

"What's that?" Marcus asks as I cross the living room. He's sitting on the couch in the shadows.

"Nothing." I keep moving.

"What is it?" he demands, uncrossing his legs and leaning forward.

I throw the crumpled up note at him and he catches it with ease before I turn and head back to my room. I don't stick around to see his reaction. Marcus never had to deal with the teasing. None of the kids dared tease him after he filled out here, grew tall and muscled. And now that he's done with the Children's Training Program, moved on to his Apprenticeship, he doesn't know what we've been left to face.

Returning to my room, I crack open my books and start studying.

Before long the door handle turns and in trots a Guardian. It settles in the corner of my room near the foot of my bed. They open doors, these strange beasts. Astrid told me about it before; it took weeks before I witnessed it myself. When I look up, there is a shadow in the hall. Marcus is there, shadowed in the night.

"You just have another year," Marcus says. "Don't let them get to you."

"Another year's not soon enough." I look down at my books and flip to a blank notebook page.

"It will pass. Enjoy the freedom while you can." His voice sounds distant.

"This is not freedom. It's oppression. I hate it here. I want to go home."

Marcus says nothing and when I look up again, he's gone.

AT BREAKFAST THIS MORNING, someone threw an apple at Isaac. It bounced off his shoulder and dropped to the floor in front of him with a splatting-thud. The darkness that flashed over his face was unmistakable. With one swift kick he sent the apple soaring into the air and broke a ceiling light. He was escorted out of the cafeteria before he could sit with us. I don't know what they do with him, or who he sees, but he's always home early on the days that he loses control.

Right now he's sitting in the living room. Alone. In the dark.

"Hello, Isaac," I say to him.

He doesn't answer and in the hazy evening light that filters through our ceilings, I can see that his fists are clenching and unclenching. No one knows what to do with him. The teachers break the rules and let him leave class early. I think it's because they can sense there is something off about him and they'd rather get rid of him than have his odd uncomfortableness in their classrooms.

"Isaac?" I ask.

His head tips, he focuses on me, smiles. A shiver runs up my back. "You're home, Lina." he responds as a different person, his hands now resting on his knees calmly.

The Guardians surround him, keeping their distance but watching. When I count them, I notice one is missing. We came here with eight; right now, I only tally seven. Maybe one is following one of the other kids around. They do that sometimes.

"So... the apple?" I ask Isaac as I cross the living space to set my bag in my room.

"I saw who did it. They'll pay." His fists ball again.

"Just forget them," I warn him.

"I can't." Isaac stands and his anger seems to radiate throughout the entire room.

"We'll be done with them soon." I stay near the door to my bedroom as he paces. "We will get our Apprenticeships and move on." Those are Marcus words. I flinch as I say them, I know it doesn't help.

"You will, Lina. You and Mark and Cash. Then Astrid. I'm one of the last to go. I have to do this for a long time." He finally stands still and focuses on me. I forget how young he actually is. A child stuck in a teenager's body, it can't be easy.

"You still have Raven. He's younger than you," I remind him.

Isaac shakes his head. "I can't do this for another six years."

I move toward him and take his hand and... I have to look up to see his face. When did that happen? Before I can ask, the door opens and Cash, Astrid, and Raven walk in. Raven's eyes zero in on my hand holding Isaac's. I give Isaac's hand a squeeze before dropping it and moving toward Astrid to see how her day was.

"Someone put a sticky rice ball in my hair at lunch," Astrid says before I get to her. When she turns, I can see her long brown hair is filled with tiny white specs. I try to run my fingers through it but find that I can't. It's tangled; the rice dried out and hard, the consistency of dried glue.

"Okay, Astrid, let's get this out." I lead her to the sink. "Raven, can you grab us a comb?" Before he leaves the room, Cash steps forward and pulls something off Raven's back. Raven keeps walking as though he didn't notice.

"Look at this," Cash says as he walks toward me. He's holding up a piece of yellow cheese with *farmer* carved into the middle of it, melted just enough to make it sticky and floppy.

When I look up at Cash, I notice he has a scrape under his eye and a bruise to his chin. "What the heck happened to you?"

Cash rubs his face. "Got hit in the face in intramurals with a... ball." His eyes flick away from mine and I sigh.

Raven returns with a comb as I'm washing Astrid's hair in the sink.

"Why won't they do anything?" Isaac asks from across the room.

"They probably don't know," I say. "We should tell them. This has gone too far."

"No," Cash warns. "It will just make it worse. And I don't think Mrs. Jones gives a crap anyways."

Here, you will follow the rules. You will do what you're told. If you don't, you'll disappear. District or Die.

Part of me wonders if keeping our mouths shut is part of her rules. Not that I'd ask her, I avoid her at all costs. Isaac doesn't follow the rules, and he hasn't disappeared, yet.

As I'm running the comb through Astrid's hair, there is a loud thudding sound; I look up to see a hole in the wall and Isaac running out of our living quarters.

Cash starts to move, like he wants to follow him.

"Let him go." I struggle with the tangles and the dried rice.

Cash and Raven sit at the table nearby and watch. The water is just making the dried rice stickier. I can't comb it out, the tangles get worse.

"Ow," Astrid cries out as I pull on her hair.

"I'm sorry," I say, truly sorry because I can see the futility of my efforts. This is getting us nowhere.

"Just cut it," Astrid says as tears well up in her eyes.

"I don't want to cut it." I pull harder on a rice encrusted tangle and she shouts. Stopping, I drop her hair and set the comb on the counter.

"Just cut it." Astrid stands and squeezes the water out of her hair. "This isn't working."

"Are you sure?" I ask. She nods, wiping at her eyes. Reaching into a nearby drawer, I take out a pair of scissors. "You're sure?" I give her one last chance to back out of the decision.

"Do it."

"Okay." I feel really bad about this, I don't know how to cut hair. Pulling out a chair, I motion for her to sit. "I'm sorry," I say.

"You didn't do it. The Hanford kids did."

I start cutting, trying to leave the pieces as long as I can, but by the time I'm done her hair is to her chin. The ends are choppy and uneven, trimming just makes it shorter, and so I stop and run my fingers through her hair to make sure I cut out all the rice.

Cash and Raven sit and watch the entire time and when I'm done, Cash nods and says, "It looks good, Astrid."

"Yeah?" She asks, her voice hopeful and her face seems to lighten up a bit as a small smile appears on her lips.

Raven nods. I move around the table to get a good look at her from the front. The short hair does look cute, and it makes her look even younger which could be a problem since the Hanford kids have already nicknamed her Baby.

I start cleaning up the floor and Astrid runs her fingers through her short hair.

"Dinner time," Cash warns. "Ten minutes."

When I'm done, we all wash up and head to the dining hall.

Isaac is already there, sitting with the Crossbenders, his plate piled with food. Maybe that's why he stormed out, maybe he was super hungry. He does tend to grow fast.

We get our plates and join them.

"Why, Astrid, honey, what happened to all of that beautiful hair?" Mrs. Crossbender asks. She reaches across the table and touches Astrid's hair.

"Someone put rice in her hair," I say. "Had to cut it all off." I look directly at Mr. Crossbender, but he's staring at his food like he could care less about how much the people here seem not to like us.

"I think it's time you children moved to the lower levels with us," Mrs. Crossbender says with a heavy sigh as her hand trails down Astrid's arm, stopping at her wrist and turning it over. "And perhaps we could do something about these marks?"

"No," Astrid speaks up, her voice shaky and low.

"What was that, dear?" Mrs. Crossbender asks, a slow smile spreading across her lips.

"No," Astrid repeats, a mere whisper this time.

"Sweetheart," Mr. Crossbender says as he pokes at his dinner. "We promised them. Can't change it now."

"There's still time." Mrs. Crossbender moves her hand away from Astrid and as we eat she asks us about our day. Cash never mentions the ball to the face, I never mention the letter I got the day before, and Raven, well, he doesn't speak so he says nothing.

Mr. Crossbender sends an escort before I even make it out of our living quarters today. Kevin shows up, looking barely awake, and walks me to his office.

"Good morning, Lina," Mr. Crossbender says, elbow deep in papers.

"Morning," I mutter as my stomach growls.

"We have something to discuss."

A cool chill consumes me as I recall what Mrs. Crossbender said at dinner last night. She's close to demanding bringing us down to their levels and covering up our Sovereign marks. I prepare myself for the blow and scan my brain for the proper response.

"There's someone I need you to meet with." Mr. Crossbender stands and walks toward me. "We have to go...above ground." He gives me a look. We're not allowed to go above ground.

"Why?" I ask.

"Our guest won't come down here." Mr. Crossbender leaves his office; I follow him down the hall and to the set of elevators. He holds the door open as I step in. "You're going to go all the way up. You remember?" he asks.

I nod and dread fills me. "You're sending me alone?" My mother's warnings of the Swamp People fill my head. "Are you kicking me out or something?" I ask, trying not to panic.

"No. Never. The person who wants to speak with you, I trust him." Mr. Crossbender pats my shoulder. "You'll be fine. Come back down when you're done."

The elevator doors start to close and Mr. Crossbender's hand moves to adjust his glasses. He makes eye contact with me just before the doors close fully and the elevator starts moving up.

With a soft *ding* the doors open and I step out into a small white room. There is one door leading outside, and as I walk toward it, I wonder who the man is on the other side waiting to greet me. Could it be Mr. Crane? My breath catches at the thought of coming face to face with him again. He scared the crap out of me as a kid and now, well, I haven't seen him in a few years but I don't want to. The hairs stand at attention on my arms with the thought of him. I twist the door handle and push. It's like stepping into a different world, a portal taking me away from the bright lights and the gray walls and out into the world. The real world.

The ruins of the abandoned high school surround me. There's a narrow hallway leading to a broken door and a set of steps. As I make my way out, shielding my eyes from the bright sun, I notice two figures standing a few hundred feet away from the building near the train platform. A lump catches in my throat as I walk down the steps. There's a man and a woman. But the man is too tall to be Crane, and his hair is dark, not red. And he's not wearing a suit. Instead, he's dressed in black military style pants like I've seen Marcus wear and an open jacket with a gray T-shirt underneath. The two notice me and stop talking. Since they don't move, I walk to them, taking a few nervous glances behind me. As I get nearer, I recognize the man. It's Adam.

Standing next to him is a woman of rather normal height and stature. More intimidating than her lack of beauty is her fierce appearance. She has blonde hair, pin-straight and long, a spattering of freckles across her nose, porcelain white skin. She's wearing green leather pants, a matching leather vest and wrapped around her arms are bands the same shade as the rest of her clothing.

Adam stills as I walk closer. "You're all grown up," he says, his voice almost a whisper. He reaches out to touch me but I take a step back.

"My mother told me never to talk to you again." I focus on his companion. "What are you doing here and who's she?"

The blonde looks right down her perfectly straight nose at me.

"She's not important," Adam says with a dire tone.

"Really?" I ask. The woman looks away, ignoring us. "I feel like I shouldn't be speaking with you. My mother forbade it. What do you want?"

Adam closes his eyes. When he opens them, they are such a bright blue, just like Raven's. "Catalina Somers," Adam starts and it sounds like a scolding, scorching me to my bones. I am not six years old anymore. "Tell me where your mother is."

I shrug. "I have no idea."

"None?"

Shaking my head, I reply, "None. Last year my parents returned to Phoenix to bring back Uncle Sam, Blithe, and their baby. They were only supposed to be gone a few days. They've never returned. Mr. Crossbender has only told us that our father died and that my mom is missing. How can that be, Adam?" I take a step toward him, so angry and looking for answers, answers no one has been able to give us. "How can my mother be missing? Of all people." I drop my voice to a whisper. "What did they do to her?"

"Lina–" Adam starts to say something but he stops midsentence and focuses behind me.

I twist around and find Raven standing there, a look of shock on his face.

"Raven?" Adam whispers.

"That child is yours–" the blonde starts, but Adam holds up a hand to silence her.

"Raven?" Adam steps around me.

Raven freezes.

"Leave him alone," I warn Adam. "You've already hurt us enough."

Adam takes two steps back so we are side by side. "Does he talk?" Adam asks.

"No.".

"Is he... okay?" he asks.

"He's a frigging genius that doesn't say a word," I whisper, hoping that Raven can't hear me. "He's just a kid. So you tell me how you think he's doing. We have been abandoned in this place. Our parents are dead."

Adam runs a hand through his hair, drops his chin. "I'm sorry, Lina. I'm so sorry. Can you tell him–"

"Why don't you?" I interrupt.

"I don't think he wants me too."

Raven starts running for the broken-down high school that holds the elevator. Somehow, he made it past Crossbender.

"I don't know where she is. But you need to find her," I beg Adam. "Can't you find her? She would never leave us here alone. Never. Something bad had to have happened to her. Find her, Adam, please."

Adam nods, places a hand on my shoulder and squeezes. "I'm going to do my best." He turns to leave, but pauses. "I'm sorry about your dad," he says. "He was a good man. A great man. He would have done anything for you."

A chill runs through me and wraps around that cog in the center of my chest where I pushed all those feelings and memories of watching my mother with the both of them, doing her best to keep me out of danger during the Reformation. Most of the other children were too young, or they didn't pay attention. But I did. She loved them both, my father and Adam. I think it ruined her. The guilt and the pain tore her apart inside. I hope to God that I never fall in love with two men.

"I think you should go," I tell him, noticing the clouds collecting in the west and remembering Kevin's warning of impending storms. "Tornado's coming."

Just as the words come out of my mouth a cool wind blows around us, picking up sand and creating a dust cloud. Within seconds, I can barely see Adam or the woman he came here with. A strong hand wraps around my upper arm. The old warning sirens from the nearby town start up.

"Come on," Adam's voice says in my ear. "Got to get you back underground before the storm hits."

And then we are running. I hold my hand in front of my face, trying to block the biting sand that's stinging my skin. Adam pulls me faster. The blowing stops. I move my hand and find we are inside the remains of the school. Adam drags me to the closet where the elevator is hidden. He pulls open the door and Raven stands there, his finger on the call button.

"How did you know this is here?" I ask Adam.

"I've been here before. Long time ago," he says. "You two need to get underground."

The elevator door opens. Adam pushes us both in just as a loud whining sound fills our ears. Raven flinches.

"The tornado!" I warn Adam.

"I know." He nods. "Take care." He reaches in and pushes the button for the lower level.

"What about you?" I ask.

"I've survived worse than a tornado. I'm going to look for your mother." He pauses. "I'm sorry, Lina and Raven. I'm sorry for everything."

And then we are descending into the earth with nothing but a promise from the man that helped Crane ruin our lives.

FIVE

CATALINA

"YOU SPOKE WITH HIM?" MR. CROSSBENDER ASKS AS I STEP into his office.

"Yes." I close the door behind me but stay standing next to it. "And I don't understand why you people keep asking me the same questions, Mr. Crossbender."

His fingers toy with the papers on his desk. "How are you all dealing with your father's death?" he asks, his voice low.

"Why are you bringing this up now? It's been over a year."

"Humor me."

"It sucks. Really, really bad." Emotion swells in my chest at the thought of my parents.

"I'm sorry."

"And the kids here are really mean to us." I add.

Mr. Crossbender's eyes flick up and he tips his head in question. "Mean?"

"Yeah. I had to cut Astrid's hair because someone put sticky rice in it."

Mr. Crossbender leans back in his chair and pushes his glasses up. "What can I do to help?"

"Make them stop."

He laughs lightly. "I may run this place, but I cannot control each and every person. It's part of growing up, learning to interact with people good or bad." He pauses. "You'll figure it out."

Tears of frustration threaten to break, and Mr. Crossbender must notice.

"How about I have some food sent to your living quarters? Will that help?"

I swallow hard and blink through my bleary vision. Is that all we are, caged animals that can be calmed with a snack? Still, it's better than nothing. "Sure," I answer.

"Well," his eyes glance up at the clock, "you'd better get back to class."

I glance up at the clock and notice I have three minutes to get to Calc. Fearing another docking of my grade, I run out the door and down the hall. The bell rings as my hand pushes on the door to Calc just as it's being pushed closed from the other side. I give it a shove and push my way inside. Ms. Smith bristles and slams the door closed as I slide into my seat.

"Catalina Somers," Ms. Smith crosses the room to her desk and jots something down in her book. "Five points."

The class erupts in murmurs and I sink down into my seat. I should have skipped this class, ran off down a hallway and taken a few minutes to myself, especially after seeing Adam.

THE REST of the day is exhausting. Seeing Adam really threw me off and by the time I get home, there's nothing more I can think of other than a long nap. One of the Guardians greets me at the door; I've only counted six of them today. As I enter our living quarters, I notice that there is a new figure sitting on the couch. Not Isaac, but Raven.

"Did you go to your classes today?" I ask him.

Raven blinks and something inside me shatters.

"Why don't you just speak already? I'm so sick of you just staring! That's all you do, Raven, you just do whatever you want and you just stare, it's so... so... strange." Tears are burning the corners of my eyes. "I just need someone to talk to."

He tips his head toward Astrid's room. She's not home yet, and even if she were I'd rather talk with someone who isn't so sensitive. She can't even handle the lunchroom.

I shake my head. "We're blood, Raven. You and me. We share her blood. You are my true brother. They've been asking me about her. Pulling me out of class. Do they pull you out of class and question you?"

Raven shakes his head no.

"They keep asking me if I've seen her. How could I see her? She's gone!"

His big blue eyes just watch me as I have a freak-out session in the middle of our living room.

The door bursts open and Marcus comes stomping in, ready for action. I get angry just seeing him, he doesn't understand, he's never around anymore. He acts like he could care less about us all.

"What's going on in here?" Marcus asks. "I could hear you yelling from down the hall."

My mouth drops open, throat tight, but I can't force out any more words. I turn and head for my bedroom door.

"Lina?" Marcus asks as he follows me.

"Go away!"

His large hand wraps around my wrist and pulls me to a stop. And in that instant it's like all my frustrations explode. I turn quick, just like my Uncle Sam taught me, snap my hand toward his throat and ram the heel of my other hand into his solar plexus. Marcus moves fast, faster than I ever remember. He deflects my hand going for his throat, but the heel of my other hand hits him, and it's like ramming it into a brick wall. My eyes flick to Marcus's. He's pissed. In half of a heartbeat he has me on the floor and detained.

"Let go of me!" I try to shrug him off, but he has my hands pinned behind my back and his knee pressing into my spine.

"Get yourself under control."

"I am!"

"You are not." He growls in my ear.

I struggle to move. "Let go!"

Marcus breathes out a huff of annoyance before standing, pulling me up and dragging me into my room. He slams the door behind us and turns to face me. I want to pummel him. I'm not sure why him, I think it's because he's the closest to me.

"What the hell is wrong with you?" he asks.

"What the hell is wrong with *you*?" I rub my wrist and my palm; both still ache from hitting him. "And what the hell are they teaching you in your Apprenticeship? I don't remember you ever moving that fast."

He crosses his arms and stares down at me. "None of your business." He's suddenly rather intimidating, the way he's looking at me right now, like I'm a bug he'd rather squash than stand in a room with.

"How is it none of my business? The only reason we are allowed to stay up here is because you're in your Apprenticeship. But you're never here, we never see you. And it still doesn't stop Crossbender's wife from threatening to bring us to the lower levels each night at dinner." I look away from him for a second and try to regain my composure. "It's like you're made of brick. Kevin isn't like that."

"Kevin isn't in the ARU," Marcus snaps. "There's a reason for that."

"What is it?"

There is a tick in Marcus's jaw before he asks, "How would you know that Kevin isn't like that?"

I blink. "I..."

"Kevin has his orders and you are *hands-off*. Do I need to report him for stepping beyond his duties?" Marcus couldn't sound more like my father on that day he smacked Marcus upside his head.

My mouth drops open and the only thing that comes out is, "You're not my father."

"You're right. I'm not." Marcus rips the door open and slams it closed behind him as he leaves.

That was... odd. Trying not to think about Marcus or Crossbender's questioning, I sit on my bed and bury my nose in my Calc notes since I now have ten points to make up on the next test. Everything consumes my mind: Adam, my mother, this place, the thought that I can't take it much longer. So, not wanting to hear any more of Mrs. Crossbender's talk of moving us to the lower levels, I skip dinner.

———

"MISSED YOU AT DINNER LAST NIGHT," Cash says as I'm getting ready for school.

"I won't be at breakfast either," I inform him. I just can't do it, face any of the Hanford people, I'd rather starve.

"Why?" he gives me a hard look. "Something going on?"

"Just... this place." Looking around the kitchen, my eyes focus on the box that's on the counter. "What's that?"

"Box of food," Cash answers, walking toward the box. "Marcus must've brought it in. Was on the counter when I got up."

I stare at the box as he pulls out a few things; a box of crackers, a loaf of bread, apples, and bananas.

"Did you have something to do with this?" he asks.

At that moment Astrid comes round the corner. "Oh!" She heads for Cash. "Real food." Astrid picks up an apple and bites into it.

"I told Mr. Crossbender about the Hanford kids."

Astrid brushes a piece of hair out of her face and tucks in behind her ear. "So we don't have to go to the cafeteria anymore?"

"I doubt this will last that long." I take a banana and some crackers. "But at least we won't have to go today."

———

"HOW WAS THE CALC EXAM TODAY?" Kevin asks as he walks me home.

"Probably failed."

He chuckles. "No one fails in Hanford. Not on your life."

"Guess I'm dead then."

Kevin is silent for a bit. "It's just kid stuff, Lina. You know that, right?"

"What's that?"

"Everything you're going through. It will be done with soon. It's different during your Apprenticeship." He motions to himself. "I didn't always look like this. A few years ago you wouldn't even recognize me."

I make a scoffing noise in my throat. "I doubt it."

"No, really." Kevin reaches out and takes my arm. "I got made fun of too. You'll get over this."

He must not know all that we are going through. I could deal with being made fun of, it's everything else piling up on my shoulders. He looks down at me and a long stretch of silence passes between us. Then a Guardian starts growling from behind me.

Kevin glances at the beast before backing away from me and removing his hand from my arm. "Take care, Lina," he says as he turns to leave.

I hesitate at the door to our living quarters. Isaac could be here. He usually is on testing days. Through the door it sounds like there is the murmuring of voices. I open the door just as Raven starts walking through the living room.

"What are you doing here?" I ask Raven. "You're supposed to be in school."

Raven looks at me. Feeling suddenly overwhelmed by hunger and knowing that dinner won't be ready in the dining hall for another three hours, I throw my bag down and head for the fridge. There's the food that Mr. Crossbender has been leaving us, but I've been trying to keep it stocked with leftovers, filling my pockets with raw vegetables and biscuits and bringing them home for later. I reach for the handle of the fridge.

"She's here," a voice says.

I pause, my hand hovering over the handle. It's a voice I've never heard before; it's deep, soft, and somehow familiar.

I turn quick. Raven stares at me.

"She's here," he says.

He speaks!

"Holy crap! Raven, you're talking!"

He gives me an annoyed look. "Did you even hear what I said?" he asks.

I stare, mouth open, shocked still.

"She's here, Lina." Raven steps toward me and grabs my hand. "Mom's here."

I blink a few rapid times to clear my head. "Who?"

"Mom."

"Mom?" I ask as he tugs me toward our parent's room.

Raven reaches for the door handle, turns it and pulls me into the room behind him.

"She's here," he says as he stops.

There is a form at the desk. The chair swivels, the person stands. It takes a moment for my eyes to focus in the dim light of the room. It looks just like her, but...younger. She's wearing jeans, a long-sleeve shirt and boots. Her hair is longer than I've ever seen it; dark brown, curly and loose around her face.

"Mom?" I ask.

"My little Catalina," she says. "You're not so little anymore."

She walks toward me, arms open, and pulls me to her chest. I feel my body stiffen, she feels so different. I'm taller than her, I realize, and as she tucks her face into my hair and breathes in deep, I do the same. What I smell is familiar, safe, comforting. It's...home. She may look younger than I remember but this is my mother, without a doubt.

"How did you get here?" I ask her.

She releases me as she answers. "Very carefully. Now," she leads me toward the bed and reaching out for Raven's hand, she pulls him along with us. "Tell me what's been happening here since I've been gone."

We sit on the edge of the bed and I fill her in on everything. The questioning, the tests, the pressure and how much we have missed her. "And then there's Isaac," I start.

"I've spoken with Isaac already. He won't be causing any more trouble, for a while at least."

"You spoke with him already?" I ask. "You spoke with him first?"

"He was already here before you two."

"Where is he now?" I ask.

"The library. Studying. Being the good boy that he has such a hard time acting as."

"Oh," I say. "What happened to Dad?"

She stills, frowns and looks away from us. "When we went to get Sam... there was an incident."

"Did Crane do it?" Raven asks, tipping his head to the side inquisitively.

She shakes her head. And in a soft voice she says, "No. Not him. It was something I did. Something I didn't know I could do." A large tear slides down her cheek. She stands, pulling me to my feet. "I have to go now."

"But you just got here," Raven argues, holding on tight to her arm.

"I know. But I have many things to do and I have many places to travel." She lets go of us and heads for the bedroom door.

"Mom," I start going after her, I don't want her to leave. I have questions, so many more questions. "How do you look so young now?"

She smiles and for a moment I think that I'm looking in the mirror. "I died."

"But you're not dead now," Raven says.

She nods her head. "Yes I am."

"Why can't you stay with us?" Raven asks, walking toward her once again.

She walks through the living quarters toward the front door. "Because I can't. I'm so sorry. But as long as Burton Crane is alive none of you are safe around me. Forget I was here." And then she whispers, "Be strong."

"What are you going to do?" I ask as she opens the door.

She just smiles as she mouths, "I love you," and closes the door.

The lock clicks, my heart sinks, and all those feelings of helplessness flood me. We had her back, just for a few minutes, and now she's gone again. Raven moves his hand to my face and rubs a finger across my cheek. He holds it up for me to see that his fingertip is damp with tears. I rub my face, not even knowing I was crying.

"It will be okay," Raven says as he hugs me tight.

When he steps back, I ask him, "Are you going to stop talking again?"

He shrugs. "Everything's easier if I don't talk."

I hear her voice on the other side of the door. "*Forget me, forget me, forget me,*" it chants.

And then, as though someone is rubbing my brain with sand, eroding everything away, I remember bits and pieces of the past few minutes, seeing my mother. It fades, scatters, disappears. She was never here.

I look at Raven; he blinks at me and scowls.

"What just happened?" I ask him, feeling suddenly hollow and empty. "Did you... did you just say something? Did you speak?"

Raven says nothing.

WEEKS PASS and in the back of my mind I feel like I'm forgetting something. Something I just can't place my finger on. I bury myself in my studies and do my best to ignore the Hanford kids.

It's while I'm lying on the living room floor, staring up at the night sky through our transparent ceiling, remembering those bonfire nights at the Pasture, I make up my mind. I'm going home. I don't believe that my mother is dead. Something deep inside my soul, is telling me it's not right. I'm going to find her.

It takes a few weeks of preparing. I take extra biscuits from the dining hall. I make excuses to meet with Mr. Crossbender and during the long silences I study the map on his wall.

He tells me about Canada, his voice dropping to a regretful tone when he says barely anyone survived the Reformation there. And then, always before I leave, says, "Don't speak of these things, Lina. They are not for the young Sovereign to hear."

I think it's strange, but I don't question him. He could tell me that cows have sprouted wings and now fly, I could care less. I just want that map in my head. I need to know where I'm going.

At night, I lie on the floor and stare up through the ceiling. Marcus comes home late. He stops when he sees me laying there in the dark.

"What are you doing?" It's the most he's spoken since he yelled at me that one night.

"Watching."

"What?"

"The night go by without me."

Marcus throws his bag on the couch and settles on the floor next to me. Close, but not touching. It wasn't so long ago that he was begging me to have my mother pair us together. Now he doesn't bring it up, can't be bothered. Maybe he's seen the futility in it. I've watched what my mother went through. Still, part of me misses the teasing and playfulness. I miss the fun Marcus that I grew up with.

He smells like fresh soap, must've showered before he came home. We've seen less and less of him every day. The deal was that we could stay together with an adult living here. Marcus is an adult but eventually he's going to find a girl and move on without us. There are no pairings here; he can choose whoever he wants. There is a sadness in my chest at the thought of that. I don't want Marcus to go. But it won't matter, I'm out of here. Soon. I'm going back to Phoenix to get answers.

"Do you ever think about home, Marcus?" I ask, already knowing the answer. It wasn't that long ago that he was ranting about wanting to find his parents. That was right before they told us my parents died.

Marcus doesn't answer. When I turn to look at him, I find he is fast asleep. I get up, go to his room and pull the blanket off his bed. He doesn't even stir when I cover him with it.

* * *

As I GET ready in the morning, I find Marcus is already gone and his blanket is back in his bedroom. The time he spent sleeping on the floor couldn't have added up to much more than a nap. Raven and Astrid leave their rooms, backpacks in hand. Then comes Cashel, and Isaac is last. He looks put together, calm. Less creepy than usual.

He smiles at me. "Good morning, sis."

"Good morning, Isaac," I say as I reach for the door.

Kevin is leaning against the railing of the Hanford divide as we leave our living quarters. "Morning, kids," he says as he pushes away and starts following us.

We start walking down the hall and I hear him talking with Cash behind me.

"Hey, what happened to all your Guardians?" Kevin asks loud enough for me to hear.

I turn to see that there are only six of them trailing us.

"Maybe they're wandering," Cash says.

"I haven't seen them anywhere else," Kevin says. "They only follow you guys around."

Isaac smiles innocently when I glance at him.

"You missed breakfast too," Kevin's continues. "Today was pancake day. My favorite."

"Those are not pancakes," Astrid says, with her usual soft voice. "Lina's mom made better pancakes."

Yes, she cooked much better than this place. As they all talk about food and whatnot, I tally off the checklist in my head. I have food, clothes, a blanket and a bag to store it all in. I think I have enough to survive out there. It's going to be a long trek, I know, but there are Survivors out there; I'll be able to find help. They can't all be bad.

When I stop at the door to my first class, the others are already gone. Kevin frowns at me.

"What?" I ask.

"You've barely talked all morning. Something wrong, Lina?"

"Everything's perfect." I force a smile. It will be perfect, when I get out of this place.

School is a waste. Since I know I'm leaving soon I don't pay attention. I don't write down one note or read one word. Instead, I'm thinking of how I'm going to get out of this place; the path I'm going to take, how long it will take me. 2,620 miles. We traveled it by train in a few days last time. This time I won't have the luxury of a train. Going by foot is going to take forever, but I'm not afraid. If anything, I'm hopeful.

Now I just need to know what the weather's going to be like. Watching it each day hasn't done much for me and the weather patterns are so chaotic, I doubt I'll be able to get much out of studying it. And I don't have much more time. But I have a plan.

Kevin shows up to escort me home and as I follow him down the hall, I unbutton the top three buttons of my shirt and unclip my hair so it falls down around my shoulders.

When we reach the elevators and Kevin presses the up button, he turns to me, looks once, and then again. His eyes widen.

"So," I start as we wait, "how much have you been learning over in the Meteorology lab? Any big storms coming?"

The elevator doors open and he looks away from me as we walk inside. I turn to face him and Kevin clears his throat and his eyes zero in on my chest. Boys. If I had known all I had to do was flash a little skin to get what I wanted, I might have tried this a long time ago.

"Um," Kevin stares as the doors close, "the weather's supposed to be good."

I crowd him into the corner of the elevator. "No tornadoes coming our way?"

Kevin's eyes get big. I move my arm and rest it on the wall near his hip.

"No. None." He licks his lips, moves his hands up like he's going to touch me but never does.

Leaning in close, I ask, "What about the next few weeks?"

"No," he replies, his voice low, eyes half-lidded.

The door opens behind us. Kevin starts to lean forward like he's going to kiss me. Before anything happens, I'm pulled backward by my backpack, out of the elevator and into the hallway. I turn my head to find Marcus there, looking super angry.

"What in the hell do you think you're doing?" he asks.

Kevin pales. "Ah... nothing." He clears his throat.

Crap. Now I've gotten him in trouble.

"Didn't look like nothing," Marcus growls at me. "Get home. Now, Lina."

"You don't have to–"

"Go!" He points down the hall toward home.

As I walk away, I hear Marcus saying something to Kevin and it doesn't sound pleasant. I make my way to the door. One of the Guardians lies there, lifting its large head as I twist the door handle. It puffs at me, long hairs flying away from its eyes.

Only a few seconds pass before Marcus comes stomping into the living room. I turn around quick. "You didn't need to do that. We weren't doing anything."

"Yes, I did." He walks right up to me, close. "And I saw exactly what you were doing."

"I don't need you pretending to be my father, bossing me around and threatening boys."

"I'm definitely not your father. And Kevin knows better. You're off limits."

"What does it matter? We were just talking."

Marcus looks me up and down and I forget for a second that my shirt is still unbuttoned. I don't miss the look in his eye; it's a lot less angry and a little more like how Kevin looked at me.

"Cover yourself up, Lina," he sneers. "Your parents didn't raise you to act like that."

No, they didn't. But my mother did raise me with the confidence to get what I need when I need it. With a huff, I turn and head to my room, buttoning my shirt up to my neck. Who cares, it worked. I got the information I need to get home. After dumping out my bag onto my bed, I find the biscuits I've been hoarding and start packing. Now is as good a time as any to get the heck out of here.

Six

CATALINA

"You can't go." Astrid looks up at me with her typical huge teary eyes.

"I have to. You stay here. Cash is going to watch over you and Raven."

"Who will watch over you, Lina?" Her voice is pleading.

Hmm. I never considered that, I only thought that I needed answers.

"I'll be fine," I assure her.

"What about Isaac?" she asks.

"Ash, he'll be fine."

She sits on my bed as I fold up a change of clothes and tuck them into my bag.

"They're always leaving," she whispers.

"Who?"

"Everyone. They always leave me. And now you're leaving, Lina. It's not fair."

I sit down next to her and hug her. "I won't be gone long. Just a few weeks. I have to find out what happened to my mother. Okay?" She nods. "If it was your mother, you'd go after her." Astrid shrugs like she's not sure she would. "Just don't tell anyone, okay?"

She nods her head. "Hey, I'm just telling you because I don't want you to be sad. We'll be together again. I promise." She nods, refusing to look up at me. I pull my backpack on. "I'll see you in a few weeks." I give her a hug and a kiss on the forehead.

"Aren't you going to tell the others?" She asks as I reach for the door. "No." I shake my head. "They'll try to stop me."

"But you told me." She fidgets with her short hair.

"You wouldn't try to stop me."

"Okay. I'll miss you, Lina."

Guilt strikes me deep in my gut. This feels wrong, but I must do something. And I can't take them all with me. "See you soon, Ash."

I leave my room and our living quarters and make my way to the elevator. I'm sure there are cameras hidden throughout here. But since it's almost dinner time, everyone will be in the dining hall eating that disgusting food. I doubt anyone is manning the cameras. The Sovereign here are trusted to just do what they're supposed to. They just trust us to do what's right here, to be good and listen. By the time they're done, I'll be long gone.

My plan is to take the stairwell that's down the hall. It will work out perfectly since two of the Guardians started following me as soon as I left. Before I open the door to the stairwell, I turn to face them and command them to stay. Who knows if they'll listen, I'm just hoping they stay put until I get the door latched. And they do.

We are so close to the surface that it's just one flight up. I climb the steps, my heart beating hard in anticipation of finally being free; I'm scared to leave my family but all that is overshadowed by the hope of seeing my mother again. Just before I push the door open, I lean over the railing and look down. The stairwell goes on forever, to the center of the earth it seems. Standing up straight, I turn, push the door open, make my way through the abandoned high school that hides the entry points into Hanford, and I step out into the sun.

Sun! I haven't seen it in so long. I miss this. I take a deep breath. Fresh air. I miss that, too.

Trying not to let my newfound freedom distract me, I remind

myself of the plan. I need to head east. After a few miles, that's where the most forest cover is. But I'll have to pass a small river. There are old roads to the south, maybe some old bridges. But I need cover, like, now. My best shot is to head directly east, the forest is closer. I just hope there will be a way to cross the river.

I take off running. My muscles burn. It's been too long since I've been this active. Running across the desert ground, my shoes slip in the sand and hard earth. The wind blows dust across my face. I've only been out here five minutes and I already feel gritty. There is a small outcropping of trees halfway to the river. I make my way toward them, stopping when I reach their shade.

It's when I stop to catch my breath that I hear the sound of running feet that are not mine. I spin around and see a small form running toward me. Crap. I focus and recognize the mop of dark hair that's blowing in the wind. It's Raven.

He catches up with me, resting one hand on a tree trunk and bending, breathing hard.

"What the heck are you doing following me, Raven?" I want to scream at him.

He just stares at me, his eyes giant but calm. "You're not going alone."

"Did you just talk? Oh my God, you can talk!"

He gives me a look before saying again, "You're not doing this alone. It's too dangerous."

"I love that you only decide to speak when I want to beat you up."

He shrugs like it's no big deal that he hasn't said a word his entire life but now he's talking to me.

"You're just going to slow me down." I cross my arms and give him an agitated look.

"You know what else would have slowed you down?" He shrugs his shoulders, dropping a backpack off them. "Your water. You wouldn't have gotten very far at all."

Hanford has made me soft and I'm a bit peeved that I forgot something so important. I'm so used to having everything where I need it, when I need it. I guess that is the comfort of living in a District. We don't have a ton, but we don't want for much.

"Thanks." I take the canteen from him and put it in my pack.

Raven nods. He peers around me. "So, you're headed across the river?"

I turn and look across the expanse of dry earth toward the river. "Somehow. There's coverage on the other side."

Raven looks back toward Hanford. "We should get moving. I'd say we have a few hours before they figure out what I did."

"What did you do?"

He smirks. "Jammed the elevator and the locks on the stairwell."

"Brat."

We run for the river and all I can think is that the trip here barely took us two days by the District rail. But on foot, it's going to take me and Raven forever. 2,620 miles. Impossible, maybe, but it doesn't matter. I have all the time in the world. I just need to get there and get answers. I itch my wrist; the Sovereign mark there feels tight and tingly. We run for two miles and we're still not under the cover of the trees. Anyone can see us. My eyes flick to the sky. It's calm. No clouds. No tornadoes. Kevin assured me there wouldn't be any for days. We stop at the banks of the river. We're sitting ducks here.

"We need cover," I warn him.

Raven is surveying the area. He looks up and down the gently flowing river, studying it. "There." Raven points to a wide area upstream.

"That will take us forever." My eyes fall on the narrowest part of the river, a few hundred feet downstream. "What about down there?"

"No," Raven says. "Narrower is deeper. There." He points upstream again. "Watch how the water flows."

I watch but I don't see whatever he's seeing. I trust him, though. "Okay." I start moving. "Let's go."

We head for the widest part upstream. I stop when Raven stops. He watches the water for just a second more before taking my hand and stepping in. I follow him and find that he's right. The water barely comes up to my shins. It's refreshing and cool, especially with all this barren land surrounding us. Off in the distance I see the mountain ranges. My stomach drops. I knew there were mountains, but from here they look huge. Impassable. Undoable. We have no choice but to try and pass them. We trudge up the embankment on the other side, water squishing in our shoes.

We cross dry, cracked earth, and a crumbling abandoned road as the sun rises higher in the sky.

"There." Raven points just south of us. There are trees. We run for them. The trees are small, but it's better than being in the open. Tall, thick grasses brush our legs.

Raven stops and bends, plucking something off the ground.

"What did you find?" I ask.

He pops whatever it is in his mouth. Chews thoughtfully before answering, "Beans."

"Beans?" If I remember correctly, the maps mom showed me at the Pasture had most of this land designated as crop lands.

"Want some?" Raven collects a few handfuls.

I take the beans. Eat a few. They're crisp and fresh.

"Home," Raven says as he closes his eyes and chews.

I do the same. "Yeah, they remind me of home too." I remember picking beans and peas in the fields. Running with Stevie before she died. Feeding the horses and alpacas. Fresh air. It's all so drastically different from the underground of Hanford.

As we walk and eat our beans the day moves on, the trees get thicker, taller, the underbrush harder to move through. Much sooner than I expected there is a cracking sound, followed by the beating of helicopter blades. We both stop and drop to the ground.

There is the shouting of voices.

They've sent the cavalry.

We get up and run.

We run hard and fast. Stumbling, I trip and fall. Raven does the same. A sound of defeat escapes my throat. Raven's hand is on my shoulder. "You go," Raven whispers to me. "I'll distract them."

"I'm not going to leave you." I grab at him, panicking. I knew they'd come after me but I wasn't expecting it to happen so soon. I'm not ready for my escape to end so close to the beginning. I wanted to at least try.

"You want answers. And they won't get any from me." He holds up his foot. The soles of his shoes are worn through and his skin is blistered.

Oh crap. We've only been walking for just over half the day and he never told me his feet hurt. I should have never let him come. I should have marched him back to Hanford.

"It will be fine." Raven hugs me quick, shakes off his backpack and tosses it in my direction. "I love you, Lina." His blue eyes are fiery and dark at the same time.

"I love you, Raven." I hug him, hard and strong and kiss his forehead. "I'll see you soon."

"They're going to find me in about ten minutes." He nods. "You better run fast."

"I will." I pick up his bag.

And then I run.

I don't make it far before my lungs are burning. Men are shouting, at Raven I assume. Probably asking him questions about where I am. I bet he's just staring at them. They don't know he can speak. I didn't know he could speak, but still, in the back of my mind, part of me knew he could. I had a feeling about it, like I've heard him speak before but couldn't remember.

Leaves crunch under my feet, twigs and fallen branches too. My shoulder hits a tree and I stumble to a stop, trying to catch my breath. It's during those few quick seconds, as I'm sucking in a breath, I hear something. Footsteps running through the forest just as fast as I was—no, faster. I start running again. Heart pounding. The ground below me starts to incline. Here come the mountains.

My foot hits a rock. I stumble again.

Before I regain my footing, something hits me from behind, dropping me to my knees and knocking the breath out of me. It's hot and heavy and breathing fast. I collapse on the ground. It must be a Volker from Hanford. I twist and claw and kick. All the muscles honed by my Uncle Sam and Elvis, I use them and more. I wish I could reach the knife in my backpack. I wish I had a gun. There is a groan, a stick stabs my in the side, hard. I gasp and roll away. On my back, a strong hand clamps over my mouth, muffling my scream as I stare into a cloth covered face. This is not one of the Volker. Whoever has found me is something else. I bite down on the hand and bring up a knee to a place where I know it will hurt.

I hear a muffled curse, another groan. And then a free hand comes up and rips the cloth away.

It's Marcus!

"Stop," he growls. "Now." He tips his head to the side, listening for a second before saying, "I'm trying to help you, goddamn it." He listens again. "Don't move." He reaches out and tugs us under some nearby brush, then starts covering us with downed branches, twigs and leaves. "Be very quiet," he warns as he lays a dense pine branch over our heads. We are thrust into darkness, surrounded by the detritus of the forest. I can feel his breath in my ear, his leg resting between both of mine. My fingers twitch and I move them to seek out something to hold onto.

Marcus moves and both of his hands cover mine, holding me tight in place. "Don't move," he whispers directly in my ear.

I shiver. I can't control it. I'm sure this is exactly the position he was thinking of us being in when my dad smacked him upside the back of the head years ago. This position, minus all our clothes.

There is movement around us. The voices of men, searching. Marcus squeezes my hand. We wait just like this for minutes, an hour or more maybe. And the entire time he's so still that I'm worried he might be sleeping. My heart is racing. I'm sure he can feel it because he's right on top of me and *heavy*. When did he get so darned big? Marcus is no longer the boy next door. No. Not even close. He's a man. Honed at the Pasture, perfected at Hanford. I try to remember our last conversation and realize I barely know who he is anymore.

I feel the temperature start to drop and less light filters through the debris covering us. Even though Marcus is covering me, I feel the cold and start shivering. His hands release mine and move to my waist. My teeth chatter.

"N-N-No touchy," I whisper into his cheek. His body makes a quick shudder. I think he's laughing. His hands move to my ribs and with his elbows resting against my sides, he's using his body to warm mine. It's not working.

"I think they're gone," he finally says and starts moving, knocking the branches and debris off us. When he stands over me, I finally get a good look at him. He's dressed in black clothes, combat boots, there's a gun on his hip and a long knife strapped to his leg. What the hell has

Marcus been learning at his Apprenticeship in the ARU? He brushes himself off before turning to me and holding out a hand. I take it and let him pull me to my feet.

"What are you doing out here?" I ask.

"I could ask you the same thing." He shrugs out of his jacket and hands it to me. "Put this on."

He's left wearing a dark, long-sleeved shirt. I take the jacket and put it on. It's warm from his heat.

"Lucky for you, I came prepared." He looks me up and down. I feel pretty much like a failure. Sam taught me better. So did Elvis. I'm not dressed for a month in the wilderness. This backpack is nothing and I forgot my canteen once already. I don't have much food. And after seeing what happened to Raven's shoes in one day, my shoes would be ruined soon. Disappointment hits me; I'd barely survive a week.

I guess it's best to give up now. "Are you going to take me back?"

"No." He looks around in the fading light, orienting himself. "Come on."

I follow Marcus through the forest. After about ten minutes, he stops at a large tree, moves some downed branches, revealing a large backpack that has a frame. I think people used to use them for hiking. Underneath the large pack is another small one, and a duffel bag. "Here." He hands me the duffel bag. "Change into these."

I open the bag to find gear just like he's wearing, heavy duty boots, dark clothes, and a jacket.

"How did you know I left?" I ask.

He gives me a smirk. "Astrid's not so good at keeping secrets."

"Astrid! When I see her again..." I instantly regret giving her the heads-up that I was leaving.

"Don't be mad at her. It's a good thing she told me." He shoulders his bag and clips it across his waist. "Get changed. I'd like to make some mileage before we camp for the night."

"Camp for the night?" With him? Great. "So, you're definitely not taking me back?"

"Nope."

I start pulling the clothes out of the bag. "Privacy."

With a chuckle, Marcus turns his back to me. I make it quick, shucking off my pants and pulling the new ones on. Then the shirt, the boots. I make sure to move the knife I brought to my belt, easier access.

"Where did you get all this?" I ask as I'm pulling the shirt over my head.

"How did you get that?" Marcus' voice is a bit worried and demanding.

My privacy's gone and he's moving toward me, lifting the shirt and pressing his hand to my side. I twist and see a deep bruise with a small puncture wound and blood. Not a lot. Just enough to draw attention.

Marcus pokes the bruise.

"Ow!" I swat at him.

"Hurts?"

"Yes."

"How did that happen?"

I think for a moment before remembering the stick that poked me in the side when he dropped me. "While we were... rolling on the ground, a stick stabbed me. I think."

"A stick?"

"Yeah."

He rubs his mouth, thinking. "How bad does it hurt?"

"I didn't notice it until you stuck your finger in it," I snap as I pull on the jacket then twist my long hair up into a ponytail. I put my old clothes and shoes into the duffel bag. Mark helps me with the backpack, pausing when I flinch as he clips the waist strap.

"Make sure you tell me if it gets worse." He straightens, looks around and then starts walking. "Come on."

I follow him. Staring at the back of his head, my eyes move to his back and focus on the large bag, it must weigh sixty pounds or more. I think about the day he was assigned to his Apprenticeship. The day Marcus found out, I came home from class and his letter was just lying on the dining table. He was standing in the kitchen, looking up at the transparent ceiling of our living quarters. I picked up the paper; across the middle of the page *ARU Apprenticeship* was simply typed. That's it. Marcus was the first of us to move on. No longer a child. I get the feeling whatever they've been teaching him at the ARU is more than whatever Kevin is learning in the Meteorology division.

Marcus starts walking directly east. "Tell me, map girl, how were you planning on getting home?"

"Walking."

"Specifics."

"There's an old highway, it runs north for a while then dips south and heads east. It cuts through the mountains."

"We're going to run into it soon?" he asks.

"Yeah, but if we keep going straight, there's plenty of old roads we can travel on before the highway comes south again and then it's almost a straight shot home if we follow it."

He shakes his head. "Staying on the roads is a bad idea. They'll send the choppers soon enough. They'll spot us."

"Well, I don't want to get lost in the wilderness."

"If we go straight, when do we hit the main highway again?"

I visualize the map and do a few mental calculations. "About four-hundred miles from here. That's when it cuts south and then east."

Marcus makes some noise; I can't tell if it's disgust or disbelief. "You were planning on doing this alone?"

"Yeah."

He makes the noise again.

"What was I supposed to do? I can't just sit around and believe what they tell me. For almost a year they asked me where she was, which means they don't believe she's dead. I'm so tired of just listening to people tell me what to do."

"Me too." His voice is low, almost drowned out by the sound of twigs and dried leaves snapping under our feet.

"Besides, I wasn't alone. Raven tagged along for a little bit." I worry about him. "They took him back, didn't they?"

"He'll be fine," Marcus says with a dismissive tone. "They won't touch him. The worst he'll see is an extra escort parked outside our living quarters. Especially now that I'm gone."

I stop in my tracks. "Marcus. Why are you here?" All I can think is that he's going to bring me back. He used to be a bit flirty and sweet on me, but since he started his Apprenticeship he's barely been around and his attitude has changed. He's all business now. "Won't they wonder where you are?"

He turns to look at me. "They'll be looking for us." He smirks and there is a sparkle in his eyes, it's like he's a boy in the fields again. "I let them think I'd bring you back. But there's something Crossbender doesn't know about me. I don't trust him or any of these people. I want answers, just like you."

My heart slows. For a second I thought I wouldn't be able to trust him. But now it seems like I am not alone in my search for the truth.

"Come on." Marcus waves me on and starts walking again. "Few more miles, then we'll camp for the night."

I think about camping for the night. It's something I've never done. I've read about it in books, seen pictures, but never experienced it.

"What's camping like?" I ask.

Marcus continues walking. "It's like living outdoors, and the only thing separating you from the wilderness is a piece of flimsy fabric."

"Sounds dangerous."

"You escape from Hanford and you think camping sounds dangerous. What did you expect to do out here? Where were you going to sleep?"

"I didn't think much about it. I just knew I had to get out of there. I have to find my mother."

"I know." He becomes suddenly silent.

The sun begins to set. Just before we break the cover of the trees, Marcus stops to survey the area.

"This should be a good spot." He drops his pack and starts pulling things out. "You want to get some wood for a fire?"

"Sure." I unclip my bag and set it next to his.

"Lina." Marcus grabs my wrist before I can turn away. "Don't go far." He shakes my arm a bit. "If you can't see me, you're too far away."

"I'll be fine," I assure him.

"Humans are no longer the most prevalent species. Wolf Creek has been restocking the land and that includes predators. I'd hate to get this far and be eaten by a bear."

I nod as I walk away, pulling the hunting knife from my pants pocket that was included in the supplies Marcus brought. Sam and Elvis trained us pretty good, but I've never been up against a bear before, the thought of it makes me nervous. I scour the land, barely making it more than two hundred feet from where Marcus is setting up camp.

I collect as many dried sticks as I can find and by the time I return to where Marcus is, he has a dome-shaped tent set up. I arrange the sticks in a pile before lighting them with a flint.

"Keep it small," Marcus warns as he pulls a few of the sticks out of the fire and sets them aside. "We don't want to draw attention. We're escapees on the run. Remember?"

"I remember."

I sit beside the fire, open my backpack and pull out the things I had packed, a bag of old biscuits and a handful of beans from earlier in the day. I pass some to Marcus.

We eat in silence before retiring to the tent.

It's a bit unnerving sharing such close quarters with Marcus. His closeness never used to bother me, but for some reason, it does now. I tell myself it's just me as I roll away from him and fall asleep.

I wake up to the sensation of someone being very close to me. It's Marcus. I can feel his breath on the back of my neck, his knee bent into the back of my thigh. And I think he wakes at the same time as I do, his breath stops and slows, his knee moves away from my leg. And then, slowly he rolls away from me before sitting up. I unzip my bag and sit to put my boots on. When I stand and bend to fold the sleeping bag, pain radiates across my abdomen, I flinch and grab my side.

"Do I need to look at that?" Marcus asks as he's tying his boots.

"No. It's just sore." I continue packing.

"You tell me if it gets worse, Lina."

"Sure." I nod as I zip my bag.

Marcus shows me how to pack up the tent. After a quick breakfast, we put on our bags and start walking east.

THIS IS how the days and nights go for close to a week. We walk during the day, camp at night. A few times we hear the Hanford choppers. We eat the hard biscuits I took from the dining hall until they're gone. And then Marcus pulls out some strange, dried meals. He tells me they're called freeze dried rations. I watch as he adds some water, purified in a canteen with its own filter, and after a few minutes he has a complete meal.

"You've let us eat those horrible biscuits for all these days and you've had these the entire time?" I ask.

"We've got a long trek. Must conserve what food we have."

I eat the meal out of the silver pack it came in, pleasantly surprised to find it tastes better than anything we've been forced to eat in Hanford over the past few years. I'm finished long before Marcus. As I'm watching the low fire burn, a shadow passes through the forest, not far from where we are.

"What?" Marcus asks.

"I thought I saw something." In slow movements, he sets down his meal, draws his weapon and stands.

"Stay here," he whispers. "And don't move."

I reach for my knife as Marcus disappears into the shadows. It seems like forever before he returns. When he does, he's carrying his knife in one hand and a rabbit in the other.

"That's not what I saw. It's too small."

"I know."

Marcus skewers the rabbit, skins it, cuts off the meatiest pieces and sets it over the fire.

"Where'd you learn that?" I ask.

"Elvis."

"He never taught me that."

"That's 'cause you're a girl. He only taught you girly things." Marcus chuckles to himself.

"That's crap."

"Nope, just the truth." He smiles and continues cooking the rabbit.

"Don't we have enough food?" I ask.

"If we find something fresh, it's best to save the freeze-dried stuff."

"Oh." I should have known that. I should have thought of it. But look at me, I forgot my darned canteen the day I left Hanford.

"Don't think too hard about it," Marcus says. The glow from the fire shows his smile. "You're not trained for this."

"And you are?" I ask.

He nods.

"What have they been teaching you during your Apprenticeship?"

Marcus shrugs. He's never talked much about it.

"Why won't you tell me?" I press him.

"Just, stuff. You know, like how Sam and Elvis used to teach us, how to use guns and self-defense and stuff. And then there are these other weapons they've developed. I mean, you could hit a squirrel in the middle of a tree from fifty miles away." Marcus moves to get the rabbit that's been cooking. He hands me a stick with the meat speared on it.

"So, what's to stop them from shooting us?" I blow on the meat to cool it. "Or finding us?"

"I'm sure they have." Marcus bites into the rabbit.

"Then why haven't they brought us back?"

Marcus swallows his bite of meat. "I'm betting they want us to find her more than they want us at the Hanford District."

"I thought we were Sovereign. They're just going to let us traipse through the wilderness?"

Marcus stills. "They don't want us in Hanford."

"What do you mean?" I eat my rabbit.

"They want your mother more. We're expendable."

"But... we're Sovereign; they're supposed to protect us."

"The only reason why we're in Hanford is because your mother and father *left* us there."

"It's not their fault. They were trying to keep us safe. It's not their fault that they died." I throw my cleaned stick into the fire before standing and stomping off into the tent.

Kicking off my boots, I'm so angry at him. My father is dead, my mother missing and most likely dead... we can't blame them. They tried to protect us; it's not their fault they failed.

Wrapped in my sleeping bag, I fume for a good long while and hold my sore side. It seemed to be getting better but over the past few days it's been hurting worse. I should tell Marcus but I'm too angry with him right now. Closing my eyes, I pretend I'm sleeping when I hear Marcus stomp out the fire and enter the tent. Without saying a word, he lays down next to me in his sleeping bag. My face is just about pressed into the fabric on the other side of the tent. I make it apparent that I am trying to get as far away from him as possible. He always has a way of bringing up my family and blaming them. It's like he doesn't care. It's not their fault. They did what they could to protect us. Him and Cash and Astrid, too, even though none of them were their biological children.

Somehow, I fall asleep only to wake in the morning to find myself pressed up against Marcus. His forehead rests on the back of my neck, his arm across my hip. I move away from him and get up. I can tell he's watching me as I tie my boots.

"Lina–" he starts. He never knows how to say sorry.

"I think we should get moving. We should reach the highway today." I shove my sleeping bag into my pack and leave the tent.

We don't discuss last night, but something's been bugging me and as Marcus folds the tent into his pack, I ask him. "Why do they treat us so differently from the other Sovereign? Crane kept my mother and father under his thumb, but us... they don't treat us the same."

"Different generations," he says quickly as he gets his pack on and clips it across his abdomen.

"What?" I ask.

"Your parents. First Generation Sovereign. You and me. Second Generation. Different generation, different rules."

"Why?"

"Think, Lina." I think for a while but come up with nothing. "Let me ask you this. Why do five Districts need an Artillery Research Unit? Why do five Districts that work together and help each other need some of the most advanced weaponry ever designed?"

"I don't know."

"Think, Lina." His finger taps my forehead. "Why do we need weapons?"

"To keep us safe."

"Why do the five Districts need weapons?"

"To...keep us safe?"

"From who?"

"Survivors?"

He shakes his head no.

"Swamp people?"

He shakes his head again.

I think for a long time. So long I'm worried that Marcus is convinced that I have brain damage. I can't figure it out. "I don't know. I give up."

"There was the Reformation. Here. Canada. Mexico. Where else?"

I shrug. "I don't know."

"You can ace an exam on quantum physics but you can't figure this out." He gives me a look, the corner of his lip tipping up. "You don't lie awake at night wondering?"

"No." Thoughts of my dead father and mother and missing uncle are the thoughts that consume my mind at night.

"I think we're the only ones. I think all those countries across the oceans, they're the same as they always were. This side of the world is the only one that's been Reformed."

I can't deal with this. He was always so busy talking about life before the Reformation, about his family, McDonald's, and shopping malls. There's no going back. I wish he'd just drop it.

"You need to stop chasing the past, Marcus."

Something snaps in him. And I watch it happen. I'm not going to lie, it scares me. He takes a few quick steps toward me, grabs my shoulders and jerks me a tiny bit. "And you need to start thinking about the future. Further than next week. Remembering the past is what shapes our future. Not repeating the same mistakes. Lina. How can you not remember? We are the last generation that will remember. After us, it all changes. Forever." His wild brown eyes drop to my lips. He licks his. Something in the pit of my stomach flutters. My father's warnings ring in my ears. They should be ringing in Marcus's also. If they are, it doesn't stop him. His big hands on my shoulders pull me to him and... he kisses me.

"Why did you do that?" I ask when he pulls away, my stomach doing this strange fluttery-thing still. My first kiss by a boy I've known almost my entire life, a boy who my father gave specific instructions to not touch me. But he's not a boy any longer and I'm not a little girl.

"I've wanted to do that for years," he whispers.

"Why?" I search his face and his big brown eyes.

"You have something special. It's right here." His fingertip settles on the corner of my right eye. "Glowing so bright."

"What?"

His voice drops to a whisper. "Freedom. Fight–"

"Da sure id freedom," a deep voice echoes from the tree line. "Das notin' wors' den freedom." A man steps out of the shadows.

Marcus turns, draws his weapon and pushes me behind him. The man is tall and lanky, with inky hair and covered in bits of mud. I've seen men like this before. They almost killed my parents years ago when Adam and Crane took us to that old school. It's the Swamp People.

"You youngins know whas worse den freedom?" He walks closer. "Curiosity."

It's strange, he says the word like it is foreign to his tongue yet practiced over and over so he can pronounce it just right.

I don't really care what he said or how he said it; I just want them to go away. "What do you want?" I ask from over Marcus's shoulder.

The man smiles. His teeth are horribly crooked and dark. "Mo swaf," he says.

The trees shudder with his people.

"I... I don't understand."

"Stop talking to him," Marcus scolds me as he backs us away.

"We hungry. An' you know wa's best eatin' on cool nights like dis? De young ones. Cook up fast, tender."

My stomach drops as more men step out of the forest. I count five, seven, ten. And then it all happens to fast. Marcus shoots, I pull my knife, the men move on us–all of them–so swift I barely see. I swipe for their necks and groins, just like Elvis said, *Aim for the balls, a man will flinch every time.* They keep their distance for a second before a few of them turn away from me and toward Marcus.

"Mark!" He drops to the ground and another one of the tall men stands over him. He licks his lips. "Don't–" I start, but the man in front of me takes a few quick steps so he's right on top of me. I squeeze my eyes shut and try to think of a way out of this. Marcus is out. They have his weapon. I'm outnumbered. I can sense him leaning closer; he sniffs me on one side of my neck, then the other. I crack an eye open as he sniffs my shoulder, my arm, my ribs.

"You been bit," he says.

I shake my head no.

"Show it."

I'm frozen in place, not moving. I'm not showing him crap.

"Now."

I do nothing and lightning fast, the man's arm moves, his finger jabbing me hard in the sore spot where I was poked with the stick. It hurts, bad, worse than anything I've ever felt. Stars explode behind my eyes and... I faint.

SEVEN

CATALINA

MARCUS IS SHOUTING. I CAN HEAR HIM AS I TRY TO OPEN MY eyes, but my body feels like it's on fire, my head heavy and foggy.

"We can't go that far!" I hear Marcus say. This is followed by the voice of the man who jabbed me in the side, except... his strange dialect is so hard to understand right now. A moan collects in the back of my throat; I try to force it out. I try to move my lips and speak but nothing seems to work and I can't seem to open my eyes. My head is burning but my body is shivering.

"She's too sick." A hand grasps mine, warming my chilled fingers.

There's the man's voice again. Most of it I can't understand, but I hear *Witch Doctor* and *swamp* and *our land*.

"No," I try to say, but I think it comes out as a moan, since I don't feel my lips move apart.

"She's feverish," Marcus says. Then it feels like hands are pressing me down, my eyelids are pried apart and all I see is darkness, hear a sharp breath inhale and then feel the stinging of sand in my eyes.

"She be fine. Few days. Den we be dere," the man's voice sounds like it's directly in front of my face. "Keep 'er warm."

Trying to blink out the sandy grit in my eyes, my head fogs even more, my thoughts spin. Something large and warm wraps itself around me and begins to warm my trembling body. There is hot breath on my neck, fingers brushing at my hair.

"I'll watch over you." It's Marcus's voice. "Just like always." He says other things, little mumblings and sweet words, like when he used to tease me when we were younger. I can't understand much of it, with that heavy feeling in my head. It's not long before I'm out again.

<hr>

WHEN I WAKE UP, I'm lying next to a small fire. Marcus is sitting at my side, looking pretty mad. His weapon is still gone. I move my arms to pat my pockets and find that my weapons are gone also. Marcus turns and reaches out, helping me to sit up. Shivering in the cool night, I move closer to him until my hip touches his. He leans toward me. "Don't say anything to them," he warns, glancing to my side. "Does it hurt?" he asks.

I twist and lift my shirt; the mark that hurt bad enough to make me pass out is covered in a rough bandage that's soaked with something foul smelling. I sniff and my shocked expression meets Marcus' eyes.

"They cut it open," he says, his voice low. "That wasn't a stick that poked you. You were bit by a snake." Marcus's gaze travels across the fire to the men standing and sitting there. "Infection had set in. They saved your life."

"Oh," escapes my lips as I tuck my shirt into my pants. "Should I thank them?" I whisper.

"Not if they're going to eat us for dinner." Marcus gives me a quick smirk before his focus turns to the men.

I move closer to him, feeling cold and weary, my side aching. My eyes scan his face; the shadows and planes that are accentuated in the glow from the fire. I stop at his lips and remember how they felt pressed against mine for that quick second. That strange fluttery feeling returns. I look away from him with a sigh and search the grounds for our packs. Finding them next to a nearby tree, I wonder how hard it would be to grab them and run for it.

"Woun't think 'bout dat, girl," a dark voice says. I look up to see the man who approached us in the forest and poked me so hard in the side that I fainted. "Dey call me Glane." He tips his head to the other men. I notice the two sticks he's carrying have meat on the end. "De fever set in. You won make it far."

I watch him warily. Marcus focuses on me as a deep shiver runs through my body. I touch my forehead, my cheeks. The Swamp Man is right, my skin feels hot but I'm shivering.

"Eat." He passes us the sticks.

"What is this?" Marcus asks.

Glane smirks. "Dis be dinner."

Marcus gives the meat an apprehensive look before sniffing it. It's not rabbit. It's not smeat from Hanford.

"Is this people?" I whisper to Marcus.

He simply stares at his stick.

"Squi'el," Glane finally says as he sits and begins eating out of a bowl.

I think he said squirrel. "What are you eating?" I ask.

"No squi'el." Glane smiles and with his rotten teeth and the darkness, it looks like his mouth is simply a dark void surrounded by thin lips.

We eat our squirrel, and the entire time Glane watches us like a wolf from across the flames. His eyes steady and body taut, ready to pounce. My stomach churns with unease before Marcus passes me a canteen full of water.

"You have to stay hydrated," he warns, taking my hand and folding it around the canteen so I can hold it. My palms shake and the canteen tips. Marcus's eyes watch me as he moves to hold the canteen to my lips.

"Thanks." I wipe my mouth with the back of my hand. "I don't know what's wrong with me."

"You're still septic." Marcus shifts and he takes off his jacket, laying it across my shoulders. I pull at the sides, trying to cover myself. Marcus looks at me for a moment before he stands. I grab at his hand, suddenly fearful that he might leave me. "It's okay," he whispers. "I'm just getting our things."

Glane watches Marcus as he makes his way to the tree where are packs are, lifts them and returns to my side. Marcus starts pulling out blankets.

"How long was I out?" I ask.

"Days."

"What?" My voice sounds too high and shocked. "How many?"

A dark lock of hair falls across Marcus's forehead as he takes a quick glance at me and nods. "I stopped counting."

Has it been days or weeks? Marcus doesn't seem interested in telling me right now.

"Why so long?"

He settles beside me, draping a blanket across my shoulders and pulling me close to him. "They cut it open, rubbed some salve and powdery stuff in the wound. It hit you quick, the sickness. They saved you. Took you to their Witch Doctor in the south."

"The south?" Closing my eyes, I focus on the map in my head. My mother said the Swamp People were from the far south, in the area that was known as Louisiana, which puts us over two-thousand miles in the wrong direction! Strategizing all the routes available for us to make it back home, I sigh. We'll never make it before winter hits.

"Just settle down," Marcus says, sensing my distress. "They said they'd guide us back to where they found us."

I stifle a yawn, asking, "So they're not going to eat us?"

"I don't think so." Marcus's hand smoothes over my feverish skin, he feels like ice. "We can trust them. For now."

My stomach churns and my head swims. "I don't feel so good," I mumble.

Marcus shifts and pulls me down so my head is resting in his lap. "You need more rest."

"How did you do it?" I ask, my eyelids feeling heavy.

"I had to make a deal," Marcus whispers just as Glane stands and walks toward us.

I have no fight left in me. The simple act of sitting up and eating has drained my energy. As my eyelids flutter shut, I feel something strange, like dirt being blown in my face. Marcus makes a soothing whispering sound, his hands stroking my hair and pulling the blanket tighter over me. And just before I'm totally out of it, I notice Glane sit cross-legged across from Marcus, and the deep tones of their voices fill the night.

I WAKE to find the sun beginning to rise, filling our tent with a bright gray hue. I don't remember getting into the tent or the sleeping bag. Those thoughts leave me as I realize that for once I am not cold but hot, so hot I'm sweating and I feel like I'm wrapped up tight and swaddled like a baby. As I wiggle, a strong arm tightens around my waist. I still and take it all in. There is a person pressed close to me, someone much larger and much warmer. My heart rate ticks up when I think of Glane and the rest of his men. As I feel soft breaths on my neck, I turn my head to find Marcus with his forehead pressed to my back and arm wrapped around me in a vice grip. He's asleep.

Relaxing against his body, I try to recall what has happened, faintly remembering what Marcus told me about being sick. I run my hands over my body and find the tender spot on my side. My clothes feel damp and the inside of the tent smells like... a barn. It smells like we spent a day in the fields and an evening rolling in the mud. I turn my head to glance at Marcus and wrinkle my nose before looking down at myself and sniffing. Oh gosh, I smell terrible. I immediately miss the showers of Hanford. It may have been oppressive there but at least we were clean.

Marcus moves and props himself up on an elbow. "You're awake." He looks down at me, his brow wrinkled in concern.

I open my mouth to speak, but instead of breathing on him I turn my head away as I say, "I smell terrible. Like death."

Marcus chuckles. "Well, you don't smell like roses. Neither of us does. But there was a time you smelled worse."

I turn to stare at him.

"Remember that time Elvis made us shovel out the pig pen?" Marcus asks. "He said it would build character. You definitely smelled worse then."

I crack a small smile remembering that. I must have been thirteen or fourteen at the time.

Marcus moves to fold up the sleeping bag and pack it. I move away to give him space. Lifting my shirt I inspect my side, peeling off the bandage to see a large open area, slightly red around the edges and oozing. I almost gag at the sight. I'm not sure when I got such a weak stomach. At the Pasture we'd watch the livestock being birthed, dealt with injuries and animal manure, but for some reason all that pales in comparison to the wound on my body. Pressing the bandage back in place, I swallow hard and close my eyes, trying to forget what I just saw.

"Please don't puke in the tent," Marcus asks absently as he zips our pack and moves around the tent. "I don't have another one."

"I think I need fresh air," I say.

"Good idea."

I reach for the zipper of the tent, fingers shaking numbly.

"Let me help you." Marcus moves my hand and as soon as he has the tent unzipped, I run out. Well, it's more like a stumble, and then I trip, nearly missing my knees as I empty out my stomach at the base of a tree.

As I'm standing, wiping my mouth and watching Marcus dismantle the tent and pack it away, a dark figure walks up beside me, so quick and silent I barely have time to react.

It's Glane. "You 'wake," he says.

"Yeah." I take a few steps toward Marcus, noticing that's he's watching us as he works.

"'bout time. We 'ave miles to make."

"Where are we?" I ask.

"Mi'souri," Glane says as he gives me a glance before sauntering off into the forest.

"How did we get to Missouri?" I ask as I walk toward Marcus.

"They move fast, Lina," Marcus says. "I could barely keep up, carrying you and all." He looks at the ground, embarrassed about something. "Sometimes they carried you," he adds.

I shiver at the thought of the Swamp men touching me. But he did what he had to do. And looking at him now, really getting a good look at him, I can see that he looks like he lost a bit of weight.

"They made a stretcher," Marcus says.

"Oh."

Looking away, I try to remember what day it is. The hot morning sun tells me it's no longer spring. "He said Missouri..."

"Yeah."

"But..." I calculate the distance in my head. "That's, like, a full month in the wilderness with them. And I was... unconscious the entire time?"

Marcus shrugs and hooks his fingers in his pockets. "You woke up a few times." He steps toward me. "And Glane had this powder he kept blowing in your face. I think it knocked you out and held the infection at bay. When we got about halfway to the swamps, his men, they had this old-school train car; it didn't run on steam or coal or electricity, but a lever. We all piled on top of the car, it took us right where we needed to go. A handcar, that's what Glane called it."

Marcus shifts on his feet. "So maybe two weeks to the swamps. And we've been traveling for another week or so now. Glane said there's another handcar coming up soon. It will take us north, almost all the way to Phoenix."

"And Hanford? Haven't they been looking for us?"

"I'm sure they have. If your mother's still alive and she finds out you're gone, I don't think it will end well for Mr. Crossbender." Marcus looks around, everywhere but at my face. I know he's not a fan of my parents, or any of the Funding Entities' workings. They took away his family, forced him to grow up with mine. He hates them for it.

"We should get moving then," I say, shrugging on my pack.

Marcus puts a black baseball cap on and pulls it low over his eyes.

"Where did you get that?" I ask.

"Swamps." Marcus snaps his pack across his stomach. "Swamp people had some things they wouldn't touch. They seemed kind of suspicious of it. Said that the blue-eyed devil left them there."

I stop and think for a moment. Adam has blue eyes and he's looking for my mom, too. "You think they were talking about Adam?"

"Don't know."

I work the straps of my pack, snapping it across my stomach and flinching when the strap tugs against my wound.

"Want me to take that?" Marcus asks.

I shake my head no. I need to regain some muscle. I've never felt so weak. Marcus starts walking slowly, waiting for me to walk by his side.

"Aren't we going to wait for Glane and his men?" I ask.

"They're already moving. Won't see much of them, they stick to the shadows. Glane will make an appearance if we get off their trail."

"Why haven't they eaten us yet?"

"I don't know."

Looking around, I don't notice much of a trail. If anything, there's a thin forest ahead of us, an opening in the trees with a rough dirt road to our right. I follow Marcus.

THE SOUND of a rushing stream fills the evening air. I'm sweating, soaked, my side aches and I think I smell worse than I did when we cleaned out the pig pens. I don't care what Marcus says. I can't stand the smell of myself any longer.

"Can we go to that stream?" I ask.

"Why?" Marcus continues walking and I sense my last shot at clean clothes and a clean body shifting away from me. Marcus should know better, letting us walk around dirty like this. Since the Districts no longer supply medications, we've been hounded on natural health, cleanliness and avoiding illness.

"I'm filthy." I head toward the sound of the stream. "I'm going to take a bath in the water and wash my clothes."

"I don't think that's a good idea." Marcus's footsteps are behind me.

"Why not, Marcus? It's a billion degrees out here. I'm sweating like a pig and we're both dirty."

He's suddenly unable to walk straight. I hear him stumble and catch himself. "There's not much... privacy out here in the open."

"I'm not getting naked," I scoff. "Just rinsing everything."

Clearing the trees, I get a good look at the stream. It's shallow, maybe a few feet deep. I unclip my pack and drop it before untying my boots and removing them. Marcus watches me, taking good look around us a few times.

Stepping into the water, I find that I was right; it's warm, just a tad bit cooler than the muggy heat. I take off my socks and rinse them before laying them out on some rocks. Next, I follow with my pants and the long sleeved shirt. I leave on my T-shirt and underwear. Marcus folds his arms across his chest and pretends to look irritated.

"Come on," I shout to him as I wade deeper into the water and settle myself in a current. "You smell worse than pigs, worse than death."

"So, what would that make me?"

"Smeat."

Marcus finally removes his pack, setting it next to mine. I look away while he takes care of business, washing my hair out in the current and moving my shirt. The material is thin and seems to dry quickly against my skin. Just as I'm contemplating removing it to get a good washing in, I glance to the side and catch a flash of skin. Marcus is just a few feet away from me, shirtless, pant-less, and floating on his back. I feel my cheeks bloom with color and look away. I guess I'll leave my shirt on.

Rinsing myself in the current, I use my fingers to get the tangles out of my hair.

"Lina…" I hear Marcus's voice.

"Yeah?" I ask without turning.

"I have soap."

Turning, I find him standing and holding his hand out to me, the river water rippling around his knees. In his palm rests a small bar of soap.

"You've had soap this entire time and you let us smell like this?"

"Keeps the bugs away." He smirks.

I reach for the soap and try to keep my eyes away from his partially naked body. Just as I take it from him, Marcus grips my fingers in his. When I glance up at him, a bit shocked, he just stares down at me, something swirling in his dark eyes.

"What?" I ask.

He looks away. "I think you should hurry up." Marcus turns and heads for the bank of the stream, water streaming down him in rivulets as I clutch the soap to my chest.

Turning away, I do my best to soap myself up under the water and under my shirt. By the time I'm done with my hair the soap is gone. I rinse and move toward the rocks where my pants and socks are. The material is already dry. It's so different than our Hanford uniforms which were a thick, stiff cotton. The pants and shirts Marcus brought are thin, quick drying and breathable. I sit on the rocks and wait for my shirt to dry.

Shadows in the woods shift and stir, agitated. It's the Swamp men, they must be bored.

I glance at the treeline and see that Marcus is simply wearing his cargo pants, slung low on his hips, his chest bare and muscled. He certainly is no longer a child. Actually, lusting after him these past few minutes makes me feel a bit like an idiot. I'm still a child. Just over seventeen–wait, I calculate the days in my head. I'll be eighteen in a few months. It looks like I've missed the last of my schooling. I wonder what Mr. Crossbender will do with me. There has never been a child who hasn't finished and gone on to their Apprenticeship. At least none that I've known of. My thoughts drift to Astrid and the boys. I miss them, all of them. I wonder if they're all right, alone without us in Hanford.

"Let's get moving, Lina," Marcus's voice interrupts.

I dress quickly. Marcus tosses me my boots to put on. And as I'm stepping over the rocks to where I left my bag he reaches out with one long arm to steady me as I step up onto the bank of the stream. We are toe-to-toe and Marcus doesn't step away, he looks down at me.

"You smell much better," he whispers, his fingers toying with the hair at my temple.

A memory of Marcus kissing me just before Glane and his men found us surfaces, and with it that fluttery feeling in the pit of my stomach returns. I discard all my father's warnings, lean in and kiss him.

He sighs deeply as I pull away. His eyes still closed, he asks, "Why did you have to go and do that, Lina?"

"What?" My head is still swimming.

"Make things so complicated."

"They're already complicated."

"Much more so now." His eyes open dreamily, hazily; brown and warm and relaxed. "So much more complicated now."

I tip my head and try to understand what he's talking about, but I can't. I have always trusted Marcus; he's always been there for me, for our family. But my mother warned me to trust no one. And now... I back away from Marcus and wait for him to say more, but he doesn't, he simply starts to turn to leave. Movement in the forest catches my eye.

"Wait." I grab Marcus's arm.

"What?"

"Look there!" A creature with a dark dreadlocked coat weaves between the trees, its eyes on us.

"I don't see anything."

"Look... it's... it's a Guardian!" I take off running toward it. I know where there is a Guardian there will be my mother, they followed her around, they followed us, always. There has to be my mother or another Sovereign who might know where she is nearby.

"Lina!" Marcus shouts after me. "Wait!"

I run faster, headed for the dark blur of a creature that seems to be running away from me.

The forest begins to thin and I hear the bustle of people, loud voices, smell smoke and fresh cooked food, hear the bleating of animals. There's a clearing ahead; I follow the Guardian. As I break the clearing a man steps in front of me, gun in my face. I stop in my tracks and raise my hands. Crap.

"Well, well, well." The man steps toward me, his gaze leering and thorough. "What have we got here?"

Instinct drives me and I don't hesitate one second. I kick him in the balls, chop him in the neck, drop a fist on the inside of his elbow and twist the gun out of his hand. The man lurches for me. I take a few quick steps away from him and aim. There is danger in his eyes, a menacing threat that warns me I will pay for what I just did.

"I will shoot you," I tell the man.

"You should listen to her," Marcus warns as he walks up behind me carrying both of our bags. "She's a great shot. Been practicing her whole life. Never misses."

The man takes one step back. "Fine," he sneers. "Didn't know she was taken. Letting her come running out of the forest like that, all alone, nothin' but trouble."

I drop the magazine out of the handgun. It's empty. He doesn't even have any bullets. I throw the gun at the man's feet and he bends to pick it up before walking away from us.

"That was interesting," I say.

Marcus looks around like it's no news to him. Makes me wonder how much he knows about the Survivors and what he's been learning in the ARU.

"Where's Glane?" I ask, looking into the forest behind us.

"They won't come through an area this populated," Marcus says. He sniffs the air. "Smells way better than squirrel." Marcus takes my hand and leads me toward the street filled with people. "Let's see if we have anything we can trade for something to eat."

I stop and pull him back to me. "Do you think this is safe?"

"Sure. Why not?"

"Because we look...different." I look up and down the street. Some people are dressed clean and nice, simple even, others wear rags and dirty clothes.

"We've always looked different." Marcus tugs at my hand. "Come on."

I follow him down a paved street, through rows of people entering and exiting storefronts. It looks like we've come upon a small town with a single paved road running through it. The pavement is cracked and uneven, but some people still drive cars, or ride horses down it.

Marcus walks toward a street vendor and as he's standing in line to talk to a man about dried meat, I get a tingle on the back of my neck. Turning, I catch sight of a short woman with long, dark curly hair. *Mom.* I start to pull away, but Marcus has a tight hold on my wrist. He's afraid to lose me in this crowd, and I can't say I'm not scared. I've never seen anything like this. I've never felt the energy in the air like this with all these people and all this freedom to mill about and do what you want. And just as soon as I see her, she disappears into the crowd like a ghost.

"What's wrong?" Marcus asks.

"I thought I saw her," I say. "My mother."

"Here?" He moves forward in line.

"Yeah." I rise up on my tip-toes and scan the crowd. That was her, it has to be.

Eight

Pulling away from Marcus, I turn to try and get another glance. I can't see the short figure or the long hair, but it felt like her, deep in my bones. I never get a glimpse of her, what I see instead is the crowd parting and a large man walking toward us. Tall and thick with muscle, eyes as blazing blue as my brother's. I saw him not too long ago in Hanford. It's Adam.

Crap.

"Oh, shit," Marcus says from behind me as he recognizes who's walking toward us. He drags us out of the line and toward a dark corner of the street, as if he could hide us, as if we could run.

Adam follows, a man on a mission, his expression most unpleasant. "Please, tell me what the *fuck* you two are doing out here?"

I can't even explain the anger I hear in his voice or the energy that ripples off him.

I swallow hard.

"Sir–" Marcus says from behind me.

Adam cuts him off. "Jesus Christ, Marcus!" Then Adam has a hold of both of our shirts, dragging us away from the crowd and the street and into an empty building that looks like an old diner. "Let me relay some rules for being a *Defector*." He reaches into a bag that's slung over his shoulder and pulls out two leather bands. "You don't seek out a crowd." He pulls my wrist forward and covers my Sovereign mark with the band. "You don't walk around all fucking doe-eyed." He reaches for Marcus's arm and slaps a band over his wrist. "You don't show up in a uniform, with a weapon in plain sight and bags packed full of supplies. You two are dressed like you're goddamned black ops. Is that..." Adam focuses on Marcus. "Is that my hat?" Adam reaches forward and rips the black baseball cap off Marcus's head. "How'd you get this?"

Marcus swallows hard. "I found it."

Adam's hands move to his hips as he glares down at us. "Now, tell me how the hell you two got out of Hanford."

Marcus tells him and takes the blame for the entire thing. Adam knows better, I can tell by the way his eyes flick to mine. He knows I'm like my mother: curious, determined, selfish.

"Your mother will..." he pauses and pinches the bridge of his nose, "*would* kill someone over this if she were still alive."

"But... I saw a Guardian. They always follow her," I say.

"They follow all the Sovereign around. It could have been following me, or you, or him." He motions to Marcus.

My heart sinks. "So it's true?"

"Yes," Adam says as he looks away from us.

"She's dead," I whisper. "Truly dead."

He gives a quick nod and just like in Mr. Crossbender's office, Marcus is at my side, catching me, holding me tight against him as I unload a bucket of tears. She's dead. We are alone.

"We are not alone," Marcus whispers in my ear as though I said the words out loud. "We have each other. We stick together. Always."

I nod into his chest.

Adam lets out a sigh. "I can't believe this shit." He opens the door and says something to someone outside the diner. The door closes. "You're going back to Hanford."

"No," I say.

"Excuse me?" Adam asks.

"No. I hate it there. I'm not going back."

"And what are you going to do, Lina? Live amongst the Survivors? You have no clue how the world runs itself. Not since the Reformation. Things aren't safe. Women aren't safe. Young women like yourself are definitely not safe out here where there are no rules, no regulations, no law." He runs a hand through his hair. "You are going back. I will not be responsible for what happens to you out here. I don't have the time to deal with the both of you. You're going back."

"No."

"Yes," Adam commands.

"NO!" I yell.

Adam pauses, shocked at the loudness of my voice I think, and gives a quick glance to Marcus. "Is she always like this?" he asks.

Marcus shrugs and gives a small nod.

"I am not!" It comes out sounding just like the way Marcus expresses his disdain for the Districts.

Adam and Marcus both break out in laughter and I just look between them, confused. "What?" I ask.

"I forget you kids are teenagers." Adam stops laughing abruptly and Marcus pauses with this confused look on his face like he's not sure what to do. "You too Marcus. These are some dumb shit decisions." Adam looks toward the door again. "You're both coming with me. I have to go talk to someone for a second. Stay right here." Adam heads to the front door, closing it behind him.

"So?" Marcus says. "Do we let him take us back?"

Still reeling from the news that my mother is actually dead and not wanting to go back, I start pacing. "I don't know. I don't know what to do any more. I had a plan and now it's all... screwed up."

Marcus stands in the middle of the empty diner and watches me. "It's dangerous out here," he warns. "You've almost died once already. And when you broke through the forest, you almost became that man's concubine or something."

"If I hadn't kicked him in the balls," I add.

"If I hadn't run out of the forest behind you," Marcus adds.

"I can handle myself." I don't want to go back.

Marcus chuckles.

"What?" I ask.

"You would be dead if I hadn't followed you when you left Hanford."

"You are so full of yourself." Picking up my pack, I run for the door, shoving it open and leaving the building.

A strong hand grabs my arm before I make it far and when I twist my eyes meet Adam's.

"Where do you think you're going?" he asks.

"Away." The hairs on the back of my neck stand at attention. I turn quick, only to see a shadowy figure run around the corner of the diner. "Who was that?" I ask.

"None of your business." Adam's fingers dig into my skin, like he's afraid I might try to take off. That was my plan. "Let's get moving." His eyes move to the sky. "It will be dark soon."

Adam pulls the door open and Marcus walks through. I scowl at him. I don't need Marcus to protect me. I can take care of myself. We start walking, Adam still holding tight to my arm, Marcus following close behind. I look and feel like a prisoner being taken into custody. The other people on the street barely glance at us and move out of the way. It seems these Survivors could care less about a girl being hauled off by two guys.

"How are we getting there?" I ask Adam, knowing that the Swamp men are around here, most likely watching us. I wonder if they will give us trouble?

"We drive to Colorado. And then from there it's a quick trip back to Hanford."

"That's not a quick trip. It's hundreds of miles," I say.

I think I hear a voice whisper something harsh. Adam skips a step, making me trip, stumble and fall right on my healing side. I let out a groan of pain as I roll to my stomach. Adam and Marcus stand over me, one of them pulling off my pack. I roll over onto my back.

"Sorry about that." Adam reaches down to help me up, but Marcus stops him.

"Wait. She's bleeding." Marcus crouches down beside me.

Running a hand over my side, it comes back wet and red. "Great," I say with an uncomfortable moan.

"What happened to you?" Adam asks, looking between me and

Marcus. "Who hurt you?" I don't miss his fists clenching and unclenching. I remember him like this, doing anything to protect us and ready to damage those who hurt us.

"She was bit by a snake," Marcus finally says. "Got infected."

"And?" Adam asks.

"Swamp people found us, they had medicine, brought us down to their land. Their Witch Doctor took care of her," Marcus continues as I lay there and wait for the pain to go away. "We were making our way back to Phoenix just now, before you found us."

"Alone? You were travelling from the swamps to Phoenix alone?" Adam asks.

"No," I say, finally able to take a deep breath. "We were travelling *with* them. But..." Wincing, I sit up. "I thought I saw a Guardian and I ran after it. That's how we wound up here."

"Where are the Swamp people now?" Adam asks.

"Probably the woods around here, waiting for us. Or else they already left," Marcus says.

"They didn't eat you?" Adam asks. "Didn't attempt?"

"No." I shake my head. "That one named Glane, he did sniff me. It was really strange," I say.

He looks us over quickly. "You shouldn't be around them. They are so far removed from humanity..." He takes a frustrated breath. "The only reason why they were put on this earth is to kill and consume. The fact that they didn't kill you both... it concerns me." Adam pauses and looks down at me, his eyes zeroing in on the blood soaking through my shirt. I can feel it trickling down my side. "We better get that bandaged."

"I have supplies here." Marcus reaches into his pack and pulls out gauze and tape. I lie back on my elbows and lift my shirt for Marcus to change the bandage. Adam watches, the entire time standing over us with his arms crossed over his chest, looking bored though his eyes are scanning the shadowed alleyways and the nearby forest.

"There," Marcus says when he's done, his fingers lingering a little too long on my skin as he presses the tape down, reminding me of the nights we spent huddled together in that small tent.

Pushing his hands away, I cover myself with my shirt. Adam offers a hand and pulls me to my feet. A memory of my time with him as a child passes through my mind; standing at the kitchen counter and making spaghetti in a strange house.

"We used to be close," I say.

Adam nods a tiny bit, just before he frowns and says, "Time to go."

I follow him, moving slower than I was earlier due to the renewed pain in my side.

Adam stops next to a rusted red truck. There is a man standing next to it, carrying a rifle and looking menacing. Adam greets him. They exchange words while Marcus and I stand near the back of the truck and wait.

"I don't want to go back to Hanford," I tell Marcus.

"It will be okay," he says.

"Doubt it," I mutter as Adam turns and opens the passenger side door to the truck.

"Hey, at least we'll all be together again. You must miss Raven and Astrid."

"Yeah," I agree. I do miss them.

Adam motions for us to get in the truck. We make our way to the passenger side. Sliding across the bench seat, I scoot to the middle as Marcus sits next to me.

Adam closes the door and walks around the back of the truck. The tailgate squeals as it opens and then closes a few moments later. Adam gets in the driver's seat.

"This thing still runs?" I ask.

"Of course," Adam answers.

"What about gas?" Marcus asks as he buckles his seat belt.

"Got plenty. And I know some people if we run out," Adam replies.

Adam drives and it's a strange sensation, watching the world fly by us as he speeds down the road. I haven't ridden in a vehicle since we were living at the Pasture. It's been years.

The truck smells oddly of home. Like fresh baked bread and sage. It smells like our little farmhouse at the Pasture making my heart heavy and my stomach growl.

The first time Adam stops to fill up, he pulls a gas can out of the bed of the truck. We've been driving for hours and he's only stopped one other time so we could relieve ourselves. Sometime between evening and night I fall asleep, lulled by the steady humming of the truck's engine.

When I wake up it's dark, the only light being the headlights of the truck illuminating the cracked road ahead of us. Adam and Marcus are in mid-conversation about his training in the ARU. I wait, my head resting against Marcus's shoulder, and listen as they speak. When they finally stop, I end a long void of silence by asking, "Don't you need to stop and take a break?"

"No," Adam says immediately.

"But you've been driving this entire time. You haven't stopped once to eat or anything." I feel the heat of Marcus's thigh as it rests against mine. Moving away from him, I try to regain a few millimeters of my personal space.

I look up at Marcus and urge, "I think you should tell him your theory, about the Reformation."

"Tell me what?" Adam asks.

Marcus shakes his head, he's not talking. So, I do. "Marcus thinks the rest of the world is normal. They were never Reformed."

"Not possible," Adam says.

"You're sure?"

"Absolutely."

"But all the weapons in Hanford. What are they for? Why all the research and everything?"

Adam gives both of us a hard look before his gaze shifts to the dash. "Gonna have to stop in a few minutes for gas." He changes the subject.

"How rare is it?" Marcus asks. "To find the gas? The people at Hanford tell us the Survivors are almost out."

Adam shakes his head. "Harder to find in the Northern areas. But down south, someone started up the drills, got a refinery running, hydroelectric plant, restarted civilization. Gasoline is expensive but if you have a good trade or a debt owed, you can find it. Worst part about driving these days are the roads. No upkeep." He motions to the other side of the road where the asphalt is crumbling and grass is growing between the cracks.

Adam slows the truck, pulling off the highway and down a dirt road. He pulls up in front of a dark house. There is a man on the front porch, sitting in a rocking chair with a lantern at his side. He stands as Adam shifts the truck into park.

"Stay here. Don't get out. Don't move. Don't anything." Adam gets out and walks toward the man. They greet each other and it seems like they know each other.

"He's not like I remember," I say.

"He's not," Marcus agrees with me. He knew Adam from his time at the Pasture when we were kids.

"Do you think we can trust him?" I turn in my seat and get a good look at the area surrounding us. "Maybe we could get away from him. Keep going, get back to Phoenix."

Marcus grips my thigh. "Lina, he confirmed our fears. She's dead. There's nothing to go back to in Phoenix."

"I just... want something different. A different reaction from Adam. Not this." He acts like he can't wait one second longer to unload us.

"How would you feel if you found two kids you knew, walking through some obscure town thousands of miles from where they're supposed to be?" Marcus asks his voice flat.

"I just wanted to find my mom."

"So, you're satisfied with his answer? That she's truly gone?"

Smoothing my hands across my pants, I say, "If my dad wasn't around, Adam was always there. I had this feeling, even when I was really little that all he wanted to do was protect her, and... us." My eyes burn like I'm going to cry. I swallow hard and sniff, holding them back. "If she's not with him right now, she must be gone. He wouldn't be without her, I don't think."

Marcus says nothing and a strange feeling prickles the back of my neck. I turn and look out the back window of the truck but all I see is dark night and a few tree branches in the glow of the moon.

"What's wrong?" Marcus asks.

"Nothing. I just... keep getting this feeling like someone is following us."

Marcus shifts to look out the back window. "They probably are," he says, turning to look directly at me. His eyes hover over my face, stopping at my lips. "It's probably Glane."

My heart thumps loudly in my chest. Even though I'm still mad at him for telling me I can't take care of myself, I want to feel his lips on mine again. "Why did you say I made things complicated?"

"Because I have to do dangerous things and I don't want you getting hurt." He brushes his thumb across my jaw. "It's safer with you in Hanford. You're not that little girl anymore who will run home when I tell her to."

"No, I'm not a little girl." I lean closer to him. "I'm grown. I can make decisions for myself."

"Not in their eyes." He leans in and I can feel his breath on my lips.

"How do they see me then?" I ask. "How do you see me, Mark?"

He shifts in his seat. "We're stuck in that place where we're not kids and not quite adults. But life is changing so fast and you just want to hold on to that one thing you've wanted all along."

I think of my family being together again, knowing it can never happen now.

"What have you wanted your whole life?" I ask, wondering if it could be so different from me, so different from wanting my family whole and my mother at my side again.

"You," Marcus whispers as leans closer and his lips brush against mine.

There is a loud rapping on the driver's side window and Adam opens the door and says, "Get a ro–" he stops sharply and clears his throat. "Actually... don't get a room. Ever." He gives us both a hard look. "You got that Marcus? No touchy. Hands off." Adam slams the door.

Marcus removes his hands from me and slides away in the few inches the truck seat has to offer him.

"Oh! I almost forgot about Uncle Sam," I say as I scoot across the bench and get out the driver's side door. "Adam?" I ask as I make my way toward him.

"Yeah." He's filling the gas tank.

"What happened to my Uncle Sam?"

Adam clears his throat but as I stand there waiting, he says nothing.

"Adam?" I ask. "Adam! What about Sam?"

"He's in Phoenix."

"Still the Volker Sovereign?"

"Yes."

"Did Blithe have the baby?" I ask.

Adam presses his lips together and looks away from me.

"I'm not some little kid anymore, Adam. Did Blithe have the baby? Tell me what happened."

"Sam's still there. But Blithe... she died in childbirth."

My hand covers my mouth. "Oh my god." I lean against the truck. "And the baby?"

Adam just shakes his head.

It must have died too. That's all I can think. If they couldn't save her, they couldn't save the baby. The Districts pulled all medications, they only want those who are strong and adaptable and agreeable to the District rules to survive. When I was little, I was so afraid of getting shots at the doctor's office; we no longer do that anymore. That's what we've been taught. They say it makes us stronger, but I'm not so sure about that, not when people who can so easily be saved die.

"Sam must be heartbroken to have his wife and child die. I miss him so much. Is he okay?" I ask.

"Haven't seen him in a long time. Not since your mother first went missing." He shifts on his feet and does this strange thing as he talks; he tips his head down and bites the inside of his mouth. My mother warned me he is a liar. But he never lied to me, so I have no reason not to trust him. But I wonder...

Gas spills down the side of the truck, leaving strong fumes in its wake.

"Shit." Adam jerks the gas can and slams the cap into place. "Get in the truck."

Slowly, I back away from him as he straps gas cans into the truck bed.

"What were you two talking about?" Marcus asks as I slide across the seat and buckle in.

"Nothing." I close my eyes, lean my head back, and feign sleep. I can't tell him Blithe died. She raised Marcus and even though he's still angry about the way things have turned out, telling him that Blithe is dead will do nothing but make things worse. I'll tell him when we get back to Hanford, where he can't do anything stupid.

Adam gets into the driver's seat, starts the truck, and drives back to the highway.

We drive for hours in utter silence. All I can feel is the heat of Marcus's body beside me, the anger radiating off Adam, and the hunger in my gut, all of it making me want to leap from this moving vehicle and run as fast and as far as I can.

"We haven't run into any Survivors," I say, needing a distraction and a break in the silence.

"No." Adam replies, not in the least bit surprised.

"Why?"

"They know better."

"Know better?"

Marcus knocks my leg with his thigh. I think it's a warning for me to stop pestering Adam with questions but I want answers. Since my world was turned upside down all I have ever done is follow the rules and do what I've been told. I'm tired of it. I want to understand. My mother's already dead, what else do I have to lose? Nothing.

"So they know better?" I press on.

"Yes. And you should too," Adam warns. "Don't fuck with me, Lina. I am not your friend. I am not a father figure. I will get you nothing but trouble, possibly killed. If you want to preserve your life you will return to Hanford and forget you ever saw me. You will forget you know me. And you will do everything that Crossbender tells you to do. Don't wind up like your mother."

My mouth snaps shut and I stare straight ahead, pressing my hands between my knees and trying to figure out what the heck just happened.

NINE

DAMN THAT HURTS, BUT I CAN'T RISK LINA TRYING anything this stupid again. I have to push her away to keep her safe.

Lina's spunky, worse than her mom when I first met her. It's probably her age. They're like twins. Every time I glance at her I think it's Andie at my side but Lina's hair is a dark blonde instead of brown, and it's less curly. She has it twisted up in a loose bun, leaving her neck exposed in this heat. It's probably keeping her cool, but Marcus can't keep his eyes off her. Damned kid. Guess the ARU didn't knock any sense into him at all. Well, maybe a little. He must have negotiated some deal with Glane to make sure they didn't get killed. That had to take some balls, I've watched grown men quiver in front of Glane, and that other one I killed, Scarface. I know they've been tracking me. Glane wants revenge, he was probably using these two and now I must get them out of here before the shit hits the fan.

The last leg of the drive is tense and uncomfortable. I think Lina's crying, but I can't look at her. It hurt too much to say those things to her, the kid that used to stand at my side making spaghetti while the world was being Reformed, all innocent and shit. She has no clue, none of them do. But that's exactly what the Entities wanted. They won't fight if they don't know the truth.

I'll drop these two in Colorado. Freddie, the guy who I got the gas from, he's a Defector and now a Transplant. Pulled out of one of the Districts by Mrs. Crossbender and placed here to help me. Freddie is getting a team together to get these kids back. And then Andie is going to have to do that thing that makes people forget. She hates doing it on her own kids but there's no choice. They can't be living in Hanford knowing what lurks outside.

Lina makes a strange noise; I almost confuse it for crying until I realize it's her stomach. They must be hungry. I forget that other people have to eat to keep up their strength.

"I'm not stopping to find food. If you brought something you'd better eat it now, before we get there," I say.

Marcus reaches in his pack and pulls out two MRE's. When he opens them, handing one to her, it smells like real food. There was a time that they smelled no better than cardboard. That was a long time ago, lifetimes ago, time that no normal human life would span.

I drive through the night until the sun starts to rise, trying to keep my mind from wandering. It's hard, I worry about her. All the time now. Worse than ever. I know she's tracking us, following close behind to ensure that her daughter makes it back to Hanford safely. I lied when I told her she didn't affect me like she does other people. She does, she affects me in the deep center of my being like no one ever has.

Crossing my last checkpoint, I slow the truck and flick my lights at my man near the gate. The Districts have their gates, we have ours. Militias who fear me as Christian but who have never seen his face, that was a past life, one I tried to relive but can never return to. I know that now. There's only so much you can bring back from the dead. They know me as Adam, what Crane created. I focus on the road, my plan. The Entities set up the inter-District rail system; they didn't expect the Survivors to get their own trains working and use them. My men will get our train ready and we'll be out of here in no time. These kids will be back in Hanford where they're safe.

I drive for five more minutes before I make it to our final destination. This place looks like a farmhouse in the middle of a field, but just like Hanford's broken-down high school, this farmhouse holds secrets and doors to important places.

Parking the truck, I reach under my seat and pull out a handgun. It's loaded, and my last one. The rest I bartered for supplies for Mack and... *Don't go there.*

I get out and slap the bench seat to wake up the kids. "We're here," I tell Marcus when he looks at me. He nods in understanding and starts to rouse Lina. Part of me wants to yell at him to wake her up fast so I can get them the hell out of here. I don't want them here one second longer than they need to be. It's not safe, especially if anyone figures out who they are.

The late summer air is hot and thick. My eyes scan the surrounding forest. We have a couple hundred yards of open grass before the privacy fence and the forest beyond. There are guards out there. But I don't trust them to protect us if Glane and his men make an appearance. My men will give their lives to protect this place, but once they're gone, we have no backup, the house will be bombed and there will be one less safe haven between the oceans surrounding North America.

I wave to the man at the gate, freezing my arm when I hear a sharp snap and see him drop to the ground. Shit.

"Marcus! Get Lina out, now!" I slam the door shut and flick the safety on my gun. "Marcus! Lina! Out now!" I run around the back of the truck, scanning the fence line. They are there. The Swamp people. I can feel them. And so is she, but she won't do anything. She wants to see me suffer, if only for a few moments. She thinks it's owed. It's actually kind of fucked up, but it is owed. I'd cut off my left arm if it would set her right again. I'd do anything to bring her back to that first day I met her on the highway, I'd take back the first lie.

"Marcus!" I shout as the passenger side door slams closed and the two of them drop to the ground. Marcus is covering Lina, his handgun ready as he takes in his surroundings. Good boy, maybe the ARU did teach him a few things. Lina peers out from behind him, her arm raised, pointing a gun at me. For a split-second I consider the possibility that she might shoot me after what I said to her. Her gun goes off and I hear a soft thud from behind me. Turning, I find a lanky Swamp man on the ground with a bullet hole in his head. That's my girl.

"Get her in the house." I turn, ready to cover them. An arrow hits me in the thigh. I shoot at a shadow in the woods. A tree shudders and limbs snap as a body falls. Got the fucker. Pulling the arrow out of my leg and tossing it aside, I head for the porch. Another arrow hits me in the shoulder. Shit.

Marcus bangs on the front door.

"Open up!" I shout to the men inside.

"It's locked!" Marcus shouts back.

With one quick glance I see he has his back pressed to Lina. He fires a shot into the surrounding forest and another body drops. I run up onto the porch and check the windows. The place is empty. It shouldn't be empty.

Shit.

The beating of helicopter blades rips through the air. I know what comes next. This comes from experience in the field. Far more experience than most think. I should have seen this coming.

"Off the porch. Off the porch!" I command.

Marcus takes off running, dragging along a petrified Lina. Arrows fly. Marcus and I aim and shoot. Glane is going to make me pay for the men he loses today. A blast from behind knocks us off our feet as the house explodes. I cover the kids, shielding them with my body as they're face down in the grass. Pieces of glass and wood from the farmhouse pepper my back. I can't be sure if this is Crane or Hanford or the Underland, but I have a strong feeling someone found the 'wanted' notice and they're looking to collect. I need to get these kids out of here and Hanford is the safest place for them.

"On the count of three, you two run, get into the chopper." Marcus nods against my shoulder. "One..." The wind whips around us as the helicopter hovers above. "Two..." I grip my weapon and get ready to move as the Chinook lands. "Thr–" Jumping to my feet, I take aim only to be met by a row of Volker and George Crossbender. Crossbender doesn't faze me; it's the Volker on each side of him. All of them are brainwashed beyond return. I know this since I headed up my own troop of them in Phoenix. No doubt Sam knows by now also.

Crossbender holds up his hand and the Volker jump out. I raise my palms and back away. At least the kids are going back to where they belong, where they'll be safe. I didn't think Crossbender had it in him to leave his underground hub, maybe his wife doesn't have his balls in a vice grip.

I wave to the kids to get them to head for the chopper. Marcus moves, dragging Lina along. She gives me a look with wide eyes. *It's okay*, I mouth to her with another wave. Backing away, I catch the sight of the forest shuddering with the movement of a full pack of Swamp men. My eyes scan the grounds, landing on the farmhouse that now has a hole the size of a tour bus in the side of it. Strange, Crossbender wouldn't blow his own wife's hideaway to kingdom come, unless... things are not all hugs and kisses at home. My eyes meet his and I know what comes next, *I know*. Shit. One Volker raises his weapon. I receive a shot in the gut, another in the leg and drop to the ground. A warning not to follow. I've had worse. The bullets don't scare me.

The helicopter lifts off, taking the kids back to Hanford and I hear Lina screaming.

What happens next is the worst part, the slow, haunted footsteps that come for me as I'm rolling toward my truck, waiting for the nanocytes to do their work. Sometimes they're slow when the stress level is high. And right now, it's through the roof. Someone betrayed me, Crossbender probably just wanted to slow me down–both Crossbenders. But Glane, he's going to make me pay for killing his father and brother. I know that.

I stop rolling to my truck, wishing Andie would leave the cover of the forest and work her magic on these bastards. She doesn't, maybe she's not here yet, she had a lot of miles to cover on foot. Even so, this is her payback. Deep down, I know it's going to fucking hurt. Worse than the Middle East, worse than what Crane did to me and Blithe as kids, worse than all these years I've spent wandering this lonely planet searching for a reason to live. Figures, about the time I find her, she hates me.

"Dis be de worst kinda man." Glane stands over me, looking taller and dirtier. If that's even possible. "'new dos' two would fin' you." He smiles, revealing rotten teeth. "Dat girl smell like her moder. De cursed one."

The nanocytes are healing the bullet wounds; I can feel them working the Volker's bullets out of me when Glane's people make their full appearance. There are twenty-two of them. Each has an arrow drawn and aimed at me.

"You goin' pay now, devil." Glane's smile widens, and with the flick of his finger, all twenty release and hit me in the gut.

TEN

CATALINA

WATCHING THEM SHOOT ADAM WAS LIKE NOTHING I'VE EVER seen before in my life. Mr. Crossbender always seems so innocent; I'd never think he'd do something like this. At least I stopped screaming. I feel like an idiot but I couldn't help it. Marcus sits at my side, his back straight, his hand clamped around my arm like I'm his prisoner or something. Maybe he's afraid I'll jump. I try to shrug him away but his hand just closes tighter over my arm. I look up at Mr. Crossbender but he seems distracted and won't look at me. Maybe he's mad because I ran away. I don't know.

My throat fills with the sudden urge to vomit as I replay the events of Colorado over and over in my head. Shooting that man... Something went very wrong back there and I don't know what to think about it.

"Settle down," Marcus whispers in my ear. The helicopter is so loud I can barely hear him. My eyes scan the Volker near us, they all seem to be wearing headsets and ignoring us. "We're fine. We'll be in Hanford soon." His grip loosens on my arm as his free arm moves to my back, rubbing the tense muscles there. I'm confused by him right now. My eyes move to the small window and I watch the endless blue sky for hours until we land.

The helicopter descends below the ground. When it lands, we are plunged into shadows. A Volker opens the door and everyone starts to get out. I step off the helicopter and look around. We are in some giant, cavernous room.

"It's the ARU," Marcus says from behind me.

"Marcus," Mr. Crossbender says as he absently looks through a handful of papers and nods to a Volker who is speaking to him at the same time. "Take her to an interrogation room."

Marcus's hand clamps around my upper arm once again and he leads me away.

"An interrogation room?" I ask as my heart beats erratic with fear.

"They're going to want to debrief us since we've been out there for so long. Just tell them the truth. We'll be fine."

Marcus leads me through a set of gray double doors and down an unrecognizable hallway. I have not seen these parts of Hanford; it's dark and dingy, older than the rest of the place. Past a gray metal door there is a narrow table. One side has a single chair, the other side has four. Marcus motions me inside, his hand on my lower back. When the door closes, he turns to face me.

I attack, releasing all the pent-up tension of the last forty-eight hours. "How could you do this to me?" I shout at Marcus. "I trusted you!"

Marcus's eyes turn dark as he sucks in a deep breath. "*You* are the one that made this so complicated. It was supposed to be easy. I was supposed to help you find your mother and then I'd be free. They were going to let me see my parents again. *My* family. You know how long I've waited for that?" He punches the wall, his knuckles splitting and leaving a red streak behind. "Only for forever. You know what they told me? I'm not even from Phoenix. I'm from some small town in California."

"But you... you grew up with *us*. You were like a brother. We all watched out for each other and you were just going to drop us? Just like that? How could you, Marcus?" I'm screaming at him now. "How could you?"

"You know what the chances are of me finding my family now?" Marcus is yelling back at me. "None! I'll never find them. So don't you ask me how *I* could have done this, you just did the same for your mother."

"People have died for you! *My* mother, *my* father, Blithe! Did you know that she's dead, Mark? And you betray us like this, during the time that we are *so* alone and have no one but each other. What the hell is wrong with you?"

His eyes lock on mine, shocked for a second. I knew her death would affect him.

Marcus moves fast, closing in on my space and backing me up against the cold wall. He whispers harshly between his teeth, "You think I don't know that? You think I don't know that I was wrong? I thought I could do it. I thought..."

"Say it," I breathe out. "Don't be a coward. Just... say it!" My heart is beating wildly in my chest, threatening to break. I have nothing left; I can push him as far away as I want now. He already hates me and my family for ruining his life, even though it was never us, it's the people who built these Districts.

"I can't do it. I can't let you go." He slams a fist into the wall near my head. "And now we are royally screwed." He slams the other fist into the wall on the other side of my head. "I hope this is what you want, Lina, because they are *never* going to let me walk away now. I was ready to leave you alone just like you've been telling me to all these years. Just like your father warned." Marcus gives a shallow laugh. "He was intuitive, really. Makes me wonder if there was something else he knew and didn't tell us about. Or maybe it was something your mother knew." Marcus looks me up and down, breathing shallow. "You're going to have so much of me that you're going to be sick of looking at my face. Just remember that *you* did this. *I* was ready to walk away."

The door opens and a Volker calls to Marcus. He gives me that look like he gave me in Adam's truck when he kissed me and told me he's wanted me for forever. But this time he doesn't act on it. Instead, he pushes himself away from the wall and stalks away, leaving me alone without another word.

Part of me wants to collapse on the floor, the rest wants to run to the door and kick it down and try for another escape. This time alone, since it seems I can't trust anyone.

Mr. Crossbender walks in the door just as Marcus is leaving. There is a Guardian pacing in the hallway. "Welcome back, Lina," Crossbender says as he pushes his glasses in place. "I have to ask you a few questions."

"Debrief me?" I ask. "That's what Mark said."

He nods, a slight smirk appearing at calling Marcus by his nickname. I shouldn't have done that. But it's too late to take it back.

"Yes. Have a seat." Mr. Crossbender sits on the side with the four chairs. I sit alone, facing him. "So you ran away?"

I nod.

"Typical thing for a teenager to do. Although, we like to think that most Sovereign here at Hanford prefer the safety here compared to the outside world. You've been thoroughly schooled on the dangers beyond our gates. Why did you do it?"

"I wanted to find my mother."

"Did you find her?"

"No."

"Well, that's too bad." He frowns. "We really need her here."

"She's dead."

"Did you know what your mother was working on? The Match-making program. We have Districts worth of Residents and Sovereign that need to be matched. Her program is set to expire soon."

"Well, that's too bad for you. Adam confirmed her death."

"And you believe him?"

I nod.

"He's the world's greatest liar. You know this, right?"

I nod again.

Mr. Crossbender smiles. "Sorry you had to see that." He waves his hand. "All the violence. But we had to make sure he remembered his place."

"So you killed him in front of us?"

Mr. Crossbender tips his head down and lowers his voice. "He never truly dies. He always comes back."

"That's impossible."

"Nothing is impossible any longer, Catalina. Crane and the Entities have changed the rules, changed the world. He's older than you and I combined. I'm sure you'll see him again one day."

There is a long stretch of silence as I try to process what he just told me. Adam is old enough to be my grandfather, maybe older. But he looks the same age as my mother. She thought he died when I was a kid, and then he was alive again and I remember her being so angry with him, calling him a liar and warning me to stay away. Something is dangerous about Adam. Maybe he was right when he warned me to stay away from him. My head is spinning with all these new ideas about him, so I try to change the subject.

"Why didn't you kill the Swamp people?" I ask.

"They are a necessary evil. As much as we despise them, they are needed. And they helped you. For that we spared them. This time."

"How do you know they helped us?"

Mr. Crossbender only offers a quick smile in place of an answer. "I think your training is complete. You've had a taste of the real world. You've seen why we do what we do. The dangers beyond our walls. You're done with your schooling."

"But..."

Mr. Crossbender folds his hands in front of him and looks directly at me. "Your Apprenticeship starts now."

"I didn't test out for anything." My fingers grip my legs. I never took my final exams or made up for all those point I lost on my Calc grade for being tardy. "I didn't even finish my classes–"

"You don't need to. We already know what you're going to do, no matter how many times you've forced yourself to fail at it." He crosses his arms and leans back in his chair. "No one fails so elegantly, Catalina. I bet it would make your mother so proud to know how hard you tried to avoid following in her footsteps."

Mr. Crossbender stands and makes his way to the door. "The other Sovereign children don't get to experience the full panel of Hanford. But you're different."

"I'm not," I argue. "I'm nothing special." I want Marcus to come back, someone, anyone, to be on my side for this. The feeling of loneliness has never felt so strong before.

"Catalina, the children of Phoenix are definitely more than special. You included."

Mr. Crossbender moves to the door and opens it. Mrs. Crossbender, Janet Jones, and an intimidating looking Volker enter. A Guardian scoots in the door just before Mr. Crossbender closes it and settles at my feet.

Mrs. Crossbender sits across from me, and having watched the Guardian enter the room she asks, "Did you take any Guardians with you?"

"No," I reply.

"Hmm. Well, there're only three left."

"Three?" I ask. There were five the day I left.

Mr. Crossbender nods in agreement.

"What happened to them?" I ask.

"They keep disappearing. Maybe your brother knows something about it," the large Volker man says.

"Which brother?" I ask.

"Isaac," the Volker answers.

"I wouldn't know. I haven't talked to him in weeks. Not since before I left."

"Before you *ran away*," Mrs. Crossbender sneers.

Mr. Crossbender raises his hand to stop her. "Dear. Not now."

Something seems off between them. They were a bit tense before I left, but now, it's much worse. The air between them is worse than it ever was between my parents, even when my father came back after those few years.

They start drilling me on all things genetics related. Mr. Crossbender brings me to the research labs here and has his scientists ask me questions. I try to give wrong answers sometimes to sway them, to make them forget about me taking my mother's place, but each time Mr. Crossbender smiles and says, "I've told you before, Lina, no one fails so elegantly. If you're going to lie, try harder."

I stop trying to lie. Crossbender takes me on as his Apprentice. He keeps me in the interrogation room, moving in a few simple pieces of bedroom furniture and a small table and chair where I eat my meals alone. They bring me clothes, simple black outfits similar to what

Marcus and I wore when we were outside the gates. I have a hard time determining if this is my punishment or my training. The only time I leave the room is with Mr. Crossbender. The wound on my side heals to a small pink scar, but nothing will heal the betrayal presented to me by Marcus.

Two weeks pass before I ask for something.

"I want to see my family," I say as I cross my arms and refuse to leave my room.

Mr. Crossbender's eyebrow ticks up. "This is not like you, Catalina."

"You've had me trapped down here for weeks. I've seen no one. None of my brothers. Not even Astrid or Cash or... Marcus." Something burns inside of me when I say his name. I'm still angry with him but I can't deny that a part of me misses him.

"Well. I guess you've earned it. Who would you like to see?"

"All of them."

"No." He shakes his head and his glasses slip down his nose. "Pick one." He presses them back in place with his index finger.

"Raven."

"You pick the only one who doesn't speak. Odd."

I keep my face pliant, trying not to reveal Raven's secret. I don't need to speak to him. I just want to find out if he's okay. Leaving him behind in that forest was one of the hardest things I've ever done and I feel like I've abandoned him.

"I'll send for him now." Mr. Crossbender leaves. I sit at my chair and wait.

Watching the clock on my nightstand tick, it's a full thirty minutes before the door opens. I hear Mr. Crossbender's voice, and then Raven walks into my room, the door closing behind him.

Springing from my seat, I run for him and wrap him in a tight hug. "Raven." My hands settle on his shoulders and I think he's grown since I last saw him, he seems taller. "Are you okay? You made it back in one piece after I left you? What's been going on up there?"

Raven smiles and takes my cheeks between his hands, resting his forehead against mind. I close my eyes and he takes two deep breaths before burying his face in my neck and whispering. "I'm fine." He continues. "They didn't do anything to me for trying to escape with you. But the kids at school have gotten worse since you disappeared. And Isaac... he's gotten worse too. Astrid hides in her room, crying all the time. Marcus doesn't know what to do with her. We need you back. Just do what they want so you can come back to us." He doesn't sound like my little brother, talking so confidently. I nod my head, my eyes stinging with tears. "We're fine. You'll be back with us soon. And... Marcus misses you. He feels bad about the last time he saw you. He didn't want to betray us, still doesn't want to. Marcus made mistakes but we can trust him. He has no one else but us."

Too soon the door opens. There is a Volker, motioning for Raven to leave. I hug him fiercely before he goes and Mr. Crossbender steps into the room.

"That was poignant," Mr. Crossbender says as he watches Raven leave. "Now. You owe me."

I cross my arms. "How can I owe you? I've been doing all this for you, bringing him here was the least you could do for me."

"There are worse things you could be doing." He motions to the door. "Let's go. We have a busy day today."

"You used to be nice." I pick a jacket off my bed and slip it on wishing I hadn't taken for granted all those days he pulled me out of class to talk to me. It's usually really warm down here, but the research labs are freezing. "I used to really like you Mr. Crossbender. But now... each day you remind me more and more of Crane."

He snaps his head away from me like I hit him in the face.

"Let's go." His voice is stern and when he pushes his glasses up the motion is quick and angry.

He brings me to the research labs, to a private room where there are boxes on a table and a computer in the corner. It looks familiar.

"Is that..." I walk toward it, recognizing the tape pressed over the tiny camera lens above the screen. "Is that my mother's computer?"

"Yes." He moves to the table. "And these are your new friends."

"Friends?"

Opening the lids on the boxes, I see that they are filled with mice. Each box holds a different species. Some are white, some brown, some tiny field mice, and larger lab bred ones that we've used in my science classes.

"A few of these mice are genetically unsound. I want you to identify them."

"How?" I ask.

"By looking."

"But... that is impossible. No one can do that."

"Your mother could."

"I am not my mother." I point at the boxes. "I can't do that."

"Have you ever tried to just give in to the one thing you want but have been warned against?"

"No." I took my mother's warning to heart. I watched what her... *gift* did to her. How they used her. How they broke her.

"I suggest you try. Might surprise yourself. I bet it will even feel good." Mr. Crossbender's eyes flick to the computer in the corner. "Take a look at her program. It might help." He closes the door and leaves.

I stare at the boxes of mice. They're squeaking and clawing at the sides of the container, trying to escape just like I've wanted to do for so long. We've never been allowed to have pets here, just the Guardians who aren't always friendly. At the Pasture there were plenty of friendly animals to play with, here we only have the Guardians and they don't play. Reaching my hand into the box with the little field mice, I pet one of the tiny species on the head. I get two strokes in before it bites my finger.

"Ow!" Pulling my hand away, I sit at the computer desk. I don't know what to do. I am not my mother. She had some voodoo genetics magic that made her special, but not me. This is impossible.

My day fluctuates between staring at the mice and fiddling with the computer. The day turns into days then into a week then two weeks.

When I'm sure that I am about to lose my mind from staring at boxes of mice all day and thinking about amino acids and chromosomes and double helices, I decide I can't take it any longer. I have to get the heck out of here. If they won't believe me, then maybe I can trick them.

I have no lab, no samples to run, no computer programs. I just have myself and these boxes of mice. I have nothing but myself and what I've learned in the classroom. I start examining the mice. I pick them up, ignoring the bite marks they leave on my fingers, and I look them over. I make it to the white ones last. White can be abnormal, but these mice don't have the red eyes like the ones they gave us to dissect in biology lab. There could be something else abnormal about them. I pick one up to examine it. Everything seems normal until my index finger rolls over a small flap of skin on the mouse's hind leg. Turning the animal over, I examine the area. It's above the paw and looks like a dew claw that a dog or a deer would have. Not a mouse. But, I guess a mouse could have one. I examine all the white mice and find that they all have the extra flap of skin on their back leg. Moving to the other boxes, I examine the other mice, they have no extra parts. I stare at the box of white mice and mill it over in my head. This could be a trick, an easy one at that. Is a flap of skin enough? What else do I have to go on? I can't believe I wasted two weeks of my life in here. I'm done.

I pick up the box, turn and knock on the door.

Mr. Crossbender opens it and waits, not letting me leave until I speak. "Lina?"

"Here." I hand him the box. "It's all of them. They're all wonky."

Mr. Crossbender's face breaks into a wide smile. "Excellent. For this you shall be rewarded."

A gentle unease settles through me. The only reward I received was running away from here, even if I almost died, at least I was free to make my own decisions and experience the world. I wonder if it was like this for my mother.

I am brought back to the lower levels of the ARU, where my room is. Mr. Crossbender stops at the end of the hallway and motions for me to continue without him. "You've earned this bit of freedom. Congratulations and good evening."

Walking down the hall alone, I decide it's nice to have a bit of freedom back. Even though walking a few hundred yards without someone at my side doesn't seem like that much of a gift. Reaching the door to my room, I find that it is already open and wonderful scents are coming from inside. My mouth waters. Okay, maybe this is a great reward; delicious food. I'll take that any day.

Entering my room, focused on the small table piled high with plates, I stop when I see another figure standing next to the table. It's Marcus.

"Lina?" he asks.

My back goes straight as I suck in a breath, all my memories of our time spent outside of Hanford and the argument when we came back, floods me. His promises, his betrayal. Marcus takes a step toward me and I hold my hands up, urging him to stop.

He frowns, and then, looking into my eyes, he smiles softly. "I told you that you'd be sick of seeing my face. It's been weeks, Lina. I'm worried about you."

Pinpricks assault the corners of my eyes. I'm going to cry, there's no way around it. The surge of emotion that comes with seeing him and smelling real food reminds me that Crossbender keeping me down here is the worst kind of punishment for having run away. I don't think there's anything worse than loneliness that comes with being taken away from your family, knowing that they are out there and you can't reach them or see them or interact in any way.

"*You...*" That's all I get out before the waterworks turn on and I can no longer form a coherent sentence.

Marcus pulls me into his arms, pressing his lips to the top of my head. "It's okay." His arms squeeze me. "Everything's going to be okay..." Marcus pauses and moves his hands to both of my shoulders, turning me to face him. "Just trust me, Lina. Please."

I want to trust him.

My fingers curl against his shirt. It's some soft material. Not like his usual ARU uniforms and not like our school uniforms. I wonder if they gave him new clothes for this... this... whatever it is. Is this a date? It doesn't matter; right now his shirt is soaked in my tears.

When I finally calm down, and remember Raven's words, I say, "I'm sorry I yelled at you."

"It's okay. I like it when you get all feisty."

"You've always said that."

"I've always meant it." Marcus smiles down at me.

There is no stronger feeling in my heart than the one that's telling me that Marcus is for me. Maybe he has been all along. Maybe he was chosen for me; maybe this was a set up. It doesn't matter. All I know is that we are meant to be together. And since I have no one else, I want to cling to him like never before. I let those feelings I had for him when we were curled up together in that tent, and bathing in that stream, and riding in that truck bloom and spread in my chest. These Districts may have taken our lives, they may be controlling us, but they are letting me keep him. They are giving me the one person I still want. I'm done pushing him away like my father warned, I'm taking him for myself.

"Lina?" Marcus asks, gripping my cheeks between his palms. "You're a bit different since I saw you last." He moves a piece of hair out of my face. "Still drop-dead gorgeous but... different."

I nod. "I've discovered a few things about myself," I whisper as I reach up on my toes and press my lips to his.

"Is that what you've been doing down here with Crossbender?" He asks when I pull away. "Self discovery? I think I like it."

I shudder at the mention of Crossbender, not wanting him occupying any space in my head right now. "Something like that," I say. "Let's not talk about Crossbender." I move my hands up his arms and across his shoulders, all thick with muscle like he never was on the farm. "I realized something while you were gone."

"What's that?"

"I think I like you. A lot."

"Is that so?"

"Um hmm."

"So does this mean I can *touchy* you all I want?" he asks.

"Within reason."

"Thank God." Marcus's hands are on me then, spanning my waist, my back, pressing me to him as he dips his head and kisses me like I'm sure he's wanted to do for years. He kisses me like I've never been kissed and, well, besides him I never have been kissed. His hands tangle in my hair and slide down my back until he grips my butt with both hands. "Jesus. You don't know how long I've wanted to do that for."

A small giggle escapes my throat and it feels out of place and wrong. Just a few minutes ago I lied to pass a test the Hanford Sovereign had set up for me. I try not to think about what comes next and what it could mean for us.

"I haven't heard you laugh since we came to Hanford." His eyes soften.

"That's because I don't like it here. They treat us..."

"I know." He wraps his arms around my shoulders. "We just do this. Just like they want. Just like we want." He pauses to look down at me. "You do want this, right?"

Do I want Marcus? He is the only boy I have ever known like this, the only boy I have ever kissed or held in my arms. But he has changed into a man while I still teeter between the lines of a girl and a woman. I have time to find someone else, to move on. But, like I saw my mother suffer, I never want to love two men. Love... is that what this is? It has to be something of the sort. You can't live through what we've lived through and not feel an undying connection to the other person. I can lie all day through my teeth at the Crossbenders, but I can't lie about this. This is a slippery slope that will hurt more than it would help. And so, I ask myself. Do I want Marcus? Because I can't lie about this, I can't turn back from this. Our lives are intertwined and I don't need some genetic voodoo to see the truth.

He looks down at me, his brown eyes clear and hopeful. "Yes," I say.

"Good." Marcus releases me and stands at arm's length. "Do you want to eat?" Marcus tips his head toward the table. "I took a bite of the turkey before you got here. It's really good. Like real food." He smirks. "Sorry. I couldn't help myself."

"Okay."

We sit across from each other and eat. This is the best meal I've ever had here. None of it has been *Hanfordized*. There's baked potatoes, steamed carrots, a small roasted turkey. All of it is unseasoned but it's still delicious.

When I'm done, I sit back in my chair and ask Marcus the question that's been nagging me. "Why are you here?"

He stops mid-chew and swallows. "Crossbender is worried about your mental health."

"Wow. Don't hold back or anything." I can't even laugh with the way he's looking at me.

"It's part of the Apprenticeship." He sets his fork down and cleans his hands and mouth on the napkins they provided us with. "This is what they do. Limit your contact with the people closest to you. The more you work, the less you care. It's pretty much a mind game. When you're too exhausted to maintain those relationships, you align with the only thing you know. It's kind of like brainwashing."

"They told you this?"

"They didn't have to. I just sat back and watched one day. Saw what they were doing to me. I never got to spend time with you guys and when I was home I was exhausted and had no patience." He stands and sets the napkin on the table. "I'm sorry for that. Some of the guys in training, they have this motto: District or Die. Repeat it enough times and you start to believe it. There's nothing there about family."

Ms. Jones said that phrase to me before. I swallow hard. I don't want that for my life.

Marcus holds out a hand to me. "Come here."

"Why?"

"I want to whisper sweet nothings in your ear." The smile that spreads across his face is infectious and I find myself smiling back. He reaches down and takes my hand, pulling me to my feet and close to him. His fingers weave between mine, clutching our hands close to his chest as his other hand circles my waist and he starts to sway, pulling my body along with his.

"What are you doing?" I ask.

"This is called dancing," he whispers in my ear.

I've seen pictures of people dancing. But I've never experienced it. "Shouldn't there be music?"

"We don't need music."

He leads me around the room, keeping our bodies close, so close I can almost feel his heartbeat. When he finally stops, he kisses my forehead, smiles and leaves.

ELEVEN

CATALINA

"ONE LAST TASK AND I THINK YOU'LL BE READY." MR. Crossbender smiles.

He brings me to the upper levels where I used to attend school. The light from the Hanford divide burns my eyes, it's been so long since I've seen actual daylight, no matter how dim. It's different than the lights in the ceilings here.

We enter a large empty room. There are no chairs, no tables, just two doors.

"While you've been deep in your Apprenticeship, your classmates have been moving on with their lives. We've had to make an executive decision. Birth rates have been at zero for years. We are going to reach a point where the gap between generations is too large to close. We need to start planning for the future."

"I don't see how I can do anything about that."

The door opens and Ms. Jones enters, a girl following behind her.

Mr. Crossbender clears his throat. "I'm sorry to have to do it like this. But we won't always have that computer program your mother wrote. We need to do it face to face."

"Do what?"

The girl steps to Ms. Jones's side and I am surprised to see Julie Rubie standing there. The note she left in my backpack blocks out all rational thought for a moment.

Matchmaker Matchmaker make me a match,
Matchmaker Matchmaker open my hatch,
Matchmaker Matchmaker scramble my brains,
Matchmaker Matchmaker... you're dead.

"THOUGHT YOU WERE DEAD," Julie says, her tone sharp. It seems the Hanford people don't hold back when they are surrounded by their own.

"Ms. Rubie," Janet Jones snaps. "I suggest you take heed to the one who will be placing you with your life partner."

Julie looks at me, her eyes large and face pale.

I know I shouldn't, but I smile at her. A sweet, farm girl smile like I have never given a soul.

Julie's eyes widen then narrow to slits. I don't think she cares about the power that I have over her life right now.

Ms. Jones moves to the other door and opens it. A row of boys walks in. Some I recognize from class. And then Kevin walks through the door. He smiles when he recognizes me, but then hides it quick, no doubt remembering the way I seduced him in the elevator to get the weather report. At the end of the line walks in Joe, the one who terrorized and bullied us with his friends. He acknowledges me by mouthing, *dirty farmer.*

My hands clench into fists, and I don't miss the look that passes between him and Julie.

"Lina," Mr. Crossbender demands my focus, even after bringing these people in here. "You need to pair her. Like your mother did."

"Okay," I whisper. Picking out a box of mice was nothing compared to this. With this, I could ruin someone's life; make them unhappy for all eternity. Make them pine after the love they never had like I would have done for Marcus.

Keeping my distance, I walk up and down the line, making a show of it. I notice Joe doesn't take his eyes off Julie. Kevin doesn't take his eyes off me. The rest of the boys, they seem quite hesitant to the whole thing.

Moment of truth: I could give her Joe. A fool could even feel the magic in the air between the two of them. Or, since they tainted the lives of my family and myself with a bit of hell, I could pair her with someone else. Karma sucks. I point at a random guy, one who looks around Kevin's age.

"Him," I say.

Julie looks less than pleased. I feel instantly guilty. The others give me hesitant looks, I'm sure the rumors have made it around school. I ran away, they caught me and dragged me back and now Crossbender is assigning me my mother's role.

"Good." Mr. Crossbender steps forward. "We're done here. Come with me, Lina."

I follow him out of the room and down the hall.

"Did I do it right?" I ask when we reach Mr. Crossbender's office, knowing inside that I faked it, just like I faked the mouse test.

"Only time will tell." After entering the room, he sits behind his desk and motions for me to sit in front of him. "It's time for the next step of your Apprenticeship."

His eyes flick to the neat stacks of papers on his desk before refocusing on me. "You had to know this was coming. I will be guiding you." He reaches for a small piece of yellowed paper on his desk and hands it to me. "This won't be like the normal Apprenticeships here, Lina. What we talk about never leaves this room. Not until the right time." It seems he's switched back to the nice Mr. Crossbender, the one I used to like. He holds out the small paper to me.

Reaching forward I take it from him. "What's this?" There are eight names written on the paper.

"Your first lesson." Leaning back in his chair, he crosses his arms. "Things are not always as they seem." I look up at him. "Trust no one."

He reaches for a stack of papers, sliding it across the desk in front of me, then tapping the sides to set it straight again.

"What's this?" I repeat.

"This is the New Mexico census from right before the Reformation. We're searching for those names." He motions to the paper in my hand. "We need to find those names. The future depends on it."

"Who are they?"

"Children. Dangerous children. Very dangerous." Mr. Crossbender slides a stack of papers toward himself. "I'll start with Arizona."

"Do you need this?" I set the list of names down on the desk, no longer wanting to hold it in my hand or have knowledge of it. I think I just dug myself a deep, deep hole.

"No. Already have them memorized. I've been searching for a long time. Check the birth dates. They must have been born before the Reformation. That's when Crane unleashed all his experiments into the world."

TWELVE

GLANE

GLANE WAS BORN OF THE SOUTHERN SWAMPS OF WHAT WAS known as Mississippi. This was before the Reformation, but not as many years before as one would expect. He was not born by the normal manner in which humans give birth, and not much of him functions in the manner that we know to be normal or even... human. He has no thoughts of what is right and what is wrong. He runs purely on need. Basic, straight-forward, cut and dry, uncomplicated need.

Glane and his people know simple fact, there is life and there is death, there is fullness and there is hunger. There is an internal force driving them. Therefore, Glane has no thoughts on his mind. He does not venture across the land thinking and theorizing and wondering. If one could spend the day listening to Glane's thoughts, the only thing they would hear is *hunger*; there would be nothing else except for a continuous drive to find more food. The need to keep his people going and the need to cleanse his land of whatever is rotting it.

Glane moves with basic instinct and skill. He knows three things: hunger, death, and procreation. If Glane senses one of his women is fertile, he takes her to his tent to continue his race and breed his genetic code. That is all. There are no hugs, no kisses, no cuddles in the dark. Freedom, affection, these are words that Glane's people do not know. This is how his people operate, stripped down to the basics of humanity, even though some would say that there is nothing human about them.

The fundamental need that Glane and his people understand the most is hunger, and it is insatiable. Glane does not know that this is what he and his people were designed to do. Consume, cleanse, filter. Beasts and man will die, and his people will strip their bones and recycle their life force.

Being one of the first families, Glane knows of the time before the Reformation when he and his people were not allowed to venture far from their swamps. The Witch Doctor forbade it. They were a small clan of people then and always hungry. And then there were the great explosions, the Swamp people felt their land shudder and quake. They were spared from harm and the Witch Doctor told them this was for a reason. Glane was just a young boy at that time; he sought council from the elder Witch Doctor, who, unlike his older brothers took him under his wing. Glane learned to trust the man as much, or more so, than he trusted his own instincts.

With the explosions came the freedom for them to venture away from their land and seek out more food. For the first time ever, Glane experienced a full stomach. But the sensation didn't last long. It seemed with each full stomach his body experienced hunger faster and stronger than ever before. And it wasn't just him, his people experienced the same thing. It was like the Reformation, as the Witch Doctor called it, had awoken something deep within the Swamp people, it intensified their need to consume. There had always been game for these people to sate their hunger, creatures of the forest that would feed two or three men. But the Reformation brought something else, troves of game in the form of humans. Flesh that was already cooked. Bodies that didn't need to be hunted.

For a member of the human race this act would seem despicable. But Glane and his people do not see themselves as human. He has no qualms in consuming humans and neither does the rest of his clan. He and his kind are an invasive species of humanity, just like the foreign pythons, disposed of in the murky waters by owners who did not know what to do with them. They have become too large, too hungry, and too dangerous, but there is something about humans that prevent them from terminating their own pets. Instead, they release them into the wild and that is exactly what Burton Crane did when he realized what he had created.

They have grown in numbers since the Reformation. Before, they were a people of just a handful, but full stomachs brought the full abdomens of their women, and soon that handful of Swamp people grew into the tens and then the hundreds. With their stomachs filled the children grew fast, much faster than those of the humans that they consumed. They were a breed of hundreds now, but tight knit in their family units and the need to protect their own young.

Glane's father, Scarface, received a slash down the side of his cheek when a child was attacked on the banks of the swamp and Scarface did just what any man would do to protect his young and ensure the future of his race. He fought the alligator. When he won the fight by ripping the soft leathered underbelly of the beast, his people feasted on the animal and made shoes from the stiff hide. Since the Swamp people had no real leader at that time, only the guidance of the Witch Doctor, Scarface was named chief. He was the first to achieve that title and held it until he was killed in the north. Not long after his death, Glane's brother took his father's position as chief and was killed by the same man. Glane was filled with feelings he'd never experienced before, and, just like when he was a child, he sought counsel from the Witch Doctor.

The Witch Doctor told Glane that his father and brother had been experiencing something the Swamp people never had before, curiosity. They wanted to breech the gates of the enclosed Districts, they were drawn to whatever was hidden there, something was not right. Glane never exhibited curiosity and that is what made him the perfect man to follow in the footsteps of his brethren. Except that, there is one sense that Glane does not realize is new to him. Revenge. His father and his brother were both killed by the same man. And although Glane's people think it strange of him to hunt a single live man when they have stomachs to feed, Glane cannot rid himself of the sentiment.

Glane and his men tracked the man. They watched him make

weekly visits to the District in the north, saw the woman arrive by train, the one he so vehemently protected by killing Glane's father.

And then she dropped out of the sky, landing at their feet in a steaming pile of cooked flesh. Glane and his men happily dragged her off into the forest, intent on filling their bellies with her hide.

That was until she woke.

There is something about that woman who woke from the dead. Glane fears none, except her. He knows, deep in his being, that waking from the dead is not possible, so he delivered the corpse to the Witch Doctor and avoided the hut in the swamps where she was. He took his men north again and began searching.

The first time Glane had a sensation which told him *not* to kill was when he and his men found the girl who looked so much like the woman who rose from the dead. He could smell that they were from the same family. And since the woman who rose from the dead is the only thing Glane fears, he hesitated, ordered his men not to kill the girl and her companion. Instead they helped her, brought her back to their land to cure the snake bite that had infected her blood.

This has never happened before.

Now that the living dead woman is gone, Glane visits the Witch Doctor more and more. Searching for answers to questions that his kind have never had before. And while the Witch Doctor tells Glane that he must learn to control his urge for revenge, he finds he cannot. It only grows stronger, just like the urge for his people to fulfill their hunger.

THIRTEEN

I NEVER KNEW THAT SEARCHING A LIST FOR NAMES COULD BE so mind numbing. There must be an easier way. I asked Mr. Crossbender if he could use a computer but he freaked out, told me we weren't even supposed to be searching for those names and if the Funding Entities did a scan of the computer systems and found out, he'd be in big trouble. Then I asked him who the Funding Entities are. I guess it's the group of people who are responsible for the Reformation. They planned it. I immediately hate them all.

After a day of Apprenticeship with Crossbender, he dismisses me, and for the first time he doesn't escort me to my living quarters. I expected this, eventually, part of the Apprenticeship is learning how to maneuver the hive–like hallways of Hanford. I can navigate the halls to my living quarters near the ARU with my eyes closed. What I really want to do is sprint up the closest stairwell to the ground level and see our old living quarters. I bet Raven and Isaac and Astrid are there. I hope they're doing okay. I haven't seen any of them in weeks.

The only interaction I get with any of the others is when Mr. Crossbender sends Marcus to walk me. But it's been days since I saw him.

Kevin has showed up a few times. He always asks me about my time outside, he seems to be fascinated with it. Many of the kids here will never know a life outside the underground passages of Hanford. Part of me feels sorry for them, even if they act despicably toward us.

But today I am alone. I would like the company of another human or anything, even a Guardian. Come to think of it, I haven't seen a Guardian in weeks. As I walk, my shoes make hollow noises on the flooring.

Sensing a presence at the end of the hall, I stop walking. It's Joe. Dread floods me. Nothing good ever happens when Joe is around, of all the Hanford kids he was the worst to us.

Joe advances toward me. Fast. I think of turning and running but I know he'll catch up with me. His legs are longer and I could tell how slow I have become when we were outside. I doubt I could outrun much any longer. I stand my ground, clench my fists. I haven't had any hand-to-hand training in a while, but I'm confident that I can handle myself.

Joe walks right up to me, coming to a sudden stop a mere two inches from my face. "Been waiting to get you alone for a long time now, *farmer*." His voice threatens and my body knows something bad is going to happen. "I still haven't made you pay for setting Julie up with that other guy." Joe moves closer and I step away, feeling the hardness of the wall against my back.

Something inside me told me that pairing her with the wrong person was a bad idea, but I wanted so badly to pay them back for all the mean crap they did to us. So, I own my flaws.

"I did what I had to do," I reply, raising my chin.

I'm not going to back down to this Joe. He's nothing and I've seen worse, much worse. I bet he'd piss his pants if he saw one of the Swamp people.

"She was mine." Joe pokes a finger into his chest. "Julie and I had plans. She loved me." Joe moves so close that his nose is almost touching mine. "You know what it's like to have someone you love taken away like that?"

He has no idea.

"You're going to pay. You and the rest of your farm-bred family. We don't want you here." He pauses, his lip tipping up into an evil smile, and he punches me in the side with a quick jab.

My knees weaken and I start to slide down the wall. Oh God, I wasn't prepared for that. He punches me again in the other side and pain radiates through my abdomen. I double over in agony, ready to drop. Uncle Sam would be so disappointed to see me go down so easily. I just didn't expect Joe to be the girl-hitting type. I mean, I knew he was a jerk, I just didn't think Hanford could break someone this bad.

Joe grabs the front of my shirt, pulling me up until I'm standing again. "This is what happens when you screw with my future." Behind him, I see two more guys step out of the shadows of the hallway. Great, he brought friends.

He kicks me in the shin. I can't stop the cry that escapes my lips. He drags me across the hall to the Hanford divide. It's seven stories down. I know that there is no surviving that. Too weak to move, I close my eyes; try to think of my next move.

The thudding sound of someone running fills the empty hallway. Joe's hand lets go of my shirt with a quick jerk and there is the thump of bodies hitting the floor. When I open my eyes I see Isaac on the ground with Joe underneath him, his face already bloodied and disfigured as Isaac punches him over and over again. Joe is kicking and punching back, but nothing he does stops Isaac.

"Isaac!" I shout. "Stop." Part of me wants Isaac to beat the crap out of Joe for all he's put us through. But I've never seen Isaac like this before, it scares me more than Joe and his goons.

Isaac doesn't stop. He keeps going. All that pent up strangeness that he's always possessed comes pouring out of him and into Joe. This is more than just childhood anger. This is rage, a rage I have only ever seen outside of the walls of Hanford. Down in the pit of my stomach I know that Isaac is going to kill Joe, he's capable of it.

"Isaac!" I move away from the railing, my abdomen throbbing from Joe's fists. "Isaac, stop!" My hand lands on his shoulder but he shrugs me away. Joe stopped moving. His legs go slack and his arms drop to the floor. "You're going to kill him!"

After a few more moments, Isaac finally stops. I move around him and press my fingers to Joe's neck, feeling for a pulse. There's nothing.

"Oh my god… What did you do?"

Isaac stands and lifts Joe's body. He carries him toward the railing of the Hanford divide, and before I can say anything, he tosses Joe over.

"No!" I scream.

Dropping to his knees, Isaac looks down at his hands. His knuckles are bleeding and cracked, coated in Joe's blood.

"Isaac…" I don't know what to say to him.

My eyes move to his face, where there are tears forming, a pained expression.

"I just want to be good, Lina." His fists clench, his voice cracks. "I just want to be good." His hands move to his face, leaving bloody streaks down his pale skin. "I just want to be good. But… without mom here, I can't control it. I can't make it stop." A sob racks his body, sounding much more like the thirteen year old boy that I know he is, but doesn't look like. "Can you make it stop? Please, Lina, can you make it stop like mom could?"

My jaw drops open and I feel the blood drain from my face. What do I say to him? What do I say when my little brother makes that kind of a confession, and after he just got done protecting me from whatever horrible injury Joe and his friends had in store? Joe was going to hurt me, but instead Isaac killed him. What am I supposed to say? My mouth moves but nothing comes out as Isaac looks up at me. He stands, towering over me now. It's just not right, not normal that he should be so large, so tall, so… wicked.

"I have to go," he says. He's taking rapid breaths and I wonder to myself if this is the first time he's killed a person.

Isaac steps by me, his hand brushing against my shoulder, leaving a streak of blood on my shirt.

Turning, I see the group of boys that were with Joe. They stare at my brother in shock as he advances toward them. Isaac grabs one by the neck and says in an almost-growl, "You stay away from them. Or I'll come back. I'll know and I'll come back and finish you off just like him." Isaac shoves the kid away, the bloody handprint on his neck standing out like a curse.

"Goodbye, Lina," Isaac says before he turns and runs down the hall.

Joe's buddies run down another hall, away from me.

Suddenly, I don't know what to do. Do I get help? Do I scream? Do I run and hide in my ARU living quarters?

I find myself dropping to my knees and staring at the blood on the floor from the dead boy who rests at the bottom of the Hanford divide. I don't move until I feel a pair of hands on my shoulders. Turning, I find Raven standing behind me. I open my mouth to say something but nothing comes out.

Raven tips his head, focusing on the blood on the floor. "I knew he would do it," Raven whispers. "Since he came to us as a kid, I knew he'd do it. I knew he'd eventually kill someone."

"How could you know?" I ask.

"Because, Lina." Raven looks directly at me. "I can read minds."

FOURTEEN

CATALINA

WHAT?!

"That's why I don't speak. That's why I always know what you're thinking and how I knew where to find you just now." Raven's eyes narrow on me.

My mouth hangs open in disbelief until I can form a thought. "You've kept this from me all this time?"

"I couldn't tell a soul, Lina. You know what they'll do to me if they find out. You know what they'll do to both of us. We are her only blood children."

Swallowing hard, I nod at him but continue to stare in disbelief.

"What can you do, Lina?" Raven asks as he kneels in front of me. "What can you do that's special?"

I shake my head. "Nothing."

"You sure?"

"I swear. I'm just... normal."

"You're not. You can't be. Don't lie to me, Lina. Tell me."

"I... there's nothing. I lied to Mr. Crossbender. I made it all up so they'd let me go. I can't do anything."

Raven presses his lips together and nods. "Okay. I can see it in your memories."

"What's wrong with us?" I ask.

"We're all special, all of us from Phoenix. We all have something that makes us... different."

Raven stands and takes my hands, pulling me to my feet.

We're all different? Not just Raven. "Like what?" I ask.

"Astrid can feel other's emotions. That's why she's always crying and upset. She's too young to filter through it all. But Cash, you know how she's always calm around him?"

I nod yes. He's always been able to soothe her.

"He blocks it, he shields her. And Marcus has strength like no one else. He holds back, though. He's still learning. We all are."

"And Isaac?"

Raven's eyes turn fierce. "Pure violence. Like a watchdog, but he's too unpredictable."

"Raven." My knees feel weak as my world has turned upside down. "What are you all?"

"You're like us too. Just wait, Lina. It will come."

I shake my head no. "I'm not..."

He shakes his head. He doesn't believe me. But I don't know what to believe anymore. He's been like this his entire life while the others are just discovering it. "I think... it's something like the last bits of humanity. Sectioned out and preserved. Now that Mom altered the Residents to be so cooperative, we've gained what they've lost."

"But how?"

"I'm not sure. You know how we've always been around the nuclear power plants? Maybe it mutated us. The radiation exposure. Something with that. I think that's the key to explaining why we are like this."

"How do you know all of this, Raven?"

"I can read minds, remember?"

"Everyone's?" I ask.

"Everyone's."

"Even..." My thoughts turn to the one man our mother has been trying to keep us from our entire lives.

"Even Crane's. He just doesn't know it. He thinks I'm messed up, a failed experiment, tried to have me tossed out of the Phoenix District. And Ms. Jones was trying for the same here."

"That's why you don't speak."

He shakes his head. "It's too hard with all the voices and thoughts from everywhere. I didn't want to mess up a conversation with details someone never told me. Then they'd know."

"Okay." A hard shiver runs through me. "This is messed up."

Raven takes my hand and starts marching me down the hallway, away from Joe's blood smeared across the floor. "We need to pack our things."

"Why?" I ask him. "We're not leaving, are we? I've been out there, with the Survivors. I don't think we can do it alone."

"No. We aren't going out there. Mr. Crossbender is sending us away."

I tug my arm back and make him stop. "Wait, away?" I ask. "Where are we going?"

"We have to get the others. Astrid, Cash." He stops to give me a sidelong glance. "And Marcus."

I haven't seen Marcus in days. I miss him but the look Raven just gave me signals that he knows there is more going on between us. "You know?"

"For years, before you even knew yourself. There's no denying it, Lina. You and him."

"Okay." I knew it, I've always known it.

"I know where Isaac's going," Raven continues. "We'll get him back. But first we need to pack."

"Pack for what?"

"We're going home. We need to go. Now."

Raven takes my hand back and starts running. I follow him through endless tunnels until I see the elevator that will bring us to our living quarters in front of us. Well, their living quarters. I haven't seen the place in months. We run toward the elevator and just as we reach it, the door opens and Mr. Crossbender is standing inside, ushering us in.

Remembering all that Mr. Crossbender put me through these past few weeks, I stop running, I don't trust him.

Raven tugs on my hand. "He had to do it, Lina. He had to get you ready, don't be mad at him for it."

Since Raven doesn't hesitate, I follow. Mr. Crossbender presses the button to bring us to the top level before turning to face us. "We have to get you all out of here," he says.

Raven squeezes my hand. I'm going to guess he's back to not talking again.

Mr. Crossbender runs a hand through his hair and pushes his glasses up on his nose. "Joe's friends have already started telling people what Isaac did. Trouble's brewing. I've barely had a hold on these Sovereign all this time."

"But you run this place. Won't they listen to you?" I ask.

"No. They've been waiting for a reason to force you all out. Especially since your parents left." He blows out a frustrated breath just as the elevator doors open on our level. "I should have let Maryam take you all to the lower levels. It would have been safer."

We leave the elevator and run for the door to the living quarters. There are no Guardians wandering the hallways like there usually are.

"Where are all of our Guardians?" I ask.

"Someone's been killing them," Mr. Crossbender replies, frowning. "I thought it was Isaac until I started following them on the District cameras. It was Joe."

Raven opens the door and we step inside. There are backpacks in the middle of the floor. Marcus is packing supplies, clothes and food like we had when we escaped. Mr. Crossbender walks toward him. "Good, Marcus. Did you get everything?"

"Almost." Marcus nods.

"Everything?"

"I didn't make it to the weapons hold."

"Oh, that's not good." Mr. Crossbender glances between all of us. "Oh well, too late now. You'll make do."

Looking around the room, I take it all in. Marcus is packing bags with a clear focus. Cash is entering and exiting the bedrooms collecting clothes and a few blankets. Raven starts helping them.

"Oh, Lina, you're back!" Astrid comes running at me and throws her arms around my waist. "I missed you so much."

"I missed you too." I hug her back and realize she's grown. Astrid shivers in my arms and she is no longer the sensitive little girl I left months ago when I decided to escape. Somewhere in that time she became a teenager; she's taller, her hair has grown out to her shoulders and her body has filled out. We are no longer children, waiting for our parents to come home. We are grown, orphans, and now we're being sent away in an effort to save us from the wrath of the Hanford Sovereign.

Astrid makes a small noise in her throat and when I look down, I see her eyes have a watery shimmer. "He can talk," she whispers to me. They must know everything that Raven has just told me.

"I know," I say.

"Astrid," Cash calls her from across the room. "Come here, I need your help."

She moves away from me and Cash gives me an understanding look and a nod.

Raven stands and moves toward the front door. He listens for a moment before turning to us all. "They're coming," he warns.

"Let's go," Mr. Crossbender says. "Now!"

Marcus hands out the packs, keeping the biggest for himself.

We run out of the living quarters and down the hall, toward the elevator.

"No. Not that, over here." Mr. Crossbender leads us away and down another hallway. He pushes open the door at the end of it, revealing stairs. "Down."

Astrid and Cash go first. When they descend the first step, I notice that Cash has her hand held tightly in his. Raven goes next and then Marcus, who stops and turns to me.

"Come on, Lina."

"Go." Mr. Crossbender motions for us to move.

We start making our way down the stairs, Mr. Crossbender following us the entire way. They seem to extend forever, deeper and deeper we run.

"How far do we go?" Cash shouts from ahead of us.

"Until they end!" Mr. Crossbender shouts back.

We run down until my sides start to ache and I am reminded of what Joe did to me before Isaac killed him. I start to slow, unable to help it.

"What's wrong?" Marcus asks.

I shake my head and try to catch my breath.

"She's injured," Mr. Crossbender motions to my abdomen. "Saw it on the camera feed."

"Where?" Marcus's voice sounds like a growl.

"I'm fine," I try to shove him away but he grabs the hem of my shirt and pulls it up. Both of them suck in a breath. Looking down, I see why: there are deep purple bruises on both sides of my stomach. My leg aches where Joe kicked me but I don't show him that.

"It's a good thing Isaac killed the bastard." Marcus drops my shirt. "If he hadn't, I would."

"I don't think we have time for this." The sounds of the other three are getting further and further away. "We need to catch up with the others," I say, ignoring the pain.

We start moving again until we catch up to Raven, Astrid, and Cash. The stairway has ended and there is only a door in front of us now.

Mr. Crossbender pauses to catch his breath before he says, "You're all going back to Phoenix. You can't stay here. Your mother would kill me if I sent you anywhere else."

"She's dead," I remind him.

Before he can respond the door opens and an oppressive heat floods the stairwell. Across the threshold there is a group of people and they're all dressed in green like the Orderly faction. Beyond them, the space looks cavernous and dimly lit.

A woman steps forward and I recognize her immediately.

"George, love, I knew you'd see it my way," Mrs. Crossbender says as she holds her arms out, welcoming us.

"Maryam, sweetheart," Mr. Crossbender replies as he ushers us out of the stairwell. "I'm trusting you with their care."

Mrs. Crossbender smiles sweetly. "Of course you are, dear. My people will see them home safely."

"Good. Goodbye, kids." Mr. Crossbender turns and leaves through the door to the stairwell.

FIFTEEN

CATALINA

A COLD CHILL FILLS ME AS WE CLUSTER TOGETHER AND THE people dressed in green surround us.

"Welcome to the Underland, children." Mrs. Crossbender smiles. "I've been trying to get you all down here for quite some time. And look, we finally have all of you. It's just too bad I have to let you all go so soon."

The people watch us and a blonde woman steps forward, her hand gripping a young man's shirt, tugging him along with her. It's Isaac; the blood has been cleaned off his hands. She shoves him toward us and Isaac moves to my side. It takes me a moment to recognize the blonde as the woman who was standing next to Adam when he first came here to ask me where my mother was.

Mrs. Crossbender takes a leisurely walk around the group of us. "All of you are finally here. Sensitive Astrid. Strong Marcus. Cashel the shield. Isaac the rogue. Lina, just like your mother, you can do so much more than memorize maps. Bet you didn't know that we knew that about you, did you?" She smiles. "And Raven..." She reaches out to touch him but he steps back. "When are you going to reveal yourself, Raven? We've been dying to find out what you can do."

Glancing around us, the people look welcoming but wary, much more welcoming than the Hanford people were to us.

"Come, children. We must have a discussion before you leave." Mrs. Crossbender waves a hand at the blonde woman and the crowd surrounding us parts.

We follow Mrs. Crossbender through the room, a giant cavern. There are windows and stairwells carved into the rocky walls that look like living quarters. On the main floor where we're standing there are tents set up, with tables resembling shops like Marcus and I saw at the settlement of Survivors. We cross the open space until we reach the far wall and Mrs. Crossbender opens a door. We file through and follow her down another set of stairs. It's hot down here, so hot I can feel sweat trickle down my back. Pushing open another door, we enter a room where all the furniture is burnt orange and dull green. There's even shaggy carpet and white and gold walls. When I glance at Marcus he winces at the décor as though it burns his eyes.

"What is this place?" I ask.

"My office," Mrs. Crossbender replies. Two men look up from their seats near another door and I'm surprised to see that they are wearing Volker uniforms. "Hello, boys. Just have a few to debrief here." She opens another door and leads us into a spacious office. "Close the door behind us, Jenn."

Turning to see who she's talking to, the blonde woman who brought Isaac to us closes the office door.

Mrs. Crossbender sits behind her desk, tapping her fingers for a moment before saying, "You were a very bad boy, Isaac. Very bad."

His entire body tenses as he stands next to me, I reach out a hand to soothe him.

"Mr. Crossbender said you were going to help us get back to Phoenix," Marcus finally says.

"Yes. I will." She smiles. "But first you need an education."

"A what?" Marcus looks like he's ready to snap.

"Don't," Mrs. Crossbender warns. "Sweet George didn't send you all down here to bust the place up. I just thought you should know what you're getting into. Thought you might like to know what your mother's been up to since she left you all behind."

"Our mother is dead," I say as I step next to Marcus.

Mrs. Crossbender's eyebrows rise. "You still think she's dead? You didn't see her when you escaped and traipsed across the countryside?" She tips her head, waiting for me to reply but I have no idea what she's talking about. "Well then. Let's watch." Focusing on her computer screen, Mrs. Crossbender taps a few keys before turning the screen to face us.

I recognize the hallway near our living quarters at Hanford, and the small woman on the screen who's speaking intently to Isaac, it's my mother. She looks younger than I remember, her hair longer than ever. After Isaac walks away, she enters the living quarters. Raven enters a short time later, followed by me. And then she leaves, alone.

Marcus turns to look at me.

"I don't remember that," I say. "I don't remember ever seeing her here after she left to get my Uncle Sam."

"You wouldn't," Mrs. Crossbender says. "Your mother has a special power also. Hers is a bit less organic, like all of yours. But, she has it nonetheless."

The image flickers and now the screen shows me and Marcus standing in line at the Survivor settlement. The crowd around us parts and Adam walks through with our mother standing at his side. I watch the replay on the screen as I turn and see her, she runs and I start to go after her but Marcus stops me. And then Adam drags us off. As we're inside she shows up again, standing outside the door. No one seems to notice she's there. The screen flickers to when Adam stopped to get gas and I can see my mother standing in the tree line, waiting.

"How did I never see her?" I ask. "Not once."

"Don't be alarmed, Catalina. That's what your mother can do. Influence you to see something else, make herself invisible, make you do things you wouldn't otherwise do."

"How did you get video of us out there?" Marcus asks.

"You know very well that Crystal River has satellite capabilities. Of all they've taught you in the ARU, I'd think you'd remember that. Sometimes they share." Mrs. Crossbender leans back in her chair looking satisfied with herself, and then she seems to become bored with looking at us. "Jenn will show you the way to Phoenix. Listen to her directions carefully."

We head for the door, each and every one of us eager to leave.

She says one last thing before the door shuts behind us. "Go, children. Run to your mother. I can guarantee that none of you are going to like what she's become." She says it quite proudly.

We follow Jenn out of the office, through the room where the two Volker sit, up the small flight of stairs, and back into the cavernous room. She turns to the left and, being this close to the wall, I can see that there truly are stairwells carved into the stone. There are doorways also, some with actual doors, others with curtains, and some with the flickering of candlelight inside. I notice a candle resting on a metal plate that's been secured into the rock wall. It all looks a bit primitive.

Jenn stops and waits until we cluster around her.

"So, I'm Jenn. That probably doesn't matter 'cause you're all leaving. What you don't know is that the Underland has been building tunnels under this country for over a century."

"How did we not know?" Isaac asks.

Jenn's eyes settle on him and seem to light up. "For decades the U.S. Presidents have had safety bunkers in case of an emergency. One of them was smart enough to expand in case there was a national emergency, so they could collect the most valuable people and tuck them away safely."

"Like the Reformation?" Marcus asks, his voice flat.

Jenn tips a finger at him. "Right-o, manchild."

"So it's complete then? This Underland?" Cash asks.

"We're still digging. Even as we speak there are crews out there expanding," Jenn replies. "We've reached every one of the Districts, we have access to them all. And more," she adds with a sly smile.

"Why?" Marcus asks.

Jenn raises a thin, blonde eyebrow as she says, "The Reformation is not complete."

The rest of us are silent, no doubt remembering what we've already lived through. We've had it mild compared to most, but that still doesn't make it any less traumatic.

"Okay," Jenn starts. "I bet the Sovereign upstairs are boiling, and since shit rolls downhill you kids need to get out of here. They'll be searching every corner of Hanford for you all and one of them is bound to find the stairwell. If they do, you don't want to be around for that." Jenn presses her hand against a large metal door that's secured into the rocky wall of the cavern. "So, this is your escape route. There will be safehouses every few hundred miles." She points her fingers at me and Marcus. "Except for that one you two got blown up."

"Why is that our fault?" I ask. "We didn't blow it up."

"The Swamp people were following you. Never lead a monster to your safehouse. If they found us under here, we'd all be dead. Eaten alive. They consume without regard."

A whimper comes from Astrid; Cash pulls her close, wrapping his arm tight around her.

Jenn continues, "The safehouses will be notified that you're on your way. They're manned by Defectors and Transplants. Don't trust them longer than you can throw them. If the trapdoor is closed, move on. You should have enough supplies to last you a few weeks at least. If you go above ground don't leave the safehouses. Any of you. This is for your own safety. You walk the route to the Phoenix District, you stay there and you wait for contact."

"There's no faster way?" Cash asks. "Can't we take a helicopter?"

Jenn smacks her palm to her forehead. "Oh, yeah, why didn't I think of that? How about all you kids pile into a helicopter that's manned by a *Hanford Sovereign*, and your freakishly tall for his age brother over here, *who just killed one of their kids,* can go with you. Right now they're scraping his body from the bottom of the Hanford divide. You know how many murders Hanford has had? Zero. Marcus knows the motto well, District or Die. Although, the ARU brainwash didn't work as well on him. You," she jabs her fingers at all of us, "violated their District. You killed one of their children, the precious next generation of Sovereign. You die. No matter what Mr. Crossbender says to them, they will hunt you down. It's ingrained in their being."

"They would have killed Lina," Isaac says, crossing his arms and straightening his back. He does look freakishly tall for his age.

"See," Jenn points a finger at him, "District or Die. You have your own alliances. They have theirs."

"And the Defectors and Transplants?" Marcus asks. "What about them, where is their alliance?"

"They could give a crap about the Districts," she replies with a bored tone. "I'd suggest getting out of here before Big Bad Burton Crane shows up to put the Hanford Sovereign back in their place. Pretty sure you kids caused a riot up there." She pulls open a heavy metal door, revealing a tunnel that's been carved out of the earth, and waves us inside. "This one will bring you straight to Phoenix."

"All this time you've had a direct route to Phoenix?" I ask.

She smiles. "Of course. But why would we tell anyone about it?"

No one seems to know what to say, and after we've all stood there for a moment, Marcus takes my arm and steps forward. "Come on, let's get moving."

Not knowing what else to say to Jenn, we start down the dimly lit passage.

"Safe travels, children," Jenn's voice echoes into the tunnel. "Oh, has anyone ever told you, Isaac, you look *exactly* like your father."

"What?" Isaac asks, but it's too late, the door slams and a loud click echoes through the tunnel as it's locked.

"She knew our father." Isaac's eyes meet mine. "He was down here?"

"She's messing with us," I warn him. "We better get moving. This is going to take a long time."

Sixteen

Catalina

THE TUNNEL IS LARGE, WIDE ENOUGH FOR US TO WALK FOUR across and tall enough that none of the boys can touch the ceiling. We walk forever, sweat trickling down our backs, until Raven finally stops to take off his shirt and roll up his pants. Cash does the same. When the pain in my side becomes too strong to ignore, I drop my pack to the ground and bend to roll my pant legs up, then I take off my outer shirt, leaving me in just a tank top.

As I'm packing my shirt into my bag, Marcus walks up to me, eyeing the red mark on my shin where Joe kicked me, and asks, "How are the bruises?"

"Fine." I lie.

I don't want to lie, I shouldn't lie. But I don't want him to worry about me.

"Not fine." He holds out his hand. "Give me your pack."

Ignoring him, I start to pull the pack on but Marcus takes it out of my hands.

"I can carry my own pack, Mark. I'm not weak." I've said these words to him before.

His lip tips up and I know it's because I called him Mark. "I know you're not weak. You're injured." He shoulders my bag as if it weighs nothing.

"I look weak to them." I motion toward Raven, Astrid, and Cash. "And it's not fair, me not pulling my own weight."

"They don't care, Lina." He takes my hand. "Can you walk?"

I like it when he touches me; he's warm, comforting.

"Yes. I don't need you to carry me or anything."

A broad smile covers his face. "I could carry you, if you want me to." He leans down and whispers in my ear. "I never let the Swamp men touch you while we were out there. I carried you the entire time."

Heat coats my body. "I'm fine." Reluctantly, I let go of his hand and start walking a little faster to catch up with the others.

"How long is this going to take?" Astrid asks.

"Weeks," Cash replies.

"We are going to be underground for weeks?" Her voice sounds shaky.

Cash settles a hand on her shoulder. "Just think Ash. The less people that are around, the less you have to feel them."

Astrid looks at all of us with wide eyes.

"They all know," Raven says. "There are no secrets between us. Not that you guys could ever keep them from me, but at least you know about it now."

"Who knows that you can actually talk?" Cash asks.

"Only you guys and Mr. Crossbender."

"Not even your mother?"

Raven shakes his head.

"Will Crossbender tell anyone?" I ask.

"No, he won't even tell his wife," Raven says. "We can trust him."

We walk in silence for a while.

"What about Ira and Lex?" Marcus asks. "We haven't seen them in years. What if they're like..." He tips his head toward Isaac and makes a face of concern.

"I saw that," Isaac growls.

"We'll find out when we see them next," Raven replies. "I couldn't gather what they can do. But they are expected to be like us."

Remembering what Mr. Crossbender told me about the other eight children he's been searching for, I find it hard to control the shiver that runs up my spine. Raven's gaze snaps to mine. If he didn't know about them before, I'm guessing he does now. I try to change the subject, since I don't think I can handle any more crazy talk right now. But it's hard, and I wind up saying the only thing I can think about right now.

"I'm not really special like you guys are though," I say. "They say I'm like Mom, but..."

"No," Raven shakes his head, "you're not like Mom. There's more to you, we just have to figure it out."

"But Mr. Crossbender locked me in a room until I could show him that I could do what she can. I lied to them, but what if it's still true?"

Raven stops walking and turns toward me. "You are nothing like her. Remember that." He grabs my shoulder and stares into my eyes. "Next time you see her, you remember that, Lina. You're not like her. You have to promise me that you'll remember that." He squeezes my shoulder.

"Okay." I nod and something inside me wilts. Maybe Mrs. Crossbender was right, maybe we won't like what she's become. Raven should know, he probably read her mind when she visited us.

"She's good with the maps," Marcus speaks up. "Maybe she has an innate sense of direction, like a shark or a bird or something."

"Shut up, Mark. That sounds stupid." Of all the things I could do.

The others seem to consider it as they walk. Distancing myself from the group, I slow my pace and hang back. My emotions are all over the place and I don't want to impact the others with the way I feel.

"Why did it take so long for us to find out about these special powers we have?" Astrid asks.

"From what I've noticed with you guys, it seems they come out in high stress situations," Raven says. "Astrid, yours started when we moved. Cash's started right after yours."

"When did mine start?" Marcus asks.

"When Lina ran away and you went after her." Raven gives him a look. "But you already knew that, Marcus."

"When did yours start?" Cash chuckles. "I mean, what high stress situation did you undergo as a baby?"

"Birth," Raven deadpans.

WE WALK until our feet are sore and we have no idea what time it is or what day it is. We sleep when we're all tired, and in an effort to conserve what little food we have, we wait until we're all starving before eating. The heat of the tunnel is incessant and all of us have cut our pants off at the knee and the sleeves off our shirts. It doesn't help, our sweat never dries. Sleeping in the tunnel is also uncomfortable. The dim lights are always on, so it never truly gets dark. We lay on top of our blankets, praying for a breeze that never comes.

When we all wake and pack our things up, we start walking again. A week could have passed by now, none of us are sure, all we really know is that we had enough water to last a few days and it's been gone for a while now. Eventually we come to a ladder that's secured into the wall. It rises up and up and up, a vertical tunnel carved around it. Next to the ladder is a small box with a speaker.

"What should we do?" I ask.

Isaac reaches forward and pushes the button.

"Wait! What if–" I start.

"Phoenix kids?" The voice that comes through the speaker asks.

We all stare at each other.

"Hello..." the speaker crackles again.

"Yes!" Astrid shouts. She turns to us with a sheepish look on her face. "Sorry, I'm just really thirsty."

The speaker crackles and the voice says, "Come up then. Leave your packs, it's a long climb."

We start shrugging off our packs and leaving them on the ground next to the ladder.

"Who goes first?" Raven asks.

"I'll go," Isaac offers and starts climbing.

Astrid goes next, followed by Cash, then Raven, then me, and Marcus is last.

The ladder is metal, cool to the touch and slightly rusted. We climb in silence until Raven shouts down, "Marcus, that's my sister whose *glorious ass* you're staring at. Control your thoughts, for God's sake, man!"

Oh my God! I stop and kick a foot out at Marcus, threatening him. My face flames red and I'm glad no one can see me.

"It's not my fault he can't keep his mind reading to himself," Marcus mutters.

When we finally reach the top, Isaac climbs out of the open trapdoor, motioning for us to wait.

His face appears over the tunnel after a few moments.

"It's safe," he says as he helps Astrid climb out.

I follow, my eyes immediately drawn to the windows surrounding us and the sunlight. I stand and move toward the brightness.

"Wouldn't get too close to them, girl," A strange voice breaks through the room. "Someone might see."

Turning, I find a man standing against the far wall with a rifle in his hand. His clothing is well-worn but clean, he looks to be middle-aged, especially with his balding head. Marcus and Isaac move in front of me and Astrid, as they try to figure out if he's a danger.

"He's not going to hurt us," Raven whispers so only we can hear him.

We all relax after that.

"You kids looking pretty pale, like you haven't seen the sun in weeks." The man snickers to himself like he just told some hilarious joke.

"We haven't," I say.

He straightens, a smile still curving his lips. "Slow walkers you all are. Got word you were on your way long time ago. Well," he pushes himself away from the wall and walks toward a doorway, "kitchen's this way. Bet you're all hungry and thirsty. You can get cleaned up after. Smell pretty ripe after being down in those blasted tunnels for so long."

We finish off two pitchers of water before a pot of stew is set on the table. We take our cues from Raven as he takes the first bite of the stew, then signals it's safe with the nod of his head. When the man tells us we can go upstairs to use the bathroom and sleep in the real beds, Raven is the first to go, and we follow.

"There's a package up there for you all," the man shouts up to us. "Been waiting here for a while now."

We find the brown paper wrapped package in one of the bedrooms. I rip it open and find clean clothes for all of us, and freeze-dried rations to replace the ones we've already consumed. We divide up the clothing. It's ARU gear like Marcus brought me when I escaped. All of it is black and lightweight.

"Who's showering first?" Astrid asks, as she combs her fingers through her short brown hair.

"We should stay in pairs, at least," Marcus offers. "Just in case."

"Okay, then, ladies first." I cross the room. "Come on Astrid. You and me."

The bathroom looks like it was fancy at one time. Someone had spent a lot of time on the tile and the shell-decorated wallpaper. Now the tiles are cracked and the wall paper peeling. Astrid starts the shower and gets in. I search the linen closet and pull out a stack of towels before waiting my turn.

"There are five more people, Astrid," I remind her. "Make it quick."

"I know. I know." I hear the sounds of soap lathering and she asks, "How much longer do you think we have before we make it home?"

Home. We haven't been home in so long. The thought of returning to the Pasture fills me with warmth and sadness; I suspect it will never be the same as it was when we were kids.

"I feel that way about it too," Astrid says with a soft voice.

This is her, sensing my emotions. "I miss it. For a long time, I've missed it."

"Me too." The water shuts off and her pale arm reaches out. I hand her a towel.

"We still have a long way to go," I say. "More weeks."

Astrid sighs as she pulls the shower curtain to the side and steps out.

"Do you remember where you're from?" I ask Astrid as I strip off my dirty clothes and get in the shower.

"I don't remember much about it. Just that it was always cold. Even in the summer." Clothes rustle as she gets dressed.

I start the water and rinse the dried sweat from my body. "Hm." I think of all the places that could be like that. "Cold like Alaska or cold like the mountains?"

"I'm not sure. I was really young. Don't even remember my parents."

I soap myself up quick and do the best I can with the trickle of water washing my long hair.

"Are you originally from Phoenix?" Astrid asks.

"Yeah."

"Why haven't we ever talked about this stuff before?"

Rinsing the soap out of my hair and shutting the water off, I say, "I don't know. I guess it's just never come up. We've all been so busy with everything else; I just assumed you guys were all from Phoenix."

"Oh."

I reach my hand outside of the curtain and Astrid hands me a towel. While drying off, I ask her, "So Cash helps?"

"Yeah. I don't know how I never noticed before. But, I've always felt better around him. You know, when he'd touch me. I just don't know why we're like this. Sometimes in Hanford, in the lunchroom, it was so hard, Lina. I thought I was going to explode from the inside out. They all hated us so much and we never did a thing to them."

Wrapping the towel around my body, I step out of the shower to find her sitting on the floor, her eyes watery.

"I don't know why they were like that." I start getting dressed and wrap my hair up in the towel.

"The strangest thing is," she sniffles, "when your mom was around they were all so calm. It was when she left that they all changed. I didn't really feel it until they left us." Her voice cracks.

There's a loud knock on the door and Cash's voice, "Ash, are you okay in there?"

"I'm fine!" she shouts back.

The floor creaks as Cash paces in front of the door.

"He's really into this whole shielding you thing, isn't he?" I ask as I squeeze the rest of the water out of my hair and twist it up into a bun.

Astrid shrugs. "He's sweet, you know. It's like he always wants to be there now, to protect me. But at times it's overkill. He can't protect me all the time. Sometimes I'm just going to have to deal with it so he can live his own life." She looks away from me, toward the door. "I mean, he can't drag me around with him forever. Someday he's going to find a girl he likes..." she trails off, her lips pressing together so hard they turn white.

"You like him?" I ask with a whisper.

Astrid looks up at me, her eyes larger than ever. "I'm like a sister to him. That's all."

"Ash..." I think she likes him, the same way I like Marcus.

She shakes her head and rolls her shoulders before standing. "Are you done? I'm sure the boys want to clean the stink off themselves. They all smell really bad."

"You should have smelled me and Marcus when we escaped. You've never smelled stink like Swamp people stink."

Astrid pulls open the door and Cash turns, his gaze focused on her. "I'm fine," she waves him away. "Go get cleaned up. I'm going to take a nap in a real bed."

The boys decide to use the bathroom one at a time, each waiting in the hallway for their turn. Astrid and I head for the bedroom at the end of the hall. She pushes open the door and inside there are two large beds on each side of the spacious room.

"This is amazing," Astrid flops down on one, her short arms and legs not quite reaching the edges of the mattress. "This is way more comfortable than that tunnel."

"And cooler," I add as I lay back on the other bed.

"Lina?" she asks after a moment of silence.

"Yeah?"

"Will you tell me what it was like outside of Hanford, when you and Marcus escaped?"

"Sure, what do you want to know?"

"Was it scary?"

"A little bit. I mean... I don't remember all of it. I got bit by a snake after Marcus found me and I wasn't awake for a lot of the trip. The Swamp people saved me."

"It's kind of romantic, Marcus going after you and all. Keeping you safe in the face of danger."

"Sure." I giggle, remembering how I thought he was going to kill me.

"I remember the Swamp people. They looked so scary the first time we saw them. I was sure they'd hurt us back then."

"They are pretty scary."

"But they saved you, so they can't be all that bad, right?"

"I don't know, Ash, everyone else seems to be petrified of them."

"So why did they save you?"

"I have no idea."

Not wanting to frighten Astrid with stories of our time with the Swamp people, I tell her what it was like after Marcus first found me. I tell her about walking through the forests that were alive with the sounds of birds chirping. We saw rabbits and deer, just like we used to see on the Pasture. I tell her about the beans that Raven and I found in the open field, and how they tasted just like home. I tell her about sleeping under the stars, arguing with Marcus about which direction to go in, and bathing in the cool stream. When I'm done, I prop myself up on my elbows and find that Astrid is curled in the fetal position and fast asleep in the other bed.

Marcus is standing in the doorway, leaning against the frame, smiling and watching me.

"What?" I ask him.

"Sounds like you had a grand old time escaping from Hanford."

I make a face and shrug. Some of it was a little bit fun.

"That's not how I remember it," Marcus says as he steps into the room.

"How do you remember it?" I ask, sitting up.

"I remember being terribly and utterly petrified that I was going to lose you forever and when your Uncle Sam found out, he was going to kick my ass."

"But you didn't."

He steps toward me, and I scoot back on the bed as he crawls across it, looking like a panther stalking its prey. "I didn't," he replies, stopping with his face just an inch from mine. "But..." His eyes graze down the length of me. "I think I just figured out what your superpower is, besides looking hot in ARU gear."

"Oh yeah? What?"

"Storytelling."

A soft laugh escapes my lips but Marcus silences me with a kiss. He pushes me back until I'm laying down and I suddenly wish that we could close every space where our bodies aren't already touching. My body feels hot, and as my hands move up Marcus's arms, I feel his is too. I press my fingers into his hair, my heartbeat racing as he kisses me senseless. It all stops when someone clears their throat loudly and Marcus pulls away, looking disappointed.

Cash is standing in the doorway. "Gross, dudes. I'd say get a room, but it looks like we're sharing." He tips his head toward where Astrid is sleeping.

Marcus just laughs quietly as he settles down next to me and pulls me against him. With the heat in the tunnel, I couldn't stand being touched but now it's nice feeling him against my skin. Within minutes I am asleep.

I wake to the feeling of Marcus suddenly shifting away from me, the movement chilling me to my bones. Rolling over, I sit up and find our host knocking on the bedroom door.

"What's wrong?" Marcus asks.

"Time for you kids to get moving again," he says.

"What's going on?" Cash asks, and I notice he's getting up from the bed that Astrid is sleeping in.

"Nothing I can't handle, but you kids can't be here any longer." He waves, motioning for us to get moving.

Cash wakes Astrid and I stand to find Isaac and Raven already awake and waiting in the hallway. Isaac has the bag with our rations slung over his shoulder; they wait as we make our way out of the room, walking down the stairs with us.

When we get to the ground level, the man already has the trapdoor open and he's lowering a rope down.

"Water jugs," he says as he stands. "Figured this would be easier than carrying it down."

"How much is there?" Cash asks.

"Enough to last you all until you get to the next stop," the man replies as he drops the rope down the tunnel. Stepping away from the hatch, he says, "Down you go, kids."

Isaac goes first, followed by Cash, who pauses before climbing down, to say, "Thanks, Mr... Wait, what's your name?"

"You don't need to know." The man leans back to look out the window. "Safe travels and all that. Don't take this personal, but I hope I never see you bunch again in these parts. Something's wrong with you all."

Isaac starts climbing first and as soon as Marcus descends the ladder, the trapdoor above us slams closed, the latch clicking loudly as it's engaged.

"That was strange," Marcus mutters.

"I didn't think we were that weird," I say.

"It was me," Isaac speaks up. "People don't like being around me."

"Or me," Raven adds. "I can read it in all their thoughts; they think I'm strange because I don't talk."

"They like me," Astrid's soft voice echoes as we climb down.

"And me," Cash adds.

"That's 'cause you make them feel all soft and gooey inside with that emotional shielding thing you do," Isaac mocks.

"I have to touch them to make it work," Cash argues back.

Well that explains why he's always touching Astrid.

"People like me," Marcus adds.

"No they don't," Raven says. "That guy thought you looked like a serial killer and the kids at Hanford were afraid of you."

"That guy looked like a serial killer, not me," Marcus adds, scoffing.

I don't think Marcus looks like a serial killer; he has dark features and that boy next door charm. I think he's quite nice to look at.

"Lina," Raven warns.

I stop thinking of what Marcus looks like. Instead, I fill my head with distracting thoughts of the Hanford lunch line.

"Think about that and I'll throw up," Raven says.

"Oh, what was she thinking about?" Marcus asks. "Was she thinking of me with my shirt off?"

Reaching up, I smack the back of his leg.

When we get to the bottom of the ladder, there are six giant jugs of water. The oppressive heat of the tunnel soaks my skin and I am grateful for the lightweight clothing that was sent for us. Somehow it remains cool, wicking the sweat off my body.

We shoulder our packs and start walking.

———

"I THINK CASH LIKES YOU," I tell Astrid.

The boys are walking ahead. Astrid and I lag behind, mostly because I want to talk to her alone.

"I don't think so." She looks at the ground as we walk.

"Why not? He's always around you, always touching you; he even slept next to you back at that safehouse."

"He does it because he feels like he must. I can tell."

"No. You have to know there's more there, Ash. What's wrong?" Reaching out I grab her arm to stop her from walking and make her face me. "Why?"

She shakes her head. "Everyone leaves me, Lina. Everyone. I didn't tell you everything when you asked me if I remembered my parents because I didn't want you to know. I never knew them. Whoever birthed me left me on the steps of an orphanage in the middle of a snowstorm. And then it was foster home to foster home, none of them wanted me because I wouldn't stop crying. Who wants a baby that cries all the time?"

"Oh..."

"You see, Lina. It's only a matter of time before something happens or he finds someone prettier or better than me. And this thing he does, his shielding, he's going to grow to hate it and then he'll hate me. And then he'll leave me, just like everyone else did. It's just easier if I don't let myself think that you all might not go away, because everyone does."

Memories of my parents leaving and the hurt I felt when Mr. Crossbender told us they were dead rush me. Astrid's face twists in pain and I realize I'm still touching her, probably making it worse, she can feel every emotion that's running through my body.

"Ash!" Suddenly Cash is running toward us. "Stop, Lina, you're hurting her," he says, slapping my hand away from her and settling his own hands on her cheeks.

"I'm fine," Astrid says.

"You're not," Cash argues as he looks into her eyes and seems annoyed.

Backing away, I say, "I'm sorry, I didn't mean it."

"Go, Lina," Cash says. "Catch up with the others. I'll take care of her."

Astrid's eyes are on mine as she softly says, "I told you."

Leaving them alone, I walk away and catch up to the others who have stopped and are watching us.

"Don't push her," Raven warns me as I get closer.

Marcus shifts the weight of the water jugs. "What's going on?" he asks.

Isaac has walked so far ahead of us that I can barely see him any longer.

"Don't worry about it," I say, walking ahead, Astrid's words echoing in my ears. Part of me knows she's right, so right it scares me. We are not safe, we've never been safe, and I think about living my life without Marcus or Raven or any of them by my side, and it hurts. I can't really imagine a life without them all. Losing my parents was hard enough, to lose them... I try not to think about it any longer, I just walk faster.

A long time has passed before I finally slow and the others catch up to me. I still haven't caught up to Isaac, he's walking too fast, keeping his distance from us. A while ago the tunnel curved and I haven't seen Isaac since.

"We should break for water," Marcus offers.

All of us stop.

"You guys want to eat too," Isaac's voice rings out and scares the crap out of me, mostly because I didn't see him anywhere. He steps out from a small alcove that's cut out of the tunnel. "I'm kind of hungry," he says.

"That was sinister, dude," Cash says. "I think I might have soiled my pants."

Isaac pulls the sack filled with rations off his shoulder and opens it, saying, "You should all be more observant."

"We're in a tunnel," Astrid says. "We can see everything."

Isaac smiles creepily. "You didn't see me."

When my eyes flick to Raven's, I know his worried gaze matches mine.

The next time we climb out of the tunnel, there is a man dressed in worn jeans and a button-down plaid shirt waiting for us.

"Hey, kids," he greets each one of us, helping us climb out of the hole in the floor. "My name's Ted. Welcome."

Being freed of the underground tunnel seems to lift a weight off my shoulders. The heat is incessant, the dim lighting is always on, and the tunnel seems to be laced with tension, especially now that Isaac is back to acting creepy again. It came on fast. He's been disappearing, finding hiding places in the tunnel, coming up behind us when we least expect it. It's become a game to him. But all it reveals to us is how easily someone could surprise us down there.

"Well," Ted starts, "reckon it's 'bout breakfast time now that the sun's up. You kids go get cleaned up and I'll start cooking'."

We follow him to the kitchen, too hungry to care about what we look like. This trek was the longest yet, so long that we ran out of food days ago for each of us to have full meals. We've been sharing ration packs and left the last jug of water miles behind us.

Ted sets a pitcher of water on the table. It doesn't last long.

This safehouse is not an old farmhouse, from what I've seen so far it looks like a mansion. Ted catches me looking out the windows at the surrounding houses.

"It's one of those fancy gated-communities," he scoops another pile of eggs onto Raven's plate. "The other houses are empty, if you're wondering."

"So you have this place all to yourself?" Marcus asks.

"Nope," Ted replies. "Got a team that comes and goes and monitors the perimeter."

"How big is the community?" Marcus asks.

"About thirty acres, twenty-two houses... well, more like mansions compared to where I'm from."

"Where are you from?" Astrid asks.

"None of your business, young lady." Ted waves the spoon at her that he's been using to scrape the eggs out of the pan with.

He piles our plates with bacon, biscuits and gravy, and sweet rolls. There's even apple juice to drink, something I haven't had since I was a little kid. Sometimes I think that the food that we've gotten on this voyage is the only thing keeping us going.

"These are the best eggs I've ever had. How did you cook them?" I ask.

"In bacon fat," Ted replies.

"Bacon fat?"

"Yeah?" Ted's brows rise. "Got a problem with that?"

I shake my head no.

"Don't care what anyone says, if you don't like eggs cooked in bacon fat, you're just not human. No part of you is."

"I like them," Astrid says quietly.

Ted smiles at her before he scrapes the last of the food out of the pans, distributing it onto our plates. After being so hungry for so long, we eat more than we should, not slowing down until Ted finishes washing the pans in the sink.

"You have running water here?" Isaac asks, moving a mouthful of food to his cheek.

"Yep." Ted shuts off the water and places the last pan in a dish drainer before drying his hands on a towel that was lying next to the sink. "Shower works too, if that's what you're wondering. There's a package of supplies. I'm guessing you kids might want to take the next twenty-four hours to clean up and rest, the next safehouse isn't for a long time. You'll be in that tunnel for a while." Ted presses his lips together and nods before saying, "Finish up here and head on upstairs. I'll be getting some supplies ready for the last leg of your trip."

We shower and change before choosing our beds. I'm staring out the window at the sunlit backyard when Marcus settles next to me. Without the heat of the tunnel, I can finally stand being touched. Marcus seems to know this, wrapping his arm around my middle and pulling me close to him, and I fall asleep.

IT's dark when I wake up with the feeling of Marcus's fingers trailing down my arm. I turn to look at him. "What?" I ask.

"Isaac is starting to act creepy again," Marcus whispers. "Like when we were in Hanford."

"I know." Him scaring the crap out of me in the tunnel is still fresh in my mind.

Marcus shakes his head and a worried look covers his face. "No, you don't. I just woke up to find him standing in the middle of the room, staring at us."

My stomach clenches.

Raven walks into the room just then, his dark hair damp and tousled. "I heard you talking," he says, tapping the side of his head.

Marcus sits up next to me. "What should we do about him?"

Ravens sits on the edge of the bed and lowers his voice. "We have to get him out of the tunnel. He's going to hurt one of us if we don't."

"But... can't we do something to help him?" I don't want to lose Isaac, even if he has been exceptionally weird the past week or so. He saved me from getting pummeled by Joe in that hallway in Hanford. And he's my brother, a brother to all of us. We can't leave him behind.

Reading my thoughts just as I'm thinking them, Raven shakes his head. "No, that's an anger and a violence that can't be helped. When he finally gave in and killed Joe, that relieved the pressure, but now it's building in him again, and worse. I agree that we can't leave him behind. We need him."

"What now?" Marcus asks.

"He needs to burn it off." Raven looks around the room. "We need to get him out of the tunnel. Maybe one of us could get him out of this safehouse for a few hours. He could kill a squirrel or something, see if that helps."

"Would he do that?" I ask, thinking it sounds absurd.

Raven nods. "He's done it before, plenty of times."

I've never known of Isaac killing animals. The Guardians at Hanford were the only things that ever went missing like that. "But Mr. Crossbender said Joe was the one killing the Guardians."

"The Guardians weren't Isaac," Raven says.

"What–"

Raven blurts out before I have a chance to ask, "The farm animals."

Oh my. A gasp escapes my lips and my hand moves to cover my heart.

"He didn't do it to hurt us. Elvis didn't tell anyone," Raven continues. "Isaac can barely control it. He can't help it."

"One of us needs to sneak him out of here tonight in hopes that he can find something to kill?" Marcus asks as he shakes his head.

Raven nods.

"And if we get caught?"

"Don't get caught." Raven blinks as though not getting caught is the easiest thing in the world.

"Who's taking him?" I ask.

Marcus stands. "I'll take him."

Worry is a string tethering me to Marcus, afraid that it's going to be snipped and taken away from me like so many others that I've loved; I reach for him, grabbing his wrist. "I don't want you to go."

"There's no one else to take him." Marcus carefully pries my fingers off his arm. "You're sure as hell not going. Raven is too young. And Cash won't let Astrid out of his sight. That leaves me." He runs his hands through his dark hair.

"They'll come back," Raven assures me as I look worriedly between the two of them. Turning to Marcus, Raven stands still for a moment, closing his eyes and tilting his head. "Ted is sleeping. We need to go now."

"You're going too?" I ask Raven.

He nods in agreement as Marcus stands and heads for the door. He stops just before leaving. "I'll be back," he promises.

Raven follows Marcus out of the room. I hear their soft footsteps in the hallway as they collect Isaac and take him downstairs.

There is no more sleeping for me. I lie in the bed, wide awake, waiting for them to return.

WHAT MUST BE HOURS LATER, I finally hear them again. The stairs creak, footsteps stop outside my door before moving down the hall to where Astrid and Cash are sleeping. More footsteps. My door flies open, much louder than Marcus would open it. The doorknob slams against the wall and I sit up straight. Before I can focus my eyes in the bright light from the hall, there are more footsteps, hands on my shoulders pull me to my feet and drag me out of the room. I can hear Cash shouting. Astrid screams and there is a thudding sound. Two men drag me through the hall, push open their bedroom door and shove me through. Cash is on the ground, knocked out cold. Astrid is being held up against the wall while a man runs his hands over her body as she screams, "Don't touch me! Don't touch me!"

Every instinct within my body is screaming at me to fight back, and I do. I drop to the floor like a dead weight. Uncle Sam used to call it the toddler-drop, arms up and knees buckle, throw your weight to the ground like a toddler having a tantrum. It puts me below these men, but it gets their hands off me for a few seconds. As they reach for me, I kick one between the legs and the other in the nose as he bends down to grab me, then I roll away from them. Scrambling to my feet, I run, leap into the air and pounce on the guy that has Astrid. Jumping up on his back I put him in a chokehold.

"Run!" I yell to Astrid as the guy scratches at my arm that's pressed to his neck.

She looks toward the bedroom door, white as a sheet, and shakes her head no. Turning, I see the other two guys getting to their feet. One is cupping his bloody nose, the other his aching man-parts.

"The window," I tell her. "Go out the window!"

Just as she starts moving, the guy I'm holding onto bends forward and flips me off his back. I land on the floor with a crack, my arms inadvertently releasing him, and I'm sure I lose consciousness for a few seconds.

Blinking rapidly, I come to and see Astrid climbing out the window. One of the guys grabs her foot but she kicks him away.

"Let her go," the one with the bloody nose says. "We'll find her later. Better get this one under control." He points at me.

The last I see of Astrid is her shadow in the moonlight as she jumps off the small space of roof below her window.

"Thought you said this would be easy," one of the guys says.

"Didn't know they could fight back," the one closest to me responds. "Frank said he was looking for girls to sell, not wrestlers."

"That little shit has some fight in her." Looking across the room, one guy is rubbing his groin where I kicked him. "Let's show her what it feels like. Knock some sense into her."

"We aren't supposed to damage them... much," the one near me says. "Bad enough we broke in here just on the word of a drunken guard. Gonna pay dearly when Whitmarsh finds out."

In a split second of silence they all look at each other and nod in unison, as though they've come to some silent decision. Then they advance on me, all three of them.

What the heck, Sam and Adam never trained us for three to one scenarios. Even if they did, I'm not sure I'd remember any of it right now. I scramble to my feet and run toward the guy who is holding his bleeding nose. Just as I had hoped, he doesn't expect it. He missteps, giving me enough room to drop to the floor and roll. I grab his ankle and knock him off his feet before I stand again. I don't get far, one of them has ahold of my shirt. Using the last of my strength I run for the door, my arms outstretched as I try to pull myself toward it; away from these men and back to my freedom which I've barely gotten a taste of since leaving Hanford. All those hopes are dashed as a thick set of arms wraps around my legs and pulls me to the ground. My knees hit hard, the breath is knocked out of my chest, my chin hits the pale oak flooring, jarring my brain.

One large hand grips my butt then my hip, rolling me onto my back, another grabs my shirt, yanking it up. "Oh yeah," the guy I kicked in the nuts drawls as he licks his lips. "Frank'll give us a pretty penny for this one. But first, it's payback time." He slaps me across the face so hard I see stars. As my body goes limp from the shock, I feel a warm hand wrap around my bare wrist. I open my eyes and see Cash lying on the floor next to me, blood trickling out of his nose, watching, as he holds onto my arm.

A tingling starts in my arm where his hand is wrapped. It travels throughout my body like a small electric current, warming and calming me until I no longer feel that adrenaline and fear that's kept me fighting for the last few minutes. This must be what he does to Astrid. It feels wonderful. I don't even notice the other men in the room. I barely hear the loud thudding of more footsteps entering the house and running up the stairs. There is shouting, bodies hit the floor but I don't look away from the dark eyes of a boy I've known for most of my life without ever knowing he could do this. Eventually he moves up on his elbows and crawls toward me, his hand never leaving my arm. He adjusts my shirt, tucking it into my pants before making eye contact again.

"Everything's fine," he whispers before releasing my arm.

Blinking, I look up and find Marcus, Isaac and Raven standing over me. Cash moves away, toward Astrid who's standing in the hall.

"Is Astrid okay?" I ask.

Marcus nods, pressing his lips together. "Are you?"

"I'm..." Marcus reaches down and offers a hand, pulling me to my feet. "I'm fine."

"You sure?"

I look around the room, to the lifeless bodies in the corner, the blood on Isaac's hands.

"Lina," Raven warns and I look away.

"Why are dudes always trying to beat you up, Lina?" Isaac asks.

"I... I don't know." I shake my head. "What happened to Ted?" I ask.

"Got hit pretty hard in the head. He's downstairs getting stuff ready for us to go." Raven takes my hand. "I think it's time to leave this place." He leads me out of the room and we walk down the stairs together, finding Ted in the same room we entered this house through.

Ted turns around as we enter the room. "You kids better get out of here." He's carrying a large sack in one hand, the other is pressing a rag to the bloody wound on his head. He holds the bag over the ladder to the tunnel and drops it. "Was warned that you might cause trouble. Just hoped it wasn't so."

"We didn't cause it," I say. "Those men attacked us."

"So you say." Ted removes the rag and fresh blood seeps down the side of his face. "You all being here is what brought it on. Either way, it's time to go."

"What was that?" Marcus asks, motioning to the tunnel where Ted had just dropped the bag down.

"Cold weather gear."

Pushing Marcus aside, I step forward. "What do we need that for? It's a thousand degrees down there."

Ted motions for us to move. "Soon the tunnel is going to get closer to ground level; you're going to lose that heat." His voice drops, sounding like a warning. "The rest of the way to your destination, the tunnel will get colder, darker, and narrower. More dirt, less rock."

"Perfect," Marcus mutters.

I don't like the sound of that. More dirt, less rock. All I can envision are miners and cave-ins and that constant pressure that was always surrounding us as we lived underground at Hanford.

"How much further do we have?" Isaac asks as he wipes his hands on his pants.

"At the pace you've been going," Ted rubs his chin. "Maybe a week."

Isaac starts climbing down the ladder, followed by Raven, then Astrid. I go next, followed by Cash and Marcus. Ted closes the trapdoor and locks it before we've reached the bottom. We continue our descent with only the dim glow of the tunnel below us.

When we reach the bottom, we divide the supplies between our packs and start moving.

"Are you okay?" Marcus asks quietly as he walks by my side.

"Fine." I smooth a hand over my sore cheek. "How did you guys get back in time to stop them?"

"Raven heard Astrid yelling as she was running away from the house. I can't imagine what would have happened if we were any later."

Shrugging my shoulders, I ask, "Did Isaac do what he needed to do?"

"Yeah. He should be good for a while. He took care of those guys too."

"I think we have a problem, though."

Raven turns to face us and slows his pace until the three of us are walking together. "One of those men said that a guard was talking about us. That's how they found out." I pause for a moment, trying to collect my thoughts. "I'm worried that others might know that we're down here. What do we do if they come looking for us?"

"We have weapons," Marcus says.

Raven adds with a quiet voice, "And Isaac."

"Isaac is just a kid," I say.

Raven looks to Marcus for a second. "You didn't see what he did, Lina. Cash made sure of it. What he did to those men who had you on the floor. He may be a kid but..." Raven struggles to find the right words. "He may be a kid but he won't let anything happen to us."

The water containers slosh as Marcus shifts them onto his opposite shoulder. "You sure they didn't hurt you?" His eyes scan my face in the dim light.

A coat of sweat seems to explode all over my body. "I'm fine."

"I don't think you are. They almost–"

"It's nothing," I cut him off. "Being manhandled by a few Survivors who wanted to sell me to the local meat-market is nothing compared to what we've already been through." I wave him away and pick up my pace to walk away.

Truthfully, I don't really want to think about what could have happened if they hadn't shown up when they did. There could have been a whole lot more than groping. I think about Cash's touch, how it made me feel so warm and safe. As we walk, I see his hand on Astrid's wrist. He treats her like some delicate flower, and that's exactly what I've thought of her my entire life also. She's always been so sensitive; it almost makes sense that she can feel the emotions rolling off people. It's a good thing she has Cash to keep her stable.

"You have someone too," Raven's voice breaks my thoughts. "Don't push him away. You're going to need each other."

"I didn't–" I start, but close my mouth. I did push him away. I cut him off and told him I was fine and then ran off, just like my mother used to do to my father. I don't want to be like that with Marcus, I don't want to hurt him. Slowing my pace until I'm walking next to him again, I say, "I'm sorry, Mark. I was really scared before you guys showed up and before Cash touched me. But... I'm just glad you got there in time. And, thanks for saving my life, again."

A small smile tips his lips up at the corners but he doesn't say anything, just shifts the packs he's carrying and stretches his free arm across my shoulders, pulling me against his side. We walk like this for a long time, until I realize that the heat isn't bothering me any longer and the ground beneath our feet has turned into a steep incline.

"I guess this is what Tim was talking about," Cash calls back to us from up ahead.

The tunnel becomes narrower, the lights strung further apart. I thought maybe we had a few days before it started to change. The tunnel floor flattens out eventually. As we walk there are places where the incline is so steep that I wish there were stairs, and then it flattens out again. The temperature drops what feels like thirty degrees. Not wanting to stop, wanting to put space between us and the last safehouse, we push ourselves to keep going long past a time when we should have stopped to rest.

"I think we all need to stop and rest," Raven finally breaks the silence, hours later. "Don't try to argue, I know you're all tired." He looks around. "Here is good."

Dropping my pack to the ground, I stretch my tired muscles and rub my fingers over my sore cheek. Marcus hands me a canteen of water and starts pulling rations out of one of his bags and handing them out to everyone.

We sit with our backs to the walls. Isaac acts relaxed, less creepy. It seems Raven was right. We eat and talk about the rest of the trek we have before us. No one seems thrilled about another week underground. Then we start getting ready for bed, rolling out our blankets and taking off our boots.

With a sigh, Astrid looks up. "I hope there aren't going to be bugs."

Isaac laughs. I shiver with the thought of waking to a spider crawling across my face. Leaning back, I wish she had never mentioned that. Cash touches her and it seems her concern with thoughts of bugs disappears.

I try to get comfortable on my blanket, but it's much colder down here now and eventually I get up to pull another blanket from my pack.

"Lina?" Marcus whispers as I'm covering myself up.

Turning my head, I look at him.

"It's okay, you can sleep." He reaches for my hand, intertwining our fingers and tugging me closer to him. He rests my palm over his heart, where I can feel the steady beating, and closes his eyes.

I lie there for a bit, studying his face, the curve of muscle under his shirt, wondering how he turned from the farmboy who used to tease me into this. Missing the warmth that always seems to radiate off him, I move closer, keeping my hand on his chest. The steady thumping of his heart is relaxing.

"You're staring," Marcus whispers so he doesn't wake the others who seem to have fallen asleep instantly.

"Wasn't."

He squeezes my hand. "You lie."

Marcus doesn't really know how much I lie. I lied to get Mr. Crossbender to think that I could be like my mother. It sits uneasy in my gut, and the thought of not knowing what I can do, that I might be just plain normal and unlike these guys, it worries me.

Eventually, I close my eyes and fall asleep.

Seventeen

A long time ago

Burton Crane had first heard about young Christian Whitmarsh when he returned to Phoenix to bury the last of his family and his secrets, secrets he hoped no one would discover until the right time. After purchasing his own gravesite and paying off the city official to complete his certificate of death, Burton Crane became a ghost.

He went back to his hotel room afterwards to eat a small dinner alone and take a call from Arthur. The experiments were running well, the first line of the genetically engineered dogs which they had decided to name Guardians turned out better than expected. Now was the time for the next step, a step that made Arthur and Andrea uneasy. Burton ignored their complaints; he was going to keep things on track. The next step was coming: human trials. It was already planned; the only thing left was to find the perfect subjects.

Burton packed his small suitcase and glanced at himself in the hotel mirror, straightening his tie and running his fingers through his hair before leaving the room. After months of intense laboratory work his hair was longer than it had ever been, and he made the decision to stop on his way out of town and get it cut. The island had one season and it was hot year-round.

The small salon didn't cater to men, exactly, but Burton usually got his hair cut at salons like this. He didn't care if he made the women uneasy with his awkwardness; they knew best how to cut his curly hair, much better than the barber shops did.

Standing at the counter, a middle-aged woman greeted him and took him to a seat. The place was full, but the woman spoke directly to him, asking about his life and sounding generally interested when he told her a tiny bit about what he used to do at Johns Hopkins.

"I feel like my son should meet you," the woman replied as she worked his hair, clipping and trimming the red curls with scissors.

"Why is that?" Burton asked.

"He's so smart, my Christian, but he wants to go into the military. I keep telling him that we're not doing what we're doing so he can run off and get himself killed. War is coming. It's only a matter of time. Taxes are sky high, they keep cutting our benefits, my husband had to pick up a second job just to make ends meet. I want better for my boy and my daughter. Don't want him going to war and getting killed. He's meant for more than that." The hairdresser's eyes met Burton's in the mirror. "Pulled him out of the local school. He's above average, they were holding him back." She shakes her head and focuses on Burton's hair again. "Tragedy really, I mean how many more kids are they holding back in these small town schools that just don't have the resources anymore? They keep laying off teachers and increasing the class sizes." She shakes her head in disgust.

"I've never thought about it," Burton replied.

"You should. Someday you'll have children of your own; you'll want what's best for them."

The woman set her scissors down and began brushing off Burton's shoulders. She unsnapped the smock that was protecting his clothing and pulled it off him in a way that ensured he did not get covered in small bits of hair.

"I can ring you out at the counter," she told him.

Burton followed her, his mind working the entire time.

"That will be fourteen twenty-seven for the cut."

Burton dug in his pockets and pulled out a twenty dollar bill, remembering the days when he could get his hair cut for fewer than ten dollars.

"Change?" she asked, and he knew she was hoping for a tip.

"Please."

"Just a sec, hon." He watched as she got out a calculator and started punching the buttons. "I'm just so terrible with math and my boss won't get one of those fancy registers that does it for you. Thank heavens for these." She held the calculator up and wiggled it before turning to the register and retrieving his change. "Here you go. Have a nice day."

Burton took his change from the smiling woman, leaving three dollar bills as the tip. The entire way to his car he wondered how that woman could effectively school her son if she couldn't even perform simple math in her head. His mind kept churning, and when he sat in his rented sedan, he never turned the key to start the engine, not until the day came close to an end and he saw the woman who had cut his hair leave the salon and head for her own vehicle. He followed her out of the parking lot, always keeping a safe distance so she wouldn't notice him, and parked a few houses down from the driveway that she pulled into.

A plan was forming in his brain, one that pushed the limits of right and wrong, but Burton Crane was teetering on the edge of those limits already.

He sat in front of the house and formulated a plan, one that his best friend would tell him was wrong, but Burton didn't care. He wasn't going to sit back and watch humanity swirl down the toilet. He had a plan and others on board, and it was time to get started.

JUST A FEW MORE YEARS, was what Burton Crane told himself each morning when he woke up. He had someone watching the boy who, against his mother's wishes, had entered the armed forces. When Crane read in his weekly report that the boy had become a Marine, he couldn't have been happier with his decision.

It was almost two years later when Christian Whitmarsh returned home for the first time. He hadn't seen his parents or sister, only spoken with them on the phone and in letters. Christian never made it to the front door of his childhood home, though. Instead, another man dressed in full military garb knocked on the door and informed Christian's family of his untimely death.

Eighteen

It's maybe two days before we get to the next safehouse. This time the ladder is significantly shorter than the others we've climbed. We used to look forward to getting out of here for a day of freedom from the tunnels. Now we're all hesitant. Now, none of us rushes to push the button and let them know we're here. We stand in a wide circle, staring.

"What should we do?" Isaac asks as he pushes the sleeves of his shirt up to his elbows. He seems antsy. Not the killing type of antsy, the let's do something type of antsy.

"I don't want to go up there," Astrid says.

Cash warily looks in my direction.

"I don't want you to go up there either." Marcus squeezes my hand. "Not after what happened last time."

"Isaac can go," Raven says.

Isaac doesn't reply but a sly smile starts to spread across his face.

"I'll go with you, if you want," Raven offers.

Isaac's smile widens. "You don't need to go, brother." The way Isaac says brother makes me uneasy. "I can handle it." Reaching forward,

Isaac presses the red button that's next to the ladder, signaling that we're here. As his hand grips the ladder, he turns. "Be back in a few." And then he's climbing up.

Marcus waits near the ladder as the rest of us wait on the other side of the tunnel. It's supposed to be so we can run if anyone tries to get down. There doesn't seem to be a problem, though. A few packs of supplies drop on the floor at Marcus's feet, there are voices, then the sound of Isaac climbing down. Jugs of water are slung over his shoulders and Marcus helps Isaac set them down.

When Isaac hops down, the jugs of water sloshing, I notice his knuckles are red, one is split and bleeding.

"What did you do up there?" I ask.

"Nothing." Isaac smiles.

The hatch door above us slams closed.

NINETEEN

CHRISTIAN WHITMARSH/ADAM WATERS

THEN

"WHERE IS MY FAMILY?" the young man with dark hair and blue eyes asked as Burton entered the room. "Where is my sister?"

"She's safe, you'll see her soon."

Burton sat down in front of the young man, admiring. The children couldn't be more ideal. Christian was the perfect specimen, tall and athletic and handsome.

"What happened to my parents?" Christian asks.

"What do you remember?" Burton clasped his hands together in his lap and waited for the young man to speak.

Bright blue eyes scanned the room before they settled on Burton's. "I was walking up the steps to my house, just made it back from..." Christian rubbed his neck. "I think I was injected with something. Then I woke up here. Where is here?" Christian demanded.

"Find out for yourself and look out the window," Burton offered.

Christian stood and made his way to the window. Pride flowed through Crane when the boy's shoulders did not slump in defeat after seeing that they were on an island surrounded by water.

Christian turned, his fists clenching. "What did you do? Where am I? Where is my sister, my family? What do you think you're going to do with us?"

Burton Crane knew enough of psychology to start with the manipulation of the young man. After all, the military had done such a proper job of preparing him for his role. He would start now; he would break him down, build him up, and mold him into perfection.

"Your parents are dead," Burton said.

Christian paled, leaned back against the windowsill. "My sister?"

"She'll be fine, we're watching her, and if you do what is required of you, then you'll get to see her. But no more wasting time, we need to get started."

"With what?"

"Your training."

"YOU'LL HAVE A NEW NAME," Crane told the young man standing in front of him.

"My current name is fine." Christian was still defiant in many ways, which lead to his current position. He was sitting in a room with two chairs and a table, strapped down to one of the chairs since there had been too many instances where he'd turned to violence and tried to escape. Crane couldn't afford to lose any more of his Volker to the young man.

There was a white button in front of Crane. Attached to it were electrical wires which were taped to Christian's arms, legs, and torso. If Crane pressed the button, a charge much like a taser, but stronger, would be delivered to Christian's body. The young man knew this already, he had endured it many times before, during what Crane referred to as *teaching sessions*.

He was teaching Christian to lie until it became believable, until everyone believed him, even himself.

"Your new name will be Adam Waters." Burton Crane smiled. "The first human."

"There are billions of humans. I am not the first," Christian replied and was rewarded with a short jolt of electricity to all the probes attached to his body.

The first time this had happened, Christian yelled, screamed, and threatened Crane with a terrible fate. But this was not the first time, Christian knew that fighting or yelling would only get more depressions of that white button.

When the electricity slowed and Christian's muscles burned from the prolonged contractions caused by the current that was forced throughout his body, the young man raised his head.

"Your name is Adam Waters," Crane repeated, his finger hovering over the button. "Say it."

"My name is Adam Waters." His voice was low, exhausted.

Crane depressed the button and the shock that ran through his body was almost unbearable, he gritted his teeth and prayed that his sister was not suffering the same fate as he was.

"Say it."

"My name is–"

Crane depressed the button.

"Again."

"My–"

"Again."

This continued until Christian Whitmarsh could say his new name with conviction. He was now Adam Waters and the young man became the best liar that Burton Crane had ever seen. He would be the perfect tool to infiltrate Crane's allies, enemies, and whoever else decided to dip their toes into the mix. Crane knew that the best way to maintain control over the rebirth of civilization that he was planning was with whispers, lies, and propaganda.

WHEN ADAM finally saw his sister again he was sitting across from her at a large dinner table. She looked much older than the last time he had seen her and this relayed to Adam that much time had passed with them in Crane's care; he hadn't seen his sister for at least a year or more.

When he called her by the name given by their parents, she just stared at him and blinked, replying with, "Don't call me that any longer. My name is now Blithe Black." It was then that Adam knew his sister had undergone the same training as he had. If his spirit wasn't broken by now, the last bits of it crumbled as he imagined what his little sister had endured and how he had not protected her from it. He would never forgive himself for letting her down. He would never forgive himself for not moving quick enough when he sensed someone was coming up behind him that night he last saw his childhood home. It seemed all his training had lagged in the shadows of excitement in finally seeing his family again. He vowed to never let something as simple as family sidetrack him again.

After seeing his sister, Adam was escorted back to his room. The building where he was kept was large, and Adam had the idea that other things went on there. He had seen workers in white coats walking the halls before, their hands filled with notebooks and minds distracted on whatever they were trying to figure out.

The long walk to his room was interrupted by the loud slamming sound of a door and the patter of small footsteps running down the hall toward them. The guard stood to the side as a little girl ran toward them. She stopped when she got close to Adam and looked up at him with wide green eyes.

"Have you seen my mommy?" the little girl asked him.

It felt like a stone was sinking in Adam's gut as he considered the small child before him undergoing the same training that he and his sister had. All he could do was stare at her.

"Have you seen her?" the girl asked again, her smile bright. She looked well cared for, loved. There were no bruises or that glaze that he knew coated his eyes during the first few months he was here.

The sound of another door opening echoed in the hallway and a feminine voice asked, "Selene, where did you go?"

The little girl smiled up at Adam. "I think I found her," she said, her voice sounding like bells and chimes and all things happiness. She went running in the direction of her mother's voice.

Adam would never forget her face, her green eyes, or the hope that swelled in his chest at the sight of her.

433

TWENTY

CATALINA

AT THE NEXT LADDER WE COME TO, THERE IS A PILE OF supplies on the ground. Astrid presses the button to communicate with whoever is at the safehouse above, but no one responds. It seems we are no longer welcome.

Marcus bends down to inspect the supplies. He hands off bags for each of us to carry. There are clothes, food, water. My stomach drops when I see what lies underneath the pile of supplies: a shovel.

TWENTY-ONE

JENN OF THE UNDERLAND

ALLIANCES SHIFT AND FALTER IN THE DAYS SINCE THE Reformation. Defectors and Transplants were born, raised, recruited. No one could be trusted.

Jenn has no last name, none of the people of the Underland do. They are known by their first names, given to them at their rebirth, a time when they leave their old lives behind to be part of something bigger. In her short life, Jenn had been many things: a young wife, a widow, a jewelry maker, a Volker, a spy.

The moment she saw Adam with Andromeda Somers, Jenn knew that they had a problem. He broke rules for her, strayed from the plan to bring her brother into the mix. Adam was always a rogue that any of them could barely trust. The majority of them didn't know his origins, but Jenn had an idea that whatever or whoever carved his past had made a mistake.

Jenn had traveled the tunnels before, stole the notebooks with all of Andie's research on the nanocytes when she fled to the Hanford District. She snuck in and out, unnoticed.

The scientists of the Underland have their own lab, be it not as shiny and new as Hanford's, but it was enough to copy Andromeda's work. Maryam Crossbender was impressed with what Andie had developed in her makeshift lab. But none of them knew if this plan would work.

Each generation had different nanocytes, and they all interacted differently with each human host. Crane was always working to improve his experiments. When Jenn passed the serum over to Adam, they knew that it might not work on Crane, but they had to try. Someone had to end him. Of all the Funding Entities, he had the majority hold on power, turned Andromeda Somers into something none of them had anticipated. She is as much a wild card as Crane now.

Therefore, Jenn gave the serum to Adam, and Adam gave the serum to Sam. What they didn't expect was for Blithe to coerce Sam into taking the serum with her. They wouldn't know that Blithe had her own plan to rid her unborn child of the things Crane had done to her. It seemed Blithe was tired of this game; she'd been involved in it too long and couldn't bear to watch another child be harmed because of it. The serum chelated the nanocytes, pulling them from her bloodstream, the combination of the serum and childbirth were more than her body could handle and without the nanocytes to heal her, she bled out.

Jenn didn't know what had happened to the child, or if Blithe's plan had worked. She suspected not. There was something strange about the Sovereign children from the Phoenix District, much stranger than any of them had initially thought. Yes, they were special, but Maryam Crossbender seemed genuinely surprised when she had found out that they had powers that reached beyond normal human abilities. This was unexpected. Someone was meddling with their plan.

There was always going to be a fight for power, always the threat of death, but now that they knew someone had taken Crane's genetic toying to the next level; it was time to act, time to make new allegiances.

Twenty-Two

Catalina

It's cold in the tunnel now. And dim, the lights stretched so far apart that there are a few feet of near blackness between them. Our jackets are zipped up to our chins as we try to sleep. On top of that there is this annoying scratching sound that has echoed throughout the tunnel for the past two nights keeping us awake. It's incessant.

"What do you think it is?" Astrid asks as we lay huddled together for warmth.

"Probably a mouse," Marcus says, his voice a joking tone.

"A bet it's a thousand beetles," Isaac says.

His comment is followed by moans of desperation from all of us and my skin tickles and itches with the thought of bugs invading the tunnel and crawling over us.

I turn to face Marcus, drop my voice to a whisper. "What do you really think it is?" I ask Marcus. He drapes his arm across me, seeking warmth.

"I don't know." He sighs. "But whatever it is, if it were after us, I'd think it wouldn't have taken so long to breach the tunnel."

We lay there, all of us trying to sleep, shivering in the coolness of the tunnel. Eventually Raven sits up and starts packing up his things.

"Might as well keep going," he says. "None of you are sleeping anyways."

We get up, eat and drink a little before setting off again.

Isaac drags the shovel behind him as he walks; the scraping drowns out the scratching sound which seems to have lessened with our walking.

"What do you think it is that you can do?" Marcus asks me as we walk at a slow pace behind the others. He stops, picking a small rock out of the wall. The loose dirt releases the rock easily then crumbles to the floor.

I shrug my shoulders. "I don't know. I haven't really thought about it."

"Maybe you're strong, like me." Marcus grips the rock in his fist; when he opens his palm there is nothing but dust left. He brushes off his hand.

"Doubt it." I adjust my pack. "I don't think I have anything. It would have manifested already."

Marcus touches my arm. "It's okay if you don't have a special power. I like you the way you are, always have. Besides," he motions to the others ahead of us. "Isaac doesn't have any super powers. Well... besides his serial killer tendencies."

"Let's hope I don't exhibit that."

I try not to think about what I could do. It brings me nothing but anxiety. Astrid, Cash and Marcus seem to have pretty mellow abilities. What if I turn out to do something terrible? I've already disappointed myself by lying, probably ruining Julie Rubie's life in the wake.

Raven slows until he is walking by my side. "Don't worry about it."

"What if I'm bad?" I ask.

"There's no way."

"But Mr. Crossbender said there are the other eight kids," I drop my voice to a whisper. "The other eight kids who are dangerous, what if one of them is me? What if he had it wrong?"

Raven shakes his head. "No. There is no way."

"You know what I did though, you saw."

"Payback sucks." Raven shoves his hands in his coat pockets. "If the Hanford kids weren't so bad to us, you would have never considered doing that. Don't dwell on it, Lina. It's just going to eat you up inside."

"Sure." I try to focus on something else, like sleeping in my own bed, seeing the farmhouse, Elvis, the fields and forests filled with Guardians.

We walk for hours and when we finally stop to eat, the scratching picks up again, this time louder than before, like something is following us from above.

Isaac presses his hands over his ears. "Is it ever going to stop?"

"Maybe we've been found," Astrid suggests as she digs in her bag.

Raven shakes his head. "No. If it were human I'd be able to read their thoughts. Whatever it is, it isn't human."

Suddenly the sound stops. There is a loud thud; dirt fills the air, clouding what little light we have.

"It broke through," Marcus says, his hand grips my jacket.

The sound of something dropping to the ground, in the darkness between the strung lighting, I count the thuds, six.

"Run." Marcus shoves me away from him.

"No. We stay together."

Soft footsteps move toward us, advancing.

It's when the glinting sheen of six sets of eyes are revealed in the light. Marcus bends to pick up the shovel we were given, wielding it as a weapon.

"Run!" Raven shouts.

We all run as fast as we can. When I turn my head to see if they're running after us, I see Isaac standing there, waiting to face those six sets of eyes alone.

We run, fast and hard. The tunnel narrows, forcing us into a single file line.

"This is not good!" Cash shouts.

"Keep running!" Marcus doesn't sound a bit out of breath.

My shoulder brushes the wall, dirt and rock falling to the ground at the impact. The tunnel feels damp, smells familiar, but before I can place it, I run into Raven's back and we all fall into a pile.

A heavy body falls on my back.

"What's going on?" Marcus shouts.

"There's nowhere else to go," Astrid says from ahead. "It just stopped."

"Looks like part of it caved in," Raven says.

"Oh no," Astrid's voice wavers. "What do we do now?"

"You have the shovel?" Cash asks.

Marcus stands and pulls me to my feet. "Yeah," he replies.

"We have to dig."

Marcus moves to the front of the tunnel, his shovel making crunching sounds as he stabs it into the earth and begins digging.

Twenty-Three

Sam

"Mr. Crane is acting strange." Richard Ruiz turns in his chair to face me.

"That little bastard always acts strange." I pace at the window.

Since Crane returned, we've been holed up at Headquarters most of the time while he begs all his contacts to help him find my sister. They all say they'll help, but no one has seen her.

"No, this is worse," Ruiz continues. "Like someone took his favorite toy and snapped it in half."

I stop pacing. "Maybe they did." Andie was his toy and now she's gone. "Where is he anyway?"

Richard spins in his chair. "Not here."

I wait.

He taps his fingers on the armrests. "We need to act now."

"We?"

"Well, you." Richard points at me. "You made a promise and it's time to deliver."

"How do you know I made a promise?"

"We have a mutual friend." Richard smiles.

"You're friends with Adam?"

"Let's just say we have a shared history. He and his sister."

I stand still at the mention of my dead wife.

"Speaking of... why would you give it to Blithe?" Richard asks.

I know he's talking about the serum. "It was her idea. She wanted me to do it."

"She had to know it would have no effect on you." Richard twists his wrist and his watch catches the sunlight, the diamonds reflecting bits of light onto the wall. "But her... Blithe had to know what it would do to her. It all sounds very *Romeo and Juliet*, no?"

I nod, the thought of what she did turns my insides to stone. I've relived those moments over and over in my head. She said she was hopeless without me, but what about me without her? I am hopeless, I miss her. There was something more going on that she didn't tell me and I am a fool for not seeing it.

"She wanted to do it for the baby," I tell Richard.

"The baby?"

"So she wouldn't pass it on to the baby. She wouldn't tell me what *it* was."

Richard presses his lips together and pauses in a moment of silence. I'm tired of silence; my life has been filled with silence since they all left. There is no more laughter from the children, no more family dinners by the fire, no more bed warmed by my wife. I have had nothing to think of besides the promise I made Adam years ago. Now is as good a time as any. Deep inside I know that I will never recover from this, you never turn back after this. I allow myself to think of Norah, for just a few minutes, happy that she's not here to see what her father has become. It's better this way.

"Let's call my people, they can use the satellites to find her," Richard offers.

He wants to find Andie just as much as I do.

Richard grips my hand before I reach the phone. "There's no going back."

I grip a cell phone in my hand. The world's last cell phone, Andie jokingly referred to it as.

"It ends here and now," he adds.

I nod. If it's the last thing I do, I'll end him.

"Pull up your satellites, Torres." I tell Emanuel.

"Colonel Salk?" Emanuel's voice is vaguely familiar; it's been so long since I was in Crystal River.

"I want to know where she is," I say.

"Um..." Keys click on a keyboard. "I wasn't expecting..." There's more clicking. He's stalling. "Just a moment. We've been busy tracking, um... a few things."

"Like Andie?"

"Well, yes."

"And?"

"We found her a few weeks ago." Emanuel clears his throat. "She was here."

"You saw her?"

"Adam too. He didn't want her to go missing again, said it took him too long to find her."

"So where is she?" I ask.

"Not far from you." Voices talk in the background. "She's headed toward the Pasture."

"What? She's here already?" I ask. "But I would have seen her... I..."

"Knew it." Richard shakes his head. "If she wanted us to see her, we'd see her."

"What..." This makes no sense.

"She's out in the forest near some abandoned buildings. Just disappeared underground."

The ruins.

Picking up the vials, I leave Headquarters.

Twenty-Four

Catalina

Something is getting closer, we can all sense it. And no matter how fast Marcus digs, he isn't going to dig us out before it gets here. Whatever those six sets of eyes are, they were advancing. There is a lone bulb hanging a few hundred feet away. I can see the shadows, the gleam from their eyes.

My heart breaks knowing that Isaac took them on for us and failed.

"They're getting closer," I say, trying to hide my panic from the others.

Astrid makes a strangled noise as Cash steps away from her. The sound of Marcus digging faster fills the tunnel.

"Wait." Raven tips his head and holds his hands out to stop Cash.

"What do you mean wait? We're going to die down here if we don't do something!" I bend, searching the loose dirt at our feet for rocks, something, anything to use to defend us. "If those are Survivors, or Swamp Men, or Hanford Sovereign, we're dead down here, Raven. All of us will be dead!"

"Lina," Raven's voice is calm. "Look, it's Isaac."

I stop, stand, and squint in the dim light. It is Isaac, his tall frame walking toward us.

"Isaac!" Cash shouts. "You okay?"

"I'm fine," he answers back.

"What are they?" Cash asks.

Before Isaac has a chance to answer, Raven answers for him. "Guardians." He laughs, almost hysterically. "They're Guardians."

He walks closer, into the light, and behind him are the large forms of six Guardians.

Twenty-Five

Mack

There is something strange with the Sovereign children from the Phoenix District, and even stranger are the ones born after the Reformation. But one would not know that unless they lived within the walls of Phoenix.

Mack wasn't sure what he was going to do with the tiny baby girl that Adam had thrust into his arms and told him to watch over and keep hidden. Mack wasn't the type of man who would settle down and have kids, not after witnessing the death and destruction of the Reformation and reading about the things people did to their kids, trading them for food at the gates of the Tonopah District. The last thing he wanted under his care was a goat named Jill and a baby girl named Norah. But both creatures wove their way into his heart over the past year and a half.

Mack didn't know much about raising a child, but he was certain that many of the things she said were abnormal. From the moment she woke up until the moment she went back to bed, Norah was talking. She talked to the goat, she talked to Mack, she talked to the men, a bird on the ground, ants, worms. The girl never stopped. There was that, and the fact that her eyes were a different color, one green and one a dark brown. It was a feature that drew eyes to her face and prevented one from looking away.

Mack tried for as long as he could to hide Norah from his men. And when the truth came out, he didn't worry about them not keeping her a secret. All of them had lived through the Skin Trades, hell, some of them took part in them, and once baby Norah had them all wrapped around her tiny finger, they did her bidding. They'd give their left arm before letting word out that they were hiding the girl. Besides, the men were living on Christian Whitmarsh's orders. They only knew that they needed to keep the girl safe and secret. They were afraid of Whitmarsh's wrath; they had heard what he was capable of. Only Mack knew that Adam was the true Christian Whitmarsh, but for fear of the tiny child he was now in charge of, Mack kept that piece of information to himself.

Mack knew that a goat wearing a pink sweater wasn't an ideal best friend for a toddler, but he had no choice, there were no other children within hundreds of miles from their location within the forests of Romney, West Virginia. The men loved them both. They gave their scraps of food to Jill and Jill provided her milk to the girl. Even in the harsh winters that were brought upon by the ever-changing climate, Jill and Norah never starved, and Mack's men would never forget the few of those who did starve to death so the goat and the girl could live.

In their darkest days, the snow was piled so high that Mack and the men had to move into the abandoned high school to conserve resources and hide from the elements of the unrelenting winter. There was room for the livestock and any supplies they could find, as well as running water and electricity. They were safe and warm and Mack could keep his promise holed up in the old building.

"Daddy Mack," Norah said one night as he was getting her ready for bed.

Mack had asked her multiple times not to call him that, but Norah never stopped, she referred to him as Daddy Mack and his men with Uncle in front of their names. And since Mack had never taught her to address them in such a way, many nights he lay wondering where she learned it from. Maybe it was the books he always found her looking at from the school library or maybe one of the men told her a story about their own lost children. Those were the only rational excuses he could come up with.

"Yes, sweetheart?" Mack asked.

"Tomorrow, we need to go on a trip."

Mack laughed as he combed her long dark hair. "On a trip to where?"

"We need to take the men and go to the north." The words were soft and serious as they left her lips, so unlike a young child.

Mack's hands stopped and he turned the small girl by her shoulders to face him. "Norah, what do you know of the north?" he asked.

Mack knew plenty of the north, he knew that was where Adam went to check on things, he knew that was where their electricity came from, and he knew that they were once in charge of keeping the Swamp people out of that area.

"That's where I came from." She smiled sweetly up at him.

Adam had never told Mack where she came from, but he had always had a feeling about the situation. Mack lifted Norah and set her on his lap. Jill shifted at his feet and her large goat eyes opened to watch them from her space on the floor.

"What makes you think that?" Mack asked.

Norah shrugged her little shoulders. "I just know."

"You just know?" Mack was smiling now, since he had heard her say things like this before. The strange part was that she was always correct with the things that she knew. For instance, she knew he wasn't her real father, she knew that these men were risking their lives to hide her, and she knew that Jill was the best goat nanny around for hundreds of miles.

"I just know, Daddy Mack." Her little face was set and determined as she repeated herself.

Mack turned Norah and continued with her hair. Since his had been kept longer than most men are comfortable with, Mack was quite skilled when it came to taking care of Norah's hair, his deft fingers loosening the tangles and working the hair into a tight braid. By the length of her hair and the amount of time that she had been in his charge, Mack guessed that she had to be around two years old, and while his time with young children was lacking, he knew that she was not a normal two year old girl. The thought came to him at least twice a day.

When he was done with her hair, he picked her up and brought her to the small bed where she slept at night, not far from his own. "Okay sweetheart, tell me why we need to go to the north, tomorrow of all days?"

Norah's eyes were wide and glinting as she looked up at him. "There is something I need to do."

Mack pulled the covers to her chin. Even though winter was over, he worried of her feeling the spring chill at night. "What could a sweet little girl like you need to do?"

"There is someone I need to meet." Her face was animated as she spoke, like she was having the most interesting conversation in the world. But that was how Norah was whether she was talking about their meager meals, the handmade clothing they had found for her, or what Jill was up to for the day.

Mack tucked the blankets tightly around her and felt the bed give as Jill jumped up onto the foot of the bed. "Who?"

"A man."

Mack's body tensed, he and his men had worked so hard to protect her from the way the world was now; introducing her to an unknown man set him on edge. "And what would this man's name be?" Mack kneeled beside her bed like he did every night, waiting for her to fall asleep.

Norah smiled as she pulled her thin arm out from under the neatly tucked blankets and placed her small hand on his cheek. A shock tore through Mack as images assaulted his brain. Mack saw what was going to happen; he saw what she needed to do.

This is what Norah could do. Sometimes she did it to soothe, sometimes to coerce, sometimes to tell the truth that none of them wanted to see. The men living with them knew of Norah's gift, and if her sweetness and innocent nature weren't enough to make them want to protect her, this gift was. They knew she was special and they were doing something that would benefit mankind. Mack and these men had seen what humans could do; the worst of it was during the early days of the Reformation. Norah gave them hope for the future and a man would go through great lengths to protect his last bit of hope during such dire times.

Norah ran her small hand over Mack's hair as his head slumped down onto her bed and he recovered from the vision she had shown him.

In the middle of the night Mack woke to find Norah sleeping soundly. He knew that when they woke in the morning, he would ready the men and the goat and they would head north. They might encounter death, but there would also be a new beginning, one that would achieve something that the Reformation couldn't.

Twenty-Six

THE LARGE CREATURES STAND BY ISAAC'S SIDE, THEIR HEADS almost reaching to his shoulders, their fur long and dreadlocked, their eyes steady and observant.

"It was them the whole time," Isaac announces proudly. "The scratching sound. They dug into the tunnel."

Marcus uses his shovel to move the loose dirt away since the tunnel is so narrow here.

The Guardians move away from Isaac to where Marcus is digging. Their large bodies knock him out of the way and they begin to dig. Their giant paws are moving the dirt faster than Marcus could ever shovel by himself.

As the Guardians work, we move back to a part of the tunnel that isn't so narrow so we can stand together.

"They've been following us all this time?" Marcus brushed the dirt off his hands. "Makes me wonder when they started."

"Makes me wonder if anyone caught onto them and followed," Cash speaks up.

Raven shakes his head. "I would have heard someone. I think we're safe."

Astrid moves away from Cash, stepping closer to the Guardians.

"Ash?" Cash asks.

"There's something on the other side of this."

A strange sound comes from one of the Guardians, like its paw hit more than dirt.

"Oh," Astrid grips the sides of her head, her face twists. "Someone on the other side is in–" Astrid falls to her knees, her face twisted, eyes closed, hand gripped to her chest. "So much pain…"

TWENTY-SEVEN

CHRISTIAN WHITMARSH/ADAM WATERS

THERE WASN'T ALWAYS PAIN ON THE ISLAND, BUT THERE WAS plenty of loneliness. Every so often a gift was given to him in the form of books or new clothing or a dinner alone with his sister. Those dinners never went as well as he had hoped; the distance between the two had become as wide as the ocean.

The days that he spent outside were his favorite, if he could enjoy something in that place. He trained with the armed guards that littered the island. Something wasn't right with the Volker and Adam could tell that they lived by their own moral code; Crane had successfully brainwashed them. His time outside was physically demanding, nothing like the way Burton Crane messed with his head when he was indoors. Adam could run mindlessly and push his body to its limit; it was the only time that he truly felt free any longer.

After another one of Crane's rigorous training sessions with the white button, he sat in front of Adam and simply watched him. The man made Adam uncomfortable, but he did as he had been taught and didn't let it influence his outward appearance.

"Your mother said that you had wanted to go into the armed forces since you were a child," Crane finally said. "She didn't want you to, but I think it was a good start for you. It's too bad you had to die on your first tour overseas."

Adam did not reply. It's not that he didn't have anything to say, it was simply that he could not allow himself to react to the mere mentioning of his parents.

Crane stood, moving further away from the white button and Adam's insides relaxed. "You leave tomorrow. I have a contact who will keep a close eye on you when you reach your destination." Crane paused and studied him before nodding. "You're ready. Don't forget the things you've been taught."

Crane stood and removed a syringe from his pocket. He walked closer to Adam and instructed him to hold out his arm. When he did, Crane proceeded to inject Adam with whatever was in the syringe. Adam didn't ask what it was, he knew better.

The next day, Adam was brought to the docks on the far side of the island. He stood there with his plainclothes guard and waited as a boat approached. When it docked, another man and a boy who couldn't be much older than Adam stepped up onto the dock and walked by him without a word. The boy was deeply tanned with dark hair and bright brown eyes that made contact with his own as they crossed paths. Adam boarded the boat and tried not to think about how many children may be experiencing the same fate as he just had.

They spent hours at sea before reaching land. There was a car waiting for him and his escort which brought them to the airport, and from there they boarded a private jet headed to the United States.

There were many opportunities in which Adam saw he could escape, but a feeling in his gut told him that this was not the time. Burton Crane still had his sister and until she was released, he would play along. But, the image of that little girl he had met in the hall haunted him. Knowing that he did nothing to get her out of there haunted him even more.

Twenty-Eight

THE GUARDIANS' DIGGING REVEALS AN OLD WOODEN DOOR. It's solid, thick, and looks like it's been here for a long time.

Astrid has fallen to the ground and even in the pale lighting I can see her whitened face as she moans.

"Cash, get her out of here." Raven motions to Astrid's trembling body.

She's mumbling something about whoever is on the other side of that wall. "They hurt," her soft voice whispers.

Cash picks her up, speaking softly in her ear. "It's okay, Ash. I've got you."

There are tears streaming down her face now. She looks so small in his arms. Cash holds her close to his chest and it's easy to see that she is special to him, even if she is intent on pushing him away.

The Guardians move away from their digging, herding Cash away as he carries Astrid from whatever is on the other side of that door.

"What is it?" I ask Raven.

He closes his eyes. "Crane is on the other side, and..."

"Who?"

"Our mother."

"Mom?" I have waited so long to see her, can't wait a moment more. How else would a child react to knowing that their parent has been brought back from the dead? I want to burst through that door and finally see her with my own eyes.

Before I have a chance to move, Raven grips my arm. "She's not the same. Lina, remember that you are nothing like her." He squeezes my arm so hard I'm sure there will be bruises.

I nod. Raven could tell me whatever he wants right now, it's all overshadowed by the need to see her again. I move to the door and try to push on it, but it doesn't budge. Running my hands over the wood, I search for a handle but don't find one. I can't figure out how to open it.

I turn to Marcus. "Can you open it?"

He motions me to move away before he runs at the door, throwing his body full force at it. The door does nothing more than creak.

"Mother..." Isaac moves to help him, slamming his body against the wood, his own need to see her apparently strong.

The door shudders under their force but never opens.

"Wait." Marcus pushes Isaac out of the way and places both of his palms on the door. "Let me try something." He closes his eyes, focusing. The muscles in his arms tense, his shoulders stiffen, and then he pushes on the door with a burst of energy.

There is a loud popping sound as the door drops backward onto the ground, revealing a dark room. Dirt starts falling from the ceiling. The narrow tunnel around us shudders.

"Get out!" Marcus pulls Isaac and Raven, shoving them into the room.

I run, shouting behind me for Cash and Astrid. They're running through the opening, Cash still carrying a frail-looking Astrid. They're followed by the Guardians, everyone making it through just as the opening to the tunnel collapses in on itself.

"What was that?" a familiar voice asks from nearby.

My mother! I run, leaving the others behind. I recognize this place, the ruins on the grounds of the Pasture. She brought me here before.

As I leave the room and turn the corner, I come face to face with Burton Crane.

"Ah, children, what an unexpected surprise."

His voice sounds the same but something is off. The tiny hairs on the back of my neck rise in anticipation. My eyes are already focused from the dim lighting of the tunnels; I see everything in the basement of the ruins. Crane looks a bit disheveled. Adam is here, looking angered and shocked. And my mother, her eyes fill with tears, but before I make my way to her she flickers, disappearing before me like a mirage.

"No!" I yell, stopping in my tracks. "Mom!" Reaching out, I grasp nothing but air.

Crane chuckles, clapping his hands together like a child. "Why don't you come out and play, Andromeda. Surely you are not afraid of your own children."

"I am not afraid of them," I hear her voice from the far corner of the room.

Even though I can't see her, I move toward the sound.

A strong hand grabs me. Adam's deep voice, a warning, "Don't, Lina, don't run after her. You'll only make it worse."

"Come now, Andromeda," Crane's voice is enthusiastic, "Show your children what you've become. It's nothing to be ashamed of."

"You did this to me!" Her voice wavers about the room, a ghost that I cannot see but want to, badly. "You did this to us. Ruined it all." Her voice flits as though she's moving fast. "Broke us."

"I made it better," Crane replies, triumphant in his declaration.

"You broke our family. Killed."

Soon the room feels like it is a thousand degrees. Sweat starts pouring down my face and back. I move a hand to wipe it out of my eyes. Adam pulls me closer to him and touches my face with the back of his hand.

"Get the children out of here." Adam looks to Marcus. "Get them all out of here. Now!"

"Perhaps you should calm down, Andromeda," Crane warns.

Raven is the first to move, tugging Cash along with him, Astrid still in his arms and writhing in pain as he grips her to his chest. "We have to go." His worried eyes meet mine. "We have to go, now."

Crane's head whips in the direction of Raven's voice. "Ah, he speaks. Finally."

Raven doesn't reply. He keeps a wary eye on Crane, the corners of the room, and his father, Adam. Crane watches him, studying Raven like a child contemplating a puzzle.

The Guardians nudge Isaac toward the wooden stairs that lead aboveground. I am the last to go, my upper arm gripped tightly in Adam's hand.

"Mom," I say, taking the first step up, my heart dropping.

"This is your last chance, Andromeda." Crane smiles. "Perhaps you should give your first-born some closure."

My mother's image flickers in the corner of the room. "Go, Lina," she says. "I am no longer your mother. I am dead to you. A ghost. A memory. Go, before I bring you death like I did your father."

My heart pinches as I look to Adam. His lips are pressed tightly together, he gives me a nod. Not so long ago he told me something similar.

I run up the stairs, swallowing the sobs that are threatening to break. I run out of the decaying old farmhouse and toward the shadows of my family and friends and Guardians, toward the daylight of the fields. As the others break the shade of the trees, Marcus turns, waiting for me, his hand extended. I run harder, swallowing it all down. Reaching out, I grasp his hand and he tugs me along, into the sunlight of the fields.

TWENTY-NINE

MACK

When the Survivor Militia men reached the gates of the Phoenix District, the Volker raised their guns and commanded the men to stop.

A goat stepped forward and on its back was a small girl.

"No, Norah," Mack reached out to stop her.

Norah's small hand caught his. "It's okay, Daddy Mack, I'm just going to ask them to let us in."

Mack hesitated, but let her speak; he knew the affect she had on people.

"Please let us in," Norah spoke like an adult, not a toddler. "I have an important message for my father."

The Volker chuckled. "And who is your father?"

Norah smiled sweetly. "I think you know him as Colonel Salk."

The Volker looked to each other in surprise. "Colonel Salk's daughter is dead," the Volker replied. "Died in childbirth with his wife."

"I am alive." Norah pulled off her mitten, rolled up her sleeve and revealed her wrist to the Volker. She bore the Phoenix District Sovereign mark, one that Mack had made her hide with long sleeves and strips of cloth.

The Volker were quick to act. They opened the gate that was usually reserved for the train and let Norah and the Survivors who accompanied her enter the Phoenix District.

The Volker did not escort the group of men to the Pasture. Somehow, Norah knew the way and led the men.

When Elvis opened the gate to the Pasture, he looked down at Norah and smiled.

"You've grown, Norah." He held a hand out for her to take and he led her into the safety of the Pasture. "Come in. We've got a full house today," Elvis said to Mack and his men.

They never responded, they were too busy taking it all in; the fields tall with crops, the pastures scattered with farm animals, the Guardians who stepped out of the shadows to observe the new visitors.

"Is he here?" Norah asked Elvis.

"Yes, dear. He's here." Elvis let go of Norah's hand. "Are you going to stop him?"

"Yes." Norah climbed onto Jill's back, dug her heels into the goat's side and trotted off.

IN THE FIELDS, Sam was a man on a mission. Walking fast, he was preparing himself to go somewhere that he would never return from. As he walked, clutching the vial in his hand and frequently patting his jacket pocket that held the syringe, he reminded himself that this moment was the reason why he sent his baby daughter away. He couldn't live with her knowing that this was what his life had come to. Sam Salk had started out good and light-hearted; he loved his family, he loved life, even with what they'd been dealt since the Reformation. But this moment was going to change all of that. Sam knew that he would never be the same person again. He had made a promise, and that promise was to kill Burton Crane.

Sam was so tall that the grass and weeds of the field barely reached his knees. He knew that he'd have no issue overpowering Crane. The man was short, soft, he hadn't honed his body over the years like Sam had. Sam walked faster, he wanted to get this moment over with, didn't know what would become of him afterwards. They might force him out, they might kill him, or maybe they'd just let him live out his days in the Pasture, dreaming of the family he once had. They were all gone now, and each day that passed took a little more of Sam's heart. He longed to be the young man he started out as, longed to relive that day he first saw Blithe, longed to relive the day he married her, first kissed her, planned their life together. But it was all a lie. That's why he was doing this. He had agreed a long time ago to help Adam but never had the chance, never had the perfect moment to slip the needle under Crane's skin and watch him writhe. There was no more perfect time than the present. Sam wasn't going to wait another day, he was going to get this over with and finally face whatever fate had planned for him afterward.

Even with all his training, Sam barely heard the galloping sound behind him. He was too focused on his mission, too focused on remembering the good and trying to forget what he was about to become. He knew the vial he held in his hand was dangerous, saw what it did to his wife but didn't understand why it had affected her like that and not him. Sam, after all, was not a scientist. He was a soldier, he gave for his country, gave for his family and now he was going to give the ultimate gift: his heart and soul.

The soft bleating from behind Sam made him stop. He turned slowly; ready to defend himself against whoever had come up behind him, but what he saw nearly caused him to laugh, if he still could laugh. There was a small girl riding on the back of a goat. The animal bleated again and the girl got down. She looked up at him and Sam recognized her immediately.

"Daddy?" Norah asked.

"Norah?"

He took in the vision before him, wondered if it was real or if he was hallucinating. Maybe he was already dead; maybe they killed him before he had even gotten here. Sam was so confused in the head that he had a hard time determining reality. He hadn't ever expected to see her again, not after he handed her over to Adam and begged the man to hide her.

Sam fully expected the child to be dead; he knew what life was like outside the gates of the Districts.

Norah walked closer.

"Daddy," she said as she held her hand out to him.

Instead of taking it, Sam dropped to his knees before her. Norah closed the distance between the two of them and took his face between her small hands. The Reformation had ruined many people and would ruin a lot more, but Norah was not going to let it drag her father as it had done to much of society. If he was the one life that she could help, then she knew she had done her job, that's what she was put on this earth for.

"You're here..." Sam searched her face, disbelieving it all.

"Yes, I am," she spoke softly to him.

She showed him her gift, what his life would become if he took this step, a step he would never recover from. She showed him a life with Burton Crane gone, one in which Sam was not responsible for ridding the planet of his existence; that was a chore for someone else, not Norah's father.

Sam dropped his arms to his sides, the vial rolled into the grass where the goat absently stepped on it while nibbling on some clover flowers, spilling the amber liquid into the soil, his mission forgotten, his fate changed.

THIRTY

THIS IS LIKE A DREAM, A MEMORY THAT I CAN BARELY recall. Tall grass brushes against our legs, our feet sink into the soft soil, burdocks and purple flowers stick to our pant legs, the bleating of farm animals in the distance calls to us. This is the Pasture, this is home.

Marcus runs faster, pulling me along with him, trying to catch up with the others and putting distance between us and the danger that lurks in the ruins. That danger is my mother, the man who helped reform society, and my brother's father. My throat burns, my muscles ache. Marcus's grip tightens on my hand and in the distance, I see a cluster of people. We run toward them. As I get closer, I recognize the tall form of my Uncle Sam, Elvis, a cluster of men surrounding them all looking exhausted and hopeful at the same time.

Sam mouths my name; I see it on his lips even from this distance. He looks past Isaac and Raven and Cash, who is still carrying Astrid, and he runs for me, his long legs propelling him in my direction. Mark's grip loosens on my hand.

"Lina!" My uncle's long, strong arms grip me, pulling me off my feet and up into a tight hug. He spins us in a circle like he did when I was a child. "Oh, Lina, you're back. I can't believe it."

When he finally sets me on my feet, I notice he looks exhausted like he's been battling something dark since we left and only recently defeated it.

"Daddy?" A soft voice asks from behind him.

Sam's face brightens as he turns, revealing a small girl standing there.

"Lina," Sam smiles as he crouches down. "I'd like you to meet Norah. Your cousin. My daughter."

I look between the small child and my large uncle. I was told she was dead, died with her mother in childbirth. But here she stands.

"She's not dead?" I ask.

The girl giggles. "I am not dead."

She's small, but her mannerisms are very adult, much like I remember Raven's being when he was young. Strangely, her eyes are each a different color. I look up and see Raven gaping at her, no doubt reading whatever is going on inside her mind.

As I reach out to touch the girl, the men behind her move, as though I am a threat they need to discharge. A man with a ponytail holds up his hand and stops them.

"What about..." I look around the grouping of people for Blithe. My eyes fall on Raven, he shakes his head. She's gone. It seems only some can be brought back from the dead in this new world.

***

WHEN I STAND, Norah takes my hand and Sam's. I notice a goat wearing a pink sweater following the girl. The man with the ponytail whistles to it, calling, "Jill." And the goat trots off in his direction.

Cash is still carrying Astrid, her arm hangs limp from her body. Elvis offers to take her but Cash pulls away from him. "No, I've got her," he says. "I need to get her some help."

"What's wrong with her?" Sam asks.

"She can..." Cash looks warily at all the people around us. "She can sense things. In the ruins... Andie..."

"Wait, wait, wait." Sam holds up his hands to stop us. "How did you kids even get in here?"

"There was a tunnel, it led to one of the basements," Marcus tells him.

"Was?" Sam asks.

"It caved in," Cash says. "Right after we came through. Marcus pushed down the door and the tunnel fell."

"He pushed it in?" Sam asks.

"Yeah, he's strong. Really strong," Cash adds.

Elvis seems to be smiling proudly; he doesn't notice the death stare coming from Raven. I've never seen Raven give Elvis such a look.

"Okay… okay, this is weird, but… Let's get her back to the houses," Sam suggests. As we start walking, Sam says, "Elvis, go call on Dr. Akiyama."

Elvis heads for his barns as we make for the cluster of houses.

Cash takes Astrid to our old house. Marcus opens the door, ushering us all inside. It's empty, stale and cold, no longer smelling like fresh baked bread and home cooked dinners. Cash carries her to our old room, sets her on her bed against the wall. I follow. He sits on the edge of the mattress, pushing her hair out of her face, adjusting her limbs and tucking the pillow under her head so she's comfortable.

I move toward them. "What's wrong with her?" I ask Cash.

"I don't know." He runs his hands through his hair and over his face. Dirt coats his clothing and skin from the tunnel collapsing. "I didn't get to her in time. Whatever your mother was doing, I could feel it." He thumps the middle of his chest with his fist. "She was making our blood boil. She did this to Astrid. I didn't get to her in time. It's my fault." Cash takes her pale hand in his, pressing it to his lips.

Reaching out, I run my fingers through her hair, brushing the soil away. "This isn't your fault, Cash," I tell him. "Can't be."

He says nothing to me, simply stares at her slackened face while rubbing her knuckles across his cheek. It's a quiet moment I don't feel like I should be a part of. I leave the room and find everyone in the living room.

Through the windows, the front porch is littered with men. Sam sits on the couch with Norah. Raven and Isaac watch them from the corners of the room. Marcus stands in the threshold to the hallway as though he's been waiting for me.

"They're Militia men, Survivors," Marcus says. "That's Mack," Marcus tips his head to the man with the pony-tail standing near the door who is watching Norah intently as though my uncle might do her harm. "From that school Adam and Crane took us to when they kidnapped us."

"How did they get in?" I ask.

"Volker at the Gateway where the train enters. They let Norah and them in after seeing her Sovereign mark." Marcus holds out his wrist, rubbing his fingers over his own.

I nod, seeing movement outside the window. The men move, the door opens, Elvis and Dr. Akiyama step into the room. Dr. Akiyama looks much older than I remember; his hair now white, his skin with deep wrinkles around his eyes and mouth.

"Where is she?" Dr. Akiyama asks.

"The bedroom." I wave him over and show him to the room.

Cash is still hunched over Astrid, his face pale with concern.

Dr. Akiyama starts with his exam, checking pulses, her pupils, listening to her breaths. The entire time he's asking Cash questions about what happened.

Finally, with a deep sigh, Dr. Akiyama says, "It's some kind of shock, I think."

"Will she come out of it?" Cash asks.

Dr. Akiyama presses his fingers to the pulse on her throat. "She's strong. We'll just have to monitor her." He stands and looks around the room. "Been a while since I was here last. Your brother was just a baby then." He sighs. "I think you should bring her down to the hospital. I could monitor her more closely there."

"No." Cash shakes his head. "No. She stays with us. We stay together." He grips Ash's hand.

Dr. Akiyama nods. "Very well. Give her a few days."

I leave them to talk as Dr. Akiyama instructs Cash on how to care for her and things to watch for.

When I return to the living room, Raven is sitting on the couch and Norah is crouched next to him on her knees. Both of their eyes are closed, their hands gripped, their foreheads touching. I watch them from the hall.

"They're communicating," Marcus whispers to me. "She can communicate with touch. Somehow."

"Did she touch you?" I ask.

Marcus shakes his head.

"Why?" I touch his arm. "Are you afraid?"

His lips tip up in a half smile.

Raven lifts his head. "It's not a true glimpse into the future. She shows you the path that your choices could lead to. It's not written in stone."

The two of them stand and walk to us. I crouch down to greet Norah.

She tips her head as she studies me. "You still don't know." Her small hand hovers close to my face.

"What don't I know?" I ask, looking into her strange eyes.

"What makes you special, like us."

I shake my head. "I don't have any special power like everyone else does. I'm normal."

"None of us are normal. Not any longer."

Norah moves her hand away from me. Refusing to touch me and show me what she's shown the others. Part of me is disappointed, part relieved.

"You're not ready to see." She smiles. "In time." Norah looks around the room before she announces. "I would like a nap now. And when I get up, a warm dinner would be nice."

Sam stands and shows her to Raven and Isaac's old room. Mack follows and the goat, who I didn't notice was sleeping in the corner of the room, trots after them all.

Marcus hugs me from behind. "We're home," he whispers into my ear.

"We are." I agree with him. "It's just too bad nothing is like I remember."

"At least we have each other." He kisses my cheek, my neck, presses his lips to my shoulder. "We're all together and out of Hanford. That must bring you some relief."

I nod. "Does it bring you relief?"

When he doesn't answer, my mind starts racing. Maybe he never wanted to leave there, maybe he liked it, maybe he's still working with them. Raven assured me Marcus was on our side, but it's hard to forget him turning me in after out escape.

Suddenly it feels like this house is crashing in on me.

"I need some air," I tell him.

We walk out of the house, stepping away from the Militia men that are crowding the porch. In the distance I see Adam walking, Crane beside him with his hands bound behind his back. The shadow of my mother trails close to them, her image flickering in and out.

Marcus stands at my side, he's always stood at my side and even though my head is a puddle of mud right now, I am grateful.

"I'm sorry," he says.

"For what?"

"That she's not like we remember."

Even with all his anger toward my family abandoning us and being part of this, it seems he misses her as well. She was a mother to all of us.

"*Forget me,*" her voice rings inside my head. "*Forget me, forget me, forget me.*"

I glance at Marcus to see if he heard her voice as well, before looking back to Adam and Crane as they make their way to the gates of the Pasture. My mother's image stops flickering as she turns to face me. Even though she's half a cornfield away, I can tell that she is not the mother I remember. Crane took her and broke her, reformed her like he and his people reformed our country, tore our family to pieces, killed our father. It was Crane and his men.

I know I shouldn't be feeling this way, the anger and hatred toward these men. I hate them for molding my mother into someone I barely recognize, for my father's death, for all we've endured. There is a struggle brewing deep inside me, one that makes me want to hide here in the Pasture for always, and that also makes me want to hunt down those who are to blame for this and put an end to all of them.

Elvis exits the Library house and makes his way toward us, his familiar smile masking his face. He said he was going to get the place ready for the Militia Men since it looks like they will be staying here with us. They refuse to leave Norah's side and since we have no Volker on the grounds of the Pasture, they are welcome to stay.

Elvis walks across the path to the courtyard. The picnic tables are still there next to the fire pit that we danced around as children. It seems this place has waited patiently for us to return. As Elvis nears us, he opens his mouth to say something but stops, his face turns shocked as he focuses behind us. The pounding of footsteps ensues, the door slams open. I turn, just slightly, to find Raven running. He leaps off the porch, rips a rifle out of the hands of one of the Militia men on the way. Flying through the air, he kicks Elvis in the chest, knocking him onto his back. Raven stands over him, gun aimed at his head.

"Why?" Raven asks through his teeth. "Why did you do it?"

Elvis stares back, raises his arms in defeat, letting them flop against the ground hear his head.

"Why would you do this to us?"

"You're just a child, Raven," Elvis replies. "You wouldn't understand."

"Try me." Raven cocks the rifle.

I move to stop them, but Marcus grabs me. "Wait," he warns. "He must've read something in Elvis's head."

"You don't know what it's like to watch your child die, boy," Elvis continues. "If she could have helped herself, she'd be here. I couldn't watch anything happen to you kids. You may be angry with me, but I did this for you." Elvis's gaze meets mine and Marcus's.

"What did he do?" I ask.

Raven backs away from Elvis, the weapon still aimed at him. "He did this to us. Our powers. Stole radioactive material from the power plant and exposed us to it. And we thought Crane was to blame. It's him who turned us into this: mutants."

"I couldn't let young lives slip through my fingers, not again, never again. I won't apologize for it. I'll never apologize for what I did. I helped them survive. I helped them live. It's a gift I couldn't give my own child. It's a surprise Crane didn't expect." Elvis's chest is heaving as he spurts the words from his mouth. "We couldn't count on your mother to get rid of him. Still can't. You kids are our only hope. Our last hope for the best future."

THIRTY-ONE

"A SURPRISE CRANE DIDN'T EXPECT?" I ASK.

Elvis nods.

"Mr. Crossbender told me that there are eight kids, kids just like us who are very dangerous. He's been searching for them for years." I look at Raven; his facial expression says he's put it all together. "Elvis, whatever you did, it was exactly what they were expecting."

Elvis's face pales and his head drops against the ground.

"Who were you working with?" I ask.

Raven aims the shotgun at Elvis's head again. "Tell her."

"Who, Elvis?"

He shakes his head, rubs his hands over his face. "President Berkley."

Before Elvis can say anything else a blast of wind hits us, knocking us off our feet.

"What the..." Marcus starts to say as he moves to stand. He reaches for me and pulls me to my feet.

"I knew I heard them nearby." Raven points the rifle at the ground.

As we stand, two boys leave the barn and start walking in our direction.

"Who are they?" Marcus asks.

"I think…" I start.

"Ira and Lex," Raven finishes for me. "Looks like they have some shiny new powers as well." He brushes some dirt off his sleeve. "Or at least one of them does."

They make their way toward us, helping Elvis to his feet when they get to him.

"Thanks, boys." Elvis brushes himself off.

Isaac runs out of the house, leaps off the porch and stands between us. "What happened?"

"Wow," Ira's tone is flat. "Looks like someone's been taking their vitamins."

Isaac's face lights up when he sees the boys, no doubt remembering a childhood with them. Or at least, part of his childhood. "Guys!" Isaac smiles and runs toward them, arms open, looking like the kid he barely resembles any longer.

Ira raises his hand and a silvery ball of light appears. He tosses it forward, striking Isaac in the chest. It throws Isaac backward onto the ground, pushing him across the grass, pulling it up and leaving a four-foot-long trail of dirt in his wake.

"What the crap!" Isaac yells.

"Boys." Elvis lays a hand on Ira's shoulder. "Play nice."

"You told us not to trust anyone," Lex says.

"We know them." Elvis moves to lend a hand to Isaac. "They haven't been gone that long. They're still our people."

Our people. I am reminded of what we faced in Hanford.

Ira holds out a hand to Isaac. "Sorry, man."

Isaac grips his hand, squeezing until Ira flinches. "No problem, brother." He pulls him in for a hug, pats him hard on the back. "Don't be surprised when I pay you back for that." Isaac pulls away and reaches for Lex, saying, "I always liked you better anyways," as they embrace.

Marcus touches my arm. "Are you okay?"

"I'm fine."

"They tossed us pretty good." Marcus looks me over. "I just want to make sure."

I look myself over, brush the dirt off my clothes. "All good."

When I look up, Adam, Crane and my mother are watching us from near the gate of the Pasture.

"She won't come over here," Raven warns me. "She's afraid."

"But we need her help," I say.

Raven shakes his head. "She's going after the world's data. In Galena."

"She's going to leave us behind for a computer filled with information?" I want to scream. Of all the times that we have needed her, now is the most important.

"She wants answers, Lina."

Ira, Lex, Elvis and Isaac close the gap until we're all standing in a circle.

"Just like us," Raven continues.

"Maybe she could make us normal again?" I ask. "Maybe she could fix the mutations?"

"This power," Ira says. "It keeps us safe."

"No, power destroys," I say. "Look at what it did to our country, our families."

"Why can't you just accept it, Lina?" Lex says. "Why can't you just be one of us? Are we so different from you? Do we scare you?"

I look at the kids I grew up with; we spent years of our lives out here on this farm, secluded from everyone, the perfect test subjects, the perfect control group.

"I like my power." A silvery ball of energy floats over Ira's palm. "I like that I'm different. That I can protect myself." He closes his palm and the ball disappears. "What's your power?" He looks at me.

"She hasn't found hers yet," Marcus speaks up for me.

"She's jealous of us," Ira says as he elbows Lex.

"I'm not jealous," I reply.

Marcus puts out a hand. "Don't be a jerk, Ira. We had enough of that in Hanford."

"How did you get out of there?" Lex asks. "We thought you were never coming back."

Raven, Marcus and I look at Isaac.

"We were forced out," Marcus says. "There was... a tragic accident."

"That's too bad," Ira says. "Well, it's nice to have you all home."

"There's more, boys." Elvis goes on to explain what Mr. Crossbender told me.

"So we fight," Ira decides.

"If we have to," Elvis says.

"We have a town full of Residents to protect," Lex points out.

"We keep training." Ira looks to Elvis. He nods in agreement.

"I'm tired of fighting," I say. "We just escaped a District backlash in Hanford."

Raven speaks up. "You have to remember, Lina, that there are eight more of us out there, somewhere in the world. Eight more kids. We need to be able to protect ourselves from them."

The door of our house opens, slamming against the wall. Norah walks out and steps down off the porch. "What is the noise interrupting my nap?" She walks to the middle of where we are standing, the goat following her. Mack watches from the porch. "And I don't even smell dinner cooking." A few of the Militia men let out soft laughs.

With tiny hands on her hips, she gives us all a good glare. "You two." She walks up to Ira and Lex, taking their hands in hers. A moment passes between them. "You see?" she asks.

The two boys nod.

"My goat is hungry." She starts walking, still holding onto the boys hands, taking them along with her.

They walk across the courtyard, the goat and Mack following after them. When I look away, to the place where my mother was standing, she is no longer there.

Marcus wraps his arms across my shoulders and I lean into him. "What are we going to do while hiding out here?" I ask.

Elvis gives a grim smile. "Prepare for war." He turns away from me to look out over the grounds of the Pasture. "I've told you, Lina. I will not let the children I love be unable to defend themselves against the evil of the world. We'll prepare for war. Continue the training that Adam and your mother started when you were all little."

Something sinks inside of me. This isn't the first time we've prepared for war. First it was for an impending war against the Survivors that never came, then the Swamp people, and now, a group of kids who George Crossbender tells me are dangerous.

It seems Burton Crane dipped his finger into the human genome and swirled. Something so simple has become something so complex. Man likes to play God, but it looks to me like being a divine entity isn't all it's cracked up to be. Maybe my mother can find the answers in Galena, maybe she can heal herself, heal us; maybe she can fix this mess. We can't turn back time but, like Marcus said, we learn from our past mistakes. But if she can't, we'll just have to keep trying to save ourselves.

Preview of Resurrection (The Phoenix Project Book 6)

Andromeda

"I was going to make a nice stew out of you," a gravelly voice breaks the silence.

My limbs are wrapped in a numbing tingle as though I've been in a dead sleep for hours—days even. My head hurts. The voice is much too loud for my comfort, even though I get the sense it is just a whisper. The sound rattles my brain, pierces my spine. An intense ringing follows with a blaring of lights and echoes in my head.

My eyelids feel dry and heavy. There is a burning brightness, as though my eyes have never been opened before. Blinking, focusing, after a few moments I realize that I am nowhere bright. Instead my surroundings are dark, hazy, and a thick smoke fills the air. It smells... strange.

I turn my head to find a man sitting on a stool. He's old; his face lined with deep wrinkles, his hair white and wiry, his eyes a fathomless black. He watches me from his perch before he reaches down and sprinkles some dirt from the floor into the bowl in his hand. The *crunch* and *whoosh* grinding motion of his pestle threatens to draw me back into a deep sleep.

My eyes move from the old man to the dark orange coals of the low fire in front of him, the hard-packed dirt floor, the rough plank walls and ceiling of the small room we are in. There are baskets lining the walls, shelves filled with an array of glass jars and bowls, and long white sticks are strung along the ceiling.

The old man stands and walks toward me, his gait awkward and stooped. The fingers of his free hand dance in the bowl. "Do you remember?" he asks.

Searching my brain, I come up with nothing. I draw no thoughts, no memories. "No," I say.

"Then go back to sleep. You are not ready to awaken." His fingers take hold of the powder in the bowl and he sprinkles it on my face, a gentle rainfall of grit. "Sleep, dead girl."

I sleep.

RESURRECTION

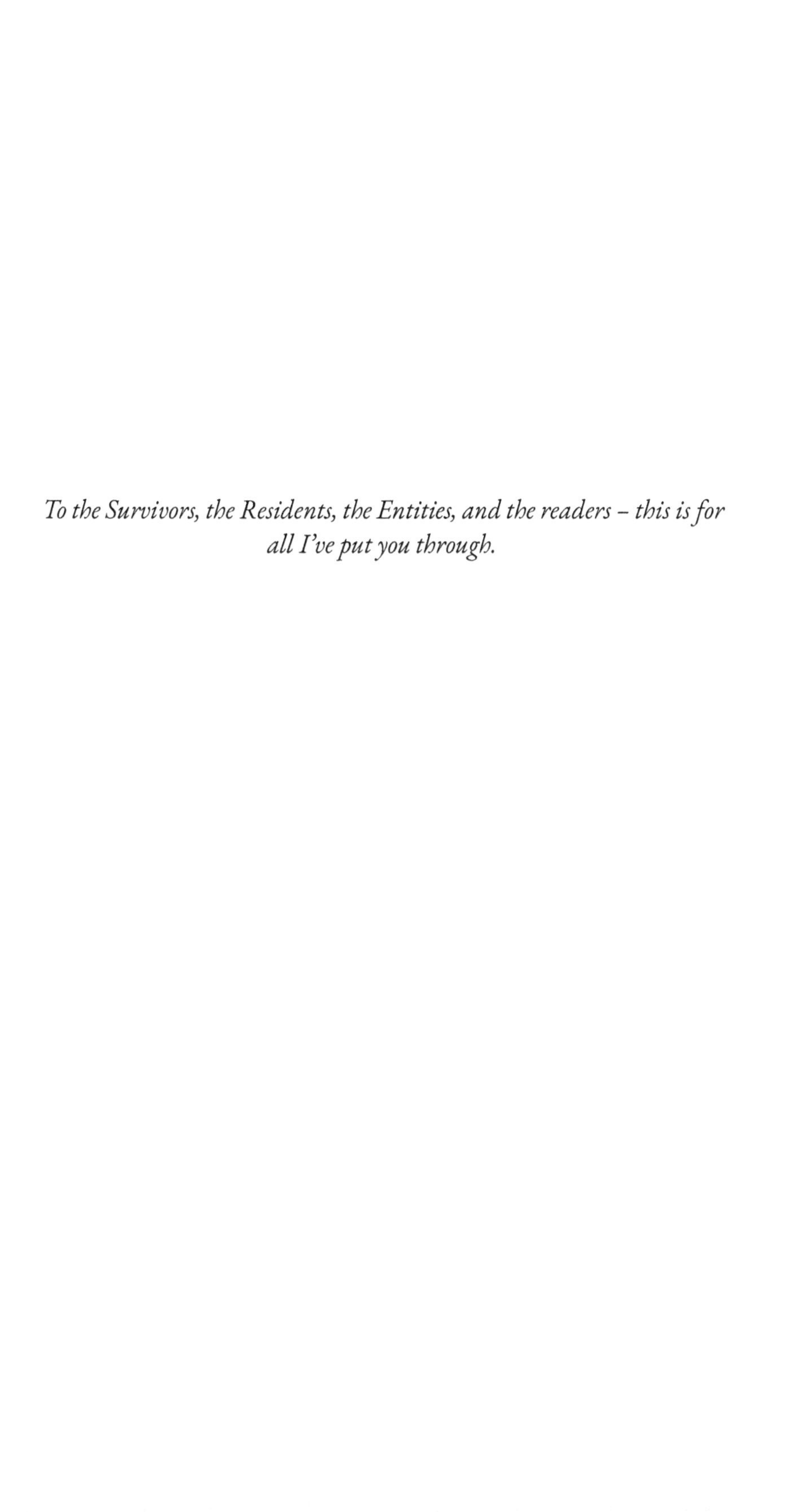

To the Survivors, the Residents, the Entities, and the readers – this is for all I've put you through.

Part One

Life
Death
Now take a breath

ONE

ANDROMEDA

"I WAS GOING TO MAKE A NICE STEW OUT OF YOU," A gravelly voice breaks the silence.

My limbs are wrapped in a numbing tingle as though I've been in a dead sleep for hours—days even. My head hurts. The voice is much too loud for my comfort, even though I get the sense it is just a whisper. The sound rattles my brain, pierces my spine. An intense ringing follows with a blaring of lights and echoes in my head.

My eyelids feel dry and heavy. There is a burning brightness, as though my eyes have never been opened before. Blinking, focusing, after a few moments I realize that I am nowhere bright. Instead my surroundings are dark, hazy, and a thick smoke fills the air. It smells... strange.

I turn my head to find a man sitting on a stool. He's old; his face lined with deep wrinkles, his hair white and wiry, his eyes a fathomless black. He watches me from his perch before he reaches down and sprinkles some dirt from the floor into the bowl in his hand. The *crunch* and *whoosh* grinding motion of his pestle threatens to draw me back into a deep sleep.

My eyes move from the old man to the dark orange coals of the low fire in front of him, the hard-packed dirt floor, the rough plank walls and ceiling of the small room we are in. There are baskets lining the walls, shelves filled with an array of glass jars and bowls, and long white sticks are strung along the ceiling.

The old man stands and walks toward me, his gait awkward and stooped. The fingers of his free hand dance in the bowl. "Do you remember?" he asks.

Searching my brain, I come up with nothing. I draw no thoughts, no memories. "No," I say.

"Then go back to sleep. You are not ready to awaken." His fingers take hold of the powder in the bowl and he sprinkles it on my face, a gentle rainfall of grit. "Sleep, dead girl."

I sleep.

Two

Norman Eckstein

A LONG TIME AGO

Norman Eckstein was a short, bald man who looked thoroughly out of place in the Middle East. He also looked less than dangerous.

When Norman Eckstein saw Adam Waters walk by him on the streets of some no name village, a sense of ownership overwhelmed him. Slavery had been abolished for over a hundred years, but he owned part of that man. His brain, his heart, his left arm, half of the nanocytes that ran through his bloodstream, it didn't matter which part. Norman was curious and ready to collect on his investment.

Few of those who had invested with B. C. Industries actually knew that Adam was on the loose. He had escaped from Burton Crane's grasp and had been rogue for years. Norman knew, just like he knew how old Adam really was, he knew Adam could live longer—much longer—than the average human. Crane had promised Norman his own nanocytes, but had yet to deliver. Time was running out. Norman had already waited over half of his life, now he was rotting away in some sand filled hellhole. He wasn't going to wait any longer. Norman knew the secret to extending his life resided in that man's body.

Norman had men of his own. Trained and paid well to ensure his longevity until his own nanocytes could be delivered. He signaled those men, sent them to collect a one Adam Waters who was currently arguing with a man at a fruit stand.

The capture was easy. Easier than it should have been. Norman figured that perhaps Crane should have spent more time on his combat training, or slipped the boy back into the Marines for another tour of duty.

No matter what they tried nothing worked. Transfusions. Transplants. They cut the man so deep that even his precious nanocytes didn't heal his body fully. But he always came back to life. Sometimes it was hours, sometimes days. Once it even took a week. But Adam always came back to life.

It was a sick joke each time he woke up. Norman would say to Adam, "I thought we killed you once already."

And Adam always replied with, "I wish you would just figure it out already."

It seemed to Norman that Crane's goldenboy was in a dark place, unthankful for the gift that had been bestowed unto him. Men would kill to have what Adam had. Men *will* kill to have what Adam has. Norman would kill. But no matter how many times he tried, Adam always came back and the nanocytes never took to Norman's body.

Norman knew he would pay dearly for what he had done, was afraid to drop the man on Crane's doorstep for fear of the retaliation. But word was that Adam had gone missing, really missing. There were no sightings and that was making Crane agitated. Norman eventually delivered Adam, more damaged than when he escaped Crane's clutches the first time.

THREE

SHIFTING, FEELING THE HARD FLOOR UNDERNEATH THE THIN cot I rest on, a rough fabric brushes over my skin and I realize I am naked under a thin burlap blanket. Was I naked before? I can't seem to remember. When I think about it I can't seem to remember much at all.

I turn to find the old man sitting on the same stool by the same burning embers. If he notices I am awake he doesn't let on.

"Could I get some clothes?" I ask and it comes out sounding like a croak.

The man stops his grinding, seemingly annoyed with my request. He stands, sets the bowl on his stool. "I will return. Do not leave," he replies.

I'm not sure where he thinks I would go naked. But I wait, eyes and limbs heavy with fatigue. I try to focus in the dim room. The only thing standing out are the white sticks strung along the wall. I give up, closing my eyes and waiting.

The old man returns with a pile of clothing in his hand and sets them next to me.

"Could I have some privacy?" I ask.

"You have nothing I haven't seen," he replies, unimpressed with my modesty. He returns to his stool, grinding whatever substance is in the bowl before he turns his back to me.

I reach out and run my fingers over the clothing. They're soft, smooth, unlike any fabric I have ever felt. The pants are a dark chocolate brown. The top, a creamy white.

"What is this made of?" I ask, pulling the clothes under the blanket to dress myself.

"Skin," he replies flatly.

I freeze with one foot in the leg of the pants. "Human skin?"

"Just put it on already." He sounds irritated. "You don't want to disappoint them by rejecting their gift."

A gift of human skin. Who does that?

Hesitantly, I push my foot the rest of the way into the pants. Pushing the blanket away, I sit up and pull the top over my head. It's fitted and a bit too tight for my liking but soft and pliable. Clasping the button behind my neck, I stand and turn to the man on the stool.

"Shoes?" I ask.

He bends, turns, and hands me a pair of tall boots.

"Are these…" I swallow hard. "Made from human skin too?"

"No. Cowhide."

"Oh." I pull the boots on and tighten the laces. When I'm done, I run my hand over my head, feeling my hair. It's a tangled mess reaching down the middle of my back, almost to my waistband. I've never had hair this long before, always preferred it short. Having no comb, I decide I'll have to cut it.

"Do you have any scissors?" I ask.

"What do you need scissors for?" He pauses from the grinding.

"To cut my hair."

He sets the bowl down, reaches for a small stool along the wall and pulls a wooden comb from a shelf. "That would be a dreadful decision." He sets the stool in front of him. "Come, living-dead girl; sit. I will fix it." He motions to the stool.

I glance at the door, thinking for a moment that I would rather run for the hills than have this strange man in this strange hut touch my hair —or any part of my body.

"Our women do not cut their hair." He motions to the chair again.

"I'm not your women."

"Do not give my people another reason to fear you. Only devils wear their hair short." I glance at the door again. "I wouldn't suggest it." He shakes his head. "If you cannot remember what happened to you, then you definitely do not want to see what is beyond these walls."

I stand, my legs feeling weak, my feet feeling heavy as I walk toward the man. I sit on the stool with my back to him and wonder if he will slit my throat instead of comb the tangles from my hair. He begins at the bottom, raking the comb through the knotted curls, much gentler than I anticipated.

While the comb catches on knots and tangles, I try to remember. Nothing comes to me and the only thing I acquire is exhaustion.

When I sense he is done, I turn on my stool and face the burning coals. "Can I have a tie?" I ask. "To put my hair up?"

"No." The old man reaches for his bowl again and resumes his grinding for a moment before his nimble fingers begin plucking things from the wall behind him and sprinkling them into the bowl.

"Why?" I ask, already annoyed with the length of hair stretching down my back, making it sweat.

He resumes his grinding. "Only our children tie back their hair." He pauses to look at me. "I suspect you are not a child. I suspect you are much older than you look."

And then the memories bombard me; of Ian, of what I did. Of Lina and Raven. Adam and his betrayal. Burton Crane. The nanocytes. A strangled sound escapes my throat as I stand, stumble away from the old man, and collapse on my cot.

"Ah." The old man tips his head. "You must be remembering." His fingers dip into the bowl. "This is not good." His fingers grasp at the powder. "You must go back to sleep. You are not ready to remember." He throws a dash of powder in my face and I am plunged into darkness.

<hr>

Sleep should have given me some reprieve but instead every

memory flashed to life. I wake sweating and gasping for air, drowning in my own torments.

The old man is sitting on his stool with his back hunched, looking more frail and older than the last time my eyes were open.

"Who are you?" I ask.

With his gritty voice low, he responds, "Witchdoctor."

"What kind of a Witchdoctor?"

"Of people from the swamp."

"So you were going to eat me?" I ask. That's what these people do, these creatures are barely human.

"Yes," the old man continues. "Would have been simple since most of your bones were already broken and your meat was tenderized from the electricity that charged through you. Would have been an easy meal. And then I could have healed many with your dried brain and ground spleen. Could have drank your blood to make my life longer." The man holds up his hand, he's missing the tip of his pinkie finger. "But that beast put a stop to it." He points to the far end of the hut. There is a Guardian lying in the corner, black as night and hidden in the shadows. I didn't notice it before. And even now I can just make out its outline and the glare of the burning coals reflecting from its pupils.

"Why am I here?" I ask, pushing the burlap blanket away. I move to the stool that's next to him.

"Fate," he responds, resuming his grinding.

I am silent, my focus moving from the fire, to the Guardian, to the old man. He taps the powder from his bowl into a glass jar and then moves to set the jar on one of the shelves that line the walls. He runs his fingers along the inside of the now empty bowl, cleaning the dust away before selecting new items from his inventory. He sits, picks his pestle from the ground and resumes the soothing *grind* and *swoosh*.

"Fate," I repeat with a whisper.

"Fate." He nods.

"I don't believe in fate." I hold my hands out to warm them by the glowing embers.

He offers a weak smile. "You have lain on that cot for months, close to a year, never rotting. So tell me, living-dead girl who does not believe in fate, tell me how is it that you are alive?"

I have been here for a year and I remember none of it. Since I have no explanation, I don't answer his question.

"How did I get here?" I ask.

"Glane brought you, from the north." *Grind, swoosh.* "Do you remember what happened?" *Grind, swoosh.* It is a mantra humming from his bowl.

I search my memories only to find nothing. "Who is Glane?" I ask.

"A leader of my people. He's young. The son of the scarred-face leader, brother of the one-eyed leader. Both are dead."

"What happened to them?"

Grind, swoosh. "They were killed by the blue-eyed ghost."

"Who is that?"

The Witchdoctor pauses his grinding. "A man with nothing left to lose. His soul is burning." He pauses, presses his lips into a thin line. "He searches for you," he finally says.

That could only be one person: *Adam.* I want nothing to do with him. Let him burn after what he did to me.

"So tell me, living-dead girl, tell me how one so young harbors so much pain. What have you been dreaming about all these months?"

Grind, swoosh.

"What makes you think that?" I ask.

The old man gives me a knowing look, the burning coals now reflected in his eyes. *Grind, swoosh.* He asks another question, "What sparked your body back to life and not all the others who have died?"

I know the answer to this. "The nanocytes." Anger nearly as strong as the anger I felt when Crane stood at my side and I killed Ian surges through my body.

The Witchdoctor winces and leans away from me. In a strangled voice, he says, "Others of my kind, they can't come within ten feet of you without being distressed within an inch of their lives." Realizing that I am the one causing his pain right now, I force my mind to clear. The Witchdoctor straightens and tilts his head. "Tell me, how does this hurt radiate off of one so young with enough strength to impact my kind? We are typically void of these emotions. Especially Glane. He will not come within a mile of my hut any longer. I must travel to see him." *Grind, swoosh.* "This is not easy for me. I do not like to leave my home."

I turn and stare at the wall that's lined with long white sticks. I think that they are actually human femurs.

"How can you be near me?" I ask. "How does it not affect you as badly?"

He shrugs. "I have seen death, I have felt pain." *Grind, swoosh.* "And I never said I didn't feel it. I have felt it all."

"I'm sorry." I look away from him, shamed for hurting this old man who seems to have done nothing but try to help me.

"Tell me, living-dead girl, tell me something about yourself." He resumes the soothing *grind* and *swoosh.*

"I'm not young." I run a finger over the tiny stitches in the seam of my pants wondering who the skin came from, how old they were before they were skinned and turned into dinner and cloth. "I'm thirty-five."

"Well, your age deceives you." The Witchdoctor stands and moves to his shelves. He digs in the shadows before holding up a misshapen piece of broken glass, the edges sharp and jagged. He moves to hold it in front of me so I can see my reflection. For a split second I think to stab the glass into my own body just to make sure I'm real. That this is real. But it can't be. There is no rational reason that the person looking back in that shard of glass is me. It's like looking into the past. And I can't even remember how old I was the last time I looked like this.

The Witchdoctor frowns. "You need more sleep. Your brain has not yet healed."

"No—" I start to protest, but before I even finish saying the word he throws a handful of powder in my face and the world goes black.

FOUR

ADAM

THEN

This was the day that they had prepared for. It had taken years to plan, hours to implement, and billions of dollars to fund. Helicopter blades thrummed loudly overhead as Adam watched the land below him pass by. He knew who he was sent to find, had the image of her face memorized and couldn't help but think that she reminded him of someone from his past. But he wasn't doing this for his past, he was doing this for the future

The pilot motioned to Adam. The helicopter dipped and hovered ten feet from the ground. Adam jumped. He fell and rolled. The helicopter was in the air and heading north before Adam had a chance to get back on his feet. The jump had damaged his ankle. He ignored the pain that sprung up his leg with each step and headed for the city.

Adam had nothing but the clothes on his back. He had survived on less and needed to make sure this looked as real as possible. She couldn't know that he was sent to find her; that would screw everything up. No, he had to look like just another pedestrian, just another survivor. He had to make sure she didn't find out how involved he really was.

The intel he received was that she had worked last night. Their guy on the inside radioed in as soon as they caught her escaping on the hospital cameras. Adam knew he didn't have much time to make it to the highway. It was the only way out of the city and it was the route she drove every day. Since humans were creatures of habit, he was ninety-nine percent certain that was where he'd find her.

Adam limped through the suburb. He walked through manicured lawns, down streets with cars parked haphazardly—the EMP had ruined them. He ignored the strange looks he got from the people he passed and those watching out their windows. He didn't offer to help anyone.

The route he traveled was familiar. In his lifetime he had visited this area. Once for a college football game, once while tracking a mole, and another time because he was on the run and trying to find the last of his family. That ended badly and reminded Adam that he didn't have much to live for any longer. There had been highs and lows, the times he had escaped Crane he had felt free but not happy. There wasn't much happiness left in this world any longer. On a daily basis he was tempted to take what he wanted and just ride this life out on his own terms.

Adam walked through a grocery store parking lot then rounded the back of the building and jumped the six-foot high chain-link fence that was the only barrier between suburbia and four-lane highway. He winced as he landed on his bruised ankle. He headed south knowing that it would take him into the center of the city. The hospital wasn't far from here and if she had already left he was bound to run into her.

Adam favored his uninjured ankle, knowing that he had many miles to walk before he could rest it and let the nanocytes do their job. He'd dealt with worse injuries and survived. Much worse.

Adam passed plenty of people on the highway; most were headed home to the suburbs and the comfort and safety of their homes. Cities held danger and these people were smart for avoiding it. They looked at him like he should know better. He did know better but Adam was on a mission and he wasn't afraid of a city that was recently plunged into chaos—other things scared him, but not that. Adam kept walking, he had a woman to find.

Approaching her was going to be the interesting part. He couldn't just walk up to her and introduce himself and drag her back to Phoenix. No, he needed a plan. He needed her trust.

Once he reached the top of the overpass, he hopped up onto the cement divide. He had almost a bird's eye view from this point, the slight weave of the highway, the people abandoning their cars, the gang of dark-skinned men that had just breached the on-ramp. They were rummaging through the empty cars. At least these men were resourceful enough to get first pick at these cars. When the rest of the people of the city finally realized that the power wouldn't be turning back on, they'd be up here looking for anything they could find as well.

Adam looked further away until he saw a small figure walking in his direction only a few hundred yards away from the gang of men in white T-shirts. She was still dressed in scrub pants and an undershirt, already soaked in sweat from the hot afternoon sun. Adam wiped at his own forehead, he didn't ever remember it being so warm this far north. But then this is what global warming was doing and it was why he had been sent on this mission.

Adam needed to think fast. He couldn't just approach the woman, he needed an *in*. He glanced at the gang. One of the men was rifling through a McDonald's bag from a big SUV. Looks like the owner left their lunch behind.

He could fake an injury, maybe that would get her to trust him, but why fake an injury when you could just create a really believable one? Adam jumped down from the cement divider and ran toward the gang, ignoring the pain shooting up his shin.

"Hey," he shouted. "Hey, get out of my car." He launched himself at the smallest of the group, a man who was currently digging through the backseat of a late model sedan.

The gang members were on him in an instant. One had a gun, another had a hearty left hook, and another knew just where to kick a man in the ribs. Adam went down like a sack of potatoes.

"This your car, man?" one asked.

The big guy had a good right hook, again and again.

Adam groaned. At this rate he'd need a long night's sleep to heal.

Suddenly they stopped.

"You see that?" one of the men asked his cohort.

The big one nodded. "Girl behind that truck?" He moved toward her. "I got this."

Adam watched from under a swollen eye.

She noticed them converging on her and backed away until she ran into the cement wall of the overpass.

Don't jump, Adam thought. *I need you alive. Very alive and able to travel.*

The big guy grabbed her. "What do you think you doin' out here, girl?"

She looked pale and scared shitless.

"Check her bag, maybe she got somethin' we be needin'!" a guy with gold teeth hollered. A third gang member stepped toward her and reached for the bag she had on her shoulder. Idiots. Adam could get up and walk away right now. They had forgotten all about him.

Her eyes flicked in Adam's direction before she recognized the one reaching for her bag.

"Ricardo?" She didn't sound scared any longer. Instead she sounded annoyed. "Are you kidding me? Is that actually you? What do you think you're doing?"

Her focus was off of Adam. He didn't want her to forget that he was there. He needed her to remember him. Let the manipulation begin. He rolled and groaned.

"What she talkin' 'bout?" the guy with the gold teeth asked.

"How's Junior doing?" she asked. "How old is he, three months? I bet he's rolling over by now, isn't he?"

The man named Ricardo finally cracked a smile and the tension on the overpass seemed to dissipate.

"He's great, Andie." Ricardo hugged her. "I never got to thank you for all you did for us. When Junior was discharged you weren't working."

"So what are you doing?"

Adam wondered how she knew a gang member and why she was making small talk with him. Whatever the reason, it worked.

"After the earthquake they closed all the stores. We're out of formula for Junior." She gave him a look. "Hey, I'm just trying to help my family. Find food for my son."

She reached into her bag. "Well, Ricardo, this is your lucky day." She pulled out a small box and held it out to Ricardo. "I will only give you this on two conditions." Ricardo was staring at that box like it was made of gold. Interesting what a man will do for his child in the middle of a disaster. "You let me walk out of this city. I have a family to take care of too, and I need to get back to them." She pointed at Adam lying on the pavement. "And, you leave that man on the ground alone."

Perfect, Adam had her attention.

Ricardo's shoulders stiffened and he said something to his men. She placed the box in his hand. They started walking away but the last guy left standing next to Adam gave him one swift kick to the foot.

"Take care of that baby, Ricardo," she said as the men headed southbound. "He needs a father to grow up with."

She stood there, refusing to turn her back on the gang until they were out of sight.

Adam groaned, unable to hold it back. The guy had kicked him in his already damaged ankle.

She moved toward him, crouched to the pavement and touched him on the shoulder, urging him to roll onto his back.

"Sit up slowly," she said. "Are you dizzy? Do you know where you are?"

Adam just stared, amazed that his plan worked so perfectly. And that this close up, she looked so young and so familiar. He had memorized her face in the picture Crane gave him, but she was different in real life. He wasn't expecting this and it stunned him into silence.

"Follow my finger." She moved her index finger from side to side in front of his face. Then she reached into her pack and pulled out a towel, pressing it to his bloody lip.

He admired her as she examined him. It was a moment he wasn't expecting. Something seemed so wrong about what he was about to do to her life.

"My name is Andie. I'm..." She looked nervous. After just talking her way out of a robbing he found it hard to believe that she was nervous of him. She should be.

She continued, "Well, I was a nurse at the hospital in the city." She pointed in the direction of the hospital but Adam already knew where she worked and where she came from. The sun gleamed on the badge hanging from her shirt.

"Who names their kid Andromeda?" It wasn't the first thing he wanted to say to her, but it was a question he'd had since he first learned of her. It was a name for a prissy princess or an ancient goddess, not some woman from a small town. Parents these days had begun naming their kids ridiculous things, what was wrong with traditional names like Billy and Joan?

She moved away from him. "How do you know my name?"

"You're wearing a badge."

She looked down, saw the hospital badge clipped to her shirt, and pulled it off. "My parents were really into mythology." She glanced at him quick. "You look like you're going to be fine, but the hospital is still open if you want to get yourself checked out. Just follow this—"

"I'm not going back into that jungle." Adam ignored her directions. He knew exactly where the hospital was and he knew he wasn't going anywhere near it. His mission was to get her back to Phoenix.

She stood. "Okay then. I have to go." She pulled her bag over her shoulder and started walking away.

Adam dropped his head. That went less than fantastic. His reaction to her didn't help, the recognition, trying to place where he had seen her before. It didn't help that she was a little awkward herself, one of those people that took a while to warm up to another person.

He watched her walk away, the sun beating down on her back, her small form hunched under the heavy bag slung over her shoulder. He had to get his head straight, couldn't approach her again until he had a plan a better plan.

When he thought he had his head together, Adam finally stood and followed her down the highway. She didn't look back, not once. Good thing it was just him and not a gang of men or someone looking to loot her. The woman was just not safe. He watched her as she stopped near her exit; she jumped up onto the hood of a car, angling herself so she could look in each direction of the highway. That was the smartest thing she'd done all day. She started eating an apple, drank some water. But when she poured water on her hands and then splashed her face, Adam had to look away. The action reminded him that she was trying to preserve some of her humanity, even in these moments of disorder, now that everything had changed.

When she looked up, she noticed Adam walking toward her. He winced exaggeratedly, favoring his uninjured foot. Catching a glimpse of himself in a car window, he was happy with what he saw. Her caring nature led her to him once and now he was hoping it would work again.

She reached in her bag as he got nearer and Adam wondered if maybe she had a weapon in there.

Adam stopped in front of her, pushed his hands into his pockets. "I never thanked you for saving my life."

"You're welcome," she snapped. She was still digging in her bag.

"My name is Adam." He held out his hand. "You're Andie, right?" It wasn't an apology, but it was the best he could summon up right now.

Andie gave up on searching her bag and stared at him hard. A moment of panic passed through Adam; had she told him that she preferred to be called Andie? Was it enough to break his cover? Adam couldn't believe he could make such a mistake this early. Shit.

Andie finally moved, reached out and shook his hand. "Yeah." She didn't seem to notice.

Something strange happened when he took her hand in his. Hers was small, warm, soft and it felt... right. Like her hand belonged in his. Adam had never felt anything like it before in his long lifetime.

"Are you headed north?" Adam asked. He already knew the answer but he couldn't let her know that.

"Yes." Her voice sounded hesitant and Adam knew he had to try harder to get her to trust him. That was the only way he was going to get her home in his care.

"So am I. How far are you going?" Adam shielded his eyes from the bright sun with his hand. He made sure he pronounced that *O* like he used to. That's how people from Phoenix talked, hard *O*'s.

She tipped her head to the side. "Do I know you from somewhere?"

Perfect. "I don't think so. Where are you from?"

"Phoenix."

"So am I." Adam smiled, showing her a row of perfectly straight teeth; it was the only part of him that was still straight, the only part that wasn't twisted and damaged.

Andie didn't move. "I'm not sure if I believe you, Mr. Adam." She crossed her arms over her chest and it was almost comical to him. She was trying to make herself look authoritative but it wasn't working for him. He had stood up against much worse men and women in his lifetime.

The next few minutes passed as a question and answer session on all things local to Phoenix. Adam hit all the right notes and aced her questions with flying colors. He should, this was only the most important task of his life.

"*Dear God*, it truly is a small world," Andie mumbled with a roll of her eyes.

"Would you mind if I walked with you?" Adam asked.

She hopped down from the hood of the car and tossed her apple core into the grass on the far side of the road. "I guess."

They walked. Adam was impressed with the speed at which she moved—being as short as she was. He limped a great deal, really soaking in the injury. It hurt, but not as bad as he was making it look. All he really needed was some rest and he'd be as good as new.

Before long Adam could tell that she was agitated with his slow pace. Her demeanor had become tense and when he let out a groan after stepping on a rock and rolling his injured ankle, she cracked. "Okay, let's take a break and I can take a look at your foot. I can't listen to your yelps of pain any longer."

Adam knew he'd be fine but he let her boss him around and sat where she told him. It was while she was inspecting his uninjured ankle that she saw the small handgun strapped there.

"Why are you carrying a weapon?" she asked, backing away from him.

Adam was instantly annoyed. Typical sheltered American. That's all she was. It made not caring easier. She was why Crane had planned this. Still, as irritated as he was, there was something about this woman that Crane wanted for himself. Adam couldn't see it. Crane had ruined enough people—including Adam—and Adam didn't understand why he needed this woman. Crane could have anyone he wanted to continue on with his experiments.

After a few minutes of silence, Andie finally got over herself and the fact that Adam was carrying a weapon. He needed the weapon. It was the only thing he brought and he needed some kind of backup plan. And to be truthful, if he couldn't get her back to Phoenix willingly and in his care then he would force her and that gun would come in handy.

She bandaged up his ankle, gave him some pain meds, and fashioned him a cane out of a stick from the side of the road. Maybe this woman was resourceful but he still didn't understand how she fit into Crane's plans.

At the halfway point, Andie was looking less than lively. Adam knew she hadn't slept in a long time. He knew he could run on no sleep for a long time, but she was just a weak normal human. She needed her rest.

"There's a hotel," Adam pointed straight ahead of them. "Looks like they have power. We can rest here for the night."

She agreed, although she seemed hesitant. She kept looking off in the distance toward the suburbs that lay past the highway. Adam remembered from reading her dossier that she had a brother that lived near here. He was grateful that she didn't ask to go find him. That would just take too much time, time that Adam didn't have. He needed to get her home before it began.

It was dark by the time they reached the front door of the hotel and the steady hum of the generator was the only noise in the night. Adam held the door open for her like the gentleman he was raised to be and not like the individual he had become.

Andie led the way, walked up to the clerk, and got two rooms. The next stop was dinner. The hotel crew had put out sparse fare, it was enough to satisfy them after a long day of walking.

They sat together and Adam bored her with some small talk of one of his lives. The time he spent in Germany wasn't exactly recent, it was actually, well, over a hundred years ago. That was back when he was known by another name, before he became Adam Waters. It was the first truth he had told her since he met her earlier this afternoon. It felt good, telling some truths and even though she was exhausted she listened to him, which was rare. He was only ever given orders or asked about intel. Rarely was he able to just talk freely about his life, past or present.

When he was done she talked about her daughter and husband.

Knowing that she belonged to another man brought about a new emotion inside of Adam's chest. It didn't feel right. Suddenly nothing about this entire situation felt right to him.

"I think it's time to get some rest." Adam interrupted her.

Andie gave him a shocked look, anger wrinkling her brow at being cut short as she spoke. He thought that maybe it was better if she didn't trust him fully. Maybe he could keep her on the fence so she didn't know exactly what to expect from him. He decided not to dwell on any of it any longer and went to his room to shower and sleep.

Injuries made Adam hungry. It was a side effect of his first generation nanocytes. After resting, his ankle was nearly healed and his bruises had lessened. Now he was simply starving.

He had gotten up early and saw the National Guard setting up along the highway. The hotel had put out a hearty breakfast bar for some of the men that came in to use the bathroom and get coffee. Adam ignored them. Sitting in a booth near a window, he ate in silence and alone, just how he liked it.

When Andie finally showed she headed straight for the coffee then started piling her plate full of food. Adam doubted that a person of her stature could hold down that much food. Maybe she liked a big breakfast.

"Are you starving to death or something?" Adam attempted to tease her but came off as sounding like a jackass. He regretted it instantly.

Andie's face twisted as she wrapped up an apple and a bagel and shoved them into her bag. Oh, she was planning for their travels. Maybe he hadn't judged her correctly.

"I'm sorry," Adam says. "I'm not really a morning person."

She raised her eyebrows at him as she scanned his face. "Neither am

I. Usually I tell people not to talk to me before I've had my coffee. I'd say you're lucky I didn't throw something at your face."

So she was spunky in the morning. The banter between them was a nice change of pace for how he usually spent his time. Alone.

"I thought nurses were healers not fighters," Adam mocked her threat to throw something at him.

Her brows lifted in jest. "I thought army guys were saviors not assholes."

Before he knew it Adam was cracking a smile only to stop with the sharp pain of his busted lip.

"You thought wrong, chuckles," she continued. "Now let's get moving. I want to make it past the county line today. I have to get home." She slung her bag over her shoulder and stood to leave.

Adam didn't argue with her. He was eager to get this show on the road as well. Being around her made him uncomfortable and comfortable, and he wasn't sure what to think of any of it.

They checked out of the hotel and as they were walking out the door a Humvee pulled up in front of the hotel vestibule. A man in fatigues dropped a stack of newspapers in front of the glass doors. Andie picked one up and started to read.

And it begins. Adam thought to himself.

This was exactly what they had planned.

Phase one: propaganda.

Phase two: physical barricades.

Phase three: total Reformation.

Adam scanned the front page of the paper from close behind Andie. He knew he shouldn't stand so near to her but being close to her was calming.

"That's almost half the population." Adam said under his breath, hoping to add to the bleak outcome supported by the propaganda in Andie's hands.

She folded the paper up. "Let's get going."

"Are you sure you want to?" Adam needed to know that she was in this for good. He couldn't have her turning around and walking back to the city before he delivered her to Crane. They were about to hit the point of no return, not that he'd let her back out. He'd drag her back there unconscious if he had to. He just didn't *want* to. He'd rather have her walk in there on her own accord. It would make him feel a little better about what he was doing to her if he didn't have to force her.

"The news report was pretty bleak. Who knows what we will find when we get there," Adam said.

"I don't care." Andie straightened her shoulders. "I broke the law when I abandoned my patients at the hospital. I will never be able to work as a nurse again. My family is all I have. Without them there is nothing." Her voice sounded sad but determined. "I'm going."

Adam was impressed with her resolve. "I was hoping you'd say that."

She was avoiding looking at him and he was hoping that it wasn't because she was crying. She had to be stronger than that if she was going to survive this.

They started walking toward the overpass to the northbound highway. Humvees and barricades blocked the exits. Armed men were scattered throughout the area.

"Wait." Andie grabbed Adam's arm to stop him. "Um..." Her fingers twitched over his bicep and, while Adam liked that she was touching him, he wished she'd stop. Her hand held onto him a few moments too long. "They won't let us by," she said. "We need to go around."

What Andie didn't know was that they'd let him go by. They had their orders just like Adam had his.

Instead of taking the highway they decided to travel through the forest that ran parallel to the main highway. Being late spring there would be mud and chill and rainfall. Adam knew that was nothing compared to what she was going to face after they make it back to Phoenix.

Adam and Andie walked around the back of the hotel and down the steep decline of tall grass that led to the forest. Andie slid on the damp ground and Adam grabbed her arm to keep her from falling. When she was busy fighting her way through the tall brush and trees, Adam held a tree branch up for her to pass. She looked back toward the hotel and noticed one of the army men at the barricades pointing in their direction.

Adam said nothing. Even if they sent troops after them it would do nothing but add excitement to their travels. Adam was up for it. He picked up a stick from the ground and chewed it; the motion helped him focus and kept his mind off of the small woman who was following behind him.

They walked for hours in the shaded forest until they came upon a road sign for Phoenix. Twenty miles was all they had left. Adam heard the sound of helicopters in the distance and he signaled for Andie to take cover. He already knew what they were doing, the helicopters and the troops. By the time they got into town Andie wouldn't recognize the place. No one would.

After the choppers passed Andie took a water break and offered some to Adam. He tried not to think too hard about the fact that she had offered up her provisions to him. He offered her nothing. He didn't really need it, after all, but he accepted the water knowing that the nanocytes would appreciate not having to rejuvenate his body from dehydration.

They walked for another long stretch before the thunder started.

"I want to go out to the road and get a better look at the sky," Andie says as she made her way toward the treeline.

Adam followed her. It was best that she get a glimpse at what they were walking into, what Crane had done.

Thunderclouds had collected ahead of them.

"There are no cars here," Adam said. Of course there were no cars here. Adam knew that they removed them overnight.

"What?" Andie asked.

He was testing her to see how observant she was. "Look around us, Andie. There's not a single car."

She looked up and down the highway until they heard the heavy low whistle in the distance. "Trains?" they both responded.

Adam knew that was Crane's preferred method of transportation. Crane had ensured all the tracks were in running order and had brought in the high-speed engine that countries overseas used.

"Why are they running the trains?" Adam started. "The paper said no travel." He needed to deepen the conspiracy, that was his job. "What about the radiation from the meltdown? They could be spreading cont-amination."

"There was no earthquake and there was no meltdown. That paper was misinformed," Andie replied.

Adam was slightly thrilled that she didn't fall into the propaganda so easily. Maybe she wasn't just like everyone else.

"What do you mean?" Adam asked.

"I overheard some colonel talking to a security guard in the basement of the hospital. He said that there is no radiation."

"This doesn't make sense. What is going on then? Is this a hoax or something?" Adam stared at Andie, waiting for her response. He ran his hand through his short dark hair then down the stubble on the side of his face.

"I don't know what's going on." Andie replied. "But I'd like to find out."

"Why didn't you tell me this before?" Adam asked.

"I'm not sure." She shrugged. "Maybe it's the same reason you didn't tell me you were carrying a gun." Then Andie turned and started walking down the empty highway toward home.

Adam followed her, pleased with the conversation. So far she seemed to think that he was just as innocent as her.

The next thing they came to was the stoplight in the small town of Oswego Falls. Adam estimated that they had about fifteen miles left. He noticed Andie's figure stiffen and he looked ahead of them. There was a chain-link fence where there wasn't before.

Adam knew what they were doing with the fencing system. He'd seen Crane's detailed plans, saw how well it had worked in Japan. But he wasn't interested in standing around and watching. He knew they needed to get to the area that they hadn't finished yet. That was the only way they could get inside undetected. And he wanted to get in undetected. He wasn't ready to give Andie up just yet. Adam had to keep up the act. If he marched her through those gates she'd catch on to him and he couldn't have that this early in the game.

"Get to the forest." He pushed her shoulder. "Run!" He pushed her harder, forcing her to move.

They ran down the embankment on the side of the highway and across a patch of tall grass. The hum of helicopters started up again. Adam noticed Andie was starting to slow and turn. He couldn't have her doing that, it would slow them down. Adam grabbed her arm and pulled her along. It was like dragging a child behind him.

Adam felt guilty as he heard the branches slapping her in the face. She slowed even more and eventually Adam gave in and stopped running. They had gone far enough and should be beyond what Crane had started.

Adam bent with his hands on his knees to catch his breath. His nanocytes weren't keeping up with this, which was strange.

"What was that all about?" Andie asked as she touched her face. Adam tried not to act alarmed when he saw the bloody scratches on her face from the tree branches. He felt guilty for hurting her.

"There were guards or something, putting that fence up. Off to the left of the road. They had guns. You didn't see them?"

"No." Andie began searching her bag. "But that means there are people here. And if they're working, then they aren't suffering from the effects of radiation poisoning. So that proves it, there can't be nuclear fallout."

Adam stilled and thought where to bring their conversation to next. "So I guess you were right, Andie." He liked saying her name. That was a problem. "Something else is going on here."

Andie pressed a towel to a cut on her forehead. "Now what do we do?"

Good girl, she was still on point. Adam was glad he didn't have to drag her back unconscious. This was more fun. "Let's stick to the woods and keep going. It may take us longer than expected to get home, but at least we can stay hidden."

"Okay," Andie agreed with him.

Pain sprung up in Adam's ankle and he cursed his blasted nanocytes. Maybe if he got this woman back in one piece, maybe then Crane will give him an upgrade. Although, for all the times Adam had tried to escape Crane, he was sure leaving him with the first generation nanocytes was nothing but punishment.

They walked through the forest, the ground soft under their feet as the sound of thunder rumbled louder in the distance. Soon the patter of raindrops falling on leaves began high above them.

Andie's stomach growled loudly. "I think we're going to have to stop soon," she warned him.

Adam couldn't agree more. He needed to get off of his feet for a few hours and heal. But, "Just a little bit further," he urged her on.

As the evening got darker and the rain poured down harder, Adam sensed Andie's unease. He kept going, hoping to find dry ground for the night soon. It was almost completely dark and Adam could hear her footsteps as she walked faster to keep up with him. She must have been disoriented or scared of the dark because she rammed right into his chest. Adam grabbed her by the shoulders, holding her up.

"Are you okay?" he asked.

"Uh, sorry." Andie blinked at him and he realized he had kept her out in the open much too long. She didn't have nanocytes, she could get sick or injured with this weather combined with the night. He needed to build a lean-to or some type of cover.

"We should camp here. There's enough branches and brush to start a small fire. No one should be able to see the smoke or the light through the thick trees. We should be safe," he said.

Andie made a face. "No offense but I'd rather not sleep on the ground."

Great, now she was back to being a prissy American. "Oh, so what are you going to do?"

"I'm going to climb that tree."

Oh, of all the bullshit he's ever heard. He started laughing. "Oh yeah, well, have fun with that. Do you know what it's like sleeping in a tree?" Adam knew, he'd done it before. Fell off of a branch one night too. Hurt like a bitch and took a week and a half for his broken arm to heal. "I'll make sure to check your pulse in the morning when I find your body on the ground." He laughed harder and although he was slightly pissed, it felt good. He couldn't remember the last time he laughed and it wasn't forced.

"Actually, chuckles, I think I see the perfect branch."

Adam looked to where she was pointing and his jaw snapped shut. For the love of Pete it was a tree house. "Nice," Adam muttered.

They walked toward the structure and climbed the ladder of rough two-by-four boards that were hammered into the trunk of the tree.

When Andie got to the top, she struggled to pull herself up inside of the dwelling.

Weakness. It agitated Adam but he pushed on her feet to get her inside. When he hauled himself up, he took in the sight. This place must be an old hunting camp or something; definitely not something a group of kids would have built. Probably some rednecks with too much money and too much time on their hands put this together.

The space was large and circular, wrapping around the thick trunk of the tree. There was a smooth floor, open areas for windows and a roof. A small bunk was built into the far wall, near some cupboards and a rough-hewn table and chair.

"Is this where you sing 'jackpot' again?" Adam asked as he passed Andie her bag.

She pulled out a bottle of soda, a bagel, and two apples that she had taken from the hotel. Adam was grateful when she offered him half of the bagel and an apple. His nanocytes would appreciate it. But he knew he needed more. Maybe a few hours sleep will be enough to get him in tip-top shape.

"You know you could be a little more grateful. After all, I have healed you, put a roof over your head, and fed you dinner." Andie held her hands open, palms up, waiting for his gratitude. It was a motion his mother used to make.

Suddenly he was thrust back in time to an era when things were much more simple.

"Thanks, mom." Adam laughed away the memories and this time it was forced.

"Not funny. And just for that I will not share this bottle of refreshing warm flat soda with you. I hope you don't choke on that bagel." The tone of her voice was a mixture of joking and serious and Adam wasn't sure how to take her.

As if a bagel could choke him. He could eat sand and survive. The thought made him laugh again.

Andie ignored him for the moment as she ate in silence. Soon the heavy patter of rain on the roof of the tree house and the deep thundering in the sky took over the night.

"Well, so much for a fire up here. At least we'll be protected from the rain but I hope it doesn't get too cold tonight," Adam said to make it sound like the cold might bother him. It wouldn't, but she was weak. It could make her sick and then he'd be in trouble, bringing her back damaged.

"Don't worry. I have that covered too." Andie rummaged through her bag and pulled out a reflective blanket.

"You want to share that?" The thought made Adam uneasy. He liked being close to her but knew that he shouldn't. She wasn't his. She was Crane's. And Adam knew that Crane broke things. It was best that he delivered her and stopped thinking about her. He was sure that the next time he saw her after delivery, he wouldn't recognize her. Just like he didn't recognize his sister or Richard after Crane was done with them.

Andie shrugged. "Or you could sleep on that cold bunk."

"No, I'm asking if you would sleep next to a stranger?" Adam said it more for himself than her. He had to remind himself that was what he was: a stranger, a bad man.

"I don't think we are complete strangers anymore. Besides, I know you're not going to try anything."

For Christ sakes he could murder her in her sleep. He'd done it before to stronger men. It was easy and she'd be even easier. She had no fight; she was too trusting of him.

"How can you be so sure?" he asked.

"Because my husband will hunt you down and kill you." She sounded so serious it was almost comical. "I'm going to sleep." She pushed her bag under her head and covered herself with the blanket. "Goodnight."

Adam settled on the floor next to her, making sure he was at the far edge of the blanket. When he saw her pull a small stuffed owl out of her bag and rub it with her thumb, something pinged deep inside his heart, something he thought was thoroughly dead.

This was a bad idea

This damn woman was confusing Adam. He thought he had it all figured out, but at that instant he wasn't sure any longer.

ADAM WAS LEANING against the tree trunk that bisected the middle of the tree house. He was watching Andie sleep. The noises she made last night led him to believe that she was having nightmares. And as he watched her now he wondered what a spoiled civilian like her would have nightmares about.

When he became bored with the watching and the thinking, he got up and checked the weapons that were displayed on the walls. There was a homemade spear, bows and arrows, weapons he knew how to use but rarely had a chance to. Next, he searched for something to eat in the cupboards and was happy to find that whoever built this place had left some staple foods; crackers, a few canned goods of corn and peaches, and some plates. Adam took the food and the table setting and laid them out on the floor near where she slept. He'd never made a woman breakfast before and he guessed this was as close as he'd ever get.

He held the simple tin cups in his hand and his eyes fell to the empty soda bottle next to her bag then to the heavy rain falling outside. Rainwater wouldn't kill him, wouldn't kill her either. But he had to eat and hydrate. His nanocytes were angry; he could tell by the way he felt when he woke up. He wasn't fully healed and for the first time in a long time his body felt like crap. He needed protein and more rest.

Adam sat down next to the food. He propped his arm on his bent knee and watched the rainfall out the window waiting for her to wake up. He made sure the sleeve of his T-shirt was up far enough for her to see his Marine Corps tattoo on his upper arm. She seemed like she placed a lot of trust in people who were in the service and while he hadn't been in the service for a long time, this was just part of the show, getting her to trust him a little bit more.

She must have been tired from their travels, the day had begun hours ago and she was still sleeping like a baby. When she finally stirred, he felt her eyes on him, taking him in. That is good, he thought to himself.

"Look what I found," Adam finally faced her and motioned to the breakfast he had laid out for them.

Andie frowned. "Where did you find that?" He gestured to the cupboard on the far wall. "Are you sure you should take this stuff? It's kind of like stealing."

Her thinking that they couldn't take what they needed didn't surprise him. If only she knew what she was in for. "I think whoever this stuff belongs to has bigger problems right now." Her stomach growled loudly. "Sounds like you're hungry too."

"Okay." She gave in. "Let's eat."

Adam pulled his knife from his boot and used it to open the cans. Then he divided up the food as she set the cups on the windowsill to catch rainwater.

Adam thought she still looked tired, and he still felt like crap. He needed more rest and judging from the soppy mess that was outside it wouldn't be hard to convince her they needed to wait another day.

"I think we're going to have to wait out the rain," Adam told her between mouthfuls of food.

She frowned again as she watched the rain out the window. "I guess you're right." She walked back to where he was sitting. "We can't walk in this." She sat on the floor in a motion that was both dramatic and comical, nearly tossing herself down in front of him.

He knew she wanted to get home and he wanted to deliver her—it was his mission—but he couldn't help but feel thankful for spending more time with her. There was just something about the woman.

Adam was curious to learn more about her than he had read in the dossier. "Have you always lived in Phoenix?" he asked.

She nodded and began telling him about her family, the death of her parents, her brother. It was all things he knew but as she sat there and spoke to him he found himself wondering what it would have been like, living a normal life with his sister, instead of having it all taken away at such a young age.

"What about you?" Andie finally asked him. "Why did you want to become a Marine?"

That decision seemed like forever ago. He had to think back to a time when he was innocent and young before he became the man he was today.

As they spoke the rain pattered on the roof of the tree house and the thunder rumbled off in the distance. Adam knew that the world outside this tree house was becoming vastly different than the one that Andie knew. He couldn't help himself but he wished there was nothing going on out there and he had nothing else to do but sit here in the middle of nowhere and talk to this woman with bright green eyes and dark curly hair. He had a crazy thought that maybe he could steal her away from all of this and protect her from the damage he knew Crane was going to inflict upon her.

He'd escaped Crane many times only to be led straight back. Adam knew better, he couldn't hide her from Crane any more than he could hide himself.

By evening the food was all gone and Adam was still hungry. His nanocytes were pissed and he was beginning to feel every part of his old age.

Andie started reading the paper that she brought from the hotel. When she was done, she handed it to Adam and he scanned the propaganda, searching for bits of truth and lies he knew would be printed for the common folk.

The rain finally stopped and Andie moved to look out the windows. Adam figured it must be a mess out there, judging from the slump of her shoulders and the sigh she emitted.

"Morning then?" he asked, knowing that he couldn't travel. He needed more rest. Leaving now would leave him almost defenseless, totally human, and he couldn't have that.

"I guess."

Adam finished the paper and saw movement out one of the tree house windows. It was a herd of deer. He moved quickly, grabbing a bow and arrow off of the wall and checking the windows for the best position.

"Can you believe they are out in this weather?" Andie asked and he wanted to tell her to shut her mouth and not scare them away but instead she noticed what he's doing. Hunting. "Adam, what are you doing?"

"I'm hungry and so are you." His voice sounded deep and low, like the killer that he was.

"I'm not going to eat a whole deer. Stop!" Her voice was getting louder. "We will have all the food we can eat tomorrow. We're almost home." Adam did his best to ignore her, he was so hungry he could eat two deer, raw. He'd suck the marrow out of their bones and his nanocytes would be happy and fully heal him. Then he'd be ready to face Crane tomorrow.

"Adam! Stop, please. You can't kill them." His body was telling him to just do it already. "Adam, stop!" Andie shouted loud enough to scare the deer off.

Now he was pissed.

"Did you seriously just sabotage my kill?" he asked. "We could have gorged for dinner and had food for tomorrow while we travel."

"We didn't need a whole deer. We'll have food in the morning."

"I hope you're happy that you got to save Bambi." He moved to replace the bow and arrow on the wall hooks. "I could have eaten half that animal myself." Adam couldn't control his anger any longer. He wanted to throttle the small woman standing in front of him. He kicked over the chair, wanted to send it flying out the window but he knew that an outburst like that would send her running away. She was just a fragile normal human; he righted the chair knowing that he was already frightening her.

"Sorry. I didn't mean to ruin your life over one little deer." Adam ignored her. She reached into her bag. "Here, I have this guide on edible plants." She held the book out to him.

Of all the ridiculous... "No thanks." Adam walked away from her and tried to regain control over himself. He was weak and tired. His first generation nanocytes were sucking at their job and worst of all he had to turn this woman over to Crane and he really didn't want to. Adam had never been so frustrated in his entire life. He stayed on the opposite side of the tree trunk and waited until he heard the sounds of her laying down.

Adam walked around the tree and watched her sleep. She seemed so innocent and stupid and awkward at times. If Crane wanted her so badly there had to be something more about her. Adam tried not to judge her based on shit she didn't know. He saw the white fluff of the stuffed owl clutched in her hand as she slept. Something gripped him in the chest. She had a child, a family that loved her, someone waiting for her, something Adam had never experienced and most likely never would. He was completely stupid for thinking he had any claim on her. Still, he enjoyed her company and wanted to get to know her better. His emotions were off, something that rarely ever happened to him; he kept them bottled up so tightly half the time he wondered if he was still human.

Andie sighed softly as she slept, and Adam moved toward her impulsively. He lay down on the floor and covered himself with the edge of the blanket. Adam didn't sleep much but when he did his head was filled with events he'd rather not remember. Strangely, here they were gone. Feeling exhausted for the first time in decades, Adam fell into a deep sleep.

WHEN ADAM WOKE, the damn chirping songbirds and sunlight were too cheery for the thoughts that had been crossing his mind as he lay next to Andie. Today was the day. He was one step closer to losing her. No, he corrected himself, closer to delivering the package, to doing his job. To doing what he was designed for, what Crane made him for.

He glanced at Andie out of the corner of his eye. Her face was soft, flexed in sleep. When she suddenly scowled and whimpered, Adam had the impulsive urge to touch her and offer comfort. He didn't like seeing her in pain. He waited for it to pass and watched as she relaxed again. Andie had a lot more to lose than he did. At least he was single when Crane took him, but his family still suffered. She had a husband and a child. If Crane allowed her to keep them it was more than he ever allowed Adam. He wasn't sure how to deal with the thoughts. He had never been allowed a family of his own, doubted he ever would. But still, thinking about it, having a family seemed normal, heck it even seemed nice. Strangely, he liked the woman lying next to him more than he had liked any other woman he had met. There was something about her that both infuriated him and made him curious.

It was best this way, he told himself. She confused the shit out of him and he couldn't have that. Today he'd get back on track, continue with the plan, and deliver her home.

He sat up abruptly and got ready without saying a word to her. He was still pissed. His body still ached. If he had eaten some venison last night his body wouldn't be taking so long to heal. Damn her for stopping him.

Andie finally woke and readied herself. They didn't speak. But just before they headed down the ladder Andie stopped. "Oh, wait, I have an idea." She pulled the book out of her bag, crossed the tree house, and left it on the bare shelf.

If she was feeling guilty for eating the food that was left here she was going to have to get over it. Things were about to get a lot worse and Andie wasn't going to have the opportunity to payback everyone whom she borrowed or took something from. She'd have to learn to let that kind of guilt go.

Adam didn't speak to her as they traveled through the soggy forest. He was still trying to focus and ignore the pain of his half-busted ankle. He heard the rushing flow of river water nearby and decided he wanted to check on Crane's progress.

"I'm going to check the road," he said.

Andie followed him to the tree line and waited as he crept through the tall grass. When he saw that Crane's plans were falling into place exactly as planned, he motioned for Andie to come look.

"Oh crap," she uttered when she got an eyeful of the large wall made of stone that was being built.

Adam was impressed with the progress of the takeover. He was also aware that anyone living near the nuke plant would be provided with their potassium iodide pill in case of a nuclear meltdown. And he knew that they weren't being given potassium iodide. Instead, it was a special medication manufactured in one of Crane's many laboratories and it did magnificent things when one was trying to control a group of people.

Adam backed away and led Andie away from the main highway leading into Phoenix. They took the long way in, past some back roads where they could maintain their cover. They passed the county jail that backed up to a graveyard.

"I think we should take a different way in," Andie argued as Adam made his way to the open area with no tree cover.

There were plenty of old trees that they could find cover under on their way through, he was about to tell her this, but then... something caught his eye. It was the gravestones. Suddenly everything came crashing in on Adam. He clenched his jaw and did his best to hold it in.

"What's wrong?" Andie whispered.

He felt his pocket for the yellowed piece of paper he'd carried around with him for decades. "There's something I have to do."

Before he knew it he was moving away from her. This was not the right time, he knew that, but he couldn't help himself. It had been so long since he'd been here, so long since Crane had allowed him to embrace his humanity. He shouldn't do it, but he'd kept it bottled up so long and now that he was here and his nanocytes were acting up and this woman was... she was driving him insane.

Adam couldn't wait any longer. This was one bit of his past he had to deal with and he had the uncontrollable urge to deal with it right now or it might ruin him.

He looked at the diagram in his hand, found where his parents were buried and, knowing that he had an alias to protect, he stopped when the names on the gravestone in front of him caught his eye. Waters was a common name in the area and it was a perfect coincidence that the fresh graves were right here right now. It would reveal nothing about him and everything he needed her to believe.

He focused a few rows away on at the headstone he was really here to visit. Whitmarsh. The resting place for his parents was the only real gift Crane had ever provided Adam with. But he had never let him visit or pay his respects. He had waited all this time.

It was hard to remember who Christian Whitmarsh was, the boy that his parents had raised. Crane had renamed him Adam because he was the first and Waters because Crane had some raging God complex. Like Crane was the water that fed the earth or some bullshit. Adam focused on the Waters gravestones and hoped to high hell that Crane had nothing to do with their deaths.

Andie was at his side again. "Adam, what are you..." Her voice trailed off as Adam was already sinking to his knees and hiding his face behind his hands. He didn't want her to see him like this, didn't want anyone to see him like this. Crane had turned him into a machine but these last few days were breaking him down.

"Oh no. I'm so sorry," Andie whispered as her small hand squeezed his shoulder.

Adam wanted to keep her there with him. Wanted to grab her wrist and pull her to the ground and hold her as he cried for the life that was stolen from him. But that wasn't what a man did, and she wasn't his. He told himself he was only feeling this way because of the exhaustion. It was making him irrational and he knew he had to get it together.

A soft wind blew the scent of her toward him. She smelled like basil, soap from the hotel, and dirt from the earth. It was enticing to him, more so than any other woman he had ever been around. He was again torn between wanting to take her away and getting her out of his possession so he could fulfill his orders. Crane had been Adam's only constant; he was the man that made him and even if Adam didn't like it he felt he owed the man his life. It was twisted and wrong but Adam knew nothing else.

"I'm sorry. I didn't know—" Andie started to tell him.

"I didn't tell you." He thought of a lie, one that was at least a half-truth. "I didn't want it to be true. I just had to see them one last time so I could move on, I guess." He set his face before looking into her eyes. "Let's get you back to your family."

She told Adam her address but he already knew it. He had been fully briefed on every aspect of her life. Her education, her career, her family, but Crane never told him exactly why she was so special. He thought it was something from her past.

They kept off of the main road and walked behind the graveyard where they were hidden by the high embankment. They heard the low dull whistle of the train as it traveled. Adam knew this was Crane moving supplies and people. He let Andie make her own assumptions as to what it was. The less she knew the better but the human brain tried to fill in the missing pieces, make everything make sense. He knew that she was currently taking in every bit of information and trying to put it together.

When they reached her street Adam added to the scheme by asking, "Where is everyone?" He already knew where they were, receiving their medication and being assigned into factions.

"There are no cars," Andie whispered.

They walked another block until she suddenly broke into a run; her house was not far ahead of them.

Adam let her go as he strolled down the street, remembering how it looked so long ago when he was a child. There were empty lots back then, now they were filled with modest homes. Even the park he used to play at as a child now held a large house. He had lived not far from here. Adam was sure that his old family home was inhabited by some other family.

Andie disappeared into her house and Adam followed. The front porch steps creaked as he climbed them. She had left the doors open so he let himself in and he looked around her house as she ran through searching for her loved ones. He saw pictures of a happy family. Of Andie and her... shit, little girl. And she looked familiar like he'd seen her before and not just as a reminiscent copy of her mother. Somewhere else, he couldn't put his finger on it.

Adam knew that Crane had a habit of stealing children in the night. And now he wondered what else the man was really up to.

FIVE

SARA THOMAS

SARA THOMAS NEVER KNEW IAN SOMERS BUT SHE BORE HIS child. Before the Reformation she was a college student at the local Phoenix campus. It was her first time living away from family, her first time living on her own. She had dreams of being a writer or maybe a librarian, she hadn't decided. What she did know was that she had already fallen in love with this place. Her dorm room overlooked Lake Ontario and was built on the outskirts of campus where it was quiet and serene. Many times she found herself staring off into the sunset in the evening time when she should have been studying. She had come from a larger city downstate, they never experienced sunsets like the ones here. She only had a few days left before heading home for the summer. Most of the campus had already emptied out, but Sara's father couldn't make the drive to pick her up until the weekend. All she had left to do was pack the remainder of her belongings and turn in her dorm room key to the resident assistant. Little did Sara know, the tiny lakefront town that she had grown to love would be the end of her, and the few of her co-eds that also remained on campus.

The tremor shook Sara's dorm in the early morning hours, when the sun was just splintering across the horizon. She sat up, shocked and disoriented. There was commotion in the hallway outside of her private dorm room, but when she looked outside her window everything seemed fine. Sara turned to look at the clock on her desk but it was blank. Pushing her blankets off of her body, Sara opened her laptop, a gift from her grandparents upon graduating high school. She pushed the power button and moved to get dressed. As she pulled on a pair of jeans someone banged on her door.

"You all right in there?"

Sara recognized John's voice, the resident assistant, and she shouted back. "I'm fine."

"Get dressed. Meet us downstairs."

Sara pulled on a sweatshirt and listened as he pounded on the door of the room next to her.

When she checked the computer, the screen was black as though she had never turned it on. She pulled her cell phone from underneath her pillow and disconnected it from its charging cord and pressed the power button. Nothing happened. Unease settled in Sara's gut. She tucked the cell phone in her pocket, took her keys from her desk and shoved them in her other pocket, then left her dorm room.

The kids on her floor were leaving their own rooms, some already headed for the stairwell. One boy stood in front of the bank of elevators.

"Don't work," one of his buddies smacked him as he walked by.

Sara followed them and more kids followed behind her as they made their way down the stairwell and to the main floor.

John was ushering everyone into the common room.

"Come on! Come on!" he waved everyone in.

Sara followed and just as she turned she caught a glimpse of men dressed in gray outside of the building. Thinking nothing of it, she chose to sit on the floor near a few of her classmates that she recognized.

John was holding a pill bottle in his hand.

"Afraid there might have been a problem at the nuke plant." He twisted open the cap of the bottle. "Potassium iodide. Your parents all signed a waiver before you came." He started handing out the pills.

Sara remembered her father telling her something about this. He had showed her the waiver, explained to her that in case of a nuclear catastrophe the pill would protect her thyroid. When she asked him about the rest of her body, her father just shrugged and replied with, "Let's hope you never have to use it." Before signing the waiver he had paused and asked, "You sure you want to go to school this close to a nuke plant?"

Since it was the only college that had awarded her a scholarship, she said yes.

Now Sara held out her hand to receive her pill.

"How are we supposed to take this?" the guy behind her asked.

"Swallow it." John continued passing out the large pills.

"Dry?" the guy sounded disgusted.

"Water's off," John replied. "Do what you can to get it down."

Groans erupted from around her as she inspected the pill. It was larger than she expected. Not wanting to risk it, Sara popped the pill in her mouth. She let saliva pool in her cheeks and rolled the pill around to dampen it, and then she swallowed.

There were only about thirty students in the room. They all watched as John did his best to swallow a pill. He coughed afterwards and his face turned pale like he was going to puke it up. He didn't though. He replaced the cap on the bottle, set it up in a cupboard on the wall, and then made his way to the door where the men in gray were now waiting.

John ran a hand through his dark hair as he glanced between the guards and the students. His normally classically handsome face was furrowed in concern. It seems no one ever thought an event like this would occur and now they were all scared.

"What do we do now?" a girl next to Sara asked.

"Yeah." A guy to her left stood up and walked to a nearby window to look out. "We can't just hang around here doing nothing. We should get moving. Head out of town. Something."

John turned back to the group. "Okay." He let out a breath. "Just sit tight until we find out what really happened. Behind these cement walls is the safest place we can be during an event like this."

Other kids around Sara stood. Some of them muttered things that sounded angry. Sara's heart sped up, she felt like she couldn't fill her lungs with enough breath. She had a history of panic attacks and prayed one wasn't coming on now.

John seemed to notice that he was losing control of the room.

"All right, guys. If you want, go back to your rooms. I'll come find you when we have some news."

A bunch of the kids happily left the common room. A few tried the exit doors that weren't near the intimidating guards in gray, but they remained tightly locked no matter how hard the kids pushed on them.

"I said stay in the building!" John shouted down the hall.

Sara stayed sitting on the floor, taking deep breaths to calm herself. She closed her eyes and tried to focus on something other than her current situation. She wanted to call her parents and tell them to come get her right now but she didn't want to put them in danger. So she sat there and practiced the deep breathing exercises her doctor taught her in case she didn't have her anxiety medicine nearby.

"Hey." She heard John's voice and her eyes fluttered open. "You okay?"

She let out a breath. "I get a little anxious sometimes."

"It'll be okay." John sat down on the floor next to her and crossed his legs. "If only this had happened a few days from now." He glanced at her. "We'd all be home. Not here."

Sara nodded before closing her eyes and trying to calm her nerves once again. It worked; after a while, she found herself becoming more and more relaxed as she sat next to John.

She finally opened her eyes and asked, "How long do you think we'll have to wait here?" Her stomach growled loudly.

"I'm not sure."

IT HAPPENED to be close to two months, that's how long they were trapped in their dormitory. The guards in gray remained outside of the building preventing any of the remaining students from leaving. Each day food and water were brought to them. And each evening when Sara lay in bed and tried to fall asleep, pressing the power button to her cell phone for the billionth time, she wished that she had departed campus when the rest of the college students had and not waited for her father to pick her up. It was too late now. All Sara could do was wait and hope that she'd get out of there soon and see her family again.

Soon never came.

Two months turned into four then five. Each day John handed out another potassium iodide pill to all of the remaining students. Sara had limited medical knowledge and her trusting nature led her to take the pill without question. Although, something ticked in the back of her mind that this whole situation seemed off. But once she swallowed her pill all was forgotten.

Sara spent her days alone in her dorm room; reading, watching the world outside her window, and spending quiet evenings with her classmates.

Conversations changed from "when we get out of here" to "wonder what they'll bring for dinner tomorrow." It seemed the lot of them had grown to accept their new arrangement and no one made an effort to change anything about their current predicament.

One day the guards in gray came inside and requested that all of them line up in the common room, side by side. They all did as requested. A tall guard walked down the row of them. He chose ten of the guys, including John.

"Volker recruits," he said as he motioned for the guys to go with another guard. He chose ten of the girls. "Fertility unit." He motioned for them to go with another guard.

Sara went with the second group. She was so excited to finally leave the confines of the dormitory that she never heard what was going to happen to the remaining ten students that were left behind.

Sara was the perfect Resident; young, healthy, fertile and oh-so compliant. But she was not needed for her fertility, only for the use of her womb. Anyone could have been chosen for the task, it just so happened that the people running this place were keeping track of their cycles and Sara was ready when they were. Poor luck chose Sara's fate.

"Everything will be fine," the doctor in the white coat told her. His smile was friendly, warm, and his fine Asian facial features lent him a trusting appearance. He was so unlike everyone else she had met during her time in the locked Fertility unit. And she trusted him. Even while he told her what he was doing between her legs in the sterile room.

"You're going to have a baby, Sara."

She heard the metal clang of medical instruments and felt a strange sensation in her lower abdomen.

"Unfortunately it's not your baby to keep," he continued.

There was pressure and a pinching sensation. A few moments later he covered her up then started cleaning up the sterile tray that was near the bed she was lying on. Afterwards she was led back to her room.

As the weeks and months passed her abdomen grew larger and larger and she began to feel the baby kick. She knew it was too soon when she began feeling the telltale signs of labor. She notified the man who stood outside her room each day and eventually the doctor showed up and informed her that she was going to be having her baby that day.

Sara had never met the man who sat next to her in the delivery room the night she delivered the child. She knew nothing about him and she only did what was instructed of her. Like when she touched his hand after the baby was born, it was the first time she had felt his skin. And when she raised her hand to his face, it was the first time she had looked into his brown eyes. Although she had never met this man before she knew that he was the father of the baby that she held in her arms.

She barely paid attention to the other woman in the room; a short nurse who she could hear crying in the hallway after the baby was born.

Afterwards she raised the child, a grandchild that her parents would never meet. And while she knew that the child wasn't truly hers, Sara imparted what love she could on the boy. He looked so much like that man who she had met in the hospital the night she delivered. But strangely, she had no urge to raise alarm about the boy's real parents and his weirdness. Sara was content to do what was asked of her until the day the boy was taken away and she was no more.

That's what the Reformation did, it broke families and it ruined dreams and it ended lives far too soon.

Six

Andromeda

"I wish you would stop doing that," I tell the Witchdoctor when I wake, rubbing the dust off of my face and out of my eyes.

"It is necessary," he answers with cool calmness.

"For who?"

"Both of us." He imparts an uneasy look in my direction. "You drain me."

The hut is dark, the air thick and murky with the tang of spice and dried herbs. I stand and move to the stool next to him, noticing the Guardian watching us from the corner.

"I'm sorry," I tell the Witchdoctor as I reach out to warm my hands by the glowing coals. I don't feel cold but the warmth is comforting.

"I forgive you." He nods, reaching to the floor and sprinkling dirt into his bowl. *Grind, swoosh.* "This time."

This time. Wonderful.

"Why do you keep putting dirt in there?" I ask.

"I take what is needed from the earth to heal my people." He pauses to poke a stick at the coals, releasing a burst of flame and smoke. "Better question, living-dead gi—"

"Please stop calling me that," I interrupt him. I am not dead. He makes me sound like a zombie and I don't like it. I'm still me, even if I fried to a crisp and came back to life.

He sets the stick down and stares at me. "Then what is your name? If it fits I shall call you by it."

"Andie."

The Witchdoctor frowns. "That is a boy's name." He shakes his head as his hands return to his bowl. *Grind, swoosh.* "You are not a boy."

"It's a nickname." I look away from him and focus on the things hanging on his walls. I can finally focus on them clearly now—those aren't sticks, those are femurs. "Andromeda is my full name."

"Ah." He sprinkles more dirt into his bowl. "Greek princess."

Grind, swoosh.

"And was your mother as arrogant as Cassiopeia?" the Witchdoctor asks.

"My mother is dead," I tell him. "And I never knew her to be arrogant. She was loving and kind. Never like the Cassiopeia in mythology."

Needing to distract myself, I pull my hair across my shoulder and begin braiding it.

"Your grandmother perhaps? Or great-grandmother? Or great-great-grandmother?" An odd grin spreads across his face as he stares into the glowing embers, avoiding my gaze.

Grind, swoosh.

"One of them—" I recall the stories Crane told me. "She wanted to better the world. Or so I've been told. I never knew her though. She developed the nanocytes that kept me alive."

The grinding stops.

"Seems the arrogance lies in technology. Perhaps that is why you were sacrificed. Our world provides for us. There is no need for what your grandmother and the Red Devil have done. The earth would have done it, within time."

"The Red Devil?" The hairs on the back of my neck stand at attention. "Do you mean Burton Crane?"

Grind, swoosh.

The Witchdoctor nods. "He is your sea monster."

I used to fear of him. Now, I simply hate him.

"Who is your Perseus?" The Witchdoctor asks.

Grind, swoosh.

Ian's lifeless body flashes to the forefront of my mind. The second person I've killed in my lifetime. "He's dead," I reply in a low voice.

"Wrong Perseus." The old man shakes his head as he grinds his pestle. "Your true Perseus cannot die."

Leaning forward, I rest my head in my hands, tired of this talk. My hair slips across my shoulder, trailing down my back. I can feel it tickle the skin that's exposed above my waistband.

"Andromeda." He pauses as he says my name as though he's tasting it for flavor. *Grind, swoosh.* "Leader of men—"

"No!" I sit up straight. "I am not a leader. I never wanted to be a leader. I never wanted any of this."

Grind, swoosh. "It's not too late, you know."

"For what?" I ask.

"For you to make a difference. Slay the sea monster." The Witchdoctor stands and moves to his shelves.

An overwhelming sadness floods me as I think of Lina and Raven. I left them in Hanford alone. I said I'd be back in two days, and it's been... it's been months according to this old man—close to a year. And I left them all behind; my children and the ones I vowed to look after.

"Please stop." The Witchdoctor grabs the shelf. Glass jars wobble and fall to the floor.

"I can't help it." Hot tears spring from my eyes. "My children..."

There is the clanking of glass, the sound of boards clattering against each other. A handful of powder is thrown in my face. I sleep once again.

I ROLL OVER, pulling the burlap blanket with me, and my eyes focus on the burning coals.

"You must learn to control your emotions." The Witchdoctor is placing jars on an empty shelf. There are broken vessels and urns and piles of odd colored dust littering the floor.

"I'm sorry," I say.

"I will only accept so many apologies. Then you must leave."

Curling my body, pulling my knees to my chest, I close my eyes and feign sleep. From a half-cracked eye, I watch the Witchdoctor mill about his home. He moves jars and adjusts his shelves. Choosing a gray colored powder, he sprinkles some in an old chipped mug, pours some water in it from the kettle near the coals, then drinks.

I try to remember the last time I ate something but I cannot.

I move to sit up. "Can I have some food?" I ask.

The Witchdoctor turns, his eyes widened in surprise. "I have never fed you." He sets his mug down. "Why do you ask for food now? Are you hungry?"

My hand moves to my abdomen. There are no hunger pangs or grumbling. "No," I reply softly. "I don't think so. But I don't know."

"You do not require food. Similar to that black beast that watches you from the shadows." The Witchdoctor points toward the Guardian. When he turns back toward me, he stares for a long moment. "For comfort maybe?"

I shrug.

"How about some tea?" he asks.

"Sure."

He moves to the shelves and selects another chipped mug then pours in water from the teakettle. Then he sprinkles one of his concoctions into the mug before handing it to me.

"Is there dirt in this?" I ask, suspiciously peering into the cup.

"What does it matter? You are made from dirt." He motions to the mug. "Drink it."

Pausing before tasting the tea, I ask, "So you're one of the Swamp People?"

He nods.

I sip, tasting the bitter tea. The warmth soothes my throat all the way down to my stomach. "But you don't talk like the others of your kind," I point out to the old man.

"I do not." The Witchdoctor returns to his stool across from me.

"Why?" I ask.

"I wasn't always who I am today." He sips from his mug.

"Who are you?"

He tips his shoulder and smiles quietly. "That is no longer important at this moment. Some other time I may tell you, but not today."

IT TAKES four days of my insistent questioning to get something out of him.

"Why are you different from the rest of them?" I ask from my mat on the floor.

He sighs heavily. The breath he blows out sends the flames in front of him dancing. "You know, we never needed to search for a cure to cancers and illness." He begins. "The earth would have found a way. What we needed to do was accept that we might die early. It was fear of death that drove the Red Devil in all of his experiments. He says he does this for mankind, but he truly fears his own mortality. What humans need to realize is that the earth gives us what we need and takes what it needs. They need to accept their death, let it be early or late in their lives; there is a reason for either timing."

"So where do I fit in?"

"Ah, you can restore the balance. You can make peace. Influence others to do good. And then, let the circle of life continue as it naturally would have." He waves a hand in the air. "Be done with all of this meddling."

"But... I need to get to Galena, to Alaska, where Crane has stored the world's data. They have a server there—"

"And what will the world's data tell you?" he interrupts me.

"How to get the nanocytes out of my body." I clutch at my chest. "I need to get them out. Live a normal life again."

"We are far beyond what you consider normal. That life is gone." He frowns. "And if you can't?"

"I will. And then I'm going to put an end to Crane."

"Yes he should be stopped. I suspect the others like him have met untimely deaths?"

"Well, there are two that I know of. Funding Entities he calls them —and himself—they died of old age it seems. I was there when one of them died. Alexander. He asked me to tell him that he was forgiven for all that he did." A somberness floods me as I recall sitting at his bedside. "I cried for him after all he did. I don't think I ever cried for Ian."

"Stop," the Witchdoctor warns. "You're doing it again."

I still, take a calming breath and try to clear the emotions.

"Better," he says as he takes a sip of his tea. "You need to learn to control what it is that you can do."

"Crane said its amplified pheromones," I tell him. "That I can influence people to do things. The nanocytes do it."

"Ah, Queen mandibular pheromone. He altered it for the human race." The Witchdoctor nods his head as though he knows exactly what I am talking about. "Queen bee. Smart and dangerous."

I hate the term. "I am a danger to my children now." There is a stinging behind my eyes. "I don't think I'll ever be able to see them again."

"Why is that?"

He's wincing again, leaning away from me.

Taking a calming breath, I tell him, "I killed my husband." The stinging grows, filling the space behind my eyes and deep in my nose. I try to take a breath, sounding like a staccato cry, it does nothing to stop the emotions.

I hear the sound of the Witchdoctor's mug falling to the floor. "Still not ready," he rasps.

And this time I pray for him to knock me out. When the handful of dust is thrown into my face, for once, I am grateful.

Seven

Adam

Then

Adam knew what Crane was doing when he threw the parties in the newly created Phoenix District. There was Christmas, Birthdays, gifts, and wine that had been forbidden to the rest of the Residents. It was all part of Crane's plan. Let them live as though not too much had changed, then take it away little by little. Let them think they're special, spoil them, sweet-talk them, and then rip it all to shreds. Crane had used this same technique on him. Bribery worked so wonderfully that Adam knew better than to accept any gift from Crane without expecting something in return.

Crane was like an emotionally abusive parent, one without true children. He only had possession of the ones he stole.

Crane had always struggled with the reproductive aspects of his experiments. He never had access to what he had now, a human population, an entire country that was about to be at his fingertips. But Crane still struggled; the only difference was that now he had Andie to help him.

"You talked to your contacts at the CIA?" Crane asked Adam as they stood in his office at the Headquarters building.

"Yes. They fear something is about to happen." Adam looked out the window, eager to get out of the room. He didn't like being this close to Crane. Nothing good ever happened when Crane had Adam locked in a room.

"Good." Crane smiled. "Because we both know something colossal is about to happen."

Adam nodded in agreement.

Crane began waltzing through the office, getting closer and closer to Adam. "You delivered the packages as well?"

"The ones marked to Sweden?" Adam nodded. "Yes. As instructed."

"Such a good dog." Crane stopped just in front of Adam and looked him up and down. "And Remington?"

"I'll take care of him. As instructed." The man was running intel for Adam. Getting him answers, digging for him. Adam had to find out how deep this project ran. But it had taken him longer than expected and now Crane was curious over what the man was doing. Adam had to clean up some loose ends.

"Perfect." Crane finally stepped away and Adam held his ground. This was a game to the man and Adam had lived through it for far too many years. "They're delivering the baby tonight," Crane told him.

"Baby?" Adam questioned.

Crane laughed. "Don't you remember?"

Adam wasn't sure, Crane had been running him ragged and while he could keep up on most days, it was getting harder and harder; there were too many distractions now.

"Ian, her long lost husband. His child will be born tonight."

Adam nodded.

"After she's going to seek comfort from you."

Adam's back straightened. Crane told him plenty to do but this was a bit much.

"You want her." It was a statement, didn't even resemble a question.

Adam shrugged. "She'll do." He tried to play it off because he knew exactly what Crane would do if he found out Adam was getting attached.

ADAM WAS WAITING near the door and he was about to go check on Lina as she slept, again. No one had ever left him in charge of a child but Adam was drawn to little girl, liked spending time with her. He worried about Crane's plans for her. Before Adam made the attempt to turn around and walk to the door to her bedroom, Andie stormed into the apartment.

"Andie." Adam reached out for her but she swerved to the side, avoiding his grasp. Adam had never seen her so mad, anger was radiating off of her in waves. She was wearing oversized scrubs and in her hands was the clothing she had left in, neatly folded. She threw them against the wall as she crossed the living room, headed for Lina's bedroom.

"Is Lina asleep?" Andie asked.

Adam grabbed the back of her top, wanting to stop her before she woke the child up, but she tore away from him.

"Yes, she's asleep. Andie, wait."

Andie peeked in the bedroom and when she was satisfied with what she saw, she closed the door. Adam was waiting for her and he reached to stop her again.

Andie slapped at his hands. "Don't touch me, Adam!" She glared at him before heading to the phone that was attached to the far wall in the living room. "Burton Crane," she demanded. She waited for a moment before she said, "I need to see you. Now."

Adam could hear the voice of Crane on the other end.

"Yes, Crane. I need to see you *now*," she said before she slammed the receiver down.

The woman was pissed and Adam knew why. After all the time they had spent together, he knew that finding out her husband was still alive would break her. He also knew that Crane made it look like he had a child with one of the other Residents. If Adam was the relationship type, if he was ever allowed to have a wife, he knew he'd be pissed to go through something similar. What Crane was doing to her wasn't right. But Crane rarely did the right thing.

Adam followed her to the Atrium where she paced, waiting for Crane. As soon as the man walked through the door, she ripped into him. For the first time, Adam thought Crane's plan might be backfiring. He expected Andie to run to Adam's arms for comfort; Andie had other plans.

Adam watched from near the elevator and Crane didn't even acknowledge him. He was amazed that Crane was letting Andie talk to him like she was, but he had always allowed it. Adam had watched similar happenings on more than one occasion. Crane lets her get away with so much.

He tells her lies and half-truths, enough to calm her down and coerce her into continuing with her job here. Adam knows that Crane needs her help.

"And now that I have completed the pairings what will I do?" she asked him.

"The population will grow, Andromeda. Children will grow up, babies will be born. You will be responsible for their pairings also. Your job will never be completed as long as the Phoenix District remains prosperous. This is excellent really, you are just in time."

"Just in time for what?" Her face twisted in question. There was fear and apprehension visible under the strain of her anger.

"Just in time to withdraw the medication and welcome the Residents fully alert into the Phoenix District." Andie's face paled as Crane continued. "I think we should continue this conversation at another time. Perhaps after you've had time to rest. Goodnight, Andromeda!" He bowed, glanced in Adam's direction, and then walked out the door.

Andie watched Crane go before storming toward the elevators. They headed back to the living quarters and the first thing Andie did was open the cupboard and pull a bottle out from behind the pans.

Adam recognized it as one of Crane's many gifts to her. He knew the woman well, knew what she liked, knew what she reached for when her stress had reached a precipice.

Andie twisted the cap off of the bottle of wine as she asked, "Do you want some of this?"

Adam knew what he had to do next, he'd promised Crane it would happen. He ran a hand through his hair. "Sure. Why not." The wine would make it easier for her and quite possibly for him.

Andie poured the wine into two coffee mugs before taking a long drink from hers. She took the bottle and handed Adam his mug as she crossed the living room and sat on the floor.

Adam sipped at the wine, grateful for how strong it was. He finally moved and sat down on the couch opposite her.

"What did you think of that conversation, Adam?" She drank more from her mug.

Adam chose his words carefully. "It's all a little much." He sipped from his mug.

"That's all you have to say? After all this time, Adam, you haven't spoken to me in months. One minute you're saving us from wolves, you're pulling out my stitches, you're kissing me in the basement, asking me to trust you, and then you're gone. I think I even called you a few weeks ago and you didn't answer. I take it all very personally." She emptied her mug and then poured herself some more.

At this rate she'd be two sheets to the wind in minutes. Adam had never seen a woman her size drink so fast.

He had to avoid her, wanted to pick up the phone when she called so badly but knew he couldn't. Crane was watching. Crane had a plan. But now, Crane wanted Adam to take their relationship a step further. Adam was trying to keep his distance, didn't like that he forgot who he was and what he was meant to do when she was around. This was all getting so tangled. Something was nipping at the forefront of his brain, a warning, but he had yet to deal with it.

"You don't understand, Andie," Adam said as he set his mug down and rubbed his hands over his face. "Crane is running me ragged. He has me out surveying the wall, the fence, the Gateway, assigning new recruits, training Remington. I barely have time to sleep." He didn't need to sleep but he didn't tell her that.

"And all this time I've been wondering what I did wrong to put you on edge." Andie paused to press her lips together, like she was having trouble feeling them. "Do you remember at Lina's birthday party? When I told you Crane slapped me across the face and split my lip?"

Adam's eyes flick to hers. Crane never mentioned this to him and he could feel his blood pressure rising at the thought of the man touching her. "He was trying to kiss me, Adam."

"What do you mean he was trying to kiss you?" Adam could barely believe what he was hearing. That was never part of the plan. But maybe Crane found out what Adam was doing while training Remington. The man always seemed to find out when Adam was betraying him. It wouldn't be the first time Adam tried to branch out on his own. But if he had found out then he would punish him, and then draw Adam right back in, just like all those years ago when Crane stole him in the night. It was a twisted relationship, one that wouldn't make sense to anyone on the outside looking in.

"Just what I said," Andie continued, "he was trying to kiss me and I pushed him away. That's why he slapped me. For *denying him*. That was right after he told me that I would be expected to reproduce and that he expects us to be paired. Me and Crane, can't you just picture it in your head like a sick putrid little love story?" Andie took another long drink of wine. "Does it make you want to vomit? Because I do. Every time I replay it in my head."

Adam stilled and watched her, trying to gauge if she was telling the truth. She usually told the truth. The woman had the outstanding ability to suck at lying.

"You're serious?" he asked.

"Unfortunately I am." She filled her mug again.

"This is bullshit." Adam paced the room, brimming with anger. "Why didn't you tell me this before?"

"You don't talk to me anymore. We've gone over this already, Adam." She waved her hand at him, dismissing the conversation.

"I can't protect you if you don't tell me these things. Crane keeps me too busy to watch you all the time like I did before."

Andie laughed as she looked into her mug. "You used to watch me?"

Adam rubbed his jaw, ran his fingers through his hair, did everything to stop his body from moving toward her and making her his. Even if it was his job, sleeping with the woman without letting strings attach was a struggle.

As Adam paced, Andie kicked off her shoes and socks and rubbed her bare feet into the carpet. Her feet were small, delicate. The thought of seeing the rest of her bare caused him to pace even more. Andie drained the last of the wine and Adam was sure that he'd never seen a woman as wasted as she currently was. Her cheeks were flushed as she stood and walked toward him.

Adam finally stopped pacing.

"What?" he asked as she stood in front of him.

"I'm tired of this, Adam. I'm tired of Crane controlling me. I'm tired of living in fear of him. I'm tired of you being gone all the time. I'm tired of being trapped up here, alone." She reached out and grabbed the front of his shirt, pulling him toward her.

This was the moment. He had to do this, he wanted to. But something felt off about the entire situation. He hesitated. "Stop. You're drunk already. It's only been like five minutes."

Her lip tipped up as she replied, "What can I say? I'm a cheap date. Most men like that in a woman." She pulled him closer. "Did you hear me, Adam? I'm done with you ignoring me all the time." She stood on her toes and wrapped her arms around him. "I need you," she breathed the words into his ear.

Adam grabbed her upper arms, trying to stop her, holding her still. He clenched his jaw, tried to remind himself of what he needed to do. But then she kissed him, hard. And he could hold back no longer. Her small hands gripped his shirt as he took control. Or at least he thought he had control, until she began leading him toward her bedroom.

Adam had to stop her, make sure she knew what she was doing.

"Are you sure you want to do this?" His eyes searched hers. He remembered the last time he revealed himself to her, she ran from his scars, ran from the monster Crane had turned him into. She'd run even further when she found out the truth about him. He knew it, didn't like it but knew nothing else. Crane had taken everything away from him and formed him into this—a monster, a liar, a thief.

Adam stood rigid in front of her waiting for her answer.

"Yes," she finally said.

Unlike the last time he allowed himself to enter the bedroom with her, this time she took control, deftly unbuttoning his shirt and pushing it away. This time she didn't run from his scars, she ran her fingers over each one of them, the slashes, the old burns, the pock marks from bullet wounds.

For a moment Adam worried that Andie could see right through his deceit and deception. But then she began to take her clothes off, her drunken fingers fumbling. She swayed on her feet before him and Adam reached out, removing the formless scrubs from her body in just a few heartbeats. He could taste the wine on her breath as he kissed her, could feel the slack of her limbs when he lifted her and set her down on the bed. When he bent down to kiss her again, Andie pressed a palm to his chest to stop him.

"What's wrong?" he asked.

She didn't answer; instead, she pushed him away, jumped to her feet and ran for the bathroom. She slammed the door behind her and Adam heard the sounds of her emptying her stomach of the wine she had consumed.

Adam sat on the edge of the bed and blew out a breath. He was close, so close to going over the edge with her. He needed to get it together. Crane was going to want him to get closer and Adam was afraid of getting too close. The more time he spent with her the harder it was for him to leave. And if she ever found out all the secrets he hid she'd never look at him again.

EIGHT

ANDROMEDA

WHEN MY EYES FLICK OPEN I FIND THAT I AM ALONE, EXCEPT for the Guardian in the corner. Usually I can see the reflection of its eyes in the burning embers of the fire but right now the fire is too low to see much. I stand, take a piece of wood off of the stack near the wall and set it on the coals. As I do, a small plume of burning ash floats up. I sit on a stool and watch the stick burn, then I add another one.

The hut is empty of the old man. Either I killed the Witchdoctor just as I killed Ian, or maybe he had to take a trip to see Glane.

Hesitant, yet wanting to leave the walls of this tiny house, I stand and make my way to the door. I reach for it, pushing the rough-hewn wood that creaks under my hand until a shadowed light filters in, falling over my booted feet. The Guardian raises its head and watches me as I step across the threshold. Gravel crunches under my feet, the sound a bit too loud in my ears. Looking up, sun filters through the canopy of large cypress trees, and even though the light is dim it registers in my brain as though the bright sun were in my face. Shielding my eyes with a hand I step forward, the gravel making another loud crunch before my feet sink into soft soundless soil.

As my eyes adjust to the outside world I realize the Witchdoctor's hut is in the center of a small island in the middle of wetlands. The swamp is alive with frogs croaking, fish flapping, birds chirping, woodpeckers drumming their bills into tree trunks. And the light, although I know it's dull it seems so bright and everything sounds so loud. Sensory overload. Ears ringing, head pounding, I cover my face and back up trying to retrace my steps to the hut. I trip, fall, sink into a rich loamy earth. Damp dirt sticks to my clothing as I try to push myself up. Panic overwhelms me as my vision blurs and the ringing in my ears gets louder.

Scrambling to my hands and knees, I crawl back into the hut and collapse on the floor. The Guardian watches me from the dark, the flames gleaming in his eyes reveals that he is unimpressed with what just happened.

I roll to my side into the shadows and take a few calming breaths. It doesn't help; even the darkest corners of this hut seem too bright at the moment. I want it all to stop. Whatever the Witchdoctor threw in my face to make me sleep has to be here somewhere. I drag myself to my feet, knocking over a stool in the process. It hits the fire and burning ash singes the exposed skin on my arms as I make my way to the Witchdoctor's shelves. I search the rows of unlabeled glass jars and bowls. Dipping my fingers into a random jar I pinch the powder and toss it in my face. It does nothing. I try another and another, wondering how the hell he knows which one to use. Finally finding a gritty powder that smells like rich soil I throw it onto my own face, then fall to the ground.

Nine

Then

"I'm not going to calm down, this is my child we are talking about," Andie hissed at Adam through gritted teeth.

He had to get her under control for fear that Crane would lash out. She didn't understand what he was capable of. "Andie, it's better than a transmitter. You remember those don't you? I know I do, because you cut one out of my arm." Adam held his forearm out for her to see. He had been reopening the wound for days so she wouldn't get suspicious if it healing so fast. "Think about it."

Adam stepped away from Andie as he sensed Crane walking toward them.

"I hear we have congratulations to give you, Andromeda," Crane said.

Andie scowled. "What?"

After threatening to force out her child, Adam thought the man was overly obnoxious for approaching her now.

"Congratulations are in order," he repeated. "I hear you are expecting." Crane clapped his hands together before looking to Adam. "It's exciting really, our first Sovereign pregnancy." He patted her hard on the shoulder before walking away, a smug smile plastered on his face.

Shit, was all Adam could think as the news overtook him. Shit. Shit. Shit. Shit. How could he be so stupid? Adam was pissed, shocked; everything he had never anticipated feeling overwhelmed him.

And when Andie finally looked at him, he could say nothing. He walked away from her at that moment. Stunned to silence, he had nothing to say.

He stood by the elevators until she walked up next to him and then they walked to his Volker SUV. Maybe this was part of Crane's plan all along. He had instructed Adam to comfort her, but this was a little much. Adam watched her out of the corner of his eye. Maybe she did it on purpose; maybe she knew she'd get pregnant. Adam shook his head as he pressed the elevator button.

Adam drove her back to the Pasture in silence, couldn't think of one word to say to her. He was shocked, pissed—a variety of emotions were fighting to take over. Worst of it all was the fact that Andie had successfully withheld information from him. She'd never done that before. Everything was so plainly written on her face or came flying out of her mouth. The woman couldn't hold a secret to save her life, but this, she'd kept this a secret and she'd kept it from him. Adam knew the day would come; he was, after all, simply doing his job. But drawing her in, getting closer, it made it harder and harder to think about the day when he'd have to turn away. He didn't want to think about it.

When Adam pulled into the drive of the Pasture he got out to open the gate. Andie got out of the SUV and walked past the threshold. Adam couldn't hold it in any longer—if she was pregnant then she was definitely no longer safe. He locked her inside the Pasture without another word, returned to his vehicle and sped off in search of answers.

Adam was an idiot, feeling this way. He knew better. He had hundreds of years worth of practice. People lied, they disappointed. Hell, he was the worst sinner of the bunch, and now this.

He let two days pass without word.

And then tattooing day had arrived. Adam received his mark on the inside of his wrist along with the rest of the Sovereign. He could barely look at Andie when she walked in to Dr. Akiyama's office. Adam warned one of the Volker guards to keep an eye on her, the woman was out of control and pregnant. He wasn't happy with her but he didn't want her hurt. Adam knew once she found out what was really going on she would fly off the handle in a heartbeat.

Adam was gone from the building before she was marked.

He wasn't expecting the call later that day; a Volker had died, attacked by someone at the Pasture. Adam made his way there as soon as he had heard the news. The place was a shit show; kids were crying, the Volker that were there didn't know what to do with themselves. They were still uneasy around the Guardians, just as most people were.

Andie had Sam and Lina held up in the Library house. Elvis had no explanation for any of the drama.

Andie was out for blood, it was perfectly clear from the way she spoke to him. Adam left the Pasture after ordering the Guardian that protected Sam to be put down. Being there was too hard.

IT WAS weeks before he returned to the Pasture. He shouldn't have gone there, wasn't on official business, but that's what five fingers worth of whiskey will get a man. Adam wanted to see her, he wanted answers, and he was struggling to keep it all together.

Adam let himself through the gate and parked his vehicle near the barn. He walked to her house knowing that the children would be asleep, but that Andie would be awake and working on Crane's project. As soon as he set foot in the house he started to sober up, then cursed his nanocytes for not letting him wallow in a drunken haze for longer.

He paced in the living room, mumbled to himself, thought to leave and escape whatever pain Crane had planned for him. Adam was never allowed a family, a child, none of it. And to be perfectly honest Adam never wanted any of it. He knew he wasn't a good man, maybe before Crane he was, but not now. He didn't deserve it, didn't want to watch the downfall.

"What are you doing here in the middle of the night?" Andie's voice broke through the night.

She was there, a light in his darkness, and Adam couldn't turn away now.

"Why didn't you tell me, Andie?" Adam barely recognized his own voice.

"I didn't tell anyone."

She was lying to him, again, and Adam hated that she could so easily be deceiving. Just like him.

"Crane knew before I did, how does that work?"

He heard her take in a breath. "The only one who knew was the doctor. Crane must have been perusing my medical file."

Adam didn't doubt the idea, it sounded like something Crane would do. He was always meddling in people's lives. Especially those he had plans for.

"Why didn't you tell me?" Adam couldn't resist walking toward her. "Why?" He wanted to touch her, lay his palm on her belly and feel the baby, his child.

"You told me yourself, you wouldn't bring a child into this. What was I supposed to do, saddle you with a child you never wanted? It was a mistake." Andie looked away from him, he could see the pain on her face illuminated by the pale moonlight that filtered through the windows. "What we did was a mistake. It should have never happened."

She was lying. This time he could tell. The truth came flying out of his mouth before he could disguise it. "You're wrong. This is not a mistake. This is so different." He couldn't hold back any longer when he reached out to touch her, brushing his hand across her cheek and bending down to kiss her. This is what real people do. He would allow himself just a glimpse of a normal life before it all ended.

Her body stiffened and she pulled away from him. "You've been drinking. Where did you even find any alcohol?"

She should have known better. Crane gifted her with wine and he'd gifted Adam with the whiskey as well. Crane liked to break the rules with his special projects; they weren't, after all, simply Residents or Survivors. They were more.

"Adam, stop it!" Andie pushed him away but it didn't work, he wanted to hold her for a moment longer, had a feeling this would be one of the last times. "Get off me, Adam!" She shoved him with all her might and he staggered back half of a step. "Come back when you've sobered up. Then we'll talk about this."

Adam stared at her for a long time before turning and leaving.

The walk to his vehicle was just as he thought it should have been, alone.

"What are you doing here?" A dark figure stepped out from next to the SUV and startled Adam. He wasn't himself right now, he knew that but he couldn't let his guard down. This was Sam, the kid was harmless, had potential to be more.

"Shit, Sam." Adam reached into his pocket to retrieve his keys, didn't bother trying to hide that he was out of sorts. The keys fell to the ground and Adam bent to search for them.

"What are you doing out here in the middle of the night?" Adam asked.

"I'd like to ask you the same thing."

Adam stood after finding his keys and simply stared at Sam. He didn't know where to start, the entire situation was beyond fucked up.

"What's your deal?" Sam asked as though he could see through Adam's bullshit.

He gave up, ran a hand through his hair and blew out a deep breath. "She's fucking pregnant."

"Who?" Sam asked.

"Your goddamned sister. Who else?"

Sam shrugged. "Who's the father?"

What a punk. Adam stepped closer to the kid, ready to pounce. "Who the hell do you think it is?" Adam stopped and leaned against the vehicle. "I fucked up. She won't talk to me. I didn't want to talk to her for a while, but I was just so... shocked. And she didn't even tell me, man. Fucking Crane told me. Of all people. She couldn't even tell me she's carrying my kid."

"So what are you going to do about it?" Sam asked.

"I have no freaking clue." Adam had yet to form a plan. He knew he needed one.

"You need to get a clue," Sam said as he stepped closer to Adam. "She needs someone. She's going to lose her shit having a baby in the middle of all this. The Reformation was bad enough. Whatever happens next with all of us... you think we'll survive? You think that baby in her belly will?"

Deep down Adam knew the kid was right. "I know." He ran two hands through his hair now, gripping it between his fingers and pulling; he had to feel something, bring him back to the present, get on track. "But this was not part of the plan—"

"Plan?" Sam asked.

Shit, he needed to shut his mouth. "Stay out of it, Sam." Adam reached for the driver's side door of the SUV.

"You brought me here." Sam stepped closer. "You brought me into this. You owe me an explanation."

"No." Adam pushed his index finger into Sam's chest. "I rescued your sorry ass from the wreckage of the Reformation. I did that. I brought you here for her. I owe you nothing. You're alive. Appreciate it."

"Yeah, you dropped me in the middle of this. And it's royally fucked up. I *appreciate* you bringing me back to my family. But when your men marked those kids. Fucking kids, man." Sam shook his head. "You weren't there. You didn't see how scared they were. It was so wrong."

"There are some things I cannot control here. Being the Volker Sovereign, I am only in charge of so much. You saw that when you were staying with me. How long did it take me to find out where this place was? Weeks. And *I'm* supposed to be in charge of the safety of the Sovereign." Adam thrust a finger into his chest. "It took me weeks to find out where the most important Sovereign of this District were being hidden. They're going to mark every Sovereign. Including the one Andie's carrying. You think I want to see my own flesh and blood go through that? I can barely stand the thought of Lina going through it." Thinking about it that second was killing him.

"What aren't you telling me?"

There was so much he wasn't telling them. Adam's eyes flicked to Blithe's house. His sister was here and he didn't like it. Andie was pregnant, everything was falling apart. Adam had tried to keep his distance, but suddenly Crane had everyone he'd ever given a shit about in his life stashed in one place.

"It's not important right now." Adam said.

"Maybe it's time for you to choose what's really important."

If only the kid knew how deep the shit ran.

Adam gave him a hard look before he wrenched open the door of his SUV, got in, and left the Pasture.

WHEN SAM CALLED Adam to tell him that Andie had collapsed at the hospital, Adam moved faster than he ever had in his entire life. Things had been bad between them over the past weeks. Adam hadn't seen much of her, he was still trying to figure out a plan, while at the same time not letting Crane see how deep his feelings for the woman ran. He cursed every moment of his time in Phoenix and for Crane sending him on this mission.

When Adam got to the hospital, he found her in a room getting lectured by Dr. Akiyama. Adam's eyes honed in on her belly, knowing his child was there drove his need to protect them deeper.

"You're having a boy, congratulations," Dr. Akiyama said.

Andie paled and looked away. She was scared and angry, and he had hurt her. Adam could tell by the way she avoided looking at him. But, a boy, she was carrying his boy.

Dr. Akiyama left the room and it was just the two of them and Sam.

"Are you going to talk to him?" Sam asked Andie. "I talked to him already. It's your turn." Sam stood up and walked across the room. "Don't open this door until you two have held a decent conversation with each other." He pointed at each of them before closing the door behind him.

Adam wanted to tell her everything, make one giant confession then get her the hell out of here. But he couldn't. He'd already put her in danger. Revealing any truths now would make it worse.

Morris was going to die. Other Entities would as well, eventually.

He could save her. He just had to take the first step.

"I'm sorry," Adam said.

"I'm sorry," Andie whispered back. "I should have told you as soon as I found out. But you said..." She sighed and seemed to search for the right words. "We both said it isn't right to bring a child into this."

It was too late for that. He'd fucked up not using protection, never risked it before. He had no more words for her, just wanted to have her close again and keep her safe. Adam reached for her, pulling her across the hospital bed and onto his lap, wrapping her in his arms. Andie's arms went around him and she buried her face in his neck. He missed this, as wrong as it was, as bad as it would turn out to be. She felt right in his arms even if he knew her husband was alive and well. Adam knew he would burn in hell for what he'd done when he finally died. Crane was going to twist this, make it burn. But right now Adam was going to take the few moments he could to remember as his own.

"It's a boy," he whispered in her ear.

Andie was crying when she pulled away from him and took his hand, placing it on her swollen belly. Adam felt movement under her skin. For the first time in his life, strange warmth filled his soul, he felt something he hadn't felt since he was a young man, before his world went to hell: pure unadulterated happiness. Adam couldn't control the smile that spread across his face and when he looked up into Andie's bright green eyes, he did the only thing that seemed natural at the moment; something real people would do, not a person like him. He kissed her.

ADAM SAT in his vehicle outside the gates to the Pasture. Andie was in there waiting for him with dinner on the table. For the first time ever Crane had let him have some semblance of family. He was never allowed this before, and Adam knew that he should keep his distance; he shouldn't have let himself fall into this comfort like he had. Having her beside him at night, having home cooked meals each evening, fresh clothes laundered for him, routine, a life, they were all the little things he thought he never wanted. He had tried not to think of what it's going to feel like when it all came crashing down. Adam wasn't trained for this and deep down he knew that Crane was teasing him.

They were slated to leave for the Tour soon and Adam expected the shit to hit the fan. He had spent the last few days making preparations and formulating a plan.

TEN

Andromeda

"You left the door open." The Witchdoctor frowns as he nudges my ribs with his foot. "And you burned my stool. Now you must sit on the ground."

Limbs stiff, I move and find that I am lying on the hard floor, my mat against the far wall. I try to remember what happened. "You were gone," I croak.

"I had to see Glane. There was... there was an ill child." The Witchdoctor grunts in dissatisfaction as he turns to his powders. "Have you recovered?" he asks mildly.

"I just...It was so bright outside and so loud."

He squats down and picks up the broken shards of glass from the floor. "I have told you that you're not ready to go outside."

Rolling to my side, I ask. "When do you think I'll be ready?"

He shrugs before pulling his mortar and pestle from a low shelf. Returning to his stool, he pokes the coals with a stick and sprinkles something over the cold coals. They ignite into a hot blue flame. "You will be ready when you can control yourself."

"I can't now?" I begin the crawl of shame to my mat.

He gives me a look, shaking his head. "How long do you think I've been gone?" he asks.

"A day or two." I pull the burlap blanket over my body.

"Try a week," he bristles.

"A week? Why so long?"

Pressing his lips together so hard they turn white, he begins the soothing *grind* and *swoosh*. "You cleared out half of the swamp with your reaction to going outside. My people felt your fear. Some of them fled."

Guilt floods me. "I'm sorry."

"I have said this before, Andromeda; you must learn to control your emotions. I can't do this for much longer." Pausing from his grinding, he glances at me with a worried look. "Perhaps when your brain is fully healed."

I lay in silence for a few minutes watching the Witchdoctor. "Why didn't you tell me we are on an island?"

"There is connecting land behind my home." He sounds bored with me and agitated.

"Aren't you afraid of your home flooding?" I ask.

"If we live in fear our entire lives what does that get us? Fear cannot drive our lives. I live where I need to be." He bends and pinches dirt from the floor between his fingers. "The richest soil in all the land is here and I require it. If I went elsewhere the land would be of no use to me and I could not do my job." He pauses his grinding. "Tell me, Andromeda, what do you fear besides your sea monster?"

I pull the blanket tighter around me. "I think everything I could ever have feared has already occurred."

"See, now you have nothing left to fear. Tell me," he says with a soothing calmness in his voice. "But use control while you speak."

"I've lost my home." I take a deep breath. "My children are without me." My eyes burn.

"Uh uh," the Witchdoctor warns.

I swallow hard, pushing the emotion down. "I killed my husband."

"Control," he whispers.

I push it away, the pain and sadness, until I feel nothing. "And now I am alone, forever."

"Good. Much better. But I have one correction for you. You will never be alone, not in all of your time on this earth."

"How can you be so sure?"

"I have already told you, someone searches for you."

Adam.

"I felt that," the Witchdoctor warns.

"What?"

"That flicker."

I push it away. I should feel nothing for him, not after what he did.

"Good. The brain controls it all. Each breath, each heartbeat, your emotional response. Control yourself, control your power."

The hut falls into a calm with the Witchdoctor grinding away at his potions and me lying on the cot staring at the burning coals and trying my damndest to feel nothing at all.

***

"Who taught you to be a Witchdoctor?" I ask.

He pauses his grinding. "My schooling began in a university much like you."

"And then?" I prod.

"And then to a laboratory. And then I met someone with the same thinking as me. He wanted to make a difference for the good of mankind. But I realized something after many years of hard work and planning. We were wasting our time."

"Who is *we*?"

The Witchdoctor stills, his grinding ceases. "I know the man who started this all. I know Crane."

I sit up straight. He knows Crane? "How?"

"I am old." I knew he was old, but...

"How old? Do you have the nanocytes too?" I ask, hopeful that he may have information for me.

He shakes his head. "I've found other ways to extend my life. I haven't fiddled in the research realm for quite some time now."

"You worked with him." I shove the blanket off of me and sit up. "Why did you leave?"

"You can't make strides without experiments, and sometimes those experiments yield the undesirable. Our ideals fell apart."

The undesirable? Everything Crane has developed seems to be desirable for plenty of people. Except for... "The Swamp people?"

He nods.

"But I thought they were just normal people, extreme but like us. That's what Crane said, he couldn't bomb the swamps."

"Crane says plenty. The truth is, in all of the experiments we did the Swamp people were created."

Oh God. Resting my head in my hands, I think long and hard about this new information. This man has been alive for a long time, without the help of the nanocytes, he worked with Crane, he knew my... Wait. "You're Arthur. Aren't you?"

He smiles.

ELEVEN

ADAM

THEN

The last thing Adam Waters remembered was that bastard Crane shooting him. Now he was strapped to a hospital bed. The lights surrounding him were bright, the liquid running through the IV in his arm was cool and there was not a damn window in the place.

"What would you do if she died?" the memory of Crane's last words to Adam came alive.

He remembered that he said, "She's not going to die."

Adam struggled against the straps that were across his biceps, legs, abdomen, and hips. He stopped when the door opened and a young blonde walked in.

He recognized her instantly. It was Jenn.

"Hey there, hero," Jenn smiled at him. Her demeanor was lighter than when she was in Phoenix acting as a Volker. "Are we feeling better yet?" She sat down on the edge of his bed. Too close for his comfort.

"Why are you dressed like an oompa loompa?" he asked her as he took in her green clothes.

"Oh this old thing?" Jenn pinched her shirt. "This is the uniform of the Underland." She leaned close to his face. "Does it look familiar? Like a faction your people organized? We are the cleaners, Colonel Waters. When you're dirty and covered in blood, we clean you up." She smirked and her blue eyes twinkled as she ran her hand seductively down Adam's arm.

The woman had a split personality. He didn't want her touching him, couldn't stand the feel of her skin on his. There was only one person he wanted to feel and that was—

"Andie!" Adam jerked against his restraints. "Where am I? Where is she? Did she survive?"

Jenn planted a hand on his chest. "Settle down, hero." She leaned in and her lips were entirely too close to his face. "We're still waiting on word from our Implants." She began loosening his restraints. "Sorry about this. We didn't want you freaking out and waking up on the wrong side of the gurney." She took her time with the strap over his left arm. "But you know he wouldn't let her die. Whatever was wrong with her? Why is it all hush-hush there?"

"She was pregnant." Adam didn't tell her that it was his child, although he was sure some knew. "And sick. You know what that medication does to pregnant women."

She nodded like she understood. "Crane already has you, and what a fine specimen you are. What would he need with her? It's a shame that he tossed you out like trash though." The fact that Jenn was currently leering at him like he was a fresh piece of meat made his skin crawl.

He gave her a look that told her to shut up, but she kept talking and when her hands moved to un-strap his other arm she trailed her fingers across his chest. "You had a nice bullet hole right here." She pressed her fingertip to his skin. "Was like a miracle watching it heal." Her fingers lingered to the old scars marring his chest. "Makes me wonder why these are still here." She traced across a light slash mark across his right pectoral. Adam knew who it was from and why he had received it. But he didn't have the patience to tell her that some scars were too deep for the nanocytes to heal.

When he pressed his lips together and stared off into the space behind her, Jenn gave up on her seduction and freed him of his bindings.

She finally stood and moved away from him. "There's some pants over there." She turned to look at him. "Although I do prefer you in all your naked glory. You're quite the specimen, Colonel Waters. No wonder that woman likes you so much."

"Shut up, Jenn," Adam growled.

She reached for the IV that was taped to his arm and ripped it off. "Oh, my dear piece of manmeat, I don't shut up for you. This is my land. You listen to me when you're down here. You see, you may sit to the right hand of the father up there, but I sit to the right hand of the mother down here." She walked out of the room, swaying her hips in a way that would make another man pant. He looked away, searching the room for something, anything to look at besides her. "Meet me in the hallway when you're dressed." She slammed the door behind her and Adam reached for the clothes that were folded on the chair near his bed.

They had provided him with what looked like SWAT gear. Black cargo pants, a black T-shirt, a black jacket and boots. Adam checked his body for anything unfamiliar. It was something that he had a habit of doing. These people he was involved with, they were always trying to implant something on a person, or dig something out. He licked his thumb and cleaned the spot of blood off of his arm where the IV was. He dressed quickly, thankful to be covered in more than half of a white sheet.

He washed his hands at the small sink near the door and looked in the mirror. His beard was no more than a half-inch scruff and his hair hadn't grown much at all. They must have loaded him up on protein and vitamins to get him to heal this fast from the bullet wound.

"Are you doing this for her or the baby?"

"Does it matter?"

"It always matters."

"There's no good answer to that question."

"Ah, but it is a question that should be asked. Are you risking your life to save her or the child in her womb? Which do you value more? Which drives you to succeed in this mission?"

"I don't value one more than the other."

"So the same then."
"Yeah, sure."
"I don't believe you."
"You don't need to believe me. You gave me a mission to complete and I'm doing it."

ADAM LEFT the small white room and found Jenn down the hall. She was talking to a Volker and Adam's heart sped up when he thought that maybe he was back in Phoenix and could get back to Andie soon.

Jenn turned around when she sensed he was close. "About time. I can shower and dress faster than that," she mocked him.

"Where am I?" Adam asked.

"The Underland. Welcome." She started walking. "Follow me."

Adam had heard of the Underland. It was what President Berkley had called his subterranean system of emergency bunkers. He hinted at it as being a safe place where Adam could hide if he needed to. He just wasn't aware that there were actually people inhabiting them. Adam followed Jenn down a long hallway. She paused before opening a door and turned to him. "Don't do anything stupid. I have some people who want to talk to you. They have a proposition."

"YOU KNOW IN SOME CULTURES, when it comes down to choosing between their spouse and their children, they always choose their spouse. Do you know what their reasoning is?"

"No."

"Because they can always make more children. But they will never be able to replace their husband or wife."

"Sounds like bullshit."

"It's the truth."

"You don't tell many truths."

EVERYONE HAD a proposition when they came to him. Adam nodded. Just once he wished that someone would ask nothing of him. Like

Andie, she had never asked for anything from him. She was the only one who had ever treated him like a real person and not some Frankenstein created by the world's greatest mastermind.

Jenn opened the door and led him out into a giant cavernous space. People milled about all dressed in green and tables were set up selling goods. There were a few Volker standing guard on the ground and the levels above them. Adam was impressed with the system of ladders, windows and doors against the far wall. Jenn didn't let him look for long, she picked up her pace and led him to another doorway.

"We're going to go up now. Hope you've got the stamina." She winked at him and opened the door.

"You see, Colonel Waters, you can tell a lot about a person by the choices they make when it comes to the ones they love, their children. And when a loved one dies sometimes people do things that they wouldn't normally do. But it's like flipping a coin. They become stronger or they become weak. They hold onto the ones that remain or they shun everyone because they cannot bear to be reminded of that long lost person they loved so much. So I wonder who will you become if she dies?"

"In case you forgot I already lost my family. They died in a car accident."

"Ah, Colonel Waters, but this is so much different. You loved them but it was a different love. No one ever gets over losing a child or the love of their life, their soulmate."

"You think she is my soulmate?"

"She is something special to you."

"You're wrong. I'm just doing my job. We ended it on the way home from the tour. We both agreed. It's over."

THEY WERE in a gray stairwell and something about it felt oddly familiar. She started her way up, Adam followed, keeping up with her pace.

When she finally stopped she was barely out of breath. "You'll recognize this place." She opened a door on the stairwell landing and led him through. They went down a long hall before turning. And what came into view shocked him.

He recognized this place. It was the ARU. He was in Hanford.

"Good to see you're doing well," George Crossbender held a hand out to Adam.

Adam was shocked for the first time in a long time, but he shook the man's hand.

"You left me on that rooftop," Adam said.

George pushed his glasses up with his index finger. "Sorry about that." He shrugged. "Had to get Crane back to Phoenix. Sent another team for you not long after. Lost quite a few men fighting the Survivors for your body." He looked Adam up and down. "Think it was worth it though."

Great, Adam thought. This was what he hated, someone doing something for him and now he felt like he owed Crossbender something for saving him.

"I'd like to introduce you to someone." George moved to the side and revealed a woman who Adam recognized as George's wife. "This is my wife, Maryam."

Adam shook her hand; she offered a firm grip on his.

"We have a proposition for you," Maryam began. "We know you're good at keeping secrets. And we know that Crane has abused you as his minion for far too long."

Adam tried not to think of what he'd endured under the man's thumb. He had escaped many times, worked the system just like Crane had taught him. The bad thing was as much as he infiltrated and promised and lied, things rarely turned in his favor. But he knew everyone and everyone knew him, all the people that mattered at least. While Crane knew all of their secrets, Adam knew their weaknesses.

"We need a man on the outside," Maryam said as she stood near her husband. "Someone to infiltrate the Survivors."

"The Funding Entities have been ordered to leave the Survivors alone," Adam reminded her.

"Yes, of course they have." Maryam smiled. "We paid our dues for the Reformation but now it's time to take back some control."

"And you want me to be a part of that?" Adam asked.

"Who better than Crane's left-hand man?"

Adam's brow tipped up in surprise. "You know I could go back and tell him. He'd want me to."

Maryam frowned. "After all he's done to you? He left you to die, Colonel Waters. And all you were trying to do was save his most prized possession and the woman you love. Doesn't it grind your gears a bit that he could do that, cut you out of his life so quickly after all he's done? After all you've done for him?"

Adam knew better than to guess that Crane did something without a hidden agenda. Crane knew Adam would heal, it was just deciding what he would do once he healed. Did Crane expect him to go crawling back to him or to venture out on his own just as he'd tried to do many times? It was just a mind game that Adam needed to figure out.

"He took you away from her," Maryam continued. "Perhaps you got too close to her and Crane didn't like that. She's his special experiment, someone you once were. It's sad really, the way he can just throw people away. Don't you think?"

Maryam was making a convincing argument. But Adam was in this for his own reasons. He would infiltrate the Survivors and set everything up and rid himself of Crane for good.

"We are fighting for something precious," Maryam reminded him.

"Are we?" Adam asked.

"Of course we are. The fate of the free world."

Adam knew better than that, the world was never free and he doubted it ever would be, not with the people who were fighting for power. There were few who made decisions for the whole. It had always been this way. Adam knew there wasn't much he could do about it. But still, he had a tiny bit of hope that he could return to the man he was raised to be so long ago.

"What do you want me to do?" Adam asked.

Twelve

"He said you died. That you were killed in—" Crap, where was it? "South America, somewhere..."

"Rio de Janero," the Witchdoctor says.

Rio de Janero, yes! They were slaughtered in Rio de Janero by a drug dealer who wasn't happy with his custom-order child. "So it was your—"

"Wife. Yes. She developed the nanocytes. Perfected them with the help of Crane."

"So she's—"

"Still dead."

"Your child?"

"Still dead."

"And me."

"Stuck in the middle of this mess." He tips his head to the side. "Although I didn't agree with what we were doing, the end result is quite spectacular."

I stand, agitated. "Does no one stay dead anymore? First Adam, then Ian, then... Jesus, you. Can't you people just stay dead and stop haunting me?" I'm ready to rip my hair out.

He leans away from me, flinching. "You need to control—"

"Why?" I yell. "Why do I need to control anything?" I pace in a line. "Why is it always me? I never asked for this. I... I..."

The Witchdoctor falls off of his stool and the force of his body hitting the ground makes the flames of the fire dance.

Oh no! I run for the door and push it open. This time it's darker outside, evening perhaps. I have to get away from him, control the flood of emotions. Make it all straight in my head. I run, round the back of the hut, my boots sinking in the soft damp soil. A tall lanky woman near the shoreline of the swamp stands suddenly as I cross. She runs away from me, her form a whisper of dark hair and long-limbed sinew. I run in the opposite direction of her and the trees shudder in my wake. It must be the rest of them trying to get away from me.

When I finally stop, the swamp is far behind me and I am surrounded by forest. With the soil under my feet finally firm, I drop to my knees with tears thick in my eyes and pray that I didn't just kill the Witchdoctor like I killed Ian. I wasn't even close to as mad as I was that day. I thought I had it under control but it seems I am still too sensitive to the past and what has been done to us.

Hearing soft footsteps behind me, I turn. There stands the Guardian from the hut. It's huge, a dreadlocked black coat with a diamond of white on its chest. Finally seeing it in the full light, it looks like a giant Stevie.

This world is just one vicious twisted cycle that I have no control over. And this is where I lose it. The tears come hot and flooding down my face, washing away the months of soot and dirt from sleeping on the floor in a hut.

The Guardian sits back on its haunches watching me, still unimpressed with anything I have to offer, which are currently just tears and desolation.

When I am done, I stand and do my best to compose myself. I push all of the anguish and anger into the recesses of my soul and save it for another time. Blowing out a calm breath, I rein in my control.

I better go check on the old man who most likely is my great grandfather. I start walking in the direction I came, the Guardian at my side now. It glances up at me when I look down at it.

"Are you my Stevie?" I ask the beast.

Of course it doesn't reply.

"Did he make you? Or are you my deceased family pet reincarnated?"

The Guardian huffs.

"I'll go with deceased family pet reincarnated." I stop and look at the animal. "I can't call you Stevie. Maybe I'll just call you Steve."

The Guardian looks annoyed and starts walking in the direction of the Witchdoctor's hut.

I follow and in the distance I can see the shadows of the Swamp people. Fires burn and figures mill about.

Now that I've got myself under control they don't seem to notice me. So I decide to test out what these amplified pheromones can do. I don't want to scare them again and I don't want them to see me, especially if I've killed their Witchdoctor.

You don't see me, you don't see me, you don't see me. I repeat under my breath as I take a deep breath and calm myself. I walk closer and the Swamp people don't seem to notice. Maybe I can do this. Maybe I can control it.

You don't see me, you don't see me, you don't see me. The Swamp people huddled around a nearby fire don't seem to notice me at all. I smile and look down to confer with my Guardian friend but... it's gone.

I walk in front of a tall man with one front tooth. He stops, looks directly at me then around me. He sees nothing. I can make myself invisible! The things I could do if people couldn't see me. The power I could take back.

All joy halts when I remember the Witchdoctor. I'd better go check on him. Heading toward the hut, out in the middle of the swamp, my trusty Guardian makes its appearance at my side once again. "Deserter," I mutter under my breath.

Rounding the back of the hut, I notice the door's still open from when I ran out. I walk inside and find the old man lying on his back, blinking up at the ceiling. He turns to look at me.

"I'm sorry," I say, glad he's still alive and I'm not responsible for killing him.

"So am I." I reach down to help him up. "If you do that again, you're out," he tells me.

"If you drop some serious shit like that on my shoulders again, I'll gladly leave," I reply.

I pull him to his feet, then right his stool and help him sit. "Fair enough."

Since my stool was burned in the fire days ago, I sit on the floor.

"How far did you go?" he asks.

"I'm not sure. Until I couldn't see the swamp any longer."

"You seem different now. Perhaps you're fully healed. The last synapse healed its connection."

"Perhaps." Maybe that's all I needed, to break down like a bumbling fool to heal the last of my brain tissue. Maybe the last synapse connected with the last tear I shed. Who knows? "I think I can make myself invisible to others."

"Show me."

You don't see me, you don't see me, you don't see me.

The Witchdoctor watches, blinks, then reaches out to touch me.

I lean away from him.

"Impressive." I let him see me again. "What you can do when you are in absolute control of it. You were completely invisible." He watches me warily. "How do you feel?"

How do I feel? I think about it for a bit. I've definitely felt worse. "Fine."

"I think you should rest. If you feel up to it, tomorrow I'll take you out to meet the ones who brought you to me."

I stand and move to my mat. As I lay down I say, "I'm sorry I almost killed you, again."

The Witchdoctor stands, finds his bowl and pestle and begins adding ingredients. "You are forgiven."

Grind, swoosh.

No MOTHER SHOULD OUTLIVE their children, or their grandchildren, and definitely not their great-grandchildren. I watch the latest two playing on the floor. The youngest one walks up to me. She is small for her age, inquisitive, steady on her tiny feet. She is the granddaughter of Raven, her hair is dark and curly, her eyes a hazel-blue. She looks like a mixture of Lina and Adam, and no doubt if she is anything like her grandfather Raven she will be a genius. This is what we breed now, the smartest and the strongest to rule. The Pasture is our castle, the District our fiefdom, the outlying land a disorganized territory struggling to survive. We live in a futuristic dark age.

"Great great Grandma," she asks me. "Why don't you have any wrinkles?" She brushes her chubby palm across my cheek. "Why do you look the same as my mommy?"

I smile at her, wishing my thirty-year-old face would wrinkle like 150-year-old skin cells should. But they won't and I hate it. I take her hand and press my lips to her fingers, to be so young and inquisitive and innocent. I miss these days.

"Because I have magic in me," I tell her as I reach down and draw her in for a hug.

"Magic?" She wrinkles her little nose. "My daddy said there's no such thing as magic."

"No such thing?" I scoff exaggeratedly.

"Uh uh." She shakes her head, sending her curls flying about her face.

I lean closer to her and whisper, "Well, if there's no such thing as magic, then what would you call this?"

You don't see me, you don't see me, you don't see me.

The little girl squeals as I disappear before her eyes and then reappear again.

"How did you do that?" she asks, her eyes wide with excitement.

I reach out and tap my finger on the tip of her nose. "Magic, my dear."

"Magic," she repeats.

"What else do we have if we don't have magic?"

"Andromeda," a male voice interrupts us.

I stand up straight and find the little girl's father standing in front of us. "You're needed at the Gateway."

I nod and send the little girl off to play with her siblings.

As I head for the gates, he stops me. "I wish you wouldn't put that in her head."

"She's just a child." I sigh, knowing that they want me to leave and live on the outskirts alone, away from what they perceive to be normal here. I just can't do it though; I can't let the last bits of family slip through my fingers, not after walking away from all of them so many years ago. "What do they need at the Gateway?"

"The usual." He motions for me to follow him.

"The usual?"

"Survivors want in. You choose, as usual."

I am filled with dread.

———

I WAKE with a start and a gasp. It's nearly pitch black in the hut, only one coal visible burning the midnight oil.

"What were you dreaming about?" the gravelly voice of the Witch-doctor breaks the night.

"The future. I think." I rub my face and roll over, pulling the blanket tighter around my body.

He grunts. "How was it?"

"Sad."

"The past was just as sad. You should go back to sleep. We have a busy day tomorrow."

"What will we be doing?"

"I'm taking you to Hanford. To see your children."

"Why?"

"You're not going to stay with us forever, Andromeda. And who better to teach you to travel through the wilderness than our own hunters?"

Thirteen

The Witchdoctor

Andromeda was a different creature. So unusual from the Swamp people. It was easy to see why Burton would want her back so badly. But she was his blood, the Witchdoctor's own flesh and he couldn't help but want to spend more time with her before she left. Because she would leave, he knew that, could sense it strengthening the longer he was with her.

He had planned this trek to help her through her last task. He knew it was going to be painful. The Witchdoctor could feel it radiating off of her every time she thought of her children. Albeit, now she had more control—she didn't clear the forest—but she still made those around her sad at times. If he could help her through this, then he had done his job when it came to his kin.

His people surround them as the Witchdoctor walked side-by-side with Andromeda. He felt a special bond with her and was thankful for the time they had together but he knew he couldn't keep her. He had to set her free and maybe she could make up for the wrongs Burton Crane and the rest of the Entities had created.

Arthur realized a long time ago that his friend had changed; he had played God for far too many years. Arthur had seen it and so had Andrea. They didn't want Selene exposed to him. Even if Burton behaved normally around their child.

While Burton and Andrea had been working on the nanocytes, Arthur had been exploring more natural ways to encourage longevity of life and he had found it. But he had never told Burton about his discoveries. Never had time. The day after he caught Andrea taking blood samples from their daughter, Arthur packed their things and left. It broke his heart to think that his wife could even consider involving their innocent daughter in anything they were working on.

During their travels she adamantly denied any wrongdoing, but Arthur knew better; his wife had become infected with the same dark desires as Burton and it was only a matter of time before she involved their own flesh in the experiments. He had seen the results of the Swamp people, and he sure as hell wasn't going to have his daughter turned into some blasted experiment.

He knew he had made the right decision when the men came after them in Rio de Janero. Arthur hated remembering that day. The pain, the loss. He was glad for one thing and that was when Burton found a pleasant foster family to raise his daughter. It seemed that was the one promise the man had kept throughout all of their friendship.

The Witchdoctor glances around him at the tall lanky men surrounding him and Andromeda. The Swamp men aren't that bad, they just need some guidance. They can't help what they are and the Witchdoctor saw no problem with them. They are what the earth needed. There were plenty of species responsible for cleaning detritus, the Swamp people were just an added benefit and their people had matured at the perfect time, cleaning up from the Reformation was a task Survivors alone couldn't handle. Hell, half of them didn't know what to do with a dead body and didn't have the energy to dig a few billion graves. The Witchdoctor is proud of his Swamp men and when he is sure that they are ready, he will leave them and move on.

The most ironic bit of it all is that Glane is scared of Andromeda. The Witchdoctor chuckles to himself when he sees the lanky man shy away from her. He wouldn't go near her, no more than a few hundred feet. But at the same time he seems enamored with her. After all, none of the bodies they had consumed had ever come back to life. She was an enigma to his people.

"What are you laughing at?" Andie asks as they sit on a handcar that is being pumped by a young Swamp man.

The Witchdoctor smiles. "At how well you are behaving."

"I'm not a child." She rests her hands on her thighs and looks away, past the fields that surround them.

"You're not. Far from it actually."

Her green stare meets his and for a moment Arthur is flung to the past, a happier time. *He was swinging Selene on the beach, her curls bounced in the tropical breeze and her laughter was the sweetest thing he had ever heard.*

When the Witchdoctor looks back at Andromeda, his eyes are glazed in sadness.

"Is it me?" she asks, worried that she has caused him pain. "Did I do something?"

He knows she is worried that she doesn't have control. She is much better, better at controlling it than she ever was but every now and then she slips up. Only time will help her perfect it, he knows this; he just has to make sure she believes in herself.

"It's not you, dear." He pats her arm. "Just an old man thinking old thoughts."

The Witchdoctor is too far from the swamps and it is taking a toll on his life force. Glane notices this one night when they stop to rest.

"Dis be de wors' idea," Glane says to the Witchdoctor.

"It is a perfectly fine idea, my boy." He pats the ground next to him and waits for Glane to sit.

Glane shakes his head and sits, watching the sleeping woman from across the fire. His men rest nearby but Glane had a hard time sleeping when she was around.

"I know you're curious, Glane."

Glane does not reply, but keeps staring at the sleeping woman.

"There is something we must talk about." The man shifts next to him. "I have been your Witchdoctor for a long time now, but in the future someone will need to take my place. You won't have me to come to anymore."

Glane almost looks distressed at this news. The Witchdoctor has known him since he was a boy and although Glane is not his true son, he feels a deep familial connection with the man.

"I know you're curious about her and others of her kind. But I must warn you to keep your distance. Curiosity is a dangerous force. It can drive a man to do thing. Things that wouldn't make him proud. Things that are dangerous, that can alter your world."

Glane turns to look at the old man now. "I be... curious." Glane pronounces the word much better than he should since their dialect was a strange one, almost inherited. To hear him speak like a normal person, that worries the Witchdoctor.

"This is a warning," the Witchdoctor says. "There is danger in curiosity. You don't need it. Your kind are special, different. Don't stray from that."

Glane nods as though he understands and the Witchdoctor is troubled if the young man truly does. There is so much that his people don't know, so much that they couldn't understand. His people were getting stronger and growing in numbers. The Witchdoctor feared for the day they found out the origins of their species, how they would react, what they would do, what they would consume.

As Andie leaves the old broken down high school that housed the elevator to Hanford, she slams the door and trudges out of the ruins. The Witchdoctor can tell that she is angry, it radiates in an aura around her small frame. His people inch away from her, deeper into the forest, in the direction of home.

Even if his people shied away from her at this moment, Arthur is proud of her and the courage it took to say goodbye to her children. He was proud of the control she had to exhibit. He remembered a time when he thought he was as bad as his old friend. But Arthur knew the difference between the two men who had played God. Arthur never saw failure and he guided his people. Crane was always looking for the next improvement, the next modification and he was eager to cast off anything that he had made that felt broken.

The Witchdoctor feels tired and weak. He is glad when Andromeda is by his side and her strange power is under control once again.

"It's not easy to leave your children to the world," he says to her as they walk.

"It makes me very sad." If Andromeda is anything with him, she is bluntly honest at all times and he appreciated that about her.

"But you're dealing well. You have control."

"For how long?" she asks.

"For as long as you can keep it." He stumbles and Andromeda catches him, helping steady the old man on his feet. Together they return to the swamps that are rich with life.

FOURTEEN

ADAM

THEN

He should have won an Emmy for his performance, the portrayal of the man he could have been. But that was what Crane had created when he reformed Adam, the world's greatest liar.

Adam knew that using his given name was a bad idea but it was one that kept him grounded, reminded him of where he came from and how he was raised, not what he had become. Adam had successfully infiltrated the Survivors. People had died but they were bad men and Adam saw that the world was better without men like that in power. He was turning a new leaf, getting rid of men like that instead of conspiring with them.

No longer head of the Volker, Adam had his own system now. He had men he trusted and he saw what civilization was capable of. Man had been stripped of most luxuries, but they were making it work. Adam had traveled North America and seen the pockets of good. He set up militias, laid ground-rules, put good people in charge. There were still bad people, but there would always be bad people, he'd deal with them in time. All he needed now was to know what was going on within the Districts.

George Crossbender was still fretting over a list of missing children. Adam was on the lookout for them, but to tell the truth it was hard to find some people these days now that things like computer databases and facial recognition software had been taken out of the equation. Big Brother had been removed from the outside world, and that made things harder when it came to searching for missing people.

When he had first heard that the trains were running, Adam was eager to learn why. Then, when he saw who Chuck and Mack had brought back to him he nearly died.

And now she was lying there, catatonic, ready to die like he had been many times. But the option of death had been taken away from him. At least she still had the opportunity. It seems she had chosen when she began refusing to eat or drink. She had lost all hope and now he was no better than Crane.

Adam was disgusted with himself for treating her this way. He couldn't watch her waste away any longer. He had to get her to talk and then he would take her home, where she would be safe from him and the rest of this wild world the Funding Entities had created.

Adam leaned back in his chair and propped his feet up on his desk. He tried to form a plan but thinking of her and knowing she was just down the hall was distracting. He had been watching her earlier that day and he remembered the first day he saw her, dripping in sweat from the hot summer sun and looking so familiar. He dropped his feet off of his desk when he realized exactly who she looked like, felt incredibly stupid that it took him this long to put two and two together.

THE GUARD STOOD to the side as a little girl ran toward them. She stopped when she got close to Adam and looked up at him with wide green eyes.

"Have you seen my mommy?" the little girl asked him.

It felt like a stone was sinking in Adam's gut as he considered the small child before him undergoing the same training that he and his sister had. All he could do was stare at her.

"Have you seen her?" the girl asked again, her smile bright. She looked well cared for, loved. There were no bruises or that glaze that he knew coated his eyes during the first few months he was here.

The sound of another door opening echoed in the hallway and a feminine voice asked, "Selene, where did you go?"

The little girl smiled up at Adam, "I think I found her." Her voice sounding like bells and chimes and all things happiness. She went running in the direction of her mother's voice.

DEAR GOD, they looked so similar. The one thing that had truly broken him, it had rotted him from the inside during all of these years, knowing that he walked away from her like a coward, not doing one thing to stop Crane from ruining that little girl.

Adam didn't know that Crane never laid a finger on Arthur and Andrea's daughter. But he saw her and did nothing, and knowing that was what drove him to do dark things.

FIFTEEN

ANDROMEDA

AFTER VISITING HANFORD, I SPEND WEEKS WITH THE SWAMP people and find that they survive on raw instinct. It's brutal at times, watching them live stripped to the basics of humanity. They go to the Witchdoctor for direction and healing but when they see me they keep their distance like wary animals. I've met Glane, their leader who seeks guidance from the Witchdoctor, he's the one who brought me here after deciding not to eat me. I'm not sure if I should thank him or curse him.

"Don't be offended by them," the Witchdoctor tells me. "They know no better."

"I'm not." I sprinkle one of his concoctions into a skin pouch for the hunters to take with them on their journey to find food and bring it back.

He makes a face as he mixes powders.

"I just..." I tie the pouch and begin filling another. "I think it's time for me to leave. I'm doing nothing here. I need to move on and do something. Put a stop to this madness."

The Witchdoctor tips his head. "You don't need my permission. If you want to go, then go. You have control." He eyes me warily. "Most of the time."

"I think I should go then." I fill another pouch. "I need to go." I decide.

He turns to face me and grasps my shoulders. "Before you leave, I have a gift for you." He turns and searches through his shelves. "Ah, here it is." Turning, he takes my hand and covers my wrist in a bracelet made of bone and metal, wide enough to hide my mark of the Phoenix District. "They made this for you. You are more than what he made you into today."

I turn my arm and admire the bracelet. "It's beautiful."

"An offering. They're afraid *you* might eat them one day."

I smile at him.

"And I would like you to remember that you are more than what Crane did to you. We all are." He kisses my cheek. "Go. Slay your sea monster, Andromeda."

"Thank you. Great Grandfather—"

"None of that." He shakes his head and I am not offended, we share a small genetic link but that is it. He takes a breath and for a man of this age, surviving on dirt and organic matter from the earth, I am simply surprised that it's not his last. "Revenge is a gift I'd like to bestow upon Crane myself, but I have my people to care for."

I too have Districts full of Residents that I altered; they are mine to look after. "And I have mine."

He nods. "Let us live in peace then."

"Okay." I agree with him. He has shown me kindness, helped me more than any of the other Entities. An outcast surviving on the fringes. Yes, I can live in peace with this man even if his Swamp people scare the crap out of me.

He collects a shoulder pack for me as well as a blanket, an old canteen, a hunting knife with sheath, and pouches of his powders. I know what most of them do now, he taught me in the time that I've been here.

"I will miss your strange presence." He glances down at the Guardian. "But I will not miss that beast." His rubs his shortened pinkie finger against his leg.

I accept the pack from him and drape it over my shoulder. "Good-bye, Witchdoctor."

"Until we meet again." He pats my arm and walks me out of his hut. The Guardian follows.

It's midday. The swamp is a damp oven and I am grateful for the light clothing these people gifted me—even if it is made of human skin.

The Witchdoctor walks me around the side of his hut, across the strip of land that leads to the mainland and then he stops, simply watching me as I head east.

The Swamp people stand and watch me go. They are not the type to offer hugs or warm words. Appreciative that I get to leave this place alive, I give them a nod of thanks as I pass.

My first stop is going to be Crystal River. I need answers from the Entities running the Districts. I need to get answers about Galena.

Eventually I need to make my way back to Phoenix. Ian gave me a piece of paper with passwords and details of the Galena District, but I lost it in the moments of Ian's death. Now I have to discover it all over again. Some of it I can remember. Bits and pieces, but I need to find that piece of paper so I can go there prepared.

SIXTEEN

THEN

Andie was standing in the same room as Adam, hurt and broken. She would never forgive him for this. Keeping her imprisoned here—she might forgive him for that—but not helping Crane kidnap her children. Adam knows he is all but dead to her now. Even if Crane promised her to Adam in order to get his help, Adam knew better. There was no way he could win her back now.

Adam hated Burton Crane with every spec of his being, especially after the man tried to kill him. But Adam knew that was Crane's modus operandi. He pushed Adam away and then reeled him in, it was just like fishing.

Crane told Andie a story of her history and Adam listened intently. Hopefully some of it was truth. Most of it sounded right from what Adam remembered.

"What about their child?" Andie asked Crane.

"Ah, Andromeda." Crane smiled. "That is a very good question, indeed. They must have had some intuition about their mortality, or maybe there was some warning. Either way, after their bodies were discovered so was a child, hiding in the back of the hotel closet. Selene was alive and well, albeit she had just witnessed the murder of her parents, my greatest friends and collaborators."

"Let me guess, you raised her as your own and everything was unicorns and rainbows?"

"No. I was—I am," Crane corrected himself, "a very selfish person. And Arthur and Andrea and I had a plan. We promised each other that we would continue to carry it out even if something happened to one of us. So because of my selfishness, I allowed Selene to go to a foster family. Being an orphan myself, despite having been placed in a poorer example of a family when my parents died, I handpicked a couple whom I thought embodied the ideas and beliefs of her parents. I have missed them terribly but I know that I have been able to keep my promise to them."

Adam was relieved to learn that the child was fine, although he still felt guilty for not doing anything to save her.

The next few events passed by in a blur. Craned promised Andie and her family a life of safety at the Pasture if she agreed to his terms. She finally agreed, and then she was on the floor, her face twisted in pain.

Adam remembered when he first received his nanocytes, how it felt like his body was on fire as they spread. He couldn't help himself when he reached for her. He didn't want her to feel pain any longer.

"Get away from me!" Andie seethed at him. Adam straightened and waited. After a few minutes Andie stood.

"Ah," Crane smiled. "It is done. Congratulations on your immortality."

"I'm not thanking you for this," Andie told him.

"I expected that," Crane replied. "So this is where we part. I will give you some time to come to terms with your new mission, Andromeda. But I will call on you again. There are things that need to be discussed."

"Where are you going?" she asked.

"I think I'll go to Hanford first. I have to have a discussion with George Crossbender. Then I will visit Sakima."

Adam hoped that Crossbender wouldn't crack when confronted by Crane. They had a deal.

"What about the Residents, the Survivors?" Andie asked.

"There will be no war," Crane said as he walked toward the door. "You have control of the Residents of Phoenix. And Adam, or dare I say Christian, has control of the Survivors. All is well." Crane pulled the door open and walked through. "Tootles." He waved.

Andie followed Crane until she saw that he left the building. Adam followed her, eager to have few minutes with her alone and explain himself.

"What does he have on you?" she finally asked, turning to face Adam.

He shook his head. There was so much—too much—and he knew that if he told her any of it, the truth would ruin her. She'd never look at him again if she knew it all and while he knew he deserved it, he couldn't tell her everything. Adam felt that if he kept her in the dark for just a little bit longer then maybe he could make things right. Adam could grow his army of Survivors and intercept Crane as he traveled. He could end it all and finally be done with Crane and all of his defunct plans.

Deep down Adam knew Maryam was right, the fate of the free world did rest in their hands, although this world was nothing like the one he was brought into. Crane had manipulated nature too much. Maybe decades from now Andie would forgive him. Maybe when she was alone and saw all that he had tried to do to protect her. Maybe then she would welcome him back into her life. There was never anyone else he had wanted as much as he had wanted her in his life. Those thoughts made him angry and confused because he had no control over what she could do.

"How could you do this, Adam? How could you agree to this and pull me into it? You're so selfish." Andie walked away from him and toward the gymnasium where her family was waiting.

"No more selfish than you." Adam needed just a few more minutes with her. He had to make her see that he wasn't the root of the cause. "All this time you've been fighting to keep your family safe. This started with *your* family." He felt like a dick saying it but it was a partial truth.

Andie turned and her glare seared him. "Don't turn this on me."

"I've escaped death twice. What happens if there's a third time? I succeeded in keeping Blithe out of trouble, keeping her safe within

Phoenix. And now there's Raven and Lina, and you." Deep down Adam knew that he'd cheated death many more times than that but she didn't need to know that right now.

"Don't include my family. Ian and I can take care of ourselves."

"You'd like to think so wouldn't you?"

Adam wanted to laugh in her face. Her husband was nothing more than a weak human. He was a good man who in a normal world could have taken care of his family, but he was out of his league with what Andie was now. Andie needed someone like her. Andie needed Adam. As much as she wouldn't admit it, they had much more in common than most these days.

"I'm done, Adam—or Christian. I don't even know what to call you anymore."

"Call me Adam."

"Whatever. I don't ever plan on seeing you again so it doesn't matter."

"And if I want to see Raven? He is my son, after all."

"Yet you've never been there for him."

That hurt, even though Adam knew the child was better off far away from him, still, he continued to argue. "I met him when we brought them here."

The child hadn't said a word to him. Adam had hoped that maybe he would speak when he met his real father, his biological father, but it seemed everything Adam had hoped for had backfired. He wanted to have a family with Andie, grow old with her and ignore the world he had helped create and all the bad decisions he had made in his life. But it seemed it was too late for any of that.

"And that's the last time. I'll be dead before I let you near him again."

The gymnasium doors crashed open, slamming against the wall. In a heartbeat, Ian was running toward Adam. He didn't stop or slow, simply ran full bore, stopping only when his fist made contact with Adam's face. A grunt of pain erupted from both men, Adam's more from surprise than anything. He didn't think Ian had it in him to pull a stunt like this.

"Stop!" Andie yelled. "Stop!"

"Who the hell do you think you are?" Ian spat out as he punched Adam.

Adam took whatever Ian had to offer, knowing that it would help, Andie seeing that her husband could try to protect them. It wouldn't be enough though, not now that Crane had made her one of them. Ian could try all he wanted.

"Ian!" Andie screamed. "Stop!"

"Don't ever come near my family again!" Ian threatened Adam, twisting the neck of Adam's shirt tight across his throat.

Adam glanced at Andie. He figured it would be the last time he could. Her hair was wild, her eyes bright—she was a sight, even after everything they'd been through.

"Don't!" Ian warned as he pulled a handgun from the back of his pants. He pressed it to Adam's lower jaw, his finger twitched near the trigger. "Don't you dare look at her or the children," Ian warned with a low voice.

Adam said nothing, he just nodded his head slightly. The barrel of the handgun was pressed so hard to his chin that it tipped his head to the side. One of the Guardians that had been waiting in the hallway began a low growl and Adam wondered if those beasts would ever make themselves useful.

"You're lucky the Guardians are standing here right now, because if they weren't, you'd be dead. Which is what will happen if I ever see your face again." Ian released Adam's shirt with a hard shove.

"Ian, let's go. We have to go," Andie was pulling at her husband's arm.

Adam knew that this was where he needed to leave her. But fate had kept drawing them back together and although Adam wanted to leave her alone for good, he knew it wouldn't be long before the universe forced their paths to cross again.

Adam walked down the hallway toward the locker rooms. He entered the men's room and waited. Emotion swelled deep within him and he punched one of the lockers so hard the door bent in on itself. The thought crossed his mind that maybe he was going about this all wrong. But that was the problem—Adam didn't know any better, he had spent so much time under Crane's thumb he had forgotten where he had left his humanity.

"So you chose the unborn child then?"

"That's not what I'm saying." I can't choose either of them. I can do this one last thing, get the medicine for Andie. "Maybe you should get some rest. We will be to Independence by morning."

"Perhaps that is a good idea. Wake me up when you need a break."

"That won't be necessary."

"Hmm, why's that?"

"I'll sleep when I get the medication back to Andie."

HE STOOD THERE FOR MINUTES, maybe an hour, he wasn't sure—didn't think of much until he heard Mack's voice shouting in the hallway.

Adam left the locker room and waved down the hall at Mack, wondered what the heck all the commotion was about.

"Swamp men on the rails! Swamp men on the rails!" his second in command shouted, gathering the Militiamen to protect their post.

Adam's chest constricted. He had a deal with the Swamp men, they could threaten the Survivors but they weren't supposed to harm them. They were only allowed to take the dead and near dead.

Fate was a bitch. Andie may hate him, her husband and family too, but he wouldn't let those creatures harm them. Not now, not ever. Adam ran out of the school and into the forest.

SEVENTEEN

GETTING THE VOLKER TO LET ME IN TO CRYSTAL RIVER IS easier than expected.

I follow the train tracks into the center of town.

The short building with the wide porch that's used for their Headquarters here looks like it's been painted since the last time I was here. There are two Volker guarding the door and Colonel Ramirez exits the building before I have a chance to cross the empty parking lot that extends between the train platform and Headquarters.

Ramirez approaches me, his Volker uniform stiff in the cool air. "How did you get in?" he asks.

"Is that a way to greet and old friend, Colonel Ramirez?"

He presses his lips together and frowns. "Do I know you?" he looks genuinely confused.

"Andromeda Somers," I remind him.

He squints before his eyes widen. "You look different from when I saw you last."

I smile. "Death does that to a person."

Emanuel Torres is the next person to exit the Crystal River Headquarters. Ramirez waves at him to stay back.

"I'm only here for answers. Then I'll go," I promise him.

Ramirez studies me for a moment before nodding and motioning for Emanuel to come closer.

"Andromeda Somers." Emanuel looks shocked. "I barely recognize you. We all thought you were dead."

"Surprise." My voice is flat.

The smell of grilled manatee is thick in the air but I see no grilling party. Maybe they got a real kitchen like Hanford has for meals together.

"Aren't you going to invite me in?" I ask.

"Maybe we should walk first," Emanuel offers.

Ramirez nods and folds his arms across his chest, watching as we wander away from him.

The heat isn't as bad as it was the last time I was here. "What month is it?" I ask.

"January." He eyes me suspiciously. "What do you want here, Andromeda?"

"You used to call me Andie," I remind him.

"You used to be an innocent pawn. People fear you now. Word got around about... Ian." He looks me up and down. "For God sakes you look like one of those Swamp people."

"Thanks for being real." I take a step toward him. "You fear me?"

He takes a step back. "That depends on what you're doing here."

"I just came to check on the Residents and get some information."

"The Residents are fine." He offers as he motions to the road ahead of us. We walk and people mill about, tending to yards and gardens, groups of children run by giggling.

"It looks good here," I say.

"It is. Much better since the last time you were here."

A group of men walk by carrying buckets suspended by ropes.

"Fishermen," he informs me. "We are quite independent now."

I nod. "The malaria?"

"Fewer and fewer casualties with each generation. Thanks to you."

So breeding the sickle-cell trait worked. Maybe it was wrong, but as a result there are a lot less dead people. "Have you taken in more Survivors?"

He gives a long pause.

I urge him on. "Tell me."

"Some. Women and children who've been on the run. We took them in." He stops to turn to me. "We aren't all that bad. I'm not going to leave people begging outside the gates. If we turn them away, that only increases our chances of being found here."

"You still feeding them Halcyon?"

He sighs. "We have to maintain control. This District has struggled from the start. We can't survive an uprising here."

I can barely control the urge to get this over and done with. The need to get away from people and return to the quiet and solace of the forests is unrelenting. "I want to see the rest of your District Development Commission."

"What do you need with them?" he asks.

"I have questions for them."

"You could simply ask me."

"Let's get this done, Emanuel. You want me gone and I want to leave." I sigh.

"Fine." He turns and heads back toward Headquarters. I follow him. When we reach the building, Colonel Ramirez holds open the door then falls in line behind me.

Inside the boardroom Mateo Pena and Javier Vega are waiting for us. They still look like they could be related with their matching tan skin and dark hair and eyes. The only one missing is Richard Ruiz.

"You look lonely without Mr. Ruiz," I say.

Mateo shoots Emanuel a sideways glance.

"What?" I ask.

"He made things uncomfortable here," Emanuel says. "To be truthful Crystal River runs better without him."

"Well thanks for sending him to my neck of the woods."

"And how is the Phoenix District treating him?" Javier asks. His glasses are now held together with mostly tape.

"I wouldn't know. I left about five minutes after he arrived. But you all know that. So let's cut to the chase. I need information."

"What kind of information?" Emanuel asks.

"About Galena," I reply.

Emanuel's face remains impassive.

"What's going on there?" I ask. "You're going to tell me some rubbish about alternative energy research but there's more."

"I can't say," Emanuel presses his lips together.

I move to sit in one of the chairs. "I need you to say."

"How do we know we can trust you?" Mateo asks.

"I'm still the same. Just because I hang out with cannibals doesn't mean I am one."

"You look like one of those Swamp men." Mateo looks uneasy.

"I think we are far beyond judging me based on my clothing. Besides," I hold up my wrist and unclasp the bracelet that covers my Sovereign mark. "I still have this." I replace the bracelet. "Now. What else is going on in Galena? I've been told that they're storing the world's data there. Why?"

Emanuel swallows loudly. "Experiments."

"What kind of experiments?" I ask.

Mateo slams his fist down on the table cursing in Spanish. "If you tell her you know what he's going to do to us."

"She'll protect us." Emanuel looks between his colleagues. "Right, Andie? You'll protect us from the backlash."

Oh, this is getting good. I fold my hands over my stomach and lean back in the chair. "What is it that I need to protect you from?"

"They're experimenting on children," Emanuel says in a sudden rush.

I sit up straight. My heart pounds in my chest. Children. What the hell? These people never cease to amaze me with how far they will go.

"What kind of experiments?" I ask.

"We're not sure." Emanuel says. "But we've seen things on the satellites." He motions to the computer we used to find Survivors years ago. "We were surveying Canada, looking for anyone who survived the Reformation there."

"Crossbender said barely anyone survived the nuclear winter," I say. "Canada is supposed to be desolate."

Emanuel nods in agreement as he continues. "We were still searching. The satellites were focused in the north-western section of the continent when there was a sudden flash of light."

"At first we thought it was a solar flare," Javier interrupts as he moves to the central computer on the table and starts typing.

"But it wasn't right. The shade of light," Emanuel continues. "It was blue."

"And the satellite didn't have any interruptions in feed." Mateo motions for me to come closer.

I push my chair back to stand and walk across the room until I'm behind Javier. He's searching through a recorded satellite feed.

"There!" Emanuel points.

Javier rewinds the feed then plays the video slow motion.

At first the images show a frozen wasteland. There are small towns frozen over and demolished, bodies frozen in the permafrost. And then a bright flash whitewashes everything. The screen jerks from left to right then zooms out. There's a small figure in the upper left hand corner. They zoom in, focus, and follow the figure. Javier presses a button to freeze the screen. It's a small boy running, his hands lit up like light bulbs.

"Where does he go?" I ask.

"Straight to Galena," Emanuel answers.

Unease twists my gut. Knowing what Crane did to me, God knows what he did to that boy.

"I'm going there," I tell them. "Keep your satellites on Galena. I'll contact you to find out what else you've seen."

I make my way for the door, but Emanuel puts out his hand to stop me. "You may want the world's data," he says. "But they're using it for something else."

Eighteen

Adam

Right now, I am no better than a nomad hopelessly wandering the desert. There's even sand under my feet. I hate sand. It reminds me of Norman Eckstein, the Middle East, the scars that are too deep for my first generation nanocytes to fix.

There is nothing great about being the first, but hopefully Andie will be the last and we can end this. I just have to find her but I have no idea where to look. There are no leads, no top-secret clues leaked to me by one of the few remaining meddlesome Entities, there is nothing. I have nothing. I have never felt so hopeless, even during my worst days.

It has been close to a year that I have scoured North America searching for her. The probability of her being alive after all this time is so small. No one survives more than a few days with the Swamp people. They've had her this long, odds can't be good. Those bastards will eat anything with a heartbeat or anything that's recently had a heartbeat. They live in the shadows and move through the forest in an effortless inky flow. I've had a hard time finding any of them recently.

Months ago I left my truck outside of a settlement near Colorado and decided to do this on foot. I bum rides off of Survivors and use horses when they're available. After all, she could be someplace where the roads don't reach. So I just walk. Walking is the easiest. Right now I'm thinking of heading to Wolf Creek. No one ever checks Wolf Creek for anything. They think it's just wildlife reintroduction going on there, but I know better. If Crane locked up a lot of land there's something wrong going on behind the walls and it's probably for no good reason.

I need a horse to get me south and I know Wolf Creek has plenty of horses. There's probably even a species they developed that doesn't need to eat or drink for a month. That's probably what they're doing there. Reintroducing animals for the good of the world? I doubt it.

Everyone knows she's missing and everyone wants to find her. Well, everyone who's important wants to find her. Crane doesn't want to lose his most prized possession. My gut aches when I think of the man and what he's done to us.

Go fetch, he said. He treats us like nothing more than lab rats. All of us.

Deep inside my chest, I know she has to be alive. I would have felt it if she had left this plane and moved on. I know this much.

NINETEEN

"Where will you go next?" Emanuel asks me.

I tip my head toward the fading light, unsure of whether I should tell him my plans or not. I'm still not ready to trust any of these people.

Before I can answer he says, "Tonopah, right? It's the only logical stop. Now that you're not dead Sakima will be expecting you. We've been worried that you were going to start looking for us. Hunting us down like some ghost seeking vengeance."

"Emanuel, you have nothing to worry about from me. The Funding Entities may be responsible for providing Crane with the means to carry out his apocalyptic plans but I don't think you had anything to do with Crane's plans for me."

Emanuel motions for the Volker to open the gates. "We weren't all on board with the nanocyte plan. There's someone looking for you," he warns before I step away from him.

"There's plenty looking for me."

"It's Adam."

I give Emanuel a look.

"He's going to make us tell him where you are." Emanuel rubs his cheek. "I don't think any of us want to suffer his wrath, he can be... unpleasant when he wants to."

"Then do your best to forget I was ever here." I walk through the gates and away from the Crystal River District.

THE SUN IS splintering across the sky in a peach haze when I turn to find a dark figure headed in my direction. I look at the Guardian by my side and point to the figure walking toward me. "Attack," I order it. The Guardian huffs before wandering away in the opposite direction. "Worthless beast," I mutter.

The figure gets closer and I'm not sure what to do until I recognize who it is. It's Adam, or Christian, or whatever name he's going by these days. He runs toward me; focused, intent. I draw my knife and hold it out at arm's length. Adam stops, the tip of the knife pressed to his chest, his eyes searching my face.

"You look like hell." Those are my first words to him. It should be something better like a holy curse word or a punch to the face or something painful akin to all the hurt he's caused me. The thought to just stab him once, really hard crosses my mind.

"And you look different." Oh, his voice, it's smooth as honey and twice as deadly. "Very different." He drops to his knees in front of me and my arm lowers with him, keeping him at a safe distance with the tip of my knife. "What happened to you, Andie? I have been searching for you for so long."

Emotion swells in my chest as I take in the sight of him. His beard is thick and down to his chest, his hair is to his shoulders, he's covered in dust, his clothing worn. He carries no pack of supplies or canteen of water. If it weren't for his intense gaze I'd think him a vagabond embracing death.

"You never should have sought me out." I point the knife at his face. "I'm going now."

In a quick movement I sheath the knife and back away from him.

"Where?" Adam asks in a low voice. He sits back on his heels, watching me as though I am a mirage or a ghost.

"Away. Goodbye."

He moves to his feet and steps toward me. "I'm going with you."

I back away fast, eager to put distance between us. "No, you're not."

"Yes." He sounds desperate.

"No! You're going wherever liars go to live out their life. And it is *nowhere* near me."

"Please." The forest debris crunches under his feet as he begins to follow me.

"I'll slit your throat as you sleep." I warn him.

"Good luck with that." His voice is dark. "I don't sleep anymore."

I turn and begin walking at as fast of a pace as I can muster at the moment. I know his stride is at least twice that of mine, being as tall as he is and as short as I am, but he stays behind me, following at an uncomfortable distance.

"I will kill you," I warn him. "Turn away now and save yourself. You're good at doing that. Tucking tail and running."

Adam says nothing but continues to follow me. I glare at Steve the Guardian and curse his worthlessness right now.

"Why do you look so different?" Adam finally asks. "I mean you look like you, just younger. A lot younger."

Stopping, I twist to face him. "This," I motion to my body, "is what happens when you touch the fence that encloses the Phoenix District. Fifty thousand volts will get you the same thing. Better than a Hollywood plastic surgeon. A lot cheaper too."

Adam's eyes widen. "How did you survive that?" He takes a step closer to me.

"The nanocytes." I take a step away from him. "I fried to a crisp. The Swamp people dragged me away expecting a fully cooked corpse." I hold up my wrist and twist it; the bracelet made of bone that covers my Sovereign tattoo gives a hollow knock. "Boy weren't they surprised when my skin sloughed off and my bones re-grew. Seems coming back to life is frowned upon by cannibals. They said I was cursed. Wouldn't touch me with a ten-foot pole. Still won't."

Adam runs a hand through his long dark hair. "You're lucky. Not much stops them when it comes to free food." He looks generally concerned. I should know better than to fall into that trap. "How did you manage to touch that fence?"

"I was running."

"From who?"

I pause. "Crane."

"Why?" He steps closer, his arms out like he might touch me.

I move away. "That's none of your concern."

"You're wrong." His gaze darkens. "I'm very concerned about it."

"Really?" I eye him skeptically before turning on my heel and continuing my trek.

"Really." He follows me. "Why were you running from Crane?" he asks.

I say nothing. I'm not about to divulge my secrets to this man at the drop of a hat just because he showed up after all of this time. It's going to take a lot more than him dropping to his knees. He's going to have to crawl through death before I tell him anything.

"Whatever he told you is probably right." I wave him away.

"He told me nothing. Just that you were missing. He asked me to find you."

"So you're my bounty hunter, huh?" I control the urge to slap him, unsure of why physically hurting him might bring me some relief from all the wrong he's done to me.

"No." Adam shakes his head. "I'm done taking orders from him. From all of them."

"So are you like a free agent now?" I snicker and it sounds strange, forced, angry.

"Something like that. I'm done with them and all the things I've done. I don't want that life any longer." He cocks his head to the side. "Do you still have that tattoo?" I scowl at him. "Those three little birds? Still reminding yourself to be brave, Andie?"

"Shut up."

He smirks.

"I will still kill you," I warn him.

"I'm not afraid of you." His smile is warm. He's not taking me the least bit serious.

"Should be. I've killed before, you'll be easy."

"I've killed plenty." He grabs my arm to stop me from walking away from him. "And it never gets easier. I can promise you that." Quicker than I've ever seen a man move he pulls the knife from the sheath at my hip and points it to his chest. Then he grabs my hand, wrapping it around the hilt and pressing it into his skin. "Don't be so quick to threaten me with death. I remember a time when I prayed for it." He drops his voice. "I remember a time when *you* prayed for it."

I rip my hands out of his grasp and re-sheath the knife. "Don't touch me." I put distance between us.

"I can't help it." He walks closer to me. "I want to touch you. I've been searching for you for so long. Scoured the country, every part of it for over a year. I've been looking for you, Andie. And here you are alive and well and..." He looks at me like he's run out of words or can't find the right ones.

"What?" All I can think is he is a traitor and a liar and he marched my ass straight into Phoenix the day the Reformation started and he has lied to me over and over and over again.

"I'm sorry." Something flashes behind his eyes. "For all of it."

For the first time in ages I laugh and it's a full-blown, from the bottom of my belly sound.

When I finally catch my breath, I say, "We are in the middle of some manmade apocalypse. I am some deus ex machina created by Crane to do his bidding and keep the world in order. And now after our sordid history you're standing in front of me and all you have to say is *I'm sorry*. It's going to take a lot more than two tiny words to make up for your royal screw ups."

I stomp off in the direction of Tonopah only to stop abruptly and turn to face him one last time. "And I just spent a year living with cannibals! Do you know what that kind of thing does to a person?"

Twenty

Adam

Shit. She's mad.

TWENTY-ONE

Andromeda

He follows me the entire way to Tonopah. It's days of walking from Florida to Arizona and I don't stop for water or food or rest. Those are things that no longer drive me and I no longer require them to live. Adam never utters a word. He stays behind me at a respectful distance while Steve the Guardian walks by my side.

I make sure the Survivors don't come near us. When I sense them, I let out a burst of *feeling* and they scatter like cockroaches.

When the giant fencing system of Tonopah finally comes into view, I am reminded that this District has greater defenses than we do in Phoenix.

The chain-link fence hums loudly but it doesn't seem to bother the people who have pitched tents outside of the District. Some stand in front of the gates begging to get in. Some wander too close to the corridor that encloses the train tracks and walk away with bloodied noses and ears. There are no singed body parts hanging off of the fencing like there was the last time I was here. Past a long stretching of sand on the other side of the fence, cement walls are visible and behind that is the secondary wall of protection where I know I will find the largest of the Districts.

As I near the fence, a thin woman hands a Volker a baby bundled in dirty rags and in return she is given a basket of food and a jug of water.

As soon as the gates close, chaos erupts. People want in, they want food and water and safety. Men follow the woman, tracking her like jackals. I know what they're going to do to her and it's going to include taking that basket of food to fill their own hollowed bellies.

I can't watch this. I walk toward them and the woman looks at me strangely, then the dark man behind me, then the Guardian. She passes in a hurry and I stop to interrupt the men.

"Stop," I tell them and they do. "You will not harm her. Go and find your own food."

They pause and slight confusion passes over their dirty faces before they scatter.

I make my way to Tonopah's gates.

"How did you do that?" Adam asks from behind me.

"Doesn't matter."

"I think it does."

I turn, the bright sun reflecting off of the golden sand, making this place look like it glows. "Go away," I tell him.

"I don't think that witchcraft works on me." Adam scowls, trying to figure out what I just did.

Turning, I continue, stopping only when I am in front of the gates.

"Let me enter," I tell the Volker. They carry large rifles in addition to the pistols. This District remains well-secured and armed.

"Who are you?" a brave Volker asks.

"Let me in," I reply calmly.

Let me in, let me in, let me in.

He opens the gate and lets us through. The other Volker watch but don't act to stop us. I have that effect on them.

"Interesting," Adam mutters from behind me.

I walk the long stretch of sand to the secondary cement wall.

"Let me in," I instruct the Volker there, and they do.

The change in scenery is just as drastic as it was the first time I was here. Rows of crops replace the sandy wilderness. A sophisticated irrigation system gleams in the desert sunlight. There are perfectly spaced rows of fruiting trees, rows of corn, and far off in the distance rows of small adobe houses.

Strangely, the fields are filled with children.

I head down the main road past perfectly spaced trailers, tents, and small homes. There are children everywhere and I only see a handful of adults.

I finally come to the Tonopah Headquarters, a small squat building that resembles an old post office. There are Volker out front who let us pass, just like I ask them to. Once inside I immediately find Colonel Yuma standing near a large circular table where Sakima sits.

Jackpot.

Sakima stands. His skin is tanned a dark brown, his Native American heritage front and present. His long black hair is secured in a braid down his back, intertwined with turquoise threading. His black suit is pressed and clean unlike my outfit of skin and dust.

"Thought the day would never come when the great Andromeda Somers would step through my gates again," Sakima says, a wide smile on his face. "I told my good friend Crane to lend you to me so I could set you straight. Seems he finally did." Sakima looks me up and down. "Although, I anticipated he'd send you looking a bit fresher."

Tonopah's Crane is just as arrogant as the original.

"Bind them," Sakima orders Colonel Yuma and the few Volker that are in the room.

"Stop," I tell them, and they do. "Bind your leader," I order.

A moment of confusion passes across the Volker's faces before they move, surround Sakima, push him to sit in a chair and bind his wrists behind his back. The action is fast and violent. His Volker don't hold back as Sakima fights them.

"What are you doing?" Adam whispers from behind me.

"Shut up. I told you not to follow me."

When he is finally subdued, Sakima chuckles from his seat.

"You shut up too." I grab a chair and move to sit in front of Sakima. "Now. I have some questions for the great Sakima."

"I bet you do, little one." His smile is wide and deceiving.

"There are things that I can do now. You don't scare me like the last time I was here."

"You sure about that?" He struggles against his bindings. "I remember your friend there detaining you for me. Is he hungry? He looks hungry. My people can get him food."

I am reminded of the dose of Halcyon Sakima fed Adam last time we were here and the way Adam treated me afterwards. He has a history of treating me like that, ordering me around and breaking my heart. I glance at Adam out of the corner of my eye to find him watching us.

"He's not hungry," I tell Sakima. "But I am."

"We can feed you. Give you some real clothes so you don't look like one of those cannibals. Is that what you're hanging around now? Crane would be so disappointed. After all the time and money he invested in you."

"I could almost care." I brush some dust off of my arm and let it fall to the floor.

"What do you want?" Sakima asks.

"You have information."

"Don't we all?" He smiles.

I pull my knife from its sheath and tap it on the back of my chair. "Let's make this quick. I'm tired of the desert heat." I focus like I would when willing someone to do what I want.

"Tell me how to get past Galena's gates?"

"Didn't Crane tell you, Andromeda? Your gift won't work on me."

It won't work on others with the nanocytes, but that doesn't mean I won't try.

"I have other gifts that will work on you." I twist the knife into the wood of my chair, making an indent. "A yearlong stay with the Swamp people will teach a person things." I watched Glane gut more than one creature during our travels to Hanford and back. "I need the codes. For the files. For the world's data. Tell me now."

Sakima laughs. Then stopping abruptly he says, "Ask Crane."

"The next time I face Crane I will be killing him." I move quick, pressing the blade to Sakima's chest. "Tell me or I stab this directly into your heart."

"You can't kill me." His face is placid, uncaring. I think at one time he was a handsome man. Now he's just pure darkness.

"I may not be able to kill you. But I can incapacitate you for a year or more. Or I could cut off your limbs and have your Volker distribute them all over the country. You'd survive. I know this." I press the knife into his chest. "Tell me what I want to hear. Now." I twist the knife the slightest bit. "Please."

Sakima scowls, a deep dark expression that might have brought me to my knees before, now it just pisses me off. I press the blade deeper into his chest.

"What are they doing with the children in Galena?" I ask.

"I won't tell you. Go there and find out for yourself."

I press the blade deeper, cutting his soft flesh.

He winces.

"You do feel pain," I mutter. "So do I. You know what hurts? Losing everyone you love. Not being able to be near your children for fear that you might kill them. I have nothing left to lose." Blood stains his skin around the blade. "Now, speak."

"Just go to Galena. I have nothing to tell you," he says as I press the knife deeper, the tip stopping against his breastbone. Feeling the point and the pressure, his eyes widen, dark pools of black, his irises void of any color. "I don't have answers for you. Crane does. Or just go to Galena. You'll figure it out or that fool Berkley will crack under pressure."

"Coward." I pull the knife out and stand, replace my chair at the table. "Leave him here for two weeks," I instruct his Volker. "Gather all of your Residents and Sovereign and meet me in the center of the District."

The men in uniform begin to move without question.

"What do you think you're doing?" Sakima asks. He scoots the chair, trying to free himself.

"Stop trying to escape or I will instruct your men to cut your limbs off and you can lie in a pool of blood until they re-grow."

He stills. "You wouldn't."

"I will." I move away from him. "Tell me, why do I only see children populating your District?"

Sakima sneers. "Halcyon. Birth rate zero. Plenty of Survivors willing to sacrifice their children for food and water. Take your pick, they all fit. You should know. *You* told us to do it!"

Sometimes I hate myself. But right now, I really hate myself. The truth is a painful reminder of all the wrongs I've committed.

They've taken too many infants and children to grow their District. I did this. I recommended this when I was last here and now they have a District of orphans.

"You haven't been following the District values, at least the ones forced upon us in Phoenix. I'm going to set your Residents and your Sovereign straight."

"They are my people. You will not interfere with my people!" Sakima spits as he screams at me.

A worried Adam looks between us but he does nothing to intervene.

"And that is where you are wrong, Sakima. They are not your people. They are mine. Treat them poorly and I treat you poorly. Remember that." Pulling open the door, I walk out into the mid-morning sun and head for the middle of the District.

"You're just going to leave him like that?" Adam asks from behind me.

"I told you not to follow me. And yes. I hope he gets a bedsore on his ass."

Now, I am just as bad as when I feared Ian hating me. What I believed before about right and wrong, heaven and hell, it doesn't apply to this life anymore; it can't. The worst part is that I am frightened by how good it feels.

WE STAND at the crossroads outside of the Tonopah Headquarters. The Volker have brought all the children and adults and the ten Sovereign.

The children look tired, dirty, uncared for. They don't look loved. It breaks my heart. I can't help but admit that Crane did something right when he formed the Phoenix District and enacted his rules: family units are necessary. And these children, they need someone to care for them.

And so I begin, telling myself that it can't be much harder than the pairings. I'm just matchmaking the few adults and grouping the children into families.

I close my eyes, focus, and move toward a man, tall and dark skinned. I take his hand. "Come with me." Standing before the women, focusing, I push through the first three rows until I stop in front of a woman with dark hair and fair skin. I press their hands together. "You are bound."

I continue until everyone is paired. Then I move to the children. The problem is that there are so many of them. When I am done the families are large, ten and twenty children in some. It's better than nothing, better than these children working in the fields and keeping this District going on their own with no one to go home to at night. No one to love them and care for them and help them grow. Even if Sakima is overseeing it all, I know he lacks the empathy to give these children the love and caring they deserve. Hopefully what I have done will help and Tonopah will no longer be a District of empty souls.

Worn out after the day's activities and the previous week's travels, I make my way for the gates.

"Let me pass," I tell the Volker.

The guards move aside and open the gates. I walk toward the hot desert sand, exhausted and drained. I haven't felt like this ever. I feel like I should sleep but not with Adam trailing me. I don't trust him. So I walk, sand stinging my eyes, across the plains and hills as the sun moves across the sky burning my skin only for it to heal again within minutes.

I head north, toward Wolf Creek. It will take me weeks and by the time I arrive Sakima will have been freed by his men and will be calling Crane to report me. Only God knows what I will encounter then.

Not nearly soon enough a sparse forest comes into view between the jutting rocky terrain. I head straight for it, rejoicing when mud clings to my boots. There's a small pond in the distance. I drop my bag at the shore and walk straight into it, dunking myself under the cool, crisp water. Coming up for air, I turn to float on my back, staring at the stars and the bright moon. This feels good, refreshing, calming. If only I weren't being watched from behind the shadows of the trees.

Collecting myself, I try and will Adam to go away.

"Stop it," he says from the edge of the forest. He must be able to sense my attempts.

"Then go away."

"I can't."

"You can't or you won't?" My moment of peace is shattered. "I don't have time for liars in my life anymore." I stand, water dripping off of my clothes, and make my way for the shoreline, shivering. I would like the comfort of a roaring fire right now, and a nap. Along with a hot shower, a warm meal, coffee, and clean clothes. But I will survive without all of that. I deserve none of it.

"Why haven't you gone to see your children?" he asks from the shadows.

A deep pang envelopes my heart. Oh, how I long to see them. "I've seen them and said my goodbyes. I won't be going back. I can't risk hurting them."

"You would never hurt them."

If only he knew. Every second of my life I relive losing my temper to Crane, causing Ian's death, trying to bring him back to life. It seems I can send people away, but I cannot bring them back from the dead. Frustrated, I pick a large stick up off of the ground and throw it in the direction of the shadows where I heard Adam's voice come from. The action is followed by a thud and a grunt.

"That was not nice," Adam groans.

"Stop following me and stop pestering me," I warn.

"I can't."

"You can and you will." I pull my bag across my shoulder. "Go away." I start walking north.

"Where are you headed?" Adam asks.

"It's none of your concern."

"You are of my concern."

"I am nothing to you."

"You are everything to me." He sounds so serious and, for the first time in forever, I think he might actually be telling the truth. I can't deal with him right now. I'm on a mission.

"Just stop," I beg him. He is finally quiet. "Now go away."

"It's too dark to travel. You should rest." His footsteps get closer. "You're tired and cold. I can tell."

"I don't need to rest. I've rested for a year."

"Where have you been? What did the Swamp people do with you?"

I pick up my pace, eager to get away from him and his questions. I don't want to talk. I don't want his company. I want nothing but the moon and the stars and the silence.

"Andie, answer me. I've been looking everywhere for you. I let you walk all the way to Tonopah without saying a word to me. I followed you silently for days on end. Now tell me."

There was a time when he was the broken one that I was trying to fix. I wonder if he still has all of his scars, or if the nanocytes healed his skin? Maybe they can only heal damage to a certain depth.

Stop, stop, stop. I have to stop myself from thinking about him.

"Go fuck yourself." I take off at a sprint, running faster than I ever have in my life.

The forest finally breaks. There is more sand, hard packed dirt, plains and empty fields. I run across it all, never stopping. I can't stop. I don't slow down until the sun rises and the earth comes alive again. And then I can feel their presence before I see them. There are at least ten Survivors. They straighten and freeze, sensing me. I have to maintain control.

"Go away." I say.

They scatter.

"How did you do that?" Adam asks. He's close behind me and sounds barely winded. "Why did they listen to you?"

I finally stop and turn to him. "Are you telling me you can't do the same?" I ask.

"No."

"Go away." I tell him. *Go away, go away, just go away!*

"No," he replies.

"Why doesn't it work on you? It works on them all so well. Just not you." I stare at him, longer than I should. I shouldn't look at him. I like the way his face looks too much, even if it is covered in scruff and dust. "So what special power did the nanocytes give you?"

"I don't know." He shakes his head. "None, actually." He wipes his mouth with a dust-caked hand.

I simply raise my eyebrows at him.

"I'm serious. I can't do anything special."

"It's been almost six years since we got the nanocytes and you don't know. What have you been doing all this time?"

He shakes his head. "It... it doesn't matter."

I scoff. "Still a liar. Now go away. For real." I turn and begin walking across the open field.

The grass is tall, not yet mowed down by the goats and cows that I can see off in the distance. I try to walk fast, feeling the eyes of the Survivors on me. I have the urge to hide in the shadows just like the Swamp people do. The Survivors won't hurt me, they can't. I just don't like it when they stare at me. I pick up the pace, staggering on the uneven ground, cursing that these blasted nanocytes couldn't give me a good sense of balance. Almost to the next tree line, I step, the lumpy ground giving, my ankle twisting and snapping.

"Shit!" I shout, trying to catch myself as I fall, but before I hit the ground I am lifted into the air.

"You're still clumsy," Adam whispers in my ear.

Heat erupts everywhere he touches me.

I struggle, twist and pound on him with my fists.

"I don't need you to save me! I don't need you! I don't need anyone!" Birds flutter out of the treetops above us. "I am on a mission. Alone!" All movement in the forest ceases.

"I see that." He squeezes me closer to his chest, the heat radiating off of him spreading comfort and unease at the same time throughout my body. "Now tell me where are you going?"

"Galena, eventually."

"What is in Galena? Why do you keep talking about the world's data? And why do you think you can kill Crane?"

I scowl. "I'm not talking to you. You'll just go back and tell him. You're a liar and a traitor." I struggle in his arms.

"I am neither of those things to you. To many others, yes. But not to you."

I struggle again, kicking my feet, my twisted ankle already healed.

Adam releases me, dropping me onto a pile of soft pine needles and leaves.

"Jerk!" I glare up at him.

"You're a jerk." He points a finger at me. "And you're out of control."

"I told you to leave."

"I can't."

"You can. You just won't." I move to stand, but Adam places one hand on my chest and pushes me back down. "Ugh! I'm not playing games with you!"

"That's good."

I move to stand and he pushes me down again. "Dick." I kick out a leg, swipe, knocking his feet out from under him. As he falls, he stumbles and twists, landing on top of me, knocking the breath out of my lungs.

"Get off of me!" I shove at him.

Adam moves, propping himself up on his elbow, still covering me, pressing me to the ground. He's warm and heavy, his body thick with muscle, igniting a deep burn throughout my body just like all those years ago. I feel my face flush. I can't control it. I shouldn't feel this way. I killed my husband. There is no happiness left for me in this world. I no longer deserve it.

It would be too easy to let myself get in trouble with Adam again but I can't let that happen. His body softens above me, giving me the chance to shove him and roll on top. Adam smiles and moves his hands to my hips.

In one quick movement I pull my knife from its sheath and hold it to his neck. I threaten, "I will kill you. Just like I killed Ian." I pause, unable to stop the tear that's collecting in the corner of my right eye. Facing the ground, my hands busy—one to his neck with the knife, the other over the steady thud of his heartbeat—I don't take the time to stop it from sliding down my face.

"I will kill you," I promise him with a shuddering breath. "Stop following me. *Please*. Please just stop."

He reaches up, wiping the tear from my face with his thumb. "Tell me what happened." His voice is so soft, like he actually cares.

"No."

"Tell me," he whispers. "Just tell me, Andie."

I press the knife harder to his throat, angry with myself for finding him so tempting even after all that's happened between us. Blinking, I push those feelings away and replace them with anger instead. "I will hurt you. That is what I do now." A small trickle of blood appears from under the knife blade. The satisfaction that fills me when I puncture his flesh scares me. I pull back and the wound heals in a matter of seconds.

"You still have that Marine Corps tattoo on your arm, Adam?" I pull up his sleeve and see the dark ink there. He smiles and it pisses me off. "Thought army guys were saviors not assholes." He drops the smile. "Seems nothing about you reveals the truth."

After wiping the blade on Adam's shirt, I secure it back in its sheath at my hip.

"Go away," I warn him as I stand. "I need to get my head straight. I can't think with you following me. You're a distraction. And I can't control myself." I straighten and put my pack on. "Stay away from me." I back away.

Adam stays on the ground where I left him. He makes no attempt to move; instead he studies me.

"Stay away," I warn one last time before turning and running.

Twenty-Two

Adam

Shit. She's really mad.
   I get up and follow her.

Twenty-Three

Andromeda

It's been miles and he's still following me. Fuming, cheeks red and emotions reeling, I turn to face him.

"What are you doing?" he asks, the corner of his lip tipped up, amused.

"I used to enjoy seeing your face," I mutter.

Crane's image flicks through my mind, the anger rising. I've never forgotten the feeling that spread throughout my body the day I killed Ian. I mimic it, imagining Crane standing near me. I feel my cheeks redden deeper, my heart pound at an angry beat. Adam remains standing in front of me perfectly fine. No blood trickling from his nose or ears, he doesn't crumple to the ground. I stop, breathe, and clear it. Just like the Witchdoctor taught me to do.

"Hmm." I start walking north again.

"Are you done with your hissy fit?" In a few short steps Adam is in front of me walking backward.

"No," I mutter.

"So what usually happens when you do that?" Adam asks.

I stop. "Death."

Adam stills. "You seriously just tried to kill me?" He looks genuinely shocked.

"I was just testing a theory."

"What's that?"

"I can't will you to go away. I can't influence your actions. I figured if none of those worked, then what I just did wouldn't work either."

"I'm not sure how I feel about you trying to kill me just now."

"Don't be so shocked. I warned you that I would. I've been warning you for weeks." I shrug. "Seems you're immune to all of my tricks. Figures." I start walking again, passing around him and head north. "Will you go away now?"

"No." Adam's voice is beside me.

"I hope you're lying. You're good at lying."

"Okay. That's enough." Adam grips my upper arm hard, dragging me to a stop and forcing me to face him. "I am not a liar by choice. I have not lied to you. I stretched the truth maybe, kept things secret."

"And why did you do all that? It's no better than lying."

He pushes a hand through his hair. "I had to protect you. I had to keep you safe."

"Why?" I scowl at him.

He opens his mouth ready to say something but it snaps shut. His bright blue eyes turn stormy and dark. "You don't know the kind of hell I've been through."

I guess that makes both of us because he doesn't know the kind of hell I've been through.

I pull away from him and walk.

The forest turns thin before rocky mountains jut up in all directions and I am forced to walk in the narrow valleys through shallow rivers and rocky paths.

"You want to stop and see the Grand Canyon?" Adam asks after a while.

"No."

"Well you're headed in the wrong direction. If you keep going that way you'll fall into it."

I stop and look around. I can't be headed in the wrong direction. I spent all that time helping Lina memorize maps. I know the lay of the land just as well as she does.

"We need to go this way." He points to the right. "Around the cliffs, through the Hopi Reservation, then the valleys of Colorado. It's the fastest route."

"How do you know?"

"I've crossed this country twice to find you." He shoves his hands in his pockets and waits, his blue eyes taking me in.

I cross my arms and orient myself. I've got nothing but time, but if he knows a faster way I'd rather not prolong this.

"Fine. But if you screw me over I swear to God I will slit your throat."

He flashes a quick smile before he begins walking again.

Now I'm following him. How quickly we change places. I'm still mad, but we cross the land. Day turns into night, then day again. Adam weaves around rocky outcroppings and mountains. The sun takes its toll on our skin but we don't stop for water or rest. We're pushing ourselves harder than we ever have and it's draining. I still haven't recovered from what I did in Tonopah.

"How are Lina and Raven?" Adam breaks the silence.

"As well as they can be now that they're orphans."

"They aren't orphans. We're alive—"

"I can't see them. I can't risk hurting them. I'll probably never see them again." A sadness flushes through me.

"I'm sorry," Adam whispers.

"It's probably best you don't see them either. It's just going to hurt them more. I willed them into believing I am dead and that what they saw when I was visiting Hanford was my ghost."

"You did what you had to," Adam seems to agree with my actions.

"I used to be a decent human being. Now I'm nothing but a monster."

"You're not a monster."

"Like you would you know?" I glare at the back of his head. Letting him take charge was a terrible idea. "Please," I beg. "Can't you just leave me alone?"

"You'd be splatter at the bottom of the Grand Canyon if I left you alone."

"Then can't you just go away?"

Adam stops and turns. "Don't you think you've punished me enough?" he asks. "I told you already that I'm sorry." He takes a step toward me and I take a step away. The prairie winds are strong at my back, as if they're telling me to stop walking away from him. I almost wish I could, but I can't.

If he wants honesty. I'll give it to him. "I'm not ready to forgive you."

He frowns, rubs his thick beard, his eyes focusing far behind me. "Your friends are trailing us."

I turn quick to see the few shrubs and trees far away shudder with movement. Swamp men.

"I didn't ask them to come."

"Well they have." Adam turns and begins walking again.

"They won't come close," I tell him. "They're afraid of me."

Adam turns as he walks, inspecting me.

"I'm telling you. Glane won't come near me."

He scowls. "You know his name?"

"Of course."

"Anything else you know about him?"

"He likes long walks on the beach and green tea with a bit of whiskey." I throw my hands in the air. "No, I barely know anything about him."

Adam makes a scoffing noise.

"Go screw yourself," I say to him. "I know Glane because he dragged my carcass back to the swamps. He brought me to their Witchdoctor. Who knows what would have happened to me if he hadn't? He pretty much saved my life."

"They have a Witchdoctor?" Adam seems surprised.

"Yes." I'll keep the details to myself for now.

"What happened with the Witchdoctor?" he asks.

"I'm not telling you."

A long moment of silence passes until I finally say, "I want you to tell me the truth. Everything you've been keeping from me."

He shakes his head.

"You want me to trust you, Adam? Tell me some truths. Because what you've shown me over the years doesn't exactly make me want to trust you."

During the silence that passes, I assume that he's agreeing.

"When did you get the nanocytes?" I ask.

"Before I ever met you."

I stop. "What?" I thought we got them at the same time, or close to it.

"Think about it." Adam turns to face me and he looks haunting in the fading light. "That first day I met you, right before the Reformation when we were making our way back to Phoenix. You think a twisted ankle can heal overnight? I should have been off my feet or had a real brace or at least crutches for weeks."

"But your lip was split. You had bruises on your face."

"I have first generation nanocytes. They take longer to work and they tire easily. I know the limitations of my nanocytes. At first they take a bit to learn your body, figure out how to work and how to heal. Everyone's are different."

This is news. My mouth opens and closes a few times as I process what he just told me.

"Mine was instant," I finally say. "The first time I cut myself it healed instantly."

Adam nods. "And who designed them?" He waits but I don't answer because I want to know if he knows. "Your own flesh and blood."

How does he know that? "I thought you were in the army?" I ask.

A dark grin spreads across Adam's face. "I have been most things at one time or another. Marine, CIA, pilot, teacher, scientist..." He trails off as I stare at him. "What?"

"You said we went to high school together."

"I said I was homeschooled and I went to your high school for filler classes. And I never said *when*."

He never ceases to surprise me.

"Liar." I brush past him and walk away.

TWENTY-FOUR

ANDROMEDA

"WHEN WILL YOU REST?" ADAM ASKS.

It's night and the cool air of the valley chills my skin.

"You can only push the nanocytes so far. You'll stop healing so fast," he warns. "You haven't rested since we left Crystal River. We've been walking for weeks. This isn't good."

I keep walking.

We've crossed the lower portion of Colorado headed for Wolf Creek in Kansas. We've passed bombed cities, abandoned towns, empty housing developments, skeletons imbedded in the dusty soil. I am tempted to stop at many of the mansions and luxury apartments we've passed. Some of the vehicles are even enticing, just to have shelter. We've walked for days and nights, through rain and hail. A few nights I even feared snow. Spring should be on its way, and the weather should be mild but I am reminded of the odd weather patterns we faced in Phoenix for years. Snow in the summer and eighty degree days in the dead of winter.

"You need to rest." His voice has a warning tone again.

"I'm fine," I say.

The moon is high over our heads as we walk near the banks of a river. Part of me wants to dive into the water and clean the dust and grime off of myself. I know I must smell terrible but it keeps the wildlife, and Adam, away. I'm also afraid the water is too cold for me to handle right now.

As we make our way to a narrow dirt road, we pass a farmhouse. Adam hasn't left my side; maybe I could trust him for a few hours if I sleep. It's dark and I'm tempted to stop. Until I hear the music.

MUSIC. Something I haven't heard since the Reformation. The sound of laughing fills the night, the twang of a guitar, the thrum of drums.

I stop in my tracks and turn toward the sound. Behind the dark farmhouse is a bar. The front doors are open and light spills out into the night. There's music and people. The Survivors are having a hoedown.

Adam looks at me, surprised. And then he takes my arm. "Come on," he says with a boyish smile as he pulls me toward the barn.

I want to hear the music but I don't want the Survivors to see us.

"I don't think this is a good idea."

"When's the last time you crashed a party?" Adam asks with a grin.

"Never."

"You haven't lived until you crash a party." He holds his hand out to me. "Come on."

I'm suddenly self-conscious of my appearance. "But we smell bad and I'm wearing clothing made of human skin."

Adam stops and turns to me. His eyes skim over my pants and top. "That's made of human skin?"

I nod.

"If they ask just tell them it's leather." He heads for the barn, tugging me along.

I'm nervous, scared, afraid that I'll scare away the Survivors and I don't want to. I want to experience the music and the laughter. It's been so long since I've heard any of it.

You don't see us, you don't see us, you don't see us.

We walk into the barn and no notices us.

Adam stops and waits.

"They won't say anything," I whisper. "I made us invisible to them. They won't see us."

"You can do that?"

I nod and bite my lip.

There is a small band in the corner playing the type of country music that I might have listened to on the radio before the Reformation. Clusters of adults and teenagers dance in the center of the barn. A few small children run across the dance floor chasing each other. There's food and drinks set up on a table to the side. It almost seems that these Survivors are doing just fine.

We watch them dance for a while. Two songs pass and still none of them notice us.

Adam starts to move. "Come on." He takes my hand and pulls me to the dance floor. "I haven't done this in decades." He looks excited.

"Crashed a party or danced in a barn?"

He flashes a quick smile. "Danced."

And then he's taking my hands and whirling me around him. This feels wrong, but right, and... fun. I can't explain the sensation. There is nothing but sound drowning out everything around us. Adam's hands grip my skin, firm and warm, leading me. The stiffness of my body gradually loosens but I still feel awkward.

Adam lets go of me when the band stops playing.

"I used to only dance when I was drunk."

His eyes move toward the table. "We can fix that." He moves, grabs a mason jar from the rough-hewn wooden table and sips at it. "Oh this is good. Homemade wine." He takes a second jar and hands it to me.

Accepting the jar, I stare into the sweet smelling liquid.

"Drink up," Adam suggests as he drains his beverage, sets it down and gulps another one.

I sip at the jar, relish the feel of moisture in my throat. The nanocytes do nothing to stop the alcohol from giving me an instant buzz. Adam must have been right, I've pushed myself too hard for too long. Who knows how long this high will last? I throw my head back and drain the jar.

Adam's smiling at me as I swallow. "That's my girl."

"I'm not your girl." The words come out dry and sharp.

Pain flashes across his face. "I know I deserve that."

"You do." Wow, this homemade wine is strong.

He looks into his empty jar. "I don't know how many times I can tell you I'm sorry."

I move away from him, set my jar down and take another, gulping the liquid courage down before I reply, "About a trillion times. Maybe more."

And for a few moments there is no one standing in the barn but us. I can only focus on Adam, this thrumming in my heart, and the anger being numbed by the wine. I should stop drinking wine. I do stupid things when I do. We simply stare at each other. His face displays a variety of emotions; pain, regret, maybe even a little sadness. Did I break his heart with my words like he broke mine with his actions? The moment is so intense that I have the urge to cry.

"You should let them see us," he suggests.

"No." I shake my head. If I let the Survivors see us, that would mean that this is real, this thing between us. I haven't yet been able to admit it to myself; I definitely cannot admit it to a room full of Survivors.

The music slows and the people around us break apart or pull their partner closer. In a sudden movement Adam grabs me, hauling me close to his body and burying his face in my neck. He sways slowly to the music, spreading his palms across my back and my waist, pulling me so close to him that there is not even a millimeter between us.

"I'm sorry," he says. "I'm sorry. I'm sorry. I'm sorry..."

He repeats it over and over and over again until I don't know how many times he's said it. As my throat grows thick and tears sting my eyes, he continues repeating the words.

When the music finally ends he loosens his hold on me. I walk away from him, out of the barn and toward the rocky road. The night is cool and fatigue finally hits me hard. Needing a place to rest, I jump a wooden fence and walk into the middle of a field where I drop down onto the ground. Tall grass surrounds me and there's a sky full of stars above.

My eyes flutter closed as I hear Adam's approaching footsteps.

"Go away," I whisper.

"I can't." He sits near me. "What do you think you're going to accomplish with this mission you're on?"

"I need answers. And I'm going to get them. What does it matter to you? I have no one and without my children I have nothing else to lose."

"Hmm," Adam grunts.

I open my bleary eyes only to glare at him.

"Someone once told me the same thing." He watches the nearby trees.

"Tell me a truth."

He sighs and the night wind plays with his dark hair. "I was never in Colorado. After Crane shot me, Hanford intercepted. They made me an offer I couldn't refuse. George and Maryam want Crane gone. Worse than ever. They wanted me to go undercover with the Survivors to build an unseen army."

The Maryam I know is nearly catatonic; I doubt she'd be involved in any of this. "Lies," I utter under my breath.

"Don't ask me questions you don't want to hear the answers to, Andie. I thought I was doing something good for my country. I thought I could protect it all from him. Change things." He makes a face of disgust. "But it all got mixed up and turned around."

He pauses and I wait to hear more since this is the first time, it seems, he's ever told me anything true.

"Christian Whitmarsh is the name I was born with. I wanted to be different. Start fresh. That's how Christian Whitmarsh was born again. It is a double identity. Bad things were happening; the Skin trades, slavery, people were doing terrible things and I had to put a stop to it. Men had to die. Crane was right when he said the Survivors would kill themselves. They were well on their way to doing just that. I had to put a stop to it. If anything I had to prove him wrong."

It seems everyone's answer is more death. "Killing people is wrong," I shake my head.

"Is it? You changed the world, altered humanity just to keep your daughter out of harm's way. Why is what I did wrong?"

He is so right that I shut my mouth.

Twenty-Five

I wake to find myself covered with the blanket that was given to me by the Witchdoctor. The air is cold, chilling my face. Sitting up, I find that I am covered in a thin layer of snow. Adam is next to me. He must have laid the blanket over us after I fell asleep.

Other than being a bit cold I feel better than I have in days. Adam must have been right, my nanocytes needed me to rest. It seems he was also telling the truth about his first generation nanocytes taking longer to recover than mine. He's out cold, so much that I want to touch him and make sure he's still alive.

Maybe I should touch him and make sure. I go for it. Just before my fingertip presses onto his thickly muscled bicep his eyes flick open and bright blue irises stare back at me.

Pulling my hand away without touching him, I say, "Good morning, princess."

He grumbles and rolls onto his back.

"If you had left me alone you could have slept someplace with a roof." I stand, find my bag and sling it over my shoulder.

Adam stands and shakes the snow off of the blanket. He steps toward me, tosses the blanket around my back and wraps it over my shoulders. He tucks it under my arms in a gesture that is completely thoughtful and gentle.

"If I had left you alone you would have slept in a field like a dog."

It's better than I deserve, especially after what I have done.

Speaking of dogs. I look around. Where is Steve the Guardian?

"What's wrong?" Adam asks.

"I had a Guardian with me. A black one. Where did he go?"

"Sometimes they wander. I'm sure it's not far. It'll make an appearance when it's needed. That's what they do."

I worry for the creature. It's been at my side for so long and now it's just wandered off. But he's right, they do tend to wander and show up when needed. Somehow they just know.

"Are you sure?" I ask just to be certain.

"Positive." Adam rubs his hands together then blows warm air between his palms. "We should get moving and warm up."

We walk and I pull the blanket tighter across my shoulders. The clothing given to me by the Swamp people is thin, human skin is not the best fabric to brave winter weather. But I'll survive. If it is one thing that I have learned from this entire ordeal, I will survive.

We walk in silence. Side by side. For miles and miles.

Twenty-Six

Andromeda

I have always wanted to see the wonders of the west. Standing here now there is not a doubt in my mind that it is the most picturesque landscape in this country. The valleys and mountains and crystal clear rivers; it's all untouched, raw, and absolutely beautiful. I could see a lot more of it if we weren't currently walking through a cold snap.

"I think we should stop and rest for the night," Adam says.

I clench my jaw to stop my teeth from chattering. "We don't—"

"Yes. We do. You do." He rubs his hands together. "It's too cold."

"March is almost over. It will be warmer soon. In a few days or so."

"Weather patterns have changed. You know this." He crosses his arms and shoves his hands in his armpits to warm them. "Cold could keep up for weeks."

"We'll be in Wolf Creek by then. We can rest there."

Adam grumbles something unintelligible as we continue.

And then the rain starts. At first it's a sprinkling shower but the further we walk the fiercer it becomes. The drops turn pelting and I have to shield my eyes. Then, as night begins to fall, the temperature plummets and the rain turns to hail, then finally a pounding sleet.

I think Kansas hates us. Or maybe it's the Gods of the West. Overnight the temperature drops, and from my time living in the northeast I'm sure it's single digits with a negative-degree wind chill.

The dampness coating our skin and clothing freezes into a layer of ice. My joints are stiff and Adam has been muttering a string of curse words for hours. Part of me knows better, wants me to stop and rest, but the rest knows that I deserve this—to suffer after all I've done. This is my purgatory and the penance is profuse.

"We should stop," Adam grumbles from my side. "We need to stop."

"Just a bit further."

His whispered curses continue.

When the dawn breaks I get a good look at him. Adam's beard, lashes, and hair are frozen in white. His clothing is stiff. I think to hand him the blanket that's cloaked over my shoulders but I fear the chill seeping through my skinwear might freeze me solid.

By midday the sky remains gray and cold. We cross a crumbling road, see the ruins that are what's left of Wichita, then walk across an abandoned overpass spanning a river.

Adam moves slower. It seems our sleep in the pasture didn't do much for him or me. I've noticed my pace has slowed considerably.

Adam's voice finally breaks the frozen day. "This is ridiculous." He grabs my arm. "We can't do this for much longer. Need to get warm and eat something."

I try to pull myself away from him but I find that my energy is sapped.

"Don't be stupid, Andie. We can't keep going on like this." His grip tightens on my arm and he begins leading me closer to him.

"Where are you going?" My teeth chatter.

"There's a place up here, few miles down the road. A settlement with food and boarding."

"I don't want to stop." I trip and stumble.

"That's 'cause you're stubborn." He hoists me up into his arms carrying me like a child.

"Put me down." I struggle.

"You might freeze to the ground if I do that." He turns down a gravel road and I hear commotion ahead of us. "Besides, this conserves body heat. Better than being naked in a sleeping bag." He starts to chuckle and I just give up, thankful to be off my feet.

As Adam walks, men, women, and children dressed in warm snow-suits pass by. Some of them nod to greet him. I close my eyes so I don't have to see them looking at me.

Finally he stops and sets me down on my feet. We are standing on the wide porch of a giant old Victorian house painted in reds and blacks. The wind blows harsh on our backs, ice and snow pelt our bare skin.

"What is this place?" I ask.

"Kind of like a hotel." He opens the door and motions for me to get inside. "We've stayed at a hotel before. Me and you." He smiles and I look away from him.

Adam walks up to a small front desk while I look around. This place looks like an inn. There's a great room, a large dining area, a small bar. Comfortable velvet upholstered couches, old paintings, and decorations furnish the place. And there's a fireplace with a roaring fire. I move to stand close to it and warm my hands near the flames.

"Lucky us. They have a room." I turn to find Adam with the ice melting off of him. It's dripping down his face and chest in rivulets, soaking his shirt and saturating the carpet beneath him.

"I don't have any money." I think of the few items I have with me. The Witchdoctor's potions might take care of a night here. "Do they take trade?"

"No need." Adam takes my arm as though I am a child. "They know me here."

He leads me across the living space and toward a sweeping stairwell, nodding at the old woman at the desk as we pass.

"You know her?" I ask as we climb the stairs.

"She knows me." He guides me to the left, down a hall of doors before stopping at the last one. He produces a key, unlocks it and enters.

The room is large and spacious, finely decorated in deep reds and black. There's already a fire roaring in the fireplace. I move toward it instinctively, wanting to be warm after being cold for so long.

A knock on the door sends Adam to answer it. Listening to the deep tones of his voice, I drop the wet blanket from across my shoulders to the floor and crouch near the fire. When the door closes I turn to see Adam roll in a cart with a ceramic pot, bowls, water and stacks of what looks like clothing.

"What's that?" I ask.

"Food and warm clothes." He pushes the cart to a small table near a window. "There's a bathroom over there. They have running water here if you want a hot shower."

A hot shower? How long has it been since I've had an actual shower? A year with the Swamp men, months walking between Districts, it's been a long time. Every fiber of my being is begging for me to take a long hot shower. So I do.

The bathroom is old with a clawfoot tub and pedestal sink, tiny square tiles and everything in white. I start the shower, strip off my clothes and throw them to the floor, then step into the water. I never thought a shower could feel so good. I crank the hot water up as far as it will go and wash my body and hair twice.

The door to the bathroom opens. "Get out," I say.

"Just leaving clean clothes on the sink." The door closes.

I turn the water off, get a towel from the shelves near the shower and get out. There's a brown ring around the base of the tub and I am further disgusted with myself.

I dry my body and hair with the towel; it's soft and fluffy and makes me wonder if they have fabric softener here. After a bit of digging around the bathroom, I find a comb in one of the drawers and start working on my hair, wishing the Witchdoctor would have just let me cut it. The mess extends down to my backside. When the tangles are gone I braid it then twist it into a bun.

The clothes Adam brought in are thick sweats, a pair of pants, wool socks, and sweatshirt. Perfect winter clothing—thick and warm. I put them on and then begin washing my outfit from the Swamp people in the sink. After scrubbing and rinsing, the skin is a few shades lighter. I leave the bathroom to set my things by the fire to dry.

When I open the bathroom door, I avoid looking around for Adam and head straight for the fireplace.

The flames are higher than when we got here. It looks like someone added a few logs to the pile. The clatter of dishes makes me turn around; Adam is sitting at the small table eating.

"There's some for you." He points to a bowl across from him. "Unless you're going to continue to starve yourself."

The thought of food is tempting. "What is it?" I ask.

"Beef stew." He takes another mouthful and glances out the window that's next to the table. "You should eat. Or I'm going to eat it all."

I can't hide the fact that the shower felt great and the fire even better. Out the window I can see plump flakes falling from the sky. As much as I hate to admit it, Adam is right. We aren't going anywhere fast, I should just eat and regain some strength.

I sit across from him and stare into the bowl. It looks like a stew I might have made a long time ago with chunks of meat, potatoes, carrots, onions, and herbs. The last time I ate a real meal was probably longer ago than the last time I showered. I eat the stew, fast. Adam fills my bowl two more times and takes more for himself.

"Happy nanocytes, happy host." He puts the top on the empty bowl pot. "If you stress them you'll live but there's a strong chance you'll feel like crap."

"I don't care," I mutter into my half-empty bowl.

"I can tell. But if you think you're going to get far in this game you need to take care of yourself." He drinks a glass of water before standing. "I'm going to shower."

I watch as he walks across the room, stops to grab the pile of clothes on the bed, then goes into the bathroom. As the water starts I eat the rest of my stew and watch the snow fall outside of the window.

Adam leaves the bathroom in record time and as he exits, my eyes fall on the turned down bed, the sheets are gray. Suddenly something seems off with this place.

"I'm not sleeping here," I say.

"Why? What's wrong with here? It's the nicest place we've come across in weeks." He's only wearing a pair of low-slung sweatpants; his chest is bare, scars front and center. He touches his finger to his chin, looking real reflective for a moment. "Let me rephrase that, this is the *only* place we've come across in weeks. I'm not counting the sleeping in a field part."

"There's only one bed. And the sheets," I point to the bed, "the sheets are gray."

"The bed is clean." He shrugs. "What's wrong with gray sheets?"

"It just seems dirty. Hidden stains."

He stares at me blankly.

"It just seems... scandalous. Dark sheets belong in a brothel." I still and look around, everything coming together. "You brought me to a damn brothel, didn't you?"

Adam shrugs. Oh, and he looks at me with those blue eyes like he's an innocent little boy who just got caught stealing a cookie.

"It's the safest place—" he starts.

"I'm not sleeping in a brothel!"

"It's the safest place in these parts."

"Forget it." I head to the door. "I don't need to rest."

Adam grabs my wrist. "Yes you do. You're walking slower. We can't go on forever. Exhaustion will hit soon and then we'll be in trouble. These nanocytes, they have their limits. I know this, I've pushed them before. It's safe here. I know the people who run it. We can have a real meal, another bath, a good night's rest in a real bed."

I shake my head in disgust. "You bring me to a brothel, with our history. That's messed up."

"Get over it." He flicks the lock on the door. "Go to bed," he orders. "Maybe after a good night's rest you'll be more rational."

I eye the large bed at the far end of the room. Even if the sheets are gray, the bed is a hell of a lot more enticing than the cot on the floor in the Witchdoctor's hut. I walk across the room, climb up onto the bed and crawl under the covers. Adam adds another log to the fire as I tuck myself in. The mattress is soft, the pillow fluffy, the sheets crisp—even if they could be hiding stains.

"How do they know you here?" I ask.

"I helped them set this place up," he says as he collects his clothing from the bathroom, sets them on the bottom shelf of the cart, and moves it out to the hall.

"So you're like a pimp or something?"

"No." He locks the door again and then sits on the velvet red couch near the fire. "I'm not a pimp."

"I can't believe you helped set up a brothel—"

"You want to know what was going on outside your safe walls of the Phoenix District?" He interrupts me before I can finish. "Women and children were being sold in lots." He looks away from me. "They called it the Skin trades. You've never seen anything like it." He shakes his head. "I've done plenty wrong but I won't apologize putting an end to that. This may be a brothel but at least women have a choice here. They're not forced into it or sold like cattle. And there's no kids. Every single time I found a young girl, all I could think of was Lina. It's better this way. Women have a choice this way." He looks at me once more and his eyes are dark as he remembers things I hope to never see in my lifetime.

Skin trades sound no better than rounding me up and bringing me back to Phoenix, keeping my family there.

"You didn't give me a choice," I mutter.

He smiles. "On the sex, you had a choice. I didn't force you."

Jesus, Lord. My face burns a bright red. "That's not... Crane taking us in like cattle to be Sovereign, that's what I meant!"

He rubs his hand through his beard. "I didn't have much of a choice either."

"I bet you did." I roll over.

"In my life I've had few choices. I just have had to figure out the best one to ensure my survival. And the best isn't always right."

He's so right.

"Tell me a truth." I scoot down under the blankets, feeling warm for the first time since I was with the Witchdoctor.

He sighs from the couch. "I was in Romney." He clears his throat. "The entire time. I kept you there."

I sit up, the warmth of the blankets dissipates as they fall to my lap. "You imprisoned me."

He looks down at his hands, refusing to look at me. "I didn't want to let you go." His voice is low. "I know it was wrong but I needed details. And I wanted you close."

I press my fingers to my lips. "You forced me to kiss you."

"It wasn't right from the beginning, how I wanted you. I can't explain it, Andie." He finally looks at me. "I'm sorry."

His words are as heartfelt as when we were dancing in the barn. But still, it hurts knowing he did that to me, pushed me so hard I was ready to give up and die. I throw myself backward onto the bed and pull the covers over my head.

***

The savory smell of bacon and eggs wakes me. I pull the covers down and sniff. Something familiar lingers in the air. Coffee!

I roll over and find that I am in an empty room. Throwing the covers back, I get up and make my way to the table near the window. There are two covered plates, mugs of coffee, sugar, crème. I sit down, use the spoon to scoop out some sugar and mix it into the mug closest to me. I add a little crème and bring the steaming cup to my nose. I haven't smelled something this wonderful in years. I take a sip and the door opens. Turning, I swallow my first sip of coffee in years down as Adam walks into the room, his arms full of what looks like coats and more clothing.

I frown at the bitterness on my tongue. This doesn't taste right.

"Chicory," Adam says as he drops his armful on the couch.

"What?" I ask, looking into the coffee cup in my hands.

"It's not coffee. It's chicory. A bit tart in these parts but it will do." He walks to the table—still shirtless and wearing the sweatpants—and sits across from me. "I thought you'd never wake up."

He lifts the lids covering our plates to reveal a real home-cooked breakfast. Scrambled eggs with pepper, thick cut bacon, and fried potatoes.

My mouth opens. "I haven't had food like this in forever."

"Me either."

Adam loads up my plate with food. We eat and I drink the chicory. It may not be real coffee but it reminds me of the luxuries I once had.

When our plates are empty Adam gets up and moves toward the pile of clothes. He starts separating everything into two piles. "Mine," he says when he's finished. "And yours." He points to a smaller pile.

"We can't take their clothes."

"They owe me." He motions to the window. "Plus I'm not going to freeze my ass off again walking through another storm. And neither are you."

"I was fine." It's a lie, I was ready to drop and I'm not sure how much longer I would have lasted if Adam hadn't taken control. I don't tell him this though.

Adam throws a pile of clothes at me and I catch them. "Sure you were." He reaches for the waistband of his sweatpants. Not wanting to get in the situation where one of us is naked, I get up and run to the bathroom.

The brothel has provided me with thermal underwear and another layer of sweats. I put it all on and wait a few more minutes before leaving to bathroom just to ensure Adam is dressed.

When I open the door he's putting on snow pants and another pair is laid out for me. There are also boots and thick parkas for each of us. I continue getting dressed. Lastly, reaching for my bag, I pack away my dried clothing from the Swamp people and cross the bag over my shoulder.

"Now we're prepared." Adam turns to look at me. "You should put your hood up." He pulls his up and ties it under his chin, then wraps a scarf around his face. He holds out another scarf for me.

"Will you tell them downstairs?" I ask.

"What's that?"

"That we didn't.... er...." My face flames. I'm too old to be embarrassed about this.

"It's a brothel, Andie. People only do one thing in a brothel." His face is dead serious.

"Well we didn't!"

He smiles. "They don't know. They don't care." He shrugs. "All they care about is us leaving. I'm sure we're bad for business."

"What did you tell them?" I ask.

"Didn't need to tell them much. They see me carrying in a young woman from a storm like that, half frozen, they can form their own opinions."

Shoving my hands in my coat pockets I find a pair of gloves in there. I pull them out and put them on. "Let's go."

Adam opens the door and motions for me to go first.

I make sure my exit from the brothel goes unnoticed.

You don't see me, you don't see me, you don't see me.

I walk out unnoticed.

"Coward," Adam says as we head down the road and I finally make myself visible. "I know what you did."

"What they can't see won't hurt them."

We walk.

WOLF CREEK LOOKS LARGER than I remember, the fence looks an insurmountable length as we walk toward it from the other side of the tracks. We find our way around the District and I stop on more than one occasion to watch the herds of wildlife.

There's something strange far off in the distance past the buffalo and the horses—animals that should have been sent out into the wild years ago. A portion of the fence looks like it's mirrored.

"What is he hiding here?" I ask Adam as we walk around a corner of fence.

"Hiding?" Adam seems uninterested. It raises a red flag in my mind.

"What else is happening in Wolf Creek?" I keep my eye on the fence in the distance, hoping to catch a glimpse of something.

Adam shrugs his shoulders and begins unwinding the scarf from around his face. "You remember the last time we were here and there were those fucked up animals? Two-heads and three eyes and all that?"

"And I killed that man." Seeing the entrance to the District a few hundred yards away, I begin unwrapping my scarf as well. "Yes. I remember."

Adam sucks in a breath and shakes his head before continuing. Maybe he doesn't want to remember or maybe those moments have scarred him as much as they scarred me.

"I think that was the beginnings of a darker plan."

"Sounds like the theme to this whole Reformation," I say.

"The Guardians are as much of a genetically engineered creature as we've ever seen." Adam gives me a look. "I doubt they're the last he's toyed with. I seriously doubt they were the first."

"But I didn't think John Blackmore was the type of man to follow along. He was ready to join the resistance against Crane last time I was here."

"John Blackmore is the type of man who will ensure his survival."

"Siding with the man playing God. I didn't think John had it in him. I thought he was good."

Adam turns to look at me. "Some cultures believe in more than one God. Some good, some bad. Blackmore isn't Crane, but he's definitely got his own demons. We all do." Adam gives me a hard look before turning and continuing on our walk.

"How can you be so sure?" I ask.

"I stopped by here not too long ago on my search for you. He showed me a few things."

THERE ARE four Volker at the gates.

"Let us in," I tell them. *Let us in, let us in, let us in.*

Adam and I wait for them to unlock the gate and let us through. As they lock the gate behind us, a figure comes running toward us from across an expanse of frozen ground.

"That's John," Adam warns me.

We walk toward him and Adam must sense my apprehension since he says, "He won't try anything, Andie. He's as much on our side as a Sovereign can be."

John slows to a stop in front of us, barely looking out of breath. He's wearing faded jeans, what looks like an old tattered Carhart jacket, and a baseball cap that's seen better days.

"You're back." He shakes hands with Adam before turning to me, tanned and rugged with his sandy-brown hair and wide smile. I wonder how he keeps his tan in this weather. "Andie," he smiles, "glad to see you're alive. You had us worried for a while there. District Matchmaker turns revolutionist." He cocks his head to the side. "You look very different. Your face that is."

"Had a makeover." I motion toward the buildings. "Can we go inside? It's incredibly cold out here."

John seems to have lost his train of thought when he shakes his head and starts walking. "Yes, yes. Come." He rubs his hands together, his rough skin making a noise like sandpaper. "You've come at an exciting time. I have something to show you."

I glance at Adam, who refuses to look at me but presses his lips together.

We walk into a large barn, one that I remember signing paperwork to transport horses across the country in. It's still a giant open space, much like an arena.

"I'm sure you'll remember this place." John sounds excited, so different from his usual business manner. "We have something special right over here."

Adam and I follow him, both of us peeling off layers of cold weather gear as we go. The heat inside the barn is stifling and it smells like hay and something else I can't quite place. In the center of the arena there are two forms, what looks like a horse lying on its side and a person wearing a white coat who's crouched down on the ground. The person stands and turns to us as we approach and I am taken aback. It's Dr. Drake, with the same paunch belly, same white tufts of hair around his balding head, but his eyes have lost the yellow hue. It's like his aging stopped.

Oh, no.

"Mrs. Somers," Dr. Drake smiles as he crosses the room. "Of all the people I would expect to see I have to say you are the last."

"The feeling's mutual." I glance down at his hands and see they are covered in blood. "What are you doing here?"

Dr. Drake's face breaks into a smile. "It's a birthday." His tone is odd, like this should be obvious.

"Come closer," John Blackmore motions us nearer to the horse that's lying on its side. "These advancements weren't slated to happen for years down the road but everything seems to be happening at a faster pace."

I step forward cautiously, taking in the horse's heavy breathing and swollen flank.

"Continue helping her," John instructs Dr. Drake.

He bends down and I notice a pair of hooves protruding from the horse's birth canal. There's blood on the hay, that's the smell I recognized when we walked in here, musky and coppery—

Suddenly I am bombarded by visions of Blithe's childbirth and death. I squeeze my eyes closed and try to will it all away, press it back into the recesses of my mind where it can't bother me. Just like I've done with so many memories.

"Yes, yes, yes, yes," John starts chanting.

Through the strange wet sounds of a horse delivering, I keep my eyes closed, no longer able to look at the miracle of birth.

Everything goes silent and I hear Adam's sharp intake of breath as he mutters under his breath, "Holy shit."

My eyes flick open and zero in on the foal lying in the hay. Its mother is currently licking it clean, nudging it around to move. There is something strange about it, more than the mother's deep brown coloring and the foal being sharp white. The coat of the foal is shaggy and long, something moves across its back, an appendage that doesn't belong. Wings. Holy crap, the foal has wings!

"Pegasus!" John slaps Dr. Drake hard on the back. "We did it!" He turns to face us. "We did it!"

I back away from him, slowly, only to step on Adam's foot and stumble. Adam grips my upper arm to stop me from falling.

And then, out of the shadows, creatures start appearing. They don't seem to care about the humans in the room but they are making their way toward the newly born foal.

A large striped tiger, a tiny pink pig, strange looking dogs, cats, birds. They look nothing like the sickly, mutated creatures that I killed an imposter over. They all look completely functional and at the same time eerily and fantastically mythological. And similar to the Guardians they seem to possess knowledge of the world around them.

I have to end this, can't let him continue. *Stop this, stop this, stop this.*

John turns sharply toward me. "Your tricks won't work on me,

Andie. You'd better just conserve your energy. There's a long road ahead of you."

"This is wrong." I glance toward Adam but he says nothing.

"To you. To me this is a life's work."

The animals, never before seen by human eyes, approach the foal and keep a respectful distance.

"You're going to keep these creatures locked up in here?" I ask.

"When the time comes they will be released. They have their own free will, much like the Guardians. The things we've done with their brain development." John throws a hand in the air in an excited movement. "They're so intelligent. Just like the Guardians but better. You'll see. You'll see, Andie. One day you'll need one of these creatures and you'll have me to thank."

I shake my head. "I don't think so."

In a sudden collective movement all of the unnatural animals look at me. Their fierce gaze is watchful, as it seems they understand that, just like them, I am no longer completely ordinary.

Adam clears his throat. "I think we should go."

"I wanted to check on their Residents," I remind him, warily watching the creatures that are watching me.

"Our Residents are fine," John Blackmore snaps. "They couldn't help care for the animals if I didn't take care of them."

"And do they know about this?" I motion to the creatures with parts that don't belong but somehow function in peculiar beauty. Wings and horns and extra appendages.

"Of course not. They're not ready. Not yet." The foal stands on skinny wobbly legs and its mother continues to lick it. "But soon. Soon we will release them. When they're ready and the world is ready to accept them.

"YOU KNEW ABOUT THAT?" I ask Adam as we walk away from Wolf Creek.

He pulls on a pair of thick gloves to ward off the chill. "Some of it."

"And you didn't warn me."

"What would you have done? I mean, I knew that little pig could fly."

"The pig could fly?" It sounds so ridiculous, but I could see why the experiments would start there.

"Yeah." A whisper of a laugh escapes his lips. "Like a tiny sparrow-pig or something. But how do you respond when you see a flying pig?"

For a moment I am speechless.

"Swine is close to human. Our skin and organs, they're close replacements. If that's where they started with adding wings and things…"

Adam reaches out and grasps my arm. "You don't think he'd go there." He shakes his head from side to side in a slow motion. "I bet it was trials for the Pegasus. Not humans. Just the Pegasus."

"How can you be so sure?" I feel the color blanch from my face. "A goddamned Pegasus. And the rest of those creatures."

"We aren't so different." Adam begins wrapping his scarf around his face and neck. "We've been changed."

"What's going on in Wolf Creek has taken it a step too far. Adding wings to things."

A sharp wind whips across the Kansas plains, stealing my breath for a moment.

"Like altering the Residents' brains?" Adam replies, his mouth tense.

Of course I know what I did and how wrong it was. I can only do what I can do; watch them, protect them, and ensure that they are taken care of. My atonement is their safety.

"I had no choice."

Adam nods. "Remember that. Sometimes we have no choice."

We walk away from the wonders of Wolf Creek and the thoughts in my head are out of control.

As suddenly as it began, the winter chill dissolves. We strip off our wintry weather wear and leave them hanging on a fencepost somewhere in the beginnings of Missouri.

"This weather pattern is strange," I say as I'm dressing in the skinwear.

Suddenly Adam's hands are on my bare shoulders as I'm pulling the vest on. I try to pull away from him.

"What happened to them?" he asks.

I can feel his breath on my bare skin and shiver.

"What?" I ask.

"Those scars." Three of his fingers trace my back where there were scars from the wolf attack years ago.

"I didn't know they were gone," I say. "I can't see my back and I haven't looked at it in a mirror."

His fingers press on my shoulder in four places. "But these are still here. The marks of the Districts." I feel him breathing and touching my hair, holding it out of the way. "Strange."

I pull away from him, unnerved by his touching my bare skin. I dress in the vest and pull a jacket over the thin material. I roll up a pair of pants and shove them in my bag. It's strange that the scars are gone but the brands of the District remain. Maybe they were too deep? Who knows?

Adam changes into a pair of dark pants and a light shirt. He stops adjusting his clothing for a moment, his gaze scanning the nearby wooded areas.

"What?" I ask.

"Swamp men were following us when we left Tonopah. Disappeared for the blizzard. But now—" He looks around. "I think they're back."

I adjust my bag across my shoulders. "They won't come near me."

The tone of Adam's voice drops. "It's not you they want." He gives a haggard breath. "We should find a settlement or market. Get some food."

"Sure," I agree with him.

He motions to the north. "There's a place near the border of Iowa. Survivors have a market."

"You seem to know a lot about what the Survivors do and don't have." I start walking.

"For a while that was my job."

A cluster of grouse scurry across the field as we walk and the Swamp men seem to keep their distance, if in fact, it is them lurking nearby.

"Tell me a truth," I ask him.

Twenty-Seven

Adam

Tell her a truth. The last time I told a truth was—damn, I can't even remember how long ago. I start at the beginning, or close enough to the beginning that I can get.

"When Crane told you about Japan being the testing ground," I swallow damn hard, "it wasn't because of their culture being so different from the American culture. It had nothing to do with their people being more accepting and grateful toward what they had and what they were given."

Andie studies me as I speak. "What was the reason then?" she asks.

"After the earthquake and the tsunami and the reactor melting down in Fukushima, the place was hot."

She nods. "A lot of people died. I saw it on the news."

"Many lived. And afterwards everything was contaminated with radioactivity. Crane had the largest radioactively tainted playground in the world."

She tips her head to the side. "And what did he do with it?"

"Genetic studies. Like he always does."

I want to reach out and touch her. After all of these years I can barely contain the urge.

She nods and looks away from me. "Like Wolf Creek?" she asks. "The animals there?"

My mouth snaps shut. That's enough for now. She's not ready to hear the rest. I know what he was doing, how far it stretched, the rules he broke.

"Tell me more."

I try to change the subject. "The Survivor market will take just about anything for trade. We can get meat maybe even some more of that homemade wine."

I glance at her, a half-smile on my lips.

She's not smiling back. Her lips are pressed in a tight line.

"Why are you always hiding things from me?" she asks.

I need to tell her more. I have to tell her more.

I take a deep breath. "I know those things will hurt you."

Andie scoffs. "Fine." She picks up her pace and advances forward.

"Wait." I take a few steps and catch up with her. "You want to hear this?"

Twenty-Eight

"What kind of experiments did he do in Fukushima?" I ask as I walk, annoyed by the fact that Adam keeps stalling.

He is silent for a long moment. "The radioactivity, it helps some of the genetic alterations stick. It also helps enhance some of them. You'll find out the details when we get to Galena. It's all there."

Of course, the information that I need so badly I have to cross the continent for.

The air around us suddenly changes. Charged with scent and activity. "I smell something," I say, sniffing the air.

Adam reaches out and grabs my arm to stop me. "Don't move," he warns as he drops to a crouch, pulling me down with him, and scans the area. "Your friends are back."

"Swamp men?" I ask.

Adam nods as he stands. "There's your Guardian." He points a few hundred yards away. I see Steve watching us.

"Trouble?" I grip the knife on my hip.

He sniffs the air. "And the settlement isn't far from here."

Releasing the knife, I stand and adjust my bag then start walking again. "You know this settlement well?" I ask.

He nods.

"Set up any brothels there?" I ask.

"Not here, specifically."

"Perfect."

"This way." He guides me along the edge of the town. We walk across a yard that backs up to the woods, then out onto a street. "We could probably trade for some supplies if we need them," he suggests.

"What else is there?" I ask.

He nods.

"If you know this place so well why don't you give me some details?" I'm starting to get annoyed with him, more so than usual.

"I know a lot of places, Andie. You don't lead the Survivors by not knowing every town, settlement, and hideaway that's left in existence."

I catch movement out of the corner of my eye and notice Steve the Guardian trailing us from the backyards of the houses we pass by.

"You hungry?" Adam asks.

"Not particularly."

He motions to a collection of people ahead of us and it looks like we're walking through a street fair or farmer's market.

"They trade goods here," Adam says. "A cooked meal would make the nanocytes happy."

We pass into the crowd of Survivors. "I'm fine."

My eyes scan the unfamiliar faces, until I notice two teenagers standing next to each other in line at a meat stand. They look so familiar and as the girl's back straightens suddenly and turns toward me, I recognize her instantly. It's Lina.

I panic. *You don't see me, you don't see me, you don't see me.*

The Survivors pass in front of me as though I'm not even there, because, well, they no longer think I'm here. I recognize the boy she's with: Marcus. How did they get out of Hanford?

"Andie?" Adam must sense something is off.

"Lina's here." I can barely control the wavering of my voice.

"Shit." Adam scans the crowd.

Lina rises up on her toes and searches, her mouth moving as she and

Marcus talk to each other. He has a tight hold on her as she tries to walk away from him. She looks tired and grown up.

"Why are they out of Hanford?" I ask Adam. Feeling the need to hold on to something to center me, I grab his shoulder and steady myself.

"Damned if I know."

"Take them back. Please, Adam. Take them back to Hanford where they'll be safe. She can't be out here with the Survivors."

Adam glances at me, his eyes softening for a moment. "I know. I'll take them back." He heads toward them, the crowd parting out of his way as he goes. "Stay invisible but stay close," he whispers over his shoulder to me.

I keep a safe distance as Adam descends on them. Marcus backs away, pulling Lina with him. Adam's posture and appearance change before my eyes. There's stiffness in his walk, his tall frame commands the attention from all around him. He lets off an electricity that fills the air.

Lina blanches as he reaches them.

"Please, tell me what the *fuck* you two are doing out here?" Adam's voice is low and threatening.

Lina swallows hard.

"Sir—" Marcus starts.

"Jesus Christ, Marcus!" Adam cuts him off before grabbing a hold of both of their shirts, dragging Lina and Marcus away from the crowd and the street. Adam seems to know where he's going when he stops at an empty building that looks like an old diner and drags the two kids inside.

I keep myself invisible as I follow them and press my ear to the door, listening.

"Let me relay some rules for being a *Defector*." I hear the sounds of Adam unzipping his bag and rummaging around. "You don't seek out a crowd. You don't walk around all fucking doe-eyed. You don't show up in a uniform, with a weapon in plain sight and bags packed full of supplies. You two are dressed like you're goddamned black ops. Is that —" The tone of his voice changes questioning. "Is that my hat? How'd you get this?"

Marcus voice responds. "I found it."

"Now, tell me how the hell you two got out of Hanford."

Marcus unloads, spilling the story of Lina's escape and him following her. Marcus takes the brunt of the blame but if I raised Lina any way it was to question these people, I'm betting she had a greater role in escaping. Marcus knows he should have brought her back, but they both wanted answers and they weren't getting them in Hanford. I instantly regret wiping Lina's memory when the Witchdoctor brought me there to test my strength.

Adam's voice comes next. "Your mother will—" he pauses and I hope they don't notice, "*would* kill someone over this if she were still alive."

"But—I saw a Guardian. They always follow her," Lina replies.

"They follow all of the Sovereign around. It could have been following me, or you, or him."

"So it's true?" Lina's voice is soft and sad.

"Yes," Adam says.

"She's dead," Lina whispers. "Truly dead."

Part of me wants to run through the door and hug her like I did when she was a child, but I can't. The closer I am to her, the more danger she's in. Crane would know and he'd target her. And I can't have that.

"We are not alone," Marcus whispers. "We have each other. We stick together. Always."

There is a moment of silence before I hear Adam's voice. "I can't believe this shit." He opens the door and I back away. "You're going back to Hanford."

"No," Lina says, her voice strong and determined.

"Excuse me?" Adam asks.

"No. I hate it there. I'm not going back."

"And what are you going to do, Lina? Live amongst the Survivors? You have no clue how the world runs itself. Not since the Reformation. Things aren't safe. Women aren't safe. Young women like yourself are definitely not safe out here where there are no rules, no regulations, no law. You are going back. I will not be responsible for what happens to you out here. I don't have the time to deal with the both of you. You're going back."

"No."

"Yes," Adam commands.

"NO!" Lina yells.

"Is she always like this?" he asks. I have to assume he's asking Marcus.

There's no reply until I hear, "I am not!"

Suddenly Adam and Marcus break out in laughter.

"What?" Lina asks, sounding confused.

"I forget you kids are teenagers." Adam stops laughing abruptly. "You too, Marcus. These are some dumb shit decisions. You're both coming with me. I have to go talk to someone for a second. Stay right here."

Adam opens the door and quickly closes it behind him. He's wearing a black baseball cap, which looks really good on him.

While the others may not be able to see me I know he can. Adam has told me more than a few times my tricks don't work on him.

"Still hiding from them?" he asks me.

"Of course."

Adam releases a frustrated breath. "This wasn't part of your plan."

"Of course not."

"So what do you want to do?" he asks.

"I need you to take them back to Hanford."

"But you were headed for Phoenix."

"I was." I nod. "We can go there after I know the kids are safe."

There's a tick in Adam's jaw as he clenches it and glances around us. "I have a guy here. Can get a truck. Drive them for a ways and then we can take an alternate route."

Before we can discuss the matter any longer the door bursts open and Lina comes running out. Adam grabs her.

"Where do you think you're going?" he asks as I move to hide behind the corner of the building.

"Away," she replies. "Who was that?"

I feel her gaze.

"None of your business. Let's get moving. It will be dark soon." The door creaks as it's opened. Marcus must be joining them. I listen for their footsteps and follow at a safe distance.

Adam is practically dragging Lina through the streets.

"How are we getting there?" she asks him.

"We drive to Colorado. And then from there it's a quick trip back to Hanford."

"That's not a quick trip. It's hundreds of miles," Lina argues.

I jog up next to Adam and whisper harshly to him, "She's right, you know." I fall into the surrounding Survivors, wondering how he's going to pull this off. But, well, I've seen him pull off worse.

Adam skips a step, which seems out of character for him. Maybe I startled him, whispering in his hear like that. Lina stumbles and falls, crying out. Marcus pulls her pack off as she rolls onto her back. Blood soaks the side of her shirt.

"Sorry about that." Adam reaches down to help her up, but Marcus puts a hand out to stop him.

"Wait. She's bleeding." Marcus crouches at her side, his face flexed in concern.

Afraid that I'll lose control of my invisibility, I step further away from them.

Lina runs a hand down her side, coating her palm in blood. "Great," she moans.

"What happened to you?" Adam asks, looking between Marcus and Lina. "Who hurt you?" His fists clench at his sides.

I listen from afar.

"She was bit by a snake," Marcus finally says. "Got infected."

"And?" Adam asks.

"Swamp people found us, they had medicine, brought us down to their land. Their Witchdoctor took care of her."

I had to see Glane. There was... there was an ill child. It was my child!

Marcus continues as Lina remains on the ground, her face flexed in pain. "We were making our way back to Phoenix just now, before you found us."

"Alone? You were travelling from the swamps to Phoenix alone?" Adam asks.

"No," Lina says. "We were travelling *with* them. But..." She winces as she sits up. "I thought I saw a Guardian and I ran after it. That's how we wound up here."

We saw the same one—Steve—who seems to be missing again.

"Where are the Swamp people now?" Adam asks.

"Probably the woods around here, waiting for us. Or else they already left," Marcus says.

"They didn't eat you?" Adam asks. "Didn't attempt?"

"No." Lina shakes her head. "That one named Glane, he did sniff me. It was really strange."

Adam looks over the kids quickly. "You shouldn't be around them. They are so far removed from humanity." He takes a frustrated breath. "The only reason why they were put on this earth is to kill and consume. The fact that they didn't kill you both... it concerns me." Adam pauses and looks down at Lina, his eyes zeroing in on the blood soaking through her shirt. "We better get that bandaged."

"I have supplies here." Marcus reaches into his pack and pulls out gauze and tape. Lina lifts her shirt and Marcus begins changing the bandage. Adam stands over them with his arms crossed over his chest, looking bored though his eyes are scanning the shadowed alleyways and the nearby forest.

His eyes finally land on me. I want to tell him that Glane wouldn't hurt her; she looks too much like me, and he fears me.

Lina lifts her shirt and Marcus pulls off the bloody dressing. He settles a clean gauze over the red wound and begins tearing pieces of tape off of the roll and securing the gauze.

"There," Marcus says when he's done, his fingers lingering a little too long on my daughter's skin as he presses the tape down. Lina looks up at him and a person would have to be blind not to see a moment pass between the two teenagers.

I tip my head and Adam notices. It seems Lina has finally noticed Marcus. I prayed this day would never come.

The moment passes and Lina covers herself. Adam pulls her up.

"We used to be close," she says to Adam quietly.

He frowns and simply says, "Time to go."

Adam conceals his pain well. I know it hurts him, losing all of us. But that was his decision. He put us all in harm's way. He died. He was part of this. Even though I want to feel for him, I tell myself I can't.

They walk until Adam stops next to a rusted red truck. There is a man standing next to it carrying a rifle and looking menacing. Adam greets him. This must be one of his men, or someone he knew while he was wrangling in the Survivors and playing dead. They exchange words while Marcus and Lina stand near the back of the truck and wait.

"I don't want to go back to Hanford," I hear Lina tell Marcus.

"It will be okay," he says.

"Doubt it," Lina replies as Adam turns and opens the passenger side door to the truck, motioning for the kids to get in.

"Hey, at least we'll all be together again. You have to miss Raven and Astrid." Marcus tells her just as Adam closes the door.

Adam rounds the back of the truck and his eyes land on me. "Want a ride?" he asks, dropping the tailgate. "There's not enough room in the cab."

I glare at him.

"Or you can run behind us." He flashes a quick smile.

"Can't be worse than walking through a blizzard." I crawl in the back of the truck.

"How long can you stay invisible to them?" Adam whispers.

"This is the longest I've tried." I give him a nervous look. "As long as I can control my emotions, I think it will be fine."

He presses his lips together and nods as he closes the tailgate.

I move against the back of the cab and lie down. Adam starts the truck and takes off. Liquid sloshes in two gas cans near the tailgate and I push one of the cap windows open to air out the fumes.

Adam drives for hours, stopping once so the kids can get out and relieve themselves, then once more to fill the tank with one of the gas cans.

He barely glances at me as he mumbles, "Few more hours."

My butt is numb from sitting on the hard metal of the truck bed. But at least I'm warm and Lina is close and safe.

The truck slows and pulls onto a gravel road. The bumps and vibrations bruise my behind. The driver's side door opens and closes. I hear

Adam's voice as he warns the kids to stay in the truck. "Stay here. Don't get out. Don't move. Don't anything."

Footsteps crunch over the gravel drive.

"Freddie," Adam says.

"Mr. Whitmarsh."

My stomach clenches as his worst lies come flooding back to me. I hate that he pretended to be dead. I hate that he is so involved with Crane. I hate that I trusted him.

"In need of some gas, Fred."

The man clucks his tongue. "Fuel is low in these parts. You'd know that if you'd been around."

I swear to God I hear Adam growl at the man before he says, "Been plenty of times that I saved your ass, now I need to claim a few favors."

"Whose kids you got in there, Whitmarsh?" the man asks.

"None of your concern." I move to peek out the window and get a good look at the man. "I need you to send word. Need the Militia train ready, near the Safe House in Colorado."

"For the kids?"

"Freddie." Adam snaps. "No questions. Just get me some gas so I can get there and get it done."

The old man picks up his lantern and walks around the side of the house. I move to get out of the back of the truck.

Adam notices. "What are you doing?" he hisses.

"Something's off here," I warn him.

Leaves rustle in the nearby trees and a chill runs up my back.

"Your friends are following us." Adam's gaze moves to the front window of the truck and he does a double take before he's stalking toward the vehicle and rapping on the window and opens the driver's side door. "Get a ro—" he stops sharply and clears his throat. "Actually. Don't get a room. Ever." He gives the kids a hard look. "You got that Marcus? No touchy. Hands off." Adam slams the door. "Damn kids."

I frown. "Please tell me she's not..."

Adam frowns. "It's just puppy love. They grew up together. They'll grow out of it."

Freddie's footsteps interrupt us and I move away, keeping myself invisible. "Who you talking to out here?" Freddie asks.

"Myself."

"Gone crazy now, have ya?" The old man hands over a gas can.

"Been crazy for a long time." He nods at Freddie. "Thanks for the gas. Now get the call in to the rail."

The man heads inside the house just as the door to the truck opens and Lina jumps out.

"Adam?" she asks as she makes her way toward him.

"Yeah." Adam moves to begin filling the gas tank.

"What happened to Uncle Sam?"

Adam clears his throat as she stands there waiting but he says nothing.

"Adam." Lina is getting agitated. "Adam! What about Sam?"

"He's in Phoenix," Adam finally replies.

"Still the Volker Sovereign?"

"Yes."

"Did Blithe have the baby?" she asks.

Adam presses his lips together and looks away, right at me. He can see me but she can't.

"I'm not some little kid anymore, Adam. Did Blithe have the baby? Tell me what happened." Lina begs.

"Sam's still there. But Blithe... she died in childbirth."

Lina's hand flies to her mouth. "Oh my God." She leans against the truck. "And the baby?"

Adam just shakes his head.

"Sam must be heartbroken to have his wife and child die. I miss him so much. Is he okay?" Lina asks.

"Haven't seen him in a long time. Not since your mother first went missing." He shifts on his feet and does this strange thing as he talks; he tips his head down and bites the inside of his mouth. I think he's lying to her. When I left the baby was still alive. Gas spills down the side of the truck, leaving strong fumes in its wake.

"Shit." Adam jerks the gas can and slams the cap into place. "Get in the truck," he orders Lina.

Slowly, she backs away from him as he straps gas cans into the truck bed.

When the door to the truck closes, Adam turns to me.

"You getting in or what?" He's pissed but I can't help but feel that something is wrong here.

"I think I need to keep an eye on your friend Freddie." I tip my head toward the house.

"We can trust him. It's fine. He's a Transplant."

"For who?" It's like there's this whole underground system in place that I have no clue about or how it works and it pisses me off to no end.

"Crossbender."

"George is involved?" I feel my body shudder and I try very hard to maintain control of myself to keep me invisible to the kids. "How deep does this run?" I demand.

"Very."

All this time I've been asking him to tell me the truth, and he's fed me tidbit by tidbit, never divulging the entire story. "You didn't feel the need to tell me?"

"I haven't had time," he argues.

"We've been traveling for weeks!" I try to keep my voice down but I want to scream at him.

"Yes, we have." Irritation is vibrating off of him. "I need you to get in, Andie. I need you to make the kids forget this before they go back to Hanford. I can't have them telling the Crossbenders what they've seen."

I press my lips together and feel the telltale signs that I'm close to losing control. I close my eyes, take a deep breath, pissed that he thinks I can just erase their memories whenever. Ludicrous.

When my eyes open, I glare at him. "This was a mistake. Travelling with you, involving you. I can't be around you, Adam, you're toxic to me."

"Don't do this—"

Before he can finish, I turn and run for the cover of the trees, unsure if I can even hold my invisibility any longer.

"I need you," he whispers and it sounds very desperate.

"I'll be watching," I say, just loud enough for him to hear.

Adam watches the shadows that I am currently hiding in for a few long moments before he gives up. He gets in the truck and pulls away.

I wait until he pulls out onto the road and then I make my way for the house. From the porch I can see the man named Freddie inside, rummaging through drawers in the kitchen. I drop the invisibility act, open the door and let myself inside.

"He was here," I hear Freddie's voice say and it takes me a moment to realize that he's on the phone. "I'm telling you he had those kids. Their wrists were wrapped up. Something special about them. No. No. I know!" He slams a drawer and reaches into a cupboard next to the sink. "He's got a bounty on his head." Freddie pauses. "Lots of people want his carcass. Just, send the team. Blow it up—"

The floorboards creak under my feet, damn.

Freddie turns. He's aiming a pistol at my face.

"Colorado Militia checkpoint, blow it up. I want the ransom. Don't care about the kids. But the girl was pretty. When Whitmarsh is dead the Skin trades will start up again. Could get a few dimes for her." He winks at me. "I gotta go," he says into the phone before hanging it up.

"Freddie."

"Do I know you?" he asks.

I smile. "Put the gun down, Freddie."

Put the gun down, put the gun down, put the gun down.

Freddie sets the gun on the table.

"Who were you talking to?"

Tell me, tell me, tell me.

"Survivor Militia in the South," he replies.

"What are they going to do, Freddie?"

"Blow the checkpoint. Kill Whitmarsh. Probably take the girl." Freddie's face is placid as he tells me everything.

"Why would you do that?"

"Power. Southern Militia wants to take control. You know, like the Civil War all over again."

"They'll never let the Survivors get that strong. Crane will never allow it."

"Crane?" Freddie tips his head in question.

Could it be that they have no idea who is responsible for the Reformation? If that's the case I don't have time to explain it.

"Pick up the phone, Freddie. I need you to call George Crossbender for me."

He turns and picks up the phone. After dialing in a number he hands me the receiver.

"Hello?" I recognize the voice on the other end.

"George Crossbender, we have a problem."

There's a long pause before I hear a door slam on the other end of the line. "Andie... Andie, is it you?"

"Yes."

"Oh my." George exhales a loud breath. "We've been searching all over."

"That's great, but we have a problem. I'm standing next to Freddie, he's a Transplant in charge of helping out Adam Waters or Christian Whitmarsh or whoever you want to call the guy."

"Adam, is what—"

"I don't really care. But, George, Freddie here just ordered a hit on Adam instead of calling you and telling you where to pick up Lina and Marcus. Because, well, you know, they escaped while under your care."

"Shit. I'm sorry. I didn't plan—"

"I know," I interrupt him. "I need you to get them. Now."

"Where are they?"

"Adam said he was headed for the Colorado Militia checkpoint. Do you know where that is?"

"Yes."

"Good. Get there before I do." I squeeze the telephone receiver in my hand. "If anything happens to them—"

"It won't."

I take a deep breath.

"Freddie needs to be taken care of. He can no longer be trusted," Crossbender warns.

"I'll take care of Freddie. I just need one thing from you."

"What's that?"

"Lina thinks I'm dead and I need you to keep it that way." There's a long pause on the other end. "Crossbender."

"Sure, Andie. But don't you think it would be better if—"

"No! They need to think I'm dead. You know it's the only way to keep them safe."

"But, wait.... There's more."

"Another time." I glance at Freddie who is patiently waiting for me to get off the phone. "It was nice talking to you, George. Take care."

I hang up and turn to Freddie.

"Where is the Colorado Militia checkpoint?" I ask.

Freddie lifts a map off of the end of the kitchen table and points. It's a straight shot down a backwoods road. Hopefully that means Adam won't be driving too fast and I can catch up with them.

"You're going to forget a lot of things now, Freddie."

I DON'T BOTHER to close the door behind me after leaving the house. And as I jog down the porch steps I kick over the lantern as I go. Hopefully the place will burn to the ground. Freddie can handle that much; I only made him forget the last year of his memories.

Running down the gravel driveway, I turn left and head in the direction of the checkpoint. I'm not a runner—never been before in my life —but if the nanocytes gave me one thing it's stamina. I'll get there eventually.

The heavy sound of something else running behind me invades the night. I turn to find my Guardian following me. Steve accelerates and runs at my side, perfect pace.

"Only show up when you want to?" I mutter to the creature.

It huffs as it runs at my side. Seems the beast doesn't like me traveling alone at night, or maybe it senses the danger. Either way I am grateful it's here.

The forest shudders and I catch a glance of movement from the corner of my eye. The Swamp people are moving, faster than me and I know I'll never catch up with them.

Seems there's a party in Colorado and everyone's invited.

TWENTY-NINE

THE ROAD IS DAMAGED AND CRUMBLING, BUT IT'S ALMOST A straight shot. Off in the distance I think I can almost see the red tail-lights of Adam's truck. It's a mirage; I know it has to be because there's no way in hell I'd catch up.

A couple of times I trip and fall, skinning my palms and knees. Steve is there, pulling on my sleeves and dragging me to my feet. I know the beast can run faster than I can and if Lina and Marcus are in danger I wish it would just run ahead and help them. But no, the darned thing stays by my side.

What happens next is sudden and loud. There's an explosion in the distance. The ground under my feet shakes and the unmistakable sound of the beating of helicopter blades fills the air. That would be Hanford. But what was the explosion?

Dread envelopes me and I try to run faster. My throat is dry and my legs weak as I push myself to get there.

It feels like an hour has passed. It's been a long time since I heard the helicopter and ahead of us is the end of the road. It's a dead-end but I can see the metal gleam of a gate. There's a man on the ground and the gate is hanging open.

Crap.

Steve the Guardian finally runs ahead of me but I slow as I take it all in. The farmhouse has a blast in the side of it. There's bodies littering the edge of the forest. The tall grass is pushed down almost flat. And then there's the truck Adam was driving with the kids. I walk toward it. The Guardian is sniffing the place and stops on the passenger side of the truck. I move closer. There's blood, a lot of blood. And lying on the ground next to the blood is a broken arrow and the black baseball hat that Adam was wearing.

Double crap.

I search the truck and find Adam's bag and the bags the kids were carrying.

The Guardian whines.

"The kids?" I ask the beast.

Since it can't answer I have to assume that Hanford took the kids. I heard the helicopter but all I have to go on is the blood.

"Show me where they took him," I tell the Guardian.

After a few moments of sniffing the Guardian takes off and I follow close behind.

The Swamp people move fast, I know this from the year I spent living with them. But they have to stop to rest; eventually I'll catch up with them.

THE DAY HAS PASSED with Steve leading me through the thickest forest I've seen in a long time. I'm sure I'm making a crapload of noise. They probably know I'm coming. Still, I do my best to hide myself, push out the pheromones that make me invisible to mankind. It must work since the Guardian slows and our pace changes to an investigative creep.

Something smells strange, a burning metallic-tinged scent hangs heavy in the air. A deep scream breaks through the night. So loud, like the person has been holding it in for a long time but has finally given up.

I stop in my tracks. The Guardian slows and paces by my side. Another scream rips through the air, this one weaker.

My gut drops as I recognize Adam's voice. His cries are pure agony.

The Guardian gives me a hesitant look. It's like the beast knows that part of me wants Adam to suffer. I'm so mad at him for all he put me through, but... I can't watch another person tear him down like this. I may be mad at him, hate him for what he did, but my soul tells me I have to save him from this. We've all suffered too much already.

"Show me," I whisper to the Guardian.

We move and the beast picks up the pace. I can sense the Swamp men in the surrounding forest, watching, keeping their distance. Adam screams again and I feel my emotions flutter. The Witchdoctor warned me to control it and push it away, but hearing this I'm having a hard time.

We step to the edge of a small clearing and I take it all in. A large piece of wood is secured in the ground, a man tied to it by his ankles and wrists. His feet are planted firmly on burning coals. His shirt is gone and his pants are smeared with soot and burning, the fabric inching toward his knees with a bright orange line. The scars that spanned his chest and back are replaced by raw muscle dripping with blood. Lanky Swamp men crowd around him, the sharp knives I've seen them gut animals with held firmly in their hands.

Jesus, they're skinning him alive.

Glane steps out of the shadows.

"The children?" I ask.

"Dey not here, dead girl. Dey flew."

I let a breath out, knowing that Hanford must have picked them up in the chopper.

With renewed focus I warn Glane, "I will stop you."

He watches me with curiosity. "Dis owed." Glane points in the direction of Adam.

"Not this. You take the dead, the dying. Not like this. I can't let you torture him."

"Dis owed." Glane repeats as he presses a finger to his chest. "Dat de worst kinda man. De most dangerous. He kill our kin'. We hunt. We kill him." The last words come out as a vicious growl. "Dis owed."

"I can't let you." I step toward Glane and he takes a step back. "He can't help himself." Another scream rips through the night as the men continue their work on Adam. "Your Witchdoctor wouldn't want this. I promised him peace between us."

Glane stiffens at the mention of his mentor. His gaze darkens. "Dis owed."

Whatever is going on between the Swamp men and Adam is deeper than what I have knowledge of. "You won't leave him alone? Even if I take him from you now?"

"Ne'er." Glane shakes his head.

I promised the Witchdoctor that I wouldn't intervene but Glane leaves me no choice. I focus and push. *Let him go. Forget him, forget him, forget him.*

Glane stills before raising his hand in the air, making a strange motion with his fingers, then turns and slithers away into the darkness.

I head toward the man burning at the stake.

THIRTY

As I get closer, Adam moans. The Swamp men that surround him still and watch me with wary eyes. One reaches out with a wicked blade, threatening to cut him again.

"Move away boys," I say. "This is my liar."

Go away, go away, go away. They scatter.

Adam's eyes are pinched closed, his teeth clenched, his damaged body covered in black soot mixed with blood. I kick the coals away, clearing them from under his feet. I pull the knife from my hip and start cutting him free. I start with his feet, using my hands to snuff out what's left of his burning pants before cutting the rope. Then I work on freeing his wrists.

"Y—you came for me?" Adam's voice is hoarse from shouting and soft with disbelief.

"Of course." Using my knife I saw through the rope that looks as though it's woven from tough vines.

"No one has ever come back for me," his voice is weak. "Not once." His voice is breathless. "Not in all of my time on this earth. Not unless they wanted something from me in return."

Well, he's got one thing right; I don't want anything in return. I didn't even want him following me around.

I pause in my cutting and look up at him. Adam's eyes are cracked open into slits; electric blue irises look down at me with disbelief. Maybe I was wrong about him and some of the things he's done. I look away and finish cutting the rope and when my knife slices through the last fiber, Adam collapses at my feet.

I just stare down at him for a minute, unsure of how to move him. Besides being twice my size, he looks like a burn victim. His raw muscle is now caked with dirt. All I can think is that he must hurt something terrible.

I pull off my jacket, leaving me in the skin vest from the Swamp people. I cut the material with my knife.

His hands still have skin on them, but his forearms are bloody and raw. I start wrapping his wrists all the way to his elbows so I have something to grip besides raw meat. I need to drag him out of here, under the cover of the trees and away from anyone who might have heard him yelling. From what I found out from Freddie, it seems there are many who want him dead, and like this he's an easy target.

When I look up, the Guardian is sitting at Adam's side, watching me. A stretcher would come in handy right now, but the Swamp men took everything when they left. The only thing that remains is the burning stake.

"You're going to have to help me," I tell the beast.

Adam groans as I roll him onto his back. "This is going to hurt like a bitch," I warn him as I grab his wrists and pull.

As I'm dragging him toward the cover of the forest, the Guardian grips Adam's waistband in its mouth and helps.

Adam is over a foot taller than me and built of solid muscle, moving his damaged body like this is akin to dragging a thousand pound sack of potatoes. I'd kill for these nanocytes to give me super strength right now.

With the help of the Guardian I get him a few hundred yards within the cover of the trees. I settle him at the base of an old pine tree. The needles that litter the ground are soft and pad the ground.

I crouch next to him and get a good look at his wounds. In addition to the lack of skin, he's got multiple puncture wounds littering his chest and a bullet wound in his thigh. If I had to guess I'd say Hanford and the Swamp people took part in what I see before me.

I sit cross-legged at his side and contemplate my next move. The Guardian lies opposite me. I wish I had a pack of medical supplies; water, clothing for him, anything. I have nothing. But I know he has the nanocytes and I know he won't die. He'll heal, eventually.

Adam's breaths are shallow, and he makes no effort to move his limbs from where I've arranged them. Eventually, his right eye cracks open and he looks up at me.

"What did you do to them to deserve this?" I ask.

"Killed their leader. And the next one after that." His eye closes and his lips press together so hard they turn white.

"Why do you always have to kill people?" I ask him.

He doesn't reply.

"I mean, not too long ago I wanted to kill you. But here I am, dragging your carcass to safety. I had things to do Adam, and it didn't include nursing you back to health. I have half a mind to cover you in dirt and go on with my business."

Both of his eyes flash open. "No grave can hold me. I'll crawl back to you. Always." He blinks and licks his dry lips. "They were going to hurt you. That's why I killed them."

Something in what's left of my soul caves.

<hr>

My back is to the tree and I'm watching the Guardian watch Adam. It's been two days and his raw muscle is finally covered in a thin pink layer of skin. The nanocytes are taking a toll on his body. He hasn't moved one millimeter and he seems to be losing muscle mass at an alarming rate. It's like his body is eating itself and healing at the same time.

When my eyes finally flick to his, I see that he's awake.

"So, you waited for me," he says quietly.

"Against my better judgment. I know what it's like to be burned, or fried, at the stake. Not fun. Hurry up and heal already, you're putting a real damper on my time frame." I look away from him, mostly because I hate seeing him so injured and not being able to do anything.

"My nanocytes are slow," he says.

I nod and stand.

"Where are you going?" he asks, moving his torso in a brief attempt to sit up. His lips split into a grimace and his teeth clench.

"Lay down. I'm going to search for supplies." The Guardian makes no attempt to follow me and I'm glad. I'd rather have it stay with him. "I'll be back," I tell Adam. "I promise."

He tips his chin down and closes his eyes again.

I head east, toward the sound of voices and smell of smoke. While I was sitting next to Adam, waiting for him to wake up, I heard Survivors nearby hunting in the forest. Now I walk in the direction they came from until I find myself on the outskirts of a small settlement.

You don't see me, you don't see me, you don't see me.

I walk down the main road. Men and women don't notice the stranger among them. I take things from the unsuspecting Survivors. I find a backpack in an empty house and fill it with a pot, a cup, a plate, a flint stone that's on the fireplace mantle, an old throw pillow from a sunken couch that's hand stitched with "Home Sweet Home."

Outside I pump a bucket of fresh water from their well and take a sack of root vegetables from the neighboring house. I fill my pockets with eggs from their chicken coop then head out onto the road, following the smell of cooking meat. There's an old man a few houses down skewering meat and cooking it over a fire. I take three skewers of meat right off of the fire when he turns his back. On my way out of town I steal clothing from a clothesline, a sheet, a blanket and a shirt and pants that look like they might fit Adam.

When I'm done pillaging I head back to where I left Adam and the Guardian, unseen.

"You came back," he whispers as I settle the bucket and sack of food next to the base of the tree.

"I left a half-honest woman and came back a thief." I motion to the things I brought back. "When they find out all of this is gone they're not going to be happy."

"They might come looking for it," he warns.

"Then I guess we better fix you up."

I search the area around us for sticks and dropped branches. After collecting a large handful and arranging it all in a cleared area, I use the stolen flint to start a fire.

I get the cup and dip it in the bucket of water.

"It's well water," I say as Adam watches me. "Should be safe to drink without boiling."

As I help him sit up, sweat beads the pink skin of his brow. I bring the cup to his lips and help him drink before filling the pot with a few inches of water. After setting the bucket near the fire to warm, I settle the eggs inside the pot and set it on the embers to boil. Reaching for the backpack, I pull out the sheet and cut some of it into strips then toss them into the bucket of water.

Adam watches me. The uncomfortable silence forces me to start talking. "Did Hanford make it to the children?" I ask.

"Yes," his voice sounds strained. "They went in the chopper. Crossbender was there. They're safe."

When I look up, I notice that Adam's face is pinched in pain and he hasn't attempted to drink from the cup that's in his hand.

I move toward him and help him drink.

"If you need to lay down just do it. I won't be ready for a little bit."

"I'm fine." Adam refuses to look at me.

I move away from him and get the sack of vegetables. There are a few potatoes, carrots, some wild onions, garlic bulbs and a rutabaga in the sack. I hit the jackpot with this. I peel the skin off the garlic and onions, use my knife to cut the other vegetables, then I toss them in the pot with the eggs and cover the pot with the plate. When that's done I lean the skewers against the pot so the meat can warm over the fire.

I stand to find a few more sticks to add to the fire. When I turn to check on Adam he's laying down, his eyes closed and his jaw tense.

I test the bucket of water and find that it's warm. I move the bucket toward Adam, drop to my knees and pull out a wet cloth.

"What are you doing?" he whispers.

"You're filthy." I hesitate before touching him. "This is probably going to hurt."

"It already does." He looks hesitantly toward the bucket and my hands.

"I'm sorry," I tell him. And I truly am. The nanocytes will heal him but the old nurse in me can't watch him lie there in filth any longer.

He nods.

I start with his face, wiping away the black ash from his cheeks. Then down his neck to his shoulders, trying my best to be careful. I use a new cloth each time, tossing it away when it's dirty to keep the bucket of water clean. I unwrap my torn shirt from his arms and clean the fresh skin and his hands, then his upper body. I avoid his gaze as my hands run over the rigid planes of his chest.

When I get to his shredded pants I hesitate and then curse myself. I'm an adult and I've seen him in less. Much less.

In a quick movement Adam reaches out and grabs my wrist. "You don't have to," he says.

When I look to his face, his eyes are still closed, his jaw clenched tight. I shake his hand off of my arm and begin to cut what's left of the pants off. I wash down his legs, to his blackened feet.

"I need you to turn on your side," I tell him as I pull the rest of the sheet from the backpack. It was large to begin with and now I have just enough left to spread underneath him.

Adam rolls to his side with a groan and I wash his back. I use the cup to rinse his hair while his head is off of the ground. After, I lay the sheet on the ground and have him roll onto it. Then I get the clothing I stole and help him dress. The flannel shirt is a little big and I leave it unbuttoned since the puncture wounds on his abdomen are still oozing. The pants are too short and the bullet wound on his thigh is already draining through the bandage. I'll have to go out for fresh clothes for him in the near future.

Lastly, I cover his legs with the blanket I stole and help him to sit up. My hands are warm from the water, and from touching his heated body. Sweat beads break out over my skin and I know I need to move away from him.

"Don't tip over," I warn him as I move toward the fire.

Pulling the pot out of the flames, I remove the plate from the top of it and check on the food inside. The vegetables are soft and the eggs have been boiled. I drain the water and pour it all out onto the plate. I pull the meat from the skewers and set the chunks on the plate. Then I begin peeling the shells off of the eggs. The Guardian watches me from across the fire. I toss it one of the peeled eggs before standing. The Guardian catches the egg in its mouth and after chewing twice, swallows it.

I bring the plate to Adam. He starts with the meat, moving as fast as his injured limbs will allow, shoving it in his mouth and swallowing after barely chewing.

"Suicide makes you hungry, huh?" I tease as I move away from him and sit near the base of the pine tree.

"I'm not usually hungry." He pauses as he swallows. "Ever."

"Me either." I look away from him. "It's the nanocytes."

Adam nods as he picks up an egg and bites into it.

"I think you're only hungry because of your injuries."

"Yes." He agrees. "I told you before, mine are first generation. I will survive but it will take a while to recover. The protein and nutrients help. Then the nanocytes don't have to waste time manufacturing them."

I toy with the lace of my boot.

"Were you—" he pauses to ask. "Were you hungry after you hit the fence?"

I shrug. "I don't know. The Witchdoctor said—"

"The Swamp people's Witchdoctor?" It's like he can't believe the guy exists.

"Yeah. He said he never fed me. I just laid in a cot until I woke up, and then things were still a bit off. He said it was my brain taking so long to heal."

"Is that what you think?" Adam asks as he finishes off another egg.

"It makes sense. The things I felt, the things I did, I couldn't control any of it. He had to be right. He had good reason to be right."

"Why's that?" Adam slows his chewing like it's exhausting him. "He had to be right. Why?"

"Because after I waited it got better. There's no other explanation," I say.

He nods, accepting my answer and continues eating. I look away, staring into the fire. And then I remember the pouch of potions the Witchdoctor gave me before I left. I get up and move to my bag.

Adam finishes and this time he brings the cup to the bucket of water and fills it himself, drinking it in one long chug. It's dark now, the only light coming from the flames of the small fire.

"Thank you," he says as I pull out the leather pouch.

I don't respond right away, because I'm not sure what to say. And I'm not sure I want to reveal to him what I learned while I was living in the Witchdoctors hut.

Adam settles on the sheet, turning to his side, facing me.

I grip the leather bag in my hand and withdraw it from my pack. "Why do you keep going back to Crane?" I ask.

"Because for some fucked up reason I felt like I owed him. He created me, made me what I am now, and I just couldn't let go of the feeling that I owed him."

"He has ruined lives. We owe him nothing."

"I know that now."

I hold the small leather bag up. "I have something that can help you."

Adam's lips press into a grim line. "I don't want it. Whatever it is I don't need it."

"It will help." I start to pull apart the leather ties.

"No." He sounds adamant.

I tie the satchel up and place it in my bag again. "If you don't start getting better faster, I'll use it on you."

The fire has burned down to coals and the only light now comes from the sliver of moonlight filtering through the branches above us.

"Come here," Adam whispers.

"I don't think that's a good idea," I warn him. "I think it's best if I stay over here."

"It's cold and dark." He insists. "Come here."

All I can see is that look he gave me as I cut him off of the stake. It's been a long time since I was warm, since I allowed someone to touch me. It's been years. He felt so warm as I washed his damaged skin just a few hours ago. Warm and alive. A chill races through my body and I shiver.

"Come here. You're cold." He opens the blanket and motions to the thin strip of sheet in front of him. When I cut the fabric up I left enough for one person to sleep on, not two. "Come," his tone turns demanding.

I give in and move to him, settling down with my back to his chest. I say, "Don't get any ideas. Just because I nursed you back to health doesn't mean anything."

He settles the blanket over us. "It means something," he whispers in my ear. "You could have finally rid me of your life. But you didn't. I told you before, Andie, no one has ever come back for me unless they wanted something in return. You're the first."

"There's nothing I want but revenge."

"That makes both of us."

I WAKE up on my back, wrapped in heat. Adam's arm is locked tightly around my abdomen, his legs pressed against my thigh. For a few moments I enjoy the feeling of being held and the closeness. Truth be told, I miss it. But then Adam's lips are suddenly on mine, his fingers buried in my hair, his tongue pressing into my mouth.

My body stiffens on its own accord. I'm not ready to go back to this; I push my hands against his shoulders.

"He said you were mine. He promised, promised me I could have you if I did it," Adam mutters between kissing me. "I finally have you."

"A—" I try to tell him to stop but he won't move. I push at his shoulders and arms. His leg moves between mine and he shifts his body over me, pressing me to the ground with his weight.

As I'm pushing at him, I notice his face is flushed and his body is pumping out an alarming amount of heat. He doesn't open his eyes once. This isn't like him—maybe once, but not now. I move my hand down his side. Feel around for the bandage wrapped around his thigh and I press my thumb into the bullet wound there.

Adam stops instantly, crying out in pain. I shove him off of me and move away. When his eyes finally open they're glazed over and his hair is soaked in sweat.

"What's wrong with you?" I ask as I reach out to touch him. The back of my hand touches his forehead and I realize he's burning up with fever.

Adam groans and grips his leg. There is a stain on his pants, fresh drainage from the wound I pushed on. I move fast, using my knife to cut the leg of his pants open and pulling off the cloth bandage I wrapped his thigh in. The bullet wound is angry red and oozing pus.

"Wonderful," I mutter.

I get a fresh cloth and water and begin washing the wound. Adam seems to come to life a bit in the middle of it.

"I have no idea how you can treat people the way you do," I start in on him.

Pressing his lips together, he scowls like he doesn't have a clue what I'm talking about.

"You're a dick. The things you've done." I shake my head. "I thought we had something. All Crane had to do was make some promise to you and that was it. You traded me for some fucked up promise from Crane. Well I hope it was a good deal!" I scrub his wound a little rougher than I need to before tossing the cloth away. "Hope it was all worth it." Pressing my fingers to each side of the wound, I squeeze out whatever is festering in there.

Adam groans. His teeth grind against each other. "It was worth it," he gets out through his clamped mouth.

"Hope so." I squeeze from the other direction and I'm surprised when a small bullet pops out of the wound. I wash it again before wrapping his thigh in a new strip of cloth.

I move to my bag and pull out the pouch from the Witchdoctor. I know which one to use, he taught me. My fingers spread the leather and I scoop a handful of the powder out.

"What are you doing?" Adam asks as he scowls at me.

"Helping you." I throw the handful of dust in his eyes.

"And now I'm going to have to find you new pants. Way to make this take so much longer than I needed it to." I tie the bag and shove it back in my pack. "You just lay here like an invalid. Hopefully this won't take too long."

Adam's eyes are closed and he's in a deep sleep before I even finish yelling at him. I stomp off in the direction of the Survivor settlement.

687

THIRTY-ONE

ADAM

SHIT.

I'm on the ground and my skin is still burning, which means that was a dream. I groan and roll to my side, remembering how perfect it was while my eyes were closed. We sure as hell weren't on the ground, we were in a bed and Andie was mine and Crane had kept his promise.

He finally let me keep her.

I wipe a strange, orange-colored dust off of my face; remember that Andie threw it at me. Rubbing it between my fingers, I wonder where she went and if she'll ever come back after what I just did.

THIRTY-TWO

I GET MORE WATER, ANOTHER PAIR OF PANTS, AND A BUNCH of eggs from the henhouse.

As I'm making my way back to where I left Adam I decide I need to ditch him. We've been camping out here for days and I need to get to Phoenix and find my notes on the nanocytes. This has already taken far too long. I've gotten distracted and off track. I need to get my notes, I need the world's data, and I need to stop whatever Cranc and the Entities are doing to those children in Galena.

I glance around the dark forest. Can I just leave him out here? Adam's fever worries me. It could just be the nanocytes working their magic but a fever that high can't be healthy. He was burning up. I make my way through the forest as quickly as possible. I'm beyond pissed at him.

When I make it back to camp, a second Guardian has showed up and is lying on the ground next to the black one I named Steve.

Only the rumpled sheet is on the ground where I left Adam. The new Guardian looks past the trees and I follow his line of sight and find

Adam standing a few feet away. If he's well enough to stand, the Witch-doctor's powder must have worked.

I set the bucket down and start making a fire to cook the eggs. When I turn around again Adam is swaying on his feet, his hands gripping tight to the trunk of a nearby tree.

"What are you doing?" I ask.

"Bathroom." He looks at me, his face flushed, his bright pink healing skin dripping with sweat. I notice his shirt is gone and he's cut the legs off of his pants.

"It's hot," he mutters as he takes a step to move and his knees buckle.

I move fast and catch him with my shoulder under his arm before he collapses. His skin is burning up. I help him back to the sheet and help him get settled.

"Why do you feel like you're on fire?" I ask as I get a cloth and dip it in the water before pressing it to his forehead.

"Healing." I fill the nearby cup and help him drink. "Sorry," he coughs out as he finishes drinking.

"For what?" I busy myself with the water and the boiling eggs.

When I turn he's looking at me, his bright blue eyes the only thing leading me to believe that he might not actually be thoroughly septic.

He blinks before looking away and closing his eyes.

Maybe there's too much that he's sorry for and he can't say it all right now.

I take the pot out of the fire and pour off the water, giving the eggs a moment to cool. I look around and find Adam's shirt discarded near where he sleeps. I stand and move toward it, picking it up off the ground, shaking the dirt and pine needles off before folding it. I set the shirt on the bag I took. Before going back to the eggs, I press the damp cloth to Adam's forehead again; it's a futile attempt to bring his fever down. I might have to use more of the powder on him.

I sit by the fire and peel the eggs, eating one before I move to sit next to Adam and wake him.

I shake his shoulder. "You need to eat."

He groans as his eyes flutter open and he waves me away.

"Eat." I nudge his shoulder until he moves up on an elbow and accepts the egg.

"I hate eggs," he tells me as he swallows.

I hand him another. "I'll get you a refund on the bill."

He grudgingly accepts the second egg and eats it.

"We need to move," I warn him.

He nods, sweat dripping down the side of his face. I can't remember the last time I saw someone who was so feverish they were sweating this profusely. "Morning," he rasps before laying down again.

My gut tells me he won't be ready by morning. I get the satchel from my backpack and scoop out a handful of the powder.

"Adam?" I call his name.

When he opens his eyes, I throw the powder in his face. In a heartbeat his body goes limp. I hated it when the Witchdoctor kept doing that to me, but it worked. Whatever he puts in here, it works well.

I clean up camp, leaving the pot, buckets, and plates near the base of a nearby tree. If the Survivors find it all out here they can have it back.

When I'm done, I crouch down next to Adam and get a good look at his wounds. The punctures are almost healed, his skin looks darker and less pink. And oddly enough, all of his scars have returned with his new skin, slashes across his chest and abdomen, pockmarks from bullet holes. The wound in his thigh is bright red but smaller. I stand before moving away from him and settling at the base of the large pine tree. I know better than to cuddle up next to him tonight.

WAKING to the sound of rustling is never good, especially when you're sleeping next to a tree. I open my eyes with a jerk and sit up straight only to find Adam getting dressed. Considering his state last night, I'd say the fact that he's standing without help is a miraculous improvement.

"We should get moving," Adam says as he buttons his flannel shirt. The pants I stole fit him a little better this time, but he's still without shoes—those burned beyond repair thanks to the Swamp men. "I need to get some better gear than this." He turns to the Guardians before looking up at the sky. He glances around the forest as though he's orienting himself to place and time. He starts walking north.

"I need to get to Phoenix," I remind him as I stand and brush the pine needles off of my pants.

Adam limps as he walks through the forest barefoot. "We'll get there." He still looks weak and pale.

"I don't need you to come with me." I shoulder my pack, now stuffed with just the blanket since that's all I need. "I know where I'm going and how to get there."

"We just need some supplies." He limps further away.

I look east because that's where I want to go. Directly east, across the plains and skim by the great lakes to home. There are things I need, answers that I was once so close to finding out.

"I don't need you." I remind him. "I think we should split up now that you can walk."

He stops, his back straightening like I just made some horrible revelation. And then he turns, stomping toward me, moving faster than I expect.

"After all of this, you'd leave me now?" He grabs my shoulders and his grip is strong.

I blink, stunned. "I have to get to Phoenix. I have to stop Crane."

"I'm going with you. You need my help. You'll never get there alone." He's glaring at me. "You wouldn't have helped me these past few days if your plan was just to run off and leave me again."

"You don't know that. And you were the one always leaving me, pretending to die, leaving me with Crane. Being part of the Reformation."

"I know." He steps closer to me so that our bodies are flush against each other. "I know I made mistakes and I will never be able to say sorry enough to get you to fully forgive me. I'm sorry, Andie. I'm sorry for all of it." His eyes search mine. "If I could have done something different..."

He's sorry. I know he's sorry, he's told me a hundred times already and I wish I could accept it but I'm just not ready. There's more he's not telling me.

"You said something when you were feverish and groping me." I clear my throat. "I could have you if I did it," I repeat his own words back to him. "What did he make you do, Adam?"

He takes one step back before running his hands through his messy hair, looking ridiculous, as he stands barefoot before me.

"I was his trillion dollar errand boy," he says. "The things he did to train me, to make me do what he wanted. You don't know brainwashing like Crane does. But you," he reaches out and tucks a strand of hair behind my ear, "he didn't brainwash you. He let you have things that he never let me have; family, children, a spouse. He dangled those in front of me. After he took it all away, made me forget who I was." Adam presses his lips together. "It's been so long."

His face twists, distorting the image of the handsome man before me who's caused me so much hurt. He's in pain. Whether it's from his healing wounds or his soul, I'm sure both. This is enough pressing him for today. I'll let him accompany me. As long as he keeps up with the soul searching. Even though I don't want to admit it, spending the night wrapped in his arms was the most comfortable and safe I've felt in years. I miss it. Even after everything that's happened between us, I miss it. I miss it just as much as I miss Ian and my children.

I have to stop thinking about them all.

"Where are you getting supplies from?" I ask.

Adam wipes a hand over his face. "The stop I made before the Colorado Militia checkpoint."

I frown. "There's a strong chance that place burned down, and Freddie won't remember you."

"I don't need the house. I have a stash nearby."

"Fine." I tug on the straps to my bag. "I'll go with you and then we'll head for Phoenix." I decide to warn him about what Freddie told me. "The Survivor Militia in the South wants you dead."

"Everyone wants me dead." He turns and starts walking.

THE HOUSE where I left Freddie is partially burned. Seems he remembered how to put out a fire. Adam has a bunker of supplies hidden in a shed behind the house. He pulls out clothing for himself, boots, weapons, a bag with canteens and food. He stockpiled like he was preparing for the apocalypse.

"I don't have clothes to fit you," he says as he tugs on a pair of black cargo pants.

"I don't need clothes."

Adam gives me a look that lets me know the skinwear from the Swamp people isn't kosher.

"We can find you something on the road. There are a few more checkpoints between here and there." He bends to tie his boots before pulling a black T-shirt over his head and then a dark jacket. He loads all the tiny pockets with tools and weapons before filling his pack and putting it on. And just like that he turns from a slightly injured Adam into the highly trained and lethal man that I remember.

We had only been walking for just over a day, but in that time his body has healed back to normal. Scars, tattoos, it's like he was never skinned by the Swamp men.

"Why did your scars come back?" I ask as I point to the Marine Corps tattoo on his arm. "And your tattoo came back."

"My nanocytes have a memory of my body." He looks away from me as he slips a sheathed knife into the loop on his pants. "And some scars are too deep to heal."

"Mine didn't do that."

"You haven't had yours as long," he replies.

Someday soon I'm betting on him telling me exactly how old he is.

"So." I look around the shed that's filled with tools and junk. "You just happened to have this place here, right where we needed it?"

"I have places like this stashed all over the northern part of the country."

Convenient. "And when did you find the time to do that?"

"I've had plenty of time." He closes the trapdoor of the shed and replaces the table that was covering it. "Let's go."

I pause before leaving the shed.

"What?" he asks.

"You're not going to do something with that beard?"

He strokes the facial hair that extends down to his chest. "Men would kill for a beard like this."

I shake my head and walk away from him. He looks good with the beard, but I'm not going to let him know that.

We head east and somewhere along the days long trek we lose the Guardians. Adam seems to know where to go to avoid Survivors. After days of walking nonstop, he finally detours toward an old farm. There is an empty house and an old barn. The roof of the barn is partially collapsed. Adam heads for it, I follow him.

He pulls open a cracked wooden door and holds it for me, motioning me inside.

"What are we doing here?" I ask.

"Getting you some real clothes."

"I'm fine. I want to keep walking."

"We're getting you some real clothes." He doesn't seem to want to take no for an answer.

I look down at myself and see that my pants are worn and dirty. There's a tear in the thigh portion of my right leg.

Sunlight filters through the damaged roof, illuminating the interior of the barn so we can see.

Adam moves some equipment before revealing another trapdoor in the flooring in the corner of the barn that isn't collapsed. He opens it to expose another space filled with suitcases and bins.

"Always be prepared," he says as he opens a bin and pulls out a stack of clothes. He hands them to me. There are pants, and a shirt and a jacket almost identical to what he's wearing. He passes me a pair of boots and socks as well.

"You just keep women's clothing lying around?" I ask as I kick off my shoes.

Adam doesn't answer as he digs through the bins.

I clear my throat.

"What?" he sounds distracted.

"I need to change."

"Go ahead."

"In private."

He laughs. "Nothing I haven't seen."

He's right. But it annoys me. So I leave and find a private corner behind some machinery and broken roofing.

As I'm stripping off my old skinwear, I'm thinking that this place reminds me of Wolf Creek. It must be the wide-open pastures and the barn. What we saw there just isn't setting right with me. It worries me, a lot.

I pull on the cargo pants and shirt, amazed at how well they fit. I hide my old clothing under some broken wood. As I'm pushing my arms through the jacket, I leave my corner to find Adam again.

He's pushing machinery over the trapdoor, hiding his stash for another time.

"Ready?" he asks.

I shoulder my pack and Adam does the same before leading me out of the barn and back on the road.

"You don't want to find a truck and drive?" I ask him, curious since he always seems to have a vehicle stashed somewhere.

Adam shakes his head. "I don't think that's a good idea." He glances at me. "If Freddie was so willing to collect on my bounty then there'll be others. I'd like to avoid any more situations like that one." He looks off in the distance. "And I like spending time with you. I get the feeling this won't last."

I would want to avoid getting skinned and burned at the stake as well. But I wonder why he thinks this won't last.

"Why is that?" I ask.

Adam shrugs. "You're ready to kill Crane and whoever else gets in your way. I've seen you angry before, Andie, but nothing like this. It's like everything is brewing just under your skin and when you explode..." He shakes his head. "It's not going to be good." Looking at me again, he says, "This is time that won't last, when we're done..." He never finishes and I just stare off in the distance and keep going.

He's right. I'm angry at the world—but mostly at Crane. I'm pissed with him for lying to me for so many years, for not just leaving me alone. I'm more angry at myself because I like Adam being around again and I know it's wrong.

"Say something," Adam finally says. "Because I'm giving up on this dream I have, this hope that's the only thing keeping me going. It's the only thing that's been keeping me going for years. I'm giving up on you."

I stop moving and turn to face him. The thought of being alone forever saddens me. And then there's this pull, this longing. It's always been there, every day since the first moment I met Adam.

I tell him a truth. "I'm just so tired of trying to hate you. I can't do it anymore." Grief and pain bubble up inside me and explode outward. I lose the control that the Witchdoctor infused in me. And I hope that we are deep enough into the countryside that no one is around to feel it because a reaction this strong has caused death before.

Adam grabs me, pulls me tight against him, hugging me tighter than anyone ever has.

"I have made so many mistakes," I whisper. "Wrong choices that I can't let go of because it changed lives. I did things I'm not proud of. I've lost people I loved. I was so stupid, a pawn to Crane and his group of Entities."

Adam grips me tighter and I can barely breathe. "I'm sorry that Ian died and that the children are gone." His hands move to press against the sides of my face and he holds me still. "Are we together in this? I need to know I can trust you."

I need to know I can trust him.

"You tell me," I whisper.

"Yes," he responds firmly.

My gut tells me it's the truth. For the first time in years, I trust the liar.

"Then yes," I reply.

Adam smiles briefly before pressing his lips to mine and pulling me closer. I grip his jacket as his hand moves to my hair, tugging just a bit to angle our mouths together.

When he finally pulls away my head is spinning and we are both out of breath.

"You had better not be lying," I warn him.

"No longer." Adam smiles and tucks my loose hair behind my ears. "Let's end this," he says as he takes my hand and we continue walking.

THIRTY-THREE

"He did very bad things to me."

Andie looks up at me, her face pale. "When?"

"When he took me from my family." I reach out and take her hand, afraid that she will run from me after I tell her what he did. "He's very good at manipulation."

"I know that." She looks away, ahead of us as we walk.

"One minute I was a kid returning home from duty, then next I was on an island and my life was gone.

I tell her everything, in detail. She pales further, sickened by truth. But this is life, many truths that no one wants to admit to.

"So you were one of them, a Funding Entity?" she asks.

"By proxy." I keep a tight hold on her hand. "I did what he told me. If not, things were very bad."

"Like Baillie did to me?" she asks.

"Worse. A hundred times worse."

"And Blithe?" she asks.

"The same."

Her body tenses. "That bastard."

Thirty-Four

Standing in front of the Phoenix District gates, this place still feels like home. I can't mistake the feeling for anything else.

Let us in, let us in, let us in.

The Volker open the gates, and then I make them forget us as we walk away.

We walk through a tunnel made of branches and leaves. It reminds me of the first time I tried to escape this place. Lina was young and we were all innocent. How times have changed.

"Where to first?" Adam asks as we step out from the cover of the brush and hit pavement.

"I'm not sure. I want to go to the Pasture. I left my research on the nanocytes there." I look at him. "Then I'm going to Galena and once I get answers on what's happening to the kids there, I'm done. I'm going to scour the world's data for answers and get the nanocytes out."

Adam nods. "I want mine out. I've been doing this long enough."

Something in my chest freezes, the same fear that Ian once had for me, I now have it for Adam. He could die in an instant. However many years old he is, his body might not be able to function once the nanocytes are removed. He could die as soon as they're out. But so could I. We could both be dead the moment they're gone from our bodies. The thought is both heartbreaking and terrifying.

"Just how long have you been doing this for?" I ask.

"Over a hundred years. Closer to two."

I have nothing to say to that. The things he must've seen, the people he lost.

We walk, the roads of the Phoenix District still familiar and worn, the forest thick with years of uninhibited growth.

"Headquarters then?" Adam asks.

I fidget with the button on my jacket. "I don't want to see Sam. I can't. I think it's best that he doesn't see me."

"He'd want to see you." Adam bends to pick a stick up off of the ground and twirls it between his fingers. "He's a good kid. He'd want to know you were still alive."

I focus off in the distance, as far as the old country road will let me see. It's just green and brown and dusty gray blacktop.

"I don't think it's a good idea. Once I see Crane I'm not sure how well I'll be able to control this... this thing I can do. No, I can't see him just like I can't see the children."

Our shoes make hollow sounds on the road as we walk. Adam turns down the road that leads to the Pasture. Birds chirp in the trees and squirrels scamper across the road in front of us. Noises that I normally fear as the Swamp people come from the dark forest bordering the road, but here I know that it is nothing but nature continuing on around us.

Adam stops at the gravel road and hidden drive that leads to the gates of the Pasture.

"We're here." He takes a deep breath. "Are you ready for this?"

I nod. The tiny hairs on my arms and the back of my neck rise. I ignore the sensation and blame it on the emotion that floods a person upon returning home after a long journey.

The drive is shadowed, the large oak and pine trees nearly blocking out the sun. It's not until we are upon the gates that we notice they're already open. We see two figures waiting just past the threshold.

One is Burton Crane, the other a Volker who I mistake for Sam at first. Crane smiles when he sees us.

"Ah, Andromeda, you've come home." Crane clasps his hands together. "Finally."

Adam stops me with his hand on my arm. The expression on his face is emotionless.

I still and wait, unsure of what to do. I know what I want to do; grab the knife at my hip and jab it into his throat—but that won't kill him. It would merely damage him for a moment until his nanocytes healed. No, I can't make any rash decisions at this moment. Instead, I need to be calculating and cold, just like him.

I don't kill Crane. I decide to do the one thing that I know might ruin him: life without control.

"Cuff him," I instruct the Volker. "And follow us."

Crane doesn't even struggle as the Volker detains him. He simply smiles and his eyes narrowed on us. "Very good, Andromeda."

Adam and I walk with the Volker leading Crane along behind us. A shadow steps out from the threshold of the largest barn as we pass. It's Elvis and he gives a strange look as we get closer. I wave at him to come out. He steps back into the shadows for a moment and I hear the deep tones of his voice speaking to someone inside the barn. He finally steps out again, following us as we make our way to the ruins.

"What are you doing here?" Elvis asks Adam with a hushed voice. He looks hesitantly at the detained Crane.

"Andie needs to get something and then we'll be leaving." Adam slows as he replies, letting me take the lead alone. "I get the feeling she's taking Crane with her though."

"You think that's a good idea?" Elvis's voice is brimming with hesitation.

"It's not my idea," Adam replies.

Tall wheat grass brushes against my legs as I walk through the field, burdocks stick to my pants, the pungent scent of wild onions and damp soil fill the air. Grasshoppers flit from blade to blade in front of us and I remember the years we spent out here, the children growing up in the middle of all of this. It was a simple life in the darkest of times and we were blessed to live with such treasures as the world outside faltered and burned. I'm torn with the memories, knowing that they bring me joy but at the same time they were nothing but a false promise, a bribe and a farce. I feel like an idiot for believing it, for living it, and the greatest pain comes from subjecting my children to this, following along blindly.

Before I know it we've passed the pond and have come upon the old farmhouses. They look worse for the wear. I step up onto the rickety porch of the middle building and walk inside, finding the trapdoor easily and propping it open.

Walking down the rickety steps to the basement under the ruins, something white catches my eye along the wall. My breath catches as I see the skeleton laying there on the dirt floor. I recognize the strips of cloth that remain, the clothing he was wearing that day, frayed pieces of fabric. The bones of his legs still shoved into his neatly laced boots. It's Ian.

This is the place where I killed my husband, the place where I became a monster in the true sense. Crane didn't even have the decency to bury him.

All I can do is stand and stare for a long moment.

I barely notice when Adam leaves, taking Elvis with him. When they return, Adam and Elvis carry a long wooden box down the stairs. A coffin. I just watch, unable to move, guilt nailing me in my place. Gentler than I've ever seen these two men move, they lift his bones and arrange them in the coffin. Boots, strips of cloth, everything that was Ian goes into the box.

"Keep Crane here," I instruct the Volker with a whispered order.

I follow Adam and Elvis through the forest, feeling the eyes of the Guardians watching us. The men head toward the water tower where we've buried the others. They dig a grave and bury the coffin. And then they leave me alone.

Ian deserved so much better than all of this. There is a hollow space in my heart that can never be filled. I will never be whole. Never again.

When I make my way back to the ruins, Adam is waiting there with Crane and the Volker.

"Where did Elvis go?" I ask.

Adam's face is flexed with concern. "He said he had chores and Ira and Lex are still here."

I nod and move through the basement that was once my secret laboratory. I find my notes, hidden in a drawer where I last left them.

Crane shifts on his feet, apparently uncomfortable with his hands being tied behind his back for so long. It's about time he's felt some discomfort, after all he's done.

"What do are you going to do with me here, Andromeda?" he asks.

A life without control, that's what I have planned for him since killing him would be too easy and there's no guarantee he'd stay dead. Deep down I know he will not die—not even without food or water or sunlight. My eyes move to the shadows of the cellar where I know there are more rooms dug out into the depths of the earth. It's more than he's ever given me. Humane even. He will just sit here.

I tell the Volker to release Crane from his bindings.

"Goodbye, Crane. Have a nice dirt-nap."

"You won't leave me here," Crane says.

"I think it's for the best," I reply.

I motion for Adam and the Volker to follow but just as I move to leave, a yellow piece of paper flutters on the ground from underneath the rough-hewn table that I once used as a lab bench.

I pick it up and find Ian's notes on Galena. And as I remember what I did, the horrors that occurred in this small dirt room, my fingers begin to tremble.

"Andie?" Adam asks.

"I'm fine, let's—" The memories of him bleeding out before me, the pale look on his face, the inability to bring him back to life; it all floods me, worse than when I was in the Witchdoctor's hut. Maybe it's because my brain is completely healed now and the emotions are stronger, maybe it's because the man who started all of this is standing in the same room with me smiling like an idiot. He thinks he's still in control.

My eyes flick to the Volker as he wipes the sweat from his face.

"Go back to Headquarters," I tell the Volker. "Run." And without hesitation, the man runs out of there faster than I've ever seen one of them move.

"Andie?" Adam asks.

I take a few deep breaths and try to regain control, try to press it to the recesses of my mind like the Witchdoctor taught me.

There's a scratching sound that starts somewhere in the back of the underground ruins, incessant, and it's hard to focus. It's not long before a loud thud interrupts us. Something hits the ground.

"What was that?" I ask.

Adam moves to stand next to me.

Footsteps, running. Before I can make a move a figure appears in the threshold between the connecting rooms.

It's Lina! I blink, swallow hard.

"Ah, children, what an unexpected surprise," Crane says with a wicked smile.

Lina! Raven! I can barely contain myself. The temperature in the space skyrockets. Adam must feel it finally since his face beads with sweat.

You don't see me, you don't see me, you don't see me.

"No!" Lina tells. "Mom!" She reaches out but I step away, out of her grasp.

Crane's laughter echoes in the small space and he claps his hands together. "Why don't you come out and play, Andromeda. Surely you are not afraid of your own children."

"I am not afraid of them." I'm afraid of hurting them.

Lina moves closer and I give Adam a begging look. He grabs her. "Don't, Lina, don't run after her. You'll only make it worse."

I step further away, pressing myself to the dirt wall, wishing it would swallow me whole and spit me out on the other side of the earth far away where I could never hurt my children again.

It gets worse, the rest of the children step out of the shadows of the room. Marcus and Cashel and... something's wrong with Astrid. Cashel is carrying her limp body.

"Come now, Andromeda." Crane's voice is enthusiastic. "Show your children what you've become. It's nothing to be ashamed of."

"You did this to me!" I shout at him feeling my voice waver. "You did this to us. Ruined it all." I move away, run along the wall, scampering like a rat, to get further from the children. "Broke us."

"I made it better," Crane replies, triumphant in his declaration.

"You broke our family. Killed."

I can't control it. I'm losing it just as bad as I did when I killed Ian. I hate the nanocytes, the pheromones that make people do things, make them do what I say, boil their blood if I can't control my emotions.

The room begins to feel hotter and hotter. Sweat starts pouring down Lina and Adam's faces. Lina wipes it out of her eyes. Adam pulls her closer to him and touches her face with the back of his hand. I don't miss the panicked look on his face. He's seen what I'm capable of; he knows the monster that Crane has turned me into.

"Get the children out of here." Adam says as he looks to Marcus. "Get them all out of here. Now!" he shouts.

"Perhaps you should calm down, Andromeda," Crane warns.

I would love to, there's nothing more that I want to do than push all of this into the recesses of my brain. But the children are a distraction, a fear, a nightmare.

Raven is the first to move, tugging Cashel along with him and Astrid is in his arms and writhing in pain as he grips her to his chest.

"We have to go." Raven says. "We have to go, now."

Crane's head whips in the direction of Raven's voice. "Ah, he speaks. Finally."

Raven doesn't reply. He keeps a wary eye on Crane, the corners of the room, and Adam. Crane watches him, studying Raven. He never knew Raven could talk. One thing actually escaped him.

Guardians make an appearance from the shadows behind the children, nudging Isaac toward the wooden stairs that lead above ground.

Adam tugs Lina away.

"Mom," she says, taking the first step of the stairs up.

The fluttering and panic in my chest ratchet up until it's overwhelming.

"This is your last chance, Andromeda." Crane smiles. "Perhaps you should give your first-born some closure."

The brain controls it all, each breath, each heartbeat, emotional response. Control yourself, control it, control it, control it.

I can't, I lose it. And feeling my image flicker, I reveal my hiding place in the corner of the room.

"Go, Lina," I say, pushing her further away. "I am no longer your mother. I am dead to you. A ghost. A memory. Go, before I bring you death like I did your father."

Lina's face blanches as she looks up to Adam. His lips are pressed tightly together. He gives her a nod and it's all the confirmation she needs to go running up the stairs, far away from her monster of a mother.

"THOUGHT YOU WERE GOING to leave me down there," Crane asks.

"Change of plans," Adam says.

I wanted to leave him down there, lock him away forever in a dirt hole, but not with the children here.

"You're flickering," Crane warns me as I trail behind him. "They can see you flickering. It's a nice trick."

"Be quiet," Adam says as he tugs Crane along.

I turn to see Lina and Marcus watching us from near the Farmhouse. Men occupy our front porch, some I recognize from Romney.

I don't want her to remember me like this, as a monster, the one who pushed her away. "Forget me." I face her one last time, knowing fully that it may be the last time I get to see her.

Forget me, forget me, forget me.

"Tragic really," Crane speaks again. "Doing that to her."

"Say one more word and I'll wire your jaw shut." Adam threatens.

"Is my guard dog turning on me now?" Crane asks.

Adam yanks Crane forward, causing him to trip and stumble. "Every method of torture you bestowed upon me, I will do it back to you. Tenfold. Now shut it."

We walk Crane to the train.

THIRTY-FIVE

CATALINA

A GLOWING BALL OF WHITE ENERGY FLIES OUT OF IRA'S OPEN palm and crashes into my side, sending me flying off of my feet.

"What the hell!" Marcus shouts at him.

"Dude, I was just testing her," Ira says. "If you push her hard enough maybe her abilities will finally show."

"I'll push you," Marcus growls as he runs for Ira.

Marcus may be strong, but Ira is small and runs fast. Marcus chases him across the fields, threatening him with bodily harm the entire way.

I stand up and brush the dirt off of my pants.

"I can hurt him if you want," Isaac is suddenly at my side and I jump back in shock.

"You have got to stop sneaking up on people," I tell him, clutching my hands to my chest and feeling my heart thundering underneath. "And I don't want you to hurt anyone."

Isaac makes a noise in his throat, like he's not satisfied with my answer. I get a good look at him for the first time in the few days that we've been here. Isaac has grown. He looks like a full-grown man, like an exact replica of my father. His presence makes everyone uneasy.

"Has Astrid woken up yet?" I ask him.

"No." Isaac shakes his head. "She's still out of it." He turns to look at me. "You should go talk to Raven."

"Why?"

"Just a suggestion."

A winded Marcus walks toward us, and Ira is nowhere to be seen. Isaac takes off, walking toward the barns.

"What did he want?" Marcus asks between deep breaths.

I shrug my shoulders. "He asked if I wanted him to hurt Ira for blasting me."

"Do you?"

"No."

Marcus waits for me to say more; it's like he knows when I'm not done, he can sense it somehow. Maybe he just knows me that well.

"He said we should see Raven."

Marcus brushes a fly off of his arm. "Why's that?"

"I don't know. Isaac was real cryptic about it. You know how strange he can be."

Marcus nods before taking my hand in his. We start walking toward the barns.

"Tell me what's wrong."

"I can't stop thinking about her," I say. "The way she looked when we met in the ruins. So scared." He squeezes my hand. "Like she was afraid of hurting us."

"You know she was," Marcus says softly. "We know what she did. I've seen you standing out there at his grave every morning."

I sigh. "He did something to her. Made her that way." Marcus nods in agreement. "She wouldn't have ever hurt my father."

"She wouldn't have hurt Astrid either." He stops and pulls me to face him. "Maybe it's best to let her go. Maybe she can come back later, in a few months or years." His eyes search mine and I know he's looking for a way to fix this.

"I want to blame her for everything. I want to hate her." I look away from Marcus angry with myself for feeling this way.

"Then let yourself." He drops my hand. "Just don't forget who the real enemy is here." His hands glide up my arms, to my shoulders, massaging the tired muscles there before trailing up my neck and into my hair.

I look into his dark brown eyes, lost for a moment, seeing what he feels for me. Maybe I'm lucky. I might have never met him if none of this had happened.

"Who will help us?" I ask. "We're just a bunch of kids."

"I think," Marcus searches my face, "I think you just might save us all." He tips his head and kisses me.

Thirty-Six

Andromeda

"You think the train is a bad idea?" I ask Adam.

He shakes his head no as he starts the engine and checks the gauges. "We'll take it straight to Galena." He looks out the window at the Volker standing there. "Tell them to let us out."

I step onto the platform and, now that I'm in control of myself, I tell the Volker to let us out, lock up, and then forget we were ever there. Afterwards I sit, watching Crane warily as Adam gets the train moving and the Gateway opens.

Crane smiles at me. "I wasn't expecting this. Both of you turning on me."

Adam stands suddenly, moving toward Crane. He punches Crane in the face, knocking him out.

"I'm so sick of listening to his bullshit." Adam says as he sits down again.

PART TWO

Trains
Planes
And nothing will ever be the same

THIRTY-SEVEN

ANDROMEDA

I WONDER IF THE OCEAN IS STILL STAINED THAT DEEP RUSTED red? Norman Eckstein had seeded it with iron, pulled the carbon dioxide out of the atmosphere, changed our weather and we're still feeling the impact. Maybe it was really terrible, him doing that, maybe he did deserve to die for what he did.

Adam shifts in his seat.

"Last time we had to fly to Galena," I say.

"The rails connect there now." Adam leans forward and rests his elbows on his knees.

Crane opens his eyes. "You've stretched the rails, have you?" He moves his jaw and winces. "That's a good idea."

The tension in the cab of the train is thick.

I pull the crumpled piece of paper out of my pocket and read Ian's handwriting.

CODE: B. C. BERTRAND, PASSWORD: 15398GENESIS

I'm not sure if this gets me into Galena or if it gets me the world's data or the children they're keeping here. I fold it back up and tuck it into my pocket.

Crane suddenly begins laughing.

"Stop," Adam warns him.

"What do you think you will accomplish?" Crane looks at Adam. "You are nothing without me. You were nothing before me. Just a poor boy from a small town. I gave you everything. I made you. Billions of dollars were spent to make you."

Adam's fists clench.

"Stop it," I warn them both, not interested in witnessing a fist-fight within these tight quarters.

"And you," Crane turns to me. "You carry within you the genetic code that can take our species to another level. You've figured out so much already with the genome, DNA migration patterns, brain development. Galena is the best place to be more. You'll have the Human Genome Project at your fingertips, all that data. Decades of research from my labs."

He disgusts me.

"Evolution did not lead us here with a gentle hand," I say. "What you did was wrong. All of this is wrong."

Crane smiles. "Ah, Andromeda, evolution is imperfect and violent. We perish or we survive."

"Bullshit, you forced this."

"It was inevitable. I just hurried us all along."

"You overstepped."

"I'm not the one who overstepped." Crane smiles as he looks at Adam.

They're keeping something from me. We promised each other the day we walked away from that barn. I was hoping I could trust Adam, especially after all the time we just spent together, all of his heartfelt truths, the hugging, the kissing.

Crane tips toward the window and looks out.

"Have you ever seen the night sky so clear?" He seems enamored with the bright stars. "You could never see this so clearly with all of the light pollution. It's better now. The milky way is a beautiful sight on a clear night like this."

I look out the window nearest to me. He's right, the night sky is brighter than it's ever been and the cosmos are on full display. It's really beautiful.

"You know what they say," he smiles to himself, "to build a new world you've got to tear the old one down."

THE GALENA DISTRICT is so far out in the middle of nowhere that it doesn't need the electrified fence or brick walls. As the small airport and building come into view, I straighten in my seat and wait for Adam to stop the train.

The place is empty. Not a Volker in sight. Adam stops the train and we step out onto the platform.

"Let's go," Adam shoves Crane forward and we descend the steps.

Before we make it to the door Berkley steps out of the building, his dark black skin is a shocking contrast to the pale blueness of his eyes. He looks at the three of us. "Colonel Waters," he salutes Adam.

"Drop the act," Adam says.

Berkley's arms fall to his sides. "What do you want Adam? And why is he here?" Berkley is pointing at Crane. He looks at me. "And who is..." His brow wrinkles

"That's our dear Andromeda," Crane speaks up. "Isn't she lovely?"

"She looks different." Berkley squints before he gives me the once over one more time.

"I came back from the dead," I explain to him.

"Amazing." Berkley reaches out to touch me but Adam slaps his hand away.

"I think she wants your databases," Crane says.

"And I need a holding cell." I start walking toward the building. "To keep him in. Preferably one without windows and plenty of locks."

I reach for the door but it opens for me. A large Volker stands in the threshold, blocking my way.

Let me in, let me in, let me in.

He steps out of the way.

"What did you just do?" Berkley makes his way toward me. "How did you—" He searches my face.

"Volker." I snap my fingers and the man faces me. "Find five of your friends and dig me an eight-foot hole just outside that door." I point to the door we just walked through.

"A hole?" Berkley asks.

"For him." I point to Crane.

BERKLEY SHOWS me the room where they keep the servers. Since he doesn't have the nanocytes, he does everything I ask of him.

Crane trails behind us, his hands still tied behind his back. Adam keeps track of him while Berkley gives me an overview of the computer system. I pull the note from my pocket and the notebook from the waistband of my pants.

"What are you planning?" Berkley asks, as I look a few things over.

"Just searching for a few answers." I jot a few notes down in the notebook. I pull Ian's note out of my pocket and hold up the code and password. "What does this do?"

Berkley's eyes widen then narrow.

Crane makes a noise from the back of the room. "You gave it to them!" he yells at Berkley. "I'll kill you!"

Berkley smiles before he reaches out and touches the paper with his fingertip. "Did Ian give this to you?"

I nod.

"He was so innocent in all of this." Berkley shakes his head from side to side.

I don't want to discuss my dead husband. "What's it do?"

"That," Berkley points to the paper, "is the beginning to the end."

"Don't—" Crane threatens. Adam growls a threat at him to get Crane to shut up.

"What end?" I ask.

Berkley narrows his gaze on me. "I think you know." He motions to the large computer and rows of hard drives.

"Shuts it down?" I ask.

Berkley nods.

"No!" Crane yells.

I could do this. Get my answers and then shut it all down. That would put an end to the Funding Entities and their future plans. It's something to think about.

"Now." I stand. "Show me the children."

Berkley frowns. "Children?"

"Crystal River's satellites saw proof of them." I push him with the power the nanocytes gave me. "Bring me to the children. Now."

Berkley looks a bit panicked before he agrees.

It's a long walk outside, through a fenced courtyard, to a guarded and secure building. We take an elevator underground and when it finally stops and the silver doors open, my mouth gapes in surprise. There's a narrow hallway stretching out before us with glass cells on each side. Children sit alone in each of them. Segregated and secure. A few of them stand as we approach, some backing away into corners, others stepping forward with looks of defiance.

"Why are they locked up?" I ask, as I take a step toward them. Raising my hand, I feel the vibration of energy coming from the glass.

"They're dangerous. These are leaded glass enclosures. Electric fields enhance them so they can't get out." Berkley looks nervously to Crane.

"They're just children," I say. "How dangerous can they be?"

"You haven't seen what they can do," Berkley replies.

"Enough," Crane warns, a clip in his voice.

Berkley's mouth snaps shut.

I turn to face him. "I will put you in the ground," I warn Crane.

A young boy stands and walks to the wall of his cell. He's pale with a mop of dark tangled hair surrounding his face.

"Let him out," I demand.

Berkley looks nervous. "I don't think you want to do tha—"

"Let him out!"

Berkley walks to an electrical panel on the wall and after pressing a few buttons the doors to the cells open.

The boy jumps out and runs toward us. Raising his hand and pointing at Crane, a bright blue stream of electric current hits Crane in the chest, knocking him on the ground.

"Stop!" I shout.

The boy stops in his tracks and focuses on me.

"Oh, Andromeda," Crane groans from his awkward position on the floor. "How perfect. You can control them."

The boy standing in front of me can't be more than eight. I crouch down so I'm at eye level with him. Suddenly, I feel Adam's presence behind me.

"What's your name?" I ask the boy.

"Milo." His voice is hard and angry for someone so young.

"Milo, I've wanted to blast that man on more than one occasion. Now, tell my why you just did that."

The boy looks warily at Crane. It is a look of fear and hatred.

"He can't hurt you now," I promise him.

"He tried to make us bad," Milo's lip quivers. "The things he's done to us—" The boy breaks down in tears.

I move forward to embrace him, glance at Adam who knows all too well the kind of torture that Crane delivers.

Adam nods, like he's read my mind. He turns, drags Crane up off of the floor and shoves him out of the room. He takes Crane away so the children don't have to see him.

"Let the rest of them out," I tell Berkley.

He presses buttons and the rest of their doors swing open.

A girl who looks just like Milo runs to his side and grasps his arm.

"This is my twin sister, Niko," Milo says as he wipes his face dry with his hands.

"It's nice to meet you." I offer her a smile.

Niko holds her hand out, palm up, and a blinding red light encompasses her hand. "It will cut through anything," she tells me proudly.

"Interesting." I nod.

The other children get closer. Their ages look to range from around eight to teenager. They're all wearing the same clothing; gray jumpsuits and white slip-on shoes.

I look up and notice on the far end of the room there is a door open but the child never leaves.

"Who's back there?" I ask as I stand.

One of the boys moves and in the blink of an eye he's standing in front of the door, guarding it.

"That's Jake," Milo says. "He can run faster than light."

"Bring them out," I call to Jake. "Whoever it is, bring them here."

A tall girl who looks to be around twelve shakes her head, her dark hair swaying. "She won't come out."

"That's Claire," Milo says. "She can manipulate fire."

On queue, Claire's arms light up with flames.

A tall boy with dark hair turns his head suddenly. "You're scaring her. I can hear her heartbeat speeding up with fear."

Milo jabs his thumb at the boy who just spoke. "That's Justice. He can hear everything."

I look at Justice. "Who's scared?" I ask.

He nods toward the cell that still holds the child. "Jesse. You're scaring her."

I shake my head. "But I didn't do anything."

A young boy with blonde hair raises both of his hands and all of the cell doors slam shut.

"That's Max," Milo says. "He can move things."

"I told you not to let them out," Berkley says from behind me. "You're going to wish you never did."

"Shut up." I shout over my shoulder to him. I focus on the children once more. "Where are your parents?"

They're all silent.

A girl with short dark hair steps forward. "My name's Elin." She holds her hand out and I move to shake it but a sly smile crosses her lips and she shakes her head from side to side. "Jesse won't come out easily." Elin closes her eyes, fists her hand and exhales a deep breath. Something above her palm starts to glisten. I watch as tiny crystals collect, stick together and form into a smooth ball. "It's ice." She smiles at me before twisting her palm and dropping the smooth ball on the floor. It breaks into a thousand pieces and begins to melt.

It's no wonder they were being hidden here, and Berkley's apprehension to letting them out can be understood. But these children don't deserve to be locked up like this.

I step around the children and make my way toward the last open cell that holds the girl.

"Jesse?" I ask.

The boy named Jake stands in front of her door, his arms crossed. "She'll come out when she's ready. She doesn't like new people."

"Why?" I ask as I lean around him to get a good look at the slight girl who is curled up on the bed.

"Milo already told you, they made us bad. And they did bad things to us." He widens his stance. "I won't let you hurt her."

I focus on Jake. "I'm not going to hurt her. I'm going to get you children out of here. You don't belong locked up like this." I turn and get a good glance at Berkley as he steps backward toward the elevator.

"They want us to be bad." Jake glares at me. "They made us do things."

"Whatever they have told you, forget it," I tell Jake as I take another step toward him. "Now, let me see her."

Let me see her, let me see her, let me see her.

Jake steps to the side.

"Jesse?" I ask as I step into the cell.

The girl lifts her head. Her eyes are dark, almost completely black. With her black hair and alabaster skin it's an eerie combination.

She extends her legs off of the bed and stands. Her arms and legs look too long for her body but she moves graceful and unhurried.

"I used to be able to fly." Jesse speaks barely above a whisper.

"You don't have to say anything," Jake says from outside the cell.

I stand in my place and wait for the girl to tell me more.

Her cheeks pale before she turns her back to me. One long arm collects her hair and pulls it to her front. "I could fly," she says again, gripping the top of her shirt. "But they took them away from me." She pulls her shirt up revealing her bare back to me.

I swallow hard, unable to control my reaction. Her pale back is marred with two sickle shaped scars extending from her shoulder blades down to the middle of her back.

My hands grip into fists at my sides. "What did they do to you?" I whisper as I am reminded of the creatures at Wolf Creek.

She drops her shirt, brushes her hair back over her shoulder, then turns to face me. "They said it wasn't the right time." Her eyes widen and glisten. "They took them." She looks away, ashamed. "Sometimes I can still feel them." Her right arm moves to brush the empty space behind her shoulder. "I know they're gone but I can still feel them there haunting me."

"That's enough," Jake says from outside the cell. "She doesn't need this. They've hurt her enough."

I nod in agreement before holding out my hand to Jesse. "Come with me. Let's get you all out of here."

BERKLEY STANDS stiff in the elevator as we take the children above ground. I find Adam and Crane standing near the fencing. I walk toward them, a million questions on my mind. He's gone too far with the Reformation, the nanocytes, the creatures in Wolf Creek, these children—all of this is too much.

"Why would you do this, Crane?" I ask as I approach.

"People need hope and they require fear to stay in line," he replies.

"Of all the bullshit—"

"Have you checked on your own children?" he asks.

"What?" My heart thuds in my chest.

"You think these are the only children?" Crane smiles. "I've been at this longer than you've been alive. Perfecting it all. There's more. They walked right past you before you had a chance to boil their blood in the Pasture."

"My children." I didn't notice anything different about my children when I left them at the Pasture. They looked the same, older but normal. I turn and glance back at the children who are enjoying the outdoors, having been freed from their cells. They look normal as well albeit pale and Jesse looks haunted.

Unease fills me. "I need to talk to Crystal River," I tell Adam. "Right now."

Thirty-Eight

Catalina

"Crane unleashed his experiments into the world," I tell Marcus. "That's what Mr. Crossbender told me. Do you think we're his experiments?"

Marcus shakes his head and sits down next to me. A bonfire burns in front of us, tall and bright. Despite the heat it's putting off, I shiver.

"Elvis didn't think Crane was in on it, but now," he shrugs, "we knew the guy was bad news when we were kids."

"What's he done to us?" I look down at my hands, wondering when I'm going to turn into someone else.

Marcus takes my hand in his. "We're still the same, just a bit different." He touches my fingers softly with each of his. "Did you think I was all that different after I found out what I could do?"

"No," I answer.

I look up at the stars, unsure of what to do next. I've been trying for weeks to figure out if I have a power like the others do. But nothing has come.

"What do you think would happen if people knew about us?" I ask Marcus. "If we just... I know it sounds crazy but what if we just evolved this way without the help of Elvis? The rest of the world would lock us up and throw away the key. We're freaks now."

"He's already locked us up." Marcus spreads his arms wide, indicating the expanse of the Pasture. "It's already been done to us."

He's right. "But we're safe here."

"For how long, Lina?" He scoots closer to me. "How long before something happens and we're no longer safe? There are thousands of Survivors, Residents in each of the Districts, the other side of the world we know nothing about. And... the Swamp people."

Our time outside the gates of a District was the most free I had ever felt.

"What did you tell those Swamp men?" I ask. "I woke up and you were talking with their leader."

Marcus clears his throat. "He was just curious, so I told him stories, just... you know, about the things we learned in school about the sun and the moon. Kid stuff." Marcus shrugs.

Curiosity, it's dangerous just like Glane said. "What else did you tell them?"

"I told him that we had a home here, but we were not free like his people."

I pluck a blade of grass out of the ground and wind it around my finger. "What did he think of that?"

"He didn't seem to know what to say," Marcus replies with a shrug.

In the moments of silence that follow Lex walks up to us, his now white shock of hair distracting, even in the dark.

"What's up?" Marcus asks him.

"They need you guys back at home." Lex shoves his hands in his pockets. He does that a lot, hides his hands. They can heal people; cuts, scrapes, bruises. The only problem is that it drains him. Sometimes he touches a person or an animal without thinking about it and drops to the ground after having healed an injury or illness that they weren't aware of.

"Did you find a way to heal her?" I ask, hopeful.

Lex nods and leads us back to the house. He's been trying to fix her since we arrived a few days ago, but he can't do too much without risking his own life.

Marcus and I get up and follow him.

When we get to the house, everyone is crammed into Astrid's room. Cash has been there the entire time, a worried look on his face. Now he sits on the bed with her.

"What's wrong with her?" I ask as I sit in a rocking chair next to the windows.

Cash is holding Astrid's hand and his lips are moving but I can't hear what he's saying.

"She's waking up," Raven says as he stands next to me.

"Why now?" I ask. "Was it Lex?"

Raven leans to whisper in my ear. "Mom's far enough away to stop affecting her. And Lex helped. And Cash."

Astrid's eyes flutter open and she locks them on Cash smiling softly before looking around the rest of the room.

"You're all staring at me," she says, her voice weak.

"That's because you've been out of it for days." Cash touches her cheek and Astrid rolls to her side.

"Is there something we can get for you, young lady?" Elvis asks.

"Something to eat." Her stomach growls loud enough for us all to hear. "And a drink."

Elvis leaves the room and I hear the floorboards creak as he walks to the kitchen.

After talking with her for a few moments, we all cycle out of the room and give her time to wake up. Before I leave her bedside, Astrid grabs my hand to stop me.

"She didn't mean to do it," Astrid says, her voice weak. Unsure of what she's talking about, I just look at her. "Your mother. She didn't mean to do it. She couldn't help it." Astrid swallows hard. "I've never felt anything like it, so strong."

"Ash," Cashel warns.

"Cash," Astrid replies. "I think you need to go help Elvis in the kitchen."

"I'm not leaving your side."

"Go. Now." She narrows her eyes at him.

With a reluctant motion, Cash stands and leaves the room.

"He's going to be insufferable now, isn't he?" Astrid says as she watches him go.

"He hasn't left this room," I tell her.

"He feels guilty." She plucks at the blanket covering her. "He couldn't help it. No one could." Astrid shifts to sit up. "I just wanted you to know..." She glances at me with hesitation. "Because I can feel what you're feeling. The confusion, loss, all of it. She was reluctant, Lina, your mom. She was so happy to see you but so scared of hurting you." Astrid pats her hand over her heart. "She was really hurting. I think that's what made her do it. She couldn't control it, the pain of losing you, all of us, it was too much." Astrid reaches out and grasps my hand. "I've never felt anything as strong as her. I can feel you struggling with it all now." She squeezes. "If you ever get to a point where you need a break, Cash can help you."

Cashel the shield, I remember his numbing warmth that comforted me when we were attacked on our travels here.

"Sure." I start to leave but Astrid grabs my arm.

"It hurts, burns hotter than anything you'll ever experience. You're mother almost killed me and I forgive her. You'll find it in yourself to forgive her as well. I know it."

A strange sensation starts in my stomach and spreads, tingling in my fingertips.

Astrid smiles softly. "It's your turn."

"My—"

The sound of Elvis and Cash returning to the room are drowned out by a shout, the sound of plates crashing to the floor and then the solid ting of the metal tray smacking me in the head and knocking me out.

THIRTY-NINE

This place is empty now that Crane has been gone. There's just myself and Ruiz, the kids, the Residents and their Factions. The District is overrun with Guardians. They used to hide out at the Pasture but now they roam the streets. And then there's my daughter, a child I thought I'd never see again. She has her own army of Militia men that never let her out of their sight. They know how special she is, what she can do. She showed me what would happen.

"There's a front of Survivors headed our way," Richard Ruiz twists the diamond-rimmed watch on his wrist.

"We're fine," I tell him. Survivors aren't a threat to us, not now. The fence is at full power and the Volker are a hundred strong. The tree line surrounding the District has grown in so thick that we can barely be seen.

Richard rubs his face and stares out the window at the lake in the distance. "We're not fine."

"Why's that?"

"They're looking for Christian Whitmarsh." He turns to look at me.

"Huge bounty. Food, fuel, a place at one of the Militia compounds. Guaranteed survival for years."

"And you know this how?"

Ruiz rubs his chin. "Got a man on the outside."

"What do you think we should do?" I ask.

Richard touches the glass with his fingertip. "I'd say call in help, but I don't think it will matter."

He's seen what Norah showed him. He knows who will come and who will run and who will ignore us.

"Everyone knows who he is now," Richard says. "They know that Adam and Christian are the same man."

I nod and turn to the Volker who is in the room with us. "I want a count on every weapon and every bullet inside the walls of this District."

The man nods then leaves.

"You already know that," Richard says, sliding his finger down the windowpane, making a squeaking noise. "And you know they are loyal to Crane. He spent a lot of effort brainwashing the Volker."

I turn and pull out the rolled up architectural plans I found in Crane's office. "I know. I just didn't want him seeing this," I say as I unroll the paper. Pointing to the corner of the Pasture where the ruins are, I say, "The kids came through a tunnel under here."

Richard moves closer. "What are you thinking?"

"If the Survivors breach our walls we need to find another way out. There's a few hundred Residents, a hundred Volker, the people at the Pasture..." I search the map like I've done for the past few days.

Richard points to the large body of water drawn on the map. "We could take boats out, cross the lake. Canada's empty. Reformation back-fired there."

"No." I shake my head. "Not enough boats for everyone."

"You're looking for another tunnel. You're not going to find anything on this map." Richard stands next to me. "Those tunnels aren't on any maps. You have to know that."

Of course I know that. I'm looking for a place where they might be able to put in one of those tunnels.

I glance at Richard. He's finally stopped wearing the full suit. Now it's just a button-down shirt and slacks. He dropped the act when Adam took off with Crane. I think my sister was there too. I couldn't see Andie, but something that Norah showed me leads me to think that she was there. I barely recognized her but it had to be her, there was no other explanation.

"He did very bad things to us, you know?" Ruiz says.

I nod. "He did very bad things to my sister as well." I still can't forget the way she looked when I first showed up here. Broken and bruised.

"Well, Norah has shown you what else he's done. We need to prepare."

Ruiz nods. "Yes. I suppose we do."

He sets his hands on the edge of the map and together we form a plan that my daughter has already informed us will go to shit in ten minutes flat. But we have nothing else to do at the moment, and planning gives us a sense of being able to change something about the future.

We fortify the two entrances to the District with Volker, contact the nuclear engineers and make sure the reactor is up to par. By the end, all hands are on deck. As long as we can keep the electricity flowing through the fencing, we could make it out of this in one piece.

FORTY

Catalina

"Lina…" Marcus's voice is worried. "Lina, wake up."

"What happened?" Lex's voice comes next.

There is a pause and the room is silent before Astrid answers. "Metal pan hit her in the head."

"How the hell did that happen?" Mark's voice is full of anger and his hands grip my shoulders harder. It hurts.

"Let go, Marcus," Astrid warns. "You're hurting her."

His large hands release me and I open my eyes, only slightly since the light hurts my head.

"Sorry," he mutters and the floorboards creak as he moves away from me.

"She only hit her head?" Lex asks, apprehensive.

"Yes," I whisper. "A metal pan hit my head." I move to sit up. "I'm fine," I say as I open my eyes the rest of the way. Lex watches me, his hands in his pockets. I know he's nervous about touching me. Healing a head injury could knock him out for hours. "You don't have to. I'll be okay."

Lex presses his lips together before nodding and leaving the room.

As I sit up I look around and find Astrid sitting on her bed, eating. Cash is sitting next to her. Marcus is a few feet away from me. Elvis is in the doorway. Raven and Norah are standing next to the window.

As Marcus helps me stand, Norah steps closer, bending to pick the metal pan up off of the floor. Her chubby fingers gripping the edge, she smiles at Raven before raising her hands in the air and throwing the pan at me with all of her strength.

My heartbeat kicks up, my eyes widen. I move my arm to block it, but... instead of the pan hitting me, it hovers in the air for a few seconds before dropping to the ground.

Norah's smile widens. "Your time has come."

"Wh—what do you mean?" I look at my hands, turning them over in front of me.

The room is silent.

"I did that?" I ask.

Raven nods from his place near the window.

"Metal," I whisper.

Marcus steps toward me and, reaching out, he brushes my hair away from my face. I feel his fingers skim over the bruise on my forehead. "You sure you're okay?" he asks.

"I don't know." I stare at the pan.

Elvis shifts on his feet from the doorway. "Maybe you should take her outside for some fresh air, young man." He tips his head at Marcus before leaving the room.

"I think that's a good idea." I wipe my hands on my shirt and start walking.

I leave the house, run down the porch steps, and make my way toward the fire that Marcus and I were sitting near earlier. I feel like I'm in a daze, remembering all that just happened.

"Lina." Marcus is behind me.

I turn to face him, holding my hands out to ward him off. I'm not sure what to think. Everyone else just dealt with their change as it came, but now, knowing full well what I can do, I feel... strange—embarrassed even.

"No. Stay away," I warn him.

"Why would I want to do that?" He steps closer.

"I..." My jaw quivers and the pressure of tears threaten.

Marcus smiles and looks at his feet for a moment, it's a boyish gesture, one that reminds me that we are still so young. "Is it because you're no longer normal?" He focuses on me again. "Is it because you stopped that metal pan from hitting your head that you think I might not want to be around you any longer?"

I feel a tear slide down my cheek.

He grips his hand into a fist and holds it out. "Did you find me any less likeable when you found out what I could do?"

I shake my head. "But all of you can do something so human. Strength, healing, all of it... all of those powers are so different from this." I look down at my hands again.

Marcus's lip tips up as he steps closer. "I don't know about that, Lina. Metal. Metallic elements are everywhere. Tiny bits are in the soil, machines, weapons, vehicles, buildings, heck, it's what surrounds the Districts. All of that is without even considering the magnetic poles of the earth and how you react to them. But I get a feeling that you've always been able to sense them. You've always been good with directions and maps." He steps closer again, taking my hands in his. "If anything you're stronger than all of us."

I grip his hands in mine. "So you don't think I'm a freak?"

"No." He shakes his head and smiles before tugging me close and wrapping me in a tight embrace. He grips me so close to him that I can barely breathe. I feel his breath on my neck as he buries his face there, his hands rubbing my back.

We stand like this until the nearby fire dies down and the evening turns into night. The sound of footsteps break the silence. Someone is running toward us. Marcus lets go of me but before he can do anything, I sense it; a large piece of scrap metal being hurled through the air at us. I stop it midair and drop it to the ground.

"Awesome!" Ira shouts before running away.

Marcus takes a step like he's going to run after him. "I will beat the stuffing out of you!" he yells after Ira. "Punk!"

"She's one of us now!" Ira hollers, his voice sounding winded and tinted with amusement as he runs away.

FORTY-ONE

ANDROMEDA

ADAM WALKS WITH ME BACK TO THE ROOM WITH THE servers, Berkley and Crane follow.

"I want to talk to Crystal River," I tell Berkley.

He picks up a phone and dials.

"How is it that all these phones still work?" I ask since the question has been gnawing at me since all of this started.

Berkley looks to Crane as though he's asking permission to tell me. It seems dumb since he already verified that I have the codes to shut everything down.

"It's a combination of satellite and cell towers," Crane says. "You should know. You're the next generation."

"Of what?" I ask.

"Me."

"I am not the next generation of you." I turn my back to Crane and accept the phone from Berkley.

"Hello?" I ask.

"Andromeda?" Emanuel's voice is on the other end.

"I need you to focus your satellites on the Pasture," I tell him.

"Sure." The sound of keystrokes in the background and hushed voices are all I hear for a few moments. "What are you looking to see?"

"I found the children in Galena," I tell him. "Crane says there's more in Phoenix."

"Oh." All sound on the other end ceases for a second.

"Have you seen something?" I ask.

"I'll patch the video through to where you are."

One of the computer screens in front of us flickers for a moment before we can clearly see an aerial view of the Pasture. Lina and Marcus are standing near the open fields talking. Ira stands not too far away, he raises his hand and a bright white bolt of energy flies off of his hand and crashes into Lina.

"What the..." I whisper in amazement.

Another phone on the desk rings and Adam answers it.

He turns to me and holds the phone out. "You're a popular person today."

"I gotta go," I say to Emanuel. "Thanks." I hang up the one receiver and take the other from Adam.

"It's Crossbender," Adam says.

"George?" I ask.

"Andie. We have a problem," he answers.

Don't I know it? Things that I thought could never happen are happening and I always seem to be in the wrong place at the wrong time.

"Maryam took a chopper. She's headed to Phoenix. After you left she always threatened to take the children underground. I think maybe it's because we lost the one and she never got over it, but..." He exhales a frustrated breath. "She's out of control. She's gotten worse since the kids left. My sources say she's been talking about getting them back, making them hers." George is talking fast and there's rustling going on in the background. "She knows about the other missing children I've been searching for. She has some twisted idea of adopting them all."

"I found the missing children," I tell him. "They're fine. A little scared after what Crane put them through but I think they'll recover."

"Oh, good. That's so good." Something slams in the background.

I grip the phone. "George, what are you doing?"

"I thought putting her in charge of the Underland would keep her mind off of it all."

"What's the Underland?" I glance at Adam.

"No time to explain. I'm going after her." Something else slams, louder this time.

"We can go—"

"It's not going to help. She took a bomb." The beating of helicopter blades starts.

"What!" Terror grips my chest.

"I can't explain now. Just... Andie, just meet me in Phoenix. And tell Adam that Jenn went with her. He'll know what that means." And then there is silence on the other end of the line.

I look up at Adam. "Did he tell you?"

Adam nods. George must've told him some of it while I was on the other line with Emanuel.

"He said Jenn went with her."

"Okay." Adam crosses his arms over his chest.

"Who's Jenn?" I ask.

"You'll recognize her when you see her," he promises. "So what's it going to be? Where do we go from here?"

I focus on the computer in front of me. The world's data, the answers to so much that I desire; solutions, decades of data.

"This is the one thing I wanted," I whisper to myself. "A cure, an end."

"It's not the only thing," Adam says as he watches me.

He's right. I've wanted more: safety for my children, peace, control over my life again. I might have achieved a small bit of that for them before the Reformation. But now, I doubt I will ever see any of it. I know what I have to do. There are only so many things we can control, and there's only so many ways to break the control that the Funding Entities have over us.

"Destroy it," I command Berkley and his crew of Volker.

Destroy it, destroy it, destroy it all.

Crane's face pales before twisting angrily.

Berkley moves to the keyboard and pulls up a red screen. He types in the code and password. After a moment it all fades to black.

"You know what this means," Adam says as he steps away from the computer system.

"Yes." It means we'll have to start from scratch, from leftover books and scavenged hard-drives and knowledge from our elders. These people, the Funding Entities, they can't be trusted with the world's data. At least this way I can give a tiny bit of power back to the people who have survived this.

The Volker begin tearing at the rows of mainframe storage. Electrical cords are ripped from their connection points; storage drives are pulled from their towers and stomped on or thrown against the cement walls. It's not long before the screens go black and the hum of electricity that occupies the room comes to a halt.

"Let's go," I tell Adam as I make my way out of the room. "We have to get the children and get home."

"And him." Adam tips his head to Crane.

"Against my better judgment, bring him."

FORTY-TWO

CATALINA

I WAKE TO SOMEONE SHAKING ME VIOLENTLY.

"Wake up! Wake up!" Astrid's voice shouts.

My eyes flash open and I take in her worried features. "What's wrong?"

"Something's coming." She stands and moves to wake Marcus. "We need to move." She's dressed in the gear we came here in. Black cargo pants, shirt, jacket and boots. She looks like she's ready for war.

"What's coming?" I rub my eyes.

Astrid stills as she turns toward me. "An awful lot of angry people."

I scramble out of bed and get dressed as quick as I can. "What kind of angry people? Residents, Survivors, who?"

"All of them," she says before running out of the room.

I hear the door of the other bedroom slam open and the sounds of her rousing Raven and Isaac. I'm not sure why I bothered asking her who was coming. Norah showed me, she showed all of us. The only problem was that my role in all of it was fuzzy. There were people that she couldn't place, rogues whose destiny ebbs and flows, she couldn't get a grasp on them. And since those people were my mother and Adam, she couldn't get a grasp on my role, she could only show me a hint of what was to come.

Marcus runs in as I'm tying my boots. "Are you ready?" he asks.

I stand. "Ready as I'll ever be."

He takes my hand, kisses me quickly on the lips, and then we're off running.

We meet Elvis at the barn with the shooting range, he's digging everything out, handing us weapons—bullets, bows, arrows, spears; everything they've ever trained us with here. He stops when his hands land on a small bow, crafted for the hands of a child. Elvis runs his fingers over the worn wood. I trained on that when I was young, it was one of the last birthday presents I received after the Reformation.

"Norah could use it," I suggest, loading a magazine into my handgun. Not that she would need it, she has an entire Militia of men who would give their lives to ensure her survival.

Elvis smiles before gripping the tiny weapon. "Guess she could." He turns and makes his way for the door. "Lets get moving."

"We aren't staying here?" Ira asks.

"No." Elvis shakes his head. "We're going to Headquarters. It's safer there. Sam's orders."

"What about the farm? The animals, the gardens?" Lex asks.

"Reckon they'll still be here after all of this." Elvis nods. "We'll have a place to come home to. Be thankful for that and get moving." Elvis ruffles Lex's hair as he passes.

We pile into three black SUVs, Norah and her group of Militia men and her pet goat as well. I can't remember the last time I was at Headquarters, I think it was when I was a little girl. Blithe would watch me while my mom met with Crane. My stomach churns as we leave the Pasture and head to town. Those are memories I do not want to relive.

The winding roads are in disrepair and the ride is a bumpy one until we make it to the outskirts of town. Inside these walls everything is as though there was never a Reformation. Streets and houses are tidy, lawns are cared for, community gardens thrive, people mill about as though there were no threat to their lives at this moment.

Marcus squeezes my hand. "They don't know what's coming," he whispers.

"Do we?" I ask.

As Elvis drives, the streets flood with Volker and an announcement plays over the town. Marcus rolls his windows down so we can hear.

"All Residents return to your homes immediately. Do not venture outside until you have been ordered to do so. Everything is under control. Return to your homes."

Without stopping to question why, all of the Residents begin moving. None ask a Volker what's going on, they simply follow the orders issued. They don't bear arms to assist us, they only go inside their homes and close the doors obediently.

"Brainwashing at its best," Marcus mutters from my side.

"Not just that," Elvis speaks up from the driver's seat. "Missing the part of their brain that makes them want to ask why."

His eyes meet mine in the rearview mirror. This is what my mother and Crane did to these people. So easily it could have been us.

<hr>

ONCE WE REACH HEADQUARTERS, Sam takes us to the Volker Headquarters in the middle section of the large building. There are twelve television screens each with a live feed of the District and the entry points of the gate.

Norah makes herself comfortable in one of those office chairs that spin, twirling herself as though it's no big deal that we are about to be attacked. The goat named Jill settles under a desk near her and nods off to sleep.

All of our eyes are on the screens.

It starts with the Volker moving toward the fence and taking aim. Then the Survivors come into view. They're not just bedraggled people on a mission, these are Militia much like the ones surrounding Norah. But the ones on the screen are wearing different colored clothing.

"Should we do something?" Marcus asks, leaning his hands on a desk near us.

Sam shakes his head. "Norah showed us what will happen. This is how it starts. You've seen it. They're looking for Adam. No point in getting them even more excited when he's not here."

Marcus nods in agreement. "I just feel like I should be out there."

"Me too," Isaac walks up behind us, startling me.

The Survivor Militia start throwing things at the fence. They start with sticks and rocks.

Within minutes a row of trees behind the Survivors shudders with movement. The Swamp men are here.

Ira stands in the back of the room, his fingertips crackling with controlled energy. It seems Isaac isn't the only one who wants to get in on the action.

The Survivors upgrade to larger objects to throw at the fence: logs, bigger rocks, someone throws a dead animal on the fence—it looks like a squirrel. And then suddenly it all stops. The Survivors turn around, then part down then middle. The Volker take aim and fire but it does nothing to stop the truck that speeds head on into the fence.

Our first line of defense is broken.

The man inside the truck opens the door and falls out onto the fencing that's underneath the tires of the vehicle. Since the electric current is still running through it, the man fries to a crisp.

I look away and cover my mouth, the image of that man being electrocuted to death forever in my mind.

"It's getting good now," Isaac steps closer to the screen. "They're going to start coming in."

"Wait," Sam warns.

The Volker at the gates start shooting but the Survivors have weapons. The men and women fight as a flood of Survivors enter the District. And now we can see that there are more than just Militia. There are haggard Survivors, eager for a chance to collect the bounty on Adam's head.

The first row of Volker are overrun and the Survivors continue on down the main road that leads into town.

"What should we do?" Astrid asks.

"Nothing." Cash takes both of her hands, shielding her from the onslaught. "We can go somewhere else. You don't need to see this, Ash."

Astrid shakes her head. "I feel like I need to."

Cash leans down to her ear and I hear him whisper, "Are you okay?"

She nods. "Just keep doing it." She grips his hand in hers and focuses on the screens once more.

We watch as the Survivors run down the street. At the fence line, the trees shudder once more before dark figures leave the shadows. They start with the man that fell out of the truck. One of the Swamp men lassos the dead man with a rope and pulls him off of the electrified metal, dragging him to the darkness of the forest.

They continue, climbing over the truck just as the Survivors did, but they don't swarm toward town, instead they start dragging the bodies away. Dead Volker, dead Survivors, they take everything that once had a heartbeat.

"So gross," Raven whispers from behind me.

"When do we start to get worried?" Ira asks.

"When they cross the bridges and breach the campus," Sam reminds him.

Isaac seems edgy; he paces the room, cracking his knuckles as he does.

Norah suddenly stops spinning in her chair. "She's here."

"Who?" I ask.

Raven makes eye contact with me and says, "Mom."

"You all need to go to the..." Norah points out the window to the open space behind the building.

"The quad?" Sam asks.

"Yes." Norah nods. "There's plenty of space out there for this."

Isaac and Ira are the first ones to run out of the building. Marcus and I follow with Elvis and Mr. Ruiz behind us. We push through the glass doors and run down the cement steps, round the building and come to a stop in the middle of the quad. Everyone else leaves the building; Norah and her goat and the Militia men. Sam stays behind to keep his eye on the camera feeds.

My heart thunders in my chest with the anticipation of what comes next. I've seen some of it, just not all of it.

From out here we can hear the shouts of the Survivors as they make their way closer.

But then it suddenly stops and a strange noise begins. A collective growling that echoes throughout the District.

"Guardians." Raven smiles.

FORTY-THREE

ANDROMEDA

WE COME UPON A WAR BETWEEN MEN AND BEASTS. THE Survivors and the Guardians are viciously battling each other just a few miles from Headquarters.

Go away, go away, go away. I urge the Survivors that are still standing. *Christian Whitmarsh is already dead. You will not find him here.*

The Survivors stop in their tracks.

Go away, go away, go away.

They start walking in the direction they came, their agenda forgotten.

"Nice trick," Crane says from the passenger seat of the Volker SUV we took from near the train platform. The children from Galena wouldn't sit anywhere near him and Adam wanted him within punching distance. So Crane got to sit shotgun.

"Be quiet," Adam warns him as he puts the vehicle into gear and speeds toward campus.

"Are you sure they're there?" I ask from the backseat.

"Only logical place," Adam says. "The Pasture was empty and Sam's a smart guy, he'd get them as far away from danger as he could. Headquarters is the best spot."

I hope he's right.

"Who's Sam?" Milo asks from the cargo area of the SUV. Not trusting the kids to drive themselves around the Phoenix District, we packed all eight of them in the vehicle with us.

"My brother," I reply.

"Can he control people too?" Niko asks.

"No," I shake my head. "He's completely normal." Completely normal but most likely completely broken after all that has happened.

Adam barrels down the campus roads before coming to a stop in front of the Phoenix District Headquarters, squealing the tires.

A figure appears from behind the building, running in our direction. As I get out of the vehicle I recognize Elvis.

"How did you get here so fast?" Elvis asks as Adam pulls Crane from the passenger seat.

I open the back hatch of the SUV and let the kids out.

"Took the train," Adam says. "At full-bore it's faster than a chopper."

Elvis nods. "Thought you weren't supposed to run them like that, bad for the parts?"

"It's probably the last time. So who cares?" Adam's tone is grim.

Crane makes a noise of disgust at this revelation.

"Right," Elvis replies. "Well, the little one has been expecting you for some time now." He does a double take when he sees the kids we brought. "Who are they?"

"Helpers," Adam replies. "From Galena."

"Who is the little one?" I ask.

Elvis tips his head. "Your niece. Norah."

"Oh." I glance at Adam and avoid Crane's gaze. "Can we see her?"

"As long as you've got yourself under control. Don't want anything happening like what happened with Astrid. Poor girl was out for days." Elvis starts walking.

We follow him around the building to the quad where everyone is waiting, it seems for us.

I recognize Lina first. "Mom?" She takes a hesitant step toward me.

This time I don't try to hide myself from her. Instead, I walk to her as fast as I can and pull her into my arms. Seeing Raven near us, I reach for him, pulling him into the hug with us.

I look around and see Astrid and Cashel standing there. "I'm sorry," I tell Astrid.

"I know." She smiles but keeps her distance.

And then a tall man steps forward. I let go of Raven and Lina and stumble away from them, running into Adam as I go.

Holy crap, it's Ian!

Adam moves to shield me.

"Mom?" Ian asks as he tips his head to the side in a questioning motion. "I thought you were dead?"

Wait, mom? Adam turns just slightly and gives a hesitant glance from the corner of his eye.

The man, who I think is Ian back from the dead, crosses his arms, smirks and tips his head down. It's intimidating. There is a flash of something in his eyes, something dark and... wrong.

"Mom?" he says again. "You don't recognize me. It's me, Isaac."

"Isaac." I whisper.

He's the spitting image of his father, younger though, like when I met him in college. Bits of *feeling* start churning. Not wanting to lose control I push it away. I push it away, plaster a smile on my face and hug the son who looks like a clone of my late husband.

Isaac's body stiffens and he pulls away. "Who are they?" his gaze is drawn on the children we brought here with us.

"They're from Galena," I say.

"The bad kids?" Lina asks. "Mr. Crossbender said there were bad kids. Like us but evil." She looks hesitantly at them.

"They're not bad." I motion for them kids to come closer. "They're here to help."

We introduce them and soon the reunion turns into a show of who can do what. Ira is quick to show off, but Lex nods shyly with his hands shoved in his pockets.

Before much else can happen, we hear the beating of helicopter blades in the distance.

"They're coming," Adam warns.

A goat bellows and I turn to see a small girl who can't be older than three with her hand on the goat, watching us all.

"I still can't see what you're going to do," she says, her voice young and sweet.

I crouch down. "Are you Norah?"

"Yes." She looks toward me, her cherub face a mixture between Sam and Blithe's handsome features.

"Andie!" Sam's tall figure leaves the back door to Headquarters and runs toward us. He stops dead in his tracks. "You look weird."

"Thanks," I reply with wry tone. "That's really no way to greet your sister after she's come back from the dead."

"I'd say more, but... they're here." Sam nods toward the sky. I catch a sadness in his eyes before I look away, and I am sure that what we lost has caused it.

We can see the helicopters now. Dark and much smaller than the Chinooks I last saw at Hanford. They look out of place in a portion of the sky that hasn't seen aircraft in quite some time. There's one headed straight for us, and another following close behind.

"The Crossbenders are here," Lina says as she stands next to me.

The other children stand side-by-side as if waiting for something to happen.

Then the Guardians show up. A dense dark line of the creatures advances from across the quad. They spread out to a half-circle, watching and waiting. There must be hundreds of them.

The first chopper hovers above the ground before landing. When the door opens, Maryam Crossbender steps out. She's holding a large box in her hands.

"She wants the children," Norah says from behind me.

The way Maryam walks, it's so different from how I knew her in Hanford. She was demure, quiet, sweet even. Now she walks with purpose.

A tall blond woman steps out of the chopper after her. And something seems familiar about her. She smiles, focused on Adam. And then I recognize her—the female Volker, this must be the Jenn that George mentioned.

"Children," Maryam starts. "I think now is the time to point out what a mistake it was letting you leave the Underland. We saw the mess created by the Survivors. The Phoenix District is no longer safe. Come with me."

Marcus steps forward. "No."

Maryam smiles before opening her box and tossing a large black object on the ground. "You were assigned to the ARU, Marcus. You know what that is." Her eyes scan the crowd, merely glancing over me as though she doesn't recognize you.

"We're not leaving," Lina says.

"You're not staying here unsupervised either," Maryam replies. "Hanford is under control. Your lives are no longer threatened there."

"There's plenty of supervision." Sam steps forward, toward the black object that Maryam threw on the ground.

Maryam scoffs. "Because you're their uncle you think you can raise them? They need a real family."

"I'm the best they've got right now," he responds. In that moment I am so proud of my little brother, standing tall in full Volker garb. He is the epitome of power in this place. And I know there is no one better for the children to be with.

Marcus grabs Lina's arm and pulls her away. "Stay away from that."

"Why?" Lina glances at the object. "What is it?"

Marcus looks at Adam but the beating of helicopter blades drowns everything out.

The second helicopter lands and George Crossbender runs out of it and toward us all.

"Maryam!" He stomps to her side and grabs her arm. "This is unacceptable." He pushes his glasses up with his index finger. Lowering his voice, he says, "There are rules and you're not following a single one of them."

Maryam rips herself out of George's grasp and stumbles backward.

"Things must not be well in paradise." Crane chuckles.

"Shut up." Adam warns him.

"I want them." Maryam's voice is agitated and sharp. "To replace what we lost. They're orphans after all. There's no reason we can't bring them back. No one loves them. No one cares for them."

"No." George reaches for her again. "It's not right."

"Why isn't it right?" Maryam scans the crowd of bystanders again. "They have no parents. We can be good to them. No one wants them anyway. Look at what they can do. No one wants them!"

George grabs Maryam by her upper arms and gives her a shake. "You can't do that. There are rules, guidelines you swore to uphold. If we can't do it right then what does that say about all we've worked to achieve?"

"I don't care." Maryam is shaking her head. "I don't care about any of it. Why should she get to keep them? Why should she be special? He didn't let us keep ours and she had so many."

"Maryam..." George's face slackens, memories softening the hardness and disappointment in his wife. "You can't do this."

Maryam glances at the black object on the ground. "Then it's too late."

"Shit." Adam leaves Crane's side. "That's a bomb," he whispers as he walks by me.

My entire body freezes.

"Mom?" Lina asks. "Are you alright?"

"Fine," I whisper.

Adam bends to inspect the object. He runs his fingers along the sides, searching for a seam or trapdoor. When he finally finds one, he takes one look at the electrical components and curses under his breath.

"Can you stop it?" I ask.

"Of course he can't." The blond woman who came with Maryam says, her tone sarcastic. "There's plenty that golden boy here can do but crackin' that sucker isn't one of them."

"No one can." Adam moves away from it. "That's pure Hanford genius." He seems agitated as George and Maryam continue to argue.

I make eye contact with Lina. "We have to get them out of here."

"There's not enough time." Adam scans the crowd.

"The choppers. We can load them in the choppers."

Adam shakes his head. "There's not enough room. Are you ready to choose who lives and who dies?"

He's right; there's sixteen kids, a goat, Militia men, this entire District. We can't leave the Residents to die like this and run to safety.

Adam takes my arm and leads me away from everyone. "We've got an hour," he warns.

What can I do? What can I do?

"Stop," Adam warns as if he were reading my mind. "You can't solve this alone."

"Just let them destroy themselves? Sit back and watch? I can't do that either."

There are only a few options, we all go down together, we send the Crossbenders off with the bomb and watch them die, or we could... I can't finish the thought.

"Andie." Adam's voice is pleading. He knows what I'm thinking and it's strange that at this moment he chooses to make the noble decision, the one that will end us and let them live. "They've been trained well. They can handle themselves."

"So we just leave?" I shake my head. "That's so selfish."

"No more selfish than trying to shield them from the world." Suddenly Adam is standing in front of me, blocking everything else out. "It's always about the next generation, trying to control it, influence it, guide them. You and Crane, you can't control the future. I've lived it. He struggled to control me and then you. And the genetic engineering, all of this." Adam waves his arm to the District. "It's all about controlling the future. It needs to end. Now."

"But I want them to have a good future." Tears sting my eyes. I don't want to leave them.

His hands hold my face and his bright blue eyes look into mine. "So do I."

Even with his lack of parenting I know he wants what's best for them. Maybe that's why he didn't push; he didn't want to run the risk of trying to control and change.

"You've guided them the best you could. They'll learn to fly alone."

"I don't want to." I want to beg him to choose another way.

Adam grips my hands. "Let them go. You've done all you can. They have learned from our mistakes. Didn't you see them just now? They're no longer children. We can't stop the rain," he says softly, tucking a piece of hair behind my ear.

I nod, understanding that this is not about the weather. It's about losing control, letting go.

"I know," I confess. "But I want to so badly."

"We can do this," Adam whispers and it's a pact.

I nod again, unable to speak.

Crane once told me a story of another culture who, when asked who they would save first, their spouse or their child, they always chose their spouse because they could make more children. This time—possibly because they are older, stronger—I know that they'll be fine without me. Just like Adam said.

I choose him. I choose Adam.

FORTY-FOUR

MARCUS MUSCLES MARYAM BACK INTO ONE OF THE choppers. The blond woman follows.

"I'm sorry about this," George says to me. "What are you going to do about that?" He nods toward the bomb.

"We'll take care of it," Adam replies.

"I couldn't stop her. I should have known she'd try this. She's been obsessed." George pushes his glasses up and the wind blows his hair around. "The things we gave up, thinking we could make the world a better place…"

Maryam struggles with Marcus at the door of the helicopter.

"It might not have been worth it. I'll take her back," George says.

"Leave the other chopper," Adam tells him.

George nods before turning and jogging toward the chopper with Maryam.

"Hey! Pretty boy," Jenn shouts as she jumps out from behind Maryam. "Every hero must learn his purpose." She smiles and tosses a metallic object to Adam.

The blonde jumps back in the chopper and slams the door closed.

Marcus backs away and the blades start circling faster. After a few moments it lifts into the air, but goes no further.

Lina steps forward, her arm extended, her brow beaded with sweat. "I don't trust them," she shouts. "What's happening with the bomb?"

Ira, Niko, and Milo's palms glow with energy waiting to be used in defense. The rest of the children look tense, ready to defend their home. Norah stands behind us all, surrounded by her Militia Men, her small hand petting the goat.

"They're going to take it," Raven shouts to Lina. "They're going to take the bomb."

I realize we never told them what we were going to do. I'm not sure I even know each detail.

My brother moves to embrace me. "He can read minds," Sam informs me as he hugs me tightly. "Half the time he knows what you're going to do before you know it."

Sam squeezes my shoulders for a moment before stepping away and standing close to Norah.

Adam moves from the place he's been standing and in once quick movement he reveals the syringe and plunges it into Burton Crane's neck. Then he nods at me before stepping away.

I recognize the amber colored serum as it empties from the syringe. That was the serum I made, the one to draw out the nanocytes. The one I wasn't sure would work.

In the moments that follow I want to scream at Adam, scream something stupid like *that was my kill!* I've only been waiting to kill him since the first day I met him, all those years ago when he tore my life apart.

He said he did this out of love, that's his reasoning. Well, Burton Crane has a pretty skewed sense of love. Love doesn't make you hurt people. Love doesn't make you force people to make horrible decisions. Love doesn't... love doesn't... I stop, snap my jaw shut, Dr. Akiyama's words ringing in my ears: *There is something honorable in taking a life so someone you love doesn't have to. There is something honorable in settling that on your conscience, so someone you love doesn't have to suffer with that guilt for the rest of their lives. You did Adam a favor.*

Adam did me a favor.

"Ah," Crane smiles. "Good dog."

Adam backs away, watching me, waiting.

"And now what will you do with me?" Crane asks.

"Nothing," I say.

"And what will you do with yourself?"

"Disappear."

"Gods don't disappear."

"Good thing I am not a God. I am nothing but a laboratory experiment."

"Your people will need you. Especially with men like Sakima loose."

I close my mouth, speaking no more to him, mostly because I have no plan. I had one goal and it is done. And part of me knows he's right. There will always be evil, bad men planning bad things. I could try to stop them.

"Mom!" Lina shouts, her brow beaded with sweat. "I can't hold them much longer!" The helicopter hovers in the air.

I've held onto the damn man for this long and couldn't do away with him. God help me, I hope that's the difference between me and Crane.

I glance at the last of my family, knowing it will be the last time. "Goodbye." I say, since there's no time for heartfelt hugs.

We run for the other chopper that George left behind. Adam drags Crane the entire way. Now he's fighting, all this time he's been so confident, but now he struggles. Crane must know that this is the end.

***

Helicopter blades beat loudly. Adam looks back at us, worried. He glances at the bomb that he set in one of the seats.

"What kind is it?" I ask him.

"The bad kind." He looks away, flipping controls and maneuvering the chopper.

"Atomic? EMP?"

"You don't really want to know."

Looking out the small window I can see Lake Ontario. He's going in a straight line, over the water, hoping to get the furthest away from Phoenix as fast as he can.

Crane suddenly comes to, looking around and taking it all in. He smiles when his eyes fall on me then the smooth, dark case of the bomb.

"You can say what you want when this is all over. But I did it. I made an Adam and Eve to survive the plague of the human race. You can think what you want, but I did it! I did it!" And he begins laughing maniacally.

"He's lost control," Adam says. "Lost control and lost his goddamned mind." Adam shakes his head.

Blood starts trickling out of Crane's nose.

The chopper jerks slightly as Adam maneuvers it, turning to the right.

"What are you doing?" I ask.

"Letting the wind blow us." He's extremely calm for someone who is about to commit suicide.

Soon we pass the lake. I look out the window and get a good glance at what was once Canada. Since the Reformation it's gone back to the wild. There are no humans below, no camps, no fires, nothing to indicate Survivors have settled here once again.

We fly over a few small towns, empty highways. Elk and bear roam the vacant streets.

"How much time is left?" Adam asks.

I glance at the bomb, my hands sweating. "Ten minutes."

Crane makes a strange noise and when I look back at him I notice there is now blood draining from his ears. It drips onto his suit and white shirt. His eyes close and his head bobs.

It looks like the serum worked. All this time it worked, but its effects are immediate. Ian was right to worry when I revealed it to him. I could have died in a day, when the children were all so young. I'm glad he stopped me.

The chopper slows and Adam lands it in open countryside. There are flowers everywhere; purples and yellows and white wildflowers. It's beautiful, heaven almost.

Adam flicks switches and the blades slow to a stop. He jumps out of the chopper, rounds it to pull me out and into his arms. He slams the door, locking a dying Crane inside of the chopper with the bomb. Without his nanocytes, I know that Crane will be turned to dust with the bomb.

"We don't have much time." His eyes are sad and intense. "I'm sorry. I wish this could have been different. I wish I could have met you at another time, when the world was different. I could have done this right."

"Me too," I whisper to him.

How endearing to hear these words from him. He's been telling me truths for miles and miles, all the time before we came to this point. How ironic that at this moment, when I can fully trust him, it is the end.

"I love you." I reach up, circle the back of his neck and pull his mouth down to mine. His lips are firm and demanding. As the kiss deepens all I can think is that we should have done this before our last moments. I should have set aside my anger as Adam had set aside his lies. And I could have set aside my guilt as he set aside his.

Adam's hands grip my body, pulling me closer, clawing at my clothes, tearing them off before dragging us to the ground.

"I wish we could have this forever." He's so intense in this moment.

The wildflowers tower over us, the sun shines bright. In this second I can't help but think that this is so beautiful. In all of the wrongness that brought us here, our final moments are picture-perfect.

I recognize this as my last chance to show him how I really feel. Like some feral animal, I tear at his clothing just as he tore at mine. His lips skim my neck as he presses himself into me. I bite down on his shoulder, centering myself. And for the last few moments I simply feel all that he has to offer me.

There is no deafening down-tic like there is in the movies before a bomb detonates. There is only silence. A thunderous void as though a vacuum sucked all of the sound away. Then there is wind and heat. I feel the weight of Adam on top of me, his lips as he presses them to mine. There is intense pleasure, pain, and warmth greater than I've ever felt in my life.

We were crafted and honed into creatures we barely recognize. Adam and I have survived so much, but I'm not sure if our nanocytes can recover from this. Perhaps this was always the best solution. We can never go back and make it right. It's too late.

Adam makes a strange noise, one of great pain as the field burns in a nanosecond. The flowers scorch and with them so do we.

My last thought is not of the defining moments of my life—the birth of my children, my first kiss, graduations, proposals, the moment I found love, my children's first steps, moments of joy, moments where I was proud. It's none of those. It is only that the Witchdoctor was wrong. Adam is not my Perseus. He is Icarus; we are forbidden, and together we have flown far too close to the sun. There is no ocean to catch us. Together we burn.

EPILOGUE

THE MOMENTS THAT ANDROMEDA WAS AWAKE AFTER THE detonation were few and far between. The few times that she opened her eyes didn't reveal much. There was one time that all she could see were gray blobs in front of her face. Another when she could feel the tightness and rawness of her skin. Then there was the time that she moved her hand and was satisfied with the feeling of Adam's hand gripping hers. There were times that she woke to find them surrounded by snow, and then by warm sunlight. And pain, there was plenty of pain. Much worse than when she touched the fence that surrounded the Phoenix District. She closed her eyes and forced her body to drift off again.

Time passed. It could have been months, it could have been years. She had no way of knowing.

She was cold when she opened her eyes again to find that she was lying in a hole of blackened earth. There were scorched pieces of metal nearby. Crane was gone, turned to dust in the wind. The only thing left was her and the form she recognized next to her. Adam was there, although his body was in a slower state of healing from hers. Feeling cold, she scooted closer to him and wrapped her arms around his frail frame. He was nothing more than bones and regenerating muscle and skin. The sight would send another running for the hills but Andromeda knew that this was part of the process. The nanocytes healing him.

Andie closed her eyes and let her body fall into a deep sleep once again. More time passed. The world rotated, the seasons changed, life went on without them.

Hearing a noise next to her, Andromeda opened her eyes to find Adam's startling blue ones looking back at her. His body was healed, his skin pale and complete. They were both naked, healed as though they were just born.

"How much time do you think has passed?" Andie asked.

"Could be five years, twenty, could be a hundred," Adam replied as he moved to his feet. Reaching for her, "Come," he said.

Andromeda took in the sight of him. Like her, he had undergone a transformation. He looked younger, his skin was taut against strong muscle and not one scar marred his body. The only thing that reminded them what they had been part of were the marks on their wrists. Andromeda focused on the phoenix as Adam held his hand out to her. She hesitated a moment before placing her hand in his. His hand was warm, alive. When she touched him she remembered everything that they had left behind, everything that they had done, what they had been a part of. They escaped. They were given a second chance.

Adam smiled as he pulled Andie to her feet and wrapped his arm around her waist. "Let's go see what the world we left behind has become," he said.

The End

Preview of "Songs for the End of Days"

Nova

I park in the closest parking spot to the door and sit in the cool air coming from the vents for an extra minute, preparing myself for the heat outside. It doesn't matter that it's been like this for over a year, nothing prepares you for that blast of burning air. Some say it's like stepping into Hell, and since I've already been to Hell and back I guess it's just like stepping into a puddle of old memories.

This is a typical mountain rest area with chipped paint, peeling window stickers, and a few shingles missing. It doesn't exactly resemble a place where people get murdered but you can't be too sure these days. The pavement is swept clean, and the "Belle's Diner" sign is still blinking, which gives the illusion that it's been kept up and gives me hope that I might find something cold to drink inside.

I doubt there will be air conditioning inside since the electricity is spotty around the Blue Ridge. I've been told the big cities have people determined to continue on with life as it once was. They have air conditioning, running water, medical facilities, and spotty cell service.

The rumor through the mountains is that there's a hospital in Charlotte still up and running. I've got a two-day travel plan, enough gas to make it there and the roads seem mostly clear. I've been to a few places with restaurants open and serving food. They took my cash with the hopes that the government can fix this mess and they'll enter the rat race once again. Other places took one look at me and gave the food for free. Pity pays. You don't see many women in my condition these days. At least none that have lasted this long. I guess I'm sort of an enigma now.

Every now and then, I have to stop in a dead town at an abandoned highway restaurant—worse than this—with the hope that they will have something unexpired on their shelves and no bodies lining their walls. I can't avoid it, since I've become an eating machine and all.

I turn the car off, grab my bag, and get out. There is a slight breeze coming through the valley. It's enough to disturb my hair, but it's just as hot as the sun-licked air. There is nothing refreshing about this breeze, nothing more than dragon's breath. Perspiration is instant. I lock the doors on my borrowed Chevy before heading inside.

"Hello?" I ask as I open the door. A tinny chime sounds. Good, the electricity is still on. "Hello?" I shout again. "Is there anyone here?"

Silence answers back.

It's hard to ignore the shiver of apprehension that slides up my spine, a sensation I've experienced more times than not since leaving the comforts of my rental. I used to watch all of those apocalyptic movies before the heat came; there's always danger lurking in the shadows, especially in empty stores that haven't been pillaged. But no one survives without facing those fears. So here I am.

I make my way to the eat-in counter.

Since there's electricity, I pull my charging cords from my bag and plug my iPhone in. Who knows when I'll have electricity again, and if I'm lucky I might get cell service once I'm closer to Charlotte.

I check the small refrigerators under the counter only to find expired milk and cottage cheese. I find a box of crackers with the packs still sealed and a variety of canned goods that I move to the counter. There's tomato paste, mustard, a half-gallon can of liquid cheese–it's tempting, if only I had some chips.

"Are ye alone, miss?" a man's voice with an odd, nearly Scottish accent asks.

I stop searching and stand, ready to fight. "What's it to you?" I never heard the door open and curse myself for not moving on when I felt that shiver of apprehension earlier. The last thing I need is a gunfight or a fistfight or a pepper spray fight — that's more my style.

He holds his hands up. "I don't mean trouble. I just want to offer ye assistance."

"Sure you do." I pick up a can of black beans, ready to pitch it at his head and run.

"I mean no harm. I promise." He smiles, showing me his hands in surrender and turning in a circle.

"I see a gun and knives." They're tucked in his belt.

"Aye, but those are not for you. They're for me." He thumbs toward the door. "For the wild yonder."

"The wild yonder?" I ask. Who talks like that on the east coast?

"Aye." He takes two steps closer. "I have concerns over the safety of this road."

A sea of tables and chairs separate us. Those will slow him down if he tries to attack. I could make it out the back door and around to my car with time to escape. He's twice my size and I'm sure I'd move faster. Even with this swollen belly.

"Didn't mean to scare ye." He sets his bag down on a nearby chair. "I was hoping for some company. It's hard to come by these days."

"It sure is," I agree as I try to figure out what to do. I knew traveling alone would be dangerous but there was no one else to come with me. And I didn't come prepared with weapons to defend myself. I was foolishly hoping I'd avoid a situation like this.

"Saw yer car out front. Haven't seen many people driving these days." He sweeps his arm over a table, clearing it of spilled salt and pepper.

"Well, it's faster than traveling on two feet." I point out the window where my car is parked. "Thankfully my neighbor left that with a full tank."

"Nice of them. Does it blow cold air?"

"Yup." I tap my fingers on the counter. "It's a nice escape from this sweltering heat."

He nods. "Reckon it is."

We no longer live in a time in which trusting strangers is customary. Still, there is something different about this guy. He has a calming vibe and I've learned to trust vibes; it's gotten me out a few situations before the shit hit the fan. I'd say in the current state of affairs with the heat blasting humanity into the dumpster, my vibe radar is my best commodity. Maybe even my superpower.

I search for a can opener on the shelves below the counter. After finding one, I grab two bowls and two spoons from the drying rack along the back wall.

"Are you hungry?" I ask.

"Aye, couldn't hurt to sit for a bit and eat." He sits at the table he cleared, with his back to the door. Then he starts digging around in his backpack.

"You're not pulling out a gun or anything, are you?" I ask.

He goes stiff, then chuckles. "Thought ye were looking for food."

I hold up the can. "I found some. It's not Chipotle, but it will do."

I drain the beans into a dry sink and then pour half in to each bowl and stick them in the microwave for a few seconds. I add some salt, some pepper, and a little cilantro. I walk around the counter and toward the table he's sitting at.

His face suddenly twists with concern when he gets a good look at me.

"What?" I ask. "Never seen a pregnant lady before?"

He pulls a bag of biscuits out of his backpack. "Aye, seen a few, but they looked different."

I sit across from him and slide a bowl his way. "How different?"

He slides a biscuit in my direction. "Well, for starters, most didn't have a belly quite that big."

"Are you calling me fat?" I joke. "Most doctors would say I'm seriously undernourished."

"Aye, sure they might. I'm just saying they didn't seem to be as far along." He takes a bite of his biscuit, chewing thoughtfully.

He's probably right; no one of good judgment would let themselves get knocked up with things like they are.

I take a bite of the beans, thankful that they're not rotten or sprouting mold. "Are you saying pregnancy looks good on me?" I talk around my mouthful of food in a quite unladylike manner. My mother would swat me if she were still alive to see it.

"Aye. Guess I am." He smiles and the sense of calm he emits intensifies.

"What's your name, sir?" I ask, leaning back in my chair to make room for my belly.

"Abraham, miss." He wipes his hands on his pant legs before holding one across the table to shake.

I lean forward. "Nice to meet you Abraham, my name's Nova."

We shake.

There is something about his hand; maybe it's the slightly foreign feeling of his smooth skin. Men should have calluses on their hands, they should be rough. And the way he smiles. There is something off, but something completely...noble. It's confusing. Maybe it's the hormones or low blood sugar?

"You should have a biscuit." He slides two my way.

"Are they better than the beans?" I ask as I take one and break it.

He shrugs as he eats. "Some say they're good. They'll fill you up."

I take a bite. The biscuit is chewy and dense, slightly sweet with something refreshing that tastes like mint. "Did you make these?" I ask. "They're good."

"Oh no, I'm not much of a cook. My sisters make them, they give them to me for my travels." He pushes his chair back and crosses his legs at the ankle, stretching out. The guy is tall and well-built. During a time when humanity is lacking fresh food and water, he looks well fed and cared for, even if his clothing is worn and strange.

"Sisters?" I ask. "Are any of them a doctor? I could use a doctor soon." I rub my stomach.

The child in my belly kicks. Abraham notices and can't stop looking.

I giggle. "Jeez, you really haven't seen a full pregnant woman before. Have you ever felt a baby kick?"

He rubs a hand over his face, strangely embarrassed. "I guess not. No." He reaches out. "Could I?"

I push my chair away from the table and stand. "Sorry, buddy, not today." I bring our empty bowls to the sink and set them down, then I find my own backpack and fill it with as much food as I can carry. Canned beans, crackers—I'm tempted by the large can of cheese, but I know the nutritional value is low and I really have nothing fried to dip in it. Instead, I slide a medium-sized steak knife into my pocket.

"Where are you headed?" Abraham asks as he stands.

I unplug my phone and coil the charging cable. "Charlotte. I have to keep moving to a bigger city, a place that still has electricity and maybe even a hospital. These little towns out here are pretty bare. Although, I feel safer out here and alone, away from the bustle of the city. But this baby is going to come soon and I prefer not to deliver it myself."

Abraham secures his backpack, which now that I get a good look at, is the strangest backpack I've ever seen; the straps crisscross across his chest and the fabric resembles suede. It was definitely made for comfort and travel, not necessarily style.

"Shouldn't you head for the mountains? A place that's safer?" he asks. "It's not as hot there."

"Nope." I sling my bag across my shoulders and head for the door. "I've been playing it safe for a while now. It's time to search out a real hospital before this belly pops and I have to cut the umbilical cord with my own teeth." I make a gagging noise. "I just can't do that. I need a professional."

Abraham follows as I push open the door. Heat greets me with a sour note. I wasn't fond of snow, but I'd kill for a day with a temperature of less than eighty degrees.

"What if I told you there was a safe place in the mountains where we could help you?" Abraham asks. "An entire city that's safe. The safest place you've ever been in your life."

I stop and turn. "Look, Abraham, you seem like a nice guy and all, but I'm not about to follow you to some 'safe place' in the mountains. I've been out past the Blue Ridge, I've seen the towns and settlements and god-fearing crazy bible groups out there. I'm headed to Charlotte, where there's normal people, educated people, *real* doctors. Civilization."

"Oh, aye, see what you're saying there." He follows me as I start to walk. "I'd be scared too, not knowing."

I stop at my car. "You'd be scared too, buddy? Last I checked you got a dick swinging between your legs and a belt loop full of weapons, not a baby sitting in your belly kicking your bladder every ten minutes and slowing you down. You're some big dude who looks like he can take a few punches. Not me. I'm better off headed for Charlotte. That's the way the world works nowadays."

Abraham pales, at a loss for words. Sometimes I do that to people. I think I might have been a bit out of line but these days I lack patience.

"You seem like a nice girl." Abraham swallows hard.

"I think I am a nice girl. If I wasn't in this position I'd probably be a whole lot nicer," I reply.

There's silence between us for a moment.

"I guess this is goodbye then." I reach for my door handle. This could be the last decent person left on earth and in all of a few minutes I've insulted him and I'm ready to run off.

"Aye, guess so." He rubs a hand across his face like he's thinking of something, or troubled or nervous.

"It was nice meeting you, Abraham. Thanks for the biscuit."

"One moment." He removes his pack and pulls out the bag of biscuits. "Take these." He holds the bag out. "They're good for you. They'll keep you full for a long time." He searches his bag again. "Do you have enough water? Humans need to drink a lot of water, especially those with child."

I can't control the confused look on my face or my mouth. "Humans? Are you not human? Are we not on planet Earth, burning to death?"

"Aye—" he pauses, surprised. "Of course I'm human," he starts muttering, "just... just... just as human as you are." He shrugs and takes a deep breath.

"Why do you talk like that?" I ask.

"I talk like I talk." There's a tick in his cheek when he smiles.

"You don't talk like people around here." I take in his odd clothing again. He could be a hippie or have been raised by wolves. Who knows these days?

"Oh, aye, suppose it's the curse of learning a thousand languages."

"A thousand?" I narrow my eyes at him. "What languages? Tell me." I've never come across a person who has known ten languages, let alone a thousand.

Abraham lists off English, Spanish, Japanese, Russian, Slavic, Arabic, Dutch, French, Scottish, Malay, and more. Many I've never heard of before. Languages I didn't know existed and some I'm sure he just plain made up.

"Wow. How long did it take you to learn all of that?"

"Oh, many years. Seems the tongue of some stuck stronger." He nods. "I guess that's why I talk the way I do. My brothers and sisters used to mock me for it. I can't change it though. It's just the way I talk now. Do ye find it hard to listen to?"

"No," I say. "It's different. A bit unusual, I guess."

I glance around the parking lot and see there is no other vehicle. "How did you get here?" I ask as sweat drips down my back.

"I walked," he replies, plain as day.

"Where are you from?" I ask.

He waves his hand in the distance, motioning to the ridges to the west. "Over there."

"Uh huh." Before I toss my bag in the back seat I pull the steak knife out that I took from the restaurant.

He seems ready to jump out of his boots, the thick air tense with nervous energy. "Charlotte, you say?" He rubs the back of his neck in a motion that's slightly endearing.

"Yup." I look away. Looking away is safe when men start doing things like rubbing their necks and giving you tips on how to take care of yourself.

"Could you give me a ride?" he asks.

"Only if you're going to Charlotte." I hold up my hand to stop him. "One more question." I clear my throat and hold up the knife. "Do you plan to kill, incapacitate, or maim me?"

His two fingers touch his breastbone. "I'd never hurt ye," he promises, seriously.

"Fine then." I set the knife in the door pocket. "Get in."

He smiles. "I guess I'm going to Charlotte."

We get in the car. I start the engine and blast the air conditioner. I buckle my seatbelt and he does the same. After plugging in my iPhone, I select "Road Trip Mix" then check my mirrors.

I pull away from Belle's Diner headed for Charlotte.

I drive the Blue Ridge Parkway, taking the loopy curves slow to be safe. There are abandoned cars parked off the road, some down embankments, their paint bubbling and cracking in the heat, tires soft, rotting corpses inside.

"This road's quite empty for miles," Abraham says.

"Have you been here before?"

"Oh, aye, came from this direction before we crossed paths."

"So you're backtracking now?" I ask.

"Not far. Usually spend most of my time along these roads and along this strip of mountainside. For now."

"Why?" I find it strange that he would travel the mountainside during a time like this. I'd think the smart ones would find a safe place and food to prep for the worst. It seems like the best thing to do, especially since the government isn't doing much to quell the violence. They dispatched the National Guard to various cities to help. They said they were going to cut carbon emissions to cool the earth. If they did anything, it's not helping. It just keeps getting hotter.

"I'm searching for people to bring back," Abraham says.

"To the mountains?" I ask.

"Aye. We have everything we need, and my people are just trying to secure the human race."

Trying to secure the human race? Now I'm wondering if he's part of one of those cults.

"You still thinking of Charlotte?" He reminds me of a car salesman about to lose a sale.

"I sure am." I push play on my iPhone screen.

He pushes pause. He's brave. I can tell because no man in his right mind would dare touch the music from the shotgun seat.

"Why are you alone in this condition?" he asks, motioning to my stomach.

I could answer him in a variety of ways. I could tell him the truth, I could tell him a lie, I could tell him a bit of both. I decide to tell him nothing. "I don't like strangers rubbing on my scars. Mind your business."

"Ah, well, figured if I was sharing about myself you might share about yourself."

I push play again. "Not today, son."

What I don't tell Abraham is there was one event that caused me to be alone in this condition. That it was the fall from grace and going splat on the ground that hurt the worst. It should have been the cancer, the loss of love, or the death. But it was none of those things. It was selling everything; the car, furniture, clothes, expensive shoes, and then the house. Each time one of those trophies fell it chipped a piece of me away. At least, that's what I try to tell myself since the pain of losing John has been just too much to focus on, even nearly a year after his death. Part of me hates him for leaving me alone to deal with the world the way it is now. We could have melted into obscurity together but instead he left me here to suffer alone.

I hate myself for being shallow and missing things, but that's the way the world was. How big was your house, your car, your cell phone memory? The days of materialism ended swiftly. My head still aches from the whiplash.

My things were gone, but the electric bill was cheaper in the rental and the top floor caught a nice breeze when all the windows were open. It was nothing compared to my old house with John. No custom cupboards, no granite countertops, no snail shower tiled with blue glass. It wasn't my old house, but I still miss it. I miss the moment of rebirth; the time spent relearning who I was without him. It seems all those years I was someone else when I was with him. I was half. He was half. Now I have no choice but to try and be whole. To fill the void. It's tough learning how to do that when the world around you starts falling apart.

The rental is gone too. A second fall. This one has nothing to do with me personally, only that I'm part of it and I'm still alive. I had to leave when the building burned and the Army came to town to help. They relocated us and brought in some entertainment to raise our spirits. It worked for a few days, until the violence got worse. And then the army men with guns, who were supposed to protect us, turned crazed. My neighbor at the time helped me. And then nearly everyone was dead.

I guess it wasn't just one event that got me here, it was a multitude of them all piling up and toppling over. The void ever deeper, threatening to never be filled again. I had a therapist once who told me I should talk about the memories that bother me. I glance at Abraham; it's rude to drop all that on a stranger.

Abraham seems to know better than to pry again for the rest of the trip.

About the Author

M. R. Pritchard writes about the elemental struggle between good and evil, and gods and monsters, and about people who turn into gods and monsters. Usually with a mix of apocalypse or post-apocalyptic setting. She also includes a spec of a love story because what is humanity without love?

M. R. Pritchard is a two-time Kindle Scout winning author, her short story "Glitch" has been featured in the 2017 winter edition of THE FIRST LINE literary journal. Her short story "Moon Lord" has been featured in Chronicle Worlds: Half Way Home (Part of the Future Chronicles) and will be time capsuled on the moon on the Lunar Codex in 2024.

M. R. Pritchard holds degrees in Biochemistry and Nursing. She is a northern New Yorker transplanted to the Gulf Coast of Florida who enjoys coffee, mint chocolate, cloudy days, and reading on the lanai.

Visit her website MRPritchard.com and sign up for her newsletter. You'll get a Work in Progress Chapters, new release alerts, and book deals.

If you enjoyed **Ashes of the Sovereign** (*The Phoenix Project Omnibus Series*), please leave a review, tell a friend, or gift to a friend. These small acts keep authors writing. Thank you.

Scarecrow

Raven King

Nightjar

Night Owl

Etched in Darkness

Embrace the Night

Shadows of Destiny

Midnight Serenade

Echoes of Treachery

Temptations of Fate

Omens of Darkness

Temptations of Fate

Veil of Shadows Omnibus 1

Veil of Shadows Omnibus 2

Veil of Shadows Omnibus 3

Veil of Shadows Omnibus 4

The Sky is Starless

The Night is Endless (2025)

<u>Standalone Fantasy</u>

Thread the Bone

<u>Fantasy/Fairy Tale Love Story/Romance:</u>

Muse

Forgotten Princess Duology

Midsummer Night's Dream: A Game of Thrones

<u>Poetry/Short Stories</u>

Consequence of Gravity